THE
HOLLYWOOD
MURDERS

THE
HOLLYWOOD
MURDERS

by ELLERY QUEEN

J. B. LIPPINCOTT COMPANY

Philadelphia   *New York*

LIBRARY OF CONGRESS CATALOG CARD NUMBER 57–10876

Contents

THE DEVIL TO PAY

I am informed that certain persons of high ego or low conscience spend all their waking hours in the soul-searching effort to find resemblances between themselves and the multifarious offspring of the literary imagination.

Consequently I feel constrained to assert the self-evident fact that what follows in these pages is a work of fiction; and that, if any character in it resembles any real person whatsoever in name, physique, idiosyncrasy, mental equipment, cultural or professional background, or general morality, such deplorable resemblance should be construed as an act of God with which the author had nothing consciously to do.

E. Q.

PART ONE

Chapter I

Much Ado About Something

HOLLYWOOD, LIKE the Land of Oz, possesses a quaint and fluty flavor: it is the place where tin Christmas trees suddenly sprout around lamp-posts in December under a ninety-degree sun, where restaurants take the shape of lighthouses and hats, ladies on Saturday nights stroll the boulevards in trousers and mink coats leading baby leopards on a leash, where morning newspapers cost five cents and evening newspapers two, and people wait in queues for unexhausting hours to witness other people pressing their hands into juicy cement.

A trivial happening in Hollywood, therefore, is hugely less trivial than if the identical event occurs in Cincinnati or Jersey City, and an important one incalculably more important.

So when the Ohippi Bubble burst, even people who were not stockholders devoured the Los Angeles dispatches, and overnight "Ohippi" became as familiar a catchword as "quintuplets" and "the nine old men."

This is not to belittle the event itself. In collapsing Ohippi paradoxically stood on its own feet as a major calamity. And while the issue was not fought in the courts, owing to little Attorney Anatole Ruhig's foresight, a veritable battle-royal raged in print and on the streets. A wonderfully martial time it was, with Solly Spaeth's lanky son firing long-range bursts from the editorial offices of the *Los Angeles Independent* and unhappy stockholders alternately howling and scowling at the iron gate of *Sans Souci*, behind which Solly sat imperturbably counting up his millions.

It was really the Eastern diagnostician's fault, for Solly would never have settled in California had the doctor not recommended its climate, its golf, and its sunbaths. Imagine Solomon Spaeth being content to do nothing but squint along the mountain-range of his belly as he lolled in the sun! It was fated that Solly should begin restlessly ruminating his capital, which was lying as idly as he in various impregnable but unexciting banks.

So Solly rose, covered his nakedness, looked hopefully about, and found Rhys Jardin and little Anatole Ruhig. And it was from their happy fusion that the celebrated and subsequently notorious Ohippi Hydro-Electric Development emerged.

(Solly met Winni Moon at the same time, but his interest in Winni was esthetic rather than commercial, so that is a different part of the story. Solly was never a man to neglect the arts. Winni became his protégée, and it is fascinating to recall that her career dated from that sensitive juxtaposition of souls.)

The organization and development of Ohippi Hydro-Electric took genius in those days, when heavy industry was prostrate and premonitory rumblings of holding-company legislation were audible in Washington; but Solly had genius. Nevertheless, he could not have succeeded without Rhys Jardin, who played the rôle of industrial angel with superb technique. Rhys, that sterling yachtsman, golfer, gymnast, and collector of *objets de sport*, was indispensable to Solly for entirely different reasons: he possessed the necessary supplemental capital, he carried the magic Jardin name, and he knew nothing whatever about big business.

When Ohippi moved from the financial pages into the offices of the Homicide Detail of the Los Angeles Central Detective Bureau the case, already precious, became a managing editor's dream; and Fitzgerald went slightly mad.

Fitz had been a classmate of Rhys Jardin's (Harvard '08) and he was also technically Walter Spaeth's employer. But the set-up was so alluring—the floods, Winni Moon and her scented chimpanzee, that provocative little detail of the molasses, the old Italian rapier, the scores of thousands of potential murderers—that Fitz shut his eyes to the ethical questions involved and let fly with both presses.

Of course, every newspaperman in Los Angeles became wall-eyed with civic pride and professional joy, and the items that flooded the papers dealt with everything from Winni's dainty bathing habits to an old still-picture of Pink, bow in hand, as Chief Yellow Pony, from that forgotten epic of the plains, *Red Indian*. They even dug out of the morgue a photograph of Rhys Jardin winning the 1928 Southern California amateur golf championship.

One feature writer, running out of material, fell back upon statistics. He pointed out that, as usual, nearly every one in the case came from anywhere but Hollywood.

Rhys Jardin was originally a Virginian, the Jardins having been one of the few first families of that great commonwealth with traditional riches as well as rich traditions.

Solly Spaeth had been spawned in New York.

Walter Spaeth—who as a result of his father's migratory instincts might have been born on mountain, plain, or sea—happened to see his first sunbeam in a Chicago hospital, where his mother saw her last.

Winni Moon had been christened Freda Möndegarde in a cold little Swed-

ish church in the South Dakota wheatfields. (Her unavoidable destination
had been Hollywood, since she was blonde and swivel-hipped, had been the
star of her high-school dramatic society, had once waited on table in an
Eatery run by a Greek named Nick, and had then won a State-fair beauty
contest, sharing honors with the prize milch-cow.)

Anatole Ruhig had been born in Vienna, an error he quickly rectified;
he passed the bar in Kansas City and was drawn to Hollywood by magnetic
attraction, like an iron filing.

Pink came from Flatbush, Brooklyn.

The reporter even included Fitzgerald, to that gentleman's wrath. Fitz,
it seemed, was a Boston Irishman with a weakness for truth and whisky who
had been called to California by chronic sinusitis and the plight of Tom
Mooney.

And so it went. Mr. Ellery Queen, himself a native of West Eighty-
seventh Street, Manhattan, amused himself once, during the darker hours of
the puzzle, by studying these interesting but futile data.

The only indigenous Californian involved in the case was Rhys Jardin's
unpredictable daughter, Valerie.

"I didn't think," said Walter Spaeth the first time he met her, which was
at a private polo game in Beverly Hills, "that any one's actually born here,
Miss Jardin."

"Is that the smallest talk you have?" sighed Val, peeling an orange.

"But why Hollywood?" insisted Walter, eying her up and down. He wondered how the felt bowler stuck on the side of her head managed to defy
the law of gravity, but that great problem was soon forgotten in a consideration of her mouth.

"I wasn't consulted," said Miss Jardin with annoyance. "Go away, you're
spoiling the—" She began to dance. "Good boy, pop! 'At' it, Pink!" she
screamed, waving the orange. "Watch that roan!"

Presumably Pink did so, for out of the mêlée shot two horsemen, the
ball preceding them in a beautiful arc.

"That's the end of that," said Miss Jardin with satisfaction. "Oh, are you
still here, Mr. Spaeth?"

The first horseman, a youngish fellow with longish legs clamped about a
brownish pony, thundered up the field smacking the ball toward the goal
with dismaying accuracy. Between him and his pursuers raced another youngish fellow with freckles, red hair, and preposterously broad shoulders. The
ball bounced between the goal-posts, the first rider brought up his mallet in
salute, and his red-haired guard completed the amenities by grinning and
putting his thumb to his nose. Then they cantered back to mid-field.

"Oh, I see," said Walter. "The first one is pop, and the second is Pink."

"A detective," said Val, looking interested. "However did you know?"

"Red hair—Pink—they seem to go together. Besides, I don't get the feeling
that your father would thumb his nose. Who's Pink?"

"Why?"

"Your boy-friend?"

"So that's the way the wind's blowing," remarked Miss Jardin shrewdly, sinking her small teeth into the orange. "Three minutes, and the man's poking his nose into my private affairs! You'll be proposing next."

"I beg your pardon," said Walter stuffily. "If I'm boring you—"

"Aren't you the one!" smiled Val. "Come here, little boy."

Walter wavered. Women of the modern school worried him. The only female he had ever known closely was Miss Titus, an aged English lady who had tutored him and tucked him into bed until he was old enough to go to Andover; and Miss Titus until her departure for a better world had deplored every feminist fad which passed her by, from smoking and knee-length skirts to suffrage and birth control.

Walter looked Miss Jardin up and down again and decided he would like to learn about women from her. He settled himself on the rail. "Your father is terribly young-looking, isn't he?"

"Isn't it disgusting? It's the vitamins and the exercise. Pop's a sports fiend. That's where Pink comes in—just," said Valerie dryly, "to relieve your mind, Mr. Spaeth. Pink's a phenomenon—can play and teach any game ever invented, and besides he's a dietitian. Vegetarian, of course."

"Very sensible," said Walter earnestly. "Are you one?"

"Heavens, no. I'm carnivorous. Are you?"

"It's a debased taste, but I'll admit I do like to sink a fang into a *filet mignon.*"

"Swell! Then you may take me to dinner tonight."

"Well—say—that would be fine," mumbled Walter, quite unconscious of how the magic had been done. He wondered with desperation how this delectable conversation might be prolonged. "Uh—he *does* look like your brother. I mean, as your brother might look if you had—"

"I'm taken for pop's older sister already," said Val tragically.

"Go on," said Walter, examining Val all over. "You're the young connubial type."

"Mr. Spaeth, you're positively clairvoyant! I sew the meanest seam, and I've always been marked A in bedmaking."

"I didn't mean exactly that." She did have the most remarkable figure, Walter thought.

Valerie eyed him sharply. "What's the matter? Am I coming out anywhere?"

"There's something wrong with the movie scouts!"

"Isn't it the truth? Just like the Yankees letting Hank Greenberg go to the Tigers—a Bronx boy, too."

"You'd photograph well," said Walter, edging closer. "I mean—you've a nose like Myrna Loy's, and your eyes and mouth remind me of—"

"*Mr.* Spaeth," murmured Val.

"My mother's," finished Walter. "I have her picture. I mean—how did they ever miss you?"

"Well, it's like this," said Valerie. "They've camped on my tail for years, but I've always turned 'em down."

"Why?"

"I'd never succeed in the movies," said Val in a hollow voice.

"That's nonsense!" said Walter warmly. "I'll bet you can even act."

"Shucks. But you see—I was born right here in Hollywood; that's one strike on me. Then I hate sables and flat heels. And I'm not a homesy girl sick of it all. So don't you see how hopeless it is?"

"You must think I'm a fool," growled Walter, whose large ears had been growing redder and redder.

"Oh, darling, forgive me," said Val contritely. "But you *are* wide open for a left hook. Finally there's kissing. Look!" She seized him, squeezed him with passion, and kissed him fiercely on the lips. "There, you see?" she sighed, biting into the orange again. "That's how it is with me."

Walter smiled a flabby smile at the polo fiends around them and wiped the lipstick off his mouth.

"What I meant to say," continued Val, "was that in the movies you've got to go through all the *motions* of passion, but when it comes right down to it they just peck at each other. When I kiss, I *kiss*."

Walter slid off the rail. "How do you spend your time?" he asked abruptly.

"Having fun," mumbled Val.

"I knew there'd be something wrong with you. You never got those hands over a wash-tub!"

"Oh, God," groaned Valerie, "a reformer." She popped the last segment into her mouth. "Listen, my lean and hungry friend. Pop and I, we live and let live. We happen to have some money, and we're trying to spend it as fast as we can before it's taken away from us."

"You're the kind of people," said Walter bitterly, "who cause revolutions."

Val stared, then burst into laughter. "Mr. Spaeth, I do believe I've misjudged you. That's the cleverest line! Isn't the next step a suggestion that we stage a private sit-down strike in the nearest park?"

"So that's what you meant by having fun!"

Valerie gasped. "Why, I'll slap your sassy face!"

"The trouble with you people," snapped Walter, "is that you're economic royalists, the pack of you."

"You just heard somebody say that!" flared Valerie. "Where do you come off lecturing me? I've heard about you and your father. You're just as fat leeches as we are, feeding on the body politic!"

"Oh, no," grinned Walter. "I don't care what you call yourself or my old man, but *I* work for a living."

"Yes, you do," sneered Val. "What's your racket?"

"Drawing. I'm a newspaper cartoonist."

"There's work for a man. Yes, sir! See tomorrow's funny section for the latest adventures of Little Billy."

"Is that so?" yelled Walter.

"Mr. Spaeth, your repartee simply floors me!"

"I draw political cartoons," yelled Walter, "for the Los Angeles Independent!"

"Communist!"

"Oh, my God," said Walter, waving his long arms, and he stamped furiously away.

Valerie smiled with satisfaction. He was a very young man, and he did look like Gary Cooper.

She examined her mouth in her hand-mirror and decided she must see Mr. Walter Spaeth again very soon.

"And tonight's date," she shouted after him, "is definitely off. But DEFINITELY!"

Chapter II

La Belle Dame Sans Souci

THERE WERE other nights, however, and other meetings; and it was not long before Mr. Walter Spaeth despairingly concluded that Miss Valerie Jardin had been set upon earth for the express purpose of making his life unbearable.

Considering Miss Jardin *in toto*, it was a pleasant curse; that was what made it so vexatious. So Walter wrestled with his conscience daily and nightly —Walter was an extremely spiritual young man—and he even plunged into Hollywood night life for a time with a variety of those beautiful females with whom Hollywood crawls.

But it all came out the same in the end—there was something about the idle, flippant, annoying Miss Jardin to which he was hopelessly allergic.

So he crept back and accepted every electric moment Miss Jardin deigned to bestow, thrashing feebly in his exquisite misery like a flea-ridden hound being scratched by his mistress.

Being totally blind to the subtleties of feminine conduct, Walter did not perceive that Miss Jardin was also going through a trying experience. But Rhys Jardin, physically a father, had had to develop the sixth sense of a mother in such matters.

"Your golf is off six strokes," he said sternly one morning as Pink mauled and pounded him on the rubbing table in the gymnasium, "and I found a wet handkerchief on the terrace last night. What's the matter, young lady?"

Val viciously punched the bag. "Nothing's the matter!"

"Filberts," jeered Pink, slapping his employer. "You had another fight with that wacky twerp last night."

"Silence, Pink," said her father. "Can't a man have a private conversation with his own daughter?"

"If that punk calls you a 'parasite' again, Val," growled Pink, digging his knuckles into Jardin's abdomen, "I'll knock his teeth out. What's a parasite?"

"Pink, you were listening!" cried Val indignantly. "This is one heck of a household, that's all I can say!"

"Can I help it if you talk loud?"

Val glared at him and plucked a pair of Indian clubs from the rack in the wall-closet.

"Now, Pink," said Rhys, "I won't have eavesdropping. . . . What else did Walter call her?"

"A lot more fancy names, and then she starts to bawl, so he hauls off and kisses her one."

"Pink," snarled Val, swishing the clubs, "you're an absolute *louse*."

"And what did my puss do?" asked Rhys comfortably. "A little more on the pectorals, Pink."

"She give him the chorus girl's salute—like she meant it, too. I mean, that was a *kiss*."

"Very interesting," said Val's father, closing an eye.

Val flung one of the Indian clubs in the general direction of the rubbing table, and Pink calmly ducked and went on kneading his employer's brown flesh. The club cracked against the far brick wall.

Val sat down on the floor and wailed: "I might as well entertain my friends in the Hollywood Bowl!"

"Nice boy," said her father. "Nice lad, Walter."

"He's an oomph!" snapped Val, jumping up. "He and his 'social consciousness'! He makes me *sick*."

"Well, I don't know," said Pink, massaging. "There's something in it. The little guy don't get much of the breaks."

"Pink, you keep out of this!"

"See what I mean?" complained Pink. "This master and man stuff. I should keep out of it. Why? Because I'm a wage slave. Turn over, Rhys."

His employer docilely turned over and Pink set about trying to crack his spine. "You don't have to see the boy, Val—ouch!"

"I should think," said Val in a frigid voice, "that I'm old enough to solve my own problems—without interference." And she flounced off.

And Walter *was* a problem. Sometimes he romped like a child, and at other times he positively snorted gloom. One moment he was trying to break her back in a movie kiss, and the next he was calling her names. And all because she wasn't interested in labor movements and didn't know a Left Wing from a Right, except in fried chicken!

It was all very confusing, because of late Val had had practically to sit on her hands; they had developed a sort of incorporeal itch. Either they wanted to muss his unruly black hair and stroke his lips and run over his sandpaper cheeks—he *always* seemed to need a shave—or they yearned to hit him on the point of his dear longish nose.

The situation was complicated by the fact that Solomon Spaeth and her father had gone into business together. Rhys Jardin in business, after all these splendid idle years! Val could not decide whether she disliked rubicund Solly more for his oozy self than for what he was doing to her father. There were tedious conferences with lawyers—especially a wet-faced little one by the name of Ruhig—arguments and contracts and negotiations and things. . . . Why, Rhys neglected his yachting, golf, and polo for three whole weeks —he barely had time for his Swedish exercises under Pink's drill-sergeant direction!

But that wasn't the worst of it. It was what happened at *Sans Souci* after the contracts were signed.

Sans Souci dated from the careless, golden days. It occupied half a dozen acres high in the Hollywood hills and was designed for exclusiveness, with a ten-foot fence of stout peeled-willow stakes all round to keep out hucksters and trailer tourists, and a secondary paling of giant royal palms to make their envious mouths water.

Inside there were four dwellings of tile, stucco, plaster, and tinted glass which were supposed to be authentic Spanish and were not.

The development was shaped like a saucer, with the four houses spacing the rim and all the rear terraces looking down upon the communal depression in the center, where the democratic architect had laid out a single immense swimming pool surrounded by rock gardens.

Rhys Jardin had bought one of the houses because the realtor was an old acquaintance in need—an empty gesture, for the bank foreclosed promptly after the depression began and the realtor shot his brains out by way of his mouth. Valerie thought the place ghastly, but their dingy expensive shack at Malibu and their bungalow-villa on the Santa Monica Palisades always seethed with people, so *Sans Souci's* promise of privacy attracted her.

The second house was occupied by a male star with a passion for Dandie Dinmonts, whose barking made life a continuous agony until their owner suddenly married an English peeress who carried him and his beasts off to dazzle the British cinema public, leaving the house happily unoccupied except for brief annual visits.

The third house was tenanted for a time by a foreign motion picture director who promptly had an attack of *delirium tremens* at the edge of the pool; so that worked out beautifully, because he was whisked off to a sanitarium and never returned.

The fourth house had never been occupied at all.

That is, until Solly Spaeth bought it from the bank "to be nearer my associate," as he beamingly told Valerie, "your worthy and charming father."

And when the insufferable Solly moved in, Walter moved in, too.

There was the rub. Walter moved in. The creature was so *inconsistent.* He didn't *have* to live there. In fact, he had been living alone in a furnished room in Los Angeles until his father took the *Sans Souci* estate. The Spaeths didn't get along—small wonder, considering Walter's ideas! But suddenly it was peaches and cream between them—for a whole week, anyway—with Solly bestowing his oleaginous benediction and Walter accepting it glumly and moving right in, drawing board, economic theories, and all.

And there he was, only yards away at any given hour of the day or night, making life miserable . . . preaching, criticizing her charge accounts and décolletage and the cut of her bathing suits, fighting with his father like an alley cat, drawing inflammatory cartoons for the *Independent* under the unpleasant *nom de guerre* of WASP, heatedly lecturing Rhys Jardin for his newly assumed "utilities overlordship," whatever that meant, scowling at poor Pink and insulting Tommy and Dwight and Joey and all the other nice boys who kept hopefully bouncing back to *Sans Souci* . . . until she was so angry she almost didn't want to return his kisses—*when* he kissed her, which wasn't often; and then only, as he hatefully expressed it, "in a moment of animal weakness."

And when Winni Moon came to live at the Spaeth house as Solly's "protégée," with her beastly beribboned chimp and a rawboned Swedish chaperon who was *supposed* to be her aunt—you would have thought a self-respecting moralist would move out *then*. But no, Walter hung on; and Valerie even suspected the impossible Winni of having designs on her benefactor's son, from certain signs invisible to the Spaeths but quite clear to the unprejudiced female eye.

Sometimes, in the sacred privacy of her own rooms, Valerie would confide in little Roxie, her Chinese maid.

"Do you know what?" she would say furiously.

"Yisss," Roxie would say, combing out Val's hair.

"It's *fantastic*. I'm in love with the beast, damn him!"

Walter leaned on his horn until Frank, the day man, unlocked the gate. The crowd in the road was silent with a rather unpleasant silence. Five State troopers stood beside their motorcycles before *Sans Souci*, looking unhappy. One little man with the aura of a tradesman leaned glassy-eyed on the shaft of a homemade sign which said: Pity The small Invester.

The crowd was composed of tradespeople, white-collar workers, laborers, small-business men. That, thought Walter grimly, accounted for the inactivity of the troopers; these solid citizens weren't the usual agitating mob. Walter wondered how many of the five troopers had also lost money in Ohippi.

Driving through the gate and hearing Frank quickly clang it shut, Walter felt a little sick. These people knew him by now, and the name he bore. He did not blame them for glaring at him. He would not have blamed them if they had tossed the troopers aside and broken down the fence.

He ran his six-cylinder coupé around to the Jardin house. More than a dozen cars were parked in the Jardin drive—sporty cars of the same breed as their owners, Walter thought bitterly. Valerie must be fiddling again—while Rome burned.

He found her in the front gardens radiantly holding off all the sad young men and their ladies with one hand and offering them *delicatessen* with the other. At first Walter blinked, for it seemed as though Val was plucking salami and sausages from the rose bushes; and he had never heard of bologna sandwiches and one-drink cocktail bottles growing on palm boles before. But then he saw that the refreshments had been artfully tied to the arboreal landscape.

"Oh, it's Walter," said Val, the radiance dimming. Then she stuck out her chin. "Walter Spaeth, if you mention one word about the starving coal-miners I'll scream!"

"Look out," giggled a young lady, "here's Amos again."

"Wasn't he the prophet who flapped his arms so much?"

"Goodbye, Val," said Tommy. "I'll see you in the first tumbril."

"Val," said Walter, "I want to talk to you."

"Why not?" said Val sweetly, and excused herself.

She maintained the sweet smile only until they were behind a cluster of palms. "Walter, don't you *dare* spoil my party. It's a brand-new idea, and I've got Tess and Nora and Wanda simply tearing their permanents—" She looked a little more closely at his face. "Walter, what's the matter?"

Walter flung himself on the grass and kicked the nearest palm. "Plenty, my feminine Nero."

"Tell me!"

"Bottom's dropped out. Hell's loose. River topped the levees last night—out of control. The whole Ohio Valley and part of the Mississippi Valley are under water. So there, may they rest in peace, go the Ohippi plants."

Valerie felt a sudden chill. It didn't seem fair that the floods in a place half a continent away should creep into her garden and spoil everything.

She leaned against the palm. "How bad is it?" she asked in a croupy little voice.

"The plants are a total loss."

"First the stock-market drop, and now— Poor pop." Val took off her floppy sunhat and began to punch it. Walter squinted up at her. It was going to be tough on the kid, at that. Well, maybe it would do her good. All this criminal nonsense—

"It's your father's fault!" cried Val, hurling the hat at him.

"Ain't it the truth?" said Walter.

Val bit her lip. "I'm sorry, darling. I know how much you hate what he stands for." She sank down and laid her head on his chest. "Oh, Walter, what are we going to do?"

"Hey, you're wetting my tie," said Walter. He kissed her curls gently.

Val jumped up, dried her eyes, and ran away. Walter heard her call out in a marvelously bright voice: "Court's adjourned, people!" and a chorus of groans.

Just then it began to drizzle, with that dreary persistence only the California clouds can achieve during the rainy season.

It's like a movie, thought Walter gloomily, or a novel by Thomas Hardy. He got to his feet and followed her.

They found Rhys Jardin patrolling the flags of his terrace at the rear of the house. Pink, in sweat-shirt and sneakers, was staring at his employer with troubled eyes.

"Oh, there you are," said her father. He immediately sat down in the porch swing. "Come here, puss. The rain's spoiled your party, hasn't it?"

"Oh, pop!" said Val, and she ran to him and put her arms about his neck.

The rain pattered on the awning.

"Well, Walter," smiled Rhys, "as a prophet you're pretty good. But not even you foresaw the floods."

Walter sat down. Pink heaved out of his deck-chair and went to the iron table and poured himself a drink of water. Then he said: "Nuts!" and sat down again.

"Is anything left?" asked Val quietly.

"Don't look so tragic, Val!"

"Is there?"

"Well, now that you ask," smiled Rhys, "not a thing. Our negotiable assets are cleaned out."

"Then why did you let me run this party today?" she cried. "All that money going to waste!"

"I never thought I'd live to see the day," said Pink lightly, "when Val Jardin would start squeezing the buffalo."

"Do we have to give up the Malibu place, the house in Santa Monica?" asked Val with difficulty.

"Now don't worry, puss—"

"This—this house, too?"

"You never liked it, anyway."

Val cradled her father's head in her arms. "Darling, you'll have to give up your yachting and golf clubs and things and go to work. How will you like that?"

The big man made a face. "We can realize a lot of money from the real estate and the furnishings—"

"And we'll get rid of Mrs. Thomson and the housemaids and Roxie—"

"No, Val!"

"Yes. And of course Pink will have to go—"

"Nuts," said Pink again.

Val became quiet and sat back in the swing, sucking her lower lip. After a while Walter said uncomfortably: "I know my anti-holding-company cartoons didn't help Ohippi, Mr. Jardin. But you understand— Newspapermen can't—"

Jardin laughed. "If I'd listened to your advice rather than your father's we'd all be a lot better off."

"The lousy part of it is," grunted Pink, "that your old man could still save Ohippi. Only he won't. There ought to be a law!"

"What do you mean?" asked Walter slowly.

Pink waved his arms. "Well, *he* cleaned up, didn't he? Why shouldn't he—"

"My father cleaned up?"

"Keep quiet, Pink," said Rhys.

"Just a moment. I've a right to know!"

"It's not important any more, Walter," said Rhys mildly. "Forget it."

"Forget your grandmother!" yelled Pink. "Go on, tell him about that cat-fight you had with Spaeth this morning!"

Jardin shrugged. "You know, your father and I were equal partners. When-ever he arranged to form a new holding company—he created seven before the government stepped in—the corporation would retain control of the com-mon stock and put the remaining forty-nine percent on the market. The preferred stock we held back, splitting share and share alike."

"Yes?" said Walter.

"Pop. Don't," said Val, looking at Walter's face.

"Go on, Mr. Jardin."

"Knowing nothing about these things, I trusted your father and Ruhig completely. Ruhig advised me to hold on to my preferred—it did seem wise, because the basic Ohippi plants were perfectly sound. Secretly, however, through agents, your father sold his preferred as the companies were cre-ated. And now, with all the stockholders caught, he's sitting back there with a fortune."

"I see," said Walter; he was pale. "And he led me to believe—"

"With the dough he's made," raved Pink, "he could rebuild those power plants and put 'em on their feet again. We got some rights, ain't we? We—"

"You lost money, too?"

Rhys Jardin winced. "I'm afraid I sucked in a lot of my friends—in my early innocence."

"Excuse me," said Walter, and he rose and went down the terrace steps into the rain.

"Walter!" cried Val, flying after him. "Please!"

"You go on back," said Walter, without stopping.

"No!"

"This is my business. Go back."

"Just the same," said Val breathlessly, "I'm coming."

She clung to his arm all the way around the pool and up the rocky slope to the Spaeth house.

Val remained nervously on the Spaeth terrace. "Walter, please don't do anything that—" But it was half a whisper, and Walter was already stalking through the glass doors into his father's study.

Mr. Solomon Spaeth sat at his oval desk the picture of baronial gravity, shaking his head a little at the rapid-fire questions of a crowd of newspapermen. His reading glasses rested on the middle of his fat nose, and with his paunch and thin gray hair and sober air he did not remotely resemble the devil and worse that the stockholders at the gate were calling him.

"Gentlemen, please," he protested.

"But how about the flood story, Mr. Spaeth?"

"Are you going on?"

"Where's that statement you promised?"

"I'll give you just this." Solly picked up a paper and fussed with it. The reporters grew quiet. Solly put the paper down. "Owing to the catastrophe in the Ohio and Mississippi Valleys," he said gravely, "our field men report the complete ruin of our equipment. That hydro-electric machinery would cost millions to replace, gentlemen. I'm afraid we shall have to abandon the plants."

There was a shocked silence. Then a man exclaimed: "But that means a loss of a hundred cents on the dollar to every investor in Ohippi securities!"

Solly spread his hands. "It's a great misfortune, gentlemen. But surely we can't be held responsible for the floods? Floods are an act of God."

The reporters did not even notice Walter in their scramble for the door. Walter stood still near the terrace doors. His lips were twisted a little. . . . His father rubbed his right jowl thoughtfully for a moment, and then began to read the afternoon papers.

Winni Moon was drifting about the study with a vague, pleased smile, touching things here and there; a small fire cracked in the grate; and Jo-Jo, Winni's chimpanzee, was whirling on her pink haunches near the hearth like a dervish, chattering crossly. Jo-Jo whirled incessantly, for she despised the smell of herself, although she was sprinkled with a scent that set Solly back fifty dollars an ounce.

On the terrace, watching, Val tingled with hostility. The Moon worm was wearing the boldest creation in burgundy crêpe, with shirrings at the wrists that "dramatize your every gesture, madame"—Val knew the line so well—and her thick wheat-colored hair was done up in a convoluted braid, like a figure eight lying on its side on top of her head.

Hostess gown. Hostess! Protégée! Val's fingers curled for something to pluck and rend.

"Oh," cried Winni, "here's Walter!" And she pounced.

Her clinging act, thought Val bitterly. True, Walter was fending her off with one arm, but that was probably because he knew Val was watching.

"Wally dear, isn't it awful? The floods, and all those people in the woad. You'd think it was the storming of the Castille, at the very weast! I've simply begged Solly—your father to make the police dwive them away—"

Walter shouted: "Lay off me!"

"Why, Walter!"

Solly took off his glasses. After a moment he said: "Get out, Winni."

Winni smiled at once. "Of course, daddy. You two men must have—" She clapped her hands prettily. "Jo-Jo!"

Oh, you—*thing!* thought Val, seeing it all from the terrace through the glass doors.

The unhappy beast leaped to Winni's shoulder and she went out with it, her hips swaying from side to side under the clinging stuff as if they were set in gimbals. She turned, smiled again, and carefully closed the study door.

Thing! THING!

Walter strode forward and faced his father across the marbled leather top of the desk.

"Let's get down to cases," said Walter. "You're a crook."

Solomon Spaeth half-rose from his chair; then, blinking, he sat back. "You can't talk to me that way!"

"You're still a crook."

Solly's complexion deepened. "Ask the United States Attorney! There's nothing illegal about my operations."

"Oh, I'm sure of that," said Walter, "with Ruhig to handle it. But that doesn't make you any the less a crook."

"If you call me that once more—" began his father balefully. Then he smiled. "Pshaw, you're excited, Walter. I forgive you. Have a drink?"

"I don't want your forgiveness!" roared Walter.

Walter, Walter, thought Val desperately.

"Before the floods our cash position was sound. It was just the government—Congress undermined the confidence of the public—"

"Look," said Walter. "How much money have you made out of the sales of your preferred stock since you began creating holding companies around Ohippi?"

"A few dollars, Walter," said Solly soothingly. "But so could Jardin, only he says he hung on to his stock."

"You got that rat Ruhig to advise him to hold on!"

"Who says so? Who says so?" spluttered Solly. "Prove that. Let him prove—"

"You weren't satisfied with swindling the investing public, you had to doublecross your partner, too!"

"If Jardin says I doublecrossed him, he's a liar!"

Val gritted her teeth. You oily rascal! she thought. If only you weren't Walter's father . . .

"Jardin's broke, and you know it!" shouted Walter.

A strange smile fattened Solly's features. "Is that so? Really? Did Jardin tell you that?"

Valerie felt her heart skip a beat. And there was almost a dazed look on Walter's face. What did the man mean? Was it possible that—

"The fact remains," muttered Walter, "you've made millions while your stockholders have been wiped out."

Spaeth shrugged. "They could have sold at peak, too."

"And now you're abandoning the plants!"

"They're useless."

"You could put them back on their feet!"

"Rubbish," said Solly shortly. "You don't know what you're talking about."

"You could put those millions back where they belong—in the plants. You could get Ohippi operating again at a profit when the floods recede!"

Spaeth pounded the desk, swallowing. "Since the Securities Act of 1934 the government is liquidating holding-company structures—"

"And a damned good thing, too!"

"The turn would have come soon, anyway, even without the floods. There's just no point in reinvesting; there's not enough money to be made. You don't know what's happening in this country!"

"You made those filthy millions out of Jardin and the public," growled Walter, "and it's your moral responsibility to save their investments."

"You're a fool," said Solly curtly. "Come back and talk when you've got some sense in your head." And he put on his glasses again and picked up a paper.

Valerie, watching Walter's face, peering around the terrace wall, felt panic. If only she dared go inside—take Walter away before he—

Walter leaned across his father's desk and gently took the paper away and tossed it into the fireplace. Solly sat very still.

"You listen to me," said Walter. "I'll overlook your crookedness, the way you took Jardin, your lie to me about how hard you were hit. But you're going to do one thing."

Solly whispered: "Walter, don't get me excited."

"You're going to save those plants."

"No!"

"It's my hard luck to own your name," said Walter thickly, "so I've got to take the stink out of it. You've ruined the father of the woman I'm going to marry, and you're going to make it up to both of them, do you hear?"

"What's that?" screamed Solly, bouncing out of his chair. "Marry? The Jardin girl?"

"You heard me!"

Val went over to the top step of the terrace and sat down limply in the rain. She felt like crying and laughing at the same time. The darling, darling idiot—proposing like that . . .

"Oh, no, you're not," panted Solly, shaking his finger in Walter's face. "Oh, no, you're not!"

Tell him, Walter, thought Val, hugging her knees ecstatically. Tell the old boa-constrictor!

"You're damned right I'm not!" shouted Walter. "Not after what you've done to her! What do you think I am?"

Val sat open-mouthed. Surprise! Oh, God, you second-hand Don Quixote. She might have known. He'd never do anything the sane and normal way. Val felt like crawling off the terrace into the rock garden and taking refuge under a stone.

In the study there was a curious silence as Solomon Spaeth scurried around his desk again and opened a drawer. He flung a handful of newspaper clippings on the desk.

"Ever since the stocks began to fall," yelled Solly, "you've been drawing these filthy cartoons in that Red rag you work for. Oh, I've been saving 'em! You've drawn me as—"

"Not you—the stinking system you stand for!"

"A rat, a vulture, a wolf, a shark, an octopus!"

"If the shoe pinches—"

Solly hurled the clippings into the fire. "I've given you your way too much! I let you pick your own vocation, childish as it is, let you brand me publicly as a damned menagerie. . . . I warn you, Walter! If you don't stop this nonsense right now—"

Walter said in a strained voice: "Put that money back into the plants."

"If you don't forget this ridiculous idea of marrying a pauper—"

"Next week *East Lynne*."

"You'll marry money!"

"Now you're thinking in terms of dynasties. Have you got the royal sow picked out yet, your Majesty?"

"By God, Walter," shrieked Solly, "if—you—don't—!"

He stopped. Their eyes locked. Val held her breath.

Solly snatched the telephone and shouted a number.

Walter waited grimly.

"Ruhig! Give me Ruhig, you fool!" Spaeth glared at his son. "I'll show *you*. I've had a bellyful of— Ruhig? . . . No, no, stop babbling! Ruhig, you come right over here with a couple of witnesses. . . . For what? To draw up a new will, that's for what!"

He hung up, panting, and adjusted his glasses with shaking fingers.

"I suppose," laughed Walter, "you think you've dealt me the mortal blow."

"You'll never get your hands on my money, damn you!"

Walter walked over to the glass doors in silence. Val got up, holding her throat. But then he went back, passed his father's desk, and opened the study door.

Winni Moon almost fell into his arms; there was a silly smile on her face. Walter brushed by her without a glance, and she disappeared.

Spaeth sat down, breathing heavily through his mouth. Val, on the terrace, felt completely numb.

A few moments later she heard Walter returning. She looked, and saw a valise in one hand and a drawing board in the other.

"I'll call for the rest of my stuff tomorrow," said Walter coldly.

His father did not reply.

"And this isn't the end of it, either," continued Walter in the same bleak way. "That money goes back to the people you took it from, do you understand? I don't know how I'll do it"—he opened the glass doors—"but by God, I'll *do* it."

Solly Spaeth sat still, only his head bobbing a little.

Walter went out onto the terrace. He nudged Val's soaked shoulders with the edge of the drawing board.

"Could you put me up tonight, Val? I can't start looking for a place until tomorrow."

Val looped her arms around his neck and clung. "Walter. Darling. Marry me."

She felt him stiffen. Then he said lightly: "I'd rather live with you in sin."

"Walter—dearest. I'm mad about you. I don't care what your father's done. We'll manage somehow. Don't keep hauling the burdens of the world around on your shoulders. Forget what's happened—"

Walter said in a gay voice: "Come on, let's run for it. You've just about ruined that precious croquignole bob of yours as it is."

Val's arms fell. "But, Walter. I asked you to *marry* me."

"No, Val," he said gently.

"But, Walter!"

"Not yet," said Walter; and there was something in the way he said it that turned the rain down her back to ice-water.

Chapter III

Design for Leaving

A GREAT FLOOD rushed down upon *Sans Souci* in the middle of the night, and Walter and Val and Winni Moon and Jo-Jo and Pink and Rhys Jardin clung shivering to the highest gable of the roof in the darkness, hearing the water gurgle hungrily as it rose.

Suddenly there was a moon, and the man in it bore the ruddy features of Solomon Spaeth. Then the moon went down into the black waters and was drowned, still leering, and the gray day began to dawn; and Val saw nothing but water, water everywhere, and she felt terribly thirsty, and she awoke with her tongue sticking to the roof of her mouth.

A pseudopod of sunlight tried to climb into her bed, but it was too weak; and soon it vanished altogether under the cold swollen clouds of the real day.

Val shivered again and crept out of bed, by habit looking around for Roxie. But Roxie was gone—Roxie and Mrs. Thomson the housekeeper and all the rest; and, as in the dream, Val felt that the end of the world had come.

She was sitting helplessly before her dressing table in the bathroom, looking at the eight-ounce crystal bottle of *Indiscret*, when Rhys knocked, and came in, and said: "What's the exact moment, puss, that bacon becomes cinders?"

Val jumped up. "Pop! You haven't been trying to make breakfast? Don't do another thing. I'll be down in a jiffy."

Rhys held her at arm's length. "I'm glad you're taking it this way, puss."

"*Will* you go downstairs?"

"If Pink goes, we'll have to get a cook."

"Don't need one. I can cook like a fiend."

"You're not going to be slave to a stove, Val. We'll be able to afford it."

Val sniffed. "Yes, until the money's eaten up. How did you make out with the real estate?"

He shrugged. "I got a fair price for the Santa Monica and Malibu places, but this one represents a considerable loss."

"Did that movie man take the yacht?"

"Literally—the pirate!"

Val kissed his brown chin. "Please don't worry, darling; *I'll* show you how to economize! Now get out."

But when she was alone again Val looked a little ill. To give up all these lovely, precious things was like facing the amputation of an arm. Val thought of the auction sale to come, mobs of curious people trampling over everything, handling their most intimate possessions . . . and stopped thinking.

She burned the toast and charred the bacon and overfried the eggs and underboiled the coffee, and Rhys gobbled it all and maintained with a plausibility that almost fooled her that he had never eaten such a delicious breakfast in his life. The only thing that really tasted good was the orange juice, and Pink had prepared that before he left. Walter was right—she *was* useless! And that made her think of Walter, and thinking of Walter made her lips quiver, and after she pushed Rhys out of the departed Mrs. Thomson's no longer spotless kitchen Val sat down and wept into the dish-washing machine. It was a sort of requiem, for Val was positive it was the last time they would ever be able to afford such a wonderful thing.

It was even worse later.

The auction people turned up and completed the details of the task begun a week before—cataloguing the furniture and art-objects. They ran all over the house like oblivious ants.

The telephones rang incessantly—the purchaser of the yacht with a complaint, a multitude of lawyers with questions about this piece of property and that, insistent reporters; Rhys kept dashing from one telephone to another, almost cheerful, followed everywhere by Pink, who looked like a house-dog which has just been kicked.

Valerie was left to her own devices in the midst of this hurly-burly; she had nothing to do but get out of the way of hurrying strangers. A man practically dumped her on the floor retrieving the antique Cape Cod rocker in which her mother had sung her to sleep; Val felt like giving him the one-two Pink had taught her, but the man was away with his loot before she could get her hands on him.

She drifted about, fingering the things she had grown up with—the heavy old silver, those precious little vessels made of old porcelain backed with pewter which Rhys had picked up on his honeymoon in Shanghai, the laces and velvets and lamps, the lovely old hunting prints. She fingered the books and stared at the pictures and spent a difficult moment before the grand old piano on which she had learned to play—never very well!—Chopin and Beethoven and Bach.

And Walter, darn him, didn't even call up *once!*

Val used up two handkerchiefs, artfully, by crying in corners.

But whenever her father bustled into view she said something gay about their new furnished apartment at the *La Salle* which Walter, who had taken rooms there, had recommended. How thrilling it was going to be living there! Yes, agreed Rhys, and different, too. Yes, said Val—that ducky little five-room place—hotel service—built-in radio—even a really fair print or two on the walls. . . . And all the while little frozen fingers crawled down her back.

She found Pink in the dismantled gymnasium, sweating powerfully over a litter of golf-bags, skis, Indian clubs, and other sporting paraphernalia.

"Oh, Pink," she wailed, "is the *La Salle* really so awful?"

"It's all right," said Pink. "Anything you want, you ask Mibs."

"Who's Mibs?"

"Mibs Austin. Girl-friend of mine."

"Why, Pincus!"

Pink blushed. "She's the telephone operator there. She'll take care of you. . . . Just *one* of 'em," he said.

"I'm sure she's sweet. . . . After all," said Val absently, "Walter does live there."

"And me," said Pink, wrapping a pair of skis. "I sort of rented me a 'phone booth there, too."

"Pink, you didn't!"

"I got to live somewhere, don't I?"

"You *darling!*"

"Anyway, who's going to cook? *You* can't. And all Rhys can make is Spanish omelet."

"But, Pink—"

"Besides, he needs his exercises. You can't give him his rubdown, either."

"But, Pink," said Val, troubled, "you know that now—we weren't figuring on extra expenses—"

"Who said anything about pay?" growled Pink. "Get out of here, squirt, and let me work."

"But how are you going to—I mean, have you any plans?"

Pink sighed. "Once I was going to start a health farm and make me some real dough out of these smart guys that run to rubber tires around the middle, but now—"

"Oh, Pink, I'm so sorry about your losing all your money!"

"I got my connections, don't worry. I can always go back to being an expert in the movies—double for some punk with a pretty pan who don't know how to hold a club but's supposed to be champ golfer of the world—that kind of hooey."

"Pink," said Val, "do you mind if I kiss you?"

Pink said gruffly: "Keep 'em for Little Boy Blue; he has 'em with cream. Val, scram!" But his nutbrown face reddened.

Val smiled a little mistily. "You're such a fraud, Pincus darling." And she kissed him without further opposition.

The auctioneer cleared his throat. "And now, ladies and gentlemen, a few announcements before the sale commences. As you know, this is not a forced sale. So the owner, Mr. Rhys Jardin, has exercised his privilege of making last-minute withdrawals. If you will kindly note these changes in your catalogue . . ."

Val, sitting beside her father in the front row of chairs, felt him tremble; she did not dare look at his face. She tried to preserve an air of "Who cares?", but she knew the attempt was a miserable failure.

". . . the sixty-foot yacht *Valerie* has been withdrawn from the auction, having been disposed of in a private sale yesterday. . . ."

Walter was here—sitting in the rear, the coward! The least he might have done was say hello—or isn't it a lovely day for an execution—or something like that. But Walter was acting very strangely. He hadn't even glanced at her before the people took seats, and he was so pale—

". . . your number one-two-six, a collection of four hundred and twenty-two assorted sporting prints. Also your number one-five-two, a collection of small arms. Also your number one-five-three, a collection of medieval arrowheads. Due to the great interest in the sporting-print collection, Mr. Jardin wishes me to announce that it has been donated to the Los Angeles public library association."

There was a little splatter of applause, which quickly died when some one hissed. Val felt like hiding her head. A man's voice behind them whispered: "I understand he's given the arrowheads to the Museum."

"He must be stony broke," whispered a female voice.

"Yeah? Maybe."

"What do you mean?"

"Shh! Isn't that him in front of us?"

Val's hands were tight in her lap. She heard her father expel a long, labored breath. People were such pigs. Vultures! Wheeling over the carrion! Even that Ruhig person had had the unadulterated gall to attend the auction. He was sitting well down front, beaming at all the hostile glances converging on his pudgy cheeks.

"Also withdrawn is number seven-three, a miscellaneous lot of sporting equipment—golf clubs, bags, fencing foils, tennis rackets, *et cetera*."

She felt Rhys stir with surprise. "No, pop," she whispered. "It's not a mistake."

"But I included them—"

"I withdrew them. You're *not* going to be stripped bare!"

He groped for her hand and found it.

"Everything else will be sold on this floor regardless of bid. Everything is in superb condition. The art-objects and antiques have all been expertized and found genuine. Each lot is fully described in your catalogue. . . ."

Come *on*. Get *started*. . . . It was worse, far worse, than Val had imagined it would be. Oh, Walter, why don't you move down here and sit by me and hold my hand, too!

"Lot number one," said the auctioneer in a brisk chant. "Lowestoft china, 1787, with the New York insignia, design female and eagle, two hundred pieces, rare antiquity and historic value, who'll start it with five thousand dollars? Do I hear five thousand on lot number one? Five thousand?"

"Two thousand," called out a cadaverous man with the predatory look of a rabid collector.

The auctioneer groaned. "Gentlemen, gentlemen. A crude imitation of these superb antiques brought seven thousand in a private sale only a few years ago—"

"Twenty-five hundred," said a calm, rather husky voice from the rear.

"Three thousand," droned the cadaverous man.

"Thirty-five," said the husky voice.

"Thirty-five! Who says four thousand?"

"Four thousand," said Mr. Anatole Ruhig.

"Five? Do I hear five?"

"Forty-five hundred," said the husky voice.

"Forty-five bid! Five, anyone? You, sir? Mr. Ruhig? Forty-five once, forty-five twice, forty-five . . . Sold to the gentleman for forty-five hundred dollars."

Robbery! screamed Val silently. The Lowestoft had come down in the family. It was worth many, many thousands. Robber!

She craned with the others to see the husky-voiced thief. He was a spare young man with a close black beard covering his cheeks and chin, and he wore *pince-nez* glasses. Val after one malevolent look turned her eyes front. Robber!

Lot number two went up; Val heard the rattle of auctioneer's patter and bids only dimly. Poor Rhys was so rigid. It was horrible having to be here. . . . When the voices stopped it appeared that the husky one belonging to the bearded young man had again prevailed. The beast—buying poor mother's b-bedroom suite!

Lot number three—history repeated itself. There were murmurs from the floor, and the auctioneer looked enchanted. Mr. Anatole Ruhig, who seemed to have a passion for antiques, looked definitely unenchanted. Black looks were hurled at the unconquerable bidder. . . . Far in the rear, Mr. Walter Spaeth sat slumped in a chair, his right hand absently sketching on the back of an envelope the head of the bearded young man, who was sitting in the row before.

Lot number four. Number five. Six. Seven. . . .

"It's a frame-up," said some one loudly. "He doesn't give any one else a chance!"

"Quiet! Please! Ladies and gentlemen—"

"This isn't an auction, it's a monologue!"

Three people rose and went out in a dudgeon. Mr. Anatole Ruhig was by this time regarding the villain of the piece thoughtfully. The cadaverous one rose and left, too. Val looked around in a panic; Rhys frowned at the greedy one.

Lot number eight, nine, number ten. . . .

"I'm going!"

"So am I!"

The bearded young man coughed. "Common courtesy compels me to warn those who still remain that you may as well leave, too, unless you choose to remain as mere spectators."

"I beg your pardon, sir—" began the auctioneer, who did not like the way things were going.

"I was about to add," the bearded young man called out to the auctioneer, "that we can all save a lot of wear-and-tear on our vocal cords if we face the fact."

"The fact?" said the auctioneer in bewilderment, rapping for order.

"The fact that I humbly intend," continued the young man, getting to his feet and revealing considerable flannel-clad length, "to buy every lot in this auction, regardless of opposition bidding."

And he sat down, smiling pleasantly at his neighbors.

"Who is he?" muttered Rhys Jardin.

"Don't you know?" whispered Val. "I can't understand—"

"This is highly irregular," said the auctioneer, wiping his face.

"In fact," said the young man hoarsely from his seat, "to save time I'm prepared to offer Mr. Jardin a lump sum for the entire catalogue!"

The man behind Val jumped up and shouted: "It's a conspiracy, that's what it is!"

"I see the whole thing," cried some one else.

"Sure! It's a trick of Jardin's!"

"He's pulling a bluff!"

"Run a fake auction to make the public think he's broke, and then plant this man to buy the whole thing back for him!"

"With his own money! *My* money!"

"Ladies and gentlemen! Please—" began Rhys, rising with a pale face.

"Sit down, you crook!" screeched a fat sweaty lady.

"No, no, he's nothing of the sort," protested the young man who had caused all the trouble. But by this time every one was shouting with indignation, and the young man's voice was lost in the noise.

"You take that back!" screamed Val, diving for the fat lady.

"Officer! Clear the room!" roared the auctioneer.

When order was restored Val scrambled over two chairs getting to the bearded young man. "You worm! Now see what you've done!"

"I'll admit," he said ruefully, "I didn't foresee a rising of the masses. . . . Mr. Jardin, I think? Of course my proposal was seriously intended."

"Breaking up auctions," grumbled the auctioneer, scowling; for obviously with such a spirited bidder on the floor he would have realized a greater gross sum and consequently a handsomer commission.

"I decided on impulse, Mr. Jardin, and didn't have time to make an offer in advance of the sale."

"Suppose we talk it over," said Jardin abruptly; and the three men put their heads together. Mr. Anatole Ruhig rose, took his hat and stick, and quietly went away.

The young man was a persuasive bargainer. In five minutes Jardin, completely mystified, had agreed to his offer, the auctioneer sat grumpily down to write out a bill of sale, and the young man dragged a large wallet out of his pocket and laid on the desk such a pile of new thousand-dollar bills that Val felt like yelling "Economic royalist!"

"Just to avoid any embarrassment about checks," he said in his hoarse voice. "And now, if there's nothing else, I have a group of vans waiting outside."

And he went out and returned a moment later with a crew of muscular gentlemen in aprons who looked around, spat on their hands, listened to their employer's whispered instructions, nodded, and went to work without conversation.

"Who is he, anyway?" demanded Pink, glaring at the beard.

"Profiteer," snapped Valerie. That made her think of Walter, so she drifted over casually to where he still sat.

"Hello."

"Hello."

Silence. Then Val said: "Aren't you ashamed of yourself?"

"Yes," said Walter.

What could you do with a creature like that? Val snatched the envelope on which he was sketching out of his hands, crumpled it, threw it at him, and flounced away.

Walter picked up the envelope and absently pocketed it.

"There you are," said a bass voice, and Walter looked up.

"Hullo, Fitz. How are you?"

Fitzgerald sat down, wheezing. "Lousy. I thought California would stop these sinus headaches of mine, but I'll be a monkey's uncle if they aren't worse." Fitz had been in California over ten years and he complained about his sinusitis on the average of a dozen times each day. "Where's the drawing?"

"Which one?"

"Today's—yesterday's—any day's," growled Fitz. "What do you think I'm paying you for—your good looks? With all this Ohippi dirt in the air, you go on a bat!"

"I was busy."

"I haven't had a cartoon for a week—I've had to fill in with old ones. Listen, Walter . . . Say, what's going on here?"

"As if you didn't know, you long-eared jackass."

"I heard outside somebody stampeded the works."

"There's nothing wrong with your nose, either."

Fitz was a bulky Irishman with eyebrows like birds' nests, embedded in which were two very glossy and restless eggs. He was also unpredictable. He left Walter like a genie.

"Hullo, Rhys. Say, Rhys, I'm damned sorry about everything. Would have come over sooner, but I thought you'd rather not jaw about it."

"Good of you." Jardin looked around; the room was getting bare. "You're in at the death, anyway," he said grimly.

"Tough break." Fitz shot sidewise glances at the bearded young man, who was watching his men calmly. "Who's the buyer? Hullo, Valerie."

Just then the young man turned his bearded face toward them, and Fitz's eyebrows almost met his puffy cheeks.

"Hello, Mr. F-Fitzgerald," said Val, watching a commode sail by. There was still a deep scratch in one leg where she had kicked it the time Mrs. Thomson had whacked her for printing "Thomson is a turkey" in yellow crayon on the drawer.

But Fitz ignored her. He lumbered over to the bearded young man and said: "Hey, you're somebody I know."

"Yes?" said the young man politely, and he moved off.

Fitz followed him. "Name's Queen, isn't it? Ellery Queen?"

"Sharp eyes," said the young man. He moved off again.

Fitz seized his arm. "Know who bought your stuff, Rhys?" he bellowed. "Ellery Queen, the master-mind!" But the master-mind was gone with a single twist. Fitz thundered after him, leaving a bewildered group behind. As he passed Walter he snapped: "Report to the office, damn you. Queen! Hey!"

He caught up with Ellery outside the house. Several of the vans had filled up and were gone; the men were packing the last two.

"Now don't be unpleasant," sighed Mr. Queen.

"I'm Fitzgerald of the *Independent*," said Fitz briskly, grasping Ellery's arm like a grappling-iron.

"You're an ass."

"What's that?"

"If I'd wanted my identity known, Mr. Fitzgerald, don't you think I'd have advertised it myself?"

"So that accounts for the phony brush!"

"Not at all. I broke out in a nasty facial rash a few months ago—probably an allergy—and I couldn't shave. Now that the rash is gone I'm so pleased with my appearance I've kept the beard."

"With me it's sinus," said Fitz. "However, it still smells. How about the voice? Got a rash on your vocal cords?"

"Very simple, my dear Watson. The moment I stepped off the train into your balmy California rains I caught a laryngitis, and I've still got it. I should be in bed," said Ellery bitterly.

"Why aren't you? What's the gag? What are you doing in Hollywood? Where'd you get the dough? Are you getting married and furnishing your love-nest?"

"If this is an interview," said Ellery, "I'm a deaf-mute overcome by complete paralysis."

"Say, who do you think you are? Managing editors don't leg it." Fitz eyed him keenly. "It isn't if you say so."

"I say so."

"Now how about satisfying my layman's curiosity?"

"It's no gag. I'm in Hollywood on a writing contract to Magna—God knows I don't know anything about writing for the screen, but they don't seem to care, so I don't either. And no, I'm not being married."

"Wait a minute! Why are you buying the Jardin stuff?"

Ellery watched the last two vans drive off. He moved out from under the porte-cochère into the drizzle and stepped hastily into his rented car.

"Goodbye, Mr. Fitzgerald," he said amiably, waving. "It's been nice seeing you." And he drove off.

The Jardins and Walter and Pink stood in silence in the denuded living-room.

"Are the—are the trunks gone?" asked Val at last in a small voice. "And . . . everything else?"

"Yes, Val."

"Then I don't suppose there's anything—"

"Come on, let's get going," growled Pink, "before I bust out crying."

They marched out of the empty house in a body, close together, like condemned criminals on their way to the wall.

Outside Val picked a rose off a bush and absently pulled it to pieces.

"Well! Here we go," said Rhys in a cheery voice. "It's goodbye to all this. I think we're going to have a lot of fun, puss." He put his arm around her.

"All the common people have fun," said Pink. "Perk up, squirt."

"I'm all right," protested Valerie. "Of course, it's a little strange. . . ."

"Let's go," said Walter in a low voice.

He preceded them down the private drive toward the pillbox at the gate, hands jammed into the pockets of his topcoat. He did not look back at either the Jardin house—or that other.

A crowd was waiting in the road beyond the gate, making mob noises; but the noises stopped as the little procession came toward them. Frank, the day man, his empty left sleeve flapping, hurried from the pillbox toward their two cars, which were parked near the gate.

It became more and more difficult to keep that steady pace. Val felt a little faint. It was like the French Revolution, with the mob of *citoyens* waiting greedily for the victims, and the guillotine looming ahead. . . .

Frank held the door of Jardin's small sedan open—the only car they had kept.

"I'm sorry, Mr. Jardin. I'm awfully sorry," said Frank. In getting into the sedan Rhys had caught his coat on the door-handle, and the camel's-hair fabric just below the right pocket ripped away in a triangular flap.

Pink said: "You tore your coat, Rhys," but Jardin paid no attention, groping blindly for the ignition-key. Valerie crept into the rear seat and slipped far down on her spine; she avoided Walter's eyes as he closed the door behind her. Pink jumped in beside Jardin.

"I'm sorry, sir," said Frank again, in a weepy voice.

"Here." Jardin leaned out and pressed a large bill into the gateman's hand. "Split it with Walewski, Frank. Goodbye."

"Thanks, thanks!" Frank scuttled off to the gate.

"Well," smiled Rhys, starting the car, "what shall it be? A snack at the Troc?"

"It's too expensive there, pop," murmured Val.

"How about Al Levy's? Or the Derby?"

"Better get going," remarked Pink dryly, "before that mob out there starts yipping for blood."

Rhys fell silent and shifted. Val looked back. Walter was getting into his coupé, slowly. Then he stopped and stepped back and looked across the lawns toward the Spaeth house. Far away, Solomon Spaeth stood alone, in motion. He was waving and his mouth was open. Apparently he was shouting something, but his voice did not carry.

Walter's lean jaw hardened. Val saw the taut whitening line. He got into his car without a sign that he had seen.

"It's like the end of a bad dream," thought Val, shivering. "For all of us."

Then they were pushing slowly through the silent crowd and she sat up straight and tried to look as she fancied Marie Antoinette had once looked in a somewhat similar situation.

Chapter IV

—And Sudden Death

AFTER LUNCH Pink said he had to see a dog about a man and Jardin dropped him at the Magna studio on Melrose.

"We may as well face it, Val," said Rhys when Pink had gone. "We'll have to go there some time."

"Why not now?" smiled Val. She felt better, because the sherry had been good and so had the chicken patties. And it was true—they might as well get used to the notion that they were proletarians just as quickly as they could. The only fly in the afternoon's ointment was Walter; he had left them abruptly, with a gloom that was odd even for him.

Val brooded about Walter as Rhys drove up to Santa Monica Boulevard and turned west on the car-tracks. She would definitely have to do something about Walter. Things couldn't go on this way. It was absurd of him to reject her proposal of marriage—absurd and a little dangerous, considering that last quarrel with his father and the look in his eye.

"Here we are," said Rhys bravely.

Val sat up. There they were, one square from Hollywood Boulevard's bedlam—in front of the *La Salle*.

"Parking," said Rhys, "is going to be a problem."

"Yes," said Val. "Won't it?"

Rhys finally found a tiny space near a curb, and he parked and they got out and looked at each other and squared their shoulders and entered the hotel.

"You must be the Jardins," said a small blonde girl with a blonde dip over one eye. "Pink 'phoned me about you. I'm Mibs Austin."

"Hello, Mibs," said Val, looking around at the lobby.

Miss Austin took the earphones off her head and leaned earnestly across the register. "Now don't let *anything* worry you, honey. I just about run this dive. Watch out for Fanny, the woman who'll clean your apartment; she skips corners. The radio needs a new thingumbob—I've told the manager about it. And, Mr. Jardin, the valay here is very high-class."

"I'm sure we'll love it," said Val.

"Oh, and your stuff came, too," said Miss Austin. "I watched myself. They didn't break a single thing."

"Stuff?" echoed Val. "What stuff? Oh, you mean the trunks. Thanks, Mibs; we're terribly grateful for everything."

They took the wheezy elevator to the third floor, rear—it was thirty dollars a month cheaper in the rear—leaving Miss Austin behind to stare. Trunks? Who said anything about trunks?

Rhys pushed the key slowly into the lock of 3-C, and slowly opened the door, and Val slowly went in and said: "Oh!"

The pseudo-modern furniture, the noisy drugget, the questionable prints—all, all had vanished. In their places were the things the moving men had carried out of *Sans Souci* under the mysterious Mr. Queen's vigilant eye only a few hours earlier.

Rhys said: "I'll be double-damned." He dropped his coat onto his own sofa and sank into his own leather chair.

Val flew to the telephone. "Mibs! Who brought our furniture here? I mean, how did—"

"Wasn't it supposed to be? The man said—"

"Mibs! Who?"

"The movers. They just brought the van loads and dumped 'em. We had orders to take out the hotel furniture this morning."

"Oh," said Val. "And who was it ordering *that?*"

"Why, the gentleman in 4-F. What's his name? That Mr. Spaeth. Oh! Miss Jardin, is that the Spaeth—?"

"Hello," said Walter from the doorway, and Val dropped the 'phone to find him grinning at her like some friendly mugwump.

"Walter, you *fiend*," sobbed Valerie, and she ran into her bedroom and slammed the door.

"Was it you?" asked Rhys.

"It's all here," said Walter gruffly. "I mean everything we could cram into five rooms. Here's the warehouse receipt for the rest, Mr. Jardin."

"Warehouse receipt?" said Rhys in an odd voice.

"I've put the leftovers in storage for you."

Rhys laughed a little blankly and rubbed the back of his neck. "I'm afraid what's happened today is getting to be a little too much for my primitive brain. And that Queen fellow—who was he?"

Walter dropped his hat and coat on the sofa and sat down to light a cigaret. "Funny thing. He's just come to the Coast on a movie-writing contract—he's a writer as well as a detective, you know—and an old school chum of mine in New York told him to look me up. So I asked him to act as my proxy. He did it well, don't you think?"

"But, Walter, why?" asked Rhys gently.

Walter scowled at his smoke. "Well . . . I know how stiff your neck is. You wouldn't have accepted money. So to avoid arguments . . ."

Jardin rose and went to the window and pulled up the Venetian blinds and threw the windows open; the drizzle had stopped and the sun was trying to shine again. Traffic noises roared into the room from the rear street below. He closed the windows at once and turned around, a little shrunken.

"It's wonderfully decent of you, Walter. But I simply can't accept it. Besides, Val has told me about your father cutting you out of his will."

"I've some money of my own from my mother's father—plenty more left."

Rhys smiled sadly. "I've deposited the cash, and it's too late today to draw it out again. But, Walter, the first thing—"

"Forget it."

"Walter, you make it awfully difficult."

They eyed each other in silence, at an impasse. Then Val sobbed from the bedroom: "The least you could do, you swine, is come in here and console me!"

Walter rose with a foolish grin.

"I think," murmured Rhys, "I'll go out for some air." He picked up his hat and left as Walter went into the bedroom.

A little later the telephone rang and Val ran into the living-room, fussing with her hair, to answer it. All trace of tears had vanished. Walter followed, looking even more foolish, if that was possible, than before.

"Yes," said Val. "Just a moment. It's for you, Walter. The telephone operator wants to know if you're up here."

Walter said: "Hullo," still looking foolish, then he said nothing at all as he listened to a voice, the foolish look slowly turning grim. Finally he muttered: "I'll be right over," and hung up.

"What's wrong?"

Walter reached for his hat and coat. "My father."

Valerie went cold. "Don't go, Walter."

"I've got to settle this thing once and for all."

She flew to him, clinging. "Please, Walter!"

Walter said gently: "Wait for me. I'll be back in half an hour and we'll drive out Wilshire to the beach for dinner." And he pushed her away and went out.

Val stood still for a long minute. The old half-quenched fears began to burn brightly again. She picked up the coat left on the sofa and took it into the foyer, hardly aware of what she was doing.

But as she was hanging the coat in the foyer closet awareness returned. She held the coat up and looked at it more closely. It was Walter's! He had taken Rhys's by mistake—they were both tan camel's-hair of the same belted style, of a size.

And as she turned the coat over in her hands, something fell out of one of the pockets and struck her foot.

It was an automatic, very black and shiny.

Val recoiled in instant reflex. But after the first horrible moment she pounced on it and thrust it hastily back into Walter's coat, unreasoningly glad her father was not there to see it. Then she took it out of the pocket and, handling it as if it were a scorpion, carried it into her bedroom and buried it in the deepest bureau drawer, her heart pounding.

A gun. Walter. . . . She was so frightened she sat down on her bed to keep from recognizing the weakness in her knees. Walter had never had a gun. Walter hated guns, as he hated war, and poverty, and injustice. . . .

She rose a little later and began to unpack her trunks, trying not to think.

Rhys returned in ten minutes, smoking a cigar and looking calmer. He called out to Val: "Where's everybody?"

"Walter's had a call from his father," said Val in a muffled voice from the bedroom.

"Oh. . . . Where do I put my hat?"

"In the foyer closet, silly. And be sure from now on you hang things up. This is going to be a co-operative joint."

Jardin chuckled, put away his hat, and went into his bedroom to unpack.

By 5.30 their clothes were hung and there was nothing left to be done.

"I wonder where Walter is," said Val worriedly.

"He's only been gone a half-hour."

Val bit her lip. "He said— Let's wait in the lobby."

"It's raining again," said Rhys, at the closet. "Val, this isn't my camel's-hair."

"Walter took it by mistake."

Jardin put on a tweed topcoat and they went downstairs. Val stared at the clock over the desk. It was 5.35.

She said nervously: "I'm going to call him."

"What's the matter with you, puss?" Jardin sat down near the potted palm and picked up a newspaper; but when he saw his photograph on the front page he put the newspaper down.

"Get me Solomon Spaeth's residence," said Val in a low voice. "I think it's Hillcrest 2411."

Mibs plugged in. "Hillcrest 2411. . . . Nice guy, Walter Spaeth. Lovely eyes, Miss Jardin, don't you think so? . . . Hello. Is that you, Mr. Spaeth? . . . This *is* Mr. Walter Spaeth, isn't it? I thought I recognized your voice, Mr. Spaeth. Miss Jardin's calling. . . . Take it right here, Miss Jardin."

Val snatched the telephone. "Walter! Is there any trouble? You said—"

Walter's voice sounded queerly thick in her ear. "Val. I've got no time now. Something awful—something awful—"

Val whispered: "Yes, Walter."

"Wait for me at the *La Salle*," said Walter's funny voice. "I'll be there as soon as I can." His voice sank. "Val. Please. Don't mention this call to any one. No one!"

Val whispered again: "Yes, Walter."

She heard the click; it sounded very loud. She hung up and said slowly: "Let's sit down."

At 6.30 Val said in a hoarse voice: "I can't stand it any longer. He told me not to tell— He's in trouble."

"Now, puss—" said Rhys uncomfortably.

She whispered: "Something awful. That's what Walter said. Something awful."

Her father looked at her with concern. "All right, Val. We'll go over there."

He drove up into the hills at fifty miles an hour. Val hung out of the car. Neither said a word.

The moment they swung into the road outside the gate of *Sans Souci* they knew something was wrong. The crowds which had swarmed there for weeks were gone. In their place were the running lights of many large, official-looking cars. It was growing dark.

"I told you," said Val. "Didn't I tell you? Something—something—"

The gate was opened by a policeman. There was no sign of Walewski, the night gateman, near his pillbox. But there were other policemen.

"What's happened, officer?" demanded Jardin. "I'm Rhys Jardin."

"Oh, are you? Hold it a minute." The policeman said something to another policeman, and the second man went into the pillbox; and they heard the tinkle of Walewski's telephone. Then he came out and jerked his finger.

Jardin shifted into first and drove through the gate. The second policeman hopped onto the running-board and stayed there.

Val, on the edge of her seat, was conscious of a long howling in her ears, as of winds.

At the Spaeth door they were met by three men, all in plain clothes. The three looked them over very coldly. Then one, taller than the rest, with a nose like an arrowhead, said: "Come in, please."

They were surrounded by the three and marched through the house. On the way they passed Winni Moon, who sat on the lowest step of the stairs which led to the upper floor staring with horror at her long feet while Jo-Jo chattered on her shoulder.

Solomon Spaeth's study was packed with men—men with cameras, men with flash-bulbs, men with tape measures, men with bottles and brushes, men with pencils. The air was thick and blue with smoke.

And there was Walter, too. Walter was sitting behind his father's desk, pushed away, with a large man over him. His face was drawn and pale. And there was a crude bandage wound around his head which would have given him a rakish look if not for the ragged blob of blood which had soaked through from his left temple.

"Walter!"

Valerie tried to run to him, but the tall arrow-nosed man put his hand on her arm. Val stopped. She felt really very calm. Everything was so water-clear—the smoke was so blue and the bandage was so red, and Walter's head moved from side to side so very definitely as he looked at her.

From side to side. Like a signal. Or a warning.

The room misted over suddenly and Val leaned back against the nearest wall.

"You're Miss Jardin?" said the tall man abruptly.

"Yes," said Val. "Of course I am." Wasn't that an absurd thing to say?

"My name is Glücke—Inspector, Detective Division."

"How do you do." That was even more absurd, but it was the strangest thing. Her brain had no control over her mouth.

"Were you looking for Mr. Walter Spaeth?"

"Inspector," began Rhys. But the tall man frowned.

"Yes," said Valerie. "Yes, of course. Why not? We had an appointment for dinner. We looked for Mr. Spaeth in his apartment but he wasn't there so we thought perhaps he had gone to his father's house and so we came over—"

"I see," said Glücke, looking elsewhere with his brilliant eyes. It seemed to Val that Walter nodded the least bit in approval. It was all so queer—everything. She mustn't lose her head. It would come out soon. Glücke—that was a funny name. Until she found out what . . .

Jardin said: "That's right, Inspector. My daughter has told you. . . . May I ask what's happened?"

"Don't you know?"

"I beg your pardon."

"Well," said the tall man dryly, "they don't send for the Homicide Detail in petit larceny cases."

He stood still. Then he made a sign, a small sign with no question in it, as a man would make it who is accustomed to be instantly obeyed. A group of men crowded together before the ell beside the fireplace separated.

A dead man was sitting on the floor in the angle of the ell, one foot doubled under him. A reddish, brownish, ragged stab-wound marred the otherwise immaculate appearance of his dove-gray gabardine jacket. As he sat there in the corner he looked like a small fat boy who has been slapped without warning; there was an expression of pure surprise on his unmoving face.

Val yelped and spun about to hide her eyes against her father's coat.

A reporter with a cigaret cached above his ear shouted into the telephone on the desk: "Benny! For the love of Mike, do I get a rewrite or not? Benny! . . . Get this. Act of God. . . . No, you dope, act of God! Solly Spaeth's just been murdered!"

PART TWO

Chapter V

Gentleman or the Tiger?

Rhys's HEART WAS a church bell resounding, a measured gong. Val pressed her head against it.

And suddenly it skipped two whole beats.

Val pushed away and looked up into her father's face. Rhys's lips parted and framed the word: "Coat."

"Coat," said Val, almost aloud.

Coat? Her father's coat!

They stood still in the bedlam. Inspector Glücke was pinching the tip of his sharp nose and regarding Walter with absorption.

Rhys's coat, that Walter had taken from the *La Salle* by mistake. *By mistake.*

Where was it?

Walter sat stonily behind dead Solly's desk. His hat, out of shape and streaked with dirt, lay near his left fist. But he was not wearing a topcoat. The camel's-hair coat, Rhys's coat, was not on the desk. Nor was it on the back of the chair.

Val no longer feared the dead man. She could return his round frog-eyed stare now without flinching. The coat. Rhys's coat. That was the important thing. That was the thing to be afraid of.

Casually, carefully, they both made a slow survey of the study. The coat was nowhere to be seen.

Where was it? What had Walter done with it?

The Jardins drew closer together by an inch. It was necessary to concentrate. Concentrate, thought Val desperately. This is murder. Keep your mind clear. Listen.

"Get that reporter out of here," Inspector Glücke was saying. "How you boys fixed?"

The Surveyor was already gone. The photographers, other men, dribbled off. The room began to enlarge. Then a gaunt young man swinging a black bag came in.

"There's the stiff, Doc. See what you get."

The coroner's physician knelt by Solly's squatting remains and detectives made a wall about the dead man and the living.

"Take their prints, Pappas."

"Prints?" said Rhys slowly. "Isn't that a bit premature, Inspector?"

"Any objection, Mr. Jardin?" rapped Glücke.

Rhys was silent.

The fingerprint man approached with his paraphernalia. Inspector Glücke pulled the tip of his nose again, almost in embarrassment. "It's only routine. We've got the whole room mugged. There are a lot of prints. Weeding 'em out, you understand."

"You'll probably find some of mine about," said Rhys.

"Yes?"

"I was in this room only this morning."

"Is that so? I'll take your statement in a minute. Go ahead, Pappas."

Pappas went ahead. Val watched her father's strong fingers deposit inky designs on paper. Then the man took her hands. His touch was cold, like the body of a fish; her flesh crawled. But all the while Val was saying over and over inside: Where is pop's coat? What has Walter done with pop's coat?

The coroner's physician broke through the living wall and looked around. He made for the desk.

"Anything the matter?" asked the Inspector.

The doctor spoke into the telephone. "Don't know exactly. Something queer. C.I. Lab, please. . . . Chemist. . . . Bronson? Polk. I've got something for you on the Spaeth murder. . . . Yes, as fast as you can."

He hurried back to the ell and the wall solidified about him once more.

"I think," began Glücke, when a husky voice said from the corridor doorway: "Hello."

Everybody turned around.

The bearded young man stood there looking grave; and also looking hard at the scene about him, as if he expected to be kicked out at once and wanted to memorize as many of the details as he could before his eviction.

For an instant Val's heart jumped. The bearded man was wearing a camel's-hair coat. But then she saw that there was no triangular tear below the right pocket.

"Here he is," said a detective beside him. "The guy that bought up all Jardin's stuff this afternoon."

"Out," said Glücke. "Later."

"Why not now?" asked the young man in a wheedling tone. And he advanced a step into the room, gazing intently at the bandage around Walter's head.

Glücke looked at him sharply. Walter said in a monotone: "Queen's all right, Inspector. He merely acted as my proxy in buying up the Jardin furnishings today. He can't possibly have anything to do with this."

"No?" said Glücke.

"Fact, he's a detective." Walter looked away. "Go on, Queen; I'll see you later."

"Queen, Queen," frowned the Inspector. "Any relation to Dick Queen of the New York police department?"

"His son," said Ellery, beaming. "Now may I stay?"

Inspector Glücke grunted. "I've heard about you. Who killed Solly Spaeth, Queen? You could save us a lot of trouble."

"Oh," said Ellery, and he made a face. "Sorry, Walter."

Walter said again: "It's all right, Queen. Go ahead. I'll see you later."

"He cost *me* eight hundred bucks," said Glücke. "All right, Phil, take this down. Let's go, Spaeth—for the book."

Val made fists. Oh, Walter, what happened?

Walter looked at Mr. Queen, and Mr. Queen looked away. Nevertheless, he did not stir.

"My father telephoned me at the *La Salle* about five o'clock," said Walter in a dreary tone. "He said he was home and wanted to see me."

"What for?"

"He didn't say. I drove up here in my car. I had a flat down the hill a way and that's why I took a half-hour for a ten-minute trip. Well, I parked and began to climb out. As I was stepping off backwards, something hit me on the side of the head. That's all."

"We found Spaeth unconscious just after we got here," explained the Inspector. "On the sidewalk near his car. So you never even got into the grounds?"

"I told you what happened," said Walter.

"Why'd you park around the corner from the entrance? Why didn't you drive right in?"

"The mob. I thought I'd stand a better chance of getting inside unrecognized if I went on foot. My name is Spaeth, Inspector." His lips twisted.

"There wasn't any mob. There wasn't a soul near the place late this afternoon, the night man says."

"I didn't know that."

"So you were bumped on the head around five-thirty?"

"Just about."

"Any idea who hit you?"

"The assault came as a complete surprise."

"Who do you think it was?"

"How the hell should I know?" growled Walter.

But it was remarkable how he kept looking at Val. Just looking, with the oddest wooden expression.

Val scuffed Solly's silky antique Indian rug with her toe. Walter didn't enter the grounds. He was attacked before he entered the grounds. That's what he said. That's what he wanted the police to believe.

But Val knew he *had* entered the grounds. She had spoken to him on the telephone, and he had been on the other end of the wire—Hillcrest 2411, his father's number. It had been Walter, all right; Val knew his voice better than—better than—

Walter had been in the house.

She studied the intricate floral design. In the house. In the house, for all she knew right at this very extension in the study, where his father had been murdered. . . .

He was lying. Lying.

"Come here without a coat, Spaeth?" asked Glücke absently, eying him.

"What?" mumbled Walter. "Oh, coat? No, I didn't wear a coat, Inspector."

And he glanced at Val again, and at her father, with that mute wooden expression.

I know! thought Val. He's hidden it. He hid the coat. He didn't want to get her father mixed up in it. Walter, you darling. . . . But then she thought: He's lying. He lied about one thing. Now he was lying about another. Where was the coat? *What had he done with that coat?*

Rhys's hand lightly brushed her skirt. She glanced up at him; his brown face was a little pale, but his lips were compressed and he shook his head ever so lightly.

"May I sit down?" asked Val in a tight voice. "Or is this part of the celebrated third degree?"

Glücke waved an indifferent arm and Val felt a chair pushed against her. She looked around; it was that Mr. Queen, smiling sympathy and encouragement. But there was something else in his smile, something that made Valerie sit down suddenly and stare straight ahead at the fireplace. He had noticed. His eyes, which were like washed gray grapes, had noticed the interplay. They would have to be careful. Watch your step. Don't make a mistake. It's like being trapped in a cave by wild animals; the least false move . . . Valerie had never been trapped in a cave by wild animals, but she thought she knew now how it must feel.

"Any clue to Spaeth's assailant, Inspector?" asked Mr. Queen amiably.

"We found one of those rustic benches up against the willow fence inside the grounds near the spot where Spaeth's car was parked. A little scraped mud on it, so it was stepped on. That looks as if whoever sloughed Spaeth came over the fence from inside. Laying for you, hey, Spaeth?"

Walter looked blank.

"He wouldn't know, of course," said Mr. Queen.

"I guess not," said Inspector Glücke. "McMahon, get Ruhig and Walewski in here."

Anatole Ruhig came in gingerly, with small arched steps, like a man walking on coals of fire. Val restrained a mad impulse to giggle; it was the first time she had ever noticed his shoes, which had built-up heels, like a cowboy's. She wondered if he wore corsets; no, she was sure of it. Oh, the coat, the coat!

As for Mr. Ruhig, his bright little eyes made one panorama of the room, resting for the merest instant on Mr. Queen, and then retreated behind their fat lids.

"Too bad, Walter," he said quickly. "Too bad, Mr. Jardin. Too bad, Miss Jardin." Then he added: "Too bad," in a generally regretful tone, and stopped, blinking.

You left out Solly. . . . Val bit her lip, for there was Walewski. Frightened. Every one was frightened. Walewski was an old round-backed man with a crown of grimy white hair which stood on end. He came into the room sidewise, like a crab, his red eyes sloshing about in his old face.

"We're taking this down now," said the Inspector, speaking to Ruhig but looking at Walewski.

The lawyer covered a courtroom cough. "Too, too bad. . . . I drove up to the entrance at a few minutes past six. Walewski opened the gate. I told him I had an appointment with Mr. Spaeth—"

"Did you have?"

"My dear Inspector! Well, Walewski telephoned the house from his booth—"

"Hearsay. Walewski, what did you do?"

The old man trembled. "I don't know nothing. I didn't do nothing. I didn't see nothing."

"Did you or didn't you 'phone the Spaeth house?"

"Yes, sir! I did. But there wasn't no answer. Not a bit of an answer."

"May I ask a stupid question?" said Ellery. "Where were the servants? In all this magnificence," he said mildly, "I assume servants."

"Please," said the Inspector. "Well, if you must know, Spaeth fired 'em last week, the whole bunch. Now—"

"Really? That's strange. Now why should he have done that?"

"Oh, for God's sake." The Inspector looked annoyed. "He received several threatening letters right after Ohippi went busted and complained to the police and a district dick spotted the writer in thirty minutes—Spaeth's own chauffeur, a Filipino named Quital. Spaeth was so scared he fired everybody working here and he hasn't had a servant since."

"The wages of high finance," murmured Ellery. "And where is Mr. Quital?"

"In jail," grinned Glücke, "where he's been for a week. So what happened when you got no answer, Walewski?"

"I told Mr. Ruhig. I said Mr. Spaeth must be home, I said," mumbled the old man. "He ain't been out for a week, I said. So I let Mr. Ruhig through."

"Spaeth called me this morning," said Ruhig helpfully. "Told me to come. So when he didn't answer I knew something must be wrong. Therefore I insisted Walewski accompany me. Which the good man did. And we found— Well, I notified the police at once, as you know."

"He was settin' down on the floor," said Walewski, wiping the spittle from his blue lips with the back of his right hand, "he was settin' and he looked so awful surprised for a minute I thought—"

"By the way, Mr. Ruhig," said Ellery with an apologetic glance at Glücke, "what was the nature of your appointment today?"

"Another change of will," said Ruhig precisely.

"Another?" Glücke glared from Ellery to Ruhig.

"Why, yes. Last Monday—yes, exactly a week ago—Mr. Spaeth had me come over with two of my assistants and I wrote out a new will, which he signed in the presence of my assistants. This will," Ruhig coughed again, "disinherited the son, Mr. Walter Spaeth."

"Oh, is that so?" said the Inspector alertly. "Did you know your old man cut you off, Spaeth?"

"We quarreled," said Walter in a weary voice, "about his abandonment of the Ohippi plants. He telephoned Ruhig while I was still here."

"Who benefited by the will he made a week ago?"

"Mr. Spaeth's protégée, Miss Moon. He left her his entire estate."

"Then what about this will business today?"

Ruhig breathed on his shiny little fingernails. "I can't say. All I know is that he wanted to change the will again. But by the time I got here," he shrugged, "it was too late."

"Then Spaeth's estate is legally Winni's," frowned the Inspector. "Nice for her that he was bumped before he could change his mind again. . . . Well, Jerry?"

"This man Frank, the day gateman. He's here."

"Bring him in."

The one-armed gateman shuffled in, his narrow features twitching nervously. "I'm Atherton F-Frank. I don't know a single blessed thing—"

"What time did you go off duty?" demanded the Inspector.

"Six o'clock he went," put in Walewski eagerly. "That's when I come on. So you see I couldn't know nothing—"

"Six o'clock," mumbled Frank. He kept looking at his misshapen shoes.

Walter was sitting forward now, staring at the one-armed man. Val noticed that Walter's hands were twitching, too, almost in rhythm with Frank's features.

Afraid, thought Val bitterly. So you're a coward, for all your brave talk. You're afraid Frank saw you. He *must* have seen you. Unless you went over the wall. Went over the wall. . . . Val closed her eyes. Now why should Walter have gone over the wall?

"Listen, Frank," said Glücke genially. "You're an important figure in this case. You know that, don't you?"

"Me?" said Frank, raising his eyes.

"Sure! There's only one entrance to *Sans Souci*, and you were on guard there all day. You were, weren't you?"

"Oh, sure I was. Certainly I was!"

"So you know every one who went in and came out this afternoon. Why, Frank old man, you might be able to clear this case up right now."

"Yeah?" said Frank.

"Think, now. Who went in and out?"

Frank drew his sparse brows together. "Well, let's see now. Let's see. Not Mr. Spaeth. I mean—him." He jerked a dirty thumb toward the ell where the coroner's physician was working. "I didn't see him all day. . . . You mean after the auction?" he asked suddenly.

"Yes."

"After the auction. . . . Well, the crowd petered out. So did the cops. A little while later Miss Moon drove out. She came back about four o'clock. Shopping, I guess; I saw packages. Her aunt, Mrs. Moon, is away in Palm Springs. Did she come back yet?"

"No," said Glücke, as man to man.

Frank scraped his lean chin. "Let's see. I guess that's all. . . . No, it ain't!" Then he stopped and looked very frightened. "I mean, I guess—"

"You mean you guess what, Frank?" asked Glücke gently.

Frank darted a hungry glance at the door. Walter sat up straighter. Val held her breath. Yes? Yes?

"Well," said Frank.

"Some one else came this afternoon!" snapped the Inspector, mask off. "Who was it?" Frank backed away. "Do you want to be held as a material witness?" thundered the Inspector.

"N-no, sir," chattered Frank. "It was him. Around half-past five. Half-past five."

"Who?"

Frank pointed a knobby forefinger at Rhys Jardin.

"No!" cried Val, springing out of the chair.

"Why, the man's simply mad," said Rhys in an astonished voice.

"Hold your horses," said Glücke. "You'll get your chance to talk. Are you sure it was Mr. Jardin, Frank?"

The gateman twisted a button on his coat. "I—I was sitting in the booth reading the paper . . . yes, I was reading the paper. I heard footsteps on the driveway, so I jumped up and ran out and there was Mr. Jardin walking up the drive toward the Spaeth house—"

"Hold it, hold it," said Glücke. "Did you leave the gate unlocked?"

"No, sir, I did not. But Mr. Jardin had a key to the gate—everybody in San Susie's got one—so that's how he must have got in."

"Was there a car outside?"

"I didn't see no car."

"This is a joke," began Rhys, very pale. The Inspector stared at him, and he stopped.

"By the way," drawled Ellery, "if you came out of your warren, Frank, and saw a man walking *away* from you, how can you be so sure it was Mr. Jardin?"

"It was Mr. Jardin, all right," said Frank stubbornly.

Glücke looked irritated. "Can't you give me a better identification? Didn't you see his face at all?"

"I won't *stand* here—" cried Val.

"You'll stand here and like it. Well, Frank?"

"I didn't see his face," mumbled Frank, "but I knew it was him, anyway. From his coat. From his camel's-hair coat, I knew him."

Walter very slowly slumped back against his chair. Val flashed a glance of pure hatred at him and Rhys sat down, jaws working, in the chair she had vacated.

"Oh, come," said Ellery with amusement. "Every second man in Hollywood wears a camel's-hair coat. I wear one myself. Are you sure it wasn't I you saw, Frank? I'm about the same size as Mr. Jardin."

Anger shone from Frank's eyes. "But your coat ain't torn," he said shortly.

"Oh," said Ellery; and the Inspector's face cleared.

"Torn, Frank?"

"Yes, sir. This afternoon, when Mr. Jardin left after the auction, his coat caught on the handle of his car and tore. Tore a flap right down under the pocket on the right side, a big piece."

"I thought you said," remarked Ellery, "that you saw only the man's back."

"He was walkin' slow," muttered Frank, with a malevolent glance at his tormentor, "like he was thinking about something, and he had his hands behind his back under his coat. So that was how I saw the pocket and the rip. So I knew it was Mr. Jardin."

"Q.E.D.," murmured Ellery.

"I even called out to him, I said: 'Mr. Jardin!' in a real loud voice, but he didn't turn around, he just kept walking. So I went back to the booth. Like he didn't hear me."

"I absolutely must insist—" began Val in an outraged voice, when a man came in and held up something.

"Look what I found," he said.

It was a long narrow strip of tan camel's-hair cloth tapering to a point.

"Where?" demanded Glücke, seizing it.

"On top of one of those stakes on the fence. Right over the spot where the bench was pushed."

The Inspector examined it with avid fingers. "It was torn already," he mumbled, "and when he climbed over the fence the torn piece caught and ripped clean away the length of the coat from the pocket down." He turned and eyed Rhys Jardin deliberately. "Mr. Jardin," he said in a cold voice, "where's your camel's-hair coat?"

The room was drowned in a silence that crushed the eardrums.

By all the rules of romantic justice Walter should have jumped up and explained what had happened, how he had taken Rhys's coat by mistake, how— But Walter sat there like a tailor's dummy.

Val saw why with acid clarity. He could not acknowledge having worn her father's coat without admitting he had lied. He had said he never entered the grounds at all. Yet it was clear now that he *had* entered the grounds with the key he also carried, that Frank had mistaken him for Rhys Jardin because of the torn coat, and that he had gone up to his father's house and . . . And what? *And what?*

Was that—Val said it to herself in a chill small voice—was that why Walter had lied? Was that why he had hidden or thrown away the telltale coat? Was that why he sat there so dumbly now, letting the police think Rhys had gone into Spaeth's house about the time Spaeth had been skewered?

Val knew without looking at him that her father was thinking exactly the same thoughts. It would be so easy for him to say—or for her—to Glücke: "Now look here, Inspector. Walter Spaeth took that coat by mistake this afternoon, and Frank mistook him for me. I haven't even got the coat. I don't know where it is. Ask Walter."

But Rhys said nothing. Nothing. And as for Val, she could not have spoken now if her life depended on one little word. Oh, Walter, why don't you explain, explain?

"So you won't talk, eh?" said the Inspector with a wry grin. "All right, Mr. Jardin. Frank, did any one but Miss Moon and Mr. Jardin enter *Sans Souci* after the auction today?"

"N-no, sir," said Frank, half out of the room.

"Walewski, when you took over from Frank, was Mr. Ruhig the only one you admitted—and then you both found the dead body of Spaeth?"

"That is the truth, sir!"

Glücke waved his hand at the gatemen with a certain grim weariness. "Let 'em go home," he said to a detective. "And get that Moon woman in here."

The thought began to pound in Val's ears now. The more she tried to shut it out the stronger it came back.

Walter, did you murder your father?

Chapter VI

Thrust and Parry

WINNI MOON had been weeping. She paused at the door in an attitude of pure despair, a black handkerchief to her eyes. Fast work, thought Mr. Ellery Queen admiringly; in mourning already!

It was Mr. Queen's habit to observe what generally escaped other people; and so he now detected a metamorphosis in Attorney Anatole Ruhig. Mr. Ruhig, who had been taking everything in with admirably restrained impersonality, suddenly with Miss Moon's tragic entrance became excited. He ran over to her and held her hand, whispering a sympathetic word—to her quickly suppressed astonishment, Mr. Queen also noticed; he ran back and pulled up a chair and took her shoulders—he had to reach up for them—and steered her gallantly to the chair, like an orthodox Chinese son. Then he took up his stand behind her, the picture of a man who means to defend beauty from contumely and calumny with his last breath.

Mr. Queen wondered ungraciously if Mr. Ruhig meant, now that Solly Spaeth had gone to join the choir invisible, to assume responsibility for Miss Moon's nebulous career.

Miss Moon began to weep afresh.

"All right, all right," said Inspector Glücke hastily. "This won't take long, and then you can cry your eyes out. Who killed Solly Spaeth?"

"I know who'd *wike* to!" cried Winni, lowering her handkerchief just long enough to glare at Rhys Jardin.

"You mean Mr. Jardin?"

At this new peril Val felt her skin tighten. That insufferable clothes-horse! But she was too steeped in more pointed miseries to do more than try to electrocute the sobbing beauty with her glance.

"Yes, I do," said Miss Moon, turning off the tears at once. "He did nothing but quawwel and quawwel with poor, darling Solly. Nothing! Last week—"

"Winni," said Walter in a choked voice, "shut that trap of yours—"

Now, thought Val, *now* he was talking!

"Your own father, too!" said Winni viciously. "I will not, Walter Spaeth. You know it's twue. Last Monday morning he and Solly had a *tewwible* battle about the floods and the factowies and ev'wything! And only this morning he came over again and thweatened him—"

"Threatened him," repeated Glücke with satisfaction.

"He said he ought to be *hanged*, he said! He said he ought to be cut up in little *pieces*, he said! He said he was a *cwook!* Then I didn't hear any more—"

"The woman was obviously listening at the door," said Rhys, his brown cheeks slowly turning crimson. "It's true, Inspector, that we had a quarrel. But—"

"It's also true," said the Inspector dryly, "that you quarreled because Spaeth caused the collapse of Ohippi."

"Yes," said Rhys, "and ruined me, but—"

"You lost everything, eh, Mr. Jardin?"

"Yes!"

"Solly made you a poor man, while he cleaned up a fortune."

"But he ruined thousands of others, too!"

"What's this ape trying to do, Rhys," yelled a familiar voice, "hang this killing on you?" And Pink bounced into the room, his red hair bristling.

"Oh, Pink," cried Val, and she fell into his arms.

"It's all right," said Rhys wearily to a panting detective. "He's a friend of mine."

"Listen, you," snarled Pink to Glücke, "I don't give a damn if you eat bombs for breakfast. If you say Rhys Jardin pulled this job you're just a dumb, one-cylinder, cock-eyed heel of a liar!" He patted Val's hair clumsily.

"I would have come sooner, only I didn't know till I got here. Mibs told me where you went."

"All right, Pink," said Rhys in a low voice, and Pink stopped talking. Inspector Glücke regarded him speculatively for a moment. Then he shrugged.

"You're a sportsman, aren't you, Mr. Jardin?"

"If you'll make your point—"

"You've won golf championships, you're a crack pistol shot, you beat this man Pink in the California Archery Tournament last spring, you've raced your yacht against the best. You see, I know all about you."

"Please come to the point," said Rhys coldly.

"You fence, too, don't you?"

"Yes."

Glücke nodded. "It isn't generally known, but you're also one of the best amateur swordsmen in the United States."

"I see," said Rhys slowly.

"He even twied to teach Solly!" shrilled Miss Moon. "He was always twying to make him exercise!"

The Inspector beamed. "Is that so?" he said. And he turned and pointedly looked up at the puce-colored wall above the fireplace.

A collection of old weapons hung there, decorative pieces—two silver-butted dueling-pistols, a long-barreled eighteenth-century rifle, an arquebus, a group of poniards and dirks and stilettos, a dozen or more time-blackened swords: rapiers, sabers, scimitars, jeweled court swords.

High above the rest lay a heavy channeled blade such as were carried by mounted men-at-arms in the thirteenth century. It lay on the wall obliquely. A thin light streak in the puce paint crossed the medieval piece in the opposite direction, as if at one time another sword had hung there.

"It's gone!" squealed Winni, pointing at the streak.

"Uh-huh," said Glücke.

"But it was there at only four o'cwock!"

"Was that when you saw Spaeth last, Miss Moon?"

"Yes, when I came back fwom shopping. . . ."

"Is it polite to inquire," murmured Mr. Queen, "what the beauteous Miss Moon was doing between four o'clock and the time Mr. Spaeth was murdered?"

"I was in my boudoir twying on new gowns!" cried Miss Moon indignantly. "How dare you!"

"And you didn't hear anything, Miss Moon?"

Ruhig glared. "If you'll tell me what right—"

"Listen, Queen," snarled Glücke. "You'll do me a big favor if you keep your nose out of this!"

"Sorry," said Ellery.

Glücke blew a little, shaking himself. "Now," he said in a calmer tone. "Let's see what that sticker was." He went to the fireplace with the air of a stage magician about to demonstrate his most baffling trick, and set a chair before it. He stepped up on the chair, craning, and loudly read the legend on a small bronze plaque set into the wall below the streak in the paint. "'Cup-hilted Italian rapier, seventeenth century,'" he announced. And he stepped down with an air of triumph.

No one said anything. Rhys sat quietly, his muscular hands resting without movement on his knees.

"The fact is, ladies and gentlemen," said the Inspector, facing them, "that Solly Spaeth was stabbed to death and an Italian rapier is missing. We've pretty well established that it's gone. It isn't in this house and so far my men haven't found it on the grounds. Stab-wound—sword missing. It looks as if Solly's killer took the rapier down from the wall, backed Solly into that corner there, gave him the works, and beat it with the sword."

In the stillness Mr. Queen's voice could clearly be heard. "That," he complained, "is precisely the trouble."

Inspector Glücke slowly passed his hand over his face. "Listen, you—" Then he turned on Jardin and snapped: "You weren't by any chance trying to teach Solly a few tricks with that sword this afternoon, were you?"

Rhys smiled his brief, charming smile; and Val was so proud of him she could have wept. And Walter, the beast, just sat there!

"Figure it out for yourself," said the Inspector amiably. "Frank says you were the only outsider to enter *Sans Souci* late this afternoon. We have the missing piece from your coat in substantiation, and we'll have the coat very shortly, I promise you."

"I'd like to see it myself," said Rhys lightly.

"You've admitted to at least two quarrels with the dead man, one only this morning."

"You left something out," said Jardin with another smile. "After our tiff in this room this morning, I saw Spaeth again. He walked over to my house— I mean the one I vacated today." Val started; she had not known that. "We had another little chat in my gymnasium, as a result of which I walked out on him."

"Thanks for the tip," said Glücke. "You'd better begin to think about keeping such facts to yourself. Got that, Phil? Well, you had a nice strong motive, too, Jardin—he ruined you and, from what I hear, he wouldn't do what you asked, which was to put his profits back in Ohippi and salvage the business. And last, you're a swordsman, and a sword was used to polish him off. You may even have got him off guard by pretending to show him some kind of fencing maneuver."

"And what was he doing," said Rhys, "parrying with his arm?"

They looked across the room at each other. "Tell you what, Jardin," said the Inspector. "You sign a full confession, and I'll get Van Every to guarantee a lesser plea. We could easily make it self-defense."

"How nice," smiled Rhys. "At that, I could almost take my chances with a jury, couldn't I? They'd probably thank me for having rid the world of a menace."

"Sure, sure! What do you say, Mr. Jardin?"

"Pop—" cried Val.

"I say I'm innocent, and you may go to hell."

Glücke eyed him again. "Suit yourself," he said shortly, and turned away. "Oh, Doc. You finished?"

Dr. Polk was visible now, rolling down the sleeves of his coat. The detectives were strung out around the room; and Val, looking out of one eye, saw that the heap in the corner near the fireplace was covered with newspapers.

"Pending autopsy findings," said Dr. Polk abruptly, "you may assume the following: The wound was made by a sharp-pointed instrument, the point at surface terminus of entry being roughly a half-inch wide. It just missed the heart. I should say it was made by the missing rapier, although I'd like to see the thing before making a positive statement."

"How about the time of death?" demanded Glücke.

"Checks with the watch."

Mr. Ellery Queen stirred restlessly. "The watch?"

"Yes," said the Inspector with impatience, "his arm banged against the wall as he sank to a sitting position in that corner, because we found his wrist-watch smashed and the pieces of shattered crystal on the floor beside him. The hands stopped at 5.32."

Rhys Jardin chuckled. Even Glücke seemed surprised at the pure happiness of it. It bothered him, for he kept eying Jardin sidewise.

But Valerie knew why her father laughed. A wave of such relief swept over her that for an instant she tasted salt in her mouth. She felt like laughing hysterically herself.

Solomon Spaeth had been murdered at 5.32. But at 5.32 Rhys Jardin had been entering the self-service elevator at the La Salle with Val, on his way from their apartment to the lobby downstairs to wait for Walter.

5.32. . . . Val's inner laughter died in a burst of panic. Rhys was all right now—nothing could touch him now, with an alibi like that. But Walter. . . . It was different in Walter's case. At 5.35, with Rhys in full view of Mibs Austin in the La Salle lobby, Val had telephoned Walter and Mibs had spoken to Walter and even recognized his voice.

If Inspector Glücke should question the little blonde telephone operator, if she should tell him about that call, where Walter was, fix the time . . .

Val caught a blurry glimpse of Walter's face as he turned away to stare out the side windows into the blackness of the grounds. There was such agony on his face that she was ready to forgive anything just to be able to take him in her arms.

He had remembered the call, too.

Walter, she cried silently, why did you lie? What are you hiding?

A tall man bustled in lugging a kit.

"Bronson!" said Dr. Polk, the wrinkles on his forehead vanishing. "Glad you're here. I want you to have a look at this."

The Bureau Chemist hurried with the coroner's physician to the ell beside the fireplace. The detectives closed in.

"Go on home," said the Inspector brusquely to Walter. "I'll talk to you again in the morning. Unless you want to stay here?"

"No," said Walter, without moving. "No, I don't."

Then he very quickly got out of the chair and groped for his hat and made for the corridor door, stumbling once over a fold in the rug. He did not look at the Jardins.

"You can go, too—Miss Moon, Mr. Ruhig. And you, there, whatever your name is."

But Pink said: "How about taking a jump in the lake?"

"Can't—can't my father and I leave, Inspector?" asked Val, staring at the doorway through which Walter had fled. Then she closed her eyes, because Mr. Ruhig was piloting the exquisite Miss Moon deferentially through the same doorway, somehow spoiling the view.

"No," said Glücke curtly.

Val sighed.

The Inspector strode over to the group near the fireplace and Mr. Queen, unable to restrain his curiosity, hurried after him and peered over his shoulder to see what was going on.

Solly Spaeth was uncovered again. The Chemist knelt over him intently studying the brownish mouth of the stab-wound. Twice he lowered his long nose to the wound and sniffed. Then he slowly shook his head, looking up at Dr. Polk.

"It's molasses, all right," he said in a wondering voice.

"That's what I thought," replied Dr. Polk. "And it's not only at the mouth of the wound, but seems to coat the sides for some way in."

"Molasses," repeated the Inspector. "That's a hell of a note. . . . Say, stop shoving me!"

Ellery rubbed his bearded cheeks. "Sorry, Inspector. Molasses? That's exciting. Did I hear you say, Doctor, the point just missed the heart?"

The doctor regarded him with curiosity. "Yes."

Ellery shouldered Glücke out of the way and pushed through the group until he was standing directly over the dead man.

"Was the stab-wound serious enough to have caused death?"

"He's dead, isn't he?" growled the Inspector.

"Undoubtedly, but I've a faint notion things aren't quite as they seem. Well, Doctor?"

"Hard to say," frowned the coroner's physician. "There wasn't much bleeding. Given an hour or so, he probably would have bled to death—that is, without medical attention. It certainly is queer."

"So queer," said Ellery, "that I'd have Mr. Bronson analyze the molasses."

"What for?" snarled Glücke.

"The molasses and its physical disposition in the wound," murmured Ellery, "suggest that it must have been smeared on the point of the blade that made the wound. Why smear molasses on a cutting edge? Well, molasses is viscid. It could be construed as the 'binder' of another substance."

"I see, I see," muttered Dr. Polk. "I hadn't thought of it just that way, but certain indications—"

"What is this?" demanded the Inspector irritably.

"It's only a suggestion, respectful and all that," said Ellery with a placative smile, "but if you'll have Mr. Bronson test that molasses for poison—some poisonous substance that comes in solid rather than liquid form—I think you'll find something."

"Poison," muttered Glücke. He stroked his nose and glanced fretfully at Ellery out of the corner of his eye.

The Chemist carefully scraped a scum of molasses from the wound and deposited it on a slide. Then he opened his kit and went to work.

Molasses. Poison. Val closed her eyes.

"Potassium cyanide," announced Bronson at last. "I'm pretty sure. Of course, I'll have to get back to my lab before I can make it official."

"Cyanide!" exclaimed Dr. Polk. "That's it."

"Comes in powder form, of course—white crystals," said the Chemist. "It was thoroughly mixed into the molasses—a good deal of it, I'd say."

"Paralyzes certain enzymes essential to cellular metabolism," muttered the doctor. "Death within a few minutes. He'd have died before complete absorption, so the tissues through which the blade passed ought to reveal traces of the poison in autopsy." He shrugged at the dead man's gray-fringed bald spot. "Well, it was a painless death, anyway."

"Isn't any one going to congratulate me?" sighed Ellery.

Glücke glared at him and turned his back. "We'll have to get busy on that cyanide," he snapped.

"I'm afraid you won't be very successful," said Bronson, packing his kit. "It's too common—used commercially in dozens of ways—film manufacture, cleaning fluids, God knows what else. And you can buy it at any drug store."

"Nuts," said the Inspector, plainly disappointed. "Well, all right, Doc, get him out of here. Let's have your report the first thing in the morning, if you can make it."

Ellery backed off as the detectives milled about and Dr. Polk superintended the removal of the body. He seemed worried about something.

"Oh, Dr. Polk," he said as the coroner's physician was about to follow Solly's remains through the doorway. "Does the condition of the body confirm the time of death as indicated by the wrist-watch?"

"Yes. The man died of cyanide poisoning, not of stabbing, and within a very short time after the blow. From the local conditions in this room and the state of the corpse, calculating roughly, he figures to have passed out around 5.30. And the watch says 5.32, which ought to be close enough for any one. . . . Smart work, Mr. Queen. Detective, eh?"

"Enough of one," sighed Ellery, "to detect traces of hostility in the official atmosphere. Thanks, Doctor." And he watched Dr. Polk and Bronson depart.

"May we go now, Inspector?" asked Val again, examining the freckle on her left ring-finger. There had been something unpleasant about Solly's quiet contour under the morgue sheet, and there was a vast desire within her to go somewhere and consume sherry frappés.

"When I'm through with you. Here," roared Glücke, "what are you doing now, damn it?"

Ellery had dragged a chair over to the fireplace and was engaged in standing on it while he made mysterious movements with his body. He looked, in fact, as if he meant to emulate Dracula and climb the fireplace wall.

"I'm trying," he said in a friendly tone, stepping down, "to find the answer to three questions."

"Listen, Queen—"

"First, why did your murderer employ that particular sword for his crime?"

"How the hell should I know? Look—"

"Why," continued Ellery, going close to the fireplace and raising his arm to the wall above it, "why didn't he take down this needle-bladed French dueling-sword?"

"I don't know," barked Glücke, "and what's more I don't give a damn. If you'll be kind enough—"

Ellery pointed. "See where that dustmark on the wall is—where the missing rapier hung. Now, no man could possibly have reached that rapier without standing on something. But why haul a chair over here to reach a cup-hilted Italian rapier of the seventeenth century when you have merely to stand on the floor and extend your arm and reach a nineteenth-century French dueling-sword which will do the work equally well?"

"That's an odd note in an unpremeditated crime," said Rhys Jardin, interested despite his preoccupation.

"Who asked you?" said the Inspector, exasperated.

"And who says it was unpremeditated?" said Ellery. "No, indeed, Mr. Jardin. Either the murderer took down the rapier and coated its tip with his molasses-and-cyanide concoction just before the crime; or else he had coated the point *some time before the crime*—prepared it, as it were. But in either event he had to mix the poison with the molasses before he killed Solly, which certainly rules out a crime of impulse."

The tips of Inspector Glücke's ears were burning by this time. "I'm not in the habit of running a forum," he said in a strangled voice, "on a case I'm investigating. So you'll all be good enough—"

"You smell from herring," said Pink, who had formed a violent dislike for Glücke.

"And then," said Ellery hastily, as if he might not be able to get it out before the catastrophe, "there's my second question. Which is: Why did he smear the sword with poison at all?"

"Why?" shouted Glücke, throwing up his arms. "What the hell is this— Quiz Night? To make sure he died, that's why!"

"Isn't that a little like the man who wears not only suspenders but a belt, too?" asked Ellery earnestly. "Don't you think you could kill a man very efficiently with merely a naked blade?"

Inspector Glücke had long since regretted his weakness in allowing the bearded young man to linger on the scene. The man was clearly one of those smart-aleck, theorizing amateurs whom Glücke had always despised. Moreover, he asked embarrassing questions before subordinates. Also, by sheer luck he might stumble on a solution and thus rob a hard-working professional of the prey, the publicity, and the departmental rewards of sensational success. All in all, a nuisance.

So the Inspector blew up. "I'm not going to have my investigation disrupted by a guy who writes *detective* stories!" he bellowed. "Your old man has to take it because he's got to live with you, but you're three thousand miles away from Centre Street, and I don't give a hoot in hell *what* you think about my case!"

Ellery stiffened. "Am I to understand that you'd like me better at a distance?"

"Understand your left tonsil! Scram!"

"I never thought I'd live to see the day," murmured Ellery, nettled but trying to preserve an Emily Postian *savoir faire*. "That's Hollywood hospitality for you!"

"Mac, get this nosey lunatic out of here!"

"Desist, Mac. I'll go quietly." Ellery went over to the Jardins and said in a loud voice: "The man's an idiot. And he's quite capable of having you in clink before you're an hour older, Mr. Jardin."

"Sorry you're leaving us," sighed Rhys. "I must say I prefer your company to his."

"Thanks for the first kind word Hollywood has bestowed. Miss Jardin, goodbye. . . . I'd advise both of you to talk as economically as possible. In fact, get a lawyer."

Inspector Glücke glared at him. Ellery went sedately to the door.

"Not, however," he added with a grimace, "Mr. Ruhig."

"Will you get out, you pest?" roared the Inspector.

"Oh, yes, Inspector," said Ellery. "I almost forgot to mention my third point. You remember I said there were three bothersome questions?" Mac approached grimly. "Now, now, Mac, I must warn you that I've just taken up ju-jutsu. The point is this, Inspector: Granting that your eccentric criminal stood on a chair to get a sword for which he had a much handier substitute, granting that he smeared the sword with poison when a good jab by a child could have dispatched Mr. Spaeth just as efficiently—granting all that, why in heaven's name did he take the sword away with him after the crime?"

Inspector Glücke was speechless.

"There," said Mr. Queen, waving adieu to the Jardins, "is something for that ossified organ you call your brain to wrestle with." And he went away.

Chapter VII

The Camel That Walked Like a Man

VAL COULD SCARCELY drag one foot after the other by the time they got back to the *La Salle*. Even the yearning for sherry frappés had dissipated. It was agony just to think.

"I'll tuck pop in, flop onto my bed, and *sleep*," she thought. "Maybe when I wake up tomorrow morning I'll find it never really happened at all."

After that strange Mr. Queen's departure Inspector Glücke had cleared the study and gone to work on Rhys with a grim enthusiasm that made Val vibrant with pure loathing. Pink became rebellious at the tone of the man's questions and was ejected by two of the larger detectives. They found him later, sitting on the sidewalk near the gate in the midst of a large section of the Los Angeles press, chewing his fingernails and growling at their pleas like a bear.

Even in the excitement of their own miraculous escape from that rapacious crew—Pink said they had the morals of a bulldog, and that they wouldn't have escaped at all if not for the greater lure still within the Spaeth house—Val's stomach lay six inches lower than its usual position merely recalling Glücke's baffled pertinacity.

Throughout the ordeal Rhys had maintained a calm that served only to infuriate the policeman. He was monosyllabic about most things; and about the important things he would not talk at all. The Inspector went over and over the ground: The Ohippi partnership, the holding companies, the collapse of the securities, Rhys's quarrels with Spaeth, his movements during the afternoon—oh, thought Val, to have been able to tell the truth!—his familiarity with the house, with swords. . . .

Her father could have cleared himself at any moment of the interminable, ferocious, accusing inquisition by merely stating his alibi. But he did not; and Val, sick and exhausted, knew why he did not. It was because of Walter. Walter. . . . She hardly heard Glücke's diatribe. Through the verbal storm leered Walter's face with its incomprehensible expression.

Rhys was deliberately allowing himself to be involved in a nasty crime because Walter meant something to her—Walter, who had always been so boyish and naïve and blunt and was now so frighteningly drawn into himself.

"I'll fix some eats," said Pink. "You must be starved."

"I couldn't eat now," said Valerie faintly.

Rhys said: "Pink's right," but he was abstracted.

"I laid in a raft of stuff from the market this afternoon," said Pink gruffly, "on my way back from the studio. If I left it to you capitalists—"

"Oh, Pink," sighed Val, "I don't know what we'd do without you."

"You'd probably die of hunger," said Pink.

Mibs Austin's place at the switchboard was occupied by the night clerk, a fat old man in a high collar; so they went through the lobby without stopping and took the cranky elevator upstairs. Val stumbled along the red carpeting of the corridor behind the two men. She wondered dully why Rhys and Pink, who had unlocked the door of 3-C, stood so still in the foyer.

But when she reached the apartment door and looked in she saw why.

Walter was sitting in the living-room on the edge of the armchair. He was sitting in a strangely stiff attitude, his dirty hat crushed on the back of his bandaged head and his eyes like two steamy pieces of glass.

They looked at Walter, and Walter looked back at them, and his head wagged from side to side as if it were too heavy for his neck.

"Stinko," said Pink, wrinkling his nose, and he went to the windows and threw them wide open.

Rhys carefully closed the corridor door and Val advanced two steps into the living-room and faltered: "Well?"

Walter's tongue licked at his lips and out of his mouth came a mumble of sounds that conveyed nothing.

"Walter. How did you get in?"

Walter placed his right forefinger to his lips. "Shh. Sh—snuck up. Sh—swiped housh-key. Deshk."

He glared up at her from the armchair in an indignant, almost a resentful, way.

"Well?" said Val again. "Haven't you anything to say to me, Walter?"

" 'Bout what? Tell me that. 'Bout what?"

"You know very well," said Val in a low voice. "About—this afternoon."

"What 'bout 'sh afternoon?" said Walter belligerently, trying to rise. "You lemme 'lone!"

Val closed her eyes. "Walter, I'm giving you your chance. You must tell me. What happened today? Where's pop's coat? Why did you—" she opened her eyes and cried—"why did you lie, Walter?"

Walter's lower lip crept forward. "None o' y'r bus'ness."

Val ran over to him and slapped his cheek twice. The marks of her fingers surged up in red streaks through the pallor beneath the stubble.

He gasped and tried to rise again, but collapsed in the armchair.

"You drunken bum," said Val passionately. "Coward. Weakling. I never want to see you again!"

Val ran into her bedroom and slammed the door.

"I'll handle him," said Pink. Rhys quietly sat down on the sofa without removing his coat. He just sat there drumming on the cushion.

Pink hauled Walter out of the chair by his collar, half strangling him. Walter sawed the air feebly, trying to fight. But Pink pushed his arm aside and dragged him into Rhys's bathroom. Rhys heard the shower start hissing and a medley of gaspy human sounds.

After a while Walter lurched back into the living-room, the shoulders of his plaid jacket drenched, his bandaged head and face dripping. Pink tossed a towel at him and went into the kitchen while Walter dropped into the arm-chair and tried with ineffectual swipes of the towel to dry himself.

Rhys drummed softly.

"Put this away, big shot," said Pink, returning with a tall glass. "What a man!"

Walter groped for the glass and gulped down the tomato juice and tabasco, shuddering.

Pink lit a cigaret and went back to the kitchen. Rhys heard the clangor of clashing pans.

"I think," said Rhys politely, "I'll go down to the drug store for a cigar. Excuse me, Walter."

Walter said nothing. After a moment Rhys rose and left the apartment.

Alone, Walter inhaled deeply and stared fog-eyed at the dusty tips of his suède sport shoes. Pink was slamming dish-closet doors in the kitchen, growling to himself.

Walter got up and tottered to Val's door. "Val," he said thickly.

There was no answer. Walter turned the knob and went in, shutting the door behind him.

Val lay, still in her hat and coat, on the bed, staring numbly at the Van Gogh on the opposite wall. Her hat, a toque, was pushed over one eye rakishly; but she did not look rakish. She looked cold and remote.

"Val."

"Go away."

Walter reached the bed by a heroic lunge and dropped. His eyes, bleared and shadowed, peered anxiously at her through a haze. He put his right hand clumsily on her slim thigh. "Know 'm drunk. Coul'n' help it, Val. Val, don' talk t'me 'at way. I love you, Val."

"Take your hand off me," said Val.

"I love you, Val."

"You've a fine way of showing it," said Val drearily.

Walter sat up with a jerk, fumbling to button his collar. "Aw right, Val. Aw right, I'll get out. 'M drunk."

He rose with an effort and stumbled toward the door.

Val lay still, watching his weaving progress across the room. . . . She jumped off the bed and flew past him to the door, setting her back against it. Walter stopped, blinking at her.

"Not yet," she said.

" 'M drunk."

"You're going to answer me. Why did you lie to Inspector Glücke? You know you were in that house at 5.35 this afternoon!"

"Yes," muttered Walter, trying to stand still.

"Walter." Val's heart sank. Her hands, spread against the door, gripped it harder. She could almost see past him through the rubbed aspen-crotch panel of her Hepplewhite bureau, where a certain automatic pistol lay hidden under a layer of chemises. She whispered: "Walter, I must know. Did you kill your father?"

Walter stopped rocking. His lower lip crept forward again in a curiously stubborn way. At the same time his bloodshot eyes shifted, almost with cunning.

"Lemme go," he muttered.

"Did you, Walter?" whispered Valerie.

"Goodbye," said Walter in a surprisingly sharp tone. He put his arm out to push her aside.

"If you didn't," cried Val, running to the bureau and digging into the drawer, "why were you carrying this?" She held up the automatic.

Walter said contemptuously: "Going through m' pockets, huh? Gimme!" Val let him take the pistol away from her. He looked at it, snorted, and dropped it into his pocket. "Threat—threat'ning letters. Dozen of 'm. Son of man who ruined thousan's. So I bought a gun." His shoulders hunched and he said painfully: "I love you, but min' y'r own bus'ness."

This wasn't Walter. Not the Walter she had known for so many years. Or was it? Wasn't it always a crisis like this that showed a man up in the true ugliness of his naked self?

"You let that Inspector think my father went to *Sans Souci* this afternoon," she cried. "Why didn't you tell him that you were the one Frank saw sneaking up the drive—that you were wearing pop's coat?"

Walter blinked several times, as if he was trying to peer through a week's collection of Hollywood's evening mists.

"Gotta trus' me," he mumbled. "Don' ask questions, Val. No questions."

"Trust you! Why?" flared Val. "After the way you've acted? Haven't I the right to ask questions when your silence implicates my own father?" But then she grasped his sodden lapels and laid her head on his chest. "Oh, Walter," she sobbed, "I don't care what you've done, if you'll only be honest about it. Trust you! Why don't you trust me?"

It was queer how humble he could be one moment and how hard, how frozen hard, the next. It was as if certain questions congealed him instantly, making him impervious to warmth or reason or appeal.

He said, trying to control his lax tongue: "Mus'n' fin' out I was in father's house. If you tell 'm . . . Don' you dare tell 'm, Val, y'un'erstan' me?"

Then it was true. Pop! goes the weasel.

Val pushed away from him. Faith was all right in its place, which was usually in drippy novels. But a human being couldn't accept certain things on faith. Appearances might be deceptive in some cases, but usually they were photographic images of the truth. Real life had a way of being harshly unsubtle.

"Apparently," she said in a remote voice, "the fact that Glücke suspects my father of murder, that one word from you would clear him, doesn't mean a thing to you. Not when your own skin is in danger."

Walter was quite steady now. He opened his mouth to say something, but then he closed it without having uttered any sound whatever.

"So you'll please me," said Val, "by getting out."

He did not know, could not know, that Rhys had an alibi for the time the crime was committed.

"Aw right," said Walter in a low tone.

And now he would never know—not through her! If she told him, how easy it would be for him to crawl out, to say he had known about her father's alibi all the time, that Rhys had never been in real danger and that it was necessary to him to protect himself. When he sobered up, he might even invent some plausible story to account for his damning actions. Walter was persuasive when he wanted to be. And in her heart Val knew she could not trust herself.

So she said again, bitterly: "Your secret, whatever it is, is safe with me. Will you get out?"

Walter plucked violently at his collar, as if he found its grip intolerable. Then he wrenched the door open, stumbled across the living-room, and zigzagged out of the apartment, leaving his hat behind.

Val picked the hat up from the living-room floor and threw it after him into the corridor.

That was that.

"Pink, I'm starved," she called out, going into the kitchen. "What's on the menu?" But then her eyes narrowed and she said: "Pink, what is that?"

Pink was guiltily hiding something in his trouser pocket.

"Nothing," he said quickly. And he got up from the chair in the breakfast nook and made for the gas range, where several pots and pans were bubbling. "Is crackpot gone?"

"Pink, what are you hiding?" Val went over to him and pulled him around. "Show me that."

"It's nothing, I tell you!" said Pink, but his tone carried no conviction.

Val thrust her hand into his pocket. He tried to dodge, but she was too quick for him. Her hand emerged with a flat, small, hard-covered pamphlet.

"Why, it's a bankbook," she said. "Oh, Pink, I'm dreadfully sorry—" But then she stopped and little schools of goose-pimples rose to the surface of her flesh.

The name on the bankbook was Rhys Jardin.

"Pop deposited Walter's money," she began, and stopped again. "But this is a different bank, Pink. The Pacific Coastal. Spaeth's bank."

"Don't bother your head with it, squirt," muttered Pink; he began to stir beans with a ladle as if his life depended on their not sticking to the pan. "Don't look inside."

Val looked inside. There was one deposit listed, no withdrawals. But the size of the deposit made her eyes widen. It was impossible. It must be a mistake. But there were the figures.

$5,000,000.00.

She seized Pink's arm. "Where did you get this? Pink, tell me the truth!"

"It was this morning," said Pink, avoiding her eyes, "in the gym over at San Susie. I was packing the golf-bags. I found it hidden under a box of tees in a pocket of that old morocco bag of Rhys's."

"Oh," said Val, and she sat down in the breakfast nook and shaded her eyes with her hand. "Pink," she went on in a muffled voice, "you mustn't— well, don't say anything about this. It will look as if . . . as if what those people said about pop not really being broke is true."

Pink stirred with absorption. "I didn't know what the hell to do, Val. There was a chance some nosey, thievin' expressman might find it. I had to take that stuff Rhys gave away over to the Museum, so—well, I just put it in my pocket."

"Thanks, Pink," said Val from stiff lips. And neither said another word as the gas hissed and Pink stirred and Val sat at the table and looked at the bankbook.

The front door banged. Rhys called out: "Val?"

Neither made a sound.

Rhys came into the kitchen smoking a cigar and shaking his wet hat. "It's raining again. Pink, that smells wonderful." He stopped, struck by the silence.

The yellow-covered bankbook lay on the maple table in full view. He glanced at it, frowning, and then studied the two stony faces.

"Is it Walter?" he asked in a puzzled way. "Wouldn't he talk?"

"No," said Val.

Rhys sat down in his soggy coat, puffing at the cigar. "Don't go off half-cocked, puss. I watched him. He's concealing something, it's true, but I have the feeling it isn't what you think. Walter's always been closemouthed— after all, he never had the benefits of a normal upbringing—he'll always depend on himself, keep things to himself. I've studied him, and I'm sure he's incapable of viciousness. I couldn't be wrong in him, darling—"

"I wonder," said Val tonelessly, "if I could be wrong in *you*."

"Val." He examined her with surprise. "Pink, what's the matter? Something's happened."

"Don't you know?" muttered Pink.

"I know," he said a trifle sharply, "that you're both being childishly mysterious."

Val pushed the bankbook an inch toward her father with the very tip of one fingernail.

He did not pick it up at once. He continued to look at Val and Pink. As he looked, a curious pallor spread under the brown of his flat cheeks.

He took the bankbook slowly, stared at his name on the cover, opened the book, stared at the figures, stared at the date, the cashier's initials. . . .

"What is this?" he asked in a flat voice. "Well, don't look at me like sticks! Pink, you know something about this. Where did it come from?"

"It's none of my business," shrugged Pink.

"I said where did it come from?"

Pink flung the ladle down. "Damn it, what do you want from me, Rhys? Don't put on an act for my benefit! It's a bankbook with a five-million-dollar deposit, and I found it this morning in your morocco golf-bag!"

Rhys rose, holding the bankbook in one hand and the fuming cigar in the other, and began to walk up and down the narrow kitchen. The brown wrinkles on his forehead deepened with each step. The paleness was gone now; the brownness had an angry red tinge.

"I never thought," said Pink bitterly, "you'd be that kind of a heel, Rhys." Rhys stopped pacing.

"I can't help being angry," he said quietly, "although I don't blame either of you. It looks damned bad. But I'm not going to deny this more than once." Pink paled. "I know nothing about this deposit. I've never had an account at Spaeth's bank. This five million dollars isn't mine. Do you understand, both of you?"

Val felt a great shame. She was so tired she could have cried for sheer exhaustion. As for Pink, his pallor, too, vanished in a blush that reached to the roots of his red hair; and he leaned against the gas range biting his fingernails.

Rhys opened the book and glanced again at the stamped date of deposit. "Pink, where was I last Wednesday?" he asked in the same quiet tone.

Pink mumbled: "We ran the yacht down to Long Beach to see that guy who decided not to buy."

"We left at six in the morning and didn't get back to town until after dark—isn't that so?"

"Yeah."

Rhys tossed the bankbook on the table. "Look at the date of that deposit. It was made last Wednesday."

Pink snatched the book. He said nothing at all. But the blush turned burning scarlet. He kept looking at the date as if he could not believe his eyes. Or perhaps because it was the only way he could cover his embarrassment.

"Pop," said Val, resting her head on her arms, "I'm sorry."

There was a long silence.

"It could only have been Spaeth," said Rhys at last. "He visited me in the gym this morning, as I told Glücke. He must have slipped it into the golf-bag when my back was turned."

"But why, for the love of Mike?" cried Pink. "My God, who gives away five million bucks? I *had* to think—"

"I see it now." Rhys flung his cigar into the drip-pan. "I've never told you before, but when things began to go wrong with Ohippi I came to my senses and had a confidential accountant and investigator look into things."

"I *had* to think—" said Pink again, miserably.

Rhys began to pace again, nibbling at his lips. "I found that friend Solly, who up to a certain point had been perfectly coached by Ruhig, had gone on his own in one connection—and slipped very badly. He issued a prospectus for the further sale of stock in which he falsified the cash position of the companies. He had to make the stocks look sound, and he did—with false figures."

Val raised her head. "He was always a thief," she said wearily.

"Suppose he did?" demanded Pink.

"Using the mails to defraud is a serious offense, Pink," said Rhys. "It was the penitentiary for Spaeth if the government ever found him out."

"Why didn't you hold him up?" asked Pink hoarsely.

"At the time there was still a chance to recoup. But later, when the floods ruined the plants completely, I threatened to send him to prison if he didn't rehabilitate them." Rhys shrugged. "He made a counter-threat. He said he had something on me which would so blacken my reputation and so completely destroy public confidence that nothing would ever save the plants. This deposit must have been the answer, making it look as if I'd cleaned up, too, and was a hypocrite besides."

"But five million dollars!"

"If paying out ten percent of fifty millions in profits would keep him out of jail," said Rhys dryly, "he was a good enough business man to pay it out."

"The dirty rat," said Pink passionately. "Mixin' people up! Why the hell do they have to look for people who bump off rats like that? It ain't fair!"

"It puts me on a spot," sighed Rhys. "I can't keep the money, of course— it isn't mine. Yet if I used it to start a fund to salvage Ohippi, nobody'd believe the story. The auction, my being broke. . . . I can't keep it, and I can't give it away. I'll have to think about it."

"Yeah," muttered Pink, "we'll have to think about it."

Rhys went heavily out of the kitchen into the foyer, taking off his coat. Pink turned blindly to the range as something began to burn. Val pulled herself to her feet and said: "I don't think I'm hungry any more, Pink. I'm going to—"

Rhys said, strangling: "Good God."

Val was paralyzed by the horror in her father's voice.

"Pop!" She found her voice and her strength at the same instant. She almost capsized Pink trying to get to the foyer first.

Rhys had turned on the overhead light. The door of the foyer closet was open. He was squatting on his heels and staring into the closet.

On the floor of the closet lay two objects.

One was a long cup-handled rapier with a red-brown stain on its point. The other, crushed into a ball, was a tan camel's-hair topcoat.

Chapter VIII

The Glory That Was Rhys

"Your coat," said Val. "Your *coat*. The—the sword!"

Rhys grasped the rapier by the hilt and brought it out of the closet, turning it this way and that in his two shaking hands, as if he were too stupefied to do more than simply look at it.

It was the Italian rapier which had hung on Solly Spaeth's wall; there was no question about that. And if there had been a question, the stained point would have answered it.

"Don't handle it. Don't touch it," whispered Val. "It's—it's poisoned. You might get a scratch!"

"Put it away," mumbled Pink. "No. Here. Gimme that. We've got to get rid of it. Rhys, for God's sake!"

But Rhys kept holding the rapier and examining it as a child might examine a strange toy.

Pink reached in and snared the coat. He shook it out; it was Rhys's coat; there was no question about that, either. For from the right pocket to the hem a narrow strip of camel's-hair cloth was missing, leaving a long gap.

"Oh, look," said Val faintly, pointing.

The breast of the coat was smeared with a dirty brown liquid which had dried and crusted.

Fresh red blood turns dirty brown under the corrupting touch of the outer world.

Rhys got to his feet, still clutching the sword; his red-streaked eyeballs were bulging slightly. "How in the name of red devils did these things get here?" he croaked.

Before Val's eyes rose the unlovely vision of Mr. Walter Spaeth, grimy, slack with drink, and pugnacious, sitting on the edge of the armchair in their living-room when they had reached the apartment after Glücke's inquisition. He had stolen the house-key from the desk downstairs; he had confessed that. He had let himself in. He had—he had—

"Walter," said Val in a still small voice. "Walter!"

Rhys rubbed his left eye with his left hand and said painfully: "Don't jump to conclusions. Don't jump, Val. It's— We'll have to sit down and think this out, too." He stood there holding the rapier, holding it because he did not seem to know what to do with it.

Pink said in an agonized treble: "Well, don't be a dope, Rhys, for God's sake. You can't just stand here with that thing. It's too risky. It's too—"

Just then some one pounded on the foyer door.

It was all so unreasonable, so theatrical, so ridiculous, that Val could only laugh. She began to laugh softly—more a titter than a laugh, and the laugh swelled until it was no longer soft and until tears rolled down her cheeks.

The buzzer rang. It rang again. Then some one leaned on it and forgot to remove his elbow.

Pink gripped Val's jaws in his iron fingers and shook her head furiously, as he might have shaken a recalcitrant puppy.

"Shut up!" he growled. "Rhys, if you don't put those things away—hide 'em. . . . In a minute!" he yelled at the door.

"Come on, open it," said a clipped voice from the other side. It was Inspector Glücke's voice.

Inspector Glücke!

"Pop, p-pop," stammered Val, looking around wildly. "Throw it out the window. Anywhere. They can't find it here. They'll— They mustn't—"

Sanity came back to her father's face. "Here," he said slowly. "This won't do."

"Open up, Jardin, or I'll have the door broken down."

"Oh, for God's sake, pop," whispered Valerie.

"No." Rhys shook his head with maddening slowness. "There's something inevitable about this. He's been tipped off. He's bound to find it. No, Val. Pink, open that door."

"Rhys, don't be a cluck!"

"Let them in, Pink."

Val shrank back. With a scowl of baffled fury Pink stepped over to the door. Rhys picked up the coat and carried it and the rapier into the living-room and laid them down on the sofa.

Men boiled in, headed by Glücke.

"Search warrant," he said curtly, waving a paper. He pushed past Val and stopped in the living-room archway.

"Is this what you want?" asked Rhys tiredly, and he sat down in the arm-chair and clasped his hands.

The Inspector pounced on the objects on the sofa. His three companions blocked the corridor door.

"Ah," said Glücke; he said nothing more.

"I suppose," murmured Rhys, "it won't do any good to assure you we just found those things on the floor of our foyer closet?"

The Inspector did not reply. He raised the coat and examined it curiously.

Then he turned and made a sign to his men, and two of them came forward with cotton bags and wrapping paper and began to stow away the coat and rapier, handling them as if they had been made of Ming porcelain.

"He's telling it to you straight," said Pink desperately. "Listen, Inspector, don't be a jackass. Listen to him, to me. We just found it—the three of us. He's being framed, Rhys is! You can't—"

"Well," said Glücke lightly, "there may be something in that, Mr. Pincus."

"Pink," muttered Pink.

"Western Union in downtown L.A. 'phoned a wire to Headquarters—anonymous—telling us to search this apartment right away. The telegram was 'phoned in to the Western Union office and we haven't been able to trace the call. So maybe all this is phony at that."

But he did not sound as if he meant what he said. He sounded as if he were merely trying to make agreeable conversation.

He nodded at his men, and two of them followed him out of the apartment. The third man set his back against the open door and just stood there, shifting from one foot to another from time to time, as if he were tired.

Val cowered against her supporting wall in the foyer, unable to move, to think. Rhys got up from the chair in the living-room and turned to go into his bathroom.

"Hold it," said the detective at the door.

Rhys looked at him. Then he sat down again.

"Hullo," said a voice from the corridor.

Pink went to the door and dug his elbow into the detective's abdomen, and the detective shoved his arm angrily away. Pink saw the two other detectives leaning against the balustrade of the emergency stairway which led down to the lobby. They were no more than five feet from the door, and they returned his glance without expression.

"Hullo," said the same voice.

Pink looked through him. It was Fitzgerald, of the *Independent*.

The detective at the door said: "Nobody in."

Fitz's eyes under their bird's-nest brows roved, took in Val before him, Rhys sitting motionless in the living-room. "I see they're keeping the death-watch here. Come on, Mac, this is the press."

"You heard him," said Pink, stepping up to him.

"I got a tip from some one I know at Headquarters," said Fitz. "It seems— Come on, mugg, out of the way."

The detective at the door closed his eyes. Pink said: "Get the hell out of here."

"Rhys," called Fitz. "I want to talk to you. This is serious, Rhys. Maybe I can give you a right steer—"

Pink put his broad palm on Fitz's chest and pushed, stepping through the doorway.

The man at the door did not open his eyes, and the two detectives across the hall did not move.

"Do you want a sock in the teeth," said Pink, "or will you go nice and quiet, like a good little man?"

Fitz laughed. He lashed out with his fist. Pink side-stepped and brought his left up in a short arc. Fitz grunted. He had been drinking, and droplets of alcoholic saliva sprayed Pink's face.

"Here, stop that," said one of the men leaning against the balustrade. "Do your brawlin' outside."

Pink grabbed Fitz by the seat of his pants and ran him down the stairs.

Val trudged into the living-room and sat down on the floor by Rhys's knee. She rested her cheek on it.

"I don't think we have much time," said Rhys in a very low voice. "Val, listen to me."

"Yes, pop."

"Glücke will be back soon." He glanced cautiously at the detective in the doorway. "Maybe in five minutes, maybe in an hour. But whenever he comes back it will be with a warrant for my arrest."

Val shivered. "But he can't do that. You didn't do it. You couldn't have done it. You were right here—"

"Val, he'll hear you." Rhys bent low over her face, speaking into her ear. "That's what I wanted to talk to you about. The police—no one—must find out about that alibi."

Val felt her forehead. It was hard to think.

"I'm in no danger," whispered Rhys. "The Austin girl will testify at any time that I was in the *La Salle* lobby when Spaeth was murdered. Don't you see?"

"Yes," said Val. "Yes."

"And there's at least one vital reason why I must let Glücke arrest me, puss. . . . No, don't make any noise, Val. That detective mustn't hear."

Val sank back, her face drawn, her eyes screwed up. They felt hot, brittle, sore; they felt like her brain.

"I don't— I can't seem to—"

"I think," whispered Rhys, "I'm in danger." He held her shoulders down. "I've just thought the whole thing through. Some one planted the sword and coat in our closet tonight, tipped the Inspector off that they were here. *Whoever did that is framing me for the murder.*"

"No," said Val. "No!"

"It must be, Val; it's the only reasonable explanation. So that means some one not only hated Spaeth, but hates me, too. He killed Spaeth and is taking his revenge on me by framing me for the crime."

"No!"

"Yes, puss. And if I produce my alibi now and the police clear me, what happens? The maniac who's doing all this, seeing that his frame-up has failed, will be more determined than ever to have his revenge. If he finds he can't get the law to kill me, he's liable to kill me himself. He committed murder once; why shouldn't he do it again?"

There's something behind this, thought Val. It's all mixed up and there's something behind it.

"I'll be safe in jail, safer than here. Don't you see?" Something. . . . "And there's another reason." Rhys paused. "It's Walter. If I produce my alibi now, Val, he'll be directly involved in the crime." Walter. That's it. That's what's behind it. Walter. "The police will learn he was wearing my coat. He certainly had a motive of revenge against his father—being cut out of the will. They'll find out he was in that house at the time of the crime. They're bound to find it out—*if* we let them know about my alibi."

"But how—?"

"Don't you see, puss?" he said patiently. "My alibi depends on the testimony of this Austin girl. She can place me in this lobby at the time of the crime, all right; but she also knows that it's tied up with that telephone call to the Spaeth house. *And she spoke directly to Walter.* The merest questioning on the part of the police would bring that out. We've got to see that she isn't questioned."

"No," said Val. "I won't let you do it. You've got to tell them about the alibi. You mustn't sacrifice yourself—"

"Walter didn't kill his father, Val. He isn't the killing kind. I'm protected, but he's not. Don't you see?"

I see. I see that I'm smaller than the smallest wiggly thing that crawls. And you're so big, so warm, so dear.

Rhys tilted her face. "Val, you've got to trust my judgment in this."

Val shivered again. Her tongue seemed tied up in knots.

"There's one other thing. I think I've got a clue that may lead somewhere. While I'm in jail covering Walter up you'll have to follow that clue, Val. Do you understand? We've got to find out who killed Spaeth before we talk!" Val turned her head slowly. "Listen, Val. Only this morning—"

"All right, Jardin," said Inspector Glücke.

Val jumped up. Rhys sat still.

The three detectives were in the room with Glücke, one of them looking hard at Pink, who was marking time, restlessly and unconsciously, with his feet, as if to inaudible music.

"So soon?" said Rhys with a faint smile.

"I had my fingerprint man waiting downstairs," said the Inspector. "Interested? Bloodstains on your coat. Your fingerprints, among others, on the rapier. And Bronson, who's also with me, says that the tip of the rapier is coated with blood and that molasses-and-cyanide goo. Have you anything to say, Jardin?"

"Will you get me my hat and coat, Pink, like a good fellow?" said Rhys, rising.

Pink went blindly into the foyer. Rhys put his arms about Valerie.

"See me tomorrow," he whispered into her ear. "The old code. Remember? We may not be able to talk. The clue may be important. Goodbye, Val. Talk to the Austin girl tonight."

"Goodbye," said Val, her lips feeling rusty and stiff.

"Thanks, Pink," said Rhys, turning around. "Take care of Val."

Pink made a strangled sound. Rhys kissed Val's cold cheek and stepped back. Pink helped him on with his coat, handed him his hat.

"Come on," said Inspector Glücke.

Two of the detectives grasped Rhys's elbows and marched him out of the apartment.

"You two," said the Inspector. "Keep on ice." He nodded to the third man and they followed the others.

Pink stood still in the middle of the living-room, blinking and blinking as if the sun were in his eyes.

He didn't do it.

Val stumbled to the door and watched Rhys go down the hall towards the elevator, walking steadily in the midst of his guard.

He didn't do it! He has an alibi!

She tried to get the words out.

Prison. Some grubby cell. Fingerprints. Arraignment. Rogues' gallery. Reporters. Sob sisters. Keepers. Trial. Murder. . . .

Please. Please.

It would be Walter marching down the hall. If she spoke it would be Walter. If she didn't . . . Oh, wait, wait, please.

Walter or pop. Pop or Walter. It wasn't fair. It wasn't a choice. He didn't do it, I tell you. He has an alibi. Stop!

But nothing came out, and the elevator swallowed the marchers, leaving the corridor bleak and empty.

PART THREE

Chapter IX

Lady of the Press

VALERIE DID NOT sleep well Monday night. The apartment was dark and cold and full of whispering voices. She tossed open-eyed on her bed until the first grilles formed through the Venetian blinds; then she dozed.

Pink pounded at the door at seven, and she crept out of bed to let him in. When she reappeared later in an old tweed sports outfit he had breakfast ready. They ate together in silence. She washed the dishes and Pink, whose broad shoulders seemed to have acquired a permanent droop, went out for the morning papers.

It occurred to Val, scrubbing the pots with aluminum wool, that she had spoken her last word aloud the night before. It had been "Goodbye," and in retrospect it seemed darkly prophetic. She said to the dripping pan: "Hello," and was so startled at the sound of her voice that she almost dropped the pan.

When Pink got back with the papers he found her powdering her nose, which had a suspiciously pink tinge.

And there it was in cold print. The coarse-screen halftone of Rhys made him look like Public Enemy Number 1. Sportsman Held As Material Witness. Arrest on Murder Charge Hinted by Van Every. Spaeth Partner Refuses to Talk. . . . "Rhys Jardin, 49, ex-millionaire and prominent Hollywood society man, is in Los Angeles City Jail this morning held as a material witness in the sensational murder yesterday of Solomon Spaeth, Jardin's business partner in the ill-fated Ohippi Hydro-Electric Development. . . ."

Val pushed the paper away. "I'm not going to read it. I won't read it."

"Why don't he hire a mouthpiece?" exclaimed Pink. "It says here he won't open his trap except to say he's innocent. Is he nuts?"

The buzzer jarred and Pink opened the door. He tried to shut it immediately, but he might have been pitting his strength against the Pacific Ocean. He vanished in a wave of arms, legs, cameras, and flash bulbs.

Val fled to her bedroom and locked the door.

"Out!" yelled Pink. "Out, you skunks! Paid parasites of the capitalist press! Get the hell out of here!"

"Where's the closet where that sword was found?"

"Is this it, punk?"

"Where was the camel's-hair coat?"

"Get that homely ape out of the way!"

"Miss Ja-a-ardin! How about a statement—Daughter Flies to Defense of Father?"

"This way, Pincus my boy. Look tough!"

Pink finally got them out. He was panting as Val cautiously peeped out of her bedroom.

"This is terrible," she moaned.

"Wait a minute. I smell a rat." Pink sneaked into Rhys's bathroom and found a knight of the lens gallantly photographing Rhys's tub. When the cameraman saw Val he hastily put a new plate into his camera.

Val bounded back to her bedroom like a gazelle.

"Funny thing about me. Either I like a guy," Pink said, knocking the photographer down, "or I don't. Scram, you three-eyed gorilla!"

The photographer scrammed.

Val peered out again. "Are they *all* gone now?"

"Unless there's one hiding in the drain," growled Pink.

"I'm going," said Val hysterically, clapping on the first hat she could find. "I'm getting out of here."

"Hey—where you going?" demanded Pink, alarmed.

"I don't know!"

Val ducked down the emergency stairway, preceded Indian-wise by Pink, who flailed through the crowd in the lobby and executed a feint by loudly warning Mibs Austin, who was barricaded behind the switchboard, to keep her mouth shut or he would break her neck, and then challenging every newspaperman in Los Angeles to a fist-fight.

He won his desire, *en masse*; and while Mibs shrieked encouragement to her red-haired gladiator and the lone policeman on duty prudently backed into the elevator, Val escaped unnoticed through the side-exit of the *La Salle*.

She almost stripped the gears of Rhys's sedan getting away from the curb.

A long time later she became conscious of the fact that the sedan was bowling along the Ocean Speedway, near Malibu Beach, the spangled Pacific glittering in the sunshine to her left and the stinging breeze lifting her hair.

The taffy sand, the chunky Santa Monica Mountains, the paintbox blue of the ocean, the salt smell and white road and warming sun did something to her; and after a while she felt quieted and comfortable, like a child dozing in its mother's lap.

Back there, in the haze-covered city, Rhys gripped gray bars, the papers whooped it up in an orgiastic war-dance, Walter sat steeped in some mysterious liquid agony of his own fermentation. But here, by the sea, in the sun, one could think things out, point by point, and reach serene, reasonable conclusions.

Oxnard slipped by, the flat white miniature Mexico of Ventura, the grove-splashed orange country where occasional fruit glowed in the trees, yellow sapphires imbedded in crushed green velvet.

Valerie drew a deep breath.

At Santa Barbara she headed for the hills. And when she got to the top she stopped the car and got out and slipped into the silence and coolness of the old Mission. She was there a long time.

Later, feeling hungry, she drove down into the sunny Spanish town and consumed *enchiladas*.

When she returned to Hollywood, in the late evening, she felt regenerated. She knew exactly what she had to do.

The Wednesday morning papers bellowed news. Inspector Glücke had decided, after a long conference with District Attorney Van Every, the Chief of Police, the Chief of Staff, and the Chief of Detectives, to charge Rhys Jardin with the premeditated murder of Solomon Spaeth.

Val drove the ten miles into downtown Los Angeles and left her sedan in a parking lot on Hill Street, near First. It was only a few steps to the City Jail. But she did not go that way. Instead, she walked southeast, crossed Broadway, turned south on Spring, and stopped before a grimy building. She hesitated only a moment. Then she went in.

The elevator deposited her on the fifth floor, and she said firmly to the reception clerk: "I want to see the managing editor."

"Who wants to see him?"

"Valerie Jardin."

The clerk said: "Wait a minute, wait a minute," and babbled into the telephone. Ten seconds later the door opened and Fitzgerald said eagerly: "Come on in, Val. Come in!"

Fitz led the way with hungry strides through the city room. Inquisitive eyes followed Val's progress through the room. But Val did not care; her lips were compressed. One man, sitting over a drawing board in a far corner, got half out of his chair and then sank down again, gripping a stick of charcoal nervously and adjusting his green eyeshade. Val suppressed a start and walked on. Walter back at work! She did not glance his way again.

Fitz slammed the door of his office. "Sit down, Val. Cigaret? Drink? Tough about the old man. What's on your mind?"

"Fitz," said Val, sitting down and clasping her hands, "how much money have you?"

"Me?" The Irishman stared. "I'm busted—Ohippi. Do you need dough? Maybe I can scare up a few C's—"

"I didn't come here for that." Valerie looked him in the eye. "Fitz, I want a job."

Fitz rubbed his black jowls. "Look, Val, if you're broke, why—"

Val said with a faint smile: "I'm a special sort of person right now, isn't that so?"

"What's the point?"

"Daughter of a famous man charged with a front-page murder?"

Fitz got out of his chair and, still rubbing his face, went to the dust-streaked window. When he turned around his bird's-nest brows almost completely concealed his eyes.

"I'm listening," he said, sitting down again.

Val smiled once more. Fitz was a little transparent. A nerve near his right eye was jumping.

"I couldn't write a news story, but you've got plenty of people who can. On the other hand, I can give you information you'd never get without my help."

Fitz flipped a switch on his communicator. "Bill. I don't want to be disturbed." He sat back. "I'm still listening."

"Well, I'm the daughter of the accused. The byline alone will sell papers."

Fitz grinned. "Oh, you want a byline, too?"

"Second, I'll be able to predict the defense before it comes out in court."

"Yes," said Fitz. "You certainly will."

"Third, I'll have inside information no other paper in town could possibly dig out. Where it won't hurt my father, you'll have an exclusive story."

Fitzgerald began to play with a paper-knife.

"And last, you can play up the human-interest angle—rich gal loses all her money, goes to work in defense of accused father." Fitz leaned forward toward his communicator again. "Wait a minute, darling," said Val. "I'm no philanthropist. I'm proposing to do something that nauseates me. It's going to take a lot of money to cure that nausea."

"Oh," said the Irishman. "All right, how much?"

Val said bravely: "A thousand dollars a yarn."

"Hey!" growled Fitz.

"I need lots of money, Fitz. If you won't give it to me, some other paper will."

"Have a heart, Val—a story a day! This thing may drag on for months."

Val rose. "I know what you're thinking. They've got pop dead to rights, no sensational news angle can come out of the case, it will be cut-and-dried, the usual story of a guilty man brought to trial. If you think that, Fitz, you're a long way off."

"What d'ye mean?"

"Do you believe pop's guilty?"

"Sure not," said Fitz soothingly. "Sit down, Val."

"I tell you he isn't."

"Sure he isn't."

"I *know* he isn't!"

Val walked to the door. Fitz shot out of his chair and ran to head her off. "Don't be so damned hasty! You mean you've got information—"

"I mean," said Val, "that I have a clue that will lead to the real criminal, Friend Scrooge."

"You have?" shouted Fitz. "Look, Val mavourneen, come here and sit

down again. What is it? Tell old Fitz. After all, I'm an old friend of your
father's—"

"Do I get my thousand a story?"

"Sure!"

"You'll let me work my own way?"

"Anything you want!"

"No questions asked, and I work alone?"

"That's not fair. How do I know you're not sandbagging me? How do I
know—"

"Take it or leave it, Mr. Fitzgerald."

"You've got the instincts of an Apache!"

"Goodbye," said Val, turning again to go.

"For God's sake, hold it, will you? Listen, Val, you haven't any experience. You may get into trouble."

"Don't worry about that," said Val sweetly.

"Or you may ruin a great story. Let me assign one of my men to double
up with you. How's that? Then I'll be protected, and so will you."

"I don't want any spies or story-stealers around," frowned Val.

"Wait a minute! I give you my word it'll be on the level, Val. You can't
gang up on me this way! A good man who knows his stuff, won't blab, and
will steer you right."

Val stood thinking. In a way, Fitz was right. She had no idea where her
investigation might lead. An experienced newspaperman to advise and assist
and even provide physical protection in the event of danger was a wise
precaution.

"All right, Fitz," she said finally.

Fitz beamed. "It's a deal! Be back here at two o'clock and I'll have my
man ready. We'll give you a press card, put you on the payroll, and you'll
be all set. You're sure you've got something?" he asked anxiously.

"You'll have to take your chances," said Val. Sure? She didn't even know
what the clue was!

"Get out of here," groaned Fitz.

When Valerie emerged into the city room Walter was standing in the
aisle, waiting.

Val tried to pass him, but he moved over to block her path.

"Please," said Val.

"I've got to talk to you," said Walter in a low voice.

"Please!"

"I've got to, Val."

Val eyed him coolly. "Well, if you must I suppose you must. I don't care
for an audience, though, so let's go into the hall."

He took her arm and hurried her through the city room. Val studied
him covertly. She was shocked by his appearance. His cheeks were sunken;
there were leaden hollows under his eyes, which were inflamed. He looked
ill, as if he were in pain and had not slept for days.

He backed her against the marble wall near the elevators. "I've read about Rhys's arrest," he said feverishly. "It muddles things for me, Val. You've got to give me time to think this over—"

"Who's stopping you?"

"Please have patience with me. I can't explain yet—"

"Nasty habit you have," said Val, "of not being able to explain. Please, Walter. You're hurting me."

Walter released her. "I'm sorry about Monday night. Getting drunk, I mean. The things I said. Val, if you'd only have a little faith in me . . ."

"I suppose you know," said Val, "that some one planted the rapier and pop's coat in our closet, and tipped off the police that they were there. Or don't you?"

"Do you believe I did that?" said Walter in a low voice.

Val stirred restlessly. Nothing could come of this. "I'm going," she said.

"Wait—"

"Oh, yes. I've just taken a job here. Special features on the case. I'm going to do a little investigating of my own. I thought you'd like to know."

Walter grew paler under his two-day growth of beard. "Val! Why?"

"Because trials cost money and lawyers are expensive."

"But you've got that money I gave you. I mean—"

"That's another thing. Of course we can't accept that, Walter. Pop has it in a bank, but I'll have him write out a check for the full amount."

"I don't want it! Oh, damn it. Val! Don't start something that might— that might bring you—"

"Yes?" murmured Valerie.

Walter was silent, gnawing his lower lip.

"Yes?" said Val again, with the merest accent of contempt. But she could not prevent a certain pity from creeping into her voice, too.

Walter did not reply.

Val pressed the elevator-button. The door slid open after a while. She got in and turned around. The operator began to pull the door shut.

Walter just stood there.

Chapter X

A Star Reporter Is Born

FITZ SAUNTERED INTO the reception room of Magna Studios and said to the man at the desk: "Hullo, Bob. Is Ellery Queen in?"

"Who?" said the man.

"Ellery Queen."

"Queen, Queen. Does he work here?" said the man, reaching for a directory.

"I believe he's under that impression," said Fitz.

"Oh, yes. Writer. Writers' Annex, Room 25. Just a second." He picked up his telephone.

Fitz stuck a cigar into the man's mouth, said: "Cut the clowning. What d'ye think I am, a trade-paper ad salesman?" and went through.

He strolled along the cement walk before the open-air quadrangle of executive buildings, past the bootblack stand, and into the alley marked "'A' Street" alongside Sound Stage One. At the end of the alley cowered a long, lean, two-story building with a red-gabled roof and stained stucco walls.

Fitz mounted the steps to the open terrace and searched along the terrace until he found an open door with the number 25 on it.

It was a magnificent room, with two magnificent desks, a magnificent rug, a magnificent central fixture, magnificent draperies, and magnificent art on the walls. And it was magnificently empty.

A typewriter stood on a mahogany worktable opposite the door; a chair with polished arms magnificently etched into curlicues by some one's penknife lay overturned on the floor before the table. From the carriage of the typewriter jutted a sheet of heavy bond paper, with words on it.

Fitz went in and read them. The words were:

"If a miracle should happen and somebody should walk into this hermit's lonely desert cell, I am currently in the office of His Holiness Seymour A. Hugger, Grand Lama of the Writers' Division of Magna Pictures, giving him a piece of what is left of my mind. For God's sake, pal, wait for me.

ELLERY QUEEN."

Fitz grinned and went out. On the way to the terrace steps he caught sight through a window of a long-legged literary person in slacks and a yellow polo shirt. The gentleman seemed fiercely intent on a toothpaste advertisement in *Cosmopolitan*. But then Fitz saw that he was asleep.

He returned to the Administration Building and hunted through the polished corridor until he discovered a door which proclaimed the presence of Mr. Hugger.

Opening the door, he found himself in a sort of glorified cubbyhole containing three large desks at which three beautiful young women sat buffing their fingernails, and a worried-looking young man who clutched a sheaf of yellow papers marked "Sequence A" which he was reading nervously.

"Yes?" said one of the young women without looking up, but Fitz opened the door lettered "Private" and strolled into Mr. Hugger's domain without stooping to conversation.

Ensconced in a throne-like chair behind a dazzling cowhide-covered desk sat a chubby young man with thin hair and a benign demeanor. The room, the rug, the desk, the radio, the draperies, the bookcases, and the *objets d'art* were even more magnificent than their generic cousins in Room 25, Writers'

Annex. Moreover, Mr. Hugger was magnificent in his happiness. Mr. Hugger seemed to want every one to know that he was happy. Particularly the bearded, purple-visaged maniac who was waving his arms and scudding up and down the room like a Sunday yacht.

"If you'll calm down for a minute, Mr. Queen," Mr. Hugger was saying in avuncular accents as Fitz walked in.

"I'll be damned if I will!" yelled Mr. Queen. "What I want to know is—why can't I see Butcher?"

"I've told you, Mr. Queen. He's *very* temperamental, Mr. Butcher is. He takes his time. Patience. Just have patience. Nobody's rushing you—"

"That's just the bloody trouble!" shouted Mr. Queen. "I want to be rushed. I want to work day and night. I want to hear a human voice. I want to engage in debates about the weather. What did you bring me out here for, anyway?"

"Excuse me," said Fitz.

"Oh, hello," said Ellery, and he sank into a ten-foot divan and plunged his hands into his beard.

"Yes?" said Mr. Hugger with an executive look.

"Oh." Ellery waved his hand wearily. "Mr. Hugger, Mr. Fitzgerald. Fitz is managing editor of the *Independent*."

"Newspaperman," said Mr. Hugger, becoming happy again. "Have a cigar, Mr. Fitzgerald. Would you be kind enough to wait outside for a moment? Mr. Queen and I—"

"Thanks, I'll wait here," said Fitz genially, licking the end of Mr. Hugger's cigar. "What's the trouble, Master-Mind?"

"I ask you," cried Ellery, bouncing up. "They brought me out here to write for the movies. They gave me twenty-four hours to get ready in New York, and they couldn't even wait for me to get off the train. I didn't have time to take a bath. Get him right down to the studio! they told my agent. So I hurried down here, full of alkali, with a running nose and a sore throat, and they gave me the Doge's Palace to work in, a mountain of foolscap, a whole school of pencils, and the offer of a beautiful stenographer, which I refused. And what do you think happened?"

"I give up," said Fitz.

"Sick as I've been, I've hung around here and hung around and hung around, waiting to be called into conference by his Lordship, Jacques Butcher, the producer I'm supposed to go to work for. You know what? After all that haste, I've sat in that damned lamasery for two solid weeks and the man hasn't so much as telephoned me. I've called him, I've haunted his office, I've tried to waylay him—nothing. I've just sat on my rump praying for the sight of a human being and slowly going mad!"

"Mr. Queen doesn't understand the Hollywood way of doing things," explained Mr. Hugger quickly. "Mr. Butcher in his own way is a genius. He has peculiar methods—"

"Oh, he has, has he?" bellowed Ellery. "Well, let me tell you something, Your Majesty. Your genius has spent the past two weeks playing golf during the day and Romeo during the night with your ingénue star, Bonnie Stuart, so what do you know about that?"

"Come on out," said Fitz, lighting the cigar, "and I'll buy you a drink."

"Yes, go on," said Mr. Hugger hastily. "You need something to quiet your nerves. Mr. Butcher will get in touch with you very shortly, I'm sure."

"You *and* Mr. Butcher," said Ellery, impaling Mr. Hugger with a terrible glance, "are from hunger."

And he stamped out, followed by Fitz.

Over the third Scotch-and-soda at Thyra's, across the street from the studio, Fitz remarked: "I see you've got your voice back."

"The sun fixed that, when he got around to it." Ellery seized his glass. "God," he said hollowly, and drained it.

"Sick of this racket already, hey?"

"If I didn't have a contract I'd take the first train out of the Santa Fe station!"

"How'd you like to get mixed up in some real excitement, not this synthetic lunacy?"

"Anything. Anything! Give me that bottle."

"It's right smack down your alley, too," murmured Fitz, obliging as he puffed at Mr. Hugger's perfecto.

"Oh," said Ellery. He put down the bottle of Scotch and looked at Fitz over the siphon. "The Spaeth case."

Fitz nodded. Ellery sat back. Then he said: "What's up?"

"You know Rhys Jardin's in the can charged with Spaeth's murder, don't you?"

"I read the papers. That's the only thing I've had to do, by God."

"You met his daughter, Valerie? Swell trick, eh?"

"Economically useless but otherwise a nice girl, I should say. Possibilities."

Fitz leaned on his elbows. "Well, they're up against it for *dinero*, and Val came to me this morning and asked for a job. I gave it to her, too."

"Nice of you," said Ellery. He wondered what had become of Walter's money, but not aloud.

"Not at all. Rhys and I boned Lit together at Harvard and all that, but the hell with sentiment. It's a business proposition. She's got something to sell, and I'm buying."

Ellery said suddenly: "Think Jardin killed Spaeth?"

"How should I know? Anyway, the kid says she's got something hot—a clue of some kind. She won't tell me what it is, but I'm playing a hunch on this one. She's going to do byline stories for me daily and meanwhile run down the clue."

"And exactly where," said Ellery, marching his fingers along the checkered cloth, "do I come in?"

Fitz coughed. "Now don't say no till you hear me out, Queen. I admit it's a screwy idea—"

"In the present state of my emotions," said Ellery, "that's in its favor."

"I told her I'd put an experienced man on with her—show her the ropes, steer her right." Fitz refilled his glass carefully. "And you're it."

"How do you know she'll work with me? After all, you spilled the beans about me at *Sans Souci* Monday."

"No, she mustn't know you're a detective," said Fitz hurriedly. "She'd tighten up like a wet rawhide in the sun."

"Oh," said Ellery. "You want me to spy on her."

"Look, Queen, if I wanted to do that I'd put one of my own men on with her. But she needs somebody familiar with murder. She ought to think her partner's just a leg-man, though; I don't want to scare her off."

Ellery frowned. "I'm not a newspaperman, and she knows what I look like."

"She wouldn't know a newspaperman if she fell over one. And how well does she know you?"

"She's seen me twice."

"Hell," said Fitz, "we can fix that."

"What do you mean?" asked Ellery, alarmed.

"Keep your pants on. The set-up's perfect, that's why I doped this out. You told me you don't normally wear a beard. So if you shaved it off Val wouldn't recognize you, would she?"

"Shave off this beautiful thing?" said Ellery in dismay, caressing it.

"Sure! It's old-fashioned, anyway. Show a clean mug, comb your hair on the side instead of straight back the way you've got it now, dress a little differently, and she'll never get wise. Even your voice will fool her—she's only heard that croak you were using Monday."

"Hmm," said Ellery. "You want me to stick to Miss Jardin, find out what she knows, and crack the case if her father's innocent?"

"Right."

"Suppose he's guilty?"

"In that case," said Fitz, taking another drink, "let your conscience be your guide."

Ellery drummed for some time on the cloth. "There are other objections. I can hardly pose as a Los Angeles reporter; I've never been here before."

"You're new from the East."

"I don't know the lingo, the habits, the hangouts—"

"Oh, my God," said Fitz. "You've been reading about reporters in your own stories. Believe it or not, newspapermen talk just like anybody else. Their habits are the same, too—maybe a little better. As far as hangouts are concerned, this is a funny town. L.A.'s the largest city in area in the United States—covers four hundred and forty-two square miles. After we go to press the boys scatter to the four winds—Tujunga, Sierra Madre, Altadena, Santa Monica Canyon, Brentwood Park. Hangouts? You don't hang out anywhere when you've got to drive sixty miles to get home to the wife and kids."

"I'm convinced. How about a name?"

"Damn. That's right. Let's see. Ellery—"

"Celery. . . ."

"Pillory. . . ."

"Hilary! That's it. Hilary what? Queen—"

"King!"

"Hilary King. Ingenious."

"Then it's all set," said Fitz, rising.

"Wait a minute. Aren't you interested in the financial aspect of the deal?"

"Are you going to blackjack me, too?" growled Fitz.

Ellery grinned. "I'll take it on for nothing and expenses, you lucky dog."

Fitz looked suspicious. "Why?"

"Because I'm sick of Messrs. Butcher and Hugger. Because there are things about the Spaeth case that positively make my mouth water. Because I like the people most directly involved. And because," said Ellery, jamming on his hat, "I've got a score to settle with the High Hocus-Pocus of the Homicide Detail!"

"An idealist, b'gorra," said Fitz. "Be in my office at two o'clock."

Chapter XI

Cards Under the Table

WHEN VAL LEFT the *Los Angeles Independent* building, she hunted up a shop, spent a few minutes there, hurried out, and made her way to the City Jail.

There was a great deal of concealed official emotion when she announced her identity. Val, holding her package casually, pretended not to notice.

It was all rather worse than she had imagined, but somehow things were different this morning. Lovelace's lines popped into her mind—what a fanatic Miss Prentiss had been on the subject of "recitations" in the ancient pigtail-and-governess days! "Minds innocent and quiet take That for an hermitage." No, stone walls do not a prison make, nor iron bars a cage.

A uniformed man said to her: "You'll have to empty your pockets and purse, Miss," and Val obeyed, raising her smooth brows. He seemed disappointed at finding no revolver underneath the vanity-case.

"What's in that bundle?" he asked suspiciously.

"Bombs," said Val.

He opened the package, glaring at her. "Okay," he said shortly.

Val gathered her purchases up and said with a sweet smile: "You have to be *so* careful with these desperate criminals, don't you?"

Another man, in an unpressed business suit, trailed along, as a guard conducted her to a remote cell block. Val's brows went up again.

And there he was, sitting on his pallet playing solitaire with a fuzzy, dirty old deck of cards which looked as if they had been used by four generations of prisoners. He did not notice their approach and Val studied his profile for a moment, trying to adjust her own expression. He was so calm, so unconcerned; he might have been lounging in his club.

"Here's your daughter," said the guard, unlocking the barred door.

Rhys looked around, startled. Then he bounced to his feet and held out his arms.

The keeper locked the door again and said to the shabby man who had followed Val: "Come on, Joe, let 'em alone. Man's got a right to talk private, ain't he?"

"Sure," said Joe heartily. "That's right, Grady."

It seemed to Val that both had spoken in unnecessarily loud voices. She looked up at her father and he grinned in answer. The keeper and the shabby man marched ostentatiously away.

"Don't you think," began Val, "that they—"

"Darling," said Rhys. He pulled her over to the pallet and sat her down. The greasy cards he pushed carelessly aside, and Val put her package down. "How's my puss?"

"How are you, pop? Like it here?" said Val, smiling.

"I don't know what those literary-minded convicts who write memoirs keep kicking about. A place like this is perfect for resting the tired business man."

"I thought those two—" began Val again.

Rhys said easily: "I do miss decent cards, though. These things must have come into California with Porciúncula."

"I've brought you a new deck," said Val, undoing her package again. She knew suddenly that he did not want her to discuss anything of possible interest to an eavesdropper. She glanced at him and he motioned meaningly toward the wall behind his pallet. So some one was planted in the next cell! Probably, thought Val, with a dictograph.

"Thanks, darling," said Rhys, as she handed him a new deck of cards with brilliant blue backs showing a schooner in full sail. "It's hell playing with fifty-two dishrags. And what's this—cigars!"

"I bought you the king size—they last longer, don't they?"

"You're simply wonderful." Rhys gathered up the old cards and began to pat them into a neat pile. "I was beginning to think you'd run out on me. In durance vile for thirty-six hours, and not a peep out of you!"

"I tried last night, but they wouldn't give you a telephone message."

"Nasty of them. Here, take these damned shingles and burn 'em." He handed her the old deck of cards and she furtively put it into her purse.

Rhys leaned back with a long sigh. Valerie closed her purse with a snap. "Did they—did they do anything to you that—"

He waved his hand. "They're cooking up an arraignment or indictment or whatever they call it, and I suppose I'll have to attend. There's been a good deal of questioning, of course."

"Questioning," said Val in a faint voice.

"Nothing brutal, you understand. You really should meet Van Every—charming fellow. I must say I like him better than that ogre Glücke."

Chit-chat, inconsequentials, to deceive the man in the next cell. To deceive her, too? Val suddenly leaned over and kissed him. They were both silent for a moment.

Then Val said: "I've got something to tell you."

He shook his head in warning. But Val reassured him with a glance and went on: "I've taken a job with Fitz."

"A job?"

She told him the story of her interview with Fitzgerald. "It's—well, it's money, pop. We've got to have some." He was silent again. "And don't you think we ought to pay back—that other money we owe?"

"Yes. Of course." He knew which money she meant, but somehow neither seemed to want to mention Walter's name. "But not now. It can wait. Naturally I won't touch it."

"Naturally." Val understood. To return Walter's money now would raise all sorts of questions. Walter's sympathy with Jardin was better kept secret—for Walter's sake. For Walter's sake! Everything, everything was for Walter's sake.

"Is there anything else I can get you?" asked Val.

"No, Val. I'm really quite comfortable."

They looked deeply into each other's eyes. Val kissed him again. Then she rose and said hurriedly: "I'll see you later," and ran to the door and began shaking the bars like a young female monkey.

"Guard!" called Rhys with a curious smile, and the keeper came running. "It's a funny feeling, isn't it, puss?"

"Goodbye, darling," said Val without looking around, and she followed the man out with her head held high but seeing very little of the massive masonry and ironwork that escorted her to the very street.

Val had taken no more than twenty steps on First Street when she knew she was being followed.

To make sure, she headed for the lot where she had parked her car. There, while the attendant hunted through the rows, Val became busy examining her face in her mirror and incidentally watching the street. Yes, there was no doubt about it. A long black sedan with two men in it had inched away from the curb across the street from the Jail and had followed her walking figure at five miles an hour. Now it was waiting unobtrusively before the parking lot, as if held up by traffic. But there was very little traffic.

The attendant brought up her car and Val got in, feeling her heart beat fast. She clutched her purse tighter and drove out of the lot with one hand.

The black sedan began to crawl again.

Val set her bag down and began to dodge in and out of traffic.

Fifteen minutes later, after a circuitous route, she found herself on Wilshire Boulevard near LaFayette Park—and the big sedan was still fifty feet behind her.

There was only one thing to do, and Val did it. She sped west on Wilshire, bound for home. North on Highland, past Third, Beverly, Melrose, Santa Monica, Sunset . . . the sedan followed grimly, maintaining its distance.

Val drove up to the *La Salle*, parked the car, snatched her purse from the seat, slipped into the lobby by the side-entrance and dodged up the stairway to 3-C. She locked her door with shaking fingers.

She flung her hat aside and sat down for a moment to catch her breath. The apartment was quiet, the Venetian blinds tipped down. She rose and went to the breakfast-room window and peered out. There, in the back street, stood the sedan; its two occupants were still sitting in it, smoking.

Val hurried back to the living-room and tore open her purse. In her nervousness the cards cascaded to the floor. She sat down cross-legged and picked them up.

She began quickly to separate the suits—clubs, diamonds, hearts, spades. When all the clubs were in one pile, she arranged them in descending order—ace on top, then king, queen, jack, down to the deuce. She repeated this curious procedure with the three other suits. When this was finished she took up the thirteen spades, then the hearts, then the diamonds, and finally the clubs.

Val turned the rearranged deck over in her hands, frowning. Something was wrong. Along both sides appeared pencil marks—dots, dashes, and on some card-edges nothing at all. It looked like a telegraph code. But that couldn't be.

Oh, she was stupid! Some cards were turned one way, the rest the other. She would have to turn each card so that its marked edge coincided with the marked edges of the cards above and below it. That was what she had had to do as a little girl, when Rhys amused her with what had then seemed a fascinating trick of secret communication.

There! The thing was done. All the marked edges lay one way, and the pencilled dots and dashes became parts of an intelligible message written in simple block letters over the tightly compressed side of the deck.

There was not enough light on the floor. Val scrambled up and ran to the breakfast-room window, careful to remain invisible to the watchers below.

She breathed a little harder as she read the clear, tiny letters. The message said:

SS PHONED AR MON AM COME
OVER URGENT BETW 5-5.30 PM

Val slowly sat down on the breakfast-nook bench. SS—that stood for Solomon Spaeth. AR—Anatole Ruhig. Solomon Spaeth had telephoned Anatole Ruhig Monday morning to call at the Spaeth house *between five and five-thirty Monday afternoon* on an urgent matter!

So that was the clue. Rhys had gone over to Spaeth's house Monday morning; they had had their argument in Spaeth's study. It must have been during this visit that Spaeth had telephoned his lawyer, and Rhys had overheard.

Between five and five-thirty Monday afternoon. But Spaeth had been murdered at five-thirty.

Val clenched her hands under her chin. What had Ruhig told Glücke? Yes, that he had appeared at *Sans Souci* a few minutes past six Monday afternoon. But that must have been true, otherwise Walewski would have called him a liar. Unless Walewski . . .

Val frowned. Spaeth had commanded his lawyer to appear between five and five-thirty, and Ruhig had simply been more than a half-hour late for the appointment. That was the reasonable explanation. Besides, had Ruhig really been on time, wouldn't Frank—on duty at the gate—have seen him and reported his visit to Inspector Glücke? Unless Frank . . .

Val was so disappointed she flung the cards from her and glowered at them as they lay strewn about the kitchen floor. She could have wept for sheer chagrin.

But she did nothing of the sort. She got down on her hands and knees and picked the cards up one by one, getting a run in one stocking in the process; and when she had them together again she rose and went into her bedroom and stowed them away in the bureau under the chemises.

Then she undressed, washed her face and hands, changed her stockings, made up, put on her black silk print with the magnolia-petal design and the last expensive hat she had bought—the one that looked so fetchingly like a modernistic soup plate—transferred her vanity and key-case and money to the alligator bag, and departed, a lady with a mission.

The information about Counselor Anatole Ruhig was the only clue she had; and, for better or worse, it had to be traced to its bitter end.

At two o'clock precisely the door of Managing Editor Fitzgerald's office flew open and an apparition appeared, making Mr. Fitzgerald choke over a hooker of eighteen-year-old whisky which he was in the process of swallowing.

"Hi, Chief," said the apparition, swaggering in.

"Who the hell do you think you're impersonating," spluttered Fitz, "a burlycue comic?"

The apparition was a tall lean young man with a clean-shaven face and features just a trifle too sharp to be handsome. But Fitzgerald was examining the costume, not the face. The young man was attired in shapeless slacks of a dingy gray hue and the loudest sport coat Fitzgerald, who had seen nearly everything, had ever laid eyes on. It was a sort of disappointed terra cotta, with wide cobalt stripes slashing through an assortment of brown plaid checks. His shoes were yellow brogues. His red-and-blue plaid socks curled around his ankles. On his head he wore a tan felt hat with the fore part of the brim sticking straight up in the air. And his eyes were covered by blue-tinted sun-glasses.

"Hilary 'Scoop' King, the demon of the city room," said the apparition, leering. "Hahzit, Fitz?"

"Oh, my God," groaned Fitz, hastily shutting his door.

"What's the matter? Don't I look the part?"

"You look like a hasheesh-eater's dream of heaven," cried Fitz. "That coat—jeeze! It must have come down to you straight from Joseph."

"Protective coloration," said Ellery defensively.

"Yeah—your own father wouldn't know you in that get-up. And with the beaver gone you don't look the same man. Only for cripe's sake don't go around telling anybody you work here. I'd be laughed out of the *pueblo*."

The door opened a little and Val said timidly: "May I come in?"

"Sure," said Fitz in a hearty voice, and he glared at Ellery, who hastily got off the desk.

Val slipped in, and Fitz shut the door behind her. "Don't let the get-up scare you, Val. This is Hilary King, the man I told you about. He's new to L.A. and he thinks the local men dress like a shopgirl's conception of Clark Gable relaxing. King, Miss Valerie Jardin."

"How do you do," said Val, trying not to giggle.

"Hi," said Ellery, removing his hat. But then he remembered that newspapermen in the movies never remove their hats, so he put it on again.

"I decided not to use a local man after all, Val," said Fitz, "because the boys would know him and get wise to what's going on. King's just in from— uh—Evansville; great record out there, especially on police work."

He bustled to his desk and Val eyed her new colleague sidewise. He looked like a perfect idiot. But then Fitz was smart, and appearances *weren't* always to be trusted. She also thought she had seen the creature before, but she couldn't decide when or where.

"Here are your credentials," said Fitz, "and yours, too, King."

"Does the gentleman from Evansville know what his job is?" asked Val.

"Oh, sure," said Ellery. "Fitz told me. Keep an eye on you, give you fatherly advice. Don't worry about me—baby."

"How," said Val, "are the gentleman's morals?"

"Who, me? I'm practically sexless."

"Not," retorted Val, "that it would do you any good if you weren't. I just wanted to avoid possible unpleasantness."

"Go on, get going, both of you," said Fitz benevolently.

"I'll have my first story," said Val, "ready for the rewrite desk tonight, Fitz."

"Not in this man's trade, you won't," grinned Fitz. "We've got a daily paper to get out. Besides, it's all written."

"What!"

"Now don't fret yourself," soothed Fitz. "You don't have to pound out the grind stuff. I've got people here who can make up a better human-interest yarn out of their heads than you could out of facts. You'll get your byline and your grand just the same."

"But I don't understand."

"Part of your value to me is your name. The other part is that clue you're battin' about. Don't worry about the writing, Val. Follow up that clue, and if you pick up any special slants, 'phone 'em in. I'll take care of the rest."

"Mr. King," said Val, eying the apparition. "For whom are you working—Fitz or me?"

"The answer to a dame," said Mr. King, "is always yes."

"Hey!" shouted Fitz.

"Now that you've learned your catechism," said Val with a kindly smile, "come along, Mr. King, and learn something else."

Chapter XII

The Affairs of Anatole

"The first thing I crave," said Hilary "Scoop" King as they paused on the sidewalk before the *Independent* building, "is lunch. Have you eaten?"

"No, but we've got an important call to make—"

"It can wait; most everything can in this world. What would you suggest?"

Val shrugged. "If you're a stranger here, you might like the Café in El Paseo."

"That sounds hundreds of miles away, to the south."

"It's in the heart of the city," laughed Val. "We can hoof it from here."

Ellery politely took the outside position, noting that a black sedan was following them slowly. Val led him up Main Street through the old Plaza, pointing out the landmarks—Pico House, the Lugo mansion plastered with placards displaying red Chinese ideographs, Nigger Alley, Marchessault Street.

When she took him into El Paseo, it was like turning a corner into old Mexico. Booths ran down the middle of the street displaying black-paper *cigarillos*, little clay toys and holy images, queer cactus plants, candles. The very stones underfoot were alien and fascinating. Along both sides of the narrow thoroughfare were *ramadas*, ovens of brick and wooden tables where fat Mexican women patted an endless array of *tortillas*. At the end of the street there was a forge, where a man sat pounding lumps of incandescent iron into cunning Mexican objects.

Ellery was enchanted. Val indicated their destination, La Golondrina Café, with its quaint overhanging balcony.

"What are those scarlet and yellow dishes I see the *señoritas* carrying about?"

They sat down at one of the sidewalk tables and Val ordered. She watched with a secret mischievousness as he bit innocently into an *enchilada*.

"*Muy caliente!*" he gasped, reaching for the water-jug. "Wow!"

Val laughed aloud then and felt better. She began to like him. And when they got down to the business of serious eating and he chattered on with the fluency of a retired diplomat, she liked him even more.

Before she knew it, she was talking about herself and Rhys and Pink and Winni Moon and Walter and Solly Spaeth. He asked guileless questions, but by some wizardry of dialectic the answers always had to be factual in order to be intelligible; and before long Val had told him nearly everything she knew about the case.

It was only the important events of Monday afternoon—Rhys's alibi, Walter's taking of Rhys's coat, the fact that Walter had really been inside his father's house at the time of the crime—that Valerie held back. Consequently there were gaps in her account, gaps of which her companion seemed casually aware—too casually, thought Val; and she sprang up and said they would have to be going.

Ellery paid the check and they sauntered out of El Paseo.

"Now where?" he said.

"To see Ruhig."

"Oh, Spaeth's lawyer. What for?"

"I have reason to believe that Ruhig had an appointment with Spaeth on Monday afternoon for five or five-thirty. He told Glücke he got there after six. You won't blab!"

"Cross my heart and hope to die a pulp-writer," said Ellery. "But suppose it's true? He could merely have been late for the appointment."

"Let's hope not," said Val grimly. "Come on—it isn't far to his office."

They made their way past the fringe of Chinatown into the business district, and after a while Ellery said in a pleasant voice: "Don't be alarmed, but we're being followed."

"Oh," said Val. "A big black sedan?"

Ellery raised his brows. "I didn't think you'd noticed. All the earmarks, incidentally, of a police car."

"So that's what it is! It followed me all morning."

"Hmm. And that's not all."

"What do you mean?"

"No, no, don't look around. There's some one else, too. A man—I've caught a blurred glimpse or two. Not enough for identification. He's on our trail like a buzzard."

"What'll we do?" asked Val in panic.

"Keep right on ambling along," said Ellery with a broad smile. "I hardly think he'll attempt assassination with all these potential witnesses around."

Val walked stiffly after that, glad that she had given in to Fitzgerald, glad that Hilary "Scoop" King, leading citizen of Evansville, was by her side. When they reached the Lawyers' Trust Building she dodged into the lobby with an exhalation of relief. But Mr. King contrived to pause and inspect the street. There was the black sedan, snuffling like a trained seal across the street; but the man on foot was nowhere to be seen. Either he was hiding in a doorway or had given up the chase.

Mr. Ruhig's office was like himself—small, neat, and deceptively ingenu-
ous. It was apparent that Mr. Ruhig did not believe in pampering his clients
with an atmosphere. There was a gaunt, worried-looking girl at the switchboard, several clerks and runners with flinty, unemotional faces, and a wall
covered with law books which had an air of being used.

There was no difficulty getting in to see the great man. In fact, he came
bustling out of his office to meet them.

"This is a pleasant surprise," he cried, bobbing and beaming. "Shocking
about your father, Miss Jardin. What can I do for you? If it's advice you
want, I'm completely at your service, although I'm not in the criminal end.
Gratis, of course. I feel like an old friend of the family."

And all the while he eyed Ellery with a puzzled, unobtrusive interest.

"Mr. Ruhig, Mr. King," said Val crisply, sitting down in the plain office.
"I hope you don't mind Mr. King's being with me, Mr. Ruhig. He's an old
college chum who's volunteered to help."

"Not at all, not at all. What are friends for?" beamed Mr. Ruhig. Apparently the Joseph's coat reassured him, for he paid no further attention to
Mr. King.

"I'll come right to the point," said Val, who had no intention of doing
any such thing. "I'm not here as Rhys Jardin's daughter but as an employee
of the *Los Angeles Independent.*"

"Well! Since when, Miss Jardin? I must say that's an unlooked-for development."

"Since this morning. My father and I need money, and it was the only
way I knew of earning a great deal quickly."

"Fitzgerald," nodded Ruhig approvingly. "Great character, Fitzgerald.
Heart as big as all outdoors. Hasn't stopped agitating for Mooney's release
in ten years."

"Now that I've got a job, I've got to earn my keep. Has anything come
up on your end, Mr. Ruhig, that might be construed as news?"

"My end?" smiled the lawyer. "Now that's putting it professionally, I'll
say that. What would my end be? Oh, you mean the will. Well, of course,
I've filed it for probate. There are certain unavoidable technicalities to go
through before it's finally probated—"

"I suppose," said Valerie dryly, "Wicious Winni is simply prostrated with
grief over the necessity of taking that fifty million dollars."

Ruhig clucked. "I should resent that remark, Miss Jardin."

"Why should you?"

"I mean the—ah—disparaging reference to Miss Moon." He clasped his
hands over his little belly and smiled suddenly. "I'll tell you what I'll do.
Suppose I start your newspaper career off with a bang, eh? Then you'll feel
a little more charitable towards Anatole Ruhig."

Mr. King lounged in his chair studying Mr. Ruhig. Beneath that bland
exterior he fancied he saw a considerable equipment for sculduggery. No,
Mr. Ruhig was not doing anything out of pure kindness of heart.

"I was going," went on the lawyer paternally, "to call in the press this afternoon and make a general announcement, but since you're here I'll give you an exclusive story. That ought to put you in solid with Fitzgerald! You know," he coughed and paused to take a drink of water from the chipped bronze carafe on his desk, "Miss Moon on the death of Solly Spaeth lost a dear friend—a dear friend. One of the few friends she had in the world. A dear friend."

"That," said Val, "is putting it mildly."

"Now I've always admired Miss Moon from afar, as you might say—the dry man of the law worshipping at the feet of unattainable beauty, ha-ha! But with Spaeth's death attainment, so to speak, becomes possible. I'm afraid I've taken advantage of dear Winni's grief-stricken condition." He coughed again. "In a word, Miss Moon has consented to be my wife."

Val, torn between astonishment and nausea, sat silent. Spaeth not even buried, and that horrible creature already accepting the advances of another man!

"If I were you, Val darling," said Mr. King in an old-college-chummy way, "I'd pick up that telephone and relate this momentous intelligence to your editor."

"Didn't I tell you it was news?" beamed Ruhig.

"Yes, yes," said Val breathlessly. "May I use your 'phone? When are you going to be married? I mean—"

A cloud passed over Mr. Ruhig's rubicund features. "Obviously there is a certain decorum that must be preserved. We haven't thought of a—ah—a date. It will not even be a formal engagement. Merely—what shall I say?—an understanding. By all means use the 'phone."

Mr. King ruminated while Val seized the instrument. Such a public announcement now would hardly endear Mr. Ruhig, already disliked, to a citizenry whose money Mr. Ruhig was proposing to marry. Obviously, then, Mr. Ruhig in making it had an important object in mind. What?

"Oh, damn," said Val into the telephone. "Fitz isn't in now. Give me . . ." She bit her lip. "Give me Walter Spaeth! . . . Walter? Val. . . . No. . . . Now, please. I've called Fitz but he isn't in, and you're the only other one. . . . It's a story. . . . Yes! Anatole Ruhig has just told me confidentially he and Winni Moon are going to be married, date uncertain. . . . Walter!" She jiggled the telephone, but Walter had hung up.

Mr. Ruhig breathed on his fingernails. "And now—" he said in the tone of a man who would like to prolong a delightful conversation but must regretfully terminate it.

Val sat down again. "There's something else."

"Something else?"

"I'm sort of checking up the day of the murder."

"Monday? Yes?"

"Did you say," asked Val, leaning forward, "that you got to *Sans Souci* a little past six Monday?"

Mr. Ruhig looked astonished. "My dear child! Certainly."

He was going to deny it. He had to deny it. Or perhaps it all wasn't true.

Val inhaled like a diver and took the plunge. "What time did Spaeth set for your appointment with him?"

"Between five and five-thirty," said Mr. Ruhig instantly.

Ellery, quietly watching, felt a backwash of admiration. No hesitation at all. Between five and five-thirty. Just like that.

"But you just said you—you got there after six!"

"So I did."

"Then you were *late*? You didn't get there between five and five-thirty at all?"

Mr. Ruhig smiled. "But I did get there between five and five-thirty. . . . How did you know?" he asked suddenly.

Val gripped her alligator bag, trying to keep calm. As for Mr. Hilary King, he saw the point. Mr. Ruhig was an old hand at questions and answers. If he was being questioned about the exact time of his arrival, then he knew Val had reason to ask the question. If she had reason, it might be based on evidence. If there was evidence, truth was safer than fiction. Mr. King's admiration for Mr. Ruhig waxed.

"Let's get this straight," said Val. "You got to *Sans Souci* when?"

"At five-fifteen, to be exact," replied Mr. Ruhig.

"Then why didn't you tell Inspector Glücke—"

"He didn't ask me when the *appointment* was for. And I merely said I drove up a bit after six, which is true. Except that it was the second time I drove up, not the first."

"A minor technicality," commented Mr. King.

"The legal training," said Mr. Ruhig with a modest downward glance. "Answer the question as asked, and don't volunteer information."

"Then you were in the house during the crime," cried Val, "and Atherton Frank lied about no one coming in but—"

"My dear child, you'll learn as you grow older never to jump at conclusions. I drove up the first time at a quarter after five, but that doesn't mean I entered the grounds."

"Oh," said Val.

"Ah," said Mr. King.

"Frank wasn't around," continued the lawyer conversationally. "You might question the one-armed gentleman, because he testified he was on duty all afternoon. But when I got there at five-fifteen the gate was locked and he wasn't in his booth, so I drove off and returned a bit after six, at which time Walewski was on duty. That's all."

"Is it?" murmured Val.

"As a matter of fact," said Ruhig, "I've been debating with myself whether to tell the Inspector about Frank's absence or not. It puts me in rather a spot. I forgot to mention it Monday night, and when I recalled it later it occurred to me that Glücke might become—uh—troublesome over my lapse of memory. However, I think now I'd better tell him."

You didn't forget anything, Mr. Ruhig, thought Mr. King. And you don't want Inspector Glücke to know even now. You're bluffing.

"No," said Val quickly. "Please don't. Just keep it to yourself for a while, Mr. Ruhig."

"But it's a criminal offense!" protested Mr. Ruhig.

"I know, but it may come in handy in the defense if—when pop goes to trial. Don't you see? They couldn't be so sure, then, that he was the *only* one—"

"You'd make a persuasive advocate," beamed Mr. Ruhig. "I'll think it over. . . . No, I shan't, either! Friendship is friendship. I won't talk until you give the word."

Well done, friend.

"Thank you," said Val, rising. "Uh . . . Hilary, let's go."

"Why not?" said Ellery-Hilary, and he uncoiled his legs from under Mr. Ruhig's uncomfortable chair.

He had scarcely got out of it when Ruhig's office-door flew open and Walter Spaeth strode in, hatless and panting, as if he had run all the way from Spring Street.

"What's this," he demanded of Ruhig, "about you and Winni?"

"Ah. Walter!"

Walter's right fist smashed down on Ruhig's desk. "So that's the game," he said in a hard voice. "All right, Ruhig, I'll get into it, too."

"What are you talking about?" asked the lawyer brusquely.

"You aren't satisfied with the hundreds of thousands you collected from my father in fees in that crooked Ohippi operation. Now that he's dead you want the big money—the millions. And you're marrying that damned empty-headed fool of a woman to get them!"

"Get out," said Ruhig. "Get out of here."

"I've been thinking it over for some time. Ruhig, there's something rotten about that will!"

"You will find," said Mr. Ruhig with a dangerous softness, "that your father had full testamentary capacity."

"I'll spike your little scheme. I'm getting a lawyer to file a protest. I'll break that will, Ruhig. You'll never live to see it probated."

"Your father," snapped Ruhig like a tormented little badger, "was entirely able to comprehend the nature and extent of his property, his relationship to the natural objects of his bounty, and the scope and effects of the contents of his will. Will you get out, or do I have to have my clerks put you out?"

Walter actually smiled. "So it's a fight, is it? By God, Ruhig, I've been itching for one."

And he strode out with no more than a passing glance at Val and Mr. King—an absent glance that sharpened momentarily and then grew absent again.

"Goodbye," said Val in a small voice.

They left Mr. Ruhig sitting still behind his desk, no longer smiling. In fact, Mr. Ruhig was immersed in thought—half-drowned in it, Mr. King would have said.

Chapter XIII

Winni the Pooh et Cetera

"THERE'S THAT MAN again," said Ellery, as they walked down the street.

"Where?"

"Somewhere behind us. I'm psychic about these things. Where's your car parked?"

"N-near Hill."

"Head for it and I'll drop behind. Let's see if we can't bag this squirrel."

Val stepped off the curb and nervously crossed the street. She was just mounting the sidewalk on the other side when she heard an outcry behind her. She whirled about.

Mr. Hilary King was struggling with a medium-sized, broad-shouldered man whose bellow could be heard as far as City Hall.

"Stop!" cried Val, racing back across the street. She yanked Ellery's arm, which was engaged in a futile-seeming maneuver that looked like ju-jutsu, and was, and then shook the other man, who had just caught Ellery flush on the nose with his freckled fist.

"*Pink!*" she screamed. "Mr. King, stop! It's Pink!"

"I'm ready to call it quits," panted Mr. King, feeling his nose with his free sleeve, "if this wildcat is."

"Who is this guy?" stormed Pink. "I spotted him for a ringer right away! Did he force you, Val? I'll tear his gizzard out!"

"Don't be an ass," said Val irritably. "Come on, they'll have the riot squad out in a minute." And indeed Old Faithful, the black sedan, had stopped and its two occupants were hastily getting out.

The three of them looked at the sedan, the gaping crowd about them, the approaching detectives, and ran. They ran all the way to Hill Street, pursued, grabbed Val's car, and shot away into the late afternoon traffic.

"There's one consolation," said Mr. King, still caressing his nose, "we've lost our escort."

Pink slumped back in the rear, trying to compress himself into the smallest possible space.

"You're an idiot," snapped Val, driving furiously. "Was it you who were following us? Pink, if you don't stop wet-nursing me—"

"How should I know?" whined Pink. "This guy looked like a phony to me. And Rhys told me to take care of you."

"That's no excuse. This is Mr. King, a—an old school chum. He's helping me on my job."

"Job!" Pink goggled.

Val told him about the events of the day, concluding with the Ruhig incident.

"Say!" exclaimed Pink. "I know why Ruhig admitted being at *San Susie* Monday at five-fifteen."

"You do?"

"I've been doin' a little snooping myself," said Pink proudly. "I got to thinking about this Ruhig menace, and I says maybe he's hiding something, so I goes up to his office this morning and I get palsy with the switchboard gal and pretty soon she spills. Ruhig and two of his gorillas left the office Monday a little past four-thirty in Ruhig's car!"

"Pink, I retract the arm-lock," said Ellery warmly. "A good job. Ruhig discovered the girl had been talking, assumed you told Valerie, and therefore came out with the truth the instant she questioned him."

"I think," murmured Val, "we've got something." She frowned, examining the road behind her in the mirror. Then she swung off the boulevard and headed the car northwest.

"Where you going now?" demanded Pink.

"To *Sans Souci*. I want to talk to Frank, and I simply must interview dear, dear Winni—the damned *Pooh!*" And she stepped viciously on the accelerator.

A detective sat dozing in the pillbox, while Frank crouched disconsolately on an empty orange-crate near the gate.

The detective opened one eye at the sound of Val's klaxon, then quickly got up and came out to the gate.

"Can't go in," he said, waving his hand. "Orders."

"Oh, dear," said Val. "Look, Lieutenant, we're not—"

"I ain't, but you can't come in."

Ellery nudged her. "Have you forgotten? You represent the massed power of the press."

"Dag my nab, yes," said Val. "Here, Captain, look at this. Press. Newspaper. Reporter."

She waggled her press card. He examined it suspiciously through the grille. "All right, you come in. But the two men stay here."

"Time," said Mr. King. "I, too, gather the news." And he exhibited his credentials. "It looks as if you're stuck, Pink."

"Not me. Where she goes, I go!"

"No, you don't," said the detective sourly; and Pink found himself back on the curb, where he had sat Monday night, glaring at the iron gate.

"Frank, come here," said Val. The one-armed gateman looked startled; the detective scowled. "Interview," said Val with a bewitching smile.

The two men were properly bewitched, and Frank followed Val some little distance from the pillbox, Ellery ambling behind lazily. But his eyes were sweeping the terrain. The place looked deserted.

"Frank," said Val sternly, when they were out of earshot of the gate, "you deliberately lied Monday night!"

The gateman paled. "Me, Miss Jardin? I didn't lie."

"Oh, didn't you? Didn't you tell Glücke no one but Miss Moon and a man wearing my father's coat entered the grounds between the time the auction ended and the time Walewski came on?"

"Sure I said that. It's the God's honest truth."

"You're a blaspheming, wicked old man!" said Val. "You *weren't* at that gate all Monday afternoon, and you know it!"

The one-armed man grew even paler. "I—I wasn't?" he faltered. Then, fearing he had given himself away, he said loudly: "I was so!"

"Come, come," sneered Val. "Where were you at a quarter past five?"

The man started. He crouched a little and peered anxiously at the detective in the distance. "Not so loud, Miss Jardin. I didn't mean nothing wrong. I just—"

"Speak up," said Ellery in an authoritative voice. "Were you at that gate, or weren't you?"

"I just sneaked down the hill a ways to Jim's Diner for a cup of coffee. I was getting awful hungry—I always do late afternoons—I got something wrong with me. . . ."

"What time was this, Frank?" asked Val excitedly.

"You won't tell nobody? I went down the hill a little after five. Maybe eight, ten after. I was back just about half-past five. Just about."

"Did you leave the gate locked?" demanded Ellery.

"Yes, sir, I did, sir. I wouldn't go away and leave—"

"Twenty minutes," breathed Val, her eyes shining. "That means *any one* could have . . . Frank, not a word about this, do you understand?"

"Oh, no, ma'am, not me. I won't say anything. If the people at the bank found out I'd lose my job. I only been on it a couple of months. I'm a poor man, Miss Jardin—"

"Let's go, babe," said "Scoop" King, *bravura*. And he linked Val's arm in his and marched her up the drive toward the Spaeth house.

Val hurried along, trying to match his long stride. "That man Ruhig is a *liar*," she panted. "He got here at five-fifteen, he says, couldn't get in, went away. And came back a few minutes past six. That's simply unbelievable. If you knew Solly Spaeth. He didn't like to be kept waiting. And Spaeth had said it was urgent. Oh, Ruhig didn't go away!"

Ellery strode on, head down, silent.

"Do you know what I think?" whispered Val.

"Certainly." Ellery lit a cigaret. "You think that when Mr. Ruhig found the gate locked but unguarded, he climbed over the fence and visited Mr. Solly Spaeth per appointment."

"Yes!"

"I'm inclined," said Ellery, "to agree." And he walked on, smoking like a demon.

"In the house. In the house between five-fifteen and five-thirty!"

"That's only theory," warned Ellery.

"I'm sure he was! The car could have been parked on the other side of

Sans Souci so that when he left, nobody—not even Frank—would have seen him. Climbed over the fence again. Got out the way he got in—" She stared at Ellery with a feverish absorption. "That means—that means—"

"Let us," murmured Mr. King, "interview the glamorous bride-to-be."

Miss Moon opened the door herself.

"So you're afraid to hire servants, too," said Val.

"What do you want?" said Miss Moon. She was flushed with anger.

"We want in, as they say," said Val, and she slipped by Miss Moon with a winning smile and skipped toward the study. Miss Moon glared at Mr. King, who spread his hands apologetically.

"After you, Miss Moon," said Mr. King. Miss Moon stamped off to the study.

"What is this, anyway?" she stormed, withering Val with one devastating look. "Can't a lady have any pwivacy?"

"Mr. King, Miss Moon," murmured Val, unwithered and undevastated. "We won't take too much of your time."

"I don't talk to murdewews!"

"If I wasn't a woiking goil," said Val, "I'd scratch those mascaraed eyes of yours out, dearie. I'm writing for a Los Angeles newspaper, however, and I want to know: Is it true what they say about you and Anatole Ruhig?"

Winni raised her pale plump arms dramatically. "I'll go mad!" she cried. "I told that nasty little— I *told* Anatole to keep his twap shut! You're the second one; a reporter was just here fwom the *Independent!*"

"Are you going to marry Anatole?"

"I've got nothing to say—especially to you!"

"I wonder what the secret of her success is, Mr. King," sighed Val. "Would you say it was charm, or manners?"

"Miss Moon," said "Scoop" King, taking out pencil and paper and pretending to write. "What are you going to do with Solly Spaeth's fifty million dollars?"

"I'll talk to *you*," cooed Miss Moon, calming magically and fussing with her wheat-colored hair. "I'm buying and buying and *buying*. It's wonderful how the shops give you cwedit when you're an heiwess, isn't it?"

She swept Val's neat costume with a scornful glance.

"And is your aunt buying and buying and buying, too?" asked Mr. King, still scribbling doodads.

Miss Moon drew herself up. "My awnt isn't here any more. My awnt has gone away."

"When do you expect her back?"

"Nevaw! She deserted me in my hour of distwess, and now she can go lump it."

"Apparently," remarked Val, "she didn't hear about the fifty million soon enough. Well, thank you, dear Miss Moon. I hope your new pearls choke you to death."

And she went out, followed meekly by Mr. King and a female glare that had the glitter of knives in it.

Mr. King grabbed Miss Jardin's arm and pulled her stealthily into the doorway of a room off the corridor. He kept peering out and back toward the study.

"What's the idea?" whispered Valerie.

He shook his head, watching. So Val watched, too. In a few moments they saw Miss Moon flounce out of the study, lifting her beige hostess-gown and scratching her naked left thigh in an inelegant manner, and mumbling crankily to herself. She clumped up the stairs, her hips rising and falling like a watery horizon in a monsoon.

Ellery took Val by the hand and tiptoed back to the study.

"There," he said, closing the study door. "Now we can reconnoiter a bit, unknown to the Presence."

"But why?" asked Val blankly.

"Sheer nosiness. This is where the last rites were administered, isn't it? Park your pretty carcass in that chair while I snoop a bit."

"You're a funny sort of newspaperman," said Val, frowning.

"I'm beginning to think so myself. Now shut up, darling."

Val shut up and sat down, watching. What she saw puzzled her. Mr. King lay down on the floor near the ell in which Mr. Solomon Spaeth had been sitting so quietly Monday night. He nosed about like Mickey's Pluto; Val could almost hear the sniffs. Then he rose and examined the wall of the alcove. After a moment he stood off and looked up at the wall above the fireplace. Then, shaking his head, he went to Solly's desk and sat down in Solly's chair and thought and thought and thought. Once he looked at his wrist-watch.

"It's an impressive act," said Val presently, "but it conveys absolutely nothing to my primitive mind."

"How do you get the gateman's booth by telephone?" he asked in reply.

"Dial one-four."

He dialed. "This is that reporter again. It's five after six, so Walewski ought to be there. Is he?"

"So what?" rasped the detective's voice.

"Put him on. What's your name?"

"David Greenberg. Say, listen, pal, if—"

"I'll remember that, Dave. Put Walewski on." He waited, saying meanwhile: "That's the hell of these post-mortem investigations. If there was any clue in this room, the police have ruined it. . . . Walewski? I'm a reporter. You remember Monday a few minutes past six, when Mr. Ruhig drove up to the gate?"

"Yes, sir, yes, sir," came Walewski's quavering voice.

"Was he alone in his car? Or were there two men with him?"

Val jumped. She ran to the desk, listening for the answer.

"No, sir," said Walewski. "He was all alone."

"Thanks."

Ellery hung up and Val stared at him. Then he rose and said lightly: "What's out here? Ah, a terrace. Let's imbibe some fresh air."

The study wall facing the terrace was completely glass. They went out through the glass doors. The terrace was deserted, and its gaily striped awning, bright furniture, cushions, rattan, wrought-iron chairs, and pastel flagstones looked a little forlorn.

Ellery handed Val gallantly into the slide-swing and stretched himself out in a long summer chair.

"I think, my brave colleague," he said, settling himself comfortably and gazing out over the rock gardens and the empty pool below, "we have our Mr. Ruhig neatly figured."

"He was alone when he came back, Walewski says!"

"Exactly. Let's see what we have. Pink discovers that Ruhig left his office around four-thirty Monday afternoon, in his car, accompanied by two assistants. This checks with other facts—that the previous week when he drew up, and Spaeth signed, the will which cut Walter Spaeth off, Ruhig also came with two assistants, to serve, as he himself said, as witnesses to the signature."

"How do you know that?" frowned Val. "You weren't present when he told that to the Inspector Monday night."

"I—uh—I read it in the papers. Now. From Ruhig's office to *Sans Souci* is a good forty-minute drive through traffic; so Ruhig probably told the truth when he said he reached here at five-fifteen Monday. With, mind you, his two assistants. He says he couldn't get in and drove away and returned at six-five or so. Why? Obviously, if he hadn't got in at five-fifteen, then he still had to handle the change of will for Spaeth. But when he returned at six-five, presumably for this purpose, his two men weren't with him! What does that suggest?"

Val wrinkled her brow. "I can't imagine."

"Obviously *that he no longer needed them.* But why had he brought his assistants in the first place? To witness a new will. Then if he no longer needed them at six-five, it seems to me highly indicative that the assistants had already served their purpose by six-five. In other words, to reduce it to specifics, that they had witnessed a new will between five-fifteen, when Ruhig first came, and five-thirty-two, when Spaeth died."

"A new will!" cried Val. "Oh, lord. Then that means—"

"Hush! We don't want Winni hearing this. We don't know exactly what this means in terms of the will. But we can be pretty sure Spaeth signed a new will before he died, and that Ruhig and his men were in this study at approximately the murder-period."

Val sat thinking furiously. It did sound logical. And it changed everything. Any new will would have affected Winni Moon's gigantic legacy. Where did Walter enter the picture? Did he find that will? Was he—was he protecting Winni? What real part did that oily little Ruhig play?

"What's that?" asked Ellery sharply, sitting up.

"What's what?" asked Val in an absent way.

Ellery pointed. Fifty yards from where they sat, directly beyond the pool, was the rear terrace of the old Jardin house. Something was winking there, flashing prismatic colors in the rays of the sinking sun.

"I can't imagine," said Val. "That's the terrace of our old house. We didn't leave anything there except an odd piece or two of porch furniture we didn't want."

Ellery rose. "Let's go look-see."

They stole down the stone steps and made their way without noise across the rock garden, around the pool, to the Jardin house. The awning still hung over the terrace, which was largely in shadow; but the sun illuminated an area several feet deep along the entire length of the terrace; and in this sunlit area stood an old wrought-iron porch table.

They saw at once what had caused the fiery flashes. A pair of battered binoculars lay on the table, its lenses facing the sun.

"Oh, shoot," said Val, disappointed. "It's just that old pair of binoculars."

"Here!" said Ellery sharply. "Don't touch that table." He was crouched over, studying its surface with narrowed eyes. "You mean you left them here when you moved?"

"Yes. One of the lenses is cracked."

"Did you leave it on this table?"

"Why, no," said Val, surprised. "It wasn't left here at that. We went over a lot of stuff—pop likes the races, and we have several pairs of binoculars— and we just threw this one out."

"Where did you leave it?"

"There's a pile of junk in the gym."

"Then what is it doing here?"

"I don't know," said Val truthfully. "But what difference does it make?"

Ellery did not reply. He indicated the glass doors which led to the vacant study; they stood slightly ajar.

"That's funny," said Val slowly. "Those doors were locked when we left. Unless the landlord had some one come in and—"

"If you'll look closely, you'll find the lock broken," said Ellery, "indicating a basic disrespect for the rights of property."

"Oh!" cried Val, pointing to the table. "Those marks!"

She bent over the table and Ellery smiled faintly. The surface was covered with mottled dust. There seemed to be two layers of dust, deposited at different times. Val was studying two oval marks—they were more like smudges—under the upper dust-stratum. One was larger than the other, and they were separated by several inches.

"Damn those rains," said Ellery. "The table didn't get the full force of it, being under the awning, but it did get a fine spray, enough to remove any fingerprints that may have been here."

"But those marks," said Val. "They *look* like fingerprints. Like the marks of two fingers—a thumb and a little finger."

"That's what they are. They were deposited on an already dusty surface.

Then more dust settled, and the rain messed things up, but they're still visible because the dust-layer is thinner where they are than on the rest of the table. However, there don't seem to be any distinguishing whorls—probably the rain."

He took out a handkerchief and carefully lifted the binoculars. Where they had lain was a slightly dusty surface, lighter than the surrounding surface. "Binoculars and fingermarks made at about the same time." He wrapped the binoculars in the folds of the handkerchief and calmly dropped the whole thing into the pocket of his sport jacket.

Val did not notice. She was striding excitedly up and down. "I've got it! It was still light at the time of the murder, and the glasses show some one stood right here on this terrace watching what was going on in Spaeth's study! He could easily see, because of the glass walls, like these here. *There was a witness to the murder!*"

"Excellently spoken," said Ellery. "I mean—you said a mouthful there, baby." But he was still studying the two finger-smudges on the table in a puzzled way.

"Then some one knows who killed Spaeth. Some one *saw!*"

"Very likely." Ellery looked around. "Did you say a lot of junk was left in the gym? Where's the gym?"

"A few doors down," said Val, hardly knowing what she was saying. Then she took a deep breath. "Here, I'll show you."

She led him along the terrace to the door of the empty gymnasium. This door, too, had been forced.

"There it is," said Val.

Ellery went over to a small pile of débris and poked it apart with his foot. But there was nothing of interest in the pile. He was about to return to the terrace when he spied a small closet set into one of the walls. The closet-door was closed. He walked over and opened it. Inside, on a rack, hung a lone Indian club. He took it out, frowning, and examined it. It was cracked.

"Funny," he said. "Very funny." He weighed the club thoughtfully, glancing over at the pile of débris.

"What is it? What's the matter now?" asked Val, waking from her trance.

"This Indian club. Indian clubs come in pairs, weighted and matched. Why on earth should you have taken along the mate to this, when this cracked one was left behind?"

"The mate?" Val wrinkled her forehead. "But we didn't. We left them both here in the closed closet."

"Really?" said Ellery dryly. "Well, one of them is gone."

Val stared, then shrugged. Ellery replaced the cracked club in the rack and, frowning, shut the closet-door.

"And another thing," said Val, as they returned to the terrace. "Whoever it was who watched, it was somebody with only two fingers on his left hand—a two-fingered man! That *is* a left-hand marking, isn't it?"

"Yes."

"Two fingers!"

Ellery smiled the same faint smile. "By the way, I think you'd better telephone police headquarters."

"What for?"

"To tell them about this table. Shocking neglect on the part of Glücke —not examining your old house!"

"Why, the binoculars are gone!" cried Val.

"Only as far as my pocket. I'd put the table in there, too, only it won't fit comfortably. Call Glücke. He ought to send a fingerprint man down here right away on the off-chance that some prints *are* left."

They went quietly back to the Spaeth house and Ellery sat down on the terrace again while Val tiptoed into the study to telephone. He heard her get her connection and ask for Inspector Glücke, but he was not listening too closely. Those marks . . .

He jumped at a choking sound from the study. He ran in and found Val staring at the telephone, her face a pale, pale gray.

"All right," she said weakly. "I'll be right down," and she replaced the instrument on its base with a thud, as if it were too heavy for her.

"What's the matter? What's happened?"

"It's Walter. Walter," said Val. It was always Walter. Whenever anything happened, it was Walter. "You know—I told you about—*him*. The one who ran into Ruhig's office—"

"Well, well?"

"Inspector Glücke just told me. . . ." She shivered suddenly and drew her coat more closely about her. "He says Walter has cleared my father. Walter's —cleared—pop!"

She began to giggle.

Ellery shook her violently. "None of that! What do you mean—cleared your father?"

Val giggled and giggled. It became a laugh, and then a shout, and finally it choked up and turned into a whisper. "He—just—confessed to Glücke that —*he* was the one—who wore my father's coat Monday afternoon . . . that he was the one—Frank saw. . . . Oh, Walter!"

And she buried her face in her hands.

Ellery pulled her hands away. "Come on," he said gruffly.

PART FOUR

Chapter XIV

Storm over Glücke

VAL LOOKED SO preoccupied that Ellery took the wheel of her sedan. She sat still, staring ahead. He could not decide whether she was frozen with stupefaction or shocked stiff by the high voltage of some more personal emotion. Her body did not sag even while the sedan squealed around corners. As for Pink, having heard the news, he kept his mouth open all the way downtown.

Inside police headquarters Val broke into a trot. And in the anteroom to Inspector Glücke's office, while the police clerk spoke into his communicator, she pranced. When he nodded she flew to the Inspector's door—and slowly opened it.

Walter sat with outstretched legs beside Glücke's big desk, blowing smoke rings.

There were two others in the office—the Inspector and a thin whippy gentleman of indecipherable age who sat quietly in a corner grasping a stylish stick. Glücke looked grim and alert, as if he were set for some emergency; but the thin man was composed and his eyes had a cynical glitter.

"Hello," grinned Walter. "Val to the rescue."

"Oh, Walter," said Val, and she went to him and put her hand on his shoulder in a proud, tender way.

"What is this," said the Inspector dryly, "Old Home Week? What d'ye want, King?"

"So I've been reported by the demon sleuth team in the black sedan, curse it," said Ellery. His name was King, was it?

"Take a powder, King. No reporters here."

"It's all right with me," said Mr. King indifferently. "I was on my way to the office anyway with the dope I've turned up."

"What's that? What dope?"

"If you'd devote less time to playing follow-the-leader and more to examining *Sans Souci* you'd show a better homicide record. Come on, Pink, let's amble."

"Just a moment," said the thin man with a smile. "I think we can manage this without ruffled feelings, Glücke." He rose. "My name is Van Every. You say you've turned up something at *Sans Souci?*"

"Ah, the D.A." They examined each other politely. "I do, but I'm not spilling till I find out what friend Spaeth's been up to."

Van Every glanced at Glücke, and Glücke growled: "Okay." He drew his brows together. "Well, here she is, Spaeth."

"Wait," said Val quickly. "Walter, I want to—"

"It's no use, Val."

"Walter, *please.*"

Walter shook his head. "I told you, Inspector, on Monday night that I didn't enter the *Sans Souci* grounds. That's not true. I did enter. I had a key to the gate, and Frank was in his booth reading a paper, so I let myself in and walked up the drive—"

"And he spotted you from the back and thought you were Rhys Jardin because you were wearing Jardin's torn coat. You've told me that already," said Glücke impatiently. "Answer some questions. So you weren't hit on the head as you got out of your car?"

"No. I was attacked after—"

"Walter!" Val put her palm over his mouth. He shook his head at her, but she kept her hand where it was. "Inspector, I want to talk to Mr. Spaeth."

Walter removed her hand gently. "Let me clear this damned thing up, Val."

"Walter, you zany! You darling idiot. . . . I insist on speaking to Walter alone, Inspector."

Glücke and the District Attorney exchanged glances, and Glücke waved his hand.

Val pulled Walter out of the chair and drew him off to a far corner. The Inspector's large ears twitched as he leaned forward, and Pink looked from Walter and Valerie to the Inspector and back again with a confused but hopeful air. But the thin man and Ellery did not stir.

Val linked her arms about Walter's neck, pressing her body close to him, her mouth an inch from his ear. Her back was toward them and they could not see her face; but they saw Walter's. As she whispered the lines of his face stretched and vanished, as if a hot iron had passed over wrinkled damp cloth.

Val stopped whispering, and for a moment she remained pressed to him. He turned his head and kissed her on the mouth.

They came forward side by side. "I want to see Rhys Jardin." His voice was fresh and untroubled.

"Jardin?" The Inspector was astonished. "What for?"

"Never mind what for. I want to talk to him."

"Quit stalling and go into your dance!"

"I don't talk until I've seen Jardin."

"I've had just about enough of this playing around," rasped Glücke. "You walked in here of your own free will with a yarn that, if it's true, cracks this case wide open. Now that you're here you'll talk—and talk fast!"

"I think," said the thin man smoothly, "that Mr. Spaeth's story will keep for an hour, Inspector. If he wants to see Jardin—why not?"

Glücke opened his mouth, closed it, opened it again. His brilliant eyes suddenly became cunning. "All right. Tell you what I'll do. You go on down to the City Jail—"

Val surreptitiously jerked Walter's jacket.

"No," said Walter. "Have him brought here."

"Listen!" roared Glücke. "Are you going—"

"Here," said Walter.

Glücke looked baffled. He turned aside and again his eyes sought the District Attorney, and again the District Attorney made a small, clear sign.

The Inspector pressed a lever of his communicator. "Boley. Have Rhys Jardin brought to my office right away."

Val looked triumphant, and Walter grinned.

Rhys Jardin appeared between two detectives, blinking as if he were unaccustomed to strong light. He stopped short on seeing Valerie and Walter but gave no other sign of recognition.

"Yes?" he said to Inspector Glücke.

The two detectives left the room and Glücke said quickly: "Just a moment, please." He hurried to District Attorney Van Every and bent over him, speaking in a vehement undertone. Ellery strolled across the room, pushed his preposterous hat back on his head, and sat down behind Glücke's desk.

"Jardin," said Glücke. "Walter Spaeth has come in with a funny story, but before he talks he wants a private confab with you."

"Story?" said Rhys, looking at Walter.

"He claims that he was the man in the camel's-hair Frank identified as you Monday afternoon."

"Did he say that, now?" said Rhys.

"Now of course," continued Glücke in a friendly way, "this is important testimony and it changes a lot of things. But we don't want to put on the squeeze. So suppose you three straighten yourselves out, and then we'll all sit down like sensible people and get to the truth, once for all."

"I have literally nothing to say," said Rhys.

"Pop," said Val. He looked at her then.

"I'll tell you what," the Inspector went on, growing more friendly with every word. "We'll clear out of here and leave you folks alone. When you're ready, sing out." He nodded to Van Every and went to one of the several doors leading out of his office. "We'll be waiting in here."

Ellery produced a cigaret, lit it, and coughed out a volcano of smoke. He leaned over Glücke's desk in a spasm.

"If you don't mind," said Walter politely, "I think we'd rather talk somewhere else." And he opened another door, looked in, nodded, and beckoned Val and her father.

THE DEVIL TO PAY

The Inspector's ears flamed. Nevertheless he said amiably: "All right. It doesn't make any difference."

Rhys Jardin crossed the room and the three of them entered the room Walter had selected. He shut the door very carefully.

"Would you gentlemen mind waiting outside?" said the District Attorney suddenly. "Inspector Glücke and I—"

"I get it," said Ellery. He rose. "Your mouth is open, Pink. Come on." He slouched over to the door at which the Inspector was standing. Pink scratched his head and followed. They entered a small room which contained four walls, three chairs, and one desk; and Ellery loudly banged the door shut.

The next instant he was at the desk opening drawers. "Transparent as cellophane," he said gleefully. "Glücke wanted them to gabble in the big office so that he could overhear their conversation. Dictograph, of course. And since this is the room he seemed so eager to wait in . . . Ah!" Pink heard the click of a switch.

He sprang about in a left-handed fighter's crouch as Van Every's voice came out of thin air: "Can you hear anything?" And then Glücke's voice, similarly disembodied: "Not a ripple. He must have smelled a rat."

Pink looked foolish. "How the hell—"

"I saw through the trick and managed to locate the machine," chuckled Ellery. "There's a switch under his desk, and it was open. Now shut up and let's hear what *they're* saying."

"Say, you're a cute finagler," growled Pink suspiciously. But Ellery was crouched over the desk, paying no attention. So Pink sat down and listened, too.

The instrument was so clear they could hear Glücke's footsteps as he walked up and down his office.

"I don't know what you gave me the high sign for, Van," said Glücke fretfully. "It's a funny way—"

"Don't be dense, Glücke," said Van Every. "This isn't an ordinary investigation. In fact, I'm beginning to think we've made a mistake in rushing matters."

"There's some secret relationship among those three," said the thin man thoughtfully, "we're not aware of. It's painted all over them. And until we know, I'm afraid—"

"That we'll have to go slow. I won't bring Jardin to trial until I've got him tied up in knots."

The Inspector cursed impotently and for a while nothing came through the transmitter. Then they heard him say: "Damn them! They're talking so low I can't hear a word through this damn' door. Cagy punks!"

"Watch your blood-pressure. Who's this man King?"

"Legman for Fitzgerald of the *Independent*. He's new to L.A."

"Any idea what he's turned up?"

"Go on, he's bluffing to get a story."

"Let's talk to him anyway. By the way."

"Yeah?"

"This afternoon one of my men discovered a bank account of Jardin's we didn't know anything about."

"I thought he was busted!"

"So did I. The auction fooled me. But he's got five million dollars salted away in the Pacific Coastal, Spaeth's old bank. So the auction must have been a cover-up."

"Five million!"

"Deposited last Wednesday."

"But cripe, Van, that blows a hole in the motive."

"I'm not so sure. Anyway, a private dick came in today, scared as the devil. Did a confidential job for Jardin not long ago; and when Spaeth was murdered he decided that maybe he'd better talk."

"Well!"

"He claims he found out that Spaeth had monkeyed with Ohippi's cash position and had sent out a prospectus falsifying their financial standing. He reported that to Jardin early last week."

Glücke stared. "Jardin was broke, threatened to expose Spaeth, black-mailed him. Spaeth gave him the five million to shut him up. Jardin thought it wasn't enough—Spaeth made ten times that. They had a couple of serious quarrels. So Jardin bumped Spaeth off to get whack. How's that?"

"It's a damn lie!" said Pink, clenching his left fist.

"Shut up," hissed Ellery.

"How's this yarn of Walter Spaeth's hit you?" mumbled the Inspector.

"I'm not sure."

"Spaeth and the girl are nuts about each other. He's screwy as hell, any-way. I wouldn't put it past that loony galoot to stick his head in a noose just to protect her old man."

"Well, let's see how they act when they come out. Our only smart course is to give them rope."

"Maybe," said the Inspector hopefully, "they'll hang one another."

"There's another angle on that five million," said the District Attorney after another pause. "Right now Jardin's a tin god to the public—it's the most popular crime this county's ever had, damn it. But they're for him only because they think he was a victim of Spaeth's rapacity, too. If we hold back the evidence of that five-million deposit until just before the trial, we'll swing public opinion against him when the swing will do us the most good."

"That's smart, Van! Hold it. Here they come."

Ellery turned the dictograph receiver off. "Finis."

Pink snarled: "The bastards!"

"Pink, did you know about that five million?"

"Found the bankbook in Rhys's golf-bag Monday morning, while I was packin' up. Hey!"

"What's the matter?" asked Ellery innocently.

"You ask too damn' many questions!"

"I'm on your side, Pink," said Ellery in a soothing voice. "What did Rhys say?"

"Well . . . Late Monday night he swore he didn't know a thing about it. And I believe him, too!"

"Of course, Pink. Of course."

"He reminded me that last Wednesday, when the deposit was made, he and I were away all day tryin' to sell the yacht to a guy down in Long Beach. The bankbook was a plant."

"Spaeth," said Ellery thoughtfully.

"That's what Rhys says, too."

"Uh—Pink, have you any idea what the Jardins and Spaeth have been talking about in there?"

"They didn't tell me anything, so it's none of my business. Or," said Pink, eying him stonily, "yours."

"But I want to help them, Pink."

Pink grabbed Ellery's red-and-blue necktie with his freckled left fist. "Listen, mugg. Lay off or I'll cripple you!"

"My, my, such muscles," murmured Ellery. "Well, let's see what the conferees have decided."

In Inspector Glücke's office the two Jardins and Walter were standing close together, like people threatened with a common peril and united in a common defense.

The Inspector was saying incredulously: "*What?*"

"You heard me," said Walter.

Glücke was speechless. District Attorney Van Every rose and said sternly: "Look here, Spaeth, you can't pull a stunt like this and hope to get away with it. You said—"

"I know what I said. I was lying."

"Why?"

Walter put his right arm about Val. "Rhys Jardin happens to be my fiancée's father."

"You don't expect me to believe that you'd deliberately say you were on the scene of a murder when you weren't—just for sentimental reasons! That happens in books."

"I'm an incurable romantic," sighed Walter.

"Well, you're not getting away with it!" shouted Glücke.

"Please," smiled Rhys. "Walter's a quixotic young fool. Naturally I can't let him sacrifice himself for me—"

"Then you admit you murdered Spaeth?" snapped the District Attorney.

"Nothing of the sort, Van Every," said Rhys coolly. "I'm not saying anything, as I've told you before. But I won't allow Walter to get himself in trouble on my account. My troubles are my own."

Van Every tapped his mouth pettishly. The Jardins, Walter, stood very still.

Then Glücke stamped to the main door. "Take Jardin back to his cell.

As for you," he went on, eying Walter malevolently, "if you ever pull a stunt like this again I'll send you up for obstructing justice. Now beat it."

The two detectives closed in on Rhys and took him away. Walter and Val, who wore a demure expression, sauntered after. Pink glared from the Inspector to the retreating figures, jammed on his hat, and ran after them.

Ellery sighed and closed the door.

"What's on your mind, King?" snapped the Inspector. "Let's have that phony information of yours and then scram."

"Don't you think we ought to discuss this new development first?"

"Who's we? Say, you're one fresh jigger!"

"You won't lose anything by letting me co-operate with you," murmured Ellery.

"I'll be damned," said Glücke in amazement.

"Let the man talk," said the thin man with a smile. "I rather like the cut of his jib. How does this retraction of Spaeth's strike you, King?"

Ellery made a face.

"Oh, he lied all right," said the Inspector disgustedly.

"On the contrary," said Ellery, "he told the exact truth. He lied when he took the admission back. If you ask me, boys, you're further from a solution of this case now than you were Monday night."

"Go on," said the District Attorney, intent.

"There aren't enough facts to play with, but I'm convinced Walter Spaeth was the man in Jardin's camel's-hair coat and furthermore that he knows enough about what went on in his father's study Monday afternoon to settle this grimy business in five minutes."

"It's all balled up," muttered the Inspector. "Jardin's attitude, how Spaeth figures, that closed corporation of theirs. By God, could they be accomplices?"

"Tell me something," said Ellery suddenly. "Did your crew search Sans Souci thoroughly, Inspector?"

"Sure."

"Then how is it," said Ellery, taking the handkerchief-wrapped binoculars out of his pocket, "that they missed this?"

He unfolded the handkerchief. Glücke licked his lips. "Where?" he asked hoarsely.

Ellery told him. Glücke turned a deep scarlet.

"Some one," said Ellery, lighting a cigaret, "was on the Jardin terrace Monday afternoon watching Spaeth's study through these glasses. Whoever it was, he left the imprint of a thumb and a little finger on that iron table. You might have that table examined."

"Yeah. Sure," said Glücke with a stricken look.

"And the binoculars."

"And the binoculars."

"I'm beginning to fill up with notions," Ellery continued. "I snooped about the grounds yesterday and tried to locate the spot where Walter Spaeth parked his car and was slugged. Wasn't it on the south side, near a sewer?"

"Yeah."

"Was the sewer searched?"

"Was the sewer searched? Well, now—"

"If I were you—of course I'm not," murmured Ellery, "but if I were, mind you, I'd open that sewer and give it the twice-over."

"Open it," said the Inspector. "Yeah."

Ellery yawned. "Goodbye," he said, and strolled out.

Glücke sat at his desk, crushed.

"Let that," said District Attorney Van Every dryly, rising, "be a lesson to you."

Chapter XV

Earthly Discourse

VAL CAME INTO Fitzgerald's office Thursday morning waving the front page of a late Wednesday night edition of the *Los Angeles Independent.*

"Who's responsible for this story?" she raged, pointing to the scarehead.

"If it's you, King," said Walter from the doorway, "you're a damned busy-body!"

"Isn't anything sacred to you?" cried Val.

"Stand up and take it," growled Pink, pushing Walter aside.

"Desist," said Ellery.

"Shut the door," said Fitz.

"What are you sore about?" said Ellery.

"This story—Walter's admission, retraction . . ."

"Is it true?" said Ellery.

"Did it happen?" said Fitz.

"I resign!" cried Val.

"Put up your mitts, lug," said Pink.

"Oh, pipe down, the lot of you," said Ellery. "You're all too damned self-righteous for your own good."

Val looked at Walter, and Walter looked at Val, and Pink looked at both of them for a clue to *his* attitude. Finally the three of them sat down.

Ellery uncoiled himself from Fitz's desk and began to stride up and down, smoking furiously.

Walter and Val hitched their chairs closer. Ellery, watching them from under his blue glasses, was reminded of their drawing together in Glücke's office the evening before. At the first hint of danger they flowed into a common meeting-place. There was mystery, secrecy, stubbornness written all over their young faces.

"I don't know what you two were up to last night," he said finally, "but I'm convinced of one thing—in a sort of inspired idiocy you're trying to solve a crime that should properly be left to trained people."

"Like you," sniffed Val.

"Like Glücke and Van Every. You are, aren't you?"

Val and Walter glanced at each other again.

"For heaven's sake," exploded Ellery, "can't you two do anything on your own? Must you have a conference before every speech?"

"What if we are trying to solve it?" said Val defiantly.

"Let him rave," said Walter. "Don't pay any attention to him, Val."

Ellery glared at them. "That's lovely. Babes in the woods! Next thing you know you'll be playing G-man with a Buck Rogers atomic pistol!"

"This is very interesting," said Walter, "but I've got work to do. Let's go, Val."

"Sit down! Where are you going? Do you know what to do? Do you know where to look? Answer me!" They were silent. Fitz beamed at the loudly dressed product of his imagination. The bewildered, sullen look was creeping over poor Pink's face again. "You don't. Well, I'll tell you. We're going after Mr. Anatole Ruhig in a big way."

"Ruhig?" frowned Val.

"We?" said Walter, raising his eyebrows.

"Do you remember what I told you yesterday about Ruhig and the will?" Val nodded despite herself. "We came to the conclusion that Ruhig had lied, that he'd got into *Sans Souci* on his first visit at five-fifteen, that it was at that time, just before Spaeth died, that Ruhig's men must have witnessed the signing of a new will."

"What's this?" exclaimed Walter.

"Oh, Walter," wailed Val, "I forgot to tell you!"

"The Moon woman is left everything," said Ellery softly, "and almost before your father's body is cold, Walter, Ruhig announces that he and she are going to be married. Why?"

"Any dope could figure that out," said Pink with a disgusted look. "He wants that dough she's falling into."

"Very lucidly put," drawled Ellery. "Any dope could figure out why *he* wants to marry *her*. But could any dope figure out why *she* wants to marry *him*?"

"I never thought of that," mumbled Val. "That's true. Why *should* she marry him?"

"There are three common reasons for relinquishing the sacred heritage of liberty," said Ellery dryly. "One, money. But the fifty millions are hers, not his. Two, to spite some one. Perhaps a reluctant swain is hanging around somewhere, but I question Miss Moon's dividing fifty million dollars just to make him feel sorry. Three, love, or whatever they call it in California. But you've seen friend Ruhig. Do you suppose any woman could feel romantically drawn to him?"

Walter jumped up and began to race up and down.

"I don't know about that," said Pink. "To look at me you wouldn't think a dame—"

"Shut up, Pithecanthropus," growled Fitz.

"The only reasonable explanation is that Winni knows her inheritance of that fifty million dollars *depends upon Ruhig*. If Ruhig could control her inheritance, if some action of his could either give her the millions or take them away, then Winni's willingness to marry him becomes understandable."

"That new will we were talking about!" cried Val.

"Exactly. With the other inferences we made yesterday, it's a cinch that Solly Spaeth signed a new will Monday afternoon, before his murder, which seriously reduced, or cut out completely, Winni's share in his estate. *That will Ruhig has suppressed.*"

"The dirty dog," said Walter. "The skunk!"

"Ruhig undoubtedly went to Winni and told her he had it in his power to see she didn't get a cent; but that if she'd marry him he'd destroy the latest will, and the older one giving her the fortune would remain in force."

"And he's holding that will over her head!" cried Walter. "He couldn't destroy it, or his hold over her would be gone. Until they're married he's got to hold on to that new will!"

"And she won't marry him until the old will is probated," said Val breathlessly.

"Certain interesting questions," murmured Ellery, "arise. For instance, exactly when did Ruhig leave the Spaeth house Monday afternoon? Before Spaeth's murder—or after?"

"You mean—"

"Nothing at all." Ellery shrugged. "But certainly Ruhig realizes that if he's caught with that new will now he's in the worst kind of jam. The police would interpret it as a Ruhig motive for murder. The will's hot—almost too hot to handle. Yet holding on to it means twenty-five million dollars to him. My guess is that he's taking a chance, at the same time safeguarding himself as much as he can."

"He certainly can't have that will in his actual possession," said Walter thoughtfully.

"Then how are we ever going to find it?" asked Val in dismay.

Fitz said briskly: "We've got to trick Ruhig into producing it. At the same time he mustn't suspect for a second that anybody knows the will exists."

"Otherwise," nodded Ellery, "rather than be tagged for a murder, he'll destroy it."

"So," said Fitz, glaring at Pink, "we've got to keep this talk a deep, dark, dirty secret. I won't print a line of it, and you're not to talk about it even in your sleep."

"Obviously," said Ellery, "strategy is called for. Mr. Ruhig's vulnerable spot is the incomparable Winni. Consequently we'll work through her."

"How?"

"It all depends on how much Ruhig has told her. It seems unlikely that he actually showed her the new will. He wouldn't carry it around with him one second longer than necessary. We'll have to assume she hasn't seen it.

"Now. If we can somehow plant the proverbial bug in her ear that little Anatole was lying all the time, that such a will has never existed, that he just invented it to make her marry him and cut himself in on the fifty million, what will Winni do?"

"Demand to see the will!" cried Val.

"Right. And Ruhig will have to show it to her or risk losing everything. When he does—we pounce."

"Smart," said Walter curtly.

"And you're the man for the job, Walter. She knows you well—I think she even likes you."

"I guess so," said Walter, flushing. Val examined her fingernails.

"Meanwhile, we've got to be in a position to follow developments. That calls for a little scientific eavesdropping."

"And that's where yours truly comes in," said Fitz. "I've got connections, and I can get hold of a dictograph under cover. We plant it in the house there and lead the wires over to the empty Jardin house."

"That's a *swell* idea," said Val, her eyes shining. "And then we keep listening on the other end—"

"Lemme in on this," pleaded Pink. "Look, guys, I can do anything. I used to be an electrician once. I can get in and plant the machine and—"

They broke into an excited gabble. Ellery opened Fitz's drawer and helped himself to the Scotch. Fitz got busy writing out a note to one of his "connections," and Pink boasted that he was as good as any second-story man that ever lived, and Val coached Walter in exactly what he was to say to the unsuspecting Winni.

"Remember!"

"Don't worry, honey."

"Walter, get the hell out there and make a stab at your cartoon, will you? They'll think it's a Cabinet meeting in here."

"Where you going?"

"To see pop."

"Gimme that note!"

Finally Walter and Val and Pink were gone, each to a different place. Ellery hastily put the bottle down on Fitz's desk and ran after Val.

"Peace," said Fitz, reaching glassy-eyed for the Scotch. "It's wonderful."

Chapter XVI

Quest for the Op

ELLERY CAUGHT UP with Val on the street.

"Mind if I tag along?"

Val stopped abruptly on the busy corner of Spring and First. The crowd flowed around them. "I certainly do!"

"That's not polite."

"See here, Mr. King," snapped Val. "We—I appreciate what you're trying to do, and all that, but there are certain things . . . I mean, please don't be annoying. I want to see my father."

"My skin," said Ellery, taking her arm, "is one part rhinoceros hide and two parts armored plate."

Val helplessly permitted herself to be pulled along. If only she could get away from him! He was too quick, too smart. He knew too much already. The way he had analyzed the Ruhig situation. He might find out everything. He might find out that Walter . . .

There was no examination at the City Jail this morning. The shabby man was on hand, but he did not follow them. And the guard unlocked Rhys's cell door and departed at once.

Rhys was calmly playing solitaire and smoking a cigar. His eyes narrowed when he saw the flamboyant figure with Valerie, but he kissed her and shook hands with Hilary "Scoop" King when Val introduced them and invited him to sit down on his pallet, brushing the cards aside.

"I don't know what's the matter," he complained with a grin. "But my friends Glücke and Van Every are ignoring me completely. Do you suppose they've got cold feet?"

He patted the scattered cards into a neat stack.

"Absolutely frozen," nodded Ellery. "Keep it up, Mr. Jardin. You've got 'em buffaloed. They've never had a prisoner who's seemed so happy with his lot."

"It's the clean life I've led. Don't worry, eat three squares a day, and get plenty of exercise. That's the only thing I miss here. Otherwise, it's ideal."

"Oh, pop," said Val.

"Why the long face, puss?"

Val said something perfunctory, and for a few minutes they chattered about inconsequentials. Ellery sucked on a cigaret. There was something in the aristocracy of blood after all. It made things difficult for a seeker after truth whose success must depend upon the agglomeration and synthesis of facts. He kept his eyes dull but aware.

And very soon after Val opened her bag and took out a handkerchief and put it to her nose in a dainty, unnecessary gesture and closed her bag and opened it again; and Ellery, squatting on the end of the pallet, knew that something was happening. He rose and turned his back.

Val kissed her father and got up, too, and Rhys offered his hand to Ellery with a charming smile, and in a moment they were out in the corridor, walking.

And Ellery thought it strange that cards which had been decorated with a schooner should, between their coming and their going, have magically changed into cards decorated with a Dutch windmill.

Now why should an otherwise honest young woman palm one deck of cards and leave another in its place?

"I wish," said Val outside, "that you would make yourself extremely scarce, Mr. King."

"Don't be that way."

"You're getting me very angry. I don't know what you think you're accomplishing by following me, but I assure you you're wasting your time."

"I like you," sighed Ellery. "You send chills down my spine. Do you call that a waste of time?"

"That's not very funny. If you don't stop following me, I'll get Fitz to. I warn you!"

She walked rapidly away, heading for the parking lot. Ellery watched her for a moment. Then he hurried around the corner.

When Val drove northwest on First Street, a small green coupé was behind her, one of that breed of rented cars which overrun Los Angeles like mice. And when Val parked outside the *La Salle* and walked into the lobby, there was Hilary "Scoop" King, his elbows on the desk, waiting for her.

Val said contemptuously: "You worm!" and made for the telephone booth in the lobby.

Mibs Austin stuck her head around the switchboard and called out. Val stopped. "Yes, Mibs?"

"Mr. Spaeth left a note for you."

Val came back. The switchboard girl handed her a hotel envelope and she tore it open.

Mr. King heaved away from the desk and quickly went to the telephone booth.

"Fitzgerald . . . Fitz? King talking," he said rapidly. "I haven't time for explanations. Do me a favor."

"For you, Master-Mind—anything!"

"In five minutes call up Val Jardin at the *La Salle*."

"Why?"

"Shut up, will you? I'm in a hurry. Call her up and tell her to come down to the *Independent* office right away."

"But what for?"

"How should I know? But make the excuse stand up. I don't want her to get wise."

"Trust me, sweetheart."

Ellery hung up and stepped out of the booth. Val was gone.

He went to the desk and said to the blonde girl: "Where did Miss Jardin go?"

"Who wants to know?" said Mibs with a hostile look.

"Give, sister. We work on the same rag."

"Oh. She went upstairs to her apartment."

"I'll show you my etchings some time."

He left the lobby ostentatiously and strolled alongside the building until he came to a tradesman's entrance. Then, with a swift look around, he ducked down the flight of stone steps, ran through an alley, and emerged into the back yard of the hotel. It took him a moment to locate the windows of the Jardin apartment. He jumped for the iron ladder of the fire-escape and clambered noiselessly to the third floor.

The Venetian blind in one of the living-room windows was raised an inch from the sill and he cautiously knelt and peered through the opening. Val was seated on the sofa, her hat still on, fumbling with the catch of her bag. She got it open, reached in, and took out a deck of cards—he saw the schooner on the top card clearly. She dropped her bag and began to spread the cards. But at that moment the telephone rang.

She jumped up, cards in her hand.

"But why?" Ellery heard her ask. There was a buzzing in the telephone. "No! Fitz, it's not possible! . . . Yes, yes. I'll be right down!"

She dropped the 'phone, threw the cards into the drawer of the refectory table—Ellery sighed with relief—grabbed her purse, and dashed out of sight. A second later he heard the front door slam.

He reached in, found the cord, yanked, and crawled over the sill.

Ellery took the loose deck of cards out of the refectory drawer, pulled a chair over to the table, and sat down.

Turning the deck curiously over in his hands he noticed odd, scattered little pencil markings on the long edges.

So that was it. The ancient playing-card code!

"The trick is," he mused, "to find the proper rearrangement of the cards. Assuming such novices in chicanery as Valerie and her father . . . some simple arrangement . . . ascending suits in bridge rotation . . ."

He separated the cards into the four suits and built the spades up from the deuce to the ace. He saw at once that he was on the wrong track. So he built them down from the ace to the deuce. The markings sprang into significant groupings.

Ellery grinned. Child's play! He rearranged the hearts, diamonds, and clubs, put them all together, and read the message.

WORRIED CAN YOU CONTINUE

KEEP OP FROM TALKING

Ellery shuffled and reshuffled the cards, shuffled them again. He spread them, pushed them together, dropped them on the floor, picked them up. No point in arousing Valerie's suspicions. He was sure she had not had time to rearrange the cards and read the message before Fitzgerald's telephone call.

Op. Op. Queer. It might mean "operative." Operative? Private investigator. Detective. Detective! Whom did Jardin mean? Could he possibly be referring to a gentleman who called himself Hilary King? Had they seen through his shrieking sport jacket? "Keep op from talking." No, that didn't gel.

He shook his head and returned the cards to the refectory drawer.

He was about to put his leg over the sill when he caught sight of a piece of white paper stuck between one of the cushions of the sofa and its back.

So he went back and pulled the paper out. It was a hotel envelope with "V. Jardin" scrawled on its face in pencil. Ellery fished under the cushion and soon found a crumpled sheet of hotel stationery.

Walter Spaeth's note to Valerie Jardin. Without qualm, and with relish, Ellery read it.

> Button-Nose: Pink got the dicto. and we're going over to Souci to plant it. Over the wall, of course—we won't let any one see us. If we're caught by the gendarmes, Godelpus.
> Darling, I love you. I LOVE you. I love YOU. Damn it, I do.

The note was signed "Walter" and at the bottom of the sheet there was a gargantuan "X" which Ellery, who knew everything, recognized as the universal lover's shibboleth for "kiss." He had the grace to feel ashamed of himself.

But only for a moment. He replaced the sheet and envelope exactly, climbed out the window, reached in and pulled the cord and lowered the Venetian blind to its precise position before his illegal entry, and thoughtfully went down the fire-escape.

Valerie trudged into the lobby of the La Salle a long time later.

"What was it, Miss Jardin?" asked Mibs Austin eagerly.

"Mibs, you listened in!" Val sighed. "It wasn't anything. Mr. Fitzgerald heard a rumor that my father was about to be released. But when I got downtown I found out nobody knew anything about it."

Ellery, hidden in the music-room off the lobby, chuckled to himself. Rather a dirty trick. But then Fitz was remorseless, with the efficiency and moral temperament of a Japanese war-lord.

He kept himself hidden while Val went to the elevator. He timed her movements. Now she was getting out at the third floor. Now she was at the door of 3-C. Now she was locking it from inside. Now she was at the refectory table. Now she was arranging the cards. Now she was reading the message. . . .

The switchboard buzzed. Ellery hid behind a drape, listening.

"What?" he heard Mibs Austin say. "Okay, Miss Jardin. I'll be right up."

There was a scrambled noise and then the blonde girl called: "Mr. Max! Take the board a minute, will you? I'll be right back."

And a moment later Mibs Austin passed the doorway of the music-room bound for the elevator.

Op . . . Operator. Telephone operator. Mibs Austin!

So it was imperative to continue to keep Mibs Austin from talking, was it?

Ellery lit a cigaret and quietly went through the lobby to the street. He was about to step into his green coupé when another coupé darted into the curb and Walter Spaeth jumped out.

"Hullo!" Walter's lean face was flushed with excitement. "King, we've pulled it off!"

"Good for you."

"It was easy. There's only one detective on duty at *Sans Souci* and Pink and I got in without being spotted. Winni was out, so we had a clear field."

"You planted the dictograph?"

"It's all set. We took along a couple of spare transmitters, just to be on the safe side. We've got one hidden in the study, one in Winni's quarters upstairs, and one in the living-room. And we led the wires over to the empty Jardin house."

"Where's Pink?"

"In the Jardin house stripped for action."

"When are you going to tackle Winni?"

"Tonight."

"Make it eight o'clock and I'll be there to listen in."

"Right." And Walter raced into the *La Salle*.

Chapter XVII

Alarums and Discursions

ELLERY SHUT Fitz's door and made for one of the five telephones on Fitz's desk. "Get me Inspector Glücke at headquarters, please."

"What's doing?" asked Fitz eagerly.

"Glücke? This is Hilary King of the *Independent*."

"What's on your mind?"

"Plenty. Can you take a friendly tip and keep your mouth shut?"

"Try me," said the Inspector.

"Investigate the telephone records of all calls from the *La Salle* switchboard on Monday afternoon, starting around five o'clock."

"What's up?"

"That's what I'm trying to find out. Work through the manager and warn him to keep it under his hat. It's especially important not to tip off the switchboard operator, a girl named Austin. She mustn't know the records are being inspected."

"I get you," said the Inspector slowly.

"Any luck with that fingerprint investigation of the iron table and the binoculars?"

"The rain spoiled the prints. Well, thanks for the tip, King."

"I'll be around to collect 'em in person."

Ellery hung up and sat down in Fitz's best chair, rubbing his chin. Fitz opened a drawer and produced a bottle and two glasses. They drank two quick ones.

"Well, Fitz," said Ellery, "your little white-haired figment of the imagination is beginning to smell a large rodent."

"You're worse than the State Department! What's on the fire, for the love of Mike?"

Ellery tipped his absurd hat over his tinted glasses. "Let me think a while."

"I want news, not ratiocination," growled Fitz. "You're beginning to get my goat."

"Ah, that reminds me," said Ellery. He reached for one of Fitz's 'phones again. "Get me the Magna Studios—Mr. Jacques Butcher."

"What's Butcher got to do with this?"

"Nothing. Hello! Butcher? . . . I don't *want* his secretary, damn it all! I want Butcher himself, in the flesh, Little Napoleon, the Genius. . . ." Ellery sat up excitedly. "My dear young lady, you haven't *heard* any language. I'm reserving my choicest words for that vanishing American you work for. Goodbye!"

He sat back, snorting, and tipped his hat over his eyes again. Fitz looked disgusted and took another drink.

When Ellery left the *Independent* building Fitz was with him, grumbling that he'd get some news if he had to leg it all over the *pueblo* himself.

They found Inspector Glücke communing darkly with his thoughts. He jumped up when he saw Ellery.

"What's behind this, King?" he exclaimed. "Oh, Fitzgerald." He scowled.

"You take a flying leap at the moon," snarled Fitz, planting himself in the best chair.

"Peace," said Ellery. "What did you turn up, Inspector?"

"The *La Salle* telephone records show that a call was made Monday *at five-thirty-five* to Hillcrest 2411!"

"The Spaeth number," said Fitz with awe. He got up and sat down again.

"To whom was the call charged?"

"3-C—the Jardins."

"So what?" asked Fitz after a moment.

"That," said Glücke, "is what I'd like to know."

But Ellery did not seem disturbed. In fact, he began to beam. "Inspector, are you game to play a long shot?"

"What's this—something else I missed?" grumbled Glücke.

"Call in Rhys Jardin and tell him the charges against him are being withdrawn."

"What!" exploded Glücke. "Do you think I'm crazy?"

Fitz stayed up this time. "Go ahead, Glücke—see what this screwball's got!"

"You don't have to mean it," said Ellery soothingly. "Just to see how he reacts. What do you say?"

"Aw, nuts," said the Inspector with bitterness, and he barked an order into his communicator.

Twenty minutes later Rhys Jardin was brought into Inspector Glücke's office. The Inspector was alone.

"I've got news for you, Jardin," said Glücke abruptly.

"Anything would be better than the Coventry I've been subjected to," said Jardin with an amiable smile.

"Van Every and I have been talking your case over and we think we've pulled a boner."

"A boner?" Glücke was astounded to see that, far from receiving the news joyfully, Jardin seemed positively depressed.

"We've just about decided to withdraw the murder charge and let you go." Jardin half-raised his hand. "As soon as the formalities—"

"Inspector—I'm going to make an unusual request."

"What?"

"Don't withdraw the charge."

"You mean you *want* to stay in the can?" asked Glücke in amazement.

"I can't explain. But there are certain reasons—"

The Inspector gaped. Then he shook his head and opened the door. The two detectives came in and Jardin's features relaxed into their usual pleasant lines.

"Thanks a lot," he said earnestly, and marched off as another man would have marched to freedom.

The Inspector closed the door and Ellery and Fitzgerald came out of one of the adjoining rooms. "Can you tie that!"

"Give," said Fitz impatiently, his thick stubby nostrils vibrating in Ellery's direction.

Glücke wagged his head. "I swear it's the first time I ever heard of a man *asking* to be kept in jail for murder!"

"This copper-rivets it," said Ellery with satisfaction. "That's all I wanted to know. The five-thirty-five telephone call Monday from the *La Salle* plus Jardin's conduct just now tell a plain story."

"It's Greek to me."

"Why should Jardin be so anxious to remain in jail? Why should he *ask* to be held on the murder count?"

Understanding leaped into Fitz's eyes. "My God!" he shouted. "He's got an out!"

The Inspector paled. "An out?" he echoed feebly.

"Certainly," said Ellery. "It's probably an ironclad alibi. I've discovered that Jardin warned his daughter to make sure Mibs Austin kept her mouth shut. Now if that five-thirty-five call Monday was made either by Jardin himself or, as seems more likely from the facts, by Val Jardin with Jardin at her side near the switchboard in sight of the Austin girl, then the whole thing becomes clear."

"Jardin would have an alibi for almost the exact moment of the murder," cried Fitz. "And if the Austin wench testified in court . . . zowie!"

Glücke looked ill. "If that's true," he muttered, "he doesn't want the alibi spilled now, so he warns his daughter to keep the Austin girl quiet. This is wonderful." But there was no appreciation on his face.

"Why the hell should he want to keep the alibi secret?" asked Fitz, frowning. "That doesn't make sense."

"It does," drawled Ellery, "if he's trying to protect some one." The two men stared at him. "Don't you see that that's the exact point? He's keeping the heat on himself while the one he's shielding remains unsuspected. He's protecting Walter Spaeth."

"Spaeth!" exclaimed the Inspector.

"Of course. Didn't Walter admit last night he was the man Frank saw wearing Jardin's coat? He was all ready to talk when Val Jardin shut him up; and after the three of them had their council of war he retracted his admission. That can only mean that Walter didn't know about Jardin's alibi until the Jardins told him about it in this office last night. He didn't know Jardin had an out. So up to last night he was protecting Jardin—at least, he thought he was."

"From what?" demanded Fitz.

"I don't know." Ellery frowned, shrugged. "And now that they've all shut up in concert, it's evident that the Jardins are protecting Walter."

"From what?" asked Fitz doggedly.

"God only knows, and I'm not His confidant. If they'd only talk, the tight-mouthed idiots! One thing is sure, though—while Jardin has his alibi to protect him, Walter Spaeth is in no such enviable position. They seem to think he's in a tough spot. Otherwise Jardin wouldn't be acting so contrary to common sense."

"Spaeth, huh," said Glücke in a savage mumble. Fitz drew his bushy brows together, shaking his head a little.

"Yes, Spaeth," snapped Ellery. "Have you stopped to ask yourself whom Valerie Jardin could have been telephoning when she called the Spaeth house Monday afternoon?"

"Cripe! If it could have been young Spaeth himself—"

"Who else? I think Walter was in his father's house at five-thirty-five and that the Jardins have known it all along!"

"If he was," cried the Inspector, "it puts him in the murder room three minutes after the killing! Well, maybe not in the room, but we could track that down. But it's a cinch now that he, not Jardin, was the only outsider to enter the grounds during the crime period. He was wearing Jardin's coat, and we've got that coat—stained with human blood." He looked sly. "And another thing—if he killed his old man, then he also tried to frame Jardin for the crime."

"Horse manure," said Fitz.

"Didn't I let him go Monday night *before* the Jardins? Couldn't he have beat it back to the *La Salle* and planted the coat and sword in Jardin's closet? Besides—I never released this—Walter Spaeth's fingerprints were found on the rapier as well as Jardin's. Prints on the weapon!"

"What!" said Ellery in a shocked voice.

"I didn't see any point," said Glücke sheepishly, "in sort of confusing the Jardin issue—"

"Walter's prints on the rapier," muttered Ellery.

"Anyway, the motive still stands—disinherited, wasn't he? And always scrapping with his old man, too." The Inspector rubbed his hands. "It's a case, boys. It's got the makings of a case. All I need for Van Every is a couple of witnesses in the right places—"

"Excuse me," said Fitz, making for the door.

Ellery pounced on him. "Where are you going?"

"To make newspaper history, my fine-feathered friend," said Fitz gleefully. "My God, this yarn will sell a million papers!"

"Fitz," said Ellery in a ferocious voice, "if you dare print one syllable of what you've just heard—" He whispered the rest in Fitz's ear.

Fitz looked pugnacious. Then he looked surprised. Then he began to grin. Ellery dragged him back to Glücke's desk.

At eight o'clock that night ghosts walked in the Jardin house at *Sans Souci*.

They were ponderable and fleshly ghosts with the air of conspirators, moving restlessly about in the room off the terrace which had served as Rhys Jardin's study. An electric-battery lantern on the floor threw long shadows to the bare walls; no light escaped through the glass wall to the terrace, for the lantern was shielded.

The chief spectre was Pink, crouched Indian-fashion on his hams with a pair of receivers over his ears, tinkering with a small apparatus before him in the light of the lantern. A pile of cans variously labeled "Soup," "Corn," and "Minced Ham" lay beside him, several open and empty.

A tall thin wraith named Queen trod the boards at one side of the room, and a large square one named Fitzgerald patrolled the other. Kneeling beside Pink was a female ghost in riding breeches—queer note in ghostly fashions—with a long tear along one thigh, as if a leg had caught on a sharp stake at the top of a fence.

"Shhh!" hissed Pink suddenly. "Here they come!"

Ellery and Fitz skittered forward. But Val was quicker. The two men fought over the last pair of earphones. Ellery won, leaving Fitz to glare and press his beefy face close to Val's ear.

Through the membranes came the sound of a door closing and Winni Moon's voice, half-frightened and half-seductive. "In here, Wally darling. We're alone here."

"Winni the Glut," whispered Val vindictively.

"Are you sure there's nobody around to overhear?" said Walter's voice.

Winni's voice was no longer frightened and altogether seductive. "Not a soul, darling. Nobody comes near me. I'm weally the loneliest person—"

"I can't stay long, Winni. No one must know I came here. So I'll have to say it fast."

"Say what, Walter?" She was frightened again.

"Do you think I'm your friend?"

They could almost see her pout. "I've twied awfully hard to *get* you to be, but you never weally showed that—"

"I'm enough a friend of yours to come out in the open, instead of skulking around in the dark like a rat!"

"I don't know what you *mean*," complained Winni.

"I've been doing some spying on my own. And I know," said Walter, accenting each word, "all about that little business arrangement between you and Ruhig."

"Oh!" said Winni. The gasp smashed against the receivers.

"I know that Ruhig told you there was a later will in existence. I know he told you that, unless you married him, he'd produce that will and you'd see those fifty millions pulled right out of your lap!"

"Walter. . . . How—how did you know that?"

The listeners let out their breaths.

"Jeeze," said Pink.

"He's wonderful," moaned Val.

"Shut up," howled Fitz. "Let's get this!"

"*Please*," groaned Ellery.

"—mind how I know. Well, I hate Ruhig's guts. I know you do, too. Winni, he's making a jackass out of you!"

She was silent.

"He's lying, Winni," said Walter gently. "There never was such a will. He's just trying to scare you into marrying him and sharing the fifty millions with him."

Her voice came through strangely distorted. "Walter, do you mean to tell me it was all—it was all—"

"He invented the whole thing," said Walter in an earnest, friendly way. "You never saw that will he spoke about, did you?"

"N-no."

"There! Doesn't that prove it? Listen, Winni. Forget that fellow; tell him to go to the devil. You and I might make some other arrangement—a settlement. Or maybe even . . ."

His voice trailed off into a mumble, as if he were whispering intimately into her ear.

Val bit a hole in the corner of her handkerchief.

The rest for the most part was inaudible. Within a short time Walter said something about having to get away, and they heard the click of the door, receding footsteps.

"Whee!" cried Val, jumping up.

"I'll be a cockeyed dinglehoofer," said Pink slowly. "It worked."

"Quiet," urged Ellery. "Let's see what happens. If I've got that blonde baby figured right, she'll make straight for the telephone."

They listened eagerly. Two minutes passed. They heard the sound of a door closing again. Whether it was the study door or some other they could not tell. There were more footsteps, quick nervous ones, for five long minutes. And then suddenly the sound of some one running and another click.

"Opewator!" It was Winni's voice, hard and angry.

"I'll be damned," said Fitz. He took a flask out of his hip pocket and drank thirstily.

"Wuhig? Anatole Wuhig! . . . Wuhig! This is Winni. . . . Never mind that gweasy line! Listen to me, you. I've been thinking things over and I think you're taking me for a wide. . . . Yes, a wide! Why should I split all that money with you? I'm not going to mawwy you, and that's final!"

There was another long silence, as if Ruhig was talking slowly, voluminously, and persuasively.

"Don't give me that will stuff! I don't think there ever *was* another will! . . . I will so discuss it. Yes, and wight this minute! You're a faker and a liar! . . . Oh, you're still twying to pull the wool over my eyes, are you? Well, if there *is* a will and you've got it, why didn't you show it to me? . . . Yes, *show* it to me! And none of your fakes, either! I know Solly's handwiting. And I don't want any what-you-call-'ems—photostatic copies. You bwing the weal thing over this second! . . . I know you don't cawwy it awound in your pocket. . . . All wight, pick your own time. *I* don't care. There's no such will, anyway. I'm fwom Missouwi, Mister Wuhig. . . . Thwee o'cwock tomowwow afternoon? In this house. . . . Yes!"

Thunder crashed—the receiver being restored to its place.

"Just goes to show," sighed Ellery. "I guess I'm a remarkable fellow."

"Do you think Ruhig's bluffing?" asked Val anxiously.

"Not at all. It's evening, which explains why he can't bring the will over now. He would if he could."

"How's that?" demanded Fitz.

"Obviously it's in a safe-deposit vault—he'll have to wait until tomorrow to get his hands on it. And he's giving himself plenty of time tomorrow to think the situation over. However, I believe Counselor Ruhig will be here per schedule."

They all started. For out of the earphones burbled a snarl scarcely recognizable as Miss Winni Moon's voice.

"Filthy little cwook!"

Chapter XVIII

Rape of the Awning

VAL AWOKE FRIDAY morning with a buzzing in her ears, which quickly turned out to be the front-door bell.

She scrambled out of bed and ran through the living-room, pulling a negligée on hastily. It might be Walter. She hoped it *was* Walter. They had sat up half the night making love and drinking sherry. There had hardly been time, between sips and kisses, to talk. As she ran, Val wondered if she oughtn't to go back and fix herself up. But then she thought he might just as well get used to seeing her fresh out of bed, with tousled hair and sleepy eyes and no powder or lipstick. Besides, she looked prettier that way. Rhys always said so. Rhys always said that she looked nicer with cold cream on her face and a tissue in her hand than most other women looked ready for presentation at the Court of St. James's. Rhys always said—

"In a minute," she called gaily, fumbling with the latch. She got the door open and smiled her most ravishing smile.

"Oh," said Val. "Oh. Mibs. Why, what's the trouble?"

Mibs leaped past her into the foyer and leaned against the wall, pressing her hand to her heart.

"Shut the door," she gasped. "Oh, shut it!"

Val shut it. "What's the matter, Mibs?"

"Wait—till—I get my breath!"

"You poor thing. Come in here and sit down. Why, you're shaking!"

The blonde girl sank into Rhys's armchair, licking her pale lips. "Miss Jardin, I—I'm scared to death."

"Nonsense," said Val, sitting down on the arm of the chair. "Why should you be? Let me get you something."

"No. No, I'll be all right. It's just that—" She looked at Val piteously. "Miss Jardin, I'm being . . . followed."

"Oh," said Val, and she got up and went to the sofa and sat down herself.

"I wish Pink were here," whimpered the girl. "He'd know what to do. Where is he? Why hasn't he been—"

"Pink's off on a special sort of job," said Val slowly. "Tell me all about it, Mibs."

Mibs drew a quavery breath. "I've been nervous ever since you spoke to me Monday night about—about your father and my seeing him Monday afternoon and speaking to Mr. Spaeth. . . . I went out to the drug store yesterday for a soda and—and I thought somebody was following me. On the way back, too. Some Hollywood wisenheimer, I thought. I didn't see him.

But last night, too. When I went home. The same thing. And now, this morning, on my way to work . . . Somebody's after me, Miss Jardin!"

Val sat still, thinking. She tried to look unconcerned, but her own heart was pounding. If Mibs was being followed, that might mean . . . Could somebody actually be . . .

"We'll have to be careful, Mibs," she said in a tone she tried to make light.

"I'm so scared I—I . . ." The girl was almost hysterical.

Val went to her again and put her arms about the girl. "Have you a family, Mibs?"

Mibs was crying. "N-no. I'm all alone. I've only got Pink. I come from St. Lou, and I've been here two years and Pink's been my only f-friend. . . ."

"Hush. You don't think we'd let anybody harm you, Mibs!" The girl sobbed. "I'll tell you what we'll do, honey," said Val in a bright voice. "Suppose you stay with me for a few days until this blows over. I mean—I'm alone here, and you can sleep in my father's bed, or with me if you'd like that better—"

"Oh, could I?" cried Mibs, raising a streaked face.

"Of course, silly. It will be lots of fun. You don't even have to go back to your own place for your things. I've got heaps of underwear and stockings and things—"

"Can I have my meals here, too?"

"Certainly. Here, here's an extra key. Now dry your eyes and fix yourself up and go downstairs as if nothing happened."

"Yes," sniffled Mibs.

"I may have to go out later, but I'm sure no one's going to do anything to you in your own lobby!"

"No. That's right," said Mibs, smiling faintly.

"There! Isn't that better? Now go wash your face." And Val led the blonde girl to her bathroom with a reassuring laugh and a stomach that felt like one vast, painful vacuum.

"Tell you why I called you," said Inspector Glücke to Ellery. He stooped over a small safe in his office.

"Nothing's happened?" began Ellery quickly.

"No, no, we're in the clear. It's this." The Inspector opened his safe and brought out something wrapped in tissue paper, something with the shape of a large bottle. "It was on your tip that we found it," he said gruffly, "so you're entitled to get in on it, King. I guess we owe you a lot."

"What is it?" asked Ellery in an avid voice.

Glücke began carefully removing the folds of tissue. "We had quite a time searching that sewer outside *Sans Souci*, but we finally fished this out of the muck. It got stuck near the bottom of the sewer."

It was an Indian club, soiled and evil-smelling. A red-brown clot adhered to part of the bulging end.

"Is that," frowned Ellery, "blood?" He flicked the clot with one fingernail.

"Nothing else but."

"Any prints?"

"Some very old ones—just traces of 'em. Jardin's, the girl's."

Ellery nodded, sucking his lower lip.

"What made you tell me to search that sewer?" asked the Inspector slowly.

"Eh? Oh—a minor reasoning process. By the way, did you find anything else of interest in the sewer?"

"Not a thing."

Ellery shook his head.

He parked his coupé outside the gate at *Sans Souci*, much to Atherton Frank's surprise. Indeed, he was even assisted by the detective on duty, who seemed oddly friendly. Frank scratched his head, swinging his half-arm in an interrogatory manner.

But no one enlightened him, and Ellery sauntered up the drive toward the Spaeth house. A sense of desolation smote him. It was like coming into the main street of a ghost-city.

But he shook his head in impatience at himself and applied his mind to the problem at hand. It was a knotty one; something told him that the key-knot was missing, the discovery of which would unravel the whole puzzle fabric.

He avoided the porte-cochère and circled the Spaeth house, trudging along under the geometric row of royal palms and wrestling with thoughts that persisted in slipping through the fingers of his brain.

He mounted the terrace steps and sat down almost against the wall in Solly Spaeth's most elaborate summer chair, putting his elbows on his knees and his chin on his palms.

A hiss brought his head up. Across the rock garden the head of Valerie Jardin protruded from the doorway of the empty Jardin study. She motioned angrily, but he shook his head, smiling. After a moment she slipped down the Jardin terrace steps and ran across to the Spaeth house.

"She'll see you!" she whispered, darting up under the protection of the terrace awning. "Are you mad?"

"Never saner," said Ellery. "Winni the Moocher is out stuffing her gullet. It seems she's sick of preparing her own meals. At least that's what the detective on duty says."

"Did you come in through the *gate*?" asked Val, horrified.

"Why not?" said Ellery innocently. "Didn't you?"

Val gazed ruefully at her ripped riding-habit. "Over the fence again. At that, Mr. King, you took an awful chance. If Ruhig should be watching—"

"He isn't."

"How do you know that?" asked Val suspiciously.

"Silence. I'm trying to concentrate."

Val looked at him in a dubious way but he merely lay back in the chair, resting his neck against the back. He folded his hands across his chest. Val experienced a twinge of bafflement. He certainly was the queerest man. Concentrate? He was just snoozing!

"Better come away from here," she said, taking a tentative step toward the stairs. "If you want to sleep, you can join Pink. He's taking a nap back there. At least Winni won't come back and find you."

"Leave this comfortable chair?" murmured Ellery. "Not on your life." He opened one eye.

"You are by all odds the most—" Val stopped, watching him in bewilderment.

The single eye, naturally invisible to her behind the tinted glasses, nevertheless contrived to communicate a certain fixity, a surface tension, to his figure. He sat up abruptly, his shoes thumping on the flagged floor.

"What's the *matter* with you?" said Val, puzzled.

It was noon, and the sun poised high. Ellery rose, looking up at the awning overhead, his Adam's apple quivering delicately. His gaze was directed toward a sliver of blinding light in the awning. He stepped on the chair and raised the blue glasses to his forehead, examining the rupture closely.

"What's wonderful about that?" demanded Val. "You're the oddest creature! It's only a rip in the awning."

He slipped the glasses back over his eyes and stepped down, smiling. "I'm sensitive to sudden flashes of light. Go away, will you, darling?"

He settled back in the chair again. Val threw up her hands and descended to the garden. He watched her from under the glasses. She darted off on a tangent bound for the far boundary of *Sans Souci*, where the bushes and trees were thick and the fence could be climbed without benefit of witness. After a moment her slender figure, boyish in the jodhpurs, disappeared beneath the palms.

Ellery lay quiet for some time, watching the palms, the terrace of the Jardin house. Cicadas sawed away somewhere; the garden before him crawled and hummed with bees. There was no sign of human life anywhere.

So he got out of the chair again and stepped up on it and once more examined the slit in the awning overhead.

The colored stripes ran from top to bottom of the awning, the slit lying neatly parallel between a yellow stripe and a green one.

"Tear roughly a half-inch long," he mumbled to himself. "Well, well," and he took a penknife out of his pocket and was about to employ surgery on the awning when he caught sight of something else, and he stopped.

On the stone wall of the house proper, not three feet to the side of the glassed area which served as the fourth and outer wall of the study, there was a sharp, clean, fresh-looking nick. Something with a keen point had chipped away a fragment of stone. He looked at the nick in the stone, and he looked at the tear in the canvas. The nick was high on the wall, and the tear was high on the awning. Tall as he was, and standing on the chair, he still had to crane directly upwards to see them closely. Yes, the tear was a little higher than the nick, and directly in front of it, judging it by the eye with the flagged floor as a base. And tear and nick were a mere four inches apart. Four inches!

Muttering excitedly to himself, he proceeded to mutilate the unoffending awning. He slashed ruthlessly away in a rough rectangle with the penknife until he was able to pull a piece about five inches square out of the awning.

He dropped to the flags, holding the canvas scrap gingerly. In the stronger light near the edge of the terrace he thought he detected a faint brown stain on the upper edges of the slit.

Golden-brown. Molasses-brown. Molasses. Molasses and potassium cyanide?

And what would an Italian rapier be doing sticking its smeared nose through a nice, clean, summery awning?

That, said Mr. Hilary-Ellery King-Queen to himself as he rolled up the canvas square with cautious fingers, was the Question.

He wrapped the roll in a handkerchief and, holding the tubular result like a twist of diamonds under his coat, he made his way from the terrace along the row of palms to the gate, trying to look unconcerned but not succeeding.

"Well, Bronson?" said Ellery, leaning over the laboratory table.

The Chemist nodded. "Molasses and cyanide, all right. Say, I've heard about you, King, around headquarters here. Where did you get hold of this piece of canvas?"

"If you're thinking of 'phoning Glücke," said Ellery hastily, rewrapping the scrap of awning with fingers that trembled a little, "don't bother. I'll be seeing him soon myself."

"But look here—" began Bronson.

"Goodbye. Oh, isn't it a lovely day?" said Ellery, hurrying out.

Chapter XIX

Blonde in the Woodpile

VALERIE CROSSED THE *La Salle* lobby, vaguely noticing that the manager of the hotel, a small dark man, was seated before the switchboard with Mibs Austin's earphones clamped about his head.

She supposed the telephone girl was upstairs and made her way to the elevator, sighing. The poor thing had been so terrified. If she only knew what really hung over her!

She unlocked the door of 3-C. "Mibs, are you here?"

The door swung to and the slam echoed. There was no other sound.

"Mibs?" Val stepped into the living-room. It was empty.

"Mibs!"

The color drained out of her cheeks. She ran into her bedroom, into Rhys's room, the bathrooms, the kitchen. . . .

Mibs was not there.

She clawed at the front door and flew down the emergency stairway to the lobby.

"Where's Miss Austin?" she cried shrilly.

The manager removed the earphones. "Why, I thought—"

"Where is she!"

"Don't you know?" asked the manager, surprised.

Val was furious in her panic. "You fool, if I knew would I ask you? Where is she!"

The man looked annoyed. "Didn't you call her up an hour or so ago? I'll have to give her a talking to. She can't make excuses like that to take time off."

"Say that again," said Val, speaking with distinctness. "She told you I telephoned her?"

"That's what the snip said. She said you called her and asked her to meet you right away at the corner of Cahuenga and Sunset on an important matter. So naturally—"

Val groped for the support of the desk. "Oh, yes," she said faintly. "Thank you." And she went over to a divan and sat down under the dwarf palm, her thighs quivery with weakness.

Call. . . . She hadn't made any call. Some one had telephoned Mibs, using her name. An appointment!

The manager went back to the switchboard, looking angry. Val felt like laughing. Angry! Oh, Mibs, you fool. . . . Val managed to get out of the divan and go to the telephone booth. It took her a long time to fish out the coins from her purse; her fingers seemed incapable of holding on to anything.

"Walter Spaeth," she said, when she was connected with the *Independent*. It was supposed to be a calm, unconcerned alto; but somehow it came out a dry croak.

"Spaeth talking," said Walter's blessed voice.

"Walter. Something terrible's happened."

"Darling! What's the matter? Has Winni—Ruhig—"

"It's—it's Mibs. Mibs Austin." Val clung to the telephone. "Walter . . . she's *gone*."

Walter made a funny little sound at the other end of the wire. "Gone? I thought you said she'd agreed not to— I mean, that she wasn't to leave—"

"You don't understand, Walter," said Val stiffly. "Somebody . . . somebody telephoned her an hour ago using my name and telling her to meet me at Cahuenga and Sunset. But—I—didn't—'phone her!"

"Oh," said Walter. Then he said: "Hold tight, funny-face. I'll be right down."

Val hung up and stood in the hot booth for a moment. Then she went out and toiled upstairs to wait for Walter. She felt like an old, old woman.

Walter was there in thirty minutes, and she let him in and bolted the door behind him. They went into the living-room and Walter sat down. Val went to the windows mechanically and let down the Venetian blinds. That done, she moved the Chinese vase a half-inch to the left on the refectory table. Then she moved it back again.

Walter sat silently, the flesh over his eyes bunched into little knots. His fist was pounding up and down on his knee.

"Do you think," said Val in a tight voice, "do you think she's—"

Walter got up and tramped around the room, red in the face. "What I can't understand is how the little fool ever let a trick like that take her in," he muttered. "Good lord, doesn't she know your voice?"

"I haven't had much to do with her, Walter," replied Val listlessly.

"The damned fool!"

"Walter." Val twisted her fingers. "She may be—she might be . . ." It was hard to say. It was impossible to say.

Walter sat down again and buried his face in his hands. "We're up against it, Val. For fair, this time." Val nodded wordlessly. How well she knew! "Now we've got blood on our hands."

"Walter," she moaned.

But it was true. Their scheming, their crazy impetuous scheming, their frantic effort to stave off the inevitable— Walter, Walter's predicament, Walter in the shadow of a tall gaunt thing made of wood. . . . It had cost the life of an innocent person.

Val said with a faint nausea: "Do you think she's—" But she could not get the word out.

Walter rubbed his palms together in a meaningless sort of way. "Whoever's behind this, hon, won't stop at anything. Somehow he found out about your father's alibi, and he's put the Austin kid out of the way to destroy it." His voice rose. "I can't, I simply can't understand such damned brutality, such savagery! How could any one hate another man so much?"

"It's our fault, Walter," whispered Val.

His face softened and he went over to her and pulled her to him. "Look, Val." He cupped her chin and made her look up at him. "Let's finish this mess here and now. We're miserable failures at this thing—we're wriggling like worms trying to get away from something that's bound to get us in the end."

"Not us," cried Val. "You!"

"You've done too much for me already, you and Rhys. And meanwhile we've done something to an innocent person we'll never be able to undo."

Val, thinking of the blonde girl, began to cry. "How could we have let her take such chances—"

"Stop crying, Val," he said gently. "The first thing we've got to do is report her disappearance to the police." Val nodded, sobbing. "Maybe it isn't too late," he said encouragingly. "Maybe she's still alive. If she is, we can't waste a second."

"But we'll have to tell them all about—all about you—"

"High time, too!" And he grinned a little.

"No, Walter." She pressed her face against his coat.

"If I don't—what about your father?" he said in the same gentle voice. "Remember, with Mibs's disappearance he has no alibi. No alibi, Val."

"Oh, Walter, what an awful, awful mess!"

"Now let's go downtown and tell Glücke the truth."

She raised her head, agonized. "But if you do, Walter, they'll arrest you! They'll say you murdered your father!"

He kissed the tip of her nose. "Did I ever tell you you're beautiful?"

"I can't let you do it!"

"And that I've dreamed about you every night for a year?"

Walter or Rhys. Rhys or Walter. It went round and round in her head like a phonograph record. It might slide off to some other place, but it always came back to the same place. . . . She dropped her arms helplessly.

PART FIVE

Chapter XX

Everything but the Truth

WALTER WENT to the telephone and called police headquarters. He waited patiently, his back to Valerie. His tall figure shimmered; and Val sat down, rubbing her eyes. She wished she could go to bed and sleep and sleep for months, years.

He spoke to Inspector Glücke in a rather listless tone, telling him about the disappearance of Mibs Austin and the false telephone call, the appointment for the corner of Cahuenga and Sunset. . . . Everything had drained out, Valerie felt. What was the use of fighting?

"Let's go, Val."

"All right, Walter."

Neither spoke on the journey downtown. There didn't seem to be anything to say. The saucy child-face of Mibs Austin with its dip and crown of blondness danced before Val, obscuring the streets. She closed her eyes, but Mibs remained there like a face on a bobbing balloon.

Glücke received them in state, with two police stenographers occupying chairs beside his desk and District Attorney Van Every enthroned to one side, all silence and alertness.

"Did you find out anything?" asked Walter abruptly.

"We're working on it now," said the Inspector. "What makes you think the girl was snatched?"

"Because she had certain information which the murderer of my father didn't want known."

Glücke laughed. "Sit down, Miss Jardin. Is this another of your fairy stories, Spaeth? If you've got anything to tell me, say it now. And make it stick this time."

"I see," said Walter, "you're all ready for me." Val looked down at her hands, and they stopped twisting. "All right. I'm glad to get this off my chest. What I said—"

A scuffling sound from an adjoining room stopped him. One of the doors burst open and Rhys Jardin appeared, struggling in the arms of a detective.

"Walter!" he cried. "It's a trick! The girl wasn't abducted at all! Glücke had her—"

"Stubborn to the end," remarked the District Attorney wryly. "Too bad, Glücke."

"Pop!" Val flew to him. The detective released Jardin, puffing.

"Do you mean to say," growled Walter, "that you cooked this up, damn you?"

The Inspector made a furious sign and the detective went back into the room and came out with Mibs Austin. The girl's eyes were red and swollen, and she kept them averted, refusing to look at the Jardins, at Walter. And suddenly she began to weep.

Rhys Jardin said curtly: "It was just a trick to make you talk, Walter. That newspaperman, King, found out about my alibi—"

"King?" cried Val. "The beast! I *knew* he'd spoil everything!"

"He told Glücke and Glücke arranged for the 'abduction' of Miss Austin. He wanted to scare Walter into talking."

"Can the chatter," said the Inspector harshly. "All right, it didn't work. But I've got this girl, and she's talked plenty. Want to hear what she said, Spaeth?"

"Oh, Miss Jardin," sobbed Mibs, "I couldn't help it. They got a police matron or—or somebody to call me, and I thought you were in trouble and went down to—to—"

"It's all right, Mibs," said Val steadily. "I'm glad you're safe."

"And they brought me up here and—and made me tell. I was so frightened I didn't know what to do. They made me tell—"

"Just a minute," said Walter. "If you know about Rhys Jardin's alibi, Inspector, then you know he's innocent."

Rhys said simply: "I'm a free man, Walter."

"That," said Walter, "is a different story."

"Miss Austin says," snapped Glücke, "that she spoke to you on the 'phone at five-thirty-five Monday afternoon, and that you were talking from your father's house. That's three minutes after the murder!"

"My advice to you, young fellow," said Van Every soberly from his corner, "is to come clean."

Walter stood facing them, hands jammed in his pockets. He wore a faint grin. The stenographers poised their pencils.

But just then the door opened and Mr. Hilary King appeared, breathing hard, as if he had been running. He was carrying a long object wrapped in brown paper which had a rather curious shape.

He stopped short on the threshold, taking in the situation at a glance. "Looks like Scene Two, Act Three," he grunted. "Well, who's said what?"

"It won't be long now," announced the Inspector triumphantly. "Spaeth's ready to talk."

"Oh," said Ellery. "Is he?"

"Am I?" murmured Walter. "And the answer is: no."

"What?" yelled Glücke. "Again?"

"I kept my mouth shut before because I didn't know about Rhys's alibi and thought I had to protect him—"

"Not knowing about his alibi," murmured Ellery, "what information did you possess which made you think Jardin killed your father?"

Walter ignored him. "Today, when I thought Miss Austin was in danger, I felt I had to talk. But now? Nuts to all of you." And he grinned.

"That's final?" demanded the Inspector.

Walter said lightly: "You'll have to speak to my lawyer."

Ellery grimaced. "You're making me do a lot of unnecessary work, Walter. Glücke, time's a-wastin'. It's two o'clock."

Glücke scowled at him. The District Attorney drew him off to a corner and they conferred earnestly. Ellery joined them, waving his package as if he were arguing.

"All right," grumbled Glücke at last. "I suppose there's plenty of time to attend to Spaeth. We'll look this Ruhig bird over and see where he fits in."

"Ruhig," said Val intensely. "You've told them!" Ellery looked guilty. "You know what you are? You're a filthy *traitor!*"

Glücke nodded to two men, and they took places on each side of Walter. "It's between you and Ruhig, Spaeth. I warn you right now, I've got two warrants in my pocket. One for you and one for Ruhig. My own hunch is you, but King seems to think we ought to give Ruhig the once-over first."

"Come on," said Ellery impatiently. "You're keeping fifty million dollars waiting."

Inspector Glücke engineered their entry into *Sans Souci* with artistic efficiency. Mr. Anatole Ruhig, who had been under secret police observation, had not yet made his unsuspecting appearance; but it was necessary to keep Miss Winni Moon, who was on the premises, in darkness. A hole had been hacked in the willow fence in a remote corner of the grounds; they crept through, constantly admonished to make no noise, and were led to the empty Jardin house from the far side, out of sight of the Spaeth house.

They caught Pink, purple-eyed and haggard from lack of sleep, completely by surprise. He jumped up with a foolish, trapped look, ready to fight; but when everybody ignored him and Glücke seized the earphones, he scratched his head and lit a cigaret and wandered about asking questions which no one bothered to answer. He did not see Rhys Jardin at first. When he did, the cigaret fell out of his mouth and Rhys stepped on it and punched his shoulder. After that Pink stayed close to Jardin with a pathetic tenacity.

Glücke's men vanished, apparently pre-instructed. There was nothing to do but wait.

Val and Walter sat down on the floor and talked to each other in undertones, ignoring the others. Ellery paced up and down, smoking tasteless cigarets. Rhys Jardin leaned against a wall, and Pink helped him lean. No one said anything.

Glücke kept looking at his watch. Two-fifty. Fifty-five. Three o'clock. The earphones were dead. He glanced at Ellery with an interrogatory scowl. Three-five. . . .

"Here he comes!"

They scrambled toward him then, listening intently.

The closing of a door.

"They're in Spaeth's study," muttered Ellery, peering through the glass wall.

Mr. Anatole Ruhig's voice grumbled through the receiver. "I'm taking a terrible chance, Winni."

"You don't fool me, Anatole Wuhig!" said Winni coldly. "If there's a will, show it to me."

"You're a fool."

"How do I know what you told me was twue? You said you got into the gwounds over the fence when you couldn't find that man Fwank—I don't even believe that. You going over a wall!"

"What's come over you?" asked the lawyer irritably. "I thought we had this all straightened out. My two assistants were with me that first time, at five-fifteen; I knew Spaeth didn't like to be kept waiting, so they boosted me over the wall and followed. I saw Spaeth, and he signed the new will and it was properly witnessed. Then we left."

"Yes," said Winni in an excited voice. "And if that's twue, maybe you and your gangsters killed him!"

"Don't get notions now," said Ruhig with a dangerous softness. "I wasn't in there more than five minutes. He had the will all made out. I was outside *Sans Souci* before five-thirty—had to go back over the wall, blast it; the gate was locked. When I left, Spaeth was very much alive."

"Then why did you come back? You came back after six."

"Spaeth told me to. There was other business he wanted to go over, and he said he expected Walter right away and wanted to talk to him alone. . . ."

Glücke glanced up at Walter with a twisted smile. Val gripped Walter's arm convulsively, and Walter went pale.

"Well, I think it's a pack of lies," sniffed Winni.

"Oh, for God's sake. I swiped the will right out of Spaeth's drawer when that fool Walewski and I found the body. I did it under his nose and he never knew the difference!"

"Well, show it to me, if you're so smart. Don't talk—just show it to me."

"One moment," said Ruhig's voice, and there was a snarling quality in it that brought a queer exclamation from the invisible Winni. "What made you think I was lying to you?"

"Keep away from me. My own mind, that's what."

"Your mind?" said the lawyer. "Isn't that a little boastful?" There was a silence, as if he were backing away, looking around. "I'm a gullible cluck. Come on, tell me! This wasn't your idea, you dumb Swede!"

"If you must know," said Winni in a frightened yet defiant little rush, "Walter Spaeth warned me!"

"It's a plant!" yelled Ruhig.

And then everything happened at once. The receivers scratched and squealed, and there were confused sounds of toppling furniture, men's hoarse exclamations, scuffling.

"Let's go!" shouted Glücke, tearing the receivers from his ears. But Ellery was already sprinting around the pool in a dash for the Spaeth terrace, the long package clamped under his arm.

The Inspector scrambled after him and the others, after a stunned moment, streamed along behind.

They found Counselor Ruhig, very pallid and pasty-faced, standing lax in the grip of two detectives; and Winni lying in a faint over Solly Spaeth's most beautifully brocaded chair.

Another detective was waving a piece of folded foolscap exultantly. "Got him with his pants down. It's the will!"

"Tried to tear it up," said one of the men holding Ruhig, "but we stopped that." He shook the little man ungently.

Glücke grabbed the paper. As he was reading it, District Attorney Van Every hurried in. "Everything under control? Ah, Ruhig. Does my heart good to see you looking so gay. Let's see that, Inspector."

He read the paper very carefully. "Chalk up one more for Mr. King. This is getting monotonous. I'm afraid, Spaeth, this will comes a little too late to do you any good."

"Is it—" began Val, but she could not go on.

"It's a will properly dated, signed, and witnessed, revoking all previous wills and leaving the entire estate to Walter Spaeth."

Winni popped out of her faint. "It's a lie!" she screamed. "Solly left it to *me!*"

"I'm afraid you're out of luck, Miss Moon."

"But I owe *thousands* to the dwess shops!" she wailed, jumping up and down. She glared spitefully at Val. "Now she'll get it—that sawed-off, pinky little wunt!" And she collapsed in the chair again in another faint.

Van Every shrugged, and Glücke said with a smack of his lips: "This gives us about all we need, Van. Motive's all clear now. And Ruhig's testimony that Spaeth told him he was expecting his son jibes perfectly—"

"I'll make a deal," jabbered Ruhig. "Forget this business and I'll testify I saw Spaeth—"

"Spaeth came," said Glücke, ignoring him "—we know he was in this house through Miss Austin's statement—his father showed him the new will, tried to make friends. But the skunk bumped his father off to get that dough."

"No!" shrieked Val, holding on to Walter.

"Inspector," pleaded Rhys, "for heaven's sake don't go off half-cocked. This boy wouldn't kill his own father. Walter, tell him what happened. He'll believe you. He's got to believe you!"

"He can talk all he wants when I get through," Glücke said coldly. "We've got his prints on the rapier, his own confession that he wore your coat, Jardin

—which has human blood on it—and he had opportunity to plant the coat and sword in your closet at the *La Salle*."

Winni opened one eye, saw that nobody was paying any attention to her, and tried to creep out unobserved. But a detective forced her into a chair and she sat there whimpering.

Walter made a helpless gesture; the flesh around his lips was oyster-white. "I suppose it won't do any good to deny I murdered my father. But I warn you, Inspector—and you, Van Every—you're heading for trouble. You don't know a quarter of what really happened in this room last Monday afternoon. You don't even know the truth about—"

"No, you don't," said a peevish voice; and they all looked around to find Ellery glaring at them. "After all the trouble you've put me to, my dear Galahad, and all the blankets of silence you've wrapped yourself up in, you're not going to rob me of the little glory I've earned."

"King, are you crazy? Keep out of this!" barked Glücke.

"And that," said Mr. King in the same peevish tone, "goes for you two as well." And he glared at Rhys and Valerie.

"King—" spluttered the Inspector threateningly.

"Relax. Walter, do you know who killed your father?" Walter shrugged. "Do you know who killed Spaeth, Jardin? You, Val?"

"I'm not speaking to you—turncoat!"

Ellery looked whimsically at the long, brown-papered object in his hands. Then he turned and went to the glass door, opened it, stepped out on the terrace.

"Come out here," he said.

Chapter XXI

The Sport of King

THERE WAS SUCH a majestic confidence in his voice that District Attorney Van Every whispered in Glücke's ear, and Glücke nodded glumly and motioned everybody out.

Ellery stood off to one side, the package tucked under one arm, waited patiently. They took positions about the terrace, some perched on the low terrace railing, others standing against the wall. Curiosity was reflected from each face—the anxious, hopeful ones of Val and Rhys; the gaping ones of the detectives, Winni, Pink; the watchful ones of Glücke and Van Every; the bitter ones of Ruhig and Walter.

The sky was blue, the garden sizzled with bees, a red hydroplane droned past high overhead. There was a strange otherworld overtone to everything, as if time had stopped still and something splendid and dreadful was about to happen.

And Ellery took a tubular object from his breast pocket and unwrapped it and said in a dreamy, mood-preserving voice: "I have here a fragment of canvas which I cut out of this awning only today." He nodded toward the rectangle of light in the awning overhead.

"In this fragment you will find a slit, or tear, or rip, or whatever you choose to call it. It is a clean sharp incision and it runs—as you can see—parallel with the green and yellow stripes. The upper edges of the rip—that is to say the edges on the side which lay exposed to the sun—are slightly stained molasses-brown."

Glücke and Van Every ran toward him.

"No," said Ellery dryly, "don't touch it. This thing is a little like Medusa's head—one careless exposure and it turns you to clay. I had Bronson—charming fellow—analyze the stain only a couple of hours ago, and he says it is composed of thoroughly mixed molasses and potassium cyanide."

"Let's see that," said Glücke excitedly, bending over the square of canvas. "That slit—it looks—"

"About a half-inch long."

"So was the incision the sword made in Spaeth's chest!"

"And the same poison—" muttered the District Attorney.

"Then this cut in the awning was made by the same rapier that killed Spaeth," exclaimed the Inspector. He looked up. He dragged a chair over and stood on it and put his nose as close to the hole in the canvas as he could get it. Then he stepped down, looking frustrated. "But how the dickens could a sword have got up there? If the stain's on top of the canvas, that means the sword came in *through* the canvas from above. That's screwy."

"It's not only screwy," said Ellery. "It didn't happen."

"Wait." Glücke jumped down the terrace steps and stared up at the house. "It could have been dropped out of one of the upper windows!"

Ellery sighed. "Come here, Inspector." Glücke came back. Ellery stood on the chair and fitted the fragment into the empty space. "See where this places the rip on the awning? Now look at the wall here. Do you notice this fresh nick in the stone? Curious place for a nick, isn't it—away over the tallest man's head? Could hardly have got there by accident, could it?"

"Well? Well?" Glücke craned with the others.

"Now observe the relative positions of the nick in the wall and the tear in the awning. About four inches apart. And the tear is slightly—not much—higher from the floor than the nick. Line up nick and tear and what have you? A sharp object with a blade width of about a half-inch which went through the awning from above and struck the wall four inches inside the awning, causing the nick.

"If the sword had been dropped from a window, it would have naturally come down in a vertical position. But since the line between the rip and nick is almost parallel with the terrace floor, it's obvious that the sharp object pierced the awning almost horizontally in relation to the floor."

He jumped down, wrapped the fragment of cloth carefully, and handed it to the Inspector, who did not seem to know what to do with it.

"I don't get this at all, King," he complained.

"Use your head, brother. Did some one stand or lie on top of the awning and stick a sword through the awning almost where it meets the wall, just for the purpose of making a nick in the stone there?"

"That's nonsense," said Van Every slowly.

"Agreed; sheer nonsense. So let's wander on. The stripes of the awning run from top to bottom; the rip is parallel with the stripes; the nick is a little lower but directly behind the rip. Therefore from what direction did the weapon come?"

"Through the air," muttered Van Every, "from a point directly facing this terrace."

"A rapier?" asked Ellery, raising his brows. "Through the air?"

"No," mumbled Glücke. "That can't be. Say—a knife! Somebody threw a knife!"

"At least," smiled Ellery, "not the rapier. We're in agreement that it's absurd to suppose somebody stood on the ground out there and hurled a sword at the awning? Very well. Then it wasn't a sword that pierced the awning. But whatever it was, it had all the characteristics of the wound in Spaeth's chest—a sharp cutting edge about a half-inch wide and coated with the same poisonous concoction that killed him."

"You mean," cried Glücke, "that Spaeth wasn't killed with that rapier at all?"

"How eloquently you put it, Inspector."

The Inspector opened his mouth wide. The others watched with a sort of horrible fascination.

"Now," said Ellery briskly, "we know one more important fact—that whatever the weapon was, it came from a point, as the District Attorney says, directly facing this terrace. What directly faces this terrace?"

"The rock garden," said Pink eagerly.

"The pool," said the Inspector.

"And beyond the pool?"

"The old Jardin house."

"Or, to be precise, the terrace of the old Jardin house, which is exactly opposite this one."

Fitzgerald came puffing around the Spaeth house. "Hey! Wait for baby! What's happened? Did Ruhig—"

"Ah, Fitz. Glad you made it. You're just in time for a little demonstration. Inspector, would you mind clearing the terrace?"

"Clear it?"

"C-l-e-a-r," said Ellery sympathetically. "A five-letter word meaning get the hell out of the way. Pink, I need you."

Pink stumbled forward with that expression of bewilderment which seemed chronic with him whenever Ellery spoke. Ellery took a leather-covered pillow from a chair and propped it up against the rear wall, resting on an iron table. Then, holding the oddly shaped package in one hand, he grasped Pink's elbow with the other and led him off the terrace, speaking earnestly. Pink ambled along, nodding. They skirted the pool and made their way toward the Jardin terrace.

"Hey!" shouted Ellery across the garden. "Didn't you hear me? Get off that terrace!"

They moved, then, leaving the terrace hurriedly. And finally they were on the ground, at the side of the house, staring out across the pool toward the two men on the opposite terrace.

Ellery unwrapped the package, still talking to Pink, who was scratching his head. Ellery turned and waved them still farther to one side.

They saw Pink pick up the thing from the package with his right hand and fit something into it and draw back his left arm. There was a queer *cwang!* and something slender flashed through the air over the Jardin rock garden, over the pool, over the nearer garden, and plunked into the leather pillow on the Spaeth terrace, striking the stone wall beyond with a vicious ping.

"Creepers," said the Inspector hoarsely.

Pink grinned as Ellery clapped him on the shoulder, and then the two of them came trotting back, Pink lugging the bow and a sheaf of arrows proudly.

Ellery ran up on the terrace and tore the arrow from the pillow. "Good shot, Pink! Damsite better than the one that hit the awning Monday afternoon."

They scurried back to the terrace again. "An *arrow?*" said Van Every incredulously.

"It was the only possible answer. Because it was the only answer which explained why the murderer of Spaeth should have smeared the point of his weapon with poison."

Ellery lit a cigaret.

"If the weapon were the rapier *in veritate,* using poison on the tip was absurd. The only purpose in poisoning the tip could have been *to make sure* Spaeth died. With the weapon an arrow, and the archer fifty yards away, the situation clarifies: while an expert archer could be pretty sure of hitting his victim at fifty yards, he couldn't be positive of striking a vital spot. But with poison on the tip of the arrow even a superficial scratch would have caused death.

"No, Spaeth wasn't killed by that rapier at all. Nor was he killed in the study. He was standing out here on the terrace and his murderer shot two poisoned arrows from the Jardin terrace across the way. The first went too high and struck the top of the awning. The second hit Spaeth squarely in the heart."

"But how can you be sure it was an arrow?" asked Van Every stubbornly. "There's something in what Glücke said about a knife. The killer could have been standing in the garden and thrown two knives. Such a theory would fill the bill just as satisfactorily as yours."

"Not by a long shot. Spaeth was killed by an archer, not a knife-thrower, and I can prove it. Pink, let me have that glove."

Pink stripped something leathery off his left hand. "I had quite a job hunting up a bow and arrows this afternoon," chuckled Ellery, "but when I located 'em—lo! the salesman brought out this glove. Look at it."

He tossed it to Glücke. It was a queer-looking glove. It had only three leather fingers—the middle three, providing no protection for the thumb and little finger. There was a strap which fastened about the wrist to hold the glove tight.

"Remember those two prints on the iron table of the Jardin terrace? A thumb and little finger. A person doesn't usually lean on just his thumb and little finger. Miss Jardin thought the two prints indicated a two-fingered man. But when you postulate an archer, the prints can only mean that they were made by some one wearing an archer's shooting glove, as it's called, the leather preventing the middle fingers from leaving an impression.

"Somebody wearing an archer's shooting glove was on the Jardin terrace. So the weapon must have been an arrow."

"That's absolutely uncanny," muttered Walter.

"Uncanny?" roared Fitzgerald. "It's colossal! Keep talking, King!"

"I'm afraid that from now on," replied Ellery with a certain grimness, "my conversation may take on a deadly tone, Fitz." There was an answering silence then of no superficial extent. "Walter."

Walter looked intensely at him, and Val felt a great shame.

"When you entered the study Monday afternoon dressed in Jardin's coat, you didn't find your father stabbed to death in that room; you found him with an arrow in his chest on this terrace. There was another arrow hanging from the tear in the awning up there.

"You removed the arrow from your father's body, you removed the arrow hanging from the awning. Then you dragged the body into the study and sat it down in the corner near the fireplace, where it was later found. The wrist-watch had probably smashed on this stone floor when your father fell dead; you swept up the fragments and deposited them near him in the study. Is that a reasonable reconstruction?"

Walter nodded wordlessly.

"You wanted it to look as if your father had been murdered with a sword. So you needed a sword with a blade-point approximately the same size and shape as the arrowhead. The only one that matched, judging by the eye, was the Italian rapier. So you ignored all the other swords and took down the rapier from the collection hanging over the fireplace.

"You took the arrows away with you, and the sword too—you knew it would be missed, and that the police would assume it had been the murder weapon; you couldn't leave it behind because you were afraid an expert comparison of the width of its blade with the width of the wound might show a discrepancy.

"And all the time you were doing this, the archer across the way was watching through the binoculars. He could even see what you were doing in the study, because of the glass wall."

Walter could not tear his gaze away.

"Why did you want it to look as if your father had been murdered with a sword? For the simplest reason imaginable: because you didn't want it known that he had been killed with an arrow! But what was so damning about an arrow?

"There can be only one answer. The arrows implicated some one you wanted to protect. And whom have you been trying to protect since Monday? Your future father-in-law." Jardin's brown face twitched. "Then those two arrows must have been identifiable as Jardin's, and you knew it. I remembered the auction catalogue, the collection of medieval arrowheads which had been withdrawn from the sale and presented to the Museum. They were museum pieces, then; as such, undoubtedly known to collectors and therefore traceable directly to their owner, Jardin.

"So you took the arrows away and tried to make it look like a sword crime because you thought Jardin had killed your father. They were his arrows and he is an expert archer. Didn't he win an archery tournament in California last spring?"

"Why should he cover up his old man's murderer?" asked Glücke plaintively. "That doesn't wash, King."

"It does," said Ellery, "if you remember that his old man ruined thousands of people, including Jardin, and that his old man's murderer is the father of the girl he wants to marry."

"You mean," frowned Van Every, "that Jardin actually—"

"I'm only telling you what Walter was thinking," said Ellery, as if that were a simple matter, "since he didn't want to tell you himself. Well, Walter, am I right?"

"Yes," muttered Walter; he looked dazed. "I recognized them as two arrowheads from Rhys's collection. Of course, whoever stole them had fitted them into modern shafts; but the arrowheads couldn't be mistaken."

"They were two identical arrowheads of polished steel," said Rhys steadily. "Japanese, dating from the fourteenth century. Like many medieval Japanese arrowheads these had decorative designs in the steel which would have identified them as mine beyond question. Walter's told me about it since. Whoever the maniac was, he stole them because he wanted to frame me for Spaeth's murder." He paused, and then said lightly: "I'd like to get my hands on his throat."

"I couldn't talk," said Walter wearily, "because my story would have implicated Rhys. I didn't know about his alibi."

"And we didn't talk," cried Val, "because we knew Walter had been in this house at the time of the murder and we thought that— Oh, Walter, Mr. King knows you didn't do it!"

"Not so fast," growled Glücke. "How do I know this man didn't shoot those arrows himself? Couldn't he have been on the Jardin terrace and then dashed over to be in here when that five-thirty-five 'phone call came in?"

"He couldn't have been," said Ellery politely, "and he wasn't. Let me go on. Walter left the house with the arrows and sword, followed by the archer, who attacked him just outside the grounds after Walter climbed the fence, using the Indian club as a weapon. The club, remember, came from the Jardin house, where the archer had been. It was the archer, of course, who dropped the club down the sewer."

"Why'd he slug Walter at all?" demanded Fitz.

"Because he wanted those arrows back. Walter had spoiled his plan—his plan to murder Spaeth and frame Jardin for the crime. He wanted to retrieve the arrows, undo what Walter had done, and leave the scene of the crime as it had been before Walter changed it. But after he struck Walter, he must have found himself unable to go through with the revised scheme. Because we did find the scene as Walter left it. Obviously, then, the arrows were gone by the time he reached Walter near the sewer."

"I'd already dropped the arrows down the sewer," said Walter, "when he hit me."

"So that was it! It puzzled me. But you hadn't had time to drop the sword through, as you intended, nor Jardin's coat. So friend archer took sword and coat, smeared both with the blood streaming out of your own head, went off, coated the sword with poison, and planted both objects in Jardin's closet. If he couldn't frame Jardin with arrows—you'd spoiled that—he was going to use your own little refinements and frame Jardin with the coat and sword. He knew Jardin would find the sword and handle it; and he was the one who wired headquarters with the tip to search Jardin's apartment, so timing his tip that discovery of the sword and coat and search by the police would be almost simultaneous. Very pretty, the whole thing."

The Inspector made a helpless gesture, like a man trying to stop an avalanche.

"His frame-up of Jardin was now complete—in a different form but still effective, even more effective. He couldn't have counted on Frank's identification of Walter as Jardin, it is true; but the rest he was almost positive of."

Ellery took the cigaret from his mouth and said calmly: "You asked before, Inspector, how I could be sure Walter hadn't killed his father. There was one conclusive reason: Walter is right-handed, as he demonstrates unconsciously all the time. But the archer wasn't. The archer was left-handed."

"How do you figure that?" demanded Glücke.

"I don't figure it; it's a fact. In archery, as in any other sport, the favored arm is called upon to do the most work. A right-handed archer will draw back the string of the bow with his right hand. Obviously a left-handed archer will draw it back with his left. Now the shooting glove is always worn on the hand which draws back the bow. On which hand did the murderer wear his shooting glove?"

"The left!" cried Val. "I remember we talked about those prints—"

"Yes, the thumb and little-finger smudges on the table from their relative shape and position came from a left hand, as you accurately observed. Then a left hand wore the shooting glove. Then the murderer was left-handed. That lets Walter out."

Walter shook his head, grinning a little, and Val ran over to him and seized him, her face shining.

"Now let me show you a little trick," murmured Ellery out of a spurt of smoke. "What do we know about the murderer?

"One—he's an expert archer. Fifty yards to hit a man in the heart is no mean feat, even after one bad shot.

"Two—he's left-handed.

"Three—and this is important—*he knew Jardin's coat had a rip in it.*"

"I don't follow, I don't follow," said the Inspector in a fit of irritable excitement.

"He took the coat from Walter and planted it on Jardin, didn't he? To do that, *he had to know it was Jardin's coat.* But how could he have known it was Jardin's coat? Walter was wearing it—a fact ordinarily sufficient to establish an assumption that it was his. Both men owned identical camel's-hairs. There were no distinguishing marks. No, the only means of identifying the coat as Jardin's was *by the rip under the pocket,* which had been made that very afternoon. The archer, then, recognized the coat by the rip. So he must have known in advance of the crime that the coat was ripped in that specific place.

"Four—and this is also a delicate point," said Ellery with a slight smile, "the murderer, in order to have been able to use the Indian club on Walter's head, *had to know where to find it.*"

"Say that again?" implored Glücke, who was having a hard time all around.

Ellery sighed. "Visualize our homicidal friend. He has just seen Walter leaving with the sword and arrows. He wants to get those arrows back. What to do? He hasn't anything against Walter personally; he's not out for Walter's blood. A tap on the head will be sufficient. What should he use for a bludgeon?

"We know he used one of the Indian clubs. That means he ran along the terrace, forced the door of the ex-gymnasium, went to the wall-closet where the two clubs hung, opened the closet, and took out the undamaged club.

"*What made him force the door of the gymnasium?* There were lots of other rooms to investigate if he wanted to find a bludgeon. Even if he went to the gymnasium first by mere chance, and forced the door, there was nothing to be seen but a small pile of débris. For Miss Jardin told me Wednesday afternoon that the closet door had been left closed when they moved out of the house.

"No, when he forced that door and went to the closed closet and opened it, *he knew what he was going to find.* He knew there were two Indian clubs in that closet."

Ellery threw away his cigaret.

"I think we have enough now to paint a picture of our 'compleat criminal.' To our knowledge, who fits all four qualifications I've laid down?

"Who is an expert archer, *and* left-handed, *and* knew Jardin's coat was ripped, *and* knew the Indian clubs were in the gymnasium closet?"

For a moment, by some communal telegraphic instinct, the very bees stopped humming; and a final silence fell that was uncomfortably not of this world.

Then Pink burst into laughter, doubling up as he clutched the bow and arrows. "But jeeze," he gasped, "you're 'way off your base. That's *me!*"

Inspector Glücke looked at Ellery with an anxiously questioning triumph, as if to say: "There, smart guy. What do you say to that?"

And Ellery said to that: "Yes, Pink. That's you."

"Oh, no," said Valerie, holding on to Walter's arm. "Oh, *no.*"

"Oh, yes," said Ellery. "I knew Pink was an expert archer—wasn't he runner-up to Jardin when Jardin won the California Archery Tournament last spring? You mentioned that yourself Monday night, Inspector. And besides, he's just beautifully demonstrated his marksmanship.

"Left-handed? Ample evidence of that, plus the fact that he just shot an arrow left-handedly.

"He was one of the five persons who were present when Jardin's coat was ripped.

"And he was one of the three who knew about the clubs being left in the closet.

"On the archery point, the only other known archer in the group is Jardin, whose alibi lets him out.

"On the coat-ripping point, the other four witnesses were Jardin, Valerie, Walter, and the gateman Frank. Jardin and Valerie are eliminated because of their alibis. Walter is right-handed. And Frank has only one arm, so he couldn't possibly have been an archer.

"And on the Indian-club point, the other two were the Jardins, eliminated before.

"Pink is the only one who fits all four characteristics. So he must have murdered Solly Spaeth." Ellery sighed. "Take it away, Inspector. I've shot my bolt, too."

During this peroration, they stood motionless, too surprised to think, to take the simplest defensive measure. As for Pink, his crimson neck grew more crimson, and the cords expanded and became visible, and the look of the hunted animal slowly emerged from the sluggish morass of his brain.

But at a certain point something snapped, and Pink demonstrated his amazing nervous and physical versatility. Before they could move a muscle he had bounded off the terrace to a point fifteen feet away and whirled like a tightly wound mechanical toy with an arrow fitted into the bow, the string taut, and the arrowhead pointed directly at Mr. Ellery Queen's petrified breast.

"Don't move," said Pink thickly. "Nobody make one little move."

They were strung out in a straggly line along the terrace, no one behind another. It was absurd, in the sun, with the bow gleaming like a plaything. And yet nobody moved.

"You can get me with a gun," said Pink in the same thick, dreary voice, "but this guy gets it through the heart first. So don't move. He's got something coming to him." He stopped, and then he said: "He *fooled* me."

And nobody laughed, even at the childish petulance, the plaintive wonder in Pink's voice. His red hair flamed. With his legs widespread and solidly planted in the earth, and the bow grotesquely arched, he was a fascinating object; and faintly in a remote chamber of his brain Mr. Ellery Queen began to recite a small, foolish prayer.

Pink's left arm drew back a little farther and his eye glared at Ellery's breast with an awful fixity.

"Pink," said Valerie. She happened to be standing with Walter near the top step of the terrace. "Pink."

Pink's eye did not waver. "Keep out of this, Val. Keep away."

"Pink," said Val again. Her cheeks were almost blue. Walter made a convulsive movement and she breathed: "Walter. Don't move. He'll kill you. He won't touch me." And slowly she stepped forward and slowly she went down the steps.

"Val," cried Pink, "Val, I swear—go back!"

"No, Pink," said Val in a quiet soothing tone. Slowly, slowly. She hardly touched the ground. She drifted toward him, never taking her eyes from him. It was as if Pink had been a sliver of gold leaf balanced on the tip of a needle; the merest quiver of the ground, the merest breath would send it tumbling. "Don't, Pink. I know there's something horribly wrong in all this. You're not a criminal. You may have killed Spaeth, but I know you must have had a good reason—in your own mind, Pink. . . ."

Fat drops appeared on Pink's red forehead. His body trembled as he stood rooted in the garden, shaken by an invisible wind.

"Pink," said Val, and she went up to him and took the bow out of his hand.

And Pink did a curious thing. He sank down among the flowers and began to weep.

When it was all over and Pink, with a dead look in his eyes, was led away to wait in a police car for Inspector Glücke, Ellery went into Solly Spaeth's study and opened a liquor cabinet and drank standing up from a full brown bottle.

Then, with the bottle in his hand, he went over to Val and kissed the tip of her ear.

"Just like a woman," he said. Val was crying bitterly in Walter's arms and Rhys was sitting, a little shrunken, and looking old. "You saved my life," said Ellery.

Val sobbed against Walter's chest. Walter glanced at Ellery significantly and he turned away. Walter drew Val off to a corner and sat her down on his lap; she clung to him. "Pink. He was . . . Oh, I can't believe it!"

"It's all right, darling. We'll get him off," crooned Walter in her ear. "No jury will ever convict him in this county."

"Oh, Walter . . ."

Ellery raised the bottle again, and Inspector Glücke said something, and Ruhig and Winni Moon were sent off in custody with their conspiracy to defraud hanging heavy over their heads. And after a while District Attorney Van Every left with a bewildered look; and Fitz, clapping his forehead like a man awakening from a trance, grabbed the telephone, spluttered into it, dashed out, dashed back, found his hat, threw it away, and dashed out again.

Glücke rubbed his jaw. "King, I don't know how to—"

Ellery lowered the bottle. "Who killed Cock Robin?" he sang. "I, said the sparrow, with my little bow and arrow. . . . It's like a resurrection! Have I sprouted any gray hairs in the last ten minutes?"

"Mr. King." Rhys Jardin rose, working his jaws. For a moment there was no sound except Val's sobbing and Walter's crooning in her ear.

Ellery sighed: "Yes?" He was not feeling terribly fit; there was a bitterness on his tongue not liquorish.

"There's one thing I'll never believe," said Rhys in a troubled voice. "I'll never believe Pink framed me for Spaeth's murder. I couldn't be wrong. He was my friend. I treated him like a member of my own family. It just can't be, Mr. King."

"Look," said Ellery. "A friend may become a greater enemy than an enemy. He was your friend, and you were his. You had advised him to put all his savings in Ohippi. When Ohippi fell, he was furious with Spaeth; and so long as he thought you were Spaeth's victim, too, he remained your friend.

"But Monday morning, in packing your things in the gym across the way, he found a bankbook in your golf-bag which seemed to indicate that you had salted away five million dollars. Were you still his friend? Not if you double-crossed him by pretending to be broke while you had five millions to keep you warm against a rainy day. Pink is a primitive soul and he didn't stop to ask questions. In his mind you became one with Spaeth—two crooks who had defrauded him of his life's savings.

"He planned things then and there. He had to take that collection of arrowheads down to the Museum, didn't he? On the way he took two of the arrowheads out of the package, delivering the rest. He fitted them out with shafts, prepared his little broth of molasses and potassium cyanide—"

"But ever since," cried Val's father, "he's been so damned—so damned solicitous! He couldn't have been acting."

"He wasn't. When you explained to him late Monday night about the five million, after the crime, after the planting of the rapier and coat in your closet—when he realized that you'd been with him the entire day on which the five millions were deposited, Pink saw what an awful thing he'd done to you. But it was too late. The crime, the frame-up, were faits accomplis. There was nothing he could do. He couldn't recall that wire he'd sent headquarters only a few minutes before—probably by dodging downstairs to the lobby while Val and Walter were in her bedroom and telephoning the wire from the public booth there.

"No, he just had to sit and take it. Every emotion of his since Monday night has been genuine."

Ellery turned to find Val and Walter before him. Val was still sniffling with her handkerchief to her nose, but she looked calmer. "I can't thank you, Mr. King. None of us can. But—"

"Feel better, Walter?"

"We're still a little dazed," said Walter, "but you might be interested to learn that Val and I have decided to do something constructive with my father's money."

"I know," sighed Ellery. "You're going to put it all back into Ohippi and rehabilitate the plants."

"How did you know?" they cried together.

"Because," said Ellery, "you're that kind of damned fool."

"That reminds me," murmured Rhys. "That five million properly belongs to you now, Walter. I'll—"

"You'll do nothing of the sort." Walter smiled faintly. "I hope you'll find me a better partner than my father was."

"Look," said Inspector Glücke, who was still hanging about. "I've got work to do. But I've got to tell you, King—"

Walter said suddenly: "King? Let me show you a trick, Inspector."

"I've had all the tricks I want. King—"

"No, no, you'll enjoy this one." Walter seized a piece of paper from the desk and with a soft pencil began to sketch a face with great rapidity. Glücke looked puzzled. "So what? That's King. I haven't time to look at pictures—"

"You have for this." Walter erased the shaded glasses and replaced them with *pince-nez*. Over the face he smudged a beard. And he put the hair-part in a different place. "Who's that?"

The Inspector gaped from the drawing to Mr. Hilary King. "My God," he screamed, "the pest!"

"I think I knew it," shrugged Walter, "from the moment I saw him. You might fool others, Queen, but you couldn't fool an artist. I sketched your face at the auction."

"Mr. Queen?" said Val, wide-eyed. "So *that's* how you knew what went on here Monday night!"

"I'll be damned," said Jardin, staring.

Ellery reached hastily for the telephone and gave the operator a number. "Magna Studios? Connect me with Mr. Jacques Butcher's office." As he waited, he said apologetically: "As long as I'm unmasked I may as well go back to work. . . . Hello, Butcher? . . . Who?" He swallowed hard. "Now look here, young woman. This is Ellery Queen, and I—want—Butcher! . . . He *is* there? Put him on!" He said exultantly: "Can you imagine? Butcher at last!" There was a buzzing noise in the receiver and he slowly sucked his lean cheeks in. "Oh, is that so?" he yelled. "So he can't see me—*yet?* Well, you tell your Mr. Butcher—" But there was a click. He stared at the dead telephone and then hurled the whole thing away.

"Uh—Queen," said the Inspector nervously. "I want to apologize—I mean, you've cracked this case and the credit is really—"

Ellery waved his hand. "Don't want any," he said grumpily. "Leave me out of it. . . . Can't see me, hey?"

"That's white of you," beamed Glücke. "Say, I take it all back. How'd you like to meet the Chief of Police and the Mayor? And we could put you up—"

"He's staying with me," said Walter. "That's definite."

"Or maybe you'd like to be appointed Honorary Chief?" glowed the Inspector. "I've got a drag—"

"Wait," said Ellery, frowning. "You're grateful, eh, Inspector?"

"What do you think?"

"You'd have the City run a banquet for me, I suppose?"

"Hell, yes. We could—"

"I wouldn't have to pay any traffic fines, either?"

"Leave it to me."

"You could even see that I met the Governor, couldn't you?"

Inspector Glücke said earnestly: "The Governor, or the President, or *anybody*."

"It's tougher than that," said Ellery in a despairing voice. "Get me in to see Butcher."

THE FOUR OF HEARTS

PART ONE

Chapter I

God's Gift to Hollywood

IT IS A well-known fact that any one exposed to Hollywood longer than six weeks goes suddenly and incurably mad.

Mr. Ellery Queen groped for the bottle of Scotch on the open trunk.

"To Hollywood, city of screwballs! Drink 'er down." He guzzled what was left of the Scotch and tossed the bottle aside, resuming his packing. "California, here I go—unwept, unhonored, and unsung. And do I care?"

Alan Clark smiled that Mona Lisa smile by which you may know any member of the fraternity of Hollywood agents, fat or thin, tall or short, dewy-eyed or soiled by life. It is the sage's, the saint's, the cynic's smile of pure wisdom.

"All you wacks act this way at first. Them that can take it snaps out of it. Them that can't—they turn yellow and go squawking back East."

"If you're trying to arouse my ire," growled Ellery, kicking his prostrate golf-bag, "desist, Alan. I cut my eyeteeth on the tactics of scheming agents."

"What the hell did you expect—a Class A assignment your first week on the lot and a testimonial dinner at the Cocoanut Grove?"

"Work," said Ellery unreasonably.

"Phooey," said his agent. "It isn't work here; it's art. Rembrandt didn't get his start knocking out the Sistine Chapel, did he? Give yourself a chance to learn the ropes."

"By burying myself in that mausoleum of an office they gave me and sucking my thumbs?"

"Sure, sure," said Clark soothingly. "Why not? It's Magna's dough, isn't it? If the studio's willing to invest six weeks' salary in you, don't you think they know what they're doing?"

"Are you asking me?" said Ellery, flinging things into the trunk. "Then I'm telling you. No!"

"You've got to get the feel of pictures, Queen, before you can wade into a script. You're not a day-laborer. You're a writer, an artist, a—a sensitive plant."

"Flapdoodle, with onions on the side."

Clark grinned and tipped his hat. "Pleased to meet you. . . . Just the same, what's the rush? You've got a future out here. You're an idea man, and that's what they pay off on in Hollywood. They need you."

"Magna gives me a six-week contract with an option for renewal, the six weeks expire today, they *don't* take up the option, and that means they need me. Typical Hollywood logic."

"They just didn't like the contract the New York office wrote. Happens out here all the time. So they let your contract lapse and now they'll offer you a new one. You'll see."

"I was brought out here to do the story and dialogue on a horse opera. Have I done a single thing in six weeks? Nobody's paid the slightest attention to me, I haven't been able to see or talk to Jacques Butcher even once. . . . Do you know how many times I've called Butcher, Alan?"

"You've got to have patience. Butch is the Boy Wonder of Hollywood. And you're just another lous— another writer."

"You can't prove it by anything I've written, because I haven't written anything. No, sir, I'm homeward bound."

"Sure, sure," said the agent. "Here, you left out this wine-colored polo shirt. I know how you feel. You hate our guts. You can't trust your best friend here; he'll use the back of your neck for a stepladder the minute you turn your head. I know. We're twerps—"

"Illogical!"

"No art—"

"Synthetic!"

"Throw our dough around—"

"Dog eat dog!"

"Just the same," grinned Clark, "you'll learn to love it. They all do. And you'll make a hell of a lot more money writing for pictures than you ever will figuring out who wrapped a meat-cleaver around Cadwallader St. Swithin's neck in Room 202. Take my advice, Queen, and stick around."

"The way I figure it," said Ellery, "the incubation period lasts six weeks. After that a man's hopelessly infected. I'm taking it on the lam while I still have my sanity."

"You've still got ten days to pick up your tickets to New York."

"Ten days!" Ellery shuddered delicately. "If it hadn't been for the Sperry murder I'd have been back East long ago."

Clark stared. "I *thought* there was something screwy in the way Glücke's been pinning medals on himself!"

"Ouch, I've let the cat out. Keep it under your hat, Alan. I promised Inspector Glücke—"

The agent pulled a gust of indignation up from his shoes. "Do you mean to stand there and tell me you cracked the Sperry case and didn't have the brains to get your pan smeared over the front page?"

"It doesn't mean anything to me. Where the devil can I put these spiked shoes?"

"Why, with that publicity you could have walked into any studio in Hollywood and written your own ticket!" Clark became quiet, and when Ellery looked up he saw the old Mona Lisa smile. "Look," said Clark. "I've got a sweet idea."

Ellery dropped the shoes. "Now wait a minute, Alan."

"Leave it to me. I absolutely guarantee—"

"I gave Glücke my word, I tell you!"

"The hell with that. Well, okay, okay. I found it out somewhere else. You'll still be the white-haired boy—"

"No!"

"I think," mused the agent, pulling his lip, "I'll try Metro first."

"Alan, absolutely no!"

"Maybe I can ring Paramount and Twentieth Century in on it, too. Play 'em off against each other. I'll have the Magna outfit eating out of my hand." He slapped Ellery's shoulder. "Why, man, I'll get you twenty-five hundred bucks a week!"

In this moral crisis the telephone rang. Ellery fled to it.

"Mr. Queen? Hold the line, please. Mr. Butcher calling."

Ellery said: "Mr. *who?*"

"Mr. Butcher."

"Butcher?"

"Butcher!" Clark yanked his hat over his ears. "See, what did I tell you? Butcho the Great! Where's your extension? Don't mention dough, now. Feel him out. Boy, oh, boy!" He dashed into the bedroom.

"Mr. Queen?" said a sharp, nervous, young man's voice in Ellery's ear. "Jacques Butcher speaking."

"Did you say Jacques Butcher?" mumbled Ellery.

"Tried to locate you in New York for four days. Finally got your address from your father at Police Headquarters. What are you doing in Hollywood? Drop in to see me today."

"What am I do—" Ellery paused. "I beg your pardon?"

"What? I say, how is it you're on the Coast? Vacation?"

"Excuse me," said Ellery. "Is this the Jacques Butcher who is executive vice-president in charge of production at the Magna Studios on Melrose, in Hollywood, California, United States of America?" He stopped. "The planet Earth?"

There was a silence. Then: "Beg pardon?"

"You're not the gag man?"

"What? Hello! Mr. Queen?" Another dead moment in Time, as if Mr. Butcher were fumbling with a memorandum. "Am I speaking to Ellery Queen, Queen the detective-story writer? Where the hell— Madge. Madge! Did you get me the wrong man, damn it?"

"Wait," said Ellery hollowly. "Madge got you the right man, all right, all right. But my brain isn't functioning at par these days, Mr. Butcher. I'm slicing 'em into the rough on every drive. Did I understand you to ask if I'm in Hollywood on a *vacation?*"

"I don't get this." The edge on the sharp voice was badly blunted. "We seem to have our wires crossed. Aren't you feeling well, Queen?"

"Well?" howled Ellery, growing red in the face. "I feel terrible! Why, you incomparable nitwit, I've been employed by your studio for six interminable weeks now—and you ask me if I'm here on a vacation?"

"What!" shouted the producer. "You've been on our lot for six weeks? *Madge!*"

"I've phoned your office twice a day, six days a week, fathead—that makes seventy-two times not counting Sundays that I've tried to talk to you, you misbegotten apology for an idiot's stand-in! And you wire New York for my address!"

"Why—doesn't—somebody *tell* me these things!"

"Here I've parked on my chassis," roared Ellery, "in that doge's palace your minions gave me to doze in—a month and a half, do you hear?—losing weight, fretting my fool head off, dying by inches not a hundred feet from your office—and *you* look for *me* in New York!" Ellery's voice grew terrible. "I'm going mad. I *am* mad. Do you know what, Mr. Butcher? Nuts to you. *Double* nuts to you!"

And he hurled the telephone majestically from him.

Clark came scurrying back, rubbing his hands. "Oh, wonderful, wonderful. We're set. We're in!"

"Go away," said Ellery. Then he screeched: "*What?*"

"Hasn't been done since Garbo gave her last interview to *Screen Squeejees*," said the agent gleefully. "Telling Butch where he gets off! Now we're getting somewhere."

"Now," said Ellery, feeling his forehead, "now—we're—getting somewhere?"

"Great guy, Butch. Biggest man in pictures. What a break! Get your lid."

"Please. *Please*. Where are we going?"

"To see the Boy Wonder, of course. Come on!"

And the agent bustled out, looking delighted with life, the world, and the whole confused, thunderous march of events.

For a moment Ellery sat still.

But when he found himself putting a match on his head, sticking his hatbrim into his mouth, and rubbing a cigaret on his shoe, he made a gibbering sound and followed his personal representative from the apartment with the fogged air of one who will never understand.

Each studio in Hollywood has its Boy Wonder. But Jacques Butcher, it was admitted by even the other Boy Wonders, was the Boy Wonder of them all.

This paragon occupied a four-room bungalow office in the heart of the quadrangle of executive buildings on the Magna lot. The bungalow, thought Ellery grimly, was some unknown architectural genius's conception of the kind of Spanish edifice a Spanish executive in charge of the production of Spanish motion pictures would erect in his native Spain amid blood, mayhem, and the belch of batteries. It was very yellow, stuccoed, Moorish, and archified; and it was tiled and roofed and patioed as no structure outside a cocaine-addicted hidalgo's nightmare had ever been. In a word, it was colossal.

The Second Secretary's office in the edifice, having been designed in the same faithful spirit to house females, resembled the interior of a Moorish prince's zenana.

Ellery, scrutinizing this plaster and silken gingerbread, nodded unpleasantly. The Sultan of Production was probably lolling on an amethyst-studded throne puffing on a golden hookah and dictating to two houris in g-strings. As for Mr. Alan Clark, his manner had grown less and less enthusiastic as Mr. Queen grew more and more steel-dignified.

"Mr. Butcher will see you in a moment, Mr. Queen," said the Second Secretary piteously. "Will you have a chair?"

"You," said Mr. Queen with a nasty inflection, "are Madge, I presume?"

"Yes, sir."

"Ha," said Mr. Queen. "I will be delighted to have a chair." And he had a chair. The Second Secretary bit her budding lip, looking as if she wanted chiefly to burst into tears.

"Maybe we'd better come back tomorrow," whispered the agent. "If you're going to have an antagonistic attitude—"

"Let me remind you, Alan," said Mr. Queen complacently, "that coming here was your idea. I'm really looking forward to this audience. I can see him now—burlap bags under his eyes, dressed like a Radio City typist's conception of Robert Taylor, with a manicurist on one hand and a eunuch on the other—"

"Some other time," said Clark, rising. "I think maybe tomorrow—"

"Sit down, friend," said Mr. Queen.

Clark sat down and began to snap at his own fingernails like a tortured turtle. A door opened; he jumped up again. But it was only a washed-out male, obviously the First Secretary.

"Mr. Butcher will see you now, Mr. Queen."

Mr. Queen smiled. The Second Secretary looked faint, the First Secretary paled, and Clark wiped his forehead.

"Nice of him," murmured Mr. Queen. He strolled into the First Secretary's domain. "Ah, quite like my preconception. In the worst of possible taste. *Le mauvais goût.*"

"Yes, Mr. Queen," said the First Secretary. "I mean—"

"By the way, what's the proper form? Does one genuflect and kiss the royal hand, or will a deep bow from the waist suffice?"

"A kick in the pants would be more like it," said a rueful voice. "*Kamerad!*"

Mr. Queen turned around. A young man was standing in the doorway holding his hands high. He wore a soiled pair of slacks, openwork sandals on bare feet, and a lumberman's plaid shirt open at the throat. More wonderful than that, he was smoking a chipped clay pipe which fumed foully; his fingers were stained with ink; and he had not shaved his heavy young beard, judging from its vigorous sprout, in at least three days.

"I thought—" began Mr. Queen.

"I certainly rate one," said the Boy Wonder. "Will you dish it out now, or can we talk things over first?"

Mr. Queen swallowed. "Are *you* Butcher?"

"Guilty. Say, that was the dumbest stunt I've ever seen pulled in this town, and we've pulled some beauties here." He shook Ellery's hand crisply. "Hello, Clark. You Queen's agent?"

"Yes, Mr. Butcher," said Clark. "Yes, sir."

"Come in, both of you," said the Boy Wonder, leading the way. "Don't mind the spurious magnificence of this dump, Queen. The damned thing was wished on me. It was built by old Sigmund in the free-lunch days, when he was tossing away the stockholders' dough like a hunyak on Saturday night. I've tried to make my own workroom livable, anyway. Come on in."

Ellery almost said: "Yes, sir." He came on in.

It wasn't fair! With his sharp green eyes and red hair and boy's smile and beautifully disreputable clothes, Butcher looked like a normal human being. And the holy of holies! From the exterior and anteroom decoration, one had a right to anticipate lushness along Latin-Oriental lines, with tapestries and tiles and inlaid woods of precious pastels. But no drapes smothered the sun; the walls had been repaneled in clean pine; an old missionwood desk bearing the scars of golf-shoes and cigaret burns stood higgledy-piggledy in the midst of a congress of deep, honest chairs; the desk was littered with clues to toil—yellow paper covered with ink-scrawls, a clay model of a ballroom set, an old typewriter with a battered face, photographs, mimeographed scripts, a can of film; books that looked as if they were being read bristled in the pine walls; and a small portable bar beside the desk stood open, crowded with bottles, and accessible to a nervous elbow, as a bar should.

"Ripped out all the junk," said the Boy Wonder cheerfully. "You should have seen it. Sit down, boys. Drink?"

"It isn't fair," moaned Mr. Queen, getting into a chair and cowering.

"What?"

"He says he needs some air," said Alan Clark hastily.

"Shouldn't wonder, after the raw deal he got," said the young man, throwing open all the windows. "Have a slug of Scotch, Queen. Do you good."

"Brandy," said Mr. Queen faintly.

"Brandy!" The Boy Wonder looked pleased. "Now there's a man with discriminating boozing habits. It gets your ticker after a while, but look at all the fun you have waiting for coronary thrombosis. Tell you what I'll do with you, Queen. I'll crack open a couple of bottles of 125-year-old Napoleon I've been saving for my wedding. Just between friends?"

Mr. Queen wavered between the demon of prejudice and the Boy Wonder's grin. While he wavered, the tempter tilted a sun-scorched bottle and poured golden liquid.

It was too, too much. The would-be avenger accepted the fat glass and buried his nose in the seductive vapors of the aged cognac.

"Here—here's to you," said Mr. Queen one bottle later.

"No, no, here's to *you*," said Mr. Butcher.

The friendly sun was beaming on the Magna lot outside, the friendly room was cloistered and cool, the friendly brandy was pure bliss, and they were old, old friends.

Mr. Queen said fervently: "My m'stake, Butchie-boy."

"No, no," said Butchie-boy, beating his breast. "*My* m'stake, El ole cock."

Clark had gone, dismissed by the Boy Wonder. He had departed with anxiety, for the magic of Butchie-boy's executive methods was legend in Hollywood and as a good and conscientious agent Clark had misgivings about leaving his client alone with the magician.

Not without cause. Already his client was prepared to do or die for dear old Magna. "Don't see how I could've mis-misjudged you, Butch," said Mr. Queen, half in tears. "Thought you were a complete an' absolute louse. You my word."

"I *yam* a louse," said Butch. "No won'er people get the wrong impression 'bout Hollywood. A yarn like that! I'll be a laughing—a laughing-stock."

Mr. Queen grasped his glass and glared. "Show me the firsht man who laughsh—laughs an' I'll kick his teeth in!"

"My pal."

"But nob'dy'll spread the story, Butch. It's jus' b'tween us an' Alan Clark." Mr. Queen snapped his fingers. "Curse it, *he'll* talk."

"Cer'nly he'll talk. Di'n't you know all agents are rats? Down with agents!"

"The dirty shkunk," said Mr. Queen ferociously, rising. "Id'll be all over *Variety* t'morrow morning."

Mr. Butcher leered. "Siddown, ole frien'. I fixed *his* wagon."

"No! How?"

"Gave the shtory to *Variety* m'self jus' before you came!"

Mr. Queen howled with admiration and pounded the Boy Wonder's back. The Boy Wonder pounded *his* back. They fell into each other's arms.

The First Secretary discovered them on the floor half a bottle later among sheets and sheets of yellow paper, planning with intense sobriety a mystery picture in which Ellery Van Christie, the world-famous detective, murders Jacques Bouchèrre, the world-famous movie producer, and pins the crime with fiendish ingenuity on one Alan Clarkwell, a scurvy fellow who skulked about making authors' lives miserable.

Chapter II

Story Conference

THE FIRST SECRETARY conferred with the Second Secretary and while the Second Secretary ran for raw eggs, Worcestershire, and tomato juice the First Secretary hauled the debaters into old Sigmund's pre-Butcher lavatory, wheedled them into undressing, pushed them respectfully under the needle-shower, turned on the cold water, and retired under a barrage of yelps to telephone the trainer in the studio gymnasium.

They emerged from the lavatory an hour later full of tomato juice and the piety of newly converted teetotalers, looking like a pair of corpses washed up on shore. Ellery groped for the nearest chair and wound his arms about his head as if he were afraid it was going to fly away.

"What happened?" he moaned.

"I think the house fell in," said the producer. "Howard, locate Lew Bascom. You'll probably find him shooting craps with the grips on Stage 12." The First Secretary vanished. "Ow, my head."

"Alan Clark will massacre me," said Ellery nervously. "You fiend, did you make me sign anything?"

"How should I know?" growled the Boy Wonder. Then they looked at each other and grinned.

For a time there was the silence of common suffering. Then Butcher began to stride up and down. Ellery closed his eyes, pained at this superhuman vitality. He opened them at the crackle of Butcher's voice to find that remarkable gentleman studying him with a sharp green look. "Ellery, I want you back on the payroll."

"Go away," said Ellery.

"This time, I promise, you'll work like a horse."

"On a script?" Ellery made a face. "I don't know a lap dissolve from a fade-in. Look, Butch, you're a nice guy and all that, but this isn't my racket. Let me crawl back to New York."

The Boy Wonder grinned. "I could really care for a mugg like you; you're an honest man. Hell, I've got a dozen writers on this lot who've forgotten more about scripts than you'll know in a million years."

"Then what the devil do you want me for?"

"I've read your books and followed your investigations for a long time. You've got a remarkable gift. You combine death-on-rats analysis with a creative imagination. And you've got a freshness of viewpoint the old-timers here, saturated in the movie tradition and technique, lost years ago. In a word, it's my job to dig up talent, and I think you're a natural-born plot man. Shall I keep talking?"

"When you say such pretty things?" Ellery sighed. "More."

"Know Lew Bascom?"

"I've heard of him. A writer, isn't he?"

"He thinks he is. He's really an idea man. Picture ideas. Gets 'em in hot flushes. Got his greatest notion—Warner's bought it for twenty-five thousand and grossed two million on it—over a poker table when he was so plastered he couldn't tell an ace from a king. The magnificent slugnut sold the idea to another writer in the game in payment of a hundred-dollar debt. . . . Well, you're going to work with Lew. You'll do the treatment together."

"What treatment?" groaned Ellery.

"Of an original he's just sold me. It's the business. If I turned Lew loose on it solo, he'd come up with the most fantastic yarn you ever saw—if he came up with anything at all, which is doubtful. So I want you to work out the plot with him."

"Does he know you're wishing a collaborator on him?" asked Ellery dryly.

"He's probably heard it by this time; you can't keep anything secret in a studio. But don't worry about Lew; he's all right. Unstable, one of Nature's screwiest noblemen, brilliant picture mind, absolutely undependable, gambler, chippy-chaser, dipsomaniac—a swell guy."

"Hmm," said Ellery.

"Only don't let him throw you. You'll be looking for him to buckle down to work and he'll probably be over in Las Vegas playing craps with silver dollars. When he does show up he'll be boiled on both sides. Nobody in town remembers the last time Lew was even relatively sober. . . . Excuse me." Butcher snapped into his communicator: "Yes, Madge?"

The Second Secretary said wearily: "Mr. Bascom just whooshed through, Mr. Butcher, and on the way he grabbed my letter-knife again. I thought you'd like to know."

"Did she say knife?" asked Ellery, alarmed.

A chunky man whizzed in like a fat thunderbolt. He wore shapeless clothes, and he had blown cheeks, nose like a boiled onion, frizzled mustache, irritated hair, eyelids too tired to sit up straight, and a gaudy complexion not caused by exposure to the great outdoors.

This apparition skidded to a stop, danced an intricate measure symbolizing indignation, and brandished a long letter-knife. Then he hopped across the rug to the Boy Wonder's desk, behind which Mr. Queen sat paralyzed, and waggled the steel under the petrified Queen nose.

"See this?" he yelled.

Mr. Queen nodded. He wished he didn't.

"Know what it is?"

Mr. Queen gulped. "A knife."

"Know where I found it?"

Mr. Queen shook his head at this inexplicable catechism. The chunky man plunged the steel into Jacques Butcher's desk-top. It quivered there menacingly.

"In *my* back!" howled Mr. Bascom. "Know who put it there—rat?"

Mr. Queen pushed his chair back an inch.

"You did, you double-crossing New York story-stealer!" bellowed Mr. Bascom; and he seized a bottle of Scotch from the Boy Wonder's bar and wrapped his lips fiercely about its dark brown neck.

"This," said Mr. Queen, "is certainly the second feature of an especially bad dream."

"Just Lew," said Butcher absently. "Always the dramatist. This happens at the start of every production. Listen, Lew, you've got Queen wrong— Ellery Queen, Lew Bascom."

"How do you do," said Mr. Queen formally.

"Lousy," said Lew from behind the bottle.

"Queen's just going to help you with the treatment, Lew. It's still your job, and of course you get top billing."

"That's right," said Ellery, with an ingratiating smile. "Just your little helper, Lew, old man."

Mr. Bascom's wet lips widened in a grin of pure cameraderie. "That's different," he said handsomely. "Here, pal, have a shot. Have two shots. You, too, Butch. Le's all have two shots."

Gentle Alan Clark, the peace and sanity of New York's quiet streets, the milieu of normal people, seemed light-years away. Mr. Queen, hangover and all, wrested the Scotch from Mr. Bascom with the artificial courage of a desperate man.

There was a spare workroom off the Boy Wonder's office which smelled slightly of disinfectant and was furnished with all the luxury of a flagellant monk's cell.

"It's where I go when I want to think," explained Butcher. "You boys use it as your office while you're on this assignment; I want you near me."

Ellery, facing the prospect of being caged within the four nude walls with a gentleman whose whimsies seemed indistinguishable from homicidal mania, appealed to the Boy Wonder with mute, sad eyes. But Butcher grinned and shut the door in his face.

"All right, all right," said Mr. Bascom irritably. "Squat and listen. You're bein' let in on the ground floor of next year's Academy prizewinner."

Eying the door which led to the patio and possible escape in an emergency, Ellery squatted. Lew lay down on the floor and spat accurately through an open window, arms behind his frowsy head.

"I can see it now," he began dreamily. "The crowds, the baby spots, the stinkin' speeches—"

"Spare the build-up," said Ellery. "Facts, please."

"What would you say," Lew went on in the same drifting way, "if M-G-M should all of a sudden make a picture out of Garbo's life? *Huh?*"

"I'd say you ought to sell the idea to M-G-M."

"Nah, nah, you don't get it. And they should *star Garbo* in it, huh? Her own life!" Lew paused, triumphantly. "Say, what's the matter with you, anyway? Don't you see it—her virgin girlhood in Sweden, the meeting with Stiller the genius, Stiller's contract in Hollywood—he takes the gawky kid along, Hollywood falls for her and gives Stiller the cold mitt, she becomes a sensation, Stiller kicks off, the Gilbert romance, the broken heart behind the dead pan—for gossakes!"

"But would Miss Garbo consent?" murmured Ellery.

"Or s'pose," continued Lew, ignoring him, "that Paramount took John and Lionel and Ethel and slung 'em together in a story of *their* lives?"

"You'd have something there," said Ellery.

Lew sprang to his feet. "See what I mean? Well, I've got a real-life yarn that's got those licked a mile! Y'know whose lives we're gonna make? The dizziest, grandest, greatest names in the American theatre! Those dynamos of the drama—the screwballs of the screen—the fightin', feudin', first families of Hollywood!"

"I suppose," frowned Ellery, "you mean the Royles and the Stuarts."

"For gossakes, who else?" groaned Lew. "Get it? Get the set-up? On one side Jack Royle and his cub Ty—on the other Blythe Stuart and her daughter Bonnie. The old generation an' the new. A reg'lar four-ring circus!"

And, overwhelmed by his own enthusiasm, Lew staggered out, returning a moment later from Butcher's office with the unfinished bottle of Scotch.

Ellery sucked his lower lip. It was an idea, all right. There was enough dramatic material in the lives of the Royles and the Stuarts to make two motion pictures, with something left over for a first-class Broadway production.

Before the War, when John Royle and Blythe Stuart had dominated the New York stage, their stormy love-affair was the romantic gossip of Mayfair and Tanktown. It was like the courtship of two jungle cats. They mauled each other from Times Square to San Francisco and back again, leaving a trail of glittering performances and swollen box-offices. But no one doubted, despite their fighting, that in the end they would marry and settle down to the important business of raising a new royal family.

Astonishingly, after the furious passion of their romance, they did nothing of the kind. Something happened; gossip-writers from that day to this had skinned their noses trying to ferret out exactly what. Whatever the cause, it broke up their romance—to such an accompaniment of tears, bellows, recriminations, escapades out of pique, and bitter professions of undying enmity as to set the whole continent to buzzing.

Immediately after the *débâcle* each married some one else. Jack Royle took to his handsome bosom a brawny Oklahoma débutante who had come to New York to give the theatre a new Duse, presented Royle with a son instead, publicly horsewhipped her husband a month later for an unexplained but easily imagined reason, and died shortly after of a broken neck as the result of a fall from a horse.

Blythe Stuart eloped with her publicity man, who fathered her daughter

Bonnie, stole and pawned the pearl necklace which had been presented to her by Jack during their engagement, fled to Europe as a war correspondent, and died in a Paris *bistro* of acute alcoholism.

When Hollywood beckoned, the Royle-Stuart feud was already in the flush of its development, its origin long forgotten in the sheer fury of the feudists' temperaments. It communicated itself to their progeny, so that the hostility of Bonnie Stuart, who was already an important screen ingénue, for Tyler Royle, who was Magna's leading juvenile, became scarcely less magnificent than that of their parents.

From Wilshire to Hollywood Boulevards the feud raged. It was said that old Sigmund, to whom Jack and Blythe had been under contract, had died not of cerebral hemorrhage but of nervous indigestion as a result of trying to keep peace on the Magna lot; and the few prematurely gray hairs at the back of Jacques Butcher's head were ascribed to his similarly futile efforts in the case of their respective issue. One studio wit stated that the Boy Wonder had proposed marriage to Bonnie Stuart as a last desperate measure, on the theory that love sometimes works miracles.

"That's right," said Ellery aloud. "Butch and Bonnie are engaged, aren't they?"

"Is that all you got to say about my idea, for gossakes?" snarled Lew, brandishing the bottle.

Butcher stuck his head into the room. "Well, Ellery, what do you think?"

"My honest opinion?"

"Give me anything else and I'll fire you out on your ear."

"I think," said Ellery, "that it's an inspired notion that will never get beyond the planning stage."

"See?" cried Lew. "You hooked me to a Jonah!"

"What makes you say that?"

"How do you propose to get those four to work in the same picture? They're mortal enemies."

Lew glared at Ellery. "The romance of the century, the most publicized cat-fight of the last twen'y years, terrific box-office appeal in four big star names, a honey of a human-int'rest story—an' *he* throws cold water!"

"Turn it off, Lew," said the Boy Wonder. "That's the major problem, of course, El. Attempts have been made before to cast them in teams, but they've always failed. This time I have a hunch it will be different."

"Love will find a way," said Lew. "The future Mrs. Butcher wouldn't throw her tootsie, would she?"

"Shut up," said Butcher, reddening. "As far as that's concerned, Lew has an in, too. He's Blythe's second cousin; aside from her father and Lew, Blythe hasn't any relatives, and I think she likes this screwball enough to listen to him."

"If she don't," grinned Lew, "I'll break her damn' neck."

"The four of them are broke, too—they always are. I'm prepared to offer them whopping big contracts. They simply won't be able to afford to turn it down."

"Listen," said Lew. "When I show 'em how they're gonna play a picture biography of themselves to an audience of millions, they'll be so damn' tickled they'll fall all over themselves grabbin' for the contracts. It's in the bag."

"I'll tackle Bonnie and Ty," said the Boy Wonder crisply, "and Lew goes to work on Blythe and Jack. Sam Vix, our publicity head, will start the ball rolling in the mags and papers."

"And I?"

"Hang around Lew. Get acquainted with the Stuarts and the Royles. Gather as much material on their personal lives as you can. The biggest job will be weeding, of course. We'll meet again in a few days and compare notes."

"*Adios*," said Lew, and he wandered out with Butcher's bottle under his arm.

A tall man with a windburned face and a black patch over one eye came strolling in. "You want me, Butch?"

"Meet Ellery Queen—he's going to work with Lew Bascom on the Royle-Stuart imbroglio. Queen, this is Sam Vix, head of our publicity department."

"Say, I heard about you," said Vix. "You're the guy worked here for six weeks and nobody knew it. Swell story."

"What's swell about it?" asked Ellery sourly.

Vix stared. "It's publicity, isn't it? By the way, what do you think of Lew's picture idea?"

"I think—"

"It's got everything. Know about Blythe's old man? There's a character for pictures! Tolland Stuart. I bet Blythe hasn't even seen the old fossil for two-three years."

"Excuse me," said the Boy Wonder, and he disappeared.

"Park the carcass," said the publicity man. "Might as well feed you dope if you're going to work on the fracas. Stuart's an eccentric millionaire—I mean he's nuts, if you ask me, but when you've got his dough you're just eccentric, see what I mean? Made it in oil. Well, he's got a million-dollar estate on top of a big butte in the Chocolate Mountains—that's below the San Bernardino range in Imperial County—forty rooms, regular palace, and not a soul on the place but himself and a doctor named Junius, who's the old man's pill-roller, nose-wiper, hash-slinger, and plug-ugly all rolled into one."

"Pardon me," said Ellery, "but I think I'd better see where Lew—"

"Forget Lew; he'll turn up by himself in a couple of days. Well, as I was saying, they spin some mighty tall yarns about old man Stuart. Hypochondriac to the gills, they say; and the wackiest personal habits. Sort of hermit, I guess you'd call him, mortifying the flesh. He's supposed to be as healthy as a horse."

"Listen, Mr. Vix—"

"Call me Sam. If there's a trail down his mountain, only a goat or an Indian could negotiate it. Doc Junius uses a plane for supplies—they've got a landing field up there; I've seen it plenty of times from the air. I'm an aviator myself, you know—got this eye shot out in a dogfight over Boileau. So naturally I'm interested in these two bugs up there flying around their eagle's nest like a couple of spicks out of the Arabian Nights—"

"Look, Sam," said Ellery. "I'd love to swap fairy tales with you, but right now what I want to know is—who in this town knows everything about everybody?"

"Paula Paris," said the publicity man promptly.

"Paris? Sounds familiar."

"Say, where do you come from? She's only syndicated in a hundred and eighty papers from coast to coast. Does the famous movie-gossip column called *Seeing Stars*. Familiar!"

"Then she should be an ideal reference-library on the Royles and the Stuarts."

"I'll arrange an appointment for you." Vix leered. "You're in for an experience, meeting Paula for the first time."

"Oh, these old female battle-axes don't feaze me," said Ellery.

"This isn't a battle-axe, my friend; it's a delicate, singing blade."

"Oh! Pretty?"

"Different. You'll fall for her like all the rest, from wubble-you-murdering Russian counts to Western Union boys. Only, don't try to date her up."

"Ah, exclusive. To whom does she belong?"

"Nobody. She suffers from crowd phobia."

"From what?"

"Fear of crowds. She hasn't left her house since she came to the Coast in a guarded drawing-room six years ago."

"Nonsense."

"Fact. People give her the willies. Never allows more than one person to be in the room with her at the same time."

"But I can't see— How does she snoop around and get her news?"

"She's got a thousand eyes—in other people's heads." Vix rolled his one eye. "What she'd be worth to a studio! Well, I'll ring her for you."

"Do that," said Ellery, feeling his head.

Vix left, and Ellery sat still. There was an eldritch chiming in his ears and the most beautiful colored spots were bouncing before his eyes.

His telephone rang. "Mr. Queen?" said the Second Secretary. "Mr. Butcher has had to go to the projection room to catch the day's rushes, but he wants you to call your agent and have him phone Mr. Butcher back to talk salary and contract. Is that all right?"

"Is what all right?" said Ellery. "I mean—certainly."

Salary. Contract. Lew. Paula. The old man of the mountains. Napoleon brandy. Gatling-gun Butch. The wild Royles and Stuarts. Crowd phobia. Chocolate Mountains. High pressure. Super-spectacle. Rushes. . . . My God, thought Ellery, is it too late?

He closed his eyes. It was too late.

Chapter III

Mr. Queen Sees Stars

AFTER TWO DAYS of trying to pin somebody into a chair within four walls, Ellery felt like a man groping with his bare hands in a goldfish bowl.

The Boy Wonder was holding all-day conferences behind locked doors, making final preparations for his widely publicized production of *Growth of the Soil*. The earth, it seemed, had swallowed Lew Bascom. And every effort of Ellery's to meet the male Royles and the female Stuarts was foiled in the one case by a nasal British voice belonging to a majordomo named Louderback and in the other by an almost incomprehensible French accent on the lips of a lady named Clotilde, neither of whom seemed aware that time was marching on and on and on.

Once, it was close. Ellery was prowling the alleys of the Magna lot with Alan Clark, who was vainly trying to restore his equilibrium, when they turned the corner of "A" Street and 1st and spied a tall girl in black satin slacks and a disreputable man's slouch hat matching pennies at the bootblack stand near the main gate with Roderick, the colored man who polished the shoes of the Magna extras.

"There's Bonnie now," said the agent. "The blonde babe. Ain't she somepin'? Knock you down. Bonnie!" he shouted. "I want you to meet—"

The star hastily dropped a handful of pennies, rubbed Roderick's humped back for luck, and vaulted into a scarlet Cord roadster.

"Wait!" roared Ellery, beside himself. "Damn it all—"

But the last he saw of Bonnie Stuart that day was a blinding smile over one slim shoulder as she shot the Cord around the corner of 1st and "B" Streets on two wheels.

"That's the last straw," stormed Ellery, hurling his Panama to the pavement. "I'm through!"

"Ever try to catch a playful fly? That's Bonnie."

"But *why* wouldn't she—"

"Look. Go see Paula Paris," said the agent diplomatically. "Sam Vix says he made an appointment for you for today. She'll tell you more about those doodlebugs than they know themselves."

"Fifteen hundred a week," mumbled Ellery.

"It's as far as Butcher would go," apologized Clark. "I tried to get him to raise the ante—"

"I'm not complaining about the salary, you fool! Here I've accumulated since yesterday almost six hundred dollars on the Magna books, and I haven't accomplished a blasted thing!"

"See Paula," soothed Clark, patting Ellery's back. "She's always good for what ails you."

So, muttering, Ellery drove up into the Hollywood hills.

He found the house almost by intuition; something told him it would be a sane, homey sort of place, and it was—white frame in a placid Colonial style surrounded by a picket fence. It stood out among the pseudo-Spanish stucco atrocities like a wimpled nun among painted wenches.

A girl at the secretary in the parlor smiled: "Miss Paris is expecting you, Mr. Queen. Go right in." Ellery went, pursued by the stares of the crowded room. They were a motley cross-section of Hollywood's floating population—extras down on their luck, salesmen, domestics, professional observers of the *scène célèbre*. He felt impatient to meet the mysterious Miss Paris, who concocted such luscious news from this salmagundi.

But the next room was another parlor in which another young woman sat taking notes as a hungry-looking man in immaculate morning clothes whispered to her.

"The weeding-out process," he thought, fascinated. "She'd have to be careful about libel, at that."

And he entered the third room at a nod from the second young woman to find himself in a wall-papered chamber full of maple furniture and sunlight, with tall glass doors giving upon a flagged terrace beyond which he could see trees, flowerbeds, and a very high stone wall blanketed with poinsettias.

"How do you do, Mr. Queen," said a pure diapason.

Perhaps his sudden emergence into the light affected his vision, for Mr. Queen indubitably blinked. Also, his ear still rang with that organ sound. But then he realized that that harmonious concord of musical tones was a human female voice, and that its owner was seated cross-kneed in a Cape Cod rocker smoking a Russian cigaret and smiling up at him.

And Mr. Queen said to himself on the instant that Paula Paris was beyond reasonable doubt the most beautiful woman he had yet met in Hollywood. No, in the world, ever, anywhere.

Now, Mr. Queen had always considered himself immune to the grand passion; even the most attractive of her sex had never meant more to him than some one to open doors for or help in and out of taxis. But at this historic moment misogyny, that crusted armor, inexplicably cracked and fell away from him, leaving him defenseless to the delicate blade.

He tried confusedly to clothe himself again in the garments of observation and analysis. There was a nose—a nose, yes, and a mouth, a white skin . . . yes, yes, very white, and two eyes—what could one say about them?—an interesting straight line of gray in her black-lacquer hair . . . all to be sure, to be sure. He was conscious, too, of a garment—was it a Lanvin, or a Patou, or a Poirot?—no, that was the little Belgian detective—a design in the silk gown; yes, yes, a design, and a bodice, and a softly falling skirt that dropped from the knee in long, pure, Praxitelean lines, and an aroma, or rather an effluvium, emanating from her person that was like the ghost of last year's honeysuckle. . . . Mr. Queen uttered a hollow inward chuckle. Honey-suckle! Damn analysis. This was a woman. No—Woman, without the pro-crusteanizing article. Or . . . was . . . it . . . *the* Woman?

"Here, here," said Mr. Queen in a panic, and almost aloud. "Stop that, you damned fool."

"If you're through inspecting me," said Paula Paris with a smile, rising, "suppose you be seated, Mr. Queen. Will you have a highball? Cigarets at your elbow."

Mr. Queen sat down stiffly, feeling for the chair.

"To tell the truth," he mumbled, "I'm—I'm sort of speechless. Paula Paris. Paris. That's it. A remarkable name. Thank you, no highball. Beautiful! Cigaret?" He sat back, folding his arms. "Will you please say something?"

There was a dimple at the left side of her mouth when she pursed her lips—not a large, gross, ordinary dimple, but a shadow, a feather's touch. It was visible now. "You speak awfully well for a speechless man, Mr. Queen, although I'll admit it doesn't quite make sense. What are you—a linguistic disciple of Dali?"

"That's it. More, please. Yahweh, thou hast given me the peace that passeth understanding."

Ah, the concern, the faint frown, the tensing of that cool still figure. Here, for heaven's sake! What's the matter with you?

"Are you ill?" she asked anxiously. "Or—"

"Or drunk. Drunk, you were going to say. Yes, I am drunk. No, delirious. I feel the way I felt when I stood on the north rim of the Grand Canyon looking into infinity. No, no, that's so unfair to you. Miss Paris, if you don't talk to me I shall go completely mad."

She seemed amused then, and yet he felt an infinitesimal withdrawing, like the stir of a small animal in the dark. "Talk to you? I thought you wanted to talk to me."

"No, no, that's all so trivial now. I must hear your voice. It bathes me. God knows I need soothing after what I've been through in this bubbling vat of a town. Has any one ever told you the organ took its tonal inspiration from your voice?"

Miss Paris averted her head suddenly, and after a moment she sat down. He saw a flush creeping down her throat. "*Et tu, Brute*," she laughed, and yet her eyes were strange. "Sometimes I think men say such kind things to me because—" She did not finish.

"On the contrary," said Ellery, out of control. "You're a gorgeous, gorgeous creature. Undoubtedly the trouble with you is an acute inferiority—"

"Mr. Queen."

He recognized it then, that eerie something in her eyes. It was fright. Before, it had seemed incredible that this poised, mature, patrician creature should be afraid of anything, let alone the mere grouping of human beings. "Crowd phobia," Sam Vix had called it; homophobia, a morbid fear of man. . . . Mr. Queen snapped out of it very quickly indeed. That one glimpse into terror had frightened him, too.

"Sorry. Please forgive me. I did it on a—on a bet. Very stupid of me."

"I'm sure you did." She kept looking at her quiet hands.

"It's the detective in me, I suppose. I mean, this clumsy leap into analysis—"

"Tell me, Mr. Queen," she said abruptly, tamping out her cigaret. "How do you like the idea of putting the Royles and the Stuarts into a biographical film?"

Dangerous ground, then. Of course. He *was* an ass. "How did you know? Oh, I imagine Sam Vix told you."

"Not at all. I have deeper channels of information." She laughed then, and Ellery drank in the lovely sound. Superb, superb! "I know all about you, you see," she was murmuring. "Your six weeks' horror at Magna, your futile scampering about the lot there, your orgy the other day with Jacques Butcher, who's a darling—"

"I'm beginning to think you'd make a pretty good detective yourself."

She shook her head ever so slowly and said: "Sam said you wanted information." Ellery recognized the barrier. "Exactly what?"

"The Royles and the Stuarts." He jumped up and began to walk around; it was not good to look at this woman too long. "What they're like. Their lives, thoughts, secrets—"

"Heavens, is that all? I'd have to take a month off, and I'm too busy for that."

"You do know all about them, though?"

"As much as any one. Do sit down again, Mr. Queen. Please."

Ellery looked at her then. He felt a little series of twitches in his spine. He grinned idiotically and sat down.

"The interesting question, of course," she went on in her gentle way, "is why Jack Royle and Blythe Stuart broke their engagement before the War. And nobody knows that."

"I understood you to know everything."

"Not quite everything, Mr. Queen. I don't agree, however, with those who think it was another woman, or another man, or anything as serious as that."

"Then you do have an opinion."

The dimple again. "Some ridiculous triviality. A lovers' spat of the most inconsequential sort."

"With such extraordinary consequences?" asked Ellery dryly.

"Apparently you don't know them. They're reckless, irresponsible, charming lunatics. They've earned top money for over twenty years, and yet both are stony. Jack was—and is—a philanderer, gambler, a swashbuckler who indulges in the most idiotic escapades; a great actor, of course. Blythe was— and is—a lovely, electric hoyden whom every one adores. It's simply that they're capable of anything, from breaking an engagement for no reason at all to keeping a vendetta for over twenty years."

"Or, I should imagine, piracy on the high seas."

She laughed. "Jack once signed a contract with old Sigmund calling for five thousand a week, to make a picture that was scheduled to take about ten weeks' shooting time. The afternoon of the day he signed the contract he dropped fifty thousand dollars at Tia Juana. So he worked the ten weeks for nothing, borrowing money from week to week for tips, and he gave the most brilliant performance of his career. That's Jack Royle."

"Keep talking."

"Blythe? She's never worn a girdle, drinks Martinis exclusively, sleeps raw, and three years ago gave half a year's salary to the Actors' Fund because Jack gave three months' income. And that's Blythe."

"I suppose the youngsters are worse than their parents. The second generation usually is."

"Oh, definitely. It's such a deep, sustained hatred that a psychologist, I suspect, would look for some frustration mechanism, like Love Crushed to Earth. . . ."

"But Bonnie's engaged to Jacques Butcher!"

"I know that," said Paula calmly. "Nevertheless—you mark my words—crushed to earth, it will rise again. Poor Butch is in for it. And I think he knows it, poor darling."

"This boy Tyler and the girl aren't on speaking terms?"

"Oh, but they are! Wait until you hear them. Of course, they both came up in pictures about the same time, and they're horribly jealous of each other. A couple of months ago Ty got a newspaper splash by wrestling with a trained grizzly at one of his father's famous parties. A few days later Bonnie adopted a panther cub as a pet and paraded it up and down the Magna lot until Ty came off a set with a gang of girls, and then somehow—quite innocently, of course—the cub came loose and began to chew at Ty's leg. The sight of Ty running away with the little animal scampering after him quite destroyed his reputation as a he-man."

"Playful, aren't they?"

"You'll love all four of them, as every one else does. In Blythe's and Bonnie's case, it's probably an inheritance from Blythe's father Tolland—that's Bonnie's grandfather."

"Vix mentioned him rather profusely."

"He's a local character—quite mad. I don't mean mentally; he was sane enough to amass a tremendous fortune in oil. Just gaga. He spent a million dollars on his estate on Chocolate Mountain, and he hasn't even a caretaker to hoe the weeds. It cost him forty thousand dollars to blast away the top of a neighboring mountain peak because he didn't like the view of it from his porch—he said it looked like the profile of a blankety-blank who had once beaten him in an oil deal."

"Charming," said Ellery, looking at her figure.

"He drinks cold water with a teaspoon and publishes pamphlets crammed with statistics crusading against stimulants, including tobacco and coffee and tea, and warning people that eating white bread brings you early to the grave."

She talked on and on, and Ellery sat back and listened, more entranced by the source than the information. It was by far the pleasantest afternoon he had spent in Hollywood.

He came to with a start. There was a shadow on Paula's face, and it was creeping higher every minute.

"Good lord!" he said, springing up and looking at his watch. "Why didn't you kick me out, Miss Paris? All those people waiting out there—"

"My girls take care of most of them, and it's a relief to be listened to for a change. And you're such a splendid listener, Mr. Queen." She rose, too, and extended her hand. "I'm afraid I haven't been much help."

He took her hand, and after a moment she gently withdrew it.

"Help?" said Ellery. "Oh, yes. Yes, you've been of tremendous service. By the way, can you suggest the surest means of treeing those four?"

"Today's Friday. Of course. You go down to the *Horseshoe Club* on Wilshire Boulevard tomorrow night."

"*Horseshoe Club*," said Ellery dutifully, watching her mouth.

"Don't you know it? It's probably the most famous gambling place in Los Angeles. Run by Alessandro, a very clever gentleman with a very dark past. You'll find them there."

"Alessandro's," said Ellery. "Yes."

"Let's see." She turned her head a little, trying to avoid his questing eyes. "There's no opening tomorrow night—yes, they'll be there, I'm sure."

"Will they let me in? I'm a stranger in town."

"Would you like me to arrange it?" she asked demurely. "I'll call Alessandro. He and I have an understanding."

"You're simply wonderful." Then he said hastily: "I mean, so— Look, Miss Paris. Or why not Paula? Do you mind? Would you— I mean, could you bring yourself to accompany—"

"Goodbye, Mr. Queen," said Paula with a faint smile.

"But would you do me the honor—"

"It's been so nice talking to you. Drop in again."

That damned phobia!

"I warn you," he said grimly. "You may live to regret that invitation." And, a little blindly, Mr. Queen made his way to the street.

What a lovely day! he thought, breathing deeply, drinking in the lovely sky, the lovely trees, even the lovely Spanish-style houses all about that supremely lovely white-frame cottage which housed surely the loveliest self-imprisoned Juliet in the history of romantic heroines.

And suddenly he remembered Vix's cynical remark two days before: "You'll fall for her like all the rest." The rest. . . . That implied a host of admirers. Well, why not? She was delectable and piquant to the jaded male palate, like a strange condiment. And what sort of figure did he cut in this land of brown, brawny, handsome men?

The loveliness went out of everything.

Crushed, Mr. Queen crept into his car and drove away.

Saturday night found him in a dinner jacket at the *Horseshoe Club*, cursing his wasted years of singleness and, his thoughts still hovering over a certain white-frame cottage in the Hollywood hills, not greatly caring if he cornered his quarry or not.

"Where can I find Alessandro?" he asked a bartender.

"In his office." The man pointed, and Ellery skirted the horseshoe-shaped bar, threaded his way across the packed dance-floor past the orchestra stand where a swaying quadroon moaned a love-song, and entered a silk-hung passage at the terminus of which stood a chrome-steel door.

Ellery went up to it and knocked. It was opened at once by a hard-looking gentleman in tails who appropriately gave him a hard look.

"Yeah?"

"Alessandro?"

"So who wants him?"

"Oh, go away," said Ellery, and he pushed the hard-looking gentleman aside. An apple-cheeked little man with China-blue eyes wearing a huge horseshoe-shaped diamond on his left hand smiled up at him from behind a horseshoe-shaped desk.

"My name is Queen. Paula Paris told me to look you up."

"Yes, she called me." Alessandro rose and offered his fat little hand. "Any friend of Paula's is welcome here."

"I hope," said Ellery not too hopefully, "she gave me a nice reference."

"Very nice. You want to play, Mr. Queen? We can give you anything at any stakes—roulette, faro, baccarat, dice, chuck-a-luck, poker—"

"I'm afraid my quarter-limit stud is too rich for your blood," grinned Ellery. "I'm really here to find the Royles and the Stuarts. Are they here?"

"They haven't turned up yet. But they will. They generally do on Saturday nights."

"May I wait inside?"

"This way, Mr. Queen." Alessandro pressed on a blank wall and the wall opened, revealing a crowded, smoky, quiet room.

"Quite a set-up," said Ellery, amused. "Is all this hocus-pocus necessary?"

The gambler smiled. "My clients expect it. You know—Hollywood? They want a kick for their dough."

"Weren't you located in New York a few years ago?" asked Ellery, studying his bland, innocent features.

The little man said: "Me?" and smiled again, and nodded to another hard-looking man in the secret passageway. "All right, Joe, let the gentleman through."

"My mistake," murmured Ellery, and he entered the gaming room.

But he had not been mistaken. Alessandro's name was not Alessandro, and he did hail from New York, and in New York he had gathered to his rosy little self a certain fame. The gossip at Police Headquarters had ascribed his sudden disappearance from Broadway to an extraordinary run of luck, during the course of which he had badly dented four bookmakers, two dice rings, and a poker clique composed of Dopey Siciliano, an assistant District

Attorney, a Municipal Court Judge, a member of the Board of Estimate, and Solly the Slob.

And here he was, running a joint in Hollywood. Well, well, thought Ellery, it's a small world.

He wandered about the place. He saw at once that Mr. Alessandro had risen in the social scale. At one table in a booth two wooden-faced house men played seven-card stud, deuces wild, with the president of a large film company, one of Hollywood's most famous directors, and a fabulously-paid radio comedian. The dice tables were monopolized—it was a curious thing, thought Ellery with a grin—by writers and gag men. And along the roulette tables were gathered more stars than Tillie the Toiler had ever dreamed on, registering a variety of emotions that would have delighted the hearts of the directors present had they been in a condition to appreciate their realism.

Ellery spied the elusive Lew Bascom, in a disreputable tuxedo, in the crowd about one of the wheels. He was clutching a stack of chips with one hand and the neck of a queenly brunette with the other.

"So here you are," said Ellery. "Don't tell me you've been hiding out here for three days!"

"Go 'way, pal," said Lew, "this is my lucky night." There was a mountain of chips before the brunette.

"Yeah," said the brunette, glaring at Ellery.

Ellery seized Lew's arms. "I want to talk to you."

"Why can't I get any peace, for gossakes? Here, toots, hang on to papa's rent," and he dropped his handful of chips down the gaping front of the brunette's décolletage. "Well, well, what's on your mind?"

"You," said Ellery firmly, "are remaining with me until the Royles and the Stuarts arrive. Then you're going to introduce me. And after that you may vanish in a puff of smoke for all I care."

Lew scowled. "What day is it?"

"Saturday."

"What the hell happened to Friday? Say, here's Jack Royle. C'mon, that wheel ain't gonna wait all night."

He dragged Ellery over to a tall, handsome man with iron-gray hair who was laughing at something Alessandro was saying. It was John Royle, all right, in the flesh, thought Ellery; the merest child knew that famous profile.

"Jack, here's a guy named Ellery Queen," grunted Lew. "Give him your autograph and lemme get back to the wheel."

"Mr. Queen," said the famous baritone voice, and the famous mustache-smile appeared. "Don't mind this lack-brain; he's probably drunk as usual. Rudeness runs in the Stuart line. Excuse me a moment." He said to Alessandro: "It's all right, Alec. I'm filthy with it tonight." The little fat man nodded curtly and walked away. "And now, Mr. Queen, how do you like working for Magna?"

"Then Butcher's told you. Do you know how hard I've tried to see you in the past three days, Mr. Royle?"

The famous smile was cordial, but the famous black eyes were roving.

"Louderback did say something. . . . Three days! Three, did you say? Lord, Queen, that's a hunch! Pardon me while I break Alessandro's heart."

And he hurried off to the cashier's cage to exchange a fistful of bills for a stack of blue chips. He dived into the crowd at the roulette table.

"Five hundred on number three," Ellery heard him chortle.

Fascinated by this scientific attack on the laws of chance, Ellery permitted Lew to wriggle away. Number 3 failed to come up. Royle smiled, glanced at the clock on the wall, noted that its hands stood at nine-five, and promptly placed stacks on numbers 9 and 5. The ball stopped on 7.

Blythe Stuart swept in, magnificent in a black evening gown, followed by a tall Hindu in tails and a turban, with a brown impassive face. Instantly she was surrounded.

"Blythe! Who's the new boy-friend?"

"I'll bet he's a prince, or a rajah, or something. Leave it to Blythe."

"Introduce me, darling!"

"Please," protested the actress, laughing. "This is Ramdu Singh, and he's a Swami from India or some place, and he has second sight or something, I'll swear, because he's told me the most amazing things about myself. The Swami is going to help me play."

"How thrilling!"

"Lew darling!" cried Blythe, spying him. "Get out of the way and let me show you how to lick that thing. Come along, Mr. Singh!"

Lew looked the Swami over blearily and shrugged. "It's your cashee, Blythe."

A Russian director gave the actress his chair and the Swami took his place behind it, ignoring the stares of the crowd. The croupier looked a little startled and glanced at Alessandro who shrugged, smiled, and moved off.

"Place your bets," said the croupier.

At this moment, across the table, the eyes of John Royle and Blythe Stuart met. And without a flicker they passed on.

With an enigmatic expression Royle placed a bet. The Swami whispered in Blythe Stuart's ear and she made no move to play, as if he had advised lying low until his Psyche could smell out the probabilities. The wheel spun, the ball clacked to a stop on a number, the croupier began raking up the chips.

"I beg your pardon," said John Royle politely, and he took the outstretched rake from the croupier's hand and poked it across the table at the Swami's turban. The turban fell off the Swami's head. His skull gleamed in the strong light—hairless, polished, pinkish-white.

The "Hindu" dived frantically for the turban. Some one gasped. Blythe Stuart gaped at the naked pink scalp.

Royle handed the rake back to the croupier with a bow. "This," he said in an amiable tone, "is Arthur William Park, the actor. You remember his Polonius, Sergei, in the Menzies *Hamlet* in 1920? An excellent performance, then—as now."

Park straightened up, murder in his eyes.

"Sorry, old man," murmured Royle. "I know you're down on your luck, but I can't permit my . . . friends to be victimized."

"You're riding high, Royle," said Park thickly, his cheeks muddy under the make-up. "Wait till you're sixty-five, unable to get a decent part, sick as a dying dog, with a wife and crippled son to support. Wait."

Alessandro signalled to two of his men.

"Come on, fella," said one of them.

"Just a moment," said Blythe Stuart in a low voice. Her hazel eyes blazed like Indian topaz. "Alessandro, call a policeman."

"Now, take it easy, Miss Stuart," said Alessandro swiftly. "I don't want any trouble here—"

Park cried out and tried to run; the two men caught him by his skinny arms. "No! Please!"

Royle's smile faded. "Don't take it out on this poor fellow, just because you're angry with me. Let him go."

"I won't be publicly humiliated!"

"Mother! What's the matter?" Bonnie Blythe, dazzling in an ermine cape, her golden curls iridescent in the light, appeared on Jacques Butcher's arm. She shook it off and ran to Blythe.

"Oh, darling, this beast put this man up to pretending to be a Swami, and he brought me here and—and the beast unmasked the Swami as an actor or something," sobbed Blythe, melting into tears at the sight of a compassionate face, "and I've never been so humiliated in my life." Then she stamped her foot. "Alessandro, will you call a policeman or must I? I'll have them both arrested!"

"Darling. Don't," said Bonnie gently, her arm about her mother's shoulders. "The man looks pretty much down in the mouth to me. I don't think you'd enjoy seeing him in jail." She nodded to Alessandro over her mother's sleek coiffure, and the gambler sighed with relief and signalled to his men, who hurried the man out. "But as for Mr. John Royle," continued Bonnie, her glance hardening, "that's—different."

"Bonnie," said the Boy Wonder warningly.

"No, Butch. It's time he was told—"

"My dear Bonnie," said Royle with a queer smile, "I assure you I didn't put Park up to his masquerade. That was his own idea."

"Don't tell me," sobbed Blythe. "I know you, John Royle. Oh, I could kill you!"

And she gathered her sweeping skirts about her and ran out of the gaming room, crying bitterly. Bonnie ran after her, followed by the Boy Wonder, whose face was red with embarrassment.

Royle shrugged with a braggadocio that did not quite come off. He pressed some bills into Lew Bascom's hand, nodding toward the door. Lew waddled out with the money.

"Place your bets," said the croupier wearily.

Lew came back after a long absence. "What a night! It's a conspiracy, damn it, to keep me from cleanin' up the joint. Just when I was goin' good!"

"I trust," sighed Ellery, "all's well that ends well? Nobody's murdered anybody?"

"Damn near. Bumped into Ty Royle outside, just comin' in. Alec's guerillas told him what happened and he tried to make Park take some dough. That kid gives away more dough to broken-down actors than half the relief-agencies in Hollywood. The old guy took it, all right. They're all outside now, raisin' hell."

"Then it wasn't a put-up job?"

"Hell, no. Though I'll bet Jack's sorry he didn't think of it."

"I doubt that," said Ellery dryly, glancing at Royle. The actor was sitting at the bar before a row of six cocktail glasses filled with Sidecars, his broad back humped.

"Park's got cancer or somepin', hasn't had more'n extra-work for two-three years. What'd he want to come around here for?" Lew made a face. "Spoiled my whole evening. Stiff old devil! I took him around the corner and bought him a couple. He wouldn't take Jack's dough, though."

"Curious ethics. And I can't say Blythe Stuart's spent a very enjoyable evening, either."

"That wacky dame! Sucker for every phony in the fortune-telling racket. She won't even take a part till she's read the tea-leaves."

Bonnie came stalking back, her face stormy. The Boy Wonder clutched her arm, looking harassed. He was talking earnestly to her; but she paid no attention, tapping the rug with her toe, glancing about. She caught sight of Jack Royle sitting Buddha-like at the bar and took a step forward.

"Hold it, me proud beauty," drawled a voice, and she stopped as if she had stepped on an electric wire.

A tall young man in evening clothes, surrounded by four beautiful young women, loomed in Alessandro's doorway. Alessandro looked positively unhappy, Ellery thought.

"You again?" said Bonnie with such colossal contempt that, had Ellery been in the young man's shoes, he would have made for the nearest crack in the wall. "You can spare that alcoholic breath of yours. He's got it coming to him, and he's going to get it."

"If this is going to be a scrap," said Ty Royle in a cold voice, "how about mixing it with me? I'm closer to your age, and dad's getting on."

Bonnie looked him up and down. "At that," she said sweetly, "he's a better man than you are. At least he doesn't flaunt *his* harem in decent people's faces."

The four young ladies surrounding Ty gasped, and for a moment Ellery thought there would be a general engagement in which the destruction of expensive coiffures would be the least of the damage.

"Ty. Bonnie," said the Boy Wonder hurriedly, stepping between them. "Not here, for the love of Mike. Here—" he glanced about desperately. "Queen! What luck. Darling, this is Ellery Queen. Queen—will you?" and Butcher dragged Ty Royle aside.

"If Butch thinks I'm going to let that conceited housemaid's hero," said Bonnie, her magnificent eyes smoking, "talk me out of giving his father a piece of my mind—"

"But would it be wise?" said Ellery hastily. "I mean—"

"Poor mother's positively *ashamed!* Of course, it's her fault for listening to every charlatan in a Hindu make-up, but a decent person wouldn't expose her that way in front of all the people she knows. She's really the dearest, sweetest thing, Mr. Queen. Only she isn't very practical, and if I didn't watch her like a nursemaid she'd get into all sorts of trouble. Especially with those detestable Royles just *watching* for a chance to humiliate her!"

"Not Tyler Royle, surely? He seems like a nice boy."

"Nice! He's loathsome! Although I'll admit he doesn't pester mother—he goes after *my* hide, and I can handle *him*. But Jack Royle. . . . Oh, I'm sure mother will cry herself to sleep tonight. I'll probably be up until dawn putting vinegar compresses on her poor head."

"Then don't you think," said Ellery cunningly, "that perhaps you'd better go home now? I mean, after all—"

"Oh, no," said Bonnie fiercely, glaring about. "I've got some unfinished business, Mr. Queen."

Ellery thought with desperation of some diversion. "I'm afraid I rather feel like an innocent Christian martyr thrown to a particularly lovely young lioness."

"*What?*" said Bonnie, looking at Ellery really for the first time.

"I talk that way sometimes," said Ellery.

She stared at him, and then burst out laughing. "Where've you *been*, Mr. Queen? That's the nicest thing I've ever been told outside a set. You must be a writer."

"I am. Hasn't Butch mentioned my name?"

"Probably." Her mouth curved and she took his arm. Ellery blushed a little. Her body felt terribly soft where it touched him, and she smelled delicious. Not quite so delicious as Paula Paris, of course, but still delicious enough to make him wonder whether he wasn't turning into a positive lecher. "I like you. You may take me over to the roulette table."

"Delighted."

"Oh, I know! You're the man who was with Alan Clark yesterday."

"So you remember!"

"Indeed I do. I thought you were an insurance agent. Did any one ever tell you you look like an insurance agent?"

"To the wheel!" groaned Ellery, "before I remind you of something you saw in your last nightmare."

He found a chair for her at the table. Butcher hurried over, looking warm but successful, and dumped two handfuls of chips before Bonnie. He winked at Ellery, wiped his face, bent over Bonnie, and kissed the nape of her neck.

Ellery, thinking instantly of a lady named Paris, sighed. Damn it, she would have to be a female hermit!

He saw Tyler Royle go over to the bar, put his arm about his father's shoulders, and say something with a cheerful expression. Jack Royle turned his head a little, and Ellery saw him smile briefly. Ty pounded his father's back affectionately and came back to herd his adoring feminine entourage over to the roulette table, opposite Bonnie. He ignored her elaborately, saying something in an undertone to his companions, who giggled.

Bonnie pursed her lips; but then she laughed and looked up at Butcher, whispering something; and Butcher laughed, not too gaily, while she turned back to place a bet. Young Mr. Royle, gazing quizzically at the board, also placed a bet. Miss Stuart smiled. Mr. Royle frowned. Miss Stuart frowned. Mr. Royle smiled.

The croupier droned on. The wheel spun. Chips made hollow, clicking sounds. Jack Royle sat imbibing Sidecars at the bar, gazing in silence at his handsome reflection in the mirror. Bonnie seemed absorbed in the play. Ty Royle placed bets carelessly.

Ellery was just beginning to feel relieved when a bray offended his left ear, and he turned to find Lew Bascom, grinning like a potbellied Pan, beside him.

"'Stoo peaceful," murmured Lew. "Watch this."

Ellery felt a premonition. The glint in Lew's bleared eye promised no advancement of the cause of peace.

The players were distributing their bets. Bonnie had pushed a stack of blue chips onto Number 19 and, scarcely paying attention, Ty shoved a similar stack on the same number. At this moment Alessandro ushered into the room a very famous lady of the screen who had just married Prince Youssov, whose royal line was reputed to stand close to the Heavenly Throne; the Prince was with her, in full panoply; and every one turned his attention from the table, including the croupier, to admire the gorgeous pair.

Lew calmly picked up Bonnie's stack and moved it from number 19 to number 9.

"My God," groaned Mr. Queen to himself. "If 19 should win . . . !"

"Nineteen," announced the croupier, and the hands of Bonnie and Ty stretched from opposite sides of the table to meet on the pile of chips shoved forward by the croupier. Bonnie did not remove her hand.

"Will somebody," she said in an ice-in-glass voice, "inform the gentleman that this is my stack?"

Ty kept his hand on hers. "Far be it from me to argue with a lady, but will somebody wise her up that it's mine?"

"The gentleman is trying to be cute. It's mine."

"The lady couldn't be if she tried. It's mine."

"Butch! You saw me cover nineteen, didn't you?"

"I wasn't watching. Look, dear—"

"Croupier!" said Ty Royle. "Didn't you see me cover number nineteen?" The croupier looked baffled. "I'm afraid I didn't see—"

"It's Ty's!" said one of his companions.

"No, it vuss Bonnie's. I see her put it there," said the Russian director.

"But I tell you I saw Ty—"

"Bonnie—"

The table was in an uproar. Ty and Bonnie glared nakedly at each other. The Boy Wonder looked angry. Alessandro ran up.

"Ladies, gentlemen. Please! You're disturbing the other players. What's the trouble?"

Ty and Bonnie both tried to explain.

"That's not true," stormed Bonnie. "You let my hand go!"

"I'm sorry," barked Ty, "but I don't see why I should. If it were anybody else I might accept her word—"

"How dare you!"

"Oh, stop mugging. You're not doing the big scene now. It's a cheap stunt."

"Mugging, am I?" cried Bonnie. "You—*comedian!*"

Ty applauded. "Keep it up, sister; you're going great."

"Pretty boy!"

That stung him. "I ought to slap your face—"

"You took the words right out of my mouth!" And Bonnie whacked his cheek resoundingly.

Ty went pale. Bonnie's bosom heaved. The Boy Wonder whispered sharply in her ear. Alessandro said something to Ty in a curt undertone.

"I don't give a damn. If she thinks she can maul me and get away with it—" said Ty, his nostrils quivering.

"Insulting pup!" raged Bonnie. "Accuse *me* of cheating—"

"I'll pay you back for that smack if it's the last thing I do!" shouted Ty across Alessandro's fat shoulders.

"There's more where that came from, Ty Royle!"

"Please!" thundered Alessandro. "I'll credit each of your accounts with the winnings on that bet. Now I'll have to ask you, Miss Stuart and Mr. Royle, either to quiet down or leave."

"Leave?" shrieked Bonnie. "I can't get away from the contaminated air surrounding that fake old lady's delight soon enough!"

And she wrenched herself from the Boy Wonder's grasp and flew to the door. Ty shook Alessandro off and ran after her. The Boy Wonder dived after both.

They all disappeared to the accompaniment of screams and bellows.

"That," said Ellery to Lew Bascom, "was one damfool trick, my playful friend."

"Ain't it the truth?" sighed Lew. "C'mon, toots, let's watch the wind-up of this bout." And he dragged his brunette companion away from the wheel and hurried her after the vanished trio.

Something made Ellery turn and look at Jack Royle. The actor still sat at the bar, motionless, as if he had not heard a word of the quarrel behind him.

But in the mirror Ellery caught a glimpse of his lips. They were twisted into a bitter smile.

Chapter IV

Battle Royle

THE SEVEN DAYS following that quiet evening at Alessandro's whistled by Mr. Ellery Queen's ears with the terrifying intimacy of bullets; it was like being caught out in No Man's Land between two blasting armies. By the end of the week he had not only collected a smoking mass of notes but several lesions of the nervous system as well.

He was entangled in a mass of old Royle-Stuart clippings in the studio library, trying to unsnarl his notes, when he was summoned by page to Jacques Butcher's office.

The Boy Wonder looked gaunt, but triumphant. "*Mirabile dictu.* We're sitting on top of the world."

"Peace, it's wonderful," grinned Lew. "It sure is."

"They've agreed?" asked Ellery incredulously.

"Absolutely."

"I refuse to believe it. What did you use—hypnosis?"

"Appeal to their vanity. I knew they'd fall."

"Blythe put up a battle," said Lew, "but when I told her Jack didn't want her but was holding out for Cornell, she got tongue-tied trying to say yes."

"How about Jaunty Jack?"

"A pushover." Lew frowned. "It was hooey about Cornell, of course. Looked to me almost as if he *wanted* to play opposite Blythe."

"He has looked peaked this week," said Ellery thoughtfully.

"Hell, he ain't had a drink in five days. That would poop up any guy. I tell you something's happened to Jack!"

"Let's not pry too deeply into the ways of Providence," said the Boy Wonder piously. "The point is—they're in."

"I shouldn't imagine, Butch, you had quite so smooth a time winning the youngsters over."

The producer shuddered. "Please. . . . Ty finally gave in because I convinced him his public was demanding a real-life rôle from him—biography's the vogue, following the Muni hits—and what could Ty Royle's public like better than Ty Royle's own life on the screen? Know what he said? 'I'll show 'em real life,' he said, 'when I get my hands around your fiancée's lily-white throat!'"

"Sounds bad," said Ellery.

"Doesn't sound good," chortled Lew.

"Bonnie," said the Boy Wonder sadly, "Bonnie was even worse. **The only** condition on which she'd give in was that the script must include at least one scene in which she had to slap, scratch, and punch Ty into insensibility."

"Who's directing?" asked Lew.

"Probably Corsi. Swell Broadway background. And you know what he did last year with the human-interest situations in *Glory Road*. Why?"

"I was thinking," said Lew dreamily; "it's going to be a lot of fun. Corsi's the most finicky retake artist in pictures. After two-three days of slapping Ty around to Corsi's satisfaction for that one scene Bonnie'll have had Ty's pound of flesh—under her fingernails."

The historic ceremony of the Great Signing took place on the 11th, which was the following Monday. From the preparations he heard and witnessed in the office adjoining his, Ellery thought whimsically of a landing-field, with a crippled plane circling above, and fire-apparatus and ambulances scurrying about below in readiness for the inevitable crack-up.

But, all things considered, the contracts were signed without the blazing wreckage the Boy Wonder apparently anticipated. Peace was achieved by a simple expedient: the signatories did not open their mouths. Jack Royle, dressed even more carefully than usual, stared out of Butcher's windows until his turn came to sign; then he signed, smiled for the photographers, and quietly walked out. Blythe, eye-filling in a silver fox-trimmed suit, preserved a queenly silence. Bonnie, it was true, stared steadily at Ty's throat throughout the ceremony, as if contemplating assault. But Ty, to whose better nature Butch had appealed beforehand, ignored the challenge in her eyes.

The trade-paper reporters and photographers were plainly disappointed.

"For gossakes," said Lew disgustedly, when they had all left, "that's a hell of a way to build up the conflict angle. Look at the chance we muffed, Butch!"

"Until they signed," said the producer calmly, "I couldn't risk one of them blowing up the whole business by backing out. You don't fumble when you're playing catch with dynamite, Lew."

"Then it's okay to shoot the works now, Butch?" asked Sam Vix.

"We're rolling, Sam."

Vix proceeded to roll. Exactly how it occurred Ellery did not discover—he suspected a conspiracy between the publicity man and Lew Bascom—but on Monday night Bonnie and Ty collided at the bar of the *Clover Club*. Lew, conveniently present, tried with suspicious gravity to affect a reconciliation "for dear old Magna." Bonnie, who was escorted by a wealthy Argentine gentleman, flared up; Ty flared back; the Argentine gentleman resented Ty's tone; Ty resented the Argentine gentleman's tone; the Argentine gentleman pulled Ty's nose vigorously; and Ty threw the Argentine gentleman over the bartender's head into the bar mirror, which did not stand up under the strain. Whereupon Bonnie had Ty arrested for assault. Bailed out in the early hours of Tuesday morning by his father, Ty swore vengeance in the presence of half the newspapermen in Hollywood.

The Tuesday papers made Sam Vix look content. "Even Goldwyn," he told Ellery modestly, "would be satisfied with that one."

But Mr. Vix did not look so content on Friday. The very patch over his eye was quivering when he burst into the Boy Wonder's office, where Lew and Ellery were shouting at each other in a "story conference," while Butcher listened in silence.

"We're sunk," panted Vix. "Never trust an actor. They've done it. Paula Paris just tipped me off!"

"Who's done what?" asked Butch sharply.

"The one thing that blows the Royle-Stuart picture higher than the Rockies. Jack and Blythe have made up!"

He sank into a chair. Lew Bascom, Ellery, goggled at him. Butcher swiveled and stared out his window.

"Go on," said Lew in a sick voice. "That's like saying Trotsky and Stalin were caught playing pinochle with J. P. Morgan."

"It's even worse than that," groaned Vix. "*They're going to be married.*"

"For gossakes!" yelled Lew, jumping up. "That screws everything!"

The Boy Wonder spun around and said into his communicator: "Madge, get Paula Paris on the wire."

"*Requiescat in pace,*" sighed Ellery. "Anybody know the dope on the next train to New York?"

Lew was racing about, declaiming to the ceiling. "Wham goes the big idea. Conflict—huh! Feud! Build up a natural for over twenty years and then they go into a clinch and kill the whole thing. They can't do this to me!"

The telephone rang. "Paula, Jacques Butcher. Is it true what Sam Vix says you say about Jack and Blythe?"

"They agreed to forgive and forget Wednesday night," answered Paula. "I heard it late yesterday. It seems Jack saw the light Saturday night at the *Horseshoe Club* after that fuss over Park, the actor, and he's been brooding over his own cussedness ever since. Seems to be true love, Mr. Butcher. They're rushing plans for the wedding."

"What happened?"

"Your guess is as good as mine."

"Well, I'm counting on you to give it a royal send-off in your column, Paula."

"Don't worry, Mr. Butcher," cooed Paula. "I shall."

Lew glared. "Is it on the level?"

And Ellery said: "Did she—did she mention me?"

"Yes to you, no to you." The Boy Wonder sat back comfortably. "Now, boys, what's the panic about?"

"I'm dying," howled Lew, "and he cracks wise!"

"It's a cinch," argued the publicity man, "this marriage knocks the feud for a loop, Butch. Where's your publicity build-up now? If they had to get hitched, blast it, why couldn't they wait till the picture was released?"

"Look," said the producer patiently, getting to his feet and beginning to walk around. "What's our story? The story of four people in a romantic conflict. Jack and Blythe as the central figures. Why?"

"Because they're crazy," yelled Lew. "This proves it."

"Because, you simpleton, they're deeply in love. You're doing a love story, gentlemen, although neither of you seems aware of it. They love, they break off, they become bitter enemies, and after twenty years they suddenly fall into a clinch."

"It's illogical," complained Ellery.

"And yet," smiled the Boy Wonder, "it's just happened. Don't you see what you've got? The natural wind-up of your picture! It follows real life like a photostat. After a generation of clawing at each other's throats, *they've made up*."

"Yes, but why?"

"How should I know the motivation? That's your job, and Lew's. You're writers, aren't you? What's the gag? What's the answer to this romantic mystery? What do you think you men are being paid for?"

"Wow," said Vix, staring.

"As for you, Sam, you've got an even bigger publicity angle now than the feud."

"They've made up," said Vix reverently.

"Yes," snapped Butcher, "and every movie fan within arm's-length of a newspaper or fan mag will wonder why the hell they did. There's your line, Sam—crack down on it!"

The publicity man slapped the desk. "Sure—why did they clinch after twenty years' scrapping around? *See the picture and find out!*"

"Now you've got it. You talk about holding up their marriage until the picture's released. Nuts! They're going to be spliced right away, and to the tune of the loudest ballyhoo you've ever blasted out of this studio."

"Leave it to me," said Vix softly, rubbing his hands.

"We'll make it a super-marriage. Shoot the works. Brass bands, high hats, press associations. . . . It's a colossal break for the production."

"Wait," whispered Lew. "I've got an idea." He rubbed his nose viciously. "Yes?"

"Everybody out here puts on the dog the same way when they take the sentence. We've got to do it different. The preacher, the ceremony don't mean nothin'; it's the build-up that gets the headlines. Why not put reverse English on the marriage?"

"Spill it, you tantalizing slug!"

"Here's the gag. Offer 'em the use of Reed Island for the honeymoon."

"Reed Island?" frowned Ellery.

"I've got a place there," explained Butcher. "It's just a hunk of rock in the Pacific—southwest of Catalina—fishing village there. Go on, Lew."

"That's it!" cried Lew. "You can have 'em flown down. Just the two of 'em—turtle-doves flying off into the setting sun, to be alone with lo-o-ove. But—before they take off, what happens? They're hitched right on the field!

We can use old Doc Erminius, the Marryin' Parson. You'll have a million people at the airport. There's more room on a flying field than in a church."

"Hmm," said the Boy Wonder. "It has its merits."

"Hell, I'll fly 'em down in my own crate," grinned Lew. "I've always thought I'd look swell in a g-string and a bow-and-arrow. Or Sam here could do it."

"Say," chuckled Vix, "the screwball's got something. Only I got a better idea. How about getting *Ty Royle* to pilot them? Son Forgives Father, Plays Cupid to Famous Film Duo. He can fly like a fool, and that's a sweet ship he's got."

"That's it," said the Boy Wonder thoughtfully. "We can really go to town on a stunt like that. Dignified, too. They want to be alone. Going to spend their honeymoon on famous producer's hideaway estate in lonely Pacific, far from the madding crowd. Newspapers, for God's sake stay away. . . . Yes, they won't! Reed Island will look like Broadway during the Lindy reception. Lew, it's in."

Lew seized a bottle. "To the bride!"

"Lemme out of here," muttered Vix, and he scrambled out.

"Pardon the small still voice," said Ellery, "but aren't you boys being a little optimistic? Suppose our friends the love-birds refuse to be exploited? Suppose Ty Royle frowns on his eminent father's hatchet-burying ritual?"

"Leave the details to me," said Butcher soothingly. "It's my job to worry. Yours is to whip that story into shape. I want an adaptation okayed by the time they get back; if possible, the first sequence of the script ready. Get going."

"You're the boss," grinned Ellery. "Coming, Lew?"

Lew waved the bottle. "Can't you see I'm celebratin' the nup-chu-als?"

So Ellery set out on his quest alone.

After a few telephone calls he headed his rented coupé towards Beverly Hills. He found the Royle estate near the grounds of the Los Angeles Country Club—an enormous castellated pile in the mediaeval English manner, faithful even unto the moat.

The portals gaped, and flunkies seemed non-existent; so Ellery followed his ears and soon came to an upper hall from which the raucous noises of a small but brisk riot were emanating. There he found the missing servants, grouped at a door in various attitudes of excited and pleasurable eavesdropping.

Ellery tapped an emaciated English gentleman on the shoulder. "Since this seems to be a public performance," he drawled, "do you think there would be any objection to my going in?"

A man gasped, and the Englishman colored, and they all backed guiltily away. "I beg pawdon. Mr. Royle—"

"Ah, Louderback," said Ellery. "You *are* Louderback?"

"I am, sir," said Louderback stiffly.

"I am happy to note," said Ellery, "that your mastiff quality of loyalty is leavened by the human trait of curiosity. Louderback, stand aside."

Ellery entered a baronial room, prepared for anything. Nevertheless, he was slightly startled. Bonnie Stuart sat campfire-girl fashion on top of a grand piano, gazing tragically into her mother's calm face. On the other side of the room Jack Royle sat sipping a cocktail while his son raced up and down the hearthstone flapping his arms like an agitated penguin.

"—won't stand for it," moaned Bonnie to her mother.

"Darling, *you* won't stand for it?"

"—hell of a note," said Ty. "Dad, are you out of your mind? It's—it's treason!"

"Just coming to my senses, Ty. Blythe, I love you."

"I love you, Jack."

"Mother!"

"Dad!"

"Oh, it's impossible!"

"—even make me set *foot* in this house," cried Bonnie. Blythe rose from the piano bench and drifted dreamy-eyed towards her fiancé. Bonnie jumped down and began to follow her. "Even that's a concession. Oh, mother darling. But I wouldn't, only Clotilde said you'd come *here* to visit that—that man, and—"

"Do you have to marry her?" pleaded Ty. "After so many years? Look at all the women you could have had!"

"Blythe dear." Jack Royle rose, too, and his son began a second chase. Ellery, watching unobserved and wide-eyed, thought they would soon need some one to direct traffic. They were weaving in and out without hand-signals, and it was a miracle no collisions occurred.

"—old enough to lead my own life, Ty!"

"Of all the women in the world—"

"The only one for me." Jack took Blythe in his arms. "Two against the world, eh, darling?"

"Jack, I'm so happy."

"Oh, my God."

"—after all the things you *said* about him, mother, I should think you'd be *ashamed*—"

"Bonnie, Bonnie. We've made up our minds. We've been fools—"

"Been?" Bonnie appealed to the beamed ceiling. "Fools, fools!"

"Who's a fool?"

"Oh, so the shoe fits!"

"You keep out of this!"

"She's my mother, and I love her, and I *won't* see her throw her life away on the father of a useless, pretty-faced, contemptible *Turk!*"

"*You* should talk, with your weakness for Argentine polo-players!"

"Ty Royle, I'll slap that hateful face of yours again!"

"Try it and I swear I'll tan your beautiful hide—yes, and where you sit, too!"

"Ty—"

"Bonnie, sweet child—"

"Oh, hello, Queen," said Jack Royle. "Have a ringside seat. Ty, you've got to cut this out. I'm old enough to know what I'm doing. Blythe and I were made for each other—"

"Page ninety-five of the script," growled Ty. "We're shooting the clinch tomorrow. For the love of Pete, dad!"

"Who *is* that man?" murmured Blythe, glancing at Ellery. "Now, Bonnie, I think you've said enough. And you need some lipstick."

"Hang the lipstick! Oh, mother, mother, how *can* you?"

"Jack darling, a Martini. Extra dry. I'm parched."

"Mr. Queen," wailed Bonnie, "isn't this *disgraceful?* They're actually making up! Mother, I simply will not allow it. Do you hear? If you insist on going through with this impossible marriage—"

"Whose marriage is this, anyway?" giggled Blythe.

"I'll—I'll disown you, that's what I'll do. I *won't* have this leering, pop-eyed, celluloid stuffed shirt for a stepbrother!"

"Disown *me?* Bonnie, you silly child."

"That's the only sane thing I've ever heard this blondined, arrow-chinned, lopsided female Gorgonzola say!" shouted Ty to his father. "Me, too. If you go through with this we're quits, dad. . . . Oh, Queen; sorry. You *are* Queen, aren't you? Help yourself to a drink. Come on, dad, wake up. It's only a bad dream."

"Ty, chuck it," said Jack Royle crisply. "Cigars in the humidor, Queen. It's settled, Ty, and if you don't like it I'm afraid you'll have to lump it."

"Then I lump it!"

"Mother," said Bonnie hollowly, "are you going to leave this hateful house with me this minute, or aren't you?"

"No, dear," said Blythe sweetly. "Now run along, like a sweet baby, and keep that appointment with Zara. Your hair's a fright."

"Is it?" asked Bonnie, startled. Then she said in a tragic voice: "Mother, this is the *end.* Goodbye, and I hope he doesn't beat you, although I know he will. Remember, you'll always be able to come back to me, because I *really* love you. Oh, mother!" And, bursting into tears, Bonnie made blindly for the door.

"Now it's Sidecars," said Ty bitterly, "but after a year with *her* it'll be absinthe and opium. Dad, goodbye."

Thus it came about that the prince and princess of the royal families endeavored to make their dramatic exists simultaneously, and in so endeavoring bumped their royal young heads royally at the door.

"Lout!" said Bonnie through the tears.

"Why don't you watch where you're going?"

"Such a gentleman. Where did you get your manners—from Jem Royle, the celebrated horse-thief of Sussex?"

"Well, this is my house, and you'll oblige me by getting out of it as quickly as those Number Eights of yours can carry you," said Ty coldly.

"*Your* house! I thought you'd just renounced it forever. As a matter of fact, Tyler Royle, you're probably behind this absurd idea of mother's. You've manipulated it some way, you—you Machiavelli!"

"I? I'd rather see my dad playing off-stage voice at Minsky's than tied up to your family! If you ask me, the whole thing is *your* doing."

"Mine? Ha, ha! And why should I engineer it, please?"

"Because you and Blythe are on the skids. While in our last picture—"

"Yes, I read those rave exhibitor reports in the *Motion Picture Herald*. And weren't those *Variety* box-office figures encouraging!"

"Ah, I see you're one of the Royle public."

"What public?"

"Mugger!"

"Camera hog!"

At this breathless moment, as Ty and Bonnie glared sadistically at each other in the doorway, and Jack and Blythe wrapped their famous arms defiantly about each other near the fireplace, and Mr. Queen sighed over a hooker of aged brandy, Louderback coughed and marched stately in bearing a salver.

"Beg pawdon," said Louderback, regarding the Fragonard on the opposite wall. "A French person has just delivered this lettah for Miss Blythe Stuart. The person says it has just arrived at Miss Stuart's domicile in the last post, and that it is marked 'important.'"

"Clotilde!" cried Bonnie, reaching for the envelope on the salver. "Delivering your mail *here?* Mother, haven't you any shame?"

"Bonnie, my child," said Blythe calmly, taking the envelope. "Since when do you read your mother's mail? I thought you were leaving me forever."

"And you, Ty," chuckled Jack Royle, sauntering over. "Have you changed your mind, too?"

Blythe Stuart said: "Oh," faintly.

She was staring at the contents of the envelope. There were two pieces of colored pasteboard in her hand, and with the other she was shaking the envelope, but nothing else came out.

She said: "Oh," again, even more faintly, and turned her back.

Mr. Queen, forgotten, approached quietly and peeped. The two pieces of pasteboard were, as far as he could see, ordinary playing-cards. One was a deuce of clubs, the other a ten of spades. As Blythe turned the cards slowly over he saw that their backs were blue and were decorated with a golden horseshoe.

"What's the matter, mother?" cried Bonnie.

Blythe turned around. She was smiling. "Nothing, silly. Somebody's idea of a joke. Are you really so concerned about your poor old mummy, whom you've just renounced forever?"

"Oh, mother, don't be tedious," said Bonnie, tossing her golden curls; and with a sniff at Mr. Tyler Royle she flounced out.

"See you later, dad," said Ty glumly, and he followed.

"That's that," said Jack with relief. He took Blythe in his arms. "It wasn't so bad, was it, darling? Those crazy kids! Kiss me."

"Jack! We've quite forgotten Mr. Queen." Blythe turned her magnificent smile on Ellery. "What must you think of us, Mr. Queen! And I don't believe we've been introduced. But Jack has mentioned you, and so has Butch—"

"Sorry," said the actor. "My dear, this is Ellery Queen, who's going to work with Lew Bascom on our picture. Well, what do you think of us, Queen? A little *meshugeh*, eh?"

"I think," smiled Ellery, "that you lead horribly interesting lives. Imagine people sending you playing-cards and things! Queer idea of humor. May I see them, Miss Stuart?"

"Really, it's nothing—" began Blythe, but somehow the cards and envelope managed to pass from her hand to Mr. Queen's; and before she could protest he was examining all three intently.

"The *Horseshoe Club*, of course," murmured Ellery. "I noticed that distinctive design on their cards the other night. And your practical joker has been very careful about the envelope. Address block-lettered by pen in that scratchy, wishy-washy blue that's so characteristic of American post-offices. Postmarked this morning. Hmm. Is this the first envelope of its kind you've received, Miss Stuart?"

"You don't think—" began Jack Royle, glancing at Blythe.

"I told you. . . ." Blythe tossed her head; Ellery saw where Bonnie had acquired the habit. "Really, Mr. Queen, it's nothing at all. People in our profession are always getting the funniest things in our fan-mail."

"But you *have* received others?"

Blythe frowned at him. He was smiling. She shrugged and went over to the piano; and as she returned with her bag she opened it and extracted another envelope.

"Blythe, there's something behind this," muttered Royle.

"Oh, Jack, it's such a fuss about nothing. I can't understand why you should be so interested, Mr. Queen. I received the first one this past Tuesday, the day after we signed the contracts."

Ellery eagerly examined it. It was identical with the one Clotilde has just brought, even to the color of the ink. It was postmarked Monday night and like the second envelope had been stamped by the Hollywood post-office. Inside were two playing-cards with the horseshoe-backed design: the knave and seven of spades.

"Puzzles and tricks amuse me," said Ellery. "And since you don't ascribe any significance to these doojiggers, surely you won't mind if I appropriate them?" He put them into his pocket. "And now," Ellery went on cheerfully, "for the real purpose of my visit. Sam Vix just got the news at the studio of your reconciliation—"

"So soon?" cried Blythe.

"But we haven't told a soul," protested Royle.

"You know Hollywood. The point is: How come?"

Jack and Blythe exchanged glances. "I suppose Butch will be on our heads soon, so we'll have to explain anyway," said the actor. "It's very simple, Queen. Blythe and I decided we've been idiots long enough. We've been in love for over twenty years and it's only pride that's kept us apart. That's all."

"When I think of all those beautiful years," sighed Blythe. "Darling, we have messed up our lives, haven't we?"

"But this isn't good story material," cried Ellery. "I've got to wangle a reason for your burying the hatchet. Plot, good people, plot! Where's the complication? Who's the other man, or woman? You can't leave it at just a temperamental spat!"

"Oh, yes, we can," grinned Royle. "Ah, there's the phone. . . . Yes, Butch, it's all true. Whoa! Wait a minute. . . . Oh! Thanks, Butch. I'm a little overwhelmed. Wait, Blythe wants to talk to you, too. . . ."

Foiled, Mr. Queen departed.

Mr. Queen emerged from the gloomy great-hall of the Royles' Elizabethan castle and spied, to his astonishment, young Mr. Royle and young Miss Stuart sitting on the drawbridge swinging their legs over the waters of the moat. Like old friends! Well, not quite. He heard Mr. Royle growl deep in his throat and for an instant Mr. Queen felt the impulse to leap forward, thinking that Mr. Royle contemplated drowning his lovely companion among the lilies below.

But then he stopped. Mr. Royle's growl was apparently animated more by disgust with himself than with Miss Stuart.

"I'm a sucker to do this," the growl said, "but I can't run out on the old man. He's all I've got. Louderback's prissy, and the agent only thinks of money, and if not for me he'd have been like old Park long ago."

"Yes, indeed," said Bonnie, gazing into the water.

"What d'ye mean? He's got more talent in his left eyebrow than all the rest of those guys in their whole bodies. I mean he's so impractical—he tosses away all his dough."

"And you," murmured Bonnie, "you're such a miser. Of course. You've got *millions*."

"Leave me out of this," said Ty, reddening. "I mean, he needs me. That's why I've agreed."

"You don't have to explain to *me*," said Bonnie coldly. "I'm not interested in you, or your father, or anything about either of you. . . . The only reason *I've* agreed is that I don't want to hurt mother. I couldn't desert her."

"Who's explaining now?" jeered Ty.

Bonnie bit her lip. "I don't know why I'm sitting here talking to you. I detest you, and—"

"You've got a run in your stocking," said Ty.

Bonnie jerked her left leg up and tucked it under her. "You nasty *thing!* You would notice such things."

"I'm sorry I said that about—I mean, about your Number Eights," mumbled Ty. "You've really got pretty fair legs, and your feet are small for such a big girl." He threw a pebble into the moat, gazing at the resulting ripples with enormous interest. "Nice figure, too—of sorts, I mean."

Bonnie gaped at him—Ellery noticed how the roses faded from her cheeks, and how suddenly little-girlish and shy she became. He noticed, too, that she furtively wet the tip of one finger and ran it over the run on the tucked-in leg; and that she looked desperately at her bag, as if she wanted more than anything else in the world to open it and take out a mirror and examine her lips—*did* they need lipstick?—and poke at her honey-gold hair and generally act like a normal female.

"Nice figure," muttered young Mr. Royle again, casting another stone.

"Well!" gasped Bonnie. And her hand did dart to her hair and begin poking with those expert pokings so meaningless to the male eye.

"So," continued the young man irrelevantly, "we'll be friends. Until the wedding, I mean. Hey?"

Mr. Queen at this psychological moment struggled to suppress a cough. But the cough insisted on erupting.

They both jumped as if he had shot off a revolver. Ty got red all over his face and scrambled to his feet. Bonnie looked guilty and then bit her lip and then opened her bag and then closed it and then said icily: "That's not the bargain. Oh, hello, Mr. Queen. I'd sooner get chummy with a polecat. No dice, my fine-feathered friend. I know *your* intentions with women. I just won't fight with you in public until mother and your father are married."

"Hello, Queen. Say, did you ever see a more disagreeable woman in your life?" Ty was busy brushing himself off. "Not a kind word in several million. All right, have it your way. I was just thinking of dad, that's all."

"And I wouldn't do a thing like this for any one else in the world but mother. Help me up, please, Mr. Queen."

"Here, I'll—"

"Mr. Queen?" cooed Bonnie.

Mr. Queen silently helped her up. Ty worked his powerful shoulders up and down several times, like a pugilist loosening his muscles. He glared at her.

"All right, damn it," growled Ty. "Till the wedding."

"You're *so* chivalrous, you great big beautiful mans."

"Can I help it if I was born handsome?" yelled Ty.

And they stalked off in opposite directions.

Mr. Ellery Queen gazed after them, mouth open. It was all too much for his simple brain.

Chapter V

Gone with the Wind

PAULA PARIS'S COLUMN gave the news to a palpitating world on Saturday morning, and on Saturday afternoon the Magna Studios doubled the guards at the main gate. The hounds were baying outside Jack Royle's mansion in Beverly Hills; Blythe had shut herself up in her mosque of a house in Glendale, its door defended by the loose-chested, tight-lipped Clotilde; and Ty and Bonnie, playing their strange rôles, granted a joint interview to the puzzled press in which they said nice things about each other and were photographed smiling into each other's eyes.

"It's all set," said Sam Vix to Ellery at the end of a furious day. He wiped his face. "But, boy, oh, boy—tomorrow!"

"Isn't Bonnie going along?" asked Ellery.

"She wanted to, but I discouraged her. I was afraid that when Ty flew her back from Reed Island, they'd strangle each other in midair."

"It's wonderful how coöperative Jack and Blythe have been," beamed the Boy Wonder. "And with Ty piloting 'em—is that a story, Sam?"

"Sweet mama," grinned Lew Bascom. "Gimme that bottle."

"Boys will handle the jamboree tomorrow at the field, Butch," said the publicity man. "I'm hopping off for Reed Island to direct the preparations for the reception. See you tomorrow night."

"Not me," said Butcher hastily. "I hate these Hollywood shindigs. I've told Jack and Blythe my doctor advised a rest, and Bonnie understands. Driving out to Palm Springs tomorrow morning for a day in the sun. Conference Monday morning."

At noon on Sunday Ellery and Lew Bascom drove out to the airport in Ellery's coupé. Los Feliz Boulevard was jammed with cars crawling bumper to bumper. They wasted an hour getting to the turn-off at Riverside and another along the Los Angeles River drive through Griffith Park to the field. After fifteen minutes of trying to park his car, Ellery abandoned it and they shouldered their way through the mob.

"Too late," groaned Lew. "There's Erminius doing his stuff!"

Ty's brilliant red-and-gold cabin monoplane, gleaming in the sun, was surrounded by a cordon of cursing police. The Royles and the Stuarts, arms locked about one another, bowed and smiled in the vortex of a maelstrom of photographers, radio men, and friends screaming above the blare of a brass band. Dr. Erminius, his sleek black whiskers flowing fluently in the wind, beamed on every one over his prayer-book and sidled closer to the crowded spot on which the cameras were trained.

"Swell work, Doc!" shouted some one.

"Boy, was that a ceremony?"

"Neat, neat. How about a snifter, Doc Erminius?"

"He'll never marry *me!*"

"It's like the Judgment Day," grinned Lew. "Hey, lemme through here! Come on, Queen. Jack! Blythe!"

The band stopped playing *Here Comes the Bride* and swung into *California, Here I Come.*

"Lew! Mr. Queen! It's all right, officer!"

"Bonnie—Bonnie Stuart! This way, please. Smile at Ty!"

"Won't you say a few words to the radio audience, Jack?"

"Dr. Erminius, how about a few shots?"

"Yes, my son," said the good man hastily, and stepped in front of Jack Royle.

"Jack! Blythe! Let's take a shot of clasped hands showing those wedding rings!"

"Get those people away from that plane, damn it!"

"Miss Blythe! Miss Blythe!" shrieked a feminine voice, and a primly attired French lady of middle age elbowed her way through to the wall of police, waving an envelope frantically.

"Clotilde!" screamed Blythe. She was radiant, her arms full of flowers, her hat askew on her head. She ran over; and as she saw the envelope she gasped aloud, going pale. Then she snatched it from Clotilde's hand over a policeman's shoulder and tore it open. Ellery saw her close her eyes, crumple the envelope convulsively. She hurled it away.

Then she put on a smile and returned to the group before the plane.

Ellery picked his way through the fruit and flower baskets littering the ground and managed to pick up the envelope unnoticed. It was another of the post-office-written envelopes, this time sent by special delivery. Inside were the torn halves of a horseshoe-backed playing-card, the eight of spades.

Torn in half. Blythe had not torn it, Ellery was certain. Queer. . . . He frowned and pocketed the envelope, looking about. The Frenchwoman had vanished in the mob.

"Ty! Kiss Bonnie for the newsreel!"

"Jack! Jack! Go into a clinch with the blushing bride!"

"What's this?" yelled some one, holding aloft a handsome wicker hamper.

"Somebody sent it!" roared Jack Royle.

"Open it!"

Bonnie straightened up with two enormous thermos bottles from the hamper. "Look what I found, people!"

"Sidecars!" bellowed Jack, unscrewing the cap of one of the bottles and sniffing. "Thanks, anonymous friend. How'd you know my weakness?"

"And mine? Martinis!" screamed Blythe over the other bottle. "Isn't that the loveliest going-away gift!"

"Toast to the bride and groom!"

The thermos bottles were hurled from hand to hand; for a few moments they were all laughing and struggling for a drink. Lew battled desperately with a large stout lady, rescued both bottles, and poured out another round in a nest of paper-cups which appeared from somewhere magically.

"Hey, save some for us," growled Jack.

"Can't you get drunk on love?"

"An old buck like you—d'ye need a *stimulant?*"

"Love—Marches—on!"

"I said save some!" howled Jack, laughing.

Lew reluctantly dropped the thermos bottles into the hamper, screwing on the caps. The hamper lay beside a pile of luggage near the plane.

Lew and Ellery were squeezed, pummeled, pushed, and mauled, stumbling over the luggage. Ellery sat down on the hamper and sighed: "No wonder Butch went to Palm Springs."

"Who swiped my helmet?" yelled Ty Royle. "Mac! Rev 'em while I get another!" And he darted into the crowd, fighting towards the nearby hangar.

"What's going on here, the Revolution?" panted a voice. Ellery, trying to save his hat from being crushed, turned to find Alan Clark, his agent, grinning down at him.

"Just a quiet Sunday in Hollywood, Alan. They're almost ready to take off."

"I gotta kiss the bride, for gossakes," shouted Lew frantically. He grabbed at Blythe, caught her, and bussed her heartily while Jack Royle, grinning, began to toss things into the cabin of the plane. Bonnie, heart-stopping in a knee-length leopard coat and Russian leopard hat, was obviously his next victim; but just then a man ran up.

"Miss Bonnie Stuart! Mr. Tyler Royle wants to see you in the hangar."

Bonnie made a face, smiled for the benefit of the staring public, and slipped after him.

Bonnie looked around inside the hangar. It seemed empty. She turned to question the man who had brought Ty's message, but he was gone.

"Ty?" she called, puzzled. Her voice echoed from the high roof.

"Here I am!" She followed the sound of Ty's voice and found him behind a tarpaulined biplane, rummaging in a steel locker.

Ty stared at her. "What do *you* want, pest?"

"What do *I* want! What do *you* want?"

"Me? Not a thing—from you."

"Look here, Ty Royle, I've stood enough from you today without playing puss-in-the-corner. You just sent a messenger to me. What do you want?"

"I sent a messenger? The hell I did."

"Ty Royle, don't stand there and be cute!"

Ty clenched his hands. "Oh, God, if only you weren't a woman."

"You seemed thankful enough just now that I was a woman," said Bonnie coldly. "That was quite a kiss you gave me."

"The cameraman asked for it!"

"Since when do you follow a cameraman's orders?"

"Listen!" yelled Ty. "I wouldn't kiss you of my own free will if I hadn't seen a woman for five years. Your lips tasted like two hunks of rouged rubber. How your leading men can keep kissing you in front of the camera . . . They ought to get medals for exceptional heroism in line of duty!"

Bonnie went white. "You— You—" she began in a fury.

Some one coughed behind them. They both turned around. They both blinked.

A tall figure in heavy flying clothes, wearing a helmet and goggles, hands gloved in fur, stood there widelegged and still. One hand pointed a revolver at them.

"All right, I'll bite," said Ty. "What's the gag?"

The revolver waved a little, with an unmistakable meaning: Silence. Ty and Bonnie drew sharp breaths simultaneously.

The figure sent a chair skittering across the hangar floor. The revolver pointed to Ty, to the chair. Ty sat down in the chair. Bonnie stood very still.

A bundle of ropes, cut in short lengths, came flying through the air from the tall figure and struck Bonnie's legs. The revolver pointed to Ty.

Ty jumped out of the chair, snarling. The revolver covered him instantly, trained on his chest.

"Ty," said Bonnie. "Please. Don't."

"You can't hope to get away with this stunt," said Ty in a thick voice. "What do you want, money? Here—"

But the weapon's weaving eye stopped him. Bonnie quickly stooped, picked up the ropes, and began to bind Ty to the back and legs of the chair.

"I see," said Ty bitterly. "I see the whole thing now. One of your little jokes. This time, by God, you've gone too far. I'll put you in clink for this."

"That revolver's no joke," whispered Bonnie, "and I may play rough, but not with guns. Can't you see he means business? I won't bind you tightly—"

The revolver poked her between the shoulder-blades. Bonnie bit her lip and bound Ty tightly. A prepared gag materialized in one gloved hand. She gagged Ty.

Things blurred. It was absurd—this deadly silence, this tongueless figure, the menace of the revolver. She opened her mouth and screamed. Only the echo answered.

The figure was upon her instantly, however. Glove over her mouth, she was forced into another chair. She fought back, kicking, biting. But soon she was strapped to the chair, as gagged and helpless as Ty; and the figure was stooping over Ty, tightening his bonds, adding others.

And then, still without a word, the figure pocketed the revolver, raised one arm in a mocking salute, and darted out of sight behind the tarpaulined biplane.

Ty's eyes were savage above the gag; he struggled against the ropes, rocking the chair. But he succeeded only in upsetting himself. He fell backwards, striking his head against the stone floor with a meaty *thunk!* that turned Bonnie's stomach.

He lay still, his eyes closed.

"Here he comes!" shouted Jack, his arm about Blythe as they stood on the movable steps of the plane. "Ty! Come on!"

"Where's Bonnie?" screamed Blythe. "Bon-NIE!"

"Crowd's got her. Ty!"

The tall goggled figure shoved his way through the mob and began to toss the remaining luggage into the cabin. Ellery stood up, helpfully handing him the hamper. He waved Blythe and Jack into the plane, raised the hamper in a farewell to the crowd, and vaulted into the cabin. The door slapped shut.

"Happy landings!" roared Lew.

Blythe and Jack pressed their faces to one of the windows, and the band struck up the *Wedding March* from *Lohengrin*.

Everybody sang.

Bonnie looked frantically about. And then she caught her breath. Through the hangar window nearest her she saw the tall goggled figure running towards Ty's plane; and for the first time Bonnie realized that the figure was dressed in a flying suit identical with Ty's. Jack . . . Blythe . . . waving, shouting . . . The brassy sounds of the band came faintly through the hangar walls.

And then, before her distended eyes, the red-and-gold plane began to move, taxiing down the field, rising . . . rising . . .

The last thing Bonnie saw before everything went black was her mother's handkerchief signalling a farewell in the cabin window.

Bonnie opened her eyes aeons later to a blank world; slowly it filled in. She was lying on her side, on the floor. A few feet away lay Ty, looking very pale, looking . . . dead. Ty!

She stirred, and thousands of needles began to shoot into her numb flesh. With the pain came full awareness. Blythe . . . Blythe was gone.

She had fallen sidewise when she fainted. How long ago? What—what time was it?

Blythe. Blythe was gone. Like smoke in thin air.

In her fall the gag had been dislodged from her mouth.

And Ty was dead.

Mother . . .

Bonnie screamed. Her own screams came screaming back at her, lying on the cold floor of the hangar behind the concealing plane.

Ty moaned.

Bonnie inched her way painfully the few feet across the floor towards him, dragging the chair to which she was bound. He opened his bloodshot eyes.

"Ty," she gasped. "They've been kidnaped! Jack—my mother. . . . That man—he flew them off the field, pretending to be you!"

Ty closed his eyes. When he opened them again Bonnie was shocked by their unnatural red color. The gag over his lips worked spasmodically, as if he were trying to speak. She could see the cords of his neck distend.

She bared her teeth, face pressed to his, gnawing at his gag like a mouse, tugging, worrying it. His cheek felt cold.

"Bonnie." His voice was unrecognizable. "Loosen these ropes."

For an instant their breaths mingled and their eyes locked. Then Bonnie looked away and Ty turned over, and with a little cry she bent her head to his bound, straining hands.

Luckily Ellery and his two companions had not left the field. Ellery had looked once at the thousands milling about the parked cars and wisely suggested procrastination. So he and Lew and Alan Clark went over to the airport restaurant for sandwiches and coffee.

They were roused out of a listless discussion of the picture story by a commotion outside, and near one of the hangars they came upon an anthill of officials and pilots and mechanics and police. They were swarming about Ty, who was rubbing his skinned hands, and Bonnie, who was seated with folded hands, paler than her own handkerchief, staring numbly at all the busy ants without seeing them.

"My father's in that plane," said Ty. There was a purplish lump on the back of his head; he looked ill. "Queen! Thank God there's one face I recognize. And Lew! Get Butch. Call Reed Island. Do something, somebody!"

"No point in calling Reed Island first," said Ellery to Lew. "That's the one place this chap *didn't* take them to. I wonder if . . ."

"Took mother," said Bonnie simply. A female attendant tried to lure her away, but she shook her head.

Ellery rang Information, then put in a call to Tolland Stuart's estate. A man with a dry, peevish voice answered after a long time.

"Is this Mr. Tolland Stuart?"

It seemed to Ellery that the voice was instantly cautious. "No, this is Dr. Junius. Who's calling Mr. Stuart?"

Ellery explained what had happened and asked if Ty's monoplane had passed near the Chocolate Mountain estate. But Tollard Stuart's physician crushed that possibility.

"Not a plane near here all day. By the way, isn't it possible that Mr. Royle and Miss Stuart merely took that way of escaping the crowds? Perhaps—it would be natural—they wanted a really private honeymoon."

"And hired some one to tie up Ty Royle and Bonnie Stuart and kidnap the plane?" said Ellery dryly. "I hardly think so, Doctor."

"Well, let me know when you get word," said Dr. Junius. "Mr. Stuart went rabbit-hunting this morning and hasn't got back yet."

Ellery thanked him, disconnected, and called Palm Springs. But Jacques Butcher could not be located. So Ellery left a message and telephoned Reed Island. Sam Vix was not about—he had flown off somewhere; Ellery could not clearly get his destination.

"Then Mr. Royle's plane hasn't landed on Reed Island?"

"No. We've been waiting. Is something the matter? They should have been here by this time."

Ellery sighed and hung up.

The police appeared, county men; swarms of newspaper reporters descended, a plague of locusts. In a short time the field was more blackly populated than at the take-off, and it was necessary to summon police reserves. Meanwhile, searching planes from the municipal airport and the nearest Army field were darkening the sky, streaming southwestward on the probable route of the red-and-gold monoplane.

The afternoon lengthened; toward sunset a small two-seater skimmed in from the west and the Boy Wonder leaped to the ground from the cockpit and ran for the hangar.

He put his arms about Bonnie and she sobbed against his chest while Ty paced up and down consuming cigaret after cigaret.

"Here it is!" shouted an airport official, dashing up. "An Army scout has just sighted a red-and-gold monoplane on a barren plateau in the Chocolate Mountains! No sign of life."

"A wreck?" asked Ty harshly.

"No. It's just grounded there."

"That's strange," muttered Ellery, but he said nothing more as he saw the expression on Bonnie's face. He had seen expressions like that on the faces of condemned criminals reprieved at the eleventh hour.

And so more planes were commandeered, and a small fleet rose from the airport in the dusk and preened their wings in the setting sun.

And soon, in the darkness, they were feeling their way over the San Bernardino Mountains, guided by radio. Then they followed a brightness in the hills to the south, which grew into flares on a flat, deserted plateau.

When they landed Army men challenged them with drawn revolvers. There seemed a curious diffidence in their manner, as if they were indisposed to talk in the evening under the white stars in the cold pale light of the flares.

"My father—" began Ty, breaking into a run. His red-and-gold plane rested quietly on the plateau, surrounded by men.

"My mother—" said Bonnie, stumbling after him.

A helmeted officer said something in a low voice to Jacques Butcher, and he made a face and instantly smiled in the most peculiar way; and he beckoned to Ellery and Lew and called out to Bonnie: "Bonnie. Just a minute."

And Bonnie stopped, her face turned sidewise in the ghostly light, looking frightened and yet trying not to look frightened; and Ty stopped, too, very abruptly, as if he had come up to a high stone wall.

And Ellery and Jacques Butcher entered the cabin of Ty's plane, and some one shut the door behind them.

Outside, Ty and Bonnie stood a few feet apart, two rigid poles in a mass of stirring humanity. Neither said anything, and both kept looking at the closed door of the monoplane. And no one came near them.

The sky was so near, thought Bonnie, so close here in the mountains at night.

The cabin door opened and Jacques Butcher came out with a strong heavy step, like a diver walking on the bottom of the sea. And he went up to Ty and Bonnie and stood between them and put his right arm about Bonnie's shoulder and his left arm about Ty's, and he said in a voice that hissed against the silence of the plateau:

"The pilot is missing. Bonnie. Ty. What can I say? Jack and Blythe are in that plane. . . ."

"In the plane," said Bonnie, taking a half-step forward. And she stopped. "Inside?" she asked in a small-child, wondering voice. "Why don't they . . . come . . . out?"

Ty turned and walked off. Then he stopped, too, his back dark and unmoving against the stars.

"Bonnie. Darling," said Butcher thickly.

"Butch." Bonnie sighed. "They're—they're not . . . ?"

"They're both dead."

The sky was so close.

PART TWO

Chapter VI

Chocolate Mountain

THE SKY WAS SO close. Because it was falling down. Down the chute of a trillion miles. Down through the pinhole stars. Down to the gorse-covered plateau. Down on Bonnie's head.

She pressed her palms to her eyes. "I don't believe it. I don't believe it."

"Bonnie," said Jacques Butcher.

"But it can't be. Not Blythe. Not mother."

"Bonnie. Darling. Please."

"She always said she'd never grow old. She always said she'd live a million, million years."

"Bonnie, let me take you away from here."

"She didn't want to die. She was afraid of death. Sometimes in the middle of the night she'd start to cry in her sleep, and I'd crawl into bed with her and she'd snuggle up to me like a baby."

"I'll get one of these Army pilots to fly you back to Los Angeles—"

Bonnie dropped her hands. "It's a horrid joke of some kind," she said slowly. "You're all in a conspiracy."

Tyler Royle came stalking back, his face blank against the pale background of the flares.

As he passed he said: "Come on, Bonnie," as if only he and Bonnie existed in a dark dead world.

And Bonnie turned from Butch and followed Ty with something of the otherworldly stiffness of a Zombie.

Lew Bascom came up to Butcher, who was standing still, and said hoarsely: "For gossakes, how do you get outa here?"

"You grow a pair of wings."

"Nah," said Lew. "I'm—pooped." He stuck his fat face out over the gorse and made a sickish, retching sound. "Butch, I gotta get off this damn' table-top. I need a drink. I need a lot o' drinks."

"Don't bother me."

"I never could stand a stiff. Are they—are they—"

Butcher walked away. Ty and Bonnie seemed to be floating in the weird aura of mingled flarelight and starshine. They merged with and were lost in the black figures about the resting plane.

Lew sank to the harsh grass, clutching his belly and shivering in the wind. After a moment he struggled to his feet and waddled towards an Army plane, its propeller roaring for a take-off.

"You gettin' outa here?" he shrieked.

The pilot nodded, and Lew scrambled into the rear cockpit. His hat flew off in the backwash of air. He sank low in the cockpit, trembling. The plane trundled off.

In the red-and-gold monoplane a man in flying togs was saying: "Hijacked by a pilot who made pretty sure he wouldn't be recognized—and then this. It looks funny, Mr. Queen."

"Funny?" scowled Ellery. "The Greeks had another word for it, Lieutenant."

John Royle and Blythe Stuart half-sat, half-lay in upholstered swivel chairs in the cabin, across the aisle from each other. Their luggage, baskets of flowers, the wicker hamper were in the aisle between them. The lid of the hamper stood open. On the floor under Royle's slack left hand lay the half-eaten remains of a ham sandwich. One of the thermos bottles from the hamper stood beside it. The empty cap-cup of the bottle was wedged between his thighs. His handsome features were composed. He looked as if he had fallen asleep.

The second thermos bottle had obviously fallen from Blythe's right hand: it lay, mouth tilted up, among the bruised blossoms of a rose-basket beside her. A wad of crumpled waxed paper, the wrappings of a consumed sandwich, was in her lap. The cup of the other thermos bottle had fallen to the floor between her feet. And she, too, eyes closed, serene of face, seemed asleep.

"It's awfully queer," remarked the Lieutenant, studying the still cold faces, "that they should both pop off around the same time."

"Nothing queer about it."

"They haven't been shot or stabbed or strangled; you can see that. Not a sign of violence. That's why I say . . . Only double heart-failure isn't—well, it's quite a coincidence."

"You could say," retorted Ellery, "that a man whose skull had been bashed into turkey-hash with a sledge-hammer died of heart-failure, too. Look here, Lieutenant."

He stooped over Royle's body and with his thumb pressed back the lid of the right eye. The pupil was almost invisible; it had contracted to a dot.

Ellery stepped across the littered aisle and opened Blythe Stuart's right eye.

"Highly constricted pupils," he shrugged. "And notice that pervasive pallor—cyanosis. They both died of morphine poisoning."

"Jack Royle and Blythe Stuart *murdered*?" The Lieutenant stared. "Wow!"

"Murdered." Bonnie Stuart stood in the cabin doorway. "No. Oh, no!"

She flung herself upon her mother's body, sobbing. Ty Royle came in then, looked down at his father. After a moment his hand felt for the cabin wall. But he did not take his eyes from that calm marble face.

Bonnie suddenly sat up, glaring at her hands where they had touched her mother's body. Although there was no mark on her white flesh, Ellery and the Lieutenant knew what she was staring at. She was staring at the invisible stain, the impalpable taint, the cold outer-space enamel of death.

"Oh, no," whispered Bonnie with loathing.

Ty said: "Bonnie," futilely, and took an awkward step across the aisle towards her.

But Bonnie sprang to her feet and screamed: "Oh, no!" and, standing there, tall and distraught, her cheeks pure gray, her breast surging, she swayed and began to fold up like the bellows of an accordion. And as she crumpled in upon herself her eyes turned completely over in their sockets.

Ty caught her as she fell.

Icy bristles of mountain wind curried the plateau. Butch took Bonnie from Ty's arms, carried her through the whipping grass to an Army plane, and threw a borrowed fur coat over her.

"Well, what are we waiting for?" said Ty in a cracked voice. "Death by freezing?"

And the Lieutenant said: "Take it easy, Mr. Royle."

"What are we waiting for?" shouted Ty. "Damn it, there's a murderer loose around here! Why doesn't somebody start tracking the scum down?"

"Take it easy, Mr. Royle," said the Lieutenant again, and he dived into a plane.

Ty began to thrash around in the knee-high grass, trampling swathes of it down in blind parabolas.

Ellery said to a pilot: "Just where are we?"

"On the north tip of the Chocolate Mountains."

He borrowed a flashlight and began to examine the terrain near the red-and-gold monoplane. But if the mysterious aviator who had borne Jack Royle and Blythe Stuart through the circumambient ether to their deaths had left tracks in making his escape from the grounded plane, the tracks had long since been obliterated by the milling feet of the Army men. Ellery wandered farther afield, skirting the rim of the plateau.

He soon saw, in the powerful beam of the electric torch, that the task of finding the unknown pilot's trail quickly was almost a hopeless one. Hundreds of trails led from the plateau down through scrub pine to the lowlands—chiefly horse-trails, as he saw from the many droppings and steel-shoe signs. To the east, as he recalled the topography, lay Black Butte; to the northwest the southern range of the San Bernardino Mountains; to the west the valley through which ran the Southern Pacific Railroad, and beyond it the Salton Sea and the San Jacinto range. The fleeing pilot could have escaped in any of the three directions, through sparsely settled country. It would take days by experienced trackers to find his trail, and by that time it would be stone-cold.

Ellery returned to the red-and-gold plane. The Lieutenant was there again. "It's a hell of a mess. We've made three-way contact by radiophone with the authorities. There's a mob of 'em on their way up."

"What's the trouble?"

"This end of the Chocolate Mountains just laps over into Riverside County —most of it lies in Imperial County to the south. The plane in coming here passed over Los Angeles County, of course, and probably the southeast tip of San Bernardino County. That makes three different counties in which these people may have died."

"So the assorted gentlemen of the law are fighting," nodded Ellery grimly, "for the right to sink their teeth into this juicy case?"

"Well, it's their oyster—let 'em scramble for it. My responsibility ends when some one shows up to claim jurisdiction."

Butcher said curtly: "I don't know about your legal responsibility, Lieutenant, but something's got to be done about Miss Stuart. She's in a bad way."

"I suppose we *could* fly you folks back to the municipal airport, but—"

"What's the trouble?" asked Ty Royle in a high-pitched voice. Ellery felt uncomfortable at the sight of his haggard face. His lips were blue and he was shivering with a cold not caused by the wind.

"Bonnie's collapsed, Ty. She's got to have a doctor."

"Well, sure," said Ty abstractedly. "Sure. I'll fly her down myself. My plane—" But then he stopped.

"Sorry," said the Lieutenant. "That's the one thing that doesn't leave this place till the police get here."

"I suppose so," mumbled Ty. "I guess so." He yelled suddenly: "Damn it to hell!"

"Here," said Ellery, grabbing his arm. "You're not far from collapse yourself. Lieutenant, have you any notion how far Tolland Stuart's place is from here? It's supposed to be on a butte in the Chocolate Mountains, somewhere below in Imperial County."

"It's only a few minutes south by air."

"Then that's where we'll take her," rasped Butcher. "If you'll be good enough to place a plane at our disposal—"

"But I don't know if I ought to."

"We'll be at Tolland Stuart's when they want us. You said yourself it's only a few minutes' hop from here."

The Lieutenant looked unhappy. Then he shrugged and shouted: "Garms! Turn 'em over."

A pilot saluted and climbed into a big Army transport. The motors began to spit and snarl. They all broke into a run.

"Where's Lew?" shouted Ellery above the din.

"He couldn't take it," Butcher shouted back. "Flew back to L. A. with one of the Army pilots."

A few minutes later they were in the air headed southeast.

The brightness on the plateau dwindled to a pale blob, then to a pinpoint, and finally blinked out altogether. Butcher held Bonnie, whose eyes were closed, tightly to his chest. Ty sat alone, forward, buried to the nose in his thin coat; he seemed to be dozing. But once Ellery caught the wild shine of his eyes.

Ellery shivered and turned to peer down at the black wrinkled face of the mountain slipping by below.

In less than ten minutes the transport was wheeling over a luminous rectangle lying flat among the crags. To Ellery it seemed no larger than a postage stamp, and he began uncomfortably to think of his own immortal soul.

As he clutched the arms of his seat he saw dimly a massive pile of stone and wood beyond the lighted field. Then they were rushing down the little landing-place bound, he could swear, for a head-on collision with a hangar.

Miraculously, however, the plane bumped and hopped to a safe stop; and Ellery opened his eyes.

A tall emaciated man was standing outside the hangar, shading his eyes from the glare of the arcs, staring at the plane. It seemed to Ellery that there was something peculiar about the man's rigidity—as if the plane were some Medusa-like monster and he had been petrified by the mere sight of it.

Then the man relaxed and ran forward, waving his arms.

Ellery shook his head impatiently at the mercurial quality of his imagination. He tapped Ty on the shoulder and said gently: "Come on, Ty." Ty started. "We're here."

Ty got up. "How is she?" Butcher shook his head. "Here. I'll—I'll give you a hand."

Between them they managed to haul Bonnie out of the plane. Her body was flaccid, as if all her bones had melted; and her eyes were open, ignoring Butcher, ignoring Ty, fixed on space with a rather terrifying blankness.

Ellery stopped to talk to the pilot. When he jumped to the ground a moment later he heard the tall thin man exclaiming in a distressed voice. "But that's not possible. Perfectly ghastly. When did it happen?"

"We can talk later," said Butch shortly. "Miss Stuart needs your professional attention now, Dr. Junius."

"Appalling," said the doctor. "And the poor child; all broken up. Naturally! This way, please."

The Army transport took to the air again as they passed the hangar, in which Ellery noted a small, stubby, powerful-looking plane, and entered a tree-canopied path leading to the dark mansion beyond. The transport circled the field once, raising echoes from the surrounding mountain walls, and then darted off towards the northwest.

"Careful. The path is rough." Dr. Junius swept the ground with the beam of a flash. "Watch these steps." Silently pursuing, Ellery made out a wide doorway. Open. A sepia cavern lay behind. The flashlight stabbed here and there; then it went out and lights sprang on.

They stood in an enormous, damp-smelling chamber, heavily raftered, with bulky oak furniture, a stone mat-strewn floor, and an immense dark fireplace.

"The settee," said Dr. Junius briskly, running back to shut the door. Except for one penetrating glance in Ellery's direction, the doctor paid no attention to him.

The man's skin was yellowed and bland, so tightly drawn over his bones that it could not wrinkle. The eyes were clever and unfriendly. The figure was stooped, even thinner than Ellery had thought at first sight. He wore a pair of shapeless grimy slacks tucked into high, laced, lumberman's shoes, and a mildew-green smoking-jacket glazed with age. Everything about the man was old—a creature who had grown old by a process of dehydration. There was something cringing about him, too, and watchful, as if he were constantly on the dodge from blows.

Ty and Butch laid Bonnie gently down on the settee.

"We weren't expecting visitors," whined Dr. Junius. "Mr. Royle, would you be good enough to start the fire?"

He scurried away, vanishing down a small side-hall, while Ty struck a match and applied it to the paper and kindling beneath the large logs in the fireplace. Butch rubbed his freezing hands, staring sombrely down at Bonnie's white face. She moaned as the fire blazed up with a great snapping and crackling.

Dr. Junius came hurrying back with an armful of blankets and a small green-black bag, its handle hanging by one link.

"Now if you gentlemen will clear out. Would one of you be kind enough to watch the coffee? Kitchen is at the end of that hall. Brandy, too, in the pantry."

"Where," asked Ellery, "is Mr. Tolland Stuart?"

Dr. Junius, on his bony knees before the settee tucking Bonnie's tossing figure into the blankets, looked up with a startled, ingratiating smile. "You're the gentleman who phoned me a few hours ago from the Griffith Park airport, aren't you? Voice has a distinctive ring. Hurry, please, Mr. Queen. We can discuss Mr. Stuart's eccentricities later."

The three men went wearily down the hall and, passing through a swinging door, found themselves in a gigantic kitchen, badly illuminated by a single small electric bulb. A pot of coffee bubbled on an old-fashioned range.

Ty sank into a chair at the worktable and rested his head on his arms. Butch blundered about until he found the pantry, and emerged with a dusty bottle of cognac.

"Drink this, Ty."

"Please. Let me alone."

"Drink it."

Ty obeyed tiredly. The Boy Wonder took the bottle and another glass and went out. He returned empty-handed, and for some time they sat around in silence. Ellery turned off the light under the coffee. The house seemed unnaturally quiet.

Dr. Junius bobbed in.

"How is she?" asked Butch hoarsely.

"Nothing to be alarmed about. She's had a bad shock, but she's coming around."

He ran out with the coffee. Ellery went to the pantry and, for lack of anything else to do, nosed about. The first thing he spied was a case of brandy on the floor. Then he remembered the ruddy bulb on Dr. Junius's nose. He shrugged.

A long time later Dr. Junius called: "All right, gentlemen," and they trooped back to the living-room.

Bonnie was sitting up before the fire, sipping the coffee. There was color in her cheeks and, while the circles under her eyes were heavy and leaden, her eyes were sane again.

She gave Butcher one hand and whispered: "I'm sorry I've been such a fuss, Butch."

"Don't be silly," said Butch roughly. "Drink that java."

Without turning her head she said: "Ty. Ty, it's so hard to say. . . . Ty, I'm sorry."

"For me?" Ty laughed, and Dr. Junius looked alarmed. "I'm sorry, too. For you. For dad. For your mother. For the whole God-damned world." He shut off the laugh in the middle of its highest note and flung himself full length on the mat before the fire at Bonnie's feet, covering his face with his hands.

Bonnie looked down at him. Her lower lip began to quiver. She set the coffee-cup down blindly.

"Oh, here, don't—" began Butcher miserably.

Dr. Junius whispered: "Let them alone. There's really nothing to do for them but let the shock and hysteria wear off naturally. A good cry will do wonders for her, and the boy is fighting it off very nicely by himself."

Bonnie wept softly into her fingers and Ty lay still before the fire. The Boy Wonder cursed and began to prowl up and down, throwing epileptic shadows on the flame-lit walls.

"Once again," said Ellery. "Dr. Junius, where the hell is Tolland Stuart?"

"I suppose you find it strange." The doctor's hands were shaking, and it occurred to Ellery that Tolland Stuart's dictum against alcohol worked a special hardship on his physician. "He's upstairs behind a barricade."

"What!"

Junius smiled apologetically. "Oh, he's quite sane."

"He must have heard our plane come down. Hasn't the man even a normal curiosity?"

"Mr. Stuart is—peculiar. He's been nursing a grudge against the world for so many years that he detests the very sight of people. And then he's a hypochondriac. And odd in other ways. I suppose you noticed the lack of central heating. He has a theory about that—that steam heat dries up your lungs. He has a theory about nearly everything."

"Very amusing," said Ellery, "but what's all this to do with the fact that his granddaughter has come calling for the first time in years? Hasn't he the decency to come downstairs to greet her?"

"Mr. Queen," said Dr. Junius, baring his false teeth in a humorless grin, "if you knew as much about Mr. Tolland Stuart as I do you wouldn't wonder at any of his vagaries." The grin became a whining snarl. "When he came back late this afternoon from his damned eternal rabbit-shooting, and I told him about your call and his daughter Blythe apparently kidnaped on her wedding day and all, he shut himself up in his room and threatened to discharge me if I disturbed him. He claims he can't stand excitement."

"Can he?"

The doctor said spitefully: "He's the healthiest man of his years I know. Damn all hypos! I have to sneak my liquor and coffee up here, go out into the woods for a smoke, and cook meat for myself when he's out hunting. He's a cunning, mean old maniac, that's what he is, and why I bury myself up here with him is more than I can understand!"

The doctor looked frightened at his own outburst; he grew pale and silent.

"Nevertheless, don't you think you might make an exception in this case? After all, a man's daughter isn't murdered every day."

"You mean go up those stairs and into his bedroom, when he's expressly forbidden it?"

"Something like that."

Dr. Junius threw up his hands. "Not I, Mr. Queen, not I. I want to live out the few remaining years of my life with a whole skin."

"Pshaw, he has you buffaloed."

"Well, you're welcome to try, if you don't mind risking a load of buckshot. He always keeps a shotgun by his bed."

Ellery said abruptly: "Ridiculous!"

The doctor made a weary gesture of invitation towards the oak staircase and trudged down the hall to the kitchen—and his cache of brandy—with sloping shoulders.

Ellery went to the foot of the staircase and shouted: "Mr. Stuart!"

Ty raised his head. "Grandfather," said Bonnie limply. "I'd forgotten about *him*. Oh, Butch, we'll have to tell him!"

"Mr. Stuart?" called Ellery again, almost angrily. Then he said: "Damn it, I'm going up."

Dr. Junius reappeared, his ruddy nose a little ruddier. "Wait, please. If you insist on being foolhardy, I'll go up with you. But it won't do you any good, I warn you."

He joined Ellery and together they began to ascend the stairs into the thickening shadows above.

And just then a low humming mutter came to their ears, growing louder with each passing moment, until it became raw thunder. They stopped short halfway up the stairs.

"A plane!" cried Dr. Junius. "Is it coming here?"

The thunder grew. It was a plane, unquestionably, and it was circling Tolland Stuart's eyrie.

"This is the last straw," moaned the doctor. "He'll be unbearable for a week. Stay here, please. I'll go out."

And without waiting for an answer he hurried down the stairs and out into the darkness.

Ellery remained uncertainly on the staircase for an instant. Then he slowly descended.

Bonnie said: "I can't understand grandfather. Is he ill? Why doesn't he come down?"

No one answered. The only sounds came from the fire. The thunder had died.

And then Dr. Junius reappeared, wringing his hands. "He'll kill me! Why did you all have to come here?"

A large man in an overcoat and fedora marched in, blinking in the firelight. He blinked at each of them, one by one.

Ellery smiled. "It seems we meet again, Inspector Glücke."

Chapter VII

The Old Man

INSPECTOR GLÜCKE GRUNTED and went to the fire, shedding his coat and rubbing his great red hands together. A man in flying togs followed him, and Dr. Junius hastily shut the outer door against a rising wind. The aviator sat quietly down in a corner. He said nothing, and Inspector Glücke did not introduce him.

"Let's get you people straight now," said Glücke, contracting his black brows. "You're Miss Stuart, I suppose, and you're Mr. Royle? You must be Butcher."

Ty scrambled to his feet. "Well?" he said eagerly. "Have you found him?"

Bonnie cried: "Who is he?"

"Now, now, all in good time. I'm half-frozen, and we've got a long wait, because the pilot says there's a storm coming up. Where's the old man?"

"Upstairs sulking," said Ellery. "You don't seem very glad to see me, old friend. And how did you horn into this case?"

Glücke grinned. "What d'ye mean? They were Angelenos, weren't they? Say, this fire feels swell."

"I take it you simply jumped in feet first and usurped the authority to handle the case?"

"Now don't start anything, Queen. When we got the flash at Headquarters that Mr. Royle and Miss Stuart had been found dead—we already knew they'd been snatched—I got me a plane and flew up to that plateau. I beat the

Riverside and San Bernardino County men by a hair. If you ask me, they were tickled to death to have L. A. step in and take over. It's too big for them."

"But not for you, eh?" murmured Ellery.

"Oh, it's simple enough," said the Inspector.

"Then you *have* found him!" cried Ty and Bonnie together.

"Not yet. But when we do, there's our man, and that's the end of it."

"When you find him?" said Ellery dryly. "Don't you mean 'if'?"

"Maybe, maybe." Glücke smiled. "Anyway, it's no case for you, Queen. Just a plain, everyday manhunt."

"How sure are you," said Ellery, lighting a cigaret, "that it *was* a man?"

"You're not suggesting it was a woman?" said the Inspector derisively.

"I'm suggesting the possibility. Miss Stuart, you and Mr. Royle saw that pilot in good light. Was it man or woman?"

"Man," said Ty. "Don't be foolish. He was a man!"

"I don't know," sighed Bonnie, trying to concentrate. "You couldn't really tell. Those flying togs were a man's, but then a woman could have worn them. And you couldn't see hair, or eyes, or even face. The goggles concealed the upper part of the face and the lower part was hidden by the turned-up collar."

"He walked like a man," cried Ty. "He was too tall for a woman."

A spirited note crept into Bonnie's voice. "Nonsense. Hollywood is full of impersonators of both sexes. And I'll bet I'm as tall as that . . . creature was."

"And nobody," put in Ellery, "heard the creature's voice, for the excellent reason that the creature took remarkable care not to speak. If it were a man, why the silence? He could have disguised his voice."

"Now listen, Queen," said Glücke plaintively, "stop throwing monkey-wrenches. All right, we don't know whether it was a man or a woman. But, man or woman, we've got the height and build—"

"Have you? Heels can be built up, and those flying suits are bulky and deceptive. No, there's only one thing you can be sure of."

"What's that?"

"That that pilot can fly an airplane."

Glücke growled deep in his throat. Dr. Junius coughed in the silence. "I don't want to seem inhospitable, but . . . I mean, don't you think it would be wise to take off now, before the storm breaks, Inspector?"

"Huh?" The Inspector turned cold eyes on Dr. Junius.

"I said—"

"I heard what you said." Glücke stared hard at the doctor's saffron face. "What's the matter with you? Nervous?"

"No. Certainly not," said the doctor, backing away.

"Who are you, anyway? What are you doing here?"

"My name is Junius, and I'm a medical doctor. I live here with Mr. Stuart."

"Where'd you come from? Did you know Blythe Stuart and Jack Royle?"

"No, indeed. I mean— I've seen Mr. Royle in Hollywood at times and

Miss Blythe Stuart used to come here. . . . But I haven't seen her for several years."

"How long have you been here?"

"Ten years. Mr. Stuart hired me to take care of him. At a very nice yearly retainer, I must say, and my own practice wasn't terribly—"

"Where'd you come from? I didn't hear you say."

"Buenavista, Colorado."

"Police record?"

Dr. Junius drew himself up. "My dear sir!"

Glücke looked him over. "No harm done," he said mildly. The doctor stepped back, wiping his face. "Now here's what we've found. You were right, Queen, about the cause of death. The coroner of Riverside County flew up there with his sheriff, examined the bodies—"

Bonnie grew pale again. Butcher said sharply: "Dr. Junius is right. We ought to clear out of here and get these kids home. You can talk to them tomorrow."

"It's all right," said Bonnie in a low voice. "I'm all right, Butch."

"As far as I'm concerned," growled Ty, "the sooner you get started the better I'll like it. Do you think I could sleep and eat and laugh and work while my father's murderer is breathing free air somewhere?"

The Inspector went on, quite as if nobody had spoken: "Well, as I was saying, preliminary examination showed they both died of very large doses of morphine."

"In the thermos bottles?" asked Ellery.

"Yes. The drinks were loaded with the stuff. The doc couldn't be sure without a chemical analysis, but he says there must easily have been five grains to each cocktail drink. I'm having Bronson, our Chemist, analyze what's left in the bottles as soon as he can lay his hands on them."

"But I don't understand," frowned Bonnie. "We all drank from the bottles just before the take-off. Why weren't we poisoned, too?"

"If you weren't, it's because the drinks were okay at that time. Does anybody remember exactly what happened to that hamper?"

"I do," said Ellery. "I was shoved about by the crowd and was forced to sit down on the hamper immediately after the last round, when the bottles were put back. And I had my eye on that hamper every instant between the time the bottles were stowed away and the time I sat down on the hamper."

"That's a break. Did you sit on the hamper till this disguised pilot hijacked the plane?"

"Better than that," said Ellery wryly. "I actually got up and handed it to him with my own hands as he got into the plane."

"So that means the drinks were poisoned inside. We've got a clear line there." Glücke looked pleased. "He swiped the plane, poisoned the drinks in the plane as he was stowing away the hamper, took off, waited for Jack and Blythe to drink—stuff's practically tasteless, the coroner said, in booze—and when they passed out he just set the plane down on that plateau and beat it. No fuss, no bother, no trouble at all. Damned neat, and damned cold-blooded."

The pilot's predicted storm broke. A thousand demons howled, and the wind lashed at the butte, pounding the old house, banging shutters and rattling windows. Suddenly lightning crashed about the exposed mountain-top and thunder roared.

Nobody spoke. Dr. Junius shambled forward to throw another log on the fire.

The thunder rolled and rolled as if it would never stop. Ellery listened uneasily. It seemed to him that he had detected the faintest undertone in the thunder. He glanced about, but none of his companions seemed conscious of it.

The thunder ceased for a moment, and Glücke said: "We've got the whole State looking for that pilot. It's only a question of time before we catch up with the guy."

"But this rain," cried Ty. "It will wipe out his trail from the plateau!"

"I know, I know, Mr. Royle," said Glücke soothingly. "Don't fret yourself. We'll collar him. Now I want you young people to tell me something about your parents. There must be a clue somewhere in their background."

Ellery took his hat and coat from the chair near the front door where he had dropped them and, unobserved, slipped down the hallway to the kitchen and out the kitchen door into the open.

The trees about the side of the house were bent over in the gale, and a downpour that seemed solid rather than liquid drenched him the instant he set foot on the spongy earth. Nevertheless he lowered his head to the wind, clutching his hat, and aided by an occasional lightning-flash fought his way toward the distant glow of the landing field.

He stumbled onto the field and stopped, gasping for breath. A commercial plane, apparently the one which had conveyed Glücke to Tolland Stuart's mountain home, strained within the hangar beside the small stubby ship; the hangar doors stood open to the wind.

Ellery shook his head impatiently, straining to see the length of the field in the badly flickering arc-lights. But the field was empty of life.

He waited for the next flash of lightning and then eagerly searched the tossing skies overhead. But if there was anything up there, it was lost in the swollen black clouds.

So it had been his imagination after all. He could have sworn he had heard the motors of an airplane through the thunder. He retraced his steps.

And then, just as he was about to break from under the trees in a dash back to the house, he saw a man.

The man was crouching in the lee of the house, to the rear, a black hunched-over figure. The friendly lightning blazed again, and Ellery saw him raise his head.

It was an old face with a ragged growth of gray beard and mustache, a deeply engraved skin, and slack blubbering lips; and it was the face of one who looks upon death, or worse. Ellery was struck by that expression of pure, stripped terror. It was as if the old man had suddenly found himself cornered against an unscalable wall by a horde of the ghastliest denizens of his worst nightmare.

In the aftermath of darkness Ellery barely made out the stooped figure creeping miserably along the side of the house to vanish somewhere behind it.

The rain hissed down, and Ellery stood still, oblivious to it, staring into the darkness. What was Mr. Tolland Stuart doing out in the storm raging about his mountain retreat at a moment when he was supposed to be shivering behind the barred door of his bedroom?

Why, indeed, only a few hours after the murder of his only child in an airplane, should he be crawling about his estate with a flyer's helmet stuck ludicrously on his head?

Ellery found the Inspector straddle-legged before the fire. He was saying: "Not much help. . . . Oh, Queen."

Ellery dashed the rain from his hat and spread his coat before the flames. "I thought I heard something on the landing-field."

"Another plane?" groaned Dr. Junius.

"It was my imagination."

Glücke frowned. "Well, we're not getting anywhere. Then aside from this down-and-outer Park you mentioned, Mr. Royle, you'd say your father had no enemies?"

"None I know of."

"I'd quite forgotten that little flare-up at the *Horseshoe Club* a couple of weeks ago," said Ellery slowly.

"Nothing to it. The man was just peeved about being found out. It's not going to be as easy as all that."

"The man's cracked," said Ty shortly. "A crackpot will do anything."

"Well, we'll check up on him. Only if he's the one, why did he kill Miss Stuart's mother as well as your father? He couldn't have had anything against *her*."

"He could have held her responsible for the whole situation," snapped Ty. "An irrational man would react that way."

"Maybe." Glücke looked at his fingernails. "By the way. It seems to me there's been a lot of talk about your two families sort of—well, not getting along."

The fire crackled, and outside the thunder and lightning went out in a spectacular finale. The rain fell to a steady patter.

The pilot got up and said: "I'll take a look at my crate, Inspector," and went out.

And then the Boy Wonder mumbled: "Nonsense."

"Did I say something wrong?" inquired Glücke innocently.

"Didn't Jack and Blythe make up? You couldn't want better proof than their reconciliation and marriage."

"But how about these two?" said Glücke. There was another silence. "Hey?" said Glücke.

Bonnie stared straight at the lowest button of the Inspector's jacket. And Ty turned his back to look at the fire.

"There's no sense smearing it, Butch. We've hated each other's guts since we were kids. We were brought up on hate. When a thing like that is fed to you morning, noon, and night from your nursery days it gets into your blood."

"You feel the same way, huh, Miss Stuart?"

Bonnie licked her dry lips. "Yes."

"But that doesn't mean," said Ty slowly, turning around, "that one of us committed those murders. Or do you think it does, Inspector Glücke?"

"But he *couldn't* think a horrible thing like that!" cried Bonnie.

"How do I know," said Glücke, "that story about the hold-up at the hangar in Griffith Park airport is on the level?"

"But we've got each other as witnesses!"

"Even if we didn't," growled Ty, "do you think I would poison my own father to revenge myself on Bonnie Stuart's mother? Or that Bonnie Stuart would murder her own mother to get even with my father? You're crazy."

"I don't know anything," said the Inspector blandly, "about anything. You might be interested to learn that the Homicide Detail's turned up the boy who brought Miss Stuart that message before the take-off. I got the news by radiophone while I was examining your plane on the plateau."

"What's he got to say for himself?"

"He says he was stopped near the hangar—he's a page, or steward, or something, at the municipal field—by a tall thin man bundled up in flying clothes, wearing goggles." The Inspector's tone was amiable, but he kept glancing from Bonnie to Ty and back again. "This man held up a piece of paper with typewriting on it in front of the kid's nose. The paper said for him to tell Miss Stuart Mr. Royle wanted her in the hangar."

"The come-on," muttered Ty. "That was the pilot, all right. What a clumsy trick!"

"Which worked nevertheless," remarked Ellery. "You're positive the boy's on the level, Inspector?"

"The airport people give him a clean bill."

"How about the typewritten note?"

"The kid never got his hands on it. It was just shown to him. Then the disguised pilot faded into the crowd, the kid says, taking the paper with him."

Bonnie rose, looking incensed. "Then how can you believe one of us had a hand in those horrible crimes?"

"I'm not saying you had," smiled Glücke. "I'm saying you could have had."

"But if we were held up and tied!"

"Suppose one of you hired that tall fellow to fake the hold-up—to make you look innocent?"

"Oh, my God," said Butch, throwing up his hands.

"You're a fool," said Ty curtly. He sat down on the settee and cupped his face in his hands.

Inspector Glücke smiled again and, going to his coat, fished in one of the pockets. He came back to the fire with a large manila envelope and slowly unwound the waxed red string.

"What's that?" demanded Ellery.

Glücke's big hand dipped into the envelope and came out with something round, thin, and blue. He held it up.

"Ever see one of these before?" he asked of no one in particular.

They crowded about him, Dr. Junius nosing with the rest. It was a blue chip, incised with a golden horseshoe.

"The *Horseshoe Club*," exclaimed Bonnie and Ty together. In their eagerness they bumped against each other. For a moment they were pressed together; then they drew apart.

"Comes from Jack Royle's pocket," said the Inspector. "It's not important." Nevertheless, Ellery noted the careful manner in which he handled it, holding it between thumb and forefinger on the thin edge of the disc, as if he were afraid of smudging a possible fingerprint.

He dropped the plaque back into the envelope and pulled out something else—a sheaf of ragged pieces of paper held together by a paper-clip.

"The clip is mine," he explained. "I found these torn scraps in Royle's pocket, too."

Ellery seized them. Separating the scraps, he spread them on the settee. It took only a few minutes to assemble the pieces. Reassembled, they constituted five small rectangles of linen memorandum paper, with the words: THE HORSESHOE CLUB, engraved in blue over a tiny golden horseshoe at the top of each sheet.

Each sheet bore a date; the dates covered roughly a period of a month, the last date being the second of the current month. In the same-colored ink, boldly scrawled, were the letters I O U, a figure preceded by a dollar-sign, and the signature *John Royle*. Each I O U noted a different sum. With a frown Ellery totaled them. They came to exactly $110,000.00.

"Know anything about these things?" asked the Inspector.

Ty studied them incredulously. He seemed baffled by the signature.

"What's the matter?" asked Ellery quickly. "Isn't that your father's signature?"

"That's just the trouble," murmured Ty. "It is."

"All five?"

"Yes."

"What d'ye mean trouble?" demanded Glücke. "Didn't you know about these debts?"

"No. At least I didn't know dad had got in so deep with Alessandro. A hundred and ten thousand dollars!" He plunged his hands into his pockets and began to walk up and down. "He was always a reckless gambler, but this—"

"You mean to say he was that broke and his own son didn't know it?"

"We rarely discussed money matters. I led my life and—" he sat slowly down on the settee, "he led his."

He fell into a deep inspection of the fire. Glücke gathered the scraps together, clipped them, and in silence stowed them away in the manila envelope.

Some one coughed. Ellery turned around. It was Dr. Junius. He had quite forgotten Dr. Junius.

Dr. Junius said nervously: "The rain's stopped, I think. You ought to be able to fly out safely now."

"Oh, it's you again, Doctor," said the Inspector. "You *are* in a fret to get rid of us, aren't you?"

"No, no," said the doctor hastily. "I was just thinking of Miss Stuart. She must have a night's rest."

"And that reminds me." Glücke looked at the staircase. "While I'm here I think I'll have a talk with the old man."

"Dr. Junius doesn't think that would be wise," said Ellery dryly. "Are you impervious to buckshot? Tolland Stuart keeps a shotgun by his bed."

"Oh, he does, does he?" said Glücke. And he strode towards the staircase.

"Be careful, Inspector!" cried Junius, running after. "He doesn't even know his daughter's dead."

"Go on," said Glücke grimly. "That shy kind have a cute habit of listening at keyholes and at the top of stairs."

He strode on. Ellery, remembering the face of the old man in the downpour outside the house, silently applauded Glücke's shrewdness. That livid old man had known the facts of death; there was no question about that.

He followed the two men up the stairs.

The light of the downstairs chamber faded as they ascended, and by the time they reached the landing upstairs they were in iced and murky darkness.

Glücke stumbled on the top step. "Aren't there any lights in this blasted morgue?" Dr. Junius brushed hurriedly and surefootedly by.

"Just a moment," he whined. "The switch is—"

"Wait," said the Inspector. Ellery waited. But, strain as he might, Ellery heard nothing but the hiss of the fire downstairs and the murmur of Butcher's voice soothing Bonnie.

"What's the matter?"

"Thought I heard some one scramble away. But I guess I was wrong. This place could drive a man nuts."

"I don't think you were wrong," said Ellery. "Our aged friend has probably been ensconced up here for some time, eavesdropping, as you suggested."

"Switch those lights on, Junius," growled Glücke, "and let's have a look at the old turkey."

The magic of sudden light after darkness materialized a wide draughty hall, thickly carpeted and hung with what seemed to Ellery a veritable gallery of old masters—lovely pictures with the rich brown patina of the Dutch period and uniformly framed in a dust no less rich and brown. There were many doors, and all were closed, and of Tolland Stuart no sign.

"Mr. Stuart!" cried Junius. There was no answer. He turned to the Inspector piteously. "There you are, Inspector. Can't you come back tomorrow? He's probably in an awful state."

"I can, but I won't," said the Inspector. "Which one is his cave?"

The doctor made a despairing gesture and, crying out: "He'll probably shoot us all!" led the way to a double door at the farthest point in the corridor. Trembling, he knocked.

An old man's voice quavered: "Keep out!" and Ellery heard scuttling sounds, as if the possessor of the voice had scrambled away from the other side of the door.

Dr. Junius yelped and fled.

Glücke chuckled: "The old guy must have something at that. Chicken-hearted mummy!" And he thundered: "Come on, open up there, Mr. Stuart!"

"Who is it?"

"The police."

"Go away. Get off my grounds. I'll have no truck with police!" The quaver was a scream now, with a curious lisping quality to the syllables which could only be effected by a toothless mouth.

"Do you know, Mr. Stuart," shouted the Inspector sternly, "that your daughter Blythe has been murdered?"

"I heard 'em. I heard you! Get out, I say!"

Bonnie came running up the hall towards them, crying: "Grandfather!"

Dr. Junius sidled after, pleading: "Please, Miss Stuart. Not now. He isn't —pleasant. He'll upset you."

"Grandfather," sobbed Bonnie, pounding on the door. "Let me in. It's Bonnie. Mother—she's dead. She's been killed, I tell you. There's only us now. Please!"

"Mr. Stuart, sir," whined Dr. Junius, "it's your granddaughter, Bonnie Stuart. She needs you, sir. Won't you open the door, talk to her, comfort her?"

There was no reply.

"Mr. Stuart, sir. This is Dr. Junius. Please!"

Then the cracked, lisping voice came. "Go away, all of you. No police. Bonnie, not—not now. There's death among you. Death! Death . . ." And the shriek was choked off on its ascending note, and they distinctly heard the thud of a body.

Bonnie bit her fingers, staring at the panels. Butcher came running up. Glücke said gently: "Stand aside, Miss Stuart. We'll have to break the door in. Get out of the way, Junius."

And Ty came up, too, and watched them from narrowed eyes as he stood quietly at the other end of the hall.

The Inspector hurled himself at the juncture of the two doors. Something snapped inside; the doors flew open. For a moment he stood still, breathing hard. The moment seemed interminable, with the infinitude of some arrested moments.

The room was vast, and gloomy, and filled with solid pieces like the great chamber downstairs; and the four-poster English bed of hand-carved antique oak, with its red fustian tester, was disheveled; and, surely enough, there stood a heavy shotgun by its side, handy to a reaching arm. And on the floor, before them, lay the crumpled body of the old man Ellery had glimpsed outdoors, clad in flannel pajamas and a woolen robe, thick socks, and carpet slippers over his bony feet. The only light came from a brown mica lamp near the bed; the fireplace was dark.

Dr. Junius hurried forward to drop on his knees beside the motionless figure.

"He's fainted. Fear—venom—temper; I don't know what. But his pulse is good; nothing to worry about. Please go now. It's useless to try to talk to him tonight."

He got to his feet, and stooped, and with a surprising strength for a man of his sparse physique and evident years, lifted the old man's body and bore him in his arms to the bed.

"He's probably shamming," said Inspector Glücke disgustedly. "Crusty old termite! Come on, folks, we'll be riding the air back to Los Angeles."

Chapter VIII

Two for Nothing

"WHERE TO?" asked the pilot.

"Municipal airport, L. A."

The plane was not large, and they sat about in a cramped silence while the pilot nosed his ship sharply northwestward. He sought altitude; and soon they were flying high above a black valley, splitting the breeze to a hairline above and between the San Bernardino and San Jacinto ranges.

"What's happened to my plane?" asked Ty, his face against a drizzle-misted window.

"It's probably in Los Angeles by this time," replied the Inspector. He paused. "Of course, we couldn't leave them . . . it there."

Bonnie stirred on Butcher's motionless shoulder. "I was in a morgue once. It was a movie set. But even in make-believe . . . It was cold. Mother didn't like—" She closed her eyes. "Give me a cigaret, Butch."

He lit one for her and stuck it between her lips.

"Thanks." She opened her eyes. "I suppose you all think I've been acting like such a baby. But it's just that it's been . . . a shock. It's even worse, now that I can think again. . . . Mother gone. It just isn't possible."

Without turning, Ty said harshly: "We all know how you feel."

"Oh! Sorry."

Ellery stared out at the stormy dark. A cluster of lights far below and ahead began to mushroom, resembling loose diamonds strewn on a black velvet cushion.

"Riverside," said the Inspector. "We'll pass over it soon, and after that it's not far to the airport."

They watched the cluster glow and grow and shrink and fade and disappear.

Ty suddenly got up. He blundered blindly up the aisle. Then he came back. "Why?" he said.

"Why what?" asked the Inspector, surprised.

"Why was dad knocked off? Why were they both knocked off?"

"If we knew that, son, it wouldn't be much of a case. Sit down."

"It doesn't make sense. Were they robbed? He had a thousand dollars in cash on him. I gave it to him only this morning as a sort of—sort of wedding gift. Or—Bonnie! Was your mother carrying much money?"

"Don't talk to me," said Bonnie.

"It's not that," said Glücke. "Their personal belongings weren't touched."

"Then why?" cried Ty. "Why? Is he a lunatic?"

"Sit down, Ty," said the Boy Wonder wearily.

"Wait!" His bloodshot eyes narrowed. "Could it have been an accident? I mean, could it have been that only one of them was meant to be killed, that the other one was a victim of some—"

"Since you're discussing it," drawled Ellery, "suppose you discuss it systematically."

"What do you mean?"

"I think motive is the keystone of this case."

"Yeah?" said the Inspector. "Why?"

"Simply because there doesn't seem to be any."

Glücke looked annoyed. Ty suddenly sat down and lit a cigaret. His eyes did not leave Ellery's face. "Go on. You've got an idea about this thing."

"He's a crazy galoot," growled Glücke, "but I admit he's got something besides sand in his skull."

"Well, look." Ellery put his elbows on his knees. "Let's begin in the proper place. Among the things I've observed in the past few weeks, Ty, is that your father never drank anything but Sidecars. Is that right?"

"Brandy, too. He liked brandy."

"Well, of course. A Sidecar is nothing but brandy with Cointreau and a little lemon juice added. And as for your mother, Bonnie, she seemed exclusively fond of dry Martinis."

"Yes."

"I seem to recall, in fact, that she recently made some disparaging remark about Sidecars, which would indicate she disliked them. Is that true?"

"She detested them."

"And dad couldn't stand Martinis, either," growled Ty. "So what?"

"So this. Some one—obviously the murderer; it could scarcely have been coincidence; the exact means of murder wouldn't have been left to chance —some one sends Blythe and Jack a going-away hamper and lo! inside are two thermos bottles and lo! in one of them is a quart of Sidecars and in the other an equal quantity of Martinis."

"If you mean," said Butch with a frown, "that in sending those bottles the murderer betrayed an intimate knowledge of Blythe's and Jack's liquor preferences, Ellery, I'm afraid you won't get far. Everybody in Hollywood knew that Blythe liked Martinis and Jack Sidecars."

Inspector Glücke looked pleased.

But Ellery smiled. "I didn't mean that. I'm attacking Ty's accident theory, improbable as it is, just to get it out of the way. It lends itself to logical disproof.

"For if, as seems indisputable, the donor of that hamper knew that Blythe liked Martinis and Jack Sidecars, then the dosing of *each* bottle of heavenly dew with a lethal amount of morphine means that *each* drinker—Jack, the drinker of Sidecars, Blythe, the drinker of Martinis—*was intended to be poisoned*. Had only Blythe been marked for death, only the bottle of Martinis would have been poisoned. And similarly if Jack were to be the sole victim." He sighed. "I'm afraid we're faced with no alternative. Neither your father, Ty, nor your mother, Bonnie, was intended ever to come out of that plane alive. It's the clearest case of a deliberate double killing."

"And where does all this folderol get you?" scowled Glücke.

"I'm sure I don't know. One rarely does at this stage of the game."

"I thought," put in the Boy Wonder shortly, "you began to talk about motive."

"Oh, that." Ellery shrugged. "If the same motive applied to both of them, as seems likely, it's even more mystifying."

"But what could it be?" cried Bonnie. "Mother wouldn't have harmed a fly."

Ellery did not reply. He looked out the window at the swirling darkness.

The Inspector said suddenly: "Miss Stuart, is your father alive?"

"He died when I was an infant."

"Your mother never remarried?"

"No."

"Any . . ." The Inspector hesitated. Then he said delicately: "Did she have any . . . romantic attachments?"

"Mother?" Bonnie laughed. "Don't be absurd." And she turned her face away.

"How about your father, Royle? Your ma's dead, too, isn't she?"

"Yes."

"Well, from all I've heard," said the Inspector, clearing his throat, "your dad was sort of a lady's man. Could there be some woman floating around who had—well, who thought she had good reason to get sore when Jack Royle announced he was going to marry Blythe Stuart?"

"How should I know? I wasn't dad's nursemaid."

"Then there could be such a woman?"

"There could," snapped Ty, "but I don't think there is. Dad was no angel, but he knew women, he knew the world, and underneath he was a right guy. The few affairs I know about ended without a fuss. He never lied to his women, and they always knew exactly what they were letting themselves in for. You're a million miles wrong, Glücke. Besides, this job was pulled by a man."

"Hmm," said the Inspector, and he slumped back. He did not seem immovably persuaded.

"I suggest," said Ellery, "we eliminate. The usual attack in theorizing about motive is to ask who stands to gain by the murder. I believe we'll make faster progress if we ask who stands to lose.

"Let's start with the principals. You, Ty, and you, Bonnie. Obviously, of every one involved you two have sustained the greatest possible loss. You've lost your sole surviving parents, to whom you were plainly tremendously attached."

Bonnie bit her lip, staring out the window. Ty crushed the burning tip of his cigaret out in his fingers.

"The studio?" Ellery shrugged. "Don't look so startled, Butch; logic knows no sentiment. The studio has suffered a large monetary loss: it has lost forever the services of two popular, money-making stars. To bring it closer home, your own unit suffers a direct and intimate loss: the big production we've been working on together will have to be abandoned."

"Wait a minute," said Glücke. "How about a studio feud? Any contract trouble with another studio, Butcher? Know anybody who wouldn't mind seeing Magna's two big stars out of pictures?"

"Oh, don't be a fool, Inspector," snapped Butch. "This is Hollywood, not mediaeval Italy."

"It didn't seem likely," grunted Glücke.

"To continue," said Ellery, glancing at the Inspector with amusement. "The agency holding contracts for Jack's and Blythe's personal services—I believe it's Alan Clark's outfit—also loses.

"So that, in a sense, every one connected with Jack and Blythe personally and professionally stands to lose a great deal."

"You're a help."

"But good lord, Ellery," protested Butch, "it stands to reason somebody gains by this crime."

"From a monetary standpoint? Well, let's see. Did Jack or Blythe leave much of an estate?"

"Mother left practically nothing," said Bonnie lifelessly. "Even her jewels were paste. She lived up to every cent she earned."

"How about Jack, Ty?"

Ty's lip curled. "What do you think? You saw those I O U's."

"How about insurance?" asked the Inspector. "Or trust funds? You Hollywood actors are always salting it away in insurance companies."

"Mother," said Bonnie tightly, "didn't believe in insurance or annuities. She didn't know the value of money at all. I was always making up shortages in her checking account."

"Dad took out a hundred-thousand-dollar policy once," said Ty. "It was in force until the second premium came due. He said to hell with it—he had to go to the race-track that afternoon."

"But for Pete's sake," exclaimed the Inspector, "there's got to be an angle somewhere. If it wasn't gain, then revenge. Something! I'm beginning to think this guy Park better be tagged right away, at that."

"Well," said Ty coldly, "how about Alessandro and those I O U's?"

"But they turned up in your father's possession," said Ellery. "If he hadn't paid up, do you think Alessandro would have returned the I O U's?"

"I don't know anything about that," muttered Ty. "All I ask is: Where would dad get a hundred and ten thousand?"

"You're absolutely sure," said Glücke slowly, "he couldn't lay his hands on that much, huh?"

"Of course not!"

The Inspector rubbed his jaw. "Alessandro's real handle is Joe DiSangri, and he's been mixed up in a lot of monkey-business in New York. He used to be one of Al's hoods, too, 'way back." Then he shook his head. "But it doesn't smell like a gang kill. Poisoned drinks! If Joe DiSangri wanted to rub out a welcher, he'd use lead. It's in his blood."

"Times have changed," snarled Ty. "That's a hell of a reason to lay off the skunk! Do I have to look him up myself?"

"Oh, we'll check him."

"At any rate," said Ellery, "did Joe DiSangri, alias Alessandro, also kill Bonnie's mother because your father welched on a gambling debt?"

Bonnie said passionately: "I knew it would only lead to trouble. I knew it. Why did she have to do it?"

Ty colored and turned aside. Glücke gnawed a fingernail. And kept looking at Bonnie and Ty.

The pilot opened his door and said: "We're here."

They looked down. The field was blackly alive, heaving with people.

Bonnie blanched and groped for Butch's hand. "It . . . it looks like a—like something big and dead and a lot of little black ants running all over it."

"Bonnie, you've been a trump so far. This won't last long. Don't spoil it. Keep your chin up."

"But I can't! All those millions of staring eyes—" She held on to his hand tightly.

"Now, Miss Stuart, take it easy," said the Inspector, getting to his feet. "You've got to face it. We're here—"

"Are we?" said Ty bitterly. "I'd say we were nowhere. And that we'd got there damned fast."

"That's why I pointed out," murmured Ellery, "that when we found out why Jack and Blythe were poisoned—when we got a clear line on the motive —we'd crack this case wide open."

Chapter IX

The Club Nine

ON WEDNESDAY THE twentieth the only completely peaceful persons in the City of Los Angeles and environs were John Royle and Blythe Stuart: they were dead.

It had been a mad three days. Reporters; cameramen, of the journalistic, artistic, and candid varieties; aging ladies of the motion picture press; State police and men of Inspector Glücke's Homicide Detail; stars; producers; directors looking for inspiration; embalmers; preachers; debtors; mortuary salesmen; lawyers; radio announcers; real estate men; thousands of glamor-struck worshipers at the shrine of the dead pair—all milled and shouted and shoved and popped in and out and made the waking hours—there were few sleeping ones—of Bonnie and Ty an animated nightmare.

"Might as well have planned services for the Bowl," cried Ty, disheveled, unshaven, purple-eyed from lack of rest. "For God's sake, somebody, can't I even send the old man out decently?"

"He was a public figure in life, Ty," said Ellery soothingly. "You couldn't expect the public to ignore him in death."

"That kind of death."

"Any kind of death."

"They're vultures!"

"Murder brings out the worst in people. Think of what poor Bonnie's going through in Glendale."

"Yes," scowled Ty. "I guess . . . it's pretty tough on a woman." Then he said: "Queen, I've got to talk to her."

"Yes, Ty?" Ellery tried not to show surprise.

"It's terribly important."

"It's going to be hard, arranging a quiet meeting now."

"I've got to."

They met at three o'clock in the morning at an undistinguished little café tucked away in a blind alley off Melrose Street, miraculously unpursued—Ty wearing dark blue glasses and Bonnie a heavy nose-veil that revealed little more than her pale lips and chin.

Ellery and the Boy Wonder stood guard outside the booth in which they sat.

"Sorry, Bonnie," said Ty abruptly, "to bring you out at a time like this. But there's something we've got to discuss."

"Yes?" Bonnie's voice startled him; it was flat, brassy, devoid of life or feeling.

"Bonnie, you're ill."

"I'm all right."

"Queen—Butch—somebody should have told me."

"I'm all right. It's just the thought of . . . Wednesday." He saw her lips quiver beneath the veil.

Ty played with a glass of Scotch. "Bonnie . . . I've never asked a favor of you, have I?"

"You?"

"I'm . . . I suppose you'll think I'm a fool, getting sentimental this way."

"You sentimental?" Bonnie's lips curved this time.

"What I want you to do . . ." Ty put the glass down. "It's not for me. It isn't even for my dad exclusively. It's as much for your mother as for dad."

Her hands crept off the table and disappeared. "Come to the point, please."

He blurted: "I think they ought to have a double funeral."

She was silent.

"I tell you it's not for dad. It's for both of them. I've been thinking things over since Sunday. Bonnie, they were in love. Before . . . I didn't think so. I thought there was something else behind it—I don't know what. But now . . . They died together. Don't you see?"

She was silent.

"They were kept apart so many years," said Ty. "And then to be knocked off just before . . . I know I'm an idiot to be talking this way. But I can't get over the feeling that dad—yes, and your mother—would have wanted to be buried together, too."

She was silent for so long that Ty thought something had happened to her. But just as he was about to touch her in alarm, she moved. Her hands appeared and pushed the veil back from her face. And she looked and looked and looked at him out of her dark-shadowed eyes, not speaking, not changing her expression; just looking.

Then she said simply: "All right, Ty," and rose.

"Thanks!"

"It's mother I'm thinking of."

Neither said another word. They went home by different routes—Ty in Ellery's coupé to Beverly Hills, Bonnie in the Boy Wonder's limousine to Glendale.

Then the coroner released the bodies, and John Royle and Blythe Stuart were embalmed, and for several hours on Wednesday morning their magnificent mahogany caskets, sheathed in purest Anaconda copper, with eighteen-carat gold handles and $50-a-yard hand-loomed Japanese silk linings stuffed with the down of black swans, were on public display in the magnificent mortuary on Sunset Boulevard which Sam Vix, who was surreptitiously superintending the production on a 2%-commission basis, persuaded Jacques Butcher to persuade Ty Royle to beg the favor of Bonnie Stuart to select, which they did, and she did; and four women were trampled, one seriously, and sixteen women fainted, and the police had to ride into the crowd on their magnificent horses, which were all curried and glossed for the occasion; and one poorly dressed man who was obviously a Communist tried to bite the stirrup of the mounted policeman who had just run over him and was properly whacked over the head with a billy and dragged off to jail; and inside the mortuary all the glittering elect, tricked out in their most gorgeous mourning clothes—Mme. Flo's and Magnin's and L'Heureuse's had had to hire mobs of seamstresses to get the special orders out in time for the funeral —remarked how beautiful Blythe looked: "Just as if she were asleep, the darling; if she weren't under glass you'd swear she was going to *move!*" "And yet she's embalmed; it's wonderful what they can do." "Yes, and to think she's got practically *nothing* left inside. I read that they performed an autopsy, and you know what they do in autopsies." "Don't be gruesome! How should I know?" "Well, but wasn't your first husband—" —and didn't Bonnie show a too, too precious taste in dressing Blythe up in that *gorgeous* white satin evening gown with that perfectly *clever* tight bodice— "She had a beautiful bust, my dear. Do you know she once told me she never wore a *girdle?* And I know for a fact that she didn't have to wear a cup-form brassière!" —with the shirring at the waist and those *thousands* of accordion pleats— "If she could only stand up, darling, you'd see what a cunning fan effect those pleats give!"—and that one dainty orchid corsage and those *exquisite* diamond clips at the shoulder-straps—"I mean they look exquisite. Are they real, do you think, dear?" And how handsome poor old Jack looked, in his starched bosom and tails, with that cynical half-smile on his face: "Wouldn't you swear he was going to get right out of that casket and put his arm around you?" "Who put that gold statuette that Jack won in thirty-three in there with him?" "I'm sure I don't know; it does seem a little like bragging, doesn't it?" "Well, there's the Academy committee and they look simply devastatingly pleased!" "He *was* a handsome devil, though, wasn't he? My second husband knocked him down once." "Don't you think that's a little indiscreet, darling?—I mean with all these detectives around? After all, Jack was *murdered.*" "Don't be funny, Nanette! You know Llewelyn ran off to Africa or some place with that snippy extra-girl with the g-string and hips two years ago." "Well, my dear, the things I could tell you about Jack Royle—not that I'm speaking ill of the dead, but in a way Blythe's better off. She'd never have been happy with him, the way he chased every chippy in town." "Oh, my darling! I'd forgotten that you knew him well, didn't you?"

And over in Glendale, in the big seething house, Bonnie stood cold and tearless and almost as devoid of life as her mother down in Hollywood being admired by thousands; while Clotilde, whose plump cheeks and Gallic nose seemed permanently puffed out from weeping, dressed her—unresisted—in soft and striking black, even though Bonnie had often said she detested public displays of grief and typical Hollywood funerals; dressed Bonnie without assistance from Bonnie, as if in truth she were dressing a corpse.

And in Beverly Hills Ty was cursing Louderback between gulps of brandy and refusing to shave and wanting to wear slacks and a blazer, just to show the damned vultures, and Alan Clark and a hastily recruited squad of husky friends finally held him down while Louderback plied the electric razor and a doctor took the decanter away and forced Ty to swallow some luminal instead.

And then Ty and Bonnie met over the magnificent twin coffins at the mortuary, framed and bowered in gigantic banks of fresh-cut flowers until they and the corpses and the mortician's assistants and the Bishop looked like figures on a float at the annual flower festival; and neither said a single word; and the Bishop read a magnificent service against the heady-sweet background, bristling with "dear Lords" and "dear departeds," and Inspector Glücke almost wore his eyes out scanning the crowd on the fundamental theory that a murderer cannot resist visiting the funeral of his victims, and saw nothing, even though he stared very hard at Joe DiSangri Alessandro, who was present looking like a solemn little Italian banker in his morning coat and striped trousers; and Jeannine Carrel, the beautiful star with the operatic voice than whom no soprano in or out of the Metropolitan sang *Ah, Sweet Mystery of Life* more thrillingly, tearfully sang *Nearer, My God, to Thee* accompanied by the entire male chorus of Magna Studio's forthcoming super-musical production, *Swing That Thing*; and Lew Bascom did not even stagger under his share of the weight of Blythe's coffin, which was a testimonial to his stamina and capacity, since he had consumed five quarts of Scotch since Sunday night and his breath would have sent a buzzard reeling in dismay.

And among the other pallbearers present were Louis X. Selvin, executive president of Magna; an ex-Mayor; an ex-Governor; three outstanding stars (selected by Sam Vix on the basis of the latest popularity poll conducted by Paula Paris for the newspaper syndicate for which she worked); the president of the Motion Picture Academy; a Broadway producer in Hollywood making comical short subjects; Randy Round, the famous Broadway columnist, to whom no set in filmland was forbidden ground; an important official of the Hays office; and a special delegate from the Friars' Club. There was a good deal of crowding.

And somehow, aeons later, the motored processional, rich with Isotta-Fraschinis, Rolls-Royces, Cords, Lincolns, and special-bodied Duesenbergs managed to reach and penetrate the memorial park—Hollywoodese for "cemetery"—where a veritable ocean of mourners surged in eye-bursting waves, mourning, to await the interment ceremonies; and the Bishop, who seemed indefatigable, read another magnificent service while a choir of freshly scrubbed angel-faced boys in cute surplices sang magnificently, and thirty-one more women fainted, and ambulances came unobtrusively and plaintively to the scene, and one headstone was knocked over and two stone angels lost their left arms, and Jack and Blythe were lowered side by side into magnificent blue spruce-trimmed graves edged in giant fern and topped off with plaits of giant lilies; and Bonnie, disdaining the Boy Wonder's arm, stood cold, lifeless, straight of back, and watched her mother make the last slow descent, magnificently dramatic, into the earth; and Ty stood alone in his own empty dimension, with incurving shoulders and a wonderfully bitter smile, watching his father's clay make the same slow descent; and finally it was practically—not quite—over, and the only part of her costume Bonnie surrendered to posterity was her dry black lawn handkerchief, snatched from her hand by a sabled fat woman with maniacal eyes as Butcher led Bonnie back to his limousine; and Ty, observing, lost the last shred of his temper and shook his fist in the fat woman's face, to be dragged off by Lew, Ellery, and Alan Clark; and stars and stars and stars wept and wept, and the sun shone blithely over Hollywood, and everybody had a lovely time, and Sam Vix said with emotion, wiping the dampness from under his black patch, that it had all been simply—there was no other word for it—magnificent.

But once safely away from the Argus-eyed mob, Bonnie gave vent to a wild sobbing in the Boy Wonder's arms as the limousine dodged through traffic trying to escape the pursuing cars of the insatiable press.

"Oh, Butch, it was so awful. People are such pigs. It was like the Rose Bowl p-parade. It's a wonder they didn't ask me to sing over the r-radio!"

"It's over now, darling. Forget it. It's all over."

"And grandfather didn't come. Oh, I hate him! I phoned him myself this morning. He begged off. He said he was ill. He said he couldn't stand funerals, and would I try to understand. His own daughter! Oh, Butch, I'm so *miserable*."

"Forget the old buzzard, Bonnie. He's not worth your misery."

"I hope I never see him again!"

And when they got to the Glendale house Bonnie begged off and sent Butcher away and instructed Clotilde to bang the door in the face of any one, friend or foe, who so much as tapped on it. And she shut herself up in her bedroom, sniffling, and tried paradoxically to find comfort in the bulky bundles of mail Clotilde had left for her.

Ty, who had to traverse the width of Hollywood to get home to Beverly Hills, changed from open rebellion to a sulky, shut-in silence; and his escort wisely left him to Louderback's stiff ministrations and departed. He had scarcely finished his third brandy when the telephone rang.

"I'm not in," he snarled to Louderback. "To any one, d'ye hear? I'm through with this town. I'm through with every one in it. It's a phony. It's mad. It's vicious. Everybody here is phony and mad and vicious. Tell whoever it is to go to hell."

Louderback raised suffering eyes ceilingward and said into the telephone: "I'm sorry, Miss Stuart, but Mr. Royle—"

"Who?" yelled Ty. "Wait. I'll take it!"

"Ty," said Bonnie in a voice so odd a cold wave swept over him. "You've got to come over at once."

"What the devil's the matter, Bonnie?"

"Please. Hurry. It's—frightfully important."

"Give me three minutes to change my clothes."

When Ty reached Bonnie's house he found Clotilde weeping at the foot of the hall staircase.

"Clotilde, where's Miss Stuart? What's the trouble?"

Clotilde wrung her fat hands. "Oh, M'siue' Royle, is it truly you? Of a surety Ma'm'selle has become demented! She is up the stairs demolishing! I desired to telephone M'sieu' Butch-erre, but Ma'm'selle menaces me. . . . *Elle est une tempête!*"

Ty took the stairs three at a time and found Bonnie, her mauve crêpe negligée flying, snatching things out of drawers like a madwoman. The boudoir, her mother's, looked as if it had been struck by lightning.

"They aren't here!" screamed Bonnie. "Or I can't find them, which is the same thing. Oh, I'm such a fool!"

She collapsed on her mother's bed. Her hair was bound loosely by a gold ribbon and cascaded like molten honey down her back where the sun caught it.

Ty twisted his hat in his hands, looking away. Then he looked at her again. "Bonnie, why did you call me?"

"Oh, because I suddenly remembered. . . . And then when I looked through the mail . . ."

"Why didn't you call Butch? Clotilde says you didn't want Butch. Why . . . me, Bonnie?"

She sat very still then and drew the negligée about her. And she looked away from the burn in his eyes.

Ty went to her and hauled her to her feet and put his arms about her roughly. "Shall I tell you why?"

"Ty . . . You look so strange. Don't."

"I feel strange. I don't know what I'm doing. This is the nuttiest thing of all. But seeing you there on the bed, alone, scared, like a lost kid. . . . Bonnie, why did you think of me first, when you had something important to tell some one?"

"Ty, please. Let go of me."

"We're supposed to hate each other."

She struggled away from him then, not very strongly. "Please, Ty. You can't. You . . . mustn't."

"But I don't hate you," said Ty in a wondering voice. His arms tightened. "I just found that out. I don't hate you at all. I love you."

"Ty! No!"

He held her fast and close to him with one arm, and with the other hand he tilted her chin and made her look up at him. "And you love me. You've always loved me. You know that's true."

"Ty," she whispered. "Let me go."

"Nothing doing."

Her body trembled against him in its rigidity, like a piece of glass struck a heavy blow; and then all at once the rigidity shivered away and her softness gave itself to him utterly.

They stood there clinging to each other, their eyes closed against the hard, unyielding vision of the disordered room.

A long time later Bonnie whispered: "This *is* insane. You said so yourself."

"Then I don't want ever to be sane."

"We're both weak now. We feel lost and— That horrible funeral. . . ."

"We're both ourselves now. Bonnie, if their deaths did nothing else—"

She hid her face in his coat. "It's like a dream. I felt naked. Oh, it *is* good to be close to you this way, when I know you and I, of all the people in the world, are—"

"Kiss me, Bonnie. Christ, I've wanted to . . ." His lips touched her forehead, her eyelids, her lashes.

Bonnie pushed away from him suddenly and sat down on the *chaise longue*. "How about Butch?" she said in an empty voice.

"Oh," said Ty. The hunger and the gladness drained out of his haggard face very quickly. "I forgot Butch." And then he cried angrily: "To hell with Butch! To hell with everybody. I've been deprived of you long enough. You've been my whole life, the wrong way—we've got to make up for that. What I thought was hate—it's been with me, you've been with me, night and day since I was a kid in knee-pants. I've thought more of you and about you and around you. . . . I've more right to you than Butch has!"

"I couldn't hurt him, Ty," said Bonnie tonelessly. "He's the grandest person in the world."

"You don't love him," said Ty with scorn.

Her eyes fell. "I'm—I can't think clearly now. It's happened so suddenly. He loves me."

"You've been my whole life, Bonnie." He tried to take her in his arms again, seeking her mouth.

"No, Ty. I want some . . . time. Oh, it does sound corny! But you can't expect . . . I've got to get used to so much." .

"I'll never let go of you."

"No, Ty. Not now. You've got to promise me you won't say anything . . . about this to any one. I don't want Butch to know, yet. Maybe I'm wrong. Maybe . . . You've got to promise."

"Don't think of any one but me, Bonnie."

She shivered. "The only thing that's really emerged these last three days has been to see mother avenged. Oh, you simply can't say real things without sounding—dramatic! But I do want that . . . badly. She was the sweetest, most harmless darling in the world. Whoever killed her is a monster. He can't be human." Her mouth hardened. "If I knew who it was I'd kill him myself, just the way I'd put a mad dog out of the way."

"Let me hold you, darling—"

She went on fiercely: "Anybody—*anybody* who was in any way involved. . . . I'd hate him just as much as I'd hate the one who poisoned her." She took his hand. "So you see, Ty, why all this . . . why we have to wait."

He did not reply.

"Don't you want to find your father's murderer?"

"Do you have to ask me that?" he said in a low voice.

"Then let's search together. It's true—I see it now—we've always had at least one thing in common. . . . Ty, look at me." He looked at her. "I'm not refusing you, darling," she whispered, close to him. "When all this happened . . . I admit it, the only one I could think of was you. Ty, they—they died and left us alone!" Her chin began to quiver.

Ty sighed, and kissed it, and led her to the bed and sat her down. "All right, partner; we're partners. A little private war on a little private crime." He said cheerfully: "Let's have it."

"Oh, Ty!"

"What's all the excitement about?"

Bonnie gazed up at him through tears, smiling back. And then the smile chilled to a bleak determination, and she withdrew an envelope from her bosom.

"For some time," Bonnie said, sniffling away the last tear, "mother'd been receiving certain letters. I thought it was the usual crank mail and didn't pay any attention to them. Now . . . I don't know."

"Threatening letters?" said Ty swiftly. "Let's see that."

"Wait. Do you know anybody who sends cards in the mail? Do cards mean anything to you? Did Jack ever get any?"

"No. Cards? You mean playing-cards?"

"Yes, from the *Horseshoe Club*."

"Alessandro again, eh?" muttered Ty.

"I've been searching for those other envelopes, the ones that came before the—accident. But they're gone. When I got back from the funeral I began going through a heap of letters and telegrams of condolence and found—this. That's what made me remember the others."

Ty seized the envelope. It was addressed in a washed-out blue ink, and the writing—block-letters crudely penned—was scratchy.

"But it's addressed to Blythe Stuart," said Ty, puzzled. "And from the postmark it was mailed in Hollywood last night, the nineteenth. That's two days *after* her death! It doesn't make sense."

"That's why," said Bonnie tensely, "I think it *is* important. Maybe when we add up all the things that don't make sense, we'll have something that does."

Ty took out what lay in the envelope and stared at it.

"And this is all there was?"

"I told you it was mad."

The only thing in the envelope was a playing-card with a golden horseshoe engraved on its blue back.

The card was the nine of clubs.

Chapter X

Freedom of the Press

WHETHER IT WAS because of the story in the paper or because banishing indecision meant seeing Paula Paris again, Mr. Ellery Queen concluded a three-day struggle with himself by driving on Thursday morning to the white house in the hills.

And there, in one of the waiting-rooms intently conning Paula's *Seeing Stars* column in the previous Sunday's night-edition of the Monday morning paper, sat Inspector Glücke. When he saw Ellery he quickly stuffed the paper into his pocket.

"Are you one of Miss Paris's doting public, too?" asked Ellery, trying to conceal his own copy of the same edition.

"Hullo, Queen." Then the Inspector growled: "What's the use of beating around the bush? I see you've spotted that column. Darned funny, I call it."

"Not at all! Some mistake, no doubt."

"Sure, that's why you're here, no doubt. This dame's got some tall explaining to do. Give me the runaround since Monday, will she? I'll break her damned neck!"

"Please," said Ellery frigidly. "Miss Paris is a lady. Don't speak of her as if she were one of your policewomen."

"So she's hooked you, too," snarled Glücke. "Listen, Queen, this isn't the first time I've locked horns with her. Whenever she comes up with something important and I ask her—in a nice way, mind you—to come down to H.Q. for a chin, I get the same old baloney about her not being able to leave this house, this crowd phobia of hers—"

"I'll thank you," snapped Ellery, "to stop insulting her."

"I've subpoenaed her from Dan to Beersheba time after time and she always wriggles out, blast her. Doctor's affidavits—God knows what! I'll show her up for a phony some day, mark my words. Crowd phobia!"

"Meanwhile," said Ellery nastily, "the mountain again approaches Mohammed. By the way, what's doing?"

"No trace of that pilot yet. But it's only a question of time. My own hunch is he cached a plane somewhere near that plateau, maybe on the plateau itself. Then when he grounded Ty's plane he simply walked over to his own ship and flew off. You don't leave much of a trail in thin air."

"Hmm. I see Dr. Polk has confirmed my guess as to the cause of death officially."

"Autopsy showed an almost equal amount of morphine, a little over five grains, in each body. That means, Doc says, that a hell of a lot of morphine was dropped into those thermos bottles. Also some stuff Bronson calls sodium allurate, a new barbiturate compound—puts you rockababy."

"No wonder there was no struggle," muttered Ellery.

"Polk says the morphine and sodium allurate would put 'em to sleep in less than five minutes. While they were sleeping that terrific dose of morphine began to get in its licks, and they must have died in less than a half-hour."

"I suppose Jack went first, and Blythe thought he was merely dozing. The soporific performed an important function. You see that? While the first victim, whichever it was, was apparently asleep although really dying or dead the second one, unsuspicious because of that sleeping appearance of the other, would drink from the other thermos bottle. The allurate was a precaution—just in case they didn't both drink at the same time. Damn clever."

"Clever or not, it did the trick. Death by respiratory paralysis, Polk calls it. The hell of it is we can't trace the stuff. Sodium allurate's now available in any drug store, and you know what a cinch it is to lay your hands on morphine."

"Anything new?"

"Well," said Glücke bashfully, "I'm not saying—much. I tried tracing the sender of that hamper, but no dice; we found the place it came from, but the order was mailed in and they threw away the letter. Phony name, of course. The plane's sterile; the only fingerprints are Jack's and Blythe's and Ty's—this guy must have worn gloves throughout. On the other hand . . ."

"Yes? You're eating my heart out."

"Well, we sort of got a line on Jack's lady-friends. I swear he was a man, that billy-goat! Got a couple of interesting leads." The Inspector chuckled. "From the way the gals in this town are running for cover you'd think—"

"I'm not in the mood for love," said Ellery sombrely. "How about this man Park? Not a word about him in the news."

"Oh, he's dead."

"What!"

"Committed suicide. It'll be in tonight's papers. We found his duds intact in the cheap flophouse in Hollywood where he bedded down, with a note saying he was dying anyway, he was no good to his wife and crippled boy back East, who are on relief, he hadn't earned enough to keep his own body and soul together for years, and so he was throwing himself to the tuna."

"Oh," said Ellery. "Then you didn't find his body?"

"Listen, my large-brained friend," grinned Glücke. "If you think that suicide note is a phony, forget it. We verified the handwriting. For another thing, we've definitely established the old guy couldn't fly a plane."

Ellery shrugged. "By the way, do something for me after you get through boiling Miss Paris in oil."

"What?" demanded the Inspector suspiciously.

"Put a night and day tail on Bonnie."

"Bonnie Stuart? What the hell for?"

"Blamed if I know. It must be my Psyche sniffing." Then he added quite without humor: "Don't neglect that, Glücke. It may be of the essence, as our French friends say."

Just then one of Paula Paris's secretaries said with an impish smile: "Will you come in now, Inspector?"

When Inspector Glücke emerged from Paula's drawing-room he looked positively murderous.

"You like that dame in there, don't you?" he panted.

"What's the matter?" asked Ellery, alarmed.

"If you do, get her to talk. Sock her, kiss her, do anything—but find out where she picked up that story!"

"So she won't talk, eh?" murmured Ellery.

"No, and if she doesn't I'll drag her out of this house by that pretty gray streak in her hair and lock her up, crowd phobia or no crowd phobia! I'll book her on a charge of—of criminal conspiracy! Hold her as a material witness!"

"Here, calm down. You wouldn't try to coerce the press in this era of constitutional sensitivity, would you? Remember the lamentable case of that newspaperman Hoover."

"I'm warning you!" yelled Glücke, and he stamped out.

"All right, Mr. Queen," said the secretary.

Ellery entered the holy of holies soberly. He found Paula finishing an apple and looking lovely, serene, and reproachful.

"You, too?" She laughed and indicated a chair. "Don't look so tragic, Mr. Queen. Sit down and tell me why you've neglected me so shamefully."

"You do look beautiful," sighed Ellery. "Too beautiful to spend the next year in jail. I wonder—"

"What?"

"Which part of Glücke's advice to take—whether to sock you or kiss you. Which would you prefer?"

"Imagine that monster playing Cupid," murmured Paula. "Disgusting! Why haven't you at least phoned me?"

"Paula," said Ellery earnestly. "You know I'm your friend. What's behind this story?" He tapped the Monday newspaper.

"I asked a question first," she said, showing the dimple.

Ellery stared hungrily. She looked ravishing in a silver lamé hostess-gown with a trailing wrap-around skirt over Turkish trousers. "Aren't you afraid I'll take Glücke's advice?"

"My dear Mr. Queen," she said coolly, "you overestimate your capacity—and his—for inspiring fear."

"I," said Ellery, still staring, "am. Damned if I'm not!"

He advanced. But the lady did not retreat. She just looked at him. "I see," she said in a pitying way, "that Hollywood's been doing nasty things to you."

Mr. Queen stopped dead, coloring. Then he said sharply: "We've strayed from the point. I want to know—"

"How it is that my column ran a story in the night-edition of the Monday paper, appearing Sunday evening, to the effect that Jack and Blythe were kidnaped on their wedding trip?"

"Don't evade the question!"

"How masterful," murmured Paula, looking down demurely.

"Damn it," cried Ellery, "don't be coy with me! You must have written that item, judging by the relative times involved, *before* the actual kidnaping!" Paula said nothing. "How did you know they were *going* to be kidnaped?"

Paula sighed. "You know, Mr. Queen, you're a fascinating creature, but what makes you think you've the right to speak to me in that tone of voice?"

"Oh, my God. Paula, can't you see the spot you're in? Where'd you get that information?"

"I'll give you the same answer," replied Paula coldly, "that I gave Inspector Glücke. And that is—none of your business."

"You've *got* to tell me. I won't tell Glücke. But I must know."

"I think," said Paula, rising, "that will be all, Mr. Queen."

"Oh, no, it won't! You're going to tell me if I have to—"

"I'm not responsible for the care and feeding of your detective instincts."

"Blast my detective instincts. It's you I'm worried about."

"Really, Mr. Queen," cooed Paula.

Ellery scowled. "I—I didn't mean to say that."

"Oh, but you did." Paula smiled at him; there was that damned dimple again! "Are you *truly* worried about me?"

"I didn't mean it that way. I meant—"

She burst into laughter suddenly and collapsed in her chair. "Oh, this is so funny!" she gasped. "The great detective. The giant intellect. The human bloodhound!"

"What's so funny about what?" asked Ellery stiffly.

"You thinking I had something to do with those murders!" She dabbed at her eyes with a Batique handkerchief.

Ellery blushed. "That's—absurd! I never said anything like that!"

"But that's what you meant. I don't think so much of your finesse, Mr. Sherlock Holmes. Trying to put it on a personal basis! I ought to be furious with you. . . . I *am* furious with you!" And Ellery, bewildered, saw that she was indeed furious with him.

"But I assure you—"

"It's *contemptible*. You overlords, you Mussolinis, you strutting men! You were going to take the poor, psychically ill little newspaperwoman and give her a delightful free ride, weren't you? Make love to her, sweep her off her silly feet, talk dizzy pretty nonsense—dash gallantly into a romantic attack, hoping all the time you'd find out something damning about her!"

"I should like to point out, in self-defense," said Ellery with dignity, "that my 'romantic attack,' as you put it so romantically, was launched long before either Jack Royle or Blythe Stuart was murdered."

Paula half-turned her shapely back, applying the handkerchief to her eyes, and Ellery saw her shoulders twitch convulsively. Damn him for a clumsy fool! He had made her cry.

He was about to go to her and act terribly sympathetic and powerful, when to his astonishment and chagrin she faced him and he saw that she was laughing.

"I *am* a fool," he said shortly, pierced to the soul. And he stalked to the door. Laughing at *him*.

She flew past him to set her back against it. "Oh, darling, you are," she choked. "No. Don't go yet."

"I don't see," he said, not mollified, but not going, "why I should stay."

"Because I want you to."

"Oh, I *see*." Not frightfully clever, that remark. What had happened to his celebrated wits? It was bewildering.

"I'll tell you what," said Paula, facing him with large, soft eyes. "I'll give you something I didn't give that lout Glücke. Now will you stay?"

"Well . . ."

"There! We're friends again." She took him by the hand and led him back to the sofa. Ellery felt suddenly pleased with himself. Not badly handled, eh? Proved something, didn't it? She liked him. And her hand was so warm and small. She did have tiny hands for a woman of her size. Not that she was so big! Well . . . she wasn't small. But not fat. Certainly not! He didn't like small women. He had always maintained a man cheated himself when he took to his bosom a small woman; man was entitled to a "generous measure of devotion." Oho, not bad, that! He looked Paula over covertly. Yes, yes, generous was the word. The richness of the cornucopia and the aristocracy of a court sword. Beautiful patrician. Quite the grand lady. Queenly, you might say.

"Queenly," he chuckled, pressing her hand ardently.

"What?" But she did not withdraw her hand.

"Oh, nothing," said Ellery modestly. "A little pun I just thought of. Queenly . . . ha, ha! I mean—what were you going to tell me?"

"You do talk in riddles," sighed Paula, pulling him down with her. "I think that's why I like you. It's so much fun just trying to keep up."

Ellery wondered what would happen if he let his arm—oh, casually, of course—slip around her shoulders. They did look so strong, and yet womanly; were they soft? Would she flee to the arms of her phobia? Science—yes, the pure spirit of science—made it mandatory to try the experiment.

"What," he mumbled, trying the experiment, "happened?"

For one delicious instant she endured the reverent pressure of his arm. Her shoulders *were* strong and yet soft; just right, just right. Mr. Queen, in a heat of scientific ardor, squeezed. She jerked away from him like a blooded mare; then she sat still, coloring.

"I'll tell you just this," said Paula to her handkerchief, in a voice barely audible. "I—" And she stopped and got up and went to the nearby table and took a cigaret from a box.

Ellery was left with his arm in empty air, feeling rather foolish.

"Yes?" he said abruptly.

She sat down in the Cape Cod rocker, busy with the cigaret. "About an hour before the plane was stolen, I received a telephone call. I was told Jack and Blythe were about to be kidnaped."

"Where was the call from?"

"I can't tell you that."

"Don't you know?" She did not reply. "Who called?" Ellery jumped up. "Paula, did you know Jack and Blythe *were going to be murdered?*"

Her eyes flashed then. "Ellery Queen, how dare you ask me such a filthy question!"

"You bring it on yourself," he said bitterly. "Paula, it's—very queer."

She was wordless for a long time. Ellery mooned down at her sleek hair with its fascinating band of gray. Teach him a lesson, he thought. The one thing he didn't know anything about was women. And this one was exceptionally clever and elusive; you just couldn't grasp her. He turned and for the second time made for the door.

"Stop!" Paula cried. "Wait. I'll—I'll tell you what I can."

"I'm waiting," he growled.

"Oh, I shouldn't, but you're so . . . Please don't be angry with me."

Her splendid eyes shed such soft, luminous warmth that Ellery felt himself beginning to melt. He said hastily: "Well?"

"I do know who called." She spoke in a very low tone, her lashes resting on her cheeks. "I recognized the voice."

"Then this man didn't give you his name?"

"Don't be clever; I didn't *say* it was a man. As a matter of fact, this—person did give a name. The right name, because the voice checked."

Ellery frowned. "Then there was no secret about this caller's identity? He—or she—made no effort to conceal it?"

"Not the slightest."

"Who was it?"

"That's the one thing I won't tell you." She cried out at his sudden movement. "Oh, can't you see I mustn't? It's against every rule of newspaper ethics. And if I betrayed an informant once, I'd lose the confidence of the thousands of people who sell me information."

"But this is murder, Paula."

"I haven't committed any crime," she said stubbornly. "I would have notified the police, except that as a precaution I had the call traced, found it came from the airport, and by the time I got my information the plane had left and the police already knew what had happened."

"The airport." Ellery sucked his lower lip.

"And besides, how was I to know it would wind up in murder? Mr. Queen . . . Ellery, don't look at me that way!"

"You're asking me to take a great deal on faith. Even now it's your duty as a citizen to tell Glücke about that call, to tell him who it was that called you."

"Then I'm afraid," she half-whispered, "you'll have to take it that way."

"All right." And for the third time Ellery went to the door.

"Wait! I— Would you like a real tip?"

"More?" said Ellery sarcastically.

"It's only for your ears. I haven't printed it yet."

"Well, what is it?"

"More than a week ago—that's the thirteenth, last Wednesday—Jack and Blythe took a quiet little trip by plane."

"I didn't know about that," muttered Ellery. "Where did they go?"

"To the Chocolate Mountain estate of Blythe's father."

"I don't see anything remarkable in that. Jack and Blythe had made up by that time. Quite natural for two people intending to be married to visit the bride-to-be's father."

"Don't say I didn't warn you."

Ellery scowled. "You possess an omniscience, Paula, that disturbs me. Who poisoned Jack and Blythe?"

"*Quien sabe?*"

"What's more to the point, *why* were they poisoned?"

"Oh," she murmured, "so that's bothering you, eh?"

"You haven't answered my question."

"Darling," she sighed, "I'm just a lonely woman shut up in a big house, and all I know is what I read in the papers. Nevertheless, I'm beginning to think . . . I could guess."

"Guess!" He wrinkled his nose scornfully.

"And I'm also beginning to think . . . you can, too." They regarded each other in sober silence. Then Paula rose and smiled and gave him her hand. "Goodbye, Ellery. Come and see me some time. Heavens, I'm starting to talk like Mae West!"

But when he had gone, definitely this time, Paula stood still, staring at the panels of the door, her hands to her flushed face. Finally she went into her bedroom, shut the door, and sat down at her vanity and stared some more, this time at her reflection.

Mae West. . . . Well, why not? she thought defiantly. It merely took courage and a—and a certain natural equipment. And he did seem . . .

She shivered all at once, all over her body. The shiver came from a sensitive spot in the area of her shoulder where Mr. Queen, in a spirit of scientific research, had squeezed it.

Chapter XI

It's in the Cards

MR. QUEEN, EVEN as he drove away from Paula's house admiring his own charms in thought, felt a premonitory chill. He had the feeling that he had not heard quite everything.

The infallibility of his intuition was demonstrated the instant he stepped into Jacques Butcher's office. The Boy Wonder was reading Paula's column in a grim silence, while Sam Vix tried to look unhappy and Lew Bascom conducted a monologue shrewdly designed to distract the Boy Wonder's mind.

"I'm like the Phoenix," Lew was chattering. "It's won'erful how I rise outa my own ashes. We'll go ahead with the original plans for the picture, see, only we'll have Bonnie and Ty double for Blythe and Jack, an'—"

"Can it, Lew," warned Sam Vix.

"Here's the master-mind," said Lew. "Looka here, Queen. Don't you think—"

Without taking his eyes from the newsprint, Butch said curtly: "It's impossible. For one thing, Bonnie and Ty wouldn't do it, and I wouldn't blame them. For another, the Hays office would crack down. Too much notoriety already. Hollywood's always sensitive about murders."

"What's the matter, Butch?" demanded Ellery.

Butch looked up then, and Ellery was startled at the expression on his face. "Nothing much," he said with an ugly laugh. "Just another little scoop of Paula Paris's."

"Oh, you mean that Monday column?"

"Who said anything about Monday? This is today's paper."

"Today?" Ellery looked blank.

"Today. Paula says here that Ty and Bonnie are on their way to honeymoonland."

"What!"

"Aw, don't believe what that halfwit writes," said Lew. "Here, Butch, have a drink."

"But I just saw Paula," cried Ellery, "and she didn't say anything about that!"

"Maybe," said Vix dryly, "she thinks you can read."

Butch shrugged. "I guess I had to wake up some time. I think I've known all along that Bonnie and I . . . She's crazy about Ty; if I hadn't been so blind I'd have realized all that bickering covered up something deep." He smiled and poured himself a water-glass full of gin. "*Prosit!*"

"It's a dirty trick," mumbled Lew. "She can't do that to my pal."

"Do they know you know?" asked Ellery abruptly.

"I guess not. What difference does it make?"

"Where are they now?"

"I just had a call from Bonnie, gay as a lark—I mean, considering. They're going down to the *Horseshoe Club* to play cops and robbers with Alessandro. Good luck to 'em."

Ellery departed in haste. He found Bonnie's scarlet roadster parked outside the *Horseshoe Club*; the interior was depressingly deserted, with charwomen scrubbing up the marks of the expensive shoes of Hollywood's élite and one bartender listlessly wiping glasses.

Bonnie and Ty were leaning side by side over the horseshoe-shaped desk in Alessandro's office, and Alessandro sat quietly before them, drumming a tune with his fingers.

"This seems to be my bad day," he remarked dryly when he saw Ellery. "It's all right, Joe; these folks don't pack rods. Well, shoot. What's on your mind?"

"Hello, Mr. Queen," cried Bonnie. She looked lovely and fresh in a tailored gabardine suit and a crimson jelly-roll of a hat tipped on her honey hair; her cheeks were pink with excitement. "We were just asking Mr. Alessandro about those I O U's."

So they didn't know yet, Ellery thought. He grinned: "Coincidence. That's why I'm here, too."

"You *and* Inspector Glücke," chuckled the little fat gambler. "The flattie! Only he was here Monday."

"I don't care about that," barked Ty. "You admit my dad owed you a hundred and ten thousand dollars?"

"Sure I admit it. It's true."

"Then how is it those I O U's were found on his body?"

"Because," said Alessandro gently, "he paid up."

"Oh, he did, did he? When?"

"On Thursday the fourteenth—just a week ago."

"And with what?"

"With good stiff American dough. Thousand-buck bills."

"You're a liar."

The man called Joe growled. But Alessandro smiled. "I've stood a lot from you people," he said amiably, "you and your folks, get me? I ought to give Joe here the office to slug you for that crack, Royle. Only your old man just got his, and maybe you're a little excited."

"You and your guerillas don't scare me."

"So you think maybe I had something to do with those murders, hey?" Alessandro snarled. "I warn you, Royle, lay off. I run a clean joint and I got a reputation in this town. Lay off, if you know what's good for you!"

Bonnie sucked in her breath. But then her eyes snapped and she snatched an envelope from her purse and tossed it on the desk. "Maybe you can explain this!"

Ellery goggled as he saw Alessandro take a blue-backed playing-card out of the envelope and stare at it. One of those cryptic messages! He groaned inwardly. They had utterly slipped his mind. He was growing senile.

Alessandro shrugged. "It comes from the Club, all right. So what?"

"That," growled Ty, "is what we're trying to find out."

The gambler shook his head. "No dice. Anybody could get hold of our cards. Hundreds play here every week, and we give dozens of packs away as souvenirs."

"I imagine," said Ellery hurriedly, "Alessandro is right. We're not learning anything here. Coming, you two?"

He herded them out before they could protest, and the instant they were in Bonnie's roadster he snapped: "Bonnie, let me see that envelope."

Bonnie gave it to him. He studied it intently, then put it into his pocket.

"Here, I want that," said Bonnie. "It's important. It's a clue."

"You're a better man than I am for spotting it as such," said Ellery. "I'll keep it, if you don't mind—as I happen to have kept the others. Oh, I'm an idiot!"

Bonnie almost ran over a Russian wolfhound. "You!" she cried. "Then it was you—"

"Yes, yes," said Ellery impatiently. "I fancy I'm better qualified for all my forgetfulness. Magna Studios, Bonnie."

Ty, who was scarcely listening, muttered: "He's lying. It couldn't be anything but a lie."

"What?"

"Alessandro. We've only got his word that those I O U's were paid. Suppose dad refused to pay, or what's more likely pointed out how impossible it was for him to pay? It would have been pie for Alessandro to get one of his plug-uglies to play the pilot and after poisoning dad and Blythe put the torn I O U's into dad's pocket."

"But why, Ty?" frowned Bonnie.

"Because he'd know he'd never get his money anyway. Because, knowing that, he'd want revenge. And planting the I O U's on dad would make it seem to the police as if the money was paid, in that way eliminating in their minds any possible motive on Alessandro's part."

"A little subtle," said Ellery, "but conceivable."

"But even if that's so," said Bonnie, "why mother? Don't you see, Ty, that's the thing that confuses everything? Why was mother poisoned, too?"

"I don't know," said Ty doggedly. "All I know is dad couldn't possibly have laid his hands on a hundred and ten grand. He had no money, and nowhere to get any."

"By the way," remarked Ellery casually, "did you people know that in today's column Paula Paris hints you two have made up rather thoroughly?"

Bonnie went slowly pale, and Ty blinked several times. Bonnie pulled up to a curb and said: "What?"

"She says you're well on your way to love and kisses."

Bonnie looked for a moment as if she were going to have a crying spell again. But then her chin came up and she turned on Ty furiously. "And you *promised* me!"

"But, Bonnie—" began Ty, still blinking.

"You—*fiend!*"

"Bonnie! You certainly don't think—"

"Don't speak to me, you publicity hound," said Bonnie with a sick, heavy, hot loathing.

That was the start of an extraordinary day, and every one was thoroughly miserable; and when they got to the Boy Wonder's office Bonnie went to him and deliberately kissed his mouth and then took up the phone and asked Madge to get Paula Paris on the wire.

Butch looked bewilderedly from Bonnie to Ty; both their faces were red with anger.

"Miss Paris? This is Bonnie Stuart speaking. I've just heard that, with your usual cleverness, you've found out that Ty Royle and I are going to be married, or something as foul and lying as that."

"I'm afraid I don't understand," murmured Paula.

"If you don't want to be sued for libel you'll please print a retraction of that story at once!"

"But, Bonnie, I had it on excellent authority—"

"No doubt. Well, I detest him as much as I detest you for listening to him!"

"But I don't understand. Ty Royle—"

"You heard me, Miss Paris." Bonnie slammed the phone down and glared at Ty.

"Well, well," chuckled Lew. "This is like old times, for gossakes. Now about that picture—"

"Then it isn't true?" asked Butcher slowly.

"Of course not! And as far as this contemptible—person is concerned . . ."

Ty turned on his heel and walked out. Ellery hurried after him. "You didn't give that story to Paula?"

"What do you think I am?"

"Hmm. Very pretty scene." Ellery glanced at him sidewise. "I shouldn't be surprised if she did it herself."

"What!" exploded Ty. He stopped short. "Well, by God, maybe you're right. She's been stringing me along. I see it all now—the whole thing, leading me on just so she could turn around and slap me down the way she's always done. What a rotten trick!"

"That's women for you," sighed Ellery.

"I thought at first it was that damned Frenchwoman. She's the only other one who could possibly have overheard."

"Oh, then you did get cuddly?"

"Well . . . But it's over now—finished! I'm through with that scheming little double-crosser for good!"

"Nobly resolved," said Ellery heartily. "Man's much better off alone. Where are you going now?"

"Hell, I don't know." They were standing before a row of pretty little stone bungalows. "That's funny. Here's dad's old dressing-room. Force of habit, eh?" Ty muttered: "If you don't mind, Queen, I think I'll sort of go in alone."

"Not a bit of it," said Ellery, taking his arm. "We've both been made fools of, so we ought to pool our misery."

And he went into John Royle's studio bungalow with Ty.

And found the key to the code.

He found it by accident, merely because he was in the dead man's room and it occurred to him that no one had disturbed it since the elder Royle's death. There was even a soiled towel, with the stains of make-up on it, lying on the make-up table beside a new-looking portable typewriter.

So Ellery poked about while Ty lay down on the couch and stared stonily at the oyster-white ceiling; and almost the first thing Ellery found in the table drawer was a creased and crumpled sheet of ordinary yellow paper, 8½ by 11 inches in size, one side blank and the other well-filled with typewritten words.

And Ellery took one look at the capitalized, underscored heading: MEANINGS OF THE CARDS, and let out a whoop that brought Ty to his feet.

"What is it? What's the matter?"

"I've found it!" yelled Ellery. "Of all the colossal breaks. The cards! All typed out. Thanks, kind Fates. Yes, here's the whole thing. . . . Wait a minute. Is it possible—"

Ty frowned over the sheet. Ellery whipped the cover off the portable typewriter, rummaged until he found a sheet of blank stationery, pushed it under the carriage, and began rapidly to type, referring to the crumpled yellow paper from time to time. And as he typed, the gladness went out of his face, and it became dark with thought.

He got up, replaced the cover of the typewriter, put the papers carefully into his pocket, picked up the machine, and said in a flat voice: "Come along, Ty."

They found Bonnie and the Boy Wonder in each other's arms, Bonnie's face still stormy and Butch looking wildly happy. Lew sat grinning at them both, like a benevolent satyr.

"We come bearing news," said Ellery. "Unhand her, Butch. This requires confabulation."

"Whassa matter?" asked Lew suspiciously.

"Plenty. I don't know whether you know it or not, Butch, but Ty and Bonnie do. Blythe for some time before last Sunday had been receiving anonymous messages."

"I didn't know that," said Butch slowly.

"What kind?" frowned Lew. "Threats?"

"Plain envelopes addressed in block letters by obviously a post-office pen, mailed in Hollywood, and containing nothing but playing-cards." He took out his wallet and tossed over a small bundle of envelopes bound by an elastic. Butch and Lew examined them incredulously.

"*Horseshoe Club*," muttered Lew.

"But what do they mean?" demanded Butch. "Bonnie, why didn't you tell me?"

"I didn't think they were important."

"I'm more to blame. I've been carrying these things around in my pocket and didn't once think of them after Sunday. But just now," said Ellery, "I found the key to those cards."

He laid down on Butcher's desk the yellow sheet. Lew and Butch and Bonnie read it with blank faces.

"I don't understand," murmured Bonnie. "It looks like some kind of fortune-telling."

"It told a remarkably grim fortune," drawled Ellery. "This—you might call it a codex—tells what each card sent through the mail means." He picked up the envelopes. "The first envelope Blythe received was mailed on the eleventh of this month and delivered on the twelfth. That was nine days ago, or five days before the murders. And what was in the envelope? Two playing-cards —the knave and seven of spades."

Automatically they craned at the yellow sheet. The meaning assigned to both the knave and seven of spades was: "An Enemy."

"Two enemies, then," said Ellery. "Just as if someone had written: 'Watch yourself. We're both after you.'"

"Two—enemies?" said Bonnie damply. There was horror in her eyes as she glanced, as if against her will, at Ty's pale face. "Two!"

"The second envelope arrived on Friday the fifteenth. And it contained two cards also—the ten of spades and the two of clubs. And what do they mean?"

"'Great Trouble,'" muttered Ty. "That's the spade ten. And 'In Two Days or Two Weeks' on the deuce of clubs."

"Two days," cried Bonnie. "Friday the fifteenth—and mother was murdered on Sunday the seventeenth!"

"And on Sunday the seventeenth, at the field," continued Ellery, "I saw Clotilde deliver the third envelope. I picked it up after your mother, Bonnie, threw it away. It was this—the eight of spades, torn in half. If you'll refer to that note at the bottom of the sheet, you'll see that the meaning is intended to become reversed when a card is torn in half. Consequently the message becomes—only a few minutes before the plane is hijacked and the murder occurs: 'Threatened Danger Will NOT Be Warded Off!'"

"This," said Butcher pallidly, "is the most childish nonsense I've ever heard of. It's completely incredible."

"Yet here it is." Ellery shrugged. "And just now Bonnie gave me the last message—the nine of clubs inclosed, meaning: 'Last Warning.' That seems

MEANINGS OF THE CARDS

	DIAMONDS	HEARTS	CLUBS	SPADES
KING	Man with Fair Hair	Man with Red Hair	Man with Dark Hair	Strange Man
QUEEN	Woman with Fair Hair	Woman with Red Hair	Woman with Dark Hair	Strange Woman
JACK	A Messenger	A Preacher	A Lawbreaker	An Enemy
TEN	Large Sum of Money	A Surprise	Gambling	Great Trouble
NINE	Lovers' Quarrel	Disappointment	Last Warning	Grief
EIGHT	A Jewel	Thoughts of Marriage	An Accident	Threatened Danger Will Be Warded Off
SEVEN	A Journey	Jealousy	Prison	An Enemy
SIX	Beware of Speculation	Beware of Scandal	Beware of Overwork	Beware of Malicious Gossip
FIVE	A Telegram	Unexpected Meeting	A Change	Unpleasant Meeting
FOUR	A Diamond Ring	Broken Engagement	A Secret	Have Nothing More to Do with a Certain Person about Whom You Are Doubtful
THREE	Quarrel over Money	Obstacles in Way of Love	Obstacles in Way of Success	Obstacles in Way of Reconciliation
TWO	Trouble Caused by Deception	An Introduction	In Two Days or Two Weeks	Tears
ACE	Telephone Call	Invitation	Wealth	Death

(The Meaning Becomes Reversed When a Card Appears Torn in Half) the most incredible nonsense of all, Butch, since this 'warning' was *sent to Blythe two days after her death.*"

The Boy Wonder looked angry. "It was bad enough before, but this . . . Damn it, how can you credit such stuff? But if we must . . . it does look as if whoever mailed this last letter didn't know Blythe was dead, doesn't it? And since all the letters were obviously the work of the same person, I can't see the relevance of any of it."

"It's ridic'lous," jeered Lew. "Plain nut stuff." Nevertheless he asked: "Say, where'd you find this sheet?"

"In Jack Royle's dressing-room." Ellery took the cover off the portable typewriter. "And what's more, if you'll examine this sample of typewriting I just made on this machine and compare it with the typing on the yellow sheet, you'll find that the small h's and r's, for instance, have identically broken serifs. Identically broken," he repeated with a sudden thoughtful note; and he seized a paperweight sun-glass on Butcher's desk and examined the keys in question. Freshly filed! But he put the glass down and merely said: "There's no doubt about it. This code-sheet was typed on Jack Royle's type-writer. It *was* your dad's, Ty?"

Ty said: "Yes. Yes, of course," and turned away.

"Jack?" repeated Butch in a dazed voice.

Lew snarled: "Aw, go on. What would Jack want to play games for?" but the snarl was somehow unconvincing. He glanced uneasily at Bonnie.

Bonnie said huskily: "On Jack Royle's typewriter. . . . You're sure of that?"

"Absolutely. Those broken keys are as good as fingerprints."

"Ty Royle, did you hear that?" asked Bonnie of his back, her eyes flashing. "Did you?"

"What do you want?" muttered Ty, without turning.

"What do I want?" screamed Bonnie. "I want you to turn around and look me in the face! Your father typed that sheet—your father sent those notes with the cards in them to mother—*your father killed my mother!*"

He turned then, defensively, his face sullen. "You're hysterical or you'd know that's a stupid, silly accusation."

"Is it?" cried Bonnie. "I *knew* there was something funny about his repent-ance, about proposing marriage to mother after so many years of hating her. Now I know he was lying all the time, playing a game—yes, Lew, but a hor-rible one!—covering himself up against the time when he expected to—to murder her. The engagement, the wedding, it was all a trap! He hired somebody to pretend to kidnap them and then poisoned my mother with his own foul hands!"

"And himself, too, I suppose?" said Ty savagely.

"Yes, because when he realized what an awful thing he'd done he had the first decent impulse of his life and put an end to it!"

"I'm not going to fight with you, Bonnie," said Ty in a low voice.

"Enemies . . . *two* enemies! Well, why not? You *and* your father! That neat little love scene yesterday . . . oh, you think you're clever, too. You *know* he killed my mother and you're trying to cover him up. For all I know you may have helped him plan it—you murderer!"

Ty made two fists and then opened them. He rubbed the back of one hand for a moment as if it itched, or pained, him. Then without a word he walked out of the office.

Bonnie flew, weeping, into Butcher's arms.

But later, when she got home and Clotilde let her in, and she crept up to her room and without undressing lay down on her bed, Bonnie wondered at herself in a dark corner of her aching head. Was it really true? Could it really be? Had he been acting yesterday when he said he loved her? Suspicions were horrible. She could have sworn . . . And yet there it was. The facts were all against him. Who could have told Paula Paris about their reconciliation? Only Ty. And after she had begged him not to! And then, finding that sheet . . . You couldn't wipe out years and years of hatred just by uttering three one-syllable words.

Oh, Ty, you monster!

Bonnie remained in her room, shut in against the world, sleepless, sick, and empty. The night passed, and it was a long night peopled with so many shadows that at three o'clock in the morning, railing at her nerves and yet twitchy with morbid thoughts, she got up and switched on all the lights. She did not close her eyes the whole night.

At eight she admitted Clotilde, who was frantic.

"Oh, Bonnie, you shall make yourself ill! See, I have brought *p'tit déjeuner. Galettes et marmelade—*"

"No, thanks, 'Tilde," said Bonnie wearily. "More letters?"

She dipped into the heap of envelopes on the tray. "Dear Bonnie Stuart: My heart goes out to you in your grief, and I want to tell you how much I feel for you. . . ." Words. Why couldn't people let her alone? And yet that was ungrateful. They *were* dears, and they had loved Blythe so. . . .

Her heart stopped.

There was an envelope—it looked so horribly familiar. . . . She tore an end off with shaking fingers. But no, it couldn't be. This one was addressed in typewriting, sloppily. But the envelope, the Hollywood postmark . . .

A blue playing-card dropped out. The seven of spades.

Nothing more.

Clotilde stared at her open-mouthed. *"Mais chérie, il semble que tu—"*

Bonnie breathed: "Go away, 'Tilde."

The seven of spades. *Again* . . . "An Enemy" . . .

Bonnie dropped the card and envelope as if they were foul, slimy things. And for the first time in her life, as she crouched in her tumbled bed with Clotilde gaping at her, she felt weak with pure fright.

An enemy. Ty . . . Ty was her only enemy.

Before Ellery left the Magna lot he went on impulse, still toting Jack

Royle's typewriter, to the studio street where the stars' stone bungalows were and quietly let himself into Blythe Stuart's dressing-room.

And there, as he had half-expected, he found a carbon copy on yellow paper of the "Meanings of the Cards." In a drawer, hidden away.

So Blythe *had* known what the cards meant! Ellery had been positive her too casual dismissal of the letters had covered a frightened knowledge.

He slipped out and made for the nearest public telephone.

"Paula? Ellery Queen."

"How nice! And so soon, too." Her voice was happy.

"I suppose," said Ellery abruptly, "it's useless for me to ask where you learned about Ty and Bonnie."

"Quite useless, Sir Snoop."

"I imagine it was that Clotilde—it couldn't have been any one else. There's loyal service for you!"

"You won't pump me, my dear Mr. Queen," she said; but from something defensive in her tone Ellery knew he had guessed the truth.

"Or why you didn't tell me this morning when I saw you. However, this is all beside the point. Paula, would you say Jack Royle killed Blythe Stuart— that his change of heart, the engagement, the wedding, were all part of a careful, murderous scheme to take his revenge on her?"

"That," said Paula crisply, "is the silliest theory of the crime I've heard yet. Why, Jack couldn't possibly . . . Is it yours?"

"Bonnie Stuart's."

"Oh." She sighed. "The poor child gave me Hail Columbia over the phone a few moments ago. I suppose running that yarn *was* a rotten trick, so soon after the funeral. But that's the trouble with newspaper work. You can't be nice, and efficient, too."

"Look, Paula. Will you do me one enormous favor? Print that retraction of the reconciliation story Bonnie demanded. Right away."

"Why?" Her voice was instantly curious.

"Because I ask you to."

"Ouch! You are possessive, aren't you?"

"Forget personalities or your job. This is—vital. Do you know the derivation of that word? Paula, you must. Swing back into the old line—their furious feud from childhood, how they detest each other, how the death of their parents has driven them farther apart. Feed them raw meat. Keep them fighting."

Paula said slowly: "Just why do you want to keep those poor mixed-up kids apart?"

"Because," said Ellery, "they're in love."

"How logical you are! Or are you a misogamist with a mission in the world? Keep them apart *because* they're in love! Why?"

"Because," replied Ellery grimly, "it happens to be very, very dangerous for them to *be* in love."

"Oh." Then Paula said with a catch in her voice: "Aren't we all?" and hung up.

PART THREE

Chapter XII

International Mailers, Inc.

ELLERY, SAM VIX, and Lew Bascom were having breakfast Friday morning in the Magna commissary when Alan Clark strolled in, sat down beside them on a stool, and said to the aged waitress behind the counter: "Coffee, beautiful."

"Oh, Alan."

"Here I am. What's on your mind?"

"I've been wondering," said Ellery. "Just what is my status now in the studio?"

"Status?" The agent stared. "What d'ye mean? You're on the payroll, aren't you?"

"His conscience is havin' an attack of the shakes," grinned Lew. "I never saw such a guy for virtue. Like the little studio steno I was out with last night. I says to her—"

"I know," protested Ellery, "but I was hired to work on the Royle-Stuart picture, and there is no Royle-Stuart picture any more."

"Isn't that too bad?" said Clark, shaking his head over the coffee. "My heart bleeds for you."

"But what am I supposed to do, Alan? After all, I'm drawing fifteen hundred a week!"

The three men shook their heads in unison. "He's drawing fifteen hundred a week," said Sam Vix pityingly. "Now that's what I call a stinking shame."

"Look, Queen," sighed the agent. "Was it your fault Jack Royle and Blythe Stuart got themselves purged?"

"I don't see what that has to do with it."

"Say, whose side are you on, anyway—labor or capital?" demanded Lew. "We writers got some rights!"

"Your contract wasn't drawn up, if I may say so," said Clark modestly, "by a cluck. You've got little Alan in there batting for you all the time, remember that. You contracted to work on a Royle-Stuart picture, and there's nothing in that immortal document about murders."

"That's just the point; the picture will never be made. It's been withdrawn from schedule. Butch announced its withdrawal only this morning."

"What of it? Your contract calls for an eight-week guarantee. So, picture or no picture, you stay here till you collect eight weeks' salary. Or, to put it crudely, till you've wrapped your bankbook around twelve thousand bucks."

"It's criminal," muttered Ellery.

"Nah, it's life," said Clark, rising. "Now forget it. Being ashamed to draw a salary! Who ever heard of such a thing?"

"But how can I take it? I can't just sit around here—"

"He can't just sit around here," exploded Lew. "Listen, drizzle-puss, I'm sittin' around here for a lot less than fifteen hundred bucks a week!"

"Me, too," sighed the publicity man.

"Work it out in detecting," suggested Clark. "You're a detective, aren't you?"

"I could use some o' that dough," Lew grumbled into his raw egg-and-tomato juice. "Say, Queen, how's about letting me have a couple o' C's till next Friday?"

"This is where I came in," said the agent hurriedly. "Got to bawl out a producer; he's knifing one of my best clients in the back."

"Just till next Friday," said Lew as Clark went away.

"If you let this pirate put the bee on you," growled Sam Vix, "you're a bigger sap than you pretend to be. Next Friday! What's the matter with this Friday? You get paid today, you fat bastard."

"Who asked you to butt in?" said Lew hotly. "You know I'm savin' up for my old age. I'm gonna start a chicken farm."

"You mean the kind that clucks 'Daddy'?" jeered Vix. "You save for your old age! You're not going to have an old age. Unless your stomach's lined with chromium."

"Anyway, I saw him first!"

"That," said the publicity man with a grin, "was one tough break—for him. Well, so long. I work for my lousy pittance."

"By the way, Sam," said Ellery absently. "I've been meaning to ask you. Where were you last Sunday?"

"Me?" The one-eyed man looked astonished. "Over at Reed Island, making arrangements for the wedding reception."

"I know, but when I phoned the Island after the plane was snatched Sunday, I was told you weren't there."

Vix scowled down at him. "What the hell you doing—taking Clark's advice seriously?"

"No offense," smiled Ellery. "I just thought I'd ask you before Glücke got around to it."

"Take a tip from me and lay off that kind of chatter. It isn't healthy." And Vix stalked off, the black patch over his eye quivering with indignation.

"What's the matter with *him*?" murmured Ellery, offering his coffee-cup to the waitress to be replenished.

Lew chuckled. "Some guys are born hatin' spinach and other guys work up a terrific peeve if you split an infinitive. Sam's weakness is he don't think it's funny to be suspected of a murder. And he thinks it's twice as not funny in the case of a double feature."

"Can't a man ask an innocent question?"

"Yeah," said Lew dryly. "Pretty soon you'll be askin' me an innocent question, too. Like: 'Was that really you standin' beside me when this masked guy hijacked Ty's plane?' "

"Well, you can't always believe your eyes," said Ellery with a grin.

"Sure not. I mighta been my twin brother."

"Have you a twin brother?" asked Ellery, startled.

"You know why I like you?" sighed Lew. "Because you're such a pushover for a gag. Of course I ain't got no twin brother!"

"I might have known that the Author of us all wouldn't repeat a mistake of *that* magnitude," said Ellery sadly. "Oh, Ty! Come over here and join us in some breakfast."

Ty Royle strode over, freshly shaven but looking as if he had spent a hectic night. "Had mine, thanks. Queen, I'd like to talk to you."

"Yes?"

Ty squatted on the stool Sam Vix had vacated, put his elbow on the counter, and ran his fingers through his hair.

"All right, all right," grumbled Lew, getting up. "I know a stage wait when I hear one."

"Don't go, Lew," said Ty wearily. "You may be able to help, too."

Ellery and Lew exchanged glances. "Sure, kid," said Lew, seating himself. "What's on your mind?"

"Bonnie."

"Oh," said Ellery.

"What's she pulled on you now?" asked Lew sympathetically.

"It's that business of yesterday afternoon." Ty fiddled with Vix's coffee-cup. "Her saying that dad was behind the—well, the whole thing. I've been up all night thinking it over. I was sore as a boil at first. But I found out something about myself last night."

"Yes?" said Ellery with a frown.

"Something's happened to me. Since Wednesday. I don't feel the way I used to about her. In fact, I feel . . . just the opposite." He banged the cup. "Oh, what the hell's the use of fighting myself any longer? I'm in love with her!"

"You feelin' good?" growled Lew.

"It's no use, Lew. I'm hooked for fair this time."

"With all the fluffs you've played!"

Ty smiled wryly. "That's almost exactly what I said to dad when I found out he'd decided he loved Blythe."

"Yes," murmured Ellery, "history has a fascinating way of repeating itself." He sent Lew a warning look, and Lew nodded.

"Listen, kid, it's your imagination and this climate," said Lew in a fatherly tone. "Jack's death sort of knocked you out of kilter, and you know what the warm sun does to young animals. Listen to your Uncle Looey. This love stuff don't get you anything but trouble. Take me, for instance. You don't see me going woozy-eyed over any one dame, do you? Hell, if I had your pan I'd make Casanova look like Cousin Hiram heavin' his first pass at the college widow!"

Ty shook his head. "No go, Lew. I don't want any woman but Bonnie. That stuff's out for good."

"Well," shrugged Lew, "it's your funeral. Don't say I didn't warn you."

"Look, Lew." Ty seemed embarrassed. "You're about as close to Bonnie as . . . I mean, I was thinking you might try to talk to her."

Ellery shook his head violently over Ty's shoulder.

"Who, me?" said Lew in a shocked voice. "What d'ye wanta make me, accessory to a crime? I wouldn't have it on my conscience. I'm no John Alden. Do your own courtin'."

"How about you, Queen? Bonnie's convinced that dad—well, you heard her yesterday. Somebody's got to show her how wrong she is. She obviously won't listen to me."

"Why don't you let matters ride for a while?" said Ellery lightly. "Give her time to cool off. She'll probably realize by herself, in time, that it's all a mistake."

"Sure, what's the rush? Give the kid a chance to get her bearings. Besides," said Lew, "there's Butch."

Ty was silent. Then he said: "Butch . . . Maybe you're right. It is less than a week."

The cashier at the commissary desk called out: "Mr. Queen, there's a call for you on this phone."

Ellery excused himself and went to the desk.

"Hello—Mr. Queen? This is Bonnie Stuart."

"Oh," said Ellery. "Yes?" He glanced at Ty, who was listening glumly as Lew waved his arms in earnest exhortation.

"I've something to show you," said Bonnie strangely. "It . . . came this morning."

"Oh, I see." Then Ellery said in a loud tone: "How about lunch?"

"But can't you come over now?"

"Sorry, I've something important to do. Shall we say the Derby on Vine at one o'clock?"

"I'll be there," said Bonnie curtly, and hung up.

Ellery strolled back to the counter. Ty interrupted Lew in the middle of a sentence. "Just the same, there's one thing we ought to do right away."

"What's that?" asked Ellery.

"I've been thinking about those anonymous letters. I think Inspector Glücke ought to be told about them."

"That nut stuff," scoffed Lew. "No one but a screw-loose would mail cards to a dame when she was dead."

Ellery lit a cigaret. "Coincidence! I've been giving the matter considerable thought, too. And I believe I've worked out a practical theory."

"You're a better man than I am, then," said Ty gloomily.

"You see, there are really only two plausible inferences to be drawn from the strange fact Lew's just mentioned—I mean, this business of mailing a letter to a dead woman. Oh, of course there's always the possibility that the sender didn't know Blythe was dead, but you'll agree we can dismiss that as a huge improbability; Sam Vix and the gentlemen of the press associations have taken care of that."

"Maybe this palooka can't read," said Lew.

"Is he deaf, too? Illiteracy is scarcely the answer in these days of news broadcasting via the radio. Besides, the envelopes were addressed by some one who could write. No, no, that can't be the answer."

"Don't you know a gag when you hear one?" said Lew disgustedly.

"The two inferences seem to me to be all-inclusive. The first is the normal, obvious inference you've already voiced, Lew: that is, that the sender is a crank; that the envelopes, the cards, the whole childish business indicate the workings of a deranged mentality. It's conceivable that such a mentality would see nothing unreasonable about continuing to send the cards even after the object of his interest has died."

"Well, that's my guess," said Lew.

"And yet I get the feeling," said Ty thoughtfully, "that while the sender of those cards may be slightly off, he isn't just a nut."

"A feeling," murmured Ellery, "I share. And if he *is* sane, the alternate inference arises."

"What's that?" demanded Lew.

Ellery rose and picked up his check. "I was going to devote the morning," he said with a smile, "to a line of investigation which would prove or disprove it. Would you care to join me, gentlemen?"

While Lew and Ty waited, mystified, Ellery borrowed the Los Angeles Classified Directory at the commissary desk and spent ten minutes poring over it.

"No luck," he said, frowning. "I'll try Information." He closeted himself in one of the telephone booths, emerging a few minutes later looking pleased.

"Simpler than I expected. We've got one shot in the dark—thank heaven there aren't dozens."

"Dozens of what?" asked Ty, puzzled.

"Shots in the dark," said Lew. "See how simple it is?"

Ellery directed Ty to drive his sport roadster down Melrose to Vine, and up Vine to Sunset, and west on Sunset to Wilcox. On Wilcox, between Selma Avenue and Hollywood Boulevard, Ellery jumped out and hurried up the steps of the new post-office, vanishing within.

Ty and Lew looked at each other.

"You got me," said Lew. "Maybe it's a new kind of treasure hunt."

Ellery was gone fifteen minutes. "The postmaster," he announced cheerfully, "says nix. I didn't have much hope."

"Then your idea is out?" asked Ty.

"Not at all. Visiting the Hollywood postmaster was a precaution. Drive around to Hollywood Boulevard, Ty. I think our destination's just past Vine Street—between Vine and Argyle Avenue."

Miraculously, they found a parking space near Hollywood's busiest intersection.

"Now what?" said Lew.

"Now we'll see. It's this building. Come on."

Ellery preceded them into the office building across the street from the bank and theatre. He consulted the directory in the lobby, nodded, and made for the elevator, Ty and Lew meekly following.

"Third," said Ellery.

They got out at the third floor. Ellery looked cautiously about, then drew a leather case out of his pocket. He took a glittering object from the case and returned the case to his pocket.

"The idea is," he said, "that I'm somebody in the L. A. police department and that you two are somebody's assistants. If we don't put up an imposing front, we'll never get the information I'm after."

"But how are you going to get away with whatever you're trying to get away with?" asked Ty with a faint smile.

"Remember the Ohippi case? I had something to do with solving it, and this"—he opened his hand—"is a token of your *pueblo's* gratitude, up to and including Glücke, poor devil. Honorary Deputy Commissioner's badge. Look tough, you two, and keep your mouths shut."

He walked down the corridor to a door with a pebbled glass front on which was daubed in unimposing black letters:

INTERNATIONAL MAILERS, INC.
T. H. LUCEY
Los Angeles Division

The office proved to be a box-like chamber with one streaky window, a scratched filing cabinet, a telephone, a littered desk, and a dusty chair. In the chair sat a depressed-looking man of forty-odd with thinning hair carefully plastered to his skull. He was sucking a lollipop morosely as he read a dog-eared copy of *True Murder Stories*.

"You Lucey?" growled Ellery, fists in his pockets.

The stick of the lollipop tilted belligerently as Mr. Lucey swung about. His fishy eyes examined the three faces.

"Yeah. So what?"

Ellery withdrew his right hand from his pocket, opened his fist, permitted the mote-choked sun to touch the gold badge in his palm for a moment, and returned the badge to his pocket.

"Headquarters," he said gruffly. "Few questions we want to ask you."

"Dicks, huh." The man took the lollipop out of his mouth. "Go peddle your eggs somewheres else. I ain't done nothin'."

"Climb down, buddy. What kind of business do you run?"

"Say, whadda ya think this is, Russia?" Mr. Lucey slammed the magazine down and rose, a vision of American indignation. "We run a legitimate racket, Mister, and you got no right to question me about it! Say," he added suspiciously, "you from the Fed'ral gov'ment?"

Ellery, who had not anticipated this sturdy resistance, felt helpless. But when he heard Lew Bascom snicker his back stiffened. "You going to talk now or do we have to take you downtown?"

Mr. Lucey frowned judiciously. Then he stuck the lollipop back into his mouth. "Aw right," he grumbled. "Though I don't see why you gotta bother me. I'm only the agent here for the company. Why don't you get in touch with the gen'ral manager? Our main office is in—"

"Don't give a hoot. I asked you what kind of business you run here?"

"We take orders from folks to mail letters, packages, greeting cards—any kind o' mailable matter—at specified dates from specified places." He jerked his thumb toward a profusely curlicued bronze plaque on the wall. "There's our motto: 'Any Time, Any Where.'"

"In other words I could leave a dozen letters with you and you would mail one from Pasadena tomorrow, the next one next week from Washington, D. C., and so on, according to my instructions?"

"That's the ticket. We got branch offices everywhere. But what's this Ogpu business? Congress pass another law?"

Ellery tossed an envelope on the man's desk. "Did you mail this envelope?"

The man looked at it, brows drawn in. Ellery watched him, trying hard to preserve the indifferent expression of the professional detective. He heard Lew and Ty breathing stertorously behind him.

"Sure thing," said Mr. Lucey at last. "Mailed it—let's see; Tuesday, I think it was. Tuesday late. So what?"

Ellery preened himself. His companions looked awed.

"So what?" said Ellery sternly. "Take a look at that name and address, Lucey!"

Mr. Lucey's lollipop stick tilted again as he bridled; but he looked, and the stick dipped like the mast of a flag being struck, and his mouth opened, and the lollipop fell out.

"B-Blythe Stuart!" he stuttered. His demeanor altered instantly to one of cringing apology. "Say, Officer, I didn't reco'nize—I didn't know—"

"Then you mailed the others, too, didn't you?"

"Yes, sir. Yes, sir, we did." Mr. Lucey betrayed liquid signs of an inner warmth. "Why, even now, even just now when you showed it to me, I read the name, but it sort of didn't register . . . I mean I spotted it because it looked familiar. The name—"

"Don't you read the names and addresses on mailable matter when you contract to take a job?"

"We don't contract. I mean—no, sir, I don't. I mean why should I? Get stuff to mail, and we mail 'em. Look, Officer, did you ever have to do the same thing day in, day out for years? Look, I don't know nothin' about these murders. I'm innocent. I got a wife and three kids. People just give us mail, see? Salesmen. People tryin' to put the dog on with their customers—as if they had branches in diff'rent cities, stuff like that—"

"And husbands supposed to be in one city but actually being in another," said Ellery. "Sure, I know. Well, keep your shirt on, Mr. Lucey; nobody's accused you of being mixed up in this thing. We just want your coöperation."

"Coöperation? That's me, that's me, Officer."

"Tell me about this transaction. You must have records."

The man swabbed his damp face. "Yes, sir," he said humbly. "Just a minute while I look it up."

The three men exchanged glances as Lucey stooped over his filing cabinet. Then they stared expectantly at the man.

"Who put this particular order through, Mr. Lucey?" asked Ellery casually. "What was the name of this customer?"

"I think," said Lucey, red-faced as he struggled with the file, "I think . . . it was . . . somebody named Smith."

"Oh," said Ellery; and he heard Ty curse under his breath. "What did this fellow Smith look like?"

"Dunno," said Lucey, panting. "He didn't come here in person, as I remember; sent the batch of letters in a package, with a note inside and a five-dollar bill. Here it is."

He straightened up, triumphant, waving a large manila envelope bearing a handwritten legend: "Egbert L. Smith."

Ellery seized the envelope, took one swift look at its contents, closed it, and tucked it under his arm.

"But it's still in our 'Open' file," protested Lucey. "There's still one letter in there to be mailed."

"Blythe Stuart won't need it any more. Did you have any further correspondence with this man Smith?"

"No, sir."

"Did he ever call up, or show up in person?"

"No, sir."

"Well, Lucey, you've been a great help. Keep your mouth shut about this. Understand?"

"Yes, sir," said Mr. Lucey eagerly.

"And if this Smith ever should write, or call up, you can get me at this number." Ellery scribbled his name and telephone number on the man's magazine. "Come on, boys."

The last thing he saw as he closed the door was Mr. Lucey stooping, dazed, to pick up his fallen lollipop.

Chapter XIII

Mr. Queen, Logician

THEY DODGED GUILTILY around the corner and hurried down Vine Street. When they were safely hidden in a private booth at the *Brown Derby* they all looked relieved.

Lew was fat with laughter. "I'd like to see Glücke's face when he hears about this," he choked, wiping his eyes dry. "That deadpan won't talk—much. He'll tell his wife and his cuties and his pals. Say, I'll bet he's on the phone right now!"

"I'll have to make it up to Glücke some way," said Ellery contritely. "He doesn't even know these letters exist."

"For God's sake, Queen," said Ty, "what's in that envelope?"

Ellery took from the manila envelope a letter, *sans* envelope; a typewritten schedule on a letterhead of International Mailers, Inc.; and a single envelope, sealed, addressed to Blythe Stuart in the scratchy, pale blue-inked block letters of the previous messages. Attached to this envelope by a steel clip was a slip of memorandum paper, bearing a typed date.

"Mr. Egbert L. Smith's letter," said Ellery, scanning it slowly. Then he passed it over to Ty.

Ty read it eagerly, Lew squinting over his shoulder. The letter had been typewritten on a sheet of white "second" paper of the flimsiest, cheapest grade. It was dated the twenty-seventh of the previous month.

International Mailers, Inc.
Hollywood Blvd. & Vine St.
Hollywood, Calif.

GENTLEMEN:—

I have seen your ad in today's paper saying you run a mailing service and wish to avail myself of this service.

I have certain letters which must be mailed to a customer of mine on certain dates, but I find I have to leave town for an indefinite period and may not be in a position to keep up my correspondence, so I am enclosing the letters in the package with a five-dollar bill, not knowing what your rates are and not having time to make inquiries. I am sure the five dollars will more than take care of stamps and your charge.

You will find the envelopes bound by an elastic. I wish them mailed in Hollywood *in the order in which they are stacked*, the top one first, the one under the top one second, and so on. This is very important. Here is a schedule of dates for mailing:

(1) Monday 11th (next month)
(2) Thursday 14th   (")
(3) Saturday 16th   (") *—special delivery*
(4) Tuesday 19th   (")
(5) Thursday 28th   (")
Thanking you in advance, I am,

Very truly yours,
EGBERT L. SMITH

P.S.—Please note letter #3 is to be mailed special delivery. This is to insure its arriving on Sunday the 17th, when there is no regular mail.

E. L. S.

"Damned Borgia didn't even *sign* his phony name," muttered Ty.

"An irritating but wise precaution," said Ellery dryly. "No handwriting, no clue. And no address. Note, too, the carefully innocuous phraseology. Neither illiterate nor erudite. With a distinct business-man flavor, as if Mr. Egbert L. Smith were exactly what he was pretending to be."

"Say, this letter was typed on Jack Royle's machine!" exclaimed Lew. "If what you said yesterday was true, Queen. Look at the broken serifs on those h's and r's. I think we ought to turn this over to Glücke pronto."

Ellery nodded, picking up the sheet of company stationery. "This is just Lucey's schedule, copied verbatim from the list in Smith's letter. Of course, the name is fictitious. And I imagine the paper will be found to be sterile of fingerprints."

A waiter came to hover over them, and Ty said absently: "Brandy."

Lew said: "Greetings, Gene."

"Double drinks, Mr. Bascom?"

"Bring the bottle, for gossakes. Can't you see I got a sucker? The fifteen-year Monnet."

The waiter grinned and padded away.

"Let's see," murmured Ellery, "what the last letter in Mr. Smith's kitbag had to say. The one that hadn't yet been mailed."

He ripped off one end of the sealed envelope and squeezed. A blue-backed playing-card dropped out.

The card was the ace of spades.

It was unnecessary to refer to the code sheet Ellery had found in John Royle's dressing-room.

All the world and his wife and children knew the cartomantic significance of the ace of spades.

"Death," said Ty nervously. "That's . . . But it came— I mean it was scheduled to come— She was killed *before* it came."

"Exactly the point," said Ellery, fingering the card.

"You and your points," snorted Lew. "How about tipping your mitt for a change?"

Ellery sat gazing at the card, and the envelope, and the memorandum slip attached to the envelope.

"One thing is sure," said Ty, his face screwed up. "It's the baldest kind of frame-up. Somebody had it in for Blythe and framed dad for the crime. Dad's feud with Blythe furnished an ideal background for a frame-up, gave him a motive. And anybody could have got to that typewriter of dad's."

"Eh?" said Ellery absently.

"It's true the date on this 'Smith's' note—twenty-seventh of last month— ought to give us a clue to where the note was typed; I mean as between the dressing-room on the lot and our house. But, damn it, dad was always lugging the machine from one place to the other. I can't remember in which place it was before the twenty-seventh."

"Why did he have a typewriter, Ty?"

"To answer fan mail. He despised secretaries and liked to correspond personally with the writers of the more interesting letters he received. Hobby of his. He wouldn't let the studio handle it at all. As a matter of fact, I do the same thing."

"You say any one could have used his machine?"

"The whole population of Hollywood," groaned Ty. "You know what our house was like, Lew, when dad was alive—a club for every hooch-hound in town."

"Am I supposed to take that personally?" chuckled Lew.

"And dad's dressing-room was a hangout for everybody on the lot. He was framed, all right—by some one who got hold of the typewriter either in the house or on the lot." He scowled. "Somebody? It could have been anybody!"

"But what I can't understand," said Lew, "is why this palooka Smith planned for two letters to be mailed to Blythe *after* she died. That in itself would screw up a frame against Jack, because Jack was knocked off, too; and dead men send no mail. And if Jack was meant to be framed, why was he murdered? It don't make sense."

"That," said Ty between his teeth, "is what I'd like to know."

"I believe," murmured Ellery, "we'll get along better if we take this problem scientifically. That alternate inference I mentioned this morning, by the way, was arrived at by mere common sense. On the assumption that the writer of those addresses was sane, not a crank, it was evident that the only sane reason ascribable to the fact that a letter was mailed to Blythe *after* Blythe's death was . . . that *the writer had no control over the source of mailing.*"

"I see," said Ty slowly. "That's what made you think of a mailing service."

"Precisely. I stopped in at the post-office on the off-chance that the writer may have arranged to have the letters mailed directly by the postmaster. But of course that was a far-fetched possibility. The only other one was an organization which made a business of mailing letters for people."

"But if Smith murdered Blythe and dad, why didn't he try to get the last two letters back from that outfit around the corner before they were mailed? Lucey said himself there's been no such attempt."

"And lay himself wide open to future identification?" jeered Lew. "Act your age, younker."

The waiter arrived bearing a bottle of brandy, a syphon, and three glasses. Lew rubbed his hands and seized the bottle.

"Of course," said Ellery, "that's perfectly true."

"As a matter of fact, why those last two letters at all?"

Ellery leaned back, clutching the glass Lew had filled. "An important question, with an important answer. Have you noticed the date, you two, on which our friend Smith intended this last letter to be mailed—the envelope bearing the unfriendly ace of spades?"

Lew looked over his glass. Ty merely looked. The date typed on the memorandum slip clipped to the envelope containing the ace of spades was "Thursday the 28th."

"I don't see the point," said Ty, frowning.

"Simple enough. What were the two cards mailed in one envelope to Blythe on Thursday the fourteenth—the envelope that arrived on Friday the fifteenth, two days before the murder?"

"I don't recall."

"The ten of spades and the deuce of clubs, meaning together: 'Great trouble in two days or two weeks.' The fact that the murders did actually occur two days after the receipt of that message was a mere coincidence. For what do we find now?" He tapped the card and envelope before him. "The ace of spades in this unmailed envelope, meaning 'Death,' is clearly marked for mailing on Thursday the twenty-eighth, or receipt by Blythe on Friday the twenty-ninth. So the murder of Blythe was obviously planned to occur not earlier than the twenty-ninth; or in other words she was scheduled to die, not two days, but two *weeks* after the Friday-the-fifteenth warning of 'Great trouble.'"

"A week from today," growled Ty. "If he hadn't changed his plans, Blythe would still be alive. And dad, too."

"Exactly the point. For what was the murderer's original plan? To murder Blythe—*Blythe alone*. Corroboration? The fact that the playing-cards were sent only to Blythe, that the ace of spades was meant to go, as you can see by the address on the envelope, only to Blythe. Also the plan included a frame-up of Jack for the murder of Blythe when it should occur—witness the use of Jack's typewriter in the typing of the code-sheet, the planting of the code-sheet in his dressing-room."

"Well?"

"But what actually happened? Blythe was murdered, all right—but NOT alone. Jack was murdered, too. What made the murderer change his plans? What made him murder not only Blythe, as originally planned, but Jack as well—the very man scheduled to take the rap for that murder?"

They were both silent, frowning back at him.

"That, as I see it, is the most significant question arising out of the whole chain of events. Answer that question and I believe you'll be well on the road to an answer to everything."

"Yeah, answer it," muttered Lew into his brandy. "I still say it's baloney."

"But what I don't understand," protested Ty, "is why the date was advanced. Why did Smith hurry up his crime? It seems to me he could have waited until the ace of spades was delivered and then murdered the two of them. But he didn't. He abandoned his own time-schedule, the whole elaborate machinery of the letters which he had set up. Why?"

"Opportunity," said Ellery succinctly. "It's more difficult, you know, to contrive the killing of two people than of one. And the honeymoon jaunt in your plane gave Smith an opportunity to kill *both* Blythe and Jack which he simply couldn't pass up."

"As the situation stands, then, the frame-up against dad is a flop and the murderer knows it."

"But there's nothing he can do about that except make an effort to get back the letters and the code list, and particularly his own telltale note in the files of the mailing company. As Lew suggested, he probably figured the relative risks involved and chose not to make the attempt."

"At least we've got enough to convince Bonnie of the absurdity of her suspicions against dad. What you've just said proves dad was another victim, that's all. Queen, would you—"

"Would I what?" Ellery emerged from a cavernous reverie.

"Would you tell that to Bonnie? Clear dad for me?"

Ellery rubbed his jaw. "And you, I take it?"

"Well . . . yes."

"Now don't worry about anything, Ty," said Ellery with a sudden briskness. "Forget this mess. Go out and get some exercise. Or go on a bat for a couple of weeks. Why not take a vacation?"

"Leave Hollywood now?" Ty looked grim. "Not a chance."

"Don't be idiotic. You're only in the way here."

"Queen's right," said Lew. "The picture's out, and I know Butch'll give you a vacation. After all, he's engaged to the girl." He giggled.

Ty smiled and got to his feet. "Coming?"

"I think I'll sit here and cogitate for a while." Ellery surreptitiously glanced at his wrist-watch. "Think it over, Ty. Here, never mind the check! I'll take care of it."

Lew clutched the bottle to his bosom, reaching with his free hand for his hat. "My pal."

Ty waved wearily and plodded off, followed a little erratically by Lew.

And Mr. Queen sat and cogitated with an unusually perturbed expression in his usually expressionless eyes.

Chapter XIV

Mr. Queen, Misogamist

AT TEN MINUTES before one o'clock Bonnie scudded into the *Brown Derby*, looked about in panic, and made for Ellery's booth with a queer little rush. She sat down and pushed herself into a corner, breathing hard.

"Here, what's the matter?" said Ellery. "You look scared to death."

"Oh, I am. I'm being followed!" She peeped over the partition at the door, her eyes wide.

"Clumsy," mumbled Ellery.

"What?"

"I mean, it's probably your imagination. Who would want to follow you?"

"I don't know. Unless . . ." She stopped inexplicably, her brows almost meeting. Then she shook her head.

"You're looking especially lovely today."

"Yet I'm *positive*. . . . A big black car. A closed car."

"You should wear bright colors all the time, Bonnie. They do remarkable things to your complexion."

Bonnie smiled vaguely, removed her hat and gloves, and passed her hands over her face like a cat. "Never mind my complexion. It isn't that. I just won't wear mourning. It's—it's ridiculous. I've never believed in mourning. Black things are like a . . . *poster*. I keep fighting with Clotilde about it. She's simply horrified."

"Yes," said Ellery encouragingly. She was carefully made up, very carefully indeed, to conceal her pallor and certain tiny fine lines around her eyes; her eyes were large and dark with lack of rest.

"I don't have to go around advertising to the world that I've lost my mother," said Bonnie in a low voice. "That funeral . . . it was a mistake. I hated it. I hate myself for having consented to it."

"She had to be buried, Bonnie. And you know Hollywood."

"Yes, but—" Bonnie smiled and said in a suddenly gay tone: "Let's not talk about it. May I have a drink?"

"So early in the day?"

She shrugged. "A daiquiri, please." She began to explore her handbag.

Ellery ordered a daiquiri, and a brandy-and-soda, and watched her. She was breathing hard again, under cover of her activity. She took out her compact and examined her face in the mirror, not looking at him, not looking at what lay plainly revealed in her open bag, picking at nonexistent stragglers of honey-hued hairs, pursing her lips, applying a dab of powder to her nose.

And suddenly, without looking at it, she took an envelope out of her bag and pushed it across the table to him.

"Here," she said in a muffled voice. "Look at this."

His hand closed over it as the waiter brought their drinks. When the waiter went away Ellery opened his hand. In it lay an envelope. Bonnie studied him anxiously.

"Our friend's renounced the post-office pen, I see," said Ellery. "Type-written address this time."

"But don't you *see?*" whispered Bonnie. "It's addressed to *me!*"

"I see quite clearly. When did it arrive?"

"In this morning's mail."

"Hollywood-posted last night, élite type, obvious characteristics three broken letters—b and d and t this time. Our friend had to use a different typewriter, since Jack's portable has been in my possession since yesterday afternoon. All of which tends to show that the letter probably wasn't written until last night."

"Look . . . at what's in it," said Bonnie.

Ellery withdrew the inclosure. It was the seven of spades.

"The mysterious 'enemy' again," he said lightly. "History seems on its way to being a bore. . . . Oh." He thrust the envelope and card into his pocket and rose suddenly. "Hello, Butch."

The Boy Wonder was standing there, looking down at Bonnie with a queer expression.

"Hello, Bonnie," he said.

"Hello," said Bonnie faintly.

He stooped, and she turned her cheek. He straightened up without kissing her, his sharp eyes veiled. "Having lunch here," he said casually. "Happened to spot you two. What's up?"

"Bonnie," said Ellery, "I think your estimable fiancé is jealous."

"Yes," said the Boy Wonder, smiling, "I think so, too." He looked ill. There were deep circles about his eyes, and his cheeks were sunken with fatigue. "I tried to get you this morning, but Clotilde said you'd gone out."

"Yes," said Bonnie. "I—did."

"You're looking better, Bonnie."

"Thank you."

"Will I see you tonight?"

"Why . . . Why don't you sit down with us?" said Bonnie, moving an inch on her seat.

"Yes, why don't you?" echoed Ellery heartily.

Those sharp eyes swept over him for an instant, stopping only long enough to touch on the pocket in which Ellery had thrust the envelope. "Thanks, no," smiled Butcher. "I've got to be getting back to the studio. Well, so long."

"So long," said Bonnie in a low voice.

He stood there for a moment more, as if hesitating over a desire to kiss her; then suddenly he smiled and nodded and walked away. They saw the droop of his shoulders as the doorman held open the door for him.

Ellery sat down and sipped at his brandy-and-soda. Bonnie jiggled her long-stemmed glass.

"Nice chap, Butch," said Ellery.

"Yes. Isn't he." Then Bonnie set down her glass with a little bang and cried: "Don't you see? Now that the cards have started coming to *me* . . ."

"Now Bonnie—"

"You don't think," she said in a shaky little voice, "you don't think . . . I'm . . . to be next?"

"Next?"

"Mother got the warnings, and she— Now I'm getting them." She tried to smile. "I'm scared silly."

Ellery sighed. "Then you've changed your mind about Jack Royle's having sent those previous letters?"

"No!"

"But, Bonnie, surely you're not afraid of a dead man?"

"No dead man mailed this letter last night," said Bonnie fiercely. "Oh, Jack Royle sent those other letters to mother. But this one to me . . ." Bonnie shivered. "I have only one enemy, Mr. Queen."

"You mean Ty?" murmured Ellery.

"I mean Ty. He's taking up where his father left off!"

Ellery was silent. He was powerfully tempted to demonstrate to Bonnie how unfounded her suspicions were; he would have given a good deal to dispel that look in her eyes. But he steeled himself. "You'll have to be careful, Bonnie."

"Then you *do* think—"

"Never mind what I think. But remember this. The most dangerous thing you can do is give yourself to Ty Royle."

Bonnie closed her eyes as she gulped down the dregs of her cocktail. When she opened them they were full of fear. "What shall I do?" she whispered.

Inwardly, Ellery cursed. But he merely said: "Watch your step. Care—care. Take care. Don't talk to Ty. Don't have anything to do with him. Avoid him as you would a leper."

"A leper." Bonnie shuddered. "That's what he is."

"Don't listen to his love-making," continued Ellery, not looking at her. "He's liable to tell you anything. Don't believe him. Remember, Bonnie."

"How could I forget?" Tears sprang into her eyes. She shook her head angrily and groped for her handkerchief.

"That car," muttered Ellery. "The one that's been following you. Don't worry about that. The men in it are protecting you. Don't try to get away from them, Bonnie."

But Bonnie scarcely heard him. "What good is my life?" she said dully. "I'm left alone in the world with a crazy beast after me, and—and—"

Ellery bit his lip, saying nothing, watching her pinch her nostrils with the handkerchief. He felt very like a beast himself.

After a while he ordered two more drinks, and when they came he urged one upon her. "Now stop it, Bonnie. You're attracting attention."

She dabbed at her reddened eyes very quickly then, and blew her little nose, and got busy with her powder-puff; and then she took up the second cocktail and began to sip it.

"I'm a fool," she sniffled. "It seems all I do is weep, like some silly heroine in a movie."

"Fine, fine. That's more like it. By the way, Bonnie, did you know that your mother and Jack Royle paid a visit to your grandfather Tolland Stuart a week ago Wednesday?"

"You mean just before their engagement was announced? Mother didn't tell me."

"That's odd."

"Isn't it." She frowned. "How do you know?"

"Paula Paris told me."

"That woman! How did *she* know?"

"Oh, she's really not so bad," said Ellery lamely. "It's just her job, Bonnie. You ought to be able to see that."

For the first time Bonnie examined him with the naked concentration of a woman seeking beneath the surface the signs of male weakness. "Oh, I see," she said slowly. "You're in love with her."

"I?" protested Ellery. "Absurd!"

Bonnie clothed the nakedness of her glance and murmured: "Sorry. I suppose it's immaterial where she found out. I do seem to recall now that mother was away all that day. I wonder why on earth she went to see grandfather. And with . . . that man."

"What's so surprising about that? After all, she'd decided to be married, and he *was* her father."

Bonnie sighed. "I suppose so, but it seems queer."

"In what way?"

"Mother hadn't visited or spoken to grandfather—oh, more than two or three times in the past dozen years. I myself hadn't been in that awful house in the Chocolate Mountains before last Sunday in at least eight years—I was wearing hair-ribbons and pinafores, so you can imagine how long ago that was. Why, if I'd passed grandfather on the street before Sunday I wouldn't have recognized him. He never came to see us, you see."

"I've meant to question you about that. Just what was the reason for the coldness between your mother and your grandfather?"

"It wasn't coldness exactly. It was . . . well, it's just that grandfather's naturally a selfish person, all wrapped up in himself. Mother used to tell me that even as a little girl she never got much affection from him. You see, my grandmother died in childbirth, when mother was born—she was an only child—and grandfather sort of . . . let go after that. I mean—"

"Cracked up?"

"He had a nervous breakdown, mother said. He was never quite the same after. He took grannie's death very hard, sort of blamed mother for it. If she hadn't been born—"

"It's not an uncommon masculine reaction."

"I don't want you to think he was brutal to mother, or anything like that," said Bonnie quickly. "He always had a sense of obligation towards her financially. He had her brought up very well, with governesses and nurses and heaps of clothes and European trips and finishing schools and all that. But when she grew up and went on the stage and got along very well by herself—why, I suppose he thought his duties as a father ended right there. And he's never paid the slightest attention to me."

"Then why did your mother visit him last Wednesday?"

"I'm sure I don't know," frowned Bonnie, "unless it was to tell him about her and Jack Royle getting married. Although certainly grandfather wouldn't care *what* she did; he took no interest in her first marriage, so why should he take any in her second?"

"Could it have been because your mother needed money? You said the other day she was always stony."

Bonnie's lip curled. "From him? Mother always said she'd beg before she'd ask him for a cent."

Ellery sat rubbing his upper lip with the tip of his finger. Bonnie finished her cocktail.

"Bonnie," said Ellery suddenly, "let's do something."

"What?"

"Let's get ourselves a plane and fly down to the Chocolate Mountains."

"After the horrible way he acted Sunday?" Bonnie sniffed. "No, indeed. Not even going to his own daughter's funeral! That's carrying eccentricity a bit *too* far, at least for me."

"I have the feeling," said Ellery, rising, "that it's important to find out why your mother and John Royle visited him nine days ago."

"But—"

Ellery looked down at her. "It may help, Bonnie, to clear away the fog."

Bonnie was silent. Then she tossed her head and got up. "In that case," she said firmly, "I'm with you."

Chapter XV

Mr. Queen, Snoop

IN THE LIGHT of blessed day the Law of Dreadful Night reversed itself and Tolland Stuart's eyrie from the sunshot air lay revealed in all its sprawling, weatherbeaten grandeur—a more fearsome scab upon the knife-edged mountain landscape than it had ever been invisible under darkness.

"It's a simply hideous place," shivered Bonnie, peering down as the hired airplane circled the landing-field.

"It's not exactly another Shangri-La," said Ellery dryly, "even though it does resemble the forbidden city at the roof of the world. Has your worthy grandfather ever visited Tibet? It might explain the geographical inspiration."

The gloomy pile crouched lifeless beneath them. And yet there was an illusion of life in the silent stones and turrets, lying still in the center of a web of power lines and telephone cables descending airily the slopes of the mountain.

"Is it my imagination," said Bonnie, "or does that thing down there look like a spider?"

"It's your imagination," replied Ellery quickly. When they trundled to a stop on the tiny field, he said to the pilot: "Wait for us. We shan't be long," and took Bonnie's arm in a casual but precautionary way. He helped her to the ground and hurried her towards the rift in the woods. As they passed the hangar he noted that its doors stood open and its interior was empty.

Bonnie noticed, too. "Do you suppose grandfather's flown off somewhere? I'd always understood he rarely left the estate."

"More likely it's Dr. Junius. I imagine the good leech has to do the shopping for cabbages and such. Picture yourself running a household up here!"

"And flying down to the grocer's for a bottle of olives," giggled Bonnie nervously.

The tree-canopied path was deserted. And when they emerged into the clearing where the house stood they saw that the front doors were shut.

Ellery knocked; there was no answer. He knocked again. Finally, he tried the knob. It turned.

"The obvious," he chuckled, "has a way of eluding me. Enter, Bonnie. The house, at least, won't bite you."

Bonnie looked doubtful; but she squared her boyish shoulders and preceded him bravely into the dim interior.

"Grandfather?" she called.

The syllables tumbled back, smothered and mocking.

"Mr. Stuart!" roared Ellery. The echo had a sneer in it. "Damn. That old man's exasperating. Do you mind if I shake some life into him?"

"Mind?" Bonnie looked angry. "I'd like to do some shaking myself!"

"Well," said Ellery cheerfully, "we'll have to find him first," and he led the way.

The living-room was empty. The kitchen, although there were breadcrumbs on the porcelain-topped table and the odor of freshly brewed tea, was also empty; so Ellery took Bonnie with him to the staircase, looking grim.

"He's up there sulking again, I'll bet a million. Mr. Stuart!"

No answer.

"Let me go first," said Bonnie firmly, and she ran up the stairs.

They found the old man lying in bed, the table by his side loaded with pill-boxes, medicine bottles, atomizers, and iron-stained spoons. His toothless jaws were doggedly munching on a cold meat sandwich, and he was gulping iced tea as he glared at them quite without surprise.

"Grandfather!" cried Bonnie. "Didn't you hear us?"

He glowered at her from under his hairy gray brows, munching without a sign he had heard her.

"Grandfather!" Bonnie looked scared. "Can't you hear me? Are you *deaf?*"

He stopped munching long enough to growl: "Go away," and then he took another swallow of tea and another bite of the white bread.

Bonnie looked relieved and furious. "How can you treat me this way? Aren't you human? What's the *matter* with you?"

The hair on his cheeks and chin stopped wiggling as his jaws suddenly clamped together. Then they wiggled again as he said curtly: "What d'ye want?"

Bonnie sat down. "I want," she said in a low voice, "a little of the affection you never gave my mother."

Studying that aged, bitter physiognomy, Ellery was astonished to see a soft expression creep into the veined and rheumy eyes. Then the expression vanished. The old man said gruffly: "Too late now. I'm an old man. Blythe should have thought of that years ago. She never was a daughter to me." The lisp grew more pronounced as his voice rose. "I don't want anybody! Go away and let me alone. If that fool Junius wouldn't hop in and out like a jack-rabbit, blast him, maybe I'd get some privacy!"

Bonnie made two tight little fists of her gloves. "You don't scare me one bit with your bellowing," she said evenly. "You know the fault was yours, not mother's. You never gave her the love she had a right to expect from you."

The old man banged down his glass and hurled the remains of the sandwich from him. "You say that to me?" he howled. "What do *you* know about it? Did she ever bring you to me? Did she ever—"

"Did you ever show her you wanted her to?"

The bony arms wavered, then fell to the coverlet with a curious weakness. "I'm not going to argue with a snip of a girl. You're after my money. I know what you want. My money. That's all children and grandchildren ever want!"

"Grandfather," gasped Bonnie, rising. "How can you say such a thing?"

"Get out, get out," he said. "That fool Junius! Going off to Los Angeles and letting this house become a Wayside Inn. Lord knows what germs you've brought in here, you and this fellow. I'm a sick old man. I'm—"

"Goodbye," said Bonnie. And she made for the door blindly.

"Wait," said Ellery. She waited, her lips trembling. Ellery faced the old man grimly. "Your life is your own to lead as you see fit, Mr. Stuart, but a capital crime has been committed and you can't shut yourself away from *that*. You're going to answer some questions."

"Who are you?" demanded the old man sourly.

"Never mind who I am. A week ago Wednesday—that's nine days ago—your daughter and John Royle paid you a visit. Why?"

It seemed to him that for an instant the old man showed astonishment; but only for an instant. "So you found that out, too, did you? You must be from the police, like that idiot Glücke who was up here early in the week. Police!"

"I asked you, Mr. Stuart—"

"You want to know why they came here, hey? All right, I'll tell you," said the old man unexpectedly, hitching himself up in bed. "Because they wanted money, that's why! That's all anybody ever wants."

"Mother asked you for money?" said Bonnie. "I don't believe it!"

"Call me a liar, do you?" said the old man venomously. "I say she asked me for money. Not for herself, I admit. But she asked me. For that good-for-nothing Royle!"

Bonnie looked at Ellery, and Ellery looked at Bonnie. So that was it. Blythe had come to her father against all her instincts—not for herself, but for the man she loved. Bonnie looked away, staring out the window at the cold sky.

"I see," said Ellery slowly. "And you gave it to her?"

"I must have been out of my mind that day," grumbled the old man. "I gave Royle a check for a hundred and ten thousand dollars and I told Blythe not to bother me again. Good-for-nothing! Something about gambling debts. She wanted to marry a gambler. Well, that was her hard luck."

"Oh, grandfather," sobbed Bonnie, "you're an old fraud." She took a step toward him.

"Don't come near me!" said the old man hastily. "You're not sterile. Full of germs!"

"You did love her. You wanted her to be happy."

"I wanted her to let me alone."

"You just pretend to be hard—"

"It was the only way I could get rid of her. Why can't people let me alone? Blythe said it would be her money some day, anyway, and all she asked was part of it before . . ." His hairy lips quivered. "Get out and don't come back."

And Bonnie's hardened. "You know," she whispered, "I believe you did give it to her just to get rid of her. Don't worry, grandfather. I'll get out and I'll never come back. I'll never speak to you again as long as you live."

The old man waved his arms again, his sallow face livid. "I won't die for a long time!" he yelled. "Don't worry about *that!* Get out, the two of you!"

"Not yet," said Ellery. He glanced at Bonnie. "Bonnie, would you mind going back to the plane? I'll join you in a few minutes. I'd like to talk to your grandfather alone."

"I can't get away from here fast enough." Bonnie stumbled out. Ellery heard her running down the stairs as if some one were after her.

He did not speak until the front door slammed. Then he said to the glowering old man: "Now, Mr. Stuart, answer one question."

"I told you why Blythe and that gambler came up here," replied the old man in a sulky voice. "I've got nothing more to say."

"But my question has nothing to do with Blythe's visit."

"Eh? What d'ye mean?"

"I mean," said Ellery calmly, "what were you doing last Sunday night outside this house in an aviator's helmet?"

For a moment he thought the man would faint; the eyes rolled alarmingly, and the large bony nose twitched with a sort of nausea. "Eh?" said the old man feebly. "What did you say?"

And as he said it the faintness and alarm disappeared, and his gray beard came up belligerently. Game old cock, thought Ellery with a grudging admiration. For all his years he absorbed punishment very quickly.

"I saw you outside in the rain with a flying helmet on your head. At a time when Junius said you were up here behind a locked door."

"Yes," nodded the old man. "Yes, I was outside. Because I wanted to breathe God's clean air. I was outside because there were strangers in my house."

"In the rain?" Ellery smiled. "I thought you had certain fears about pneumonia and such."

"I'm a sick man," said the old man stolidly. "But I'd rather risk pneumonia than be mixed up with strangers."

"You almost said 'a murder,' didn't you? Why should you be so timid about being mixed up in this one, Mr. Stuart?"

"Any one."

"Your own daughter's? You don't feel—I almost made the mistake of calling it 'natural'—you don't feel a desire for vengeance?"

"I want only to be let alone."

"And the helmet on your head—that had nothing to do with . . . let us say . . . airplanes, Mr. Stuart?"

"There are a few helmets about. They're good protection against rain."

"Ah, amiable now. I wonder why? People who have something to conceal generally are anxious to talk amiably, Mr. Stuart. Just what are you concealing?"

For answer the old man reached over and snatched the shotgun from its position beside the testered bed. Without speaking, he placed the shotgun in his lap. He looked at Ellery steadily.

Ellery smiled, shrugged, and strolled out.

He made a deliberate clatter as he went down the stairs, and he set one foot loudly after another on the floor of the living-room as he went to the front door. The door he banged.

But he remained inside, listening. There was no sound from above. Frowning, he looked about. That door. . . . Tiptoeing, he crossing the living-room, opened the door carefully, glanced in, nodded, and slipped through, shutting the door behind him with the same caution.

He stood in a library, or study, vast and raftered and gloomy, like all the rooms in the house. This one, too, had a brooding atmosphere, as if it had stood too long untenanted. There was a thick layer of dust over everything, mute reflection on Dr. Junius's housekeeping talents.

Ellery went without hesitation to the huge flat-topped desk in the center of the room, a piece of solid carved oak with an ancient patina. But he was not interested in the antiquity of Tolland Stuart's desk; he was interested in its contents. A rapid glance about had convinced him there was no safe in the room; and the desk seemed the most likely repository for what he was seeking.

He found it in the second drawer he opened, sepultured in an unlocked green-painted steel box, although a lock with a key in it lay beside the box.

It was Tolland Stuart's will.

Ellery read it avidly, one ear cocked for sounds from the old man's room above.

The date on the will was nine and a half years old, and the paper was a sheet of heavy bond bearing the imprint of an old, solid banking house in Los Angeles. It was a holograph will, handwritten in ink by a crabbed fist— Ellery could visualize the old terrorist twisting his tongue in his withered cheek and refusing to allow any one at his bank to catch a glimpse of what he was writing. The will was signed with Tolland Stuart's signature, which had been witnessed by names meaningless to Ellery, obviously employees of the bank.

The will said:

"I, Tolland Stuart, being this day sixty years of age and of sound mind, make my last will and testament.

"The sum of one hundred thousand dollars in cash or negotiable bonds is hereby left to Dr. Henry F. Junius, of my employ, but only on the following conditions:

"(1) That until my death Dr. Junius shall have been continuously in my employ for not less than ten years from the date of this will, except for periods of illness or other such interruptions in his service to me which shall be reasonably beyond his control; at all other times he is to act as my physician and exclusive guardian of my health; and

"(2) That I, Tolland Stuart, shall have survived this ten-year period; that is to say, that my death shall have occurred after my 70th birthday.

"In the event of my death before the age of 70 from any cause whatsoever, or in the event that Dr. Junius shall have left my employ either voluntarily or by dismissal before the expiration of the ten-year period noted above, my bequest to him of $100,000.00 shall be considered cancelled; and my estate shall then go free and clear of any participating bequest to my legal heirs.

"I direct also that my just debts be paid, also the expenses of my funeral.

"The residue of my estate I leave to be divided as follows: One-half

(½) to go to my only child and daughter, Blythe, or in the event that she pre-deceases me, to her heirs. The other half (½) to go to my granddaughter Bonita, Blythe's daughter, or in the event that Bonnie pre-deceases me, to Bonnie's heirs."

Except for an additional short paragraph in which the junior vice-president of the bank where the will had been drawn up and witnessed was named executor of the estate, there was nothing more.

Ellery replaced the document in its green box, shut the drawer, and stole out of the house.

As he stepped onto the landing-field he spied the stubby airplane which he had seen Sunday night in the nearby hangar. It was gliding down to a landing. It taxied to a stop beside the commercial plane which had flown Ellery and Bonnie up into the mountains. Dr. Junius jumped to the ground, looking like an elderly condor in the helmet which flapped about his ears.

He waved to Bonnie, who was waiting in the other plane, and hurried forward to greet Ellery.

"Paying us a visit, I see," he said companionably. "I would be out shopping! What's happening on the Hollywood front?"

"It's all quiet." Ellery paused. "We've just had the honor of an interview with your worthy benefactor."

"Since your skin is still whole," smiled the doctor, "it can't have been so terrifying." Then he said in quite a different tone: "Did you say 'benefactor'?"

"Why, yes," murmured Ellery. "Isn't he?"

"I don't know what you mean." The doctor's bright eyes retreated into their old yellow sockets.

"Oh, come, doctor."

"No. Really."

"Don't tell me you're unaware that the old crank has set aside a little something for your old age!"

Dr. Junius threw back his head and laughed. "Oh, that!" The laugh turned bitter. "Of course I'm aware of it. Why do you think I've buried myself up here?"

"I thought," said Ellery dryly, "there must be a sound reason."

"I assume he told you."

"Mmm."

"I'm not so sure," said Dr. Junius, shrugging, "that I got the better of the bargain. It's cheap at a hundred thousand, dirt cheap. Living with that old pirate and putting up with his tantrums and whims for ten years is worth closer to a million, even at a conservative estimate."

"How did he ever come to make such an odd arrangement with you, Doctor?"

"When we met he'd just been given a rather thorough going-over by a pair of quack 'specialists' who'd got hold of him and were milking him for thousands in fees. They told him he had cancer of the stomach, scared him into believing he had only a year or two at the most to live."

"You mean a deliberately false diagnosis?"

"I imagine so. I suppose they were afraid the sacred cow would stop giving milk sooner or later and thought they'd get much more out of him by concentrating their 'services' over a short period than by trying to pander to his hypochondria over a longer one. Anyway, some one recommended me to him, and I examined him and found he merely had ulcers. I told him so, and the quacks discreetly vanished."

"But I still don't see—"

"I told you you don't know Tolland Stuart," said the doctor grimly. "He was suspicious of them, but he couldn't get it out of his mind that perhaps there *was* a cancer in his stomach. My insistence that he hadn't, and that I could cure his ulcers very easily—he was in perfectly sound condition otherwise—gave him an idea. He remembered what the quacks had said about his having only a year or so to live. So, in view of my confidence, he engaged me to keep him alive for a minimum of ten years—he liked my honesty, he said, and if I kept him in reasonably good health five times longer than the other men had claimed he would live, I was entitled to a large fee."

"The Chinese system. You collect during the good health of your patient."

"Good health!" snorted Dr. Junius. "The man's as sound as a nut. It took me only a short time to heal the ulcers, and he hasn't had so much as a cold since."

"But all those medicines and pills by his bed—"

"Colored water and sugar-coated anodynes. It's a disgusting but essential therapy. I haven't used a legitimate drug from my little pharmacy in there in eight years. I've got to treat him for his imaginary ailments or he'd kick me out of the house."

"And then you wouldn't collect your hundred thousand when he dies."

The doctor threw up his hands. "When he dies! As far as I can tell, he'll live to be ninety. The chances are all in favor of his surviving me, and I'll get for my long years of martyrdom up here just two lines in an obituary column."

"But isn't he paying you a yearly retainer besides?"

"Oh, yes, quite handsome." The doctor shrugged. "But unfortunately I haven't any of it. I'd go crazy if I didn't sneak down into L. A. once in a while. When I do, it's only to lose money at roulette, or at the race-track—I've dropped some in the stock market. . . ."

"Not Alessandro's?" said Ellery suddenly.

The doctor scowled at the jagged skyline. "Did you ever want something very badly?"

"Often."

"I recognized early in my career that I wouldn't make a go of medicine. Haven't the proper temperament. What I've always wanted more than anything else, and couldn't have for lack of money, was leisure."

"Leisure? To what purpose?"

"Writing! I've got a story to tell the world. Lots of stories!" He tapped his breast. "They're locked up in here, and they won't come free until my mind is relieved of financial worry and I've got time and a sense of security."

"But up here—"

"What about up here?" demanded Junius fiercely. "Security? Time? I'm a prisoner. I'm on my feet from morning to night, catering to that old fool, cooking for him, wiping his nose, running his errands, cleaning his house. . . . No, Mr. Queen, I can't write up here. All I can do up here is run my feet off and hope he'll break his neck some day while he's out rabbit-hunting."

"At least," murmured Ellery, "you're frank."

The doctor looked frightened. He said hastily: "Goodbye," and plodded off towards the tree-masked house.

"Goodbye," said Ellery soberly, and he climbed into the waiting plane.

Chapter XVI

Mr. Queen, Rat

ELLERY WAS SITTING at his kitchenette table Saturday morning clad in pajamas and robe and giving his divided attention simultaneously to a sooty slab of toast, the morning paper announcing the latest developments, which were nil, in the Royle-Stuart case, and a paper-backed book entitled *Fortune Telling by Cards*, when his telephone rang.

"Queen!" Ty's voice was eager. "What did she say?"

"What did who say?"

"Bonnie. Did you fix it up for me?"

"Oh, Bonnie." Ellery thought furiously. "Well, now, Ty, I've got bad news for you."

"What do you mean?"

"She won't believe a word of it. She's still convinced your father wrote those notes to her mother."

"But she can't!" howled Ty. "It's not reasonable. Didn't you tell her about that mailing company and the rest of it?"

"Oh, certainly," lied Ellery. "But you can't expect reasonableness from a woman, Ty; a man of your experience ought to know that. Why don't you give Bonnie up as a hopeless job?"

Ty was silent; Ellery could almost see him grinding his teeth together and sticking out his lean jaw. "I couldn't be mistaken," said Ty at last, in a sort of stubborn despair. "She gave herself to me too completely. She loves me. I know she does."

"Pshaw, the girl's an actress. Every woman has something of the mime in her, but when it's also her profession—"

"Since when do you know so much about women? I tell you she *wasn't* acting!"

"Look, Ty," said Ellery with simulated impatience, "I'm a sorely harassed man, and I'm not at my best at this hour of the morning. You asked me, and I told you."

"I've kissed too many girls in my time," muttered Ty, "not to recognize the real thing when it's dished out to me."

"Thus spake Casanova," sighed Ellery. "I still think you ought to take a vacation. Hop an Eastern plane. A whirl around Broadway's hot spots will get Bonnie out of your system."

"I don't want her out of my system! Damn it, if it's that bad I'll face the music in person. I should have done it in the first place."

"Wait," said Ellery, alarmed. "Don't go looking for trouble, Ty."

"I know if I talk to her, take her in my arms again—"

"Do you want a knife in your back when you do? She's been receiving letters again."

"More?" said Ty incredulously. "But I thought we bagged the whole batch in that mailing office!"

"She showed me one that came yesterday. Addressed to her."

"To *her?*"

"Yes, and with the seven of spades inclosed. 'An Enemy.'"

"But if it was mailed Thursday night—and we know it couldn't have come from that fellow Lucey's office—why, that *proves* dad couldn't have sent it!"

Ellery said desperately: "Oh, she knows your father couldn't have mailed this one. It's worse. She thinks *you* sent it."

"I?" Ty sounded dazed.

"Yes, she's convinced now the whole series of card messages has been inspired by the Royle family. The ones to Blythe by your father and now this one, apparently the first of a fresh series, by you."

"But that's . . . why, that's mad! By me? Does she actually think I . . . ?"

"I told you she was past reasoning with. You'll never rehabilitate this affair, Ty. Stop wasting your time."

"But she mustn't think I'm hounding her! I ought to be able to do something to convince her—"

"Don't you know that the only truly inert material in the universe is an idea rooted in a woman's skull? The winds do blow, but to no avail. I don't want to seem to be changing the subject, but do you own a typewriter?"

"What?" mumbled Ty.

"I said: Do you own a typewriter?"

"Why, yes. But—"

"Where is it?"

"In my dressing-room on the lot."

"Where are you going now?"

"To see Bonnie."

"Ty." Ellery winced at his own perfidy. "Don't. Take my advice. You may be . . . in danger."

"Danger? What do you mean?"

"You understand English perfectly well."

"Look here," said Ty sharply, "are you trying to tell me that Bonnie would . . . You're joking, or crazy."

"Will you do me one favor? Don't talk to Bonnie until I tell you it's safe to."

"But I don't understand, Queen!"

"You've got to promise."

"But—"

"I can't explain now. Have I your word?"

Ty was silent. Then he said wearily: "Oh, very well," and hung up.

Ellery did likewise, swabbing his moist brow. A close shave. Raw apprentice himself in the laboratory of love, he was just beginning to discover what powerful magnetic properties the grand passion possessed. Damn that stubborn kid! At the same time, far and deep inside, Mr. Queen felt a great, consuming shame. Of all the black tricks he had ever played in the interests of ultimate truth, this was certainly the blackest!

Sighing, he plodded towards his kitchenette for a further perusal of the book on fortune-telling and a Star Chamber session with his own dark thoughts.

The doorbell rang.

Absently he turned about and went to the door and opened it.

And there stood Bonnie.

"Bonnie! Well, well. Come in."

Bonnie was radiant. She flew by, hurled herself on his sofa, and looked up at him with dancing eyes.

"What a lovely day! Isn't it? And that's the most fetching robe you're wearing, Mr. Queen. And I've just been followed by that same closed black car, and I don't care—whoever it is—and oh, the most wonderful thing's happened!"

Ellery closed the door slowly. What now?

Nevertheless, he managed to smile. "There's one pleasant feature of this case, anyway—it's thrown me into daily contact with one of the loveliest damsels of our time."

"One of the happiest," laughed Bonnie. "And are you trying to seduce me with that mustachioed old technique? Oh, I feel so chipper it's indecent!" She bounced up and down on the sofa like a gleeful little girl. "Aren't you going to ask me what it is?"

"What what is?"

"The wonderful thing that's happened?"

"Well," said Ellery, without elation, "what is it?"

She opened her bag. Ellery studied her. Her pixie features were ravaged to a degree that neither her present gaiety nor the art of make-up as taught by its most celebrated impresarios could conceal. There were gray hollows in her cheeks and her eyes were underscored by violet shadows. She looked like a sufferer from a serious ailment who has just been informed by her physician that she would live and get well.

She took an envelope out of her bag and offered it to him. He took it, frowning; why should the receipt of another warning note have this extraordinary effect on her spirits? Apprehension ruffled his spine as he removed the enclosed card. It was a four of spades.

He stared at it gloomily. So that was it. If he recalled the code sheet correctly . . .

"You needn't go looking for the yellow sheet," said Bonnie gaily. "I know all those meanings by heart. The four of spades means: 'Have Nothing More to Do with a Certain Person about Whom You Are Doubtful.' Isn't it scrumptious?"

Ellery sat down opposite her, scrutinizing the envelope.

"You don't look pleased," said Bonnie. "I can't imagine why."

"Perhaps," muttered Ellery, "it's because I don't understand in what way it's so scrumptious."

Bonnie's eyes widened. "But it says: 'Have Nothing More to Do with a Certain Person about Whom You Are Doubtful.' Don't you see?" she said happily. "And I thought Ty sent that card yesterday!"

Bonnie, Bonnie. Ellery felt savage. First Ty, now Bonnie. Only the meanest man in the world would even attempt to wipe that blissful look from her drawn face, the first expression of pure happiness it had exhibited in the century-long week of doubts and torments and sorrow and death.

And yet, it had to be done. It was vitally important to wipe that look off her face. For an instant Ellery toyed with the notion to tell Bonnie the truth. That would stop her, if he gauged her character accurately. But then she wouldn't be able to keep it from Ty. And if Ty knew . . .

He steeled himself. "I don't see why you're so cheerful," he said, injecting a sneer into his voice.

Bonnie stared. "What do you mean?"

"You said you thought Ty sent that card yesterday. Apparently you don't think so any more. What's made you change your mind?"

"Why, this card—the one you're holding!"

"I fail," said Ellery coldly, "to follow your reasoning."

Her smile faded. "You mean you don't see—" She tossed her head. "You're teasing me. There's only one person in this world I could have been, and was, doubtful about. That was Ty."

"What of it?"

"No matter who sent this card, its meaning is plain—it warns me not to have anything more to do with Ty. Don't you see?" she cried, her cheeks pink again. "Don't you see that that clears Ty—that he couldn't have sent it? *Would he warn me against himself* if he were behind all this?" She paused triumphantly.

"He would under certain circumstances."

The smile flickered and went out for good. She lowered her gaze and began to pick aimlessly at the handle of her bag.

"I suppose," she said in a small voice, "you know what you're talking about. I'm—I'm not much at this sort of thing. It just seemed to me that . . ."

"He's been terribly clever," said Ellery in a flat tone. "He knows you suspect him, and therefore he's sent you the one message calculated to dispel your suspicions. As it did."

He rose, suddenly unable to endure the sight of her steady picking at the bag. At the same time he became conscious that she had raised her eyes again and was looking at him with a queer directness—a sad, sharp, questioning look that made him feel he had committed a great crime.

"You really believe that?" murmured Bonnie.

Ellery snapped: "Wait for me. I'll prove it." He went into his bedroom, shut the door, and quickly began to dress. Because it made things easier, he kept his mind blank.

Bonnie drove him to the Magna Studios, and when she had parked her roadster in the studio garage he said: "Where's Ty's dressing-room?"

"Oh," she said.

And without another word she led him to the little tree-shaded street of the stone bungalows and up the three steps to a door with Ty's name on it. The door was unlocked, and they went in.

A standard-sized typewriter stood on a table beside a chair. Bonnie was perfectly motionless at the door. Ellery went to the typewriter, took a sheet of clean paper from his pocket, and rapidly typed a few lines.

That he returned to Bonnie with the sheet, pulling out of his pocket the envelope which she had just received.

"Open and shut," he said tonelessly. "Here, Bonnie, compare these specimens. Notice the b's and d's and t's? Broken type." He did not mention that, like the h's and r's on John Royle's portable, the imperfect keys on Ty's machine had been freshly—and obviously—filed to make them so. "Also élite, which is unusual for a non-portable typewriter."

Bonnie moved then and looked, not at the paper specimens, but directly at the keys. She poked the b and examined the key, and the d, and the t. And then she said: "I see."

"Little doubt about it. This envelope and the one that came yesterday were both addressed on this machine."

"How did you know?" she asked, looking at him with that same queer, questioning gaze.

"It seemed likely."

"Then there ought to be a carbon copy of the yellow code sheet, too. It wouldn't be complete without that."

"Clever girl." Ellery rummaged through the table drawer. "And here it is, too! Looks like a third or fourth carbon." He offered it for her inspection, but she kept looking at him.

"What are you going to do?" Bonnie's voice was chill. "Expose Ty to Inspector Glücke?"

"No, no, that would be premature," said Ellery hastily. "No real evidence for a prosecutor." She said nothing. "Bonnie, don't say anything about this to any one. And keep away from Ty. Do you hear?"

"I hear," said Bonnie.

"As far away as you can." Bonnie opened the door. "Where are you going now?" Bonnie did not answer. "Be careful!" She looked at him, once, a long hard look that had in its depths a gleam of—that was strange—fright.

Her stride lengthened. Half a block away she was running.

Ellery watched her with grim eyes. When she vanished around a corner he closed the door and sank into the chair.

"I wonder," he thought miserably, "what the penalty is for murdering love."

Chapter XVII

Danse Amoureuse

MR. QUEEN SAT in Ty's cool room and cogitated. He sat and cogitated for a considerable time. In many ways things were satisfactory; yes, quite satisfactory. In one important way, however, they were unquestionably not satisfactory. The most important way.

"Same old story," reflected Mr. Queen. "Find the nut and there's nothing to crack it with. Is it possible there's nothing to do but wait? Think, man, think!"

Mr. Queen thought. An hour passed; another. Mr. Queen kept on thinking. But it was no use.

He got to his feet, stretching to iron the kinks out of his muscles. It all gelled; the case lay smooth and shiny and whole before his critical appetite. The problem, which he found himself unable to solve, was how to wrap his fingers around it without causing it to disintegrate into a sticky, ruined, quivering mess.

Hoping fervently for an inspiration, Mr. Queen left the bungalow and the studio and took a taxi back to his hotel. In his apartment he called the desk clerk and instructed him to have his coupé brought around from the garage. While he was gathering the various letters in his collection and placing them under the lid of John Royle's portable typewriter, the telephone rang.

"Queen?" bellowed Inspector Glücke. "You come down to my office right away! Right away, d'ye hear?"

"Do I hear? I can't very well help myself, Glücke."

"I'm not saying anything now. You just get down here as fast as those smart legs of yours can carry you!"

"Mmm," said Ellery. "Shall I take a toothbrush and pajamas?"

"You ought to be in clink, damn you. Step on it!"

"As a matter of fact, I was on my way, Glücke—"

"You'd double-cross your own father," roared the Inspector. "I give you a half-hour. Not a minute more!" He hung up.

Ellery frowned, sighed, snapped down the lid of the typewriter, went downstairs, got into his coupé, and headed for downtown Los Angeles.

"Well?" said Mr. Queen, precisely a half-hour later.

Inspector Glücke sat behind his desk blowing out his hard cheeks and contriving to look both vexed and wounded at once. Also, he breathed hard and angrily.

"What's that you've got there?" he growled, pointing to the typewriter.

"I asked first," said Ellery coyly.

"Sit down and don't be so damned funny. Did you see Paula Paris's paper today?"

"No."

"Can't you read English, or aren't our newspapers classy enough for you? After all, you *are* a literary man."

"Ha, ha," said Ellery. "That, I take it, was meant to positively gore me. You see how much I love you, darling? I even split an infinitive with you! Come on, spill." Glücke hurled a newspaper at Ellery. Ellery caught it, raising his brows, and began to read a passage marked in red pencil in Paula Paris's column.

"What you got to say for yourself?"

"I say she's wonderful," said Ellery dreamily. "My lady Paula! A woman with brains. Glücke, tell me truthfully: Have you ever met a woman who combined intellect, beauty, and charm so perfectly?"

The Inspector smote his desk with the flat of his hand, making things jump and tremble. "You think you're damned cute—you and that pest of a newspaperwoman! Queen, I don't mind telling you I'm raving mad. Raving! When I read that piece I had a good mind to issue a warrant for your arrest. I mean it!"

"Looking for a goat, eh?" said Ellery sympathetically.

"Collecting all those letters! Holding out on me all week! Posing as a Headquarters dick!"

"You've worked fast," said Ellery with admiration. "All she says here, after all, is that Blythe Stuart was receiving anonymous letters and that they were mailed through the agency of a mailing service. Good work, Glücke."

"Don't salve me! There's only one mailing service in town, and I had this guy Lucey on the carpet just a while ago. He told me all about you—recognized you from his description. And you left your name and hotel phone number with him. The cheek of it! That proved his story. I suppose the other two were Ty Royle and Lew Bascom, from Lucey's description."

"Wonderful."

"I've been having the Stuart house searched—no letters—so I know you have 'em." The Inspector looked as if he were about to cry. "To think you'd pull a lousy trick like that on *me*." He jumped up and shouted: "Fork over!"

Ellery frowned. "Nevertheless, the inevitability of secrets finally coming to rest in Paula's column is beginning to give me the willies. Where the devil does she get her information?"

"I don't care," yelled Glücke. "I didn't even call her this morning on it—what the hell good would it do? Listen, Queen, are you going to give me those letters or do I have to slap you in the can?"

"Oh, the letters." Ellery kicked the typewriter between his legs. "You'll find them in here, with the cards and the machine the scoundrel used to type his code sheet, and his letter to International Mailers."

"Cards? Code sheet?" gaped Glücke. "Machine? Whose machine?"

"Jack Royle's."

The Inspector sank back, feeling his brow. "All right," he choked. "Let's have the story. I'm just in charge of the Homicide Detail. Just give me a break, a handout." He bellowed: "Damn it, man, GIVE!"

Ellery gave, chuckling. He launched into a long exposition, beginning at the beginning—the very beginning, which was his acquisition of the first two cards from Blythe Stuart herself in Jack Royle's house—and concluding with the story of the new series of letters sent to Bonnie.

The Inspector sat glowering at the typewriter, the yellow sheets, the cards, the envelopes.

"And when I found that the two letters to Bonnie were typed on Ty's machine," shrugged Ellery, "that was the end of it. Honestly, Glücke, I was on my way to give you all this stuff when you phoned me."

The Inspector rose, grunting, and took a turn about the room. Then he summoned his secretary. "Take all this stuff down to Bronson and have him check it, along with the fingerprint detail." When the man left, he resumed his pacing.

Finally, he sat down. "To tell you the truth," he confessed, "it doesn't mean an awful lot to me. That letter signed Smith is a phony, of course; just a neat way of wiping out the trail to himself. The only thing I get out of the whole set-up is that the original plan was to bump Blythe off, and that something happened to make this Smith give Jack the works, too."

"The essential point," murmured Ellery.

"But why *was* Jack knocked off? Why were the warnings sent at all?" The Inspector waved his arms. "And what's the idea of starting on Bonnie Stuart now? Say!" His eyes narrowed. "So that's why you had me put a day-and-night tail on her!"

"If you'll recall, I asked you to have her watched before the first warning was sent to her."

"Then why—"

"Call it a hunch. The cards to Bonnie later confirmed it."

"So now she's elected," muttered Glücke. "No savvy."

"Have you seen her today?"

"I tried to locate her when I found out about the anonymous letters, but she's not home, and my men haven't reported. Matter of fact, Royle isn't around, either."

A chilly finger pressed on Ellery's spine. "You haven't been able to locate Ty?"

"Nope." The Inspector looked startled. "Say, you don't think *he's* behind these letters? That he's the one—!" He jumped up again. "Sure! You say yourself these last messages to Bonnie were typed on his machine!" He grabbed his phone. "Miller! Hop down to the Magna Studios on the double and bring back the typewriter in Ty Royle's dressing-room. Careful with it— prints." He hung up, rubbing his hands. "We'll have to go easy, of course. Proving he sent the cards doesn't prove he pulled the double murder. But just the same it's a start. Motive galore—"

"You mean he killed his father, too?"

Glücke looked uncomfortable. "Well, I said we'd go easy. There's a lot of questions to clear up. Keep this under your hat, Queen, while I start the ball rolling."

"Oh, I will," said Ellery dryly.

The Inspector grinned and hurried out. Ellery mused over a cigaret. When the Inspector came back he was beaming.

"We'll locate him in short order, of course. Then a day-and-night tail without his knowledge. I'm having his house finecombed. Maybe we'll turn up something on that morphine and sodium allurate, too—check over his movements for a couple of weeks, drug purchases, and so on. It's a start; it's a start."

"Of course, you know Ty physically couldn't have been that masked pilot," Ellery pointed out.

"Sure not, but he could have hired some one as a blind. Swell blind, too, having himself held up with a gun and tied like a rooster. With the girl as witness, too."

Ellery sighed. "I hesitate to dampen your enthusiasm, Glücke, but you're all wrong."

"Hey? Wrong? How's that?" Glücke looked startled.

"Ty never wrote those letters—no, any more than Jack wrote the ones that came to Blythe."

The Inspector sucked his finger. "How come?" He looked disappointed.

"You might examine," drawled Ellery, "the faces of the h and r keys on this machine."

Glücke did so, frowning. The frown disappeared magically, to be replaced by a scowl. "Filed!"

"Exactly. And, when you examine Ty's typewriter, you'll find that the b and d and t are similarly filed. There could be only one purpose in a deliberate mutilation of typewriter keys—identification of the machine from a sample of its writing. Well, who would want Jack Royle's machine to be easily identified as the machine which typed the code sheet behind the anonymous letters? Jack Royle? Hardly, if he was sending them. And the same goes for Ty and his machine."

"I know, I know," said Glücke irritably. "Framed, by God."

"So we can be sure of several things. First, that Jack Royle did *not* send those card messages to Blythe. Second, that Ty Royle did *not* send those card messages to Bonnie. And third—this follows a pattern of probability— from the fact that the same method of mutilation was used on both machines, filing of keys, a conclusion that *the same person* mutilated both, and consequently the same person sent both series of messages."

"But a frame of *two* men!"

"See what we have. Originally a plan to murder Blythe, and in doing so to frame Jack for the murder by the device of sending those otherwise infantile messages, leaving a trail to them through Jack's typewriter."

"But Jack was killed, too."

"Yes, but we also know the murderer had to change his original plans. Somehow that change necessitated the killing of Jack and the abandonment of the frame-up against him by virtue of the very fact that he had to be murdered."

"But the cards kept coming."

"Because the murderer had set up the machinery for having them mailed and didn't want to risk stopping it. Think now, Glücke. We have a change of plan. Jack's murder. Then the cards start coming to Bonnie. Had the original plans been followed through, it's reasonable to assume that Jack would continue to be framed. But with Jack dead, some one else must be framed for the threats against Bonnie. Who? Well, we know now it's Ty being framed for those threats. It all adds up to one thing."

"Keep talking," said the Inspector intently.

"Some one is using the Royle-Stuart feud as a motive background for his crime. He's throwing you a ready-made motive. So the feud can't be the motive at all."

"The pilot!"

Ellery looked thoughtful. "Any trace of the pilot yet?"

"Damned shadow simply vanished. We're still plugging along on it. I've sort of become discouraged myself." He eyed Ellery. "Did you know I've cleared Alessandro?"

"Cleared?" Ellery elevated his brows.

"That hundred and ten grand Jack owed him was really paid. No doubt about it."

"Was there ever any?"

The Inspector looked suspicious. "You knew it!"

"As a matter of fact, I did. How did you find out?"

"Checked over bank accounts. Found that Jack had cashed a check for a hundred and ten thousand dollars in the bank on the morning of Thursday, the fourteenth."

"Not his bank, surely; they wouldn't honor a check of that size for him so quickly. Tolland Stuart's bank?"

"How'd you know that?" exploded Glücke.

"Guessed. I do know the check was signed by old man Stuart and was dated the thirteenth. I know because I asked the terrible-tempered old coot just yesterday."

"How come Stuart forked over all that dough to Jack? Jack didn't mean anything to him. Or did he?"

"I think not. It was Blythe's work. She took Jack with her that Wednesday to see her father, pleaded for the money for Jack's sake, not for her own. He says he gave it to her to get rid of both of them."

"Sounds screwy enough to be true. Even if it wasn't the reason, the signature's genuine; we know the old gent did make out a check for that amount."

"Anything else turn up?"

"Nope. Our leads on Jack's lady-friends petered out; every one of 'em had an alibi. And the poison—not a trace." Ellery drummed on the arm of his chair. Glücke scowled. "But this frame-up, now. If Ty's being framed, this last card was an awfully dumb one to send the girl! What kind of cluck are we dealing with, anyway?"

"A cluck who puts morphine into people's cocktails and sends 'em dumb messages. Perplexing, isn't it?"

"Maybe," muttered the Inspector hopefully, "maybe there's a lead in this fortune-telling stuff after all. I do know Blythe was a little cracked on the subject, like most of the wacky dames out here."

"No self-respecting fortune-teller would tolerate the salmagundi of which that yellow code sheet is the recipe."

"Come again?"

"I've been delving into the occult art. The little I've read convinces me that those cards simply couldn't have been sent by a professional fortune-teller, or even by one who knew much about fortune-telling."

"You mean those meanings for each card were just made up?"

"Oh, the meanings are authentic enough, one by one. The only liberty the poisoner took that I could find was in the meaning of the nine of clubs, which in one system of divination means 'warning.' Our friend Egbert improved that; he made it 'last warning.' Otherwise, the meanings can be found in any work on the subject.

"The trouble is that the ones on the yellow sheet represent a haphazard mixture of meanings from a number of *different* systems—there are lots of them, you know. Some from the fifty-two card system, some from the thirty-two, one from the so-called 'tableau of 21' system; and so on. Also, no account is taken of the different meanings for upright cards as against reversed; there's no mention of specific method such as Incantation, Oracle, Old English, Romany, Witch, Gypsy; or of specific arrangement, such as Rows of Nine, Lover's Tableau, Lucky Horseshoe, Pyramid, Wheel of Fortune. Also, the tearing of a card in two to reverse its meaning—absolute innovation on the part of friend Egbert; can't find it mentioned anywhere. Also—"

"For God's sake, I've had enough hocus-pocus!" cried the Inspector, seizing his head.

"I trust," said Ellery, "I've made my point?"

"The whole damned thing," groaned Glücke, "adds up to one beautiful headache."

"*La vie*," said Ellery philosophically, and he strolled out.

He made straight for the Hollywood hills, like a faithful homing-pigeon. The very sight of the white frame house calmed his ruffled spirit and laid a blanket over his tossing thoughts.

Paula kept him cooling his heels for twenty minutes, succeeding admirably in undoing all the good work achieved by her house.

"You can't do that to me," he said in reproach, when her secretary sent him in. He devoured her with his eyes. She was gowned in something svelte and clinging; she looked delectable. Remarkable how every time he saw her he discovered something new to admire! Her left eyelid, now; there was a tiny mole on it. Simply adorable. Gave her eyes interest, character. He seized her hands.

"Can't do what to you?" Paula murmured.

"Keep me waiting. Paula, you look so tasty I could eat you."

"Cannibal." She laughed, squeezing his hands. "What can you expect if you don't tell a lady in advance you're coming?"

"What difference does that make?"

"Difference! Are you really as stupid as you sound? Don't you know that every woman looks forward to an excuse to change her dress?"

"Oh, that. You don't have to primp for me."

"I'm *not* primping for you! This is one of my oldest rags—"

"The ancient plaint. And you're using lipstick. I don't like lipstick."

"*Mr.* Queen! I'll bet you still wear long underwear."

"A woman's lips are infinitely more attractive in their natural state." He pulled her toward him.

"Well, it stays on," said Paula hurriedly, backing away. "Oh, you infuriate me! I always say to myself I'm going to be as cool and remote as a queen with you, and you always manage to make me feel like a silly little girl on her first date. Sit down, you beast, and tell me why you've come."

"To see you," said Ellery tenderly.

"Don't give me *that*. You never had a decent, honest, uncomplicated impulse in your life. What is it this time?"

"Uh . . . there *was* a little matter of an item in your column today. I mean, about those letters—"

"I knew it! You are a beast."

"You don't begin to fathom how true that is."

"You're not even polite. You might lie about it, just once. Make me think you've come for no other reason than to see me."

"But that is the reason. In fact," said Ellery, brightening, "the letter business was just an excuse. That's what it was, an excuse."

She sniffed. "*You* needing an excuse for anything!"

"Paula, did I ever tell you how beautiful you are? You're the woman I've dreamed about since the days when I mooned over movie actresses. The perfect supplement to my soul. I think—"

"You think?" she breathed.

Ellery ran his finger under his collar. "I think it's warm in here."

"Oh."

"Warm in here, all right. Where are your cigarets? Ah. My brand, too. You're a jewel." He nervously lit a cigaret.

"You were about to say?"

"I was about to say? Oh, yes. That item in your column about the letters to Blythe."

"Oh," she said again.

"Where'd you dig up that nugget?"

She sighed. "Nothing up my sleeve. One of my informants was told about your visit to International Mailers, Inc., by a friend of a friend of your friend Mr. Lucey. And so it got to me, as almost everything that happens in this town does. I put two and two together—"

"And got three."

"Oh, no, a cool and accurate four. The description was too, too perfect. A lean and hungry galoot with a rapacious glint in his eye. Besides, you left your name." She eyed him curiously. "What's it all about?"

He told her. She listened in perfect quiet. When he had finished she reached for a cigaret. He held a match to it and she thanked him with a glance. Then she frowned into space.

"It's a frame-up, of course. But why did you ask me to keep peppering away in my column at the Ty-Bonnie feud?"

"Don't you know?"

"If Bonnie's in danger, it seems to me that Ty, being innocent . . ." She stopped. "Look here, Ellery Queen, you've got something up your sleeve!"

"No, no," said Ellery hastily.

"You just told me yourself you've done everything short of kidnaping to keep those two apart. Why?"

"A—whim. At any rate, if I must say so myself, I think I've done it very well."

"Oh, have you? Well, I don't know why you've done it, but I don't think you've done it well, Mister."

"Eh?"

"You've handled that part of it very badly."

Ellery regarded her with some annoyance. "I have, have I? Tell me, my omniscient Minerva, how you would have handled it?"

She gazed at him, her beautiful eyes mocking. "How true to type," she murmured. "Such magnificent sarcasm, arising from such magnificent egoism. The great man himself condescending to listen to a mere layman. And a woman, at that. Oh, Ellery, sometimes I think you're either the smartest man in the world or the dumbest!"

Ellery's cheeks took on a strong reddish cast. "That's not fair," he said angrily. "I admit I've been a good deal of an ass in my conduct towards you, but as far as the Ty-Bonnie situation is concerned—"

"You've been even more of an ass, darling."

"Damn it all," cried Ellery, springing to his feet, "where? How? You're the most exasperating female I've ever known!"

"In the first place, Mr. Queen," smiled Paula, "don't shout at me."

"Sorry! But—"

"In the second place, you should have asked my advice, confided in me—"

"In you?" said Ellery bitterly. "When you could have cleared up that business of the mess at the airport so easily?"

"That was different. A question of professional ethics—"

"There's woman's logic for you! That was different, she says. Let me tell you, Paula, it was precisely the same in principle. Besides, why should I confide in you? What reason have I to believe—" He stopped very suddenly.

"For that," said Paula with a glint in her eye, "you'll suffer. No, I think I'll give you the benefit of my wisdom after all. It may reduce the swelling above your ears. You bungled that Ty-Bonnie situation because you don't know women."

"What has that to do with it?"

"Well, Bonnie's very much the woman, and from what you've told me about the exact nature of your lies and her reaction to them . . . Mr. Queen, you are due to get the surprise of your life, I think very shortly."

"I think," said Mr. Queen nastily, "you're talking through your hat."

"Brr! don't we look mean! Smile, darling. Come, come. You look as if you wanted to eat me up, all right—but not from amorous motives."

"Paula," said Mr. Queen through his teeth, "I can stand just so much and no more. You need a lesson. Even the rat stands and fights at last."

"Such a humble metaphor!"

"Paula," thundered Mr. Queen, "I challenge you!"

"My, how formal," smiled Paula. "Touch a man's vanity and you send it screaming into the night. Challenge me to what?"

Mr. Queen seated himself again, smiling a wintry smile. "To tell me who killed Jack Royle and Blythe Stuart." Nevertheless, his eyes were curiously intent.

She raised her brows. "Don't you know—you, who know everything?"

"I asked *you*. Have you figured it out?"

"How tedious." She wrinkled her little nose. "Oh, I imagine I could guess if I wanted to."

"Guess." Ellery sneered. "Of course, it wouldn't stand to reason. I mean, that's the point. A woman doesn't reason. She guesses."

"And you, you great big powerful man, you've arrived at it by simply herculean efforts of the mind, haven't you?"

"Who is it?" said Ellery.

"You tell me first."

"Good lord, Paula, you sound like Fanny Brice doing Baby Snooks!"

"Why should I trust you?" murmured Paula. "You'd only claim it was your guess, too. Only you wouldn't use the word 'guess.' You'd say 'ratioci-nation,' or something like that."

"But for Pete's sake," said Ellery irritably, "I *don't* do these things by guesswork. It's a science with me!"

"Nothing doing." Again mockery. "You write your name down—the name you've guessed—and I'll do the same, and we'll exchange papers."

"Very well," groaned Ellery. "You've disrupted my whole intellectual life. It's childish, but you've got to be taught that lesson I mentioned."

Paula laughed, and procured two sheets of stationery, and gave him a pen-cil, and turned her back and wrote something quickly on her paper. Ellery hesitated. Then, with heavy strokes, he wrote a name, too. His eyes were veiled as she turned around.

"Wait," said Ellery. "I have an improvement to suggest. Get two enve-lopes."

She looked perplexed, but obeyed.

"Put yours in that envelope, and I'll put mine in this."

"But why?"

"Do as I say."

She shrugged and sealed the envelope over her sheet. Ellery did likewise. Then he stowed her envelope away in his wallet and handed his envelope to her.

"Not to be opened," he said grimly, "until our friend's ears are pinned back."

She laughed again. "Then I'm afraid they'll never be opened."

"Why?"

"Because," said Paula, "the criminal will never be caught."

"Is that so?" said Ellery softly.

"Oh, I know it's so," murmured Paula.

They looked at each other for a long time in silence. The mockery in her eyes had deepened.

"And what makes you so sure?" asked Ellery at last.

"No proof. Not a shred of evidence you could take into court. Unless you've been holding out on me."

"If I snap the trap," said Ellery with bright eyes, "on friend Egbert, will you admit you were wrong?"

"That would prove me wrong, wouldn't it?" she murmured. "But you won't."

"Willing to stake something on that?"

"Certainly. If you'll assure me," she looked at him through her long lashes, "you've got no evidence at this moment."

"I haven't."

"Then I can't lose—unless the creature goes completely haywire and con-fesses for no reason at all."

"I have an idea," said Ellery, "this creature won't do any such thing. You'll bet, eh?"

"Anything you say."

"Anything?"

She lowered her lashes. "Well . . . that's a broad term. Anything within reason."

"Would it be reasonable," murmured Ellery, "to make the loser take the winner out to the *Horseshoe Club?*"

Once before he had seen that terrified glimmer in her eyes. It almost made him contrite. But not quite. And then it passed very quickly.

"No guts," jeered Ellery. "If that disgusting term may be applied to a lady's anatomy. Well, I knew you wouldn't."

"I didn't . . . say . . . I wouldn't."

"Then it's a bet!"

She began to laugh softly. "Anyway, there's not the slightest danger of your winning."

"Either a bet's a bet, or it isn't."

"And either a bet has two hazards, or it's no bet either. What are *you* giving up if you lose, as you will?"

"Probably my . . ."

Something new leaped into Paula's eyes, and it was not terror. "Your what?" she asked swiftly.

"Uh—"

"What were you going to say?"

"You know, Paula," said Ellery, avoiding her eager gaze, "I really have you to thank for my solution of this case."

"But you were about to say—"

"You were the one who supplied me with the vital clues." His tone dried out and became impersonal. "The two vital clues."

"Ellery Queen, I could shake you! Who cares about that?"

"Consequently," said Ellery in the same dry way, "I'll be grateful to you for those tips all my life."

"All your life?" said Paula tenderly. "*All* your life?"

And she went slowly up to him and stood so close that the sweet odor of her filled his nose, and his head began to swim, and he began to back away like a dog sniffing danger.

"All your life?" she whispered. "Oh, Ellery . . ."

One of the telephones on her desk rang.

"Damn!" cried Paula, stamping her foot; and she ran to the desk.

Mr. Queen wiped his damp cheeks with his handkerchief.

"Yes?" said Paula impatiently into the telephone. And then she said nothing at all. As she listened everything live went out of her face, leaving it a blank and set as a *papier-mâché* mask. She hung up in the same odd silence.

"Paula, what's the matter?"

She sank into the Cape Cod chair. "I knew your *modus operandi* was wrong, and I was sure Bonnie saw through your transparent masculine tactics. But I never thought—"

"Bonnie?" Ellery stiffened. "What's happened?"

"My dear Mr. Know-It-All, prepare for a shock." Paula smiled vaguely.

"You've been trying to keep Bonnie and Ty at each other's throats. Why? You've got to tell me."

"So that a—certain person should see, believe, and be content." Ellery gnawed his lip. "Paula, for heaven's sake. Don't torment me. Who was that, and what did he say?"

"That was a friend of mine, a U.P. man. I'm afraid your certain person, unless afflicted by total paralysis, including eyes and ears, will in a matter of minutes learn the awful truth."

"What awful truth?" asked Ellery hoarsely.

"An hour ago Bonnie Stuart, hanging onto Ty Royle's neck as if she were afraid he'd fly away, gave an interview to the press—called 'em all in to her house in Glendale—in which she made a certain announcement to the world."

"Announcement?" Ellery said feebly. "What announcement?"

"To the effect that tomorrow, Sunday the twenty-fourth, she, Bonita Stuart, intends to become Mrs. Tyler Royle."

"My God!" howled Ellery, and he dived for the door.

Chapter XVIII

The Sorcerer's Apprentices

ELLERY, SCRAPING the fender of his coupé in his haste to park outside Bonnie's house in Glendale, caught sight of three men, patently detectives, speaking to a tall familiar figure who had just descended from a police car.

"Glücke! Is anything—has anything—"

"What brings you here?"

"I just heard the news. Is she still alive? There's been no attack on her?"

"Attack? Alive? Who you talking about?"

"Bonnie Stuart."

"Of course not." The Inspector grunted. "Say, what's the matter with you? I just got the flash myself."

"Thank the lord." Ellery swabbed his neck. "Glücke, you'll have to put a cordon around this house. As many men as you can scrape up."

"Cordon? But I've got three men—"

"Not enough. I want the place surrounded. I want it so well guarded that not even a mouse will get through. But it mustn't be obvious. The men are to stay out of sight. Get those flatfeet off this sidewalk!"

"Sure, but—"

"But nothing." Ellery raced for the gate.

Inspector Glücke ran back to the police car, rasped something, and pounded the pavement to the gate again. The police car shot away, and the three detectives strolled off.

Glücke caught up with Ellery, puffing. "What's this all about?"

"Something's wrong somewhere. Of all the idiotic stunts!"

The buxom, mousy Clotilde admitted them, her woman's black eyes sparkling with romantic excitement.

"Oh, but *Messieurs*, they cannot be—"

"Oh, but *Ma'm'selle*, they can, and they shall be," said Ellery rudely. "Ty! Bonnie!"

A muffled noise came from the nearest room, and he and the Inspector hurried towards its source. They burst into the drawing-room to find young Mr. Royle and his fiancée, considerably disheveled, disengaging themselves from each other's arms. Mr. Royle's mouth looked as if it were bleeding all round. But it was only Bonnie's lip-rouge.

"So here you are," said Ellery. "What the devil's the idea?"

"Oh, it's you," said Mr. Royle, in a grim tone, removing his lady's hands from about his neck.

"Hell of a mess," said Ellery, glaring at them. "Can't you two keep out of each other's hair for so much as two consecutive days? And if you can't, can't you at least keep your pretty mouths shut? Did you have to shout your goo-goo to the whole damned world?"

Mr. Royle rose purposefully from the sofa.

"Ty, your mouth," said Bonnie. "Oh, there's the Inspector. Inspector Glücke, I *demand*—"

"I think," said Ty in the same grim tone, "I know how to handle the situation."

"Oh, you do," said Ellery bitterly. "That's what comes of dealing with a couple of empty-headed kids who—"

A bomb exploded against his chin. It exploded, and little colored stars all gold and blue and scarlet, dancing like mad, filled the range of his vision, and the world swam languidly, and the next thing he knew it was a long long time after and he was lying on the floor blinking up at the chandelier and wondering when the war had broken out. The ceiling was insubstantial, too, heaving and rippling like a spread sail in a gale.

And he heard Ty blowing on his knuckles and saying in a hot, faraway voice: "There's your man, Inspector!"

"Don't be a jackass," said the Inspector's voice remotely. "Come on, Queen, get up. You'll dirty your nice pants."

"Where am I?" murmured Mr. Queen.

"He is, too!" shrieked Bonnie. "Sock him again, Ty. The sneaky devil!" Squinting for better visibility, Mr. Queen received a wavering impression of two slim ankles, a billowing skirt like a smaller sail, and a tiny stamping alligator. No, it was an alligator shoe. "I *knew* there was something wrong! When he took me to Ty's dressing-room . . . oh, it was so *pat*! That typewriter, and his smart 'deductions,' and Ty would *never* have sent me that warning against himself if he were the one, and then I saw with my own eyes how that b and d and t were *filed* down, so I knew Ty wouldn't do that if he really sent them, and everything." Bonnie paused for breath, but not for long. "You see? He was lying all the time! And so I went right to Ty, that's what I did, and—"

It went on and on, and Mr. Queen lay there surveying the ceiling. Why did it shift and sway so? He had it. It was an earthquake, a temblor. California was doing the Big Apple!

"Yes," growled Ty, "and we compared notes—should have done it a long time ago—and, Inspector, you'd be amazed at the things this fellow told us separately. Why, he actually tried to get each one of us to believe the other was a killer!"

"Yes, he told *me*—"

"The damned murderer told *me*—"

It went on and on and on. Somebody was making a fuss about something, Mr. Queen decided, but for the life of him he could not make out what it was. He groaned, trying to rise.

"Come on, come on," said Glücke in the most unfeeling way. "It was just a clout on the whiskers. Not that you don't deserve it, you lone wolf, you." And the detestable creature actually chuckled as he hauled Mr. Queen to a sitting position. "How you feeling? Terrible, I hope."

"My jaw is broken," mumbled Mr. Queen, waggling the organ in question. "Ooh, my head." He struggled to his feet.

"Try to tell Bonnie I sent those notes, hey?" snarled Ty, cocking his fist again.

"Why would he do that," cried Bonnie triumphantly, linking her arms about her hero's neck, "if he didn't send them himself? Answer that one!"

"Well, I had a reason," said Ellery shortly. "Where's a mirror?"

He wabbled to the mirror in the hall and examined his physiognomy. As he tenderly surveyed the damage, which was concentrated in a rapidly swelling heliotrope lump at the point of his chin, the doorbell rang and Clotilde hurried past him to admit two men. To Ellery's foggy gaze one was slow and grim and the other quick and excited. He rubbed his eyes and leaned against the wall, dizzy.

"Let 'em through," he muttered. "Glücke, didn't I tell you—"

Apparently the Inspector had the same notion, for he hurried out to talk to his men.

The slow one went slowly past Ellery, with no sign of recognition, into the drawing-room; and the quick one went quickly. Mr. Queen, satisfied that his jaw was still in one piece, tottered to the drawing-room doorway and closed his eyes.

The slow one stood just inside the room, looking at Bonnie. Looking. There was a sort of permanent flush under the topmost layer of his skin.

"It's Butch," said Bonnie faintly.

"Oh, say, Butch," began Ty in a defiant mutter. "We were going to tell you, call you, sort of—"

"The hell with that!" yelled the quick one. "I don't care a hoot about how you two bedbugs conduct your private lives, but I'll be damned if I see why you played such a dirty trick on your own studio!"

"Lay off, you," said Ty. "Butch, we really owe you—"

"Lay off?" Sam Vix glared out of his one eye. "He says lay off. Listen, me fine bucko, you haven't *got* a private life, see? You're a piece of property, like this house. You belong to Magna Studios, see? When Magna says jump—"

"Oh, go away, Sam," said Bonnie. She took one step towards the Boy Wonder, who stood exactly where he had stopped on entering the room and was still regarding her with that fixed and awful sadness of a man who sees the coffin-lid being screwed down over the face of his child, or mother, or sweetheart.

"Butch dear." Bonnie pinched her dress. "We were both so excited. . . . You know, I think, how I've always felt towards you. I never really told you I loved you, did I, Butch? Oh, I know I've treated you shamefully, and you've been a perfect angel about everything. But something happened today. . . . Ty is the only man I'll ever love, Butch, and I'm going to marry him just as quickly as I can."

Jacques Butcher took off his hat, looked around, put on his hat, and then sat down. He did not cross his legs, but sat stiffly, like a ventriloquist's dummy; and as he began to talk the only part of his face that moved was his lips.

"I'm sorry to have to intrude at such a time," he said, and stopped. Then he started again. "I wouldn't have come at all. Only Louis Selvin asked me to. Louis is—well, a little put out. Especially by you, Ty."

"Oh, Butch—" began Bonnie, but she stopped helplessly.

"By me?" said Ty.

Butcher cleared his throat. "Damn it all, I wouldn't—I've got to talk to you not as myself but as vice-president of Magna, Ty. I've just come from a long talk with Selvin. As president of Magna he feels it his duty to warn you— not to get married."

Ty blinked. "You don't mean to tell me he's going to hold me to that ridiculous marriage clause in my contract!"

"Marriage clause?" Bonnie stared. "Ty! What marriage clause?"

"Oh, Selvin stuck an anti-marriage clause into my contract the last time," said Ty disgustedly. "Prevents me from getting married."

"Sure, why not?" said Vix. "Great lover. You don't think the studio's going to build you up into a national fem-killer and let you spoil it by getting hitched!"

"I didn't know that, Ty," said Bonnie, distressed. "You didn't tell me."

"Forgot all about it. Anyway, it doesn't make any difference. Louis X. Selvin isn't going to tell me how to run my life!"

"Selvin asked me to point out," said Butcher in his cold, flat voice, "that you'll breach your contract if you marry Bonnie."

"The hell with Selvin! There are plenty of other studios in Hollywood."

"All Hollywood studios respect one another's star-contracts," said Butcher drearily. "If you breach a Magna contract you're through, Ty."

"Then I'm through!" Ty waved his arms angrily.

"But, Ty," cried Bonnie, "you *can't!* I won't let you throw away your career. We can wait. Maybe when you sign your next contract—"

"I don't want to wait. I've waited long enough. I'm marrying you tomorrow, and if Selvin doesn't like it he can go to hell."

"No, Ty!"

"No more arguments." Ty turned away with a stubborn, final gesture.

"All right, then," said Butcher in the same dreary way. "Louis anticipated that you might be stubborn. He could break you, Ty, but he admits you're too valuable a piece of property. So he's prepared to dicker."

"Oh, he is, is he?"

"But he warns you that his proposal is final. Take it or leave it."

"What proposal?" said Ty abruptly.

"If you insist on being married to Bonnie, he's willing to waive the anti-marriage clause. But only on the following conditions. First, you are to let Magna handle the details of your wedding. Second, after your wedding you and Bonnie are to co-star in a picture biography of Jack and Blythe, taking the rôles of your parents."

"Wait a minute, wait a minute," said Ty. "Does that wedding stunt mean a lot of this noisy publicity?"

"It means whatever Magna wants to do."

"And the picture—does that mean the murders, too?" asked Bonnie, looking ill at the very thought.

"The story," said Butcher, "is entirely up to me. You will have nothing to say about it."

"Oh, yes, we have," shouted Ty. "We say no—right now!"

Butcher rose. "I'm sorry. I'll tell Selvin."

"No—wait, Butch," cried Bonnie. She ran over to Ty and shook him. "Ty, please. You can't throw everything away like this. If—if you're stubborn I won't marry you!"

"Let 'em make monkeys out of us with one of those studio weddings?" growled Ty. "Make us put dad and Blythe on the screen in God knows what? Nothing doing."

"Ty, you've *got* to. I don't like it any more than you do; you know that. I'm fed up with—with all this. But we've got to look to the future, darling. Neither of us has anything. We can't throw up the only thing we've got. It won't be so bad. The wedding won't take long, and then we'll go away somewhere by ourselves—"

Ty glowered at the rug. He lifted his head and said sharply to Butcher: "If we go through with this, do we get a rest? A vacation? A honeymoon without brass bands?"

"Hell, no," said Vix quickly. "We can use that honeymoon swell. We can—"

"Please, Sam," said Butcher. Vix fell silent. "Yes, I can promise you that, Ty. Our wedding, your honeymoon. We realize that you're both upset, not yourselves, won't be able to do your best work immediately. So you may have as long for your honeymoon as you feel you need."

"And privacy!"

"And privacy."

Ty looked at Bonnie, and Bonnie looked pleadingly at Ty. Finally Ty said: "All right. It's a deal."

The Boy Wonder said: "Revised contracts will be in your hands in the morning. Sam here will handle all the details of the wedding." He turned on his heel and quietly went to the door. At the door he hesitated; then he turned around. "I'll convey my congratulations—tomorrow." And he walked out.

"Swell," said Sam Vix briskly. "Now look. You want to tie the knot to-morrow?"

"Yes," sighed Ty, sitting down. "Anything. Just get out of here."

"I've figured it all out on the way down. Here's the angle. We use the Jack-Blythe marriage as a model, see?"

"Oh," began Bonnie. Then she said: "Yes."

"Only we smear it on, see? Go the whole hog. You won't be married on the field. You'll—"

"You mean another airplane shindig?" growled Ty.

"Yeah, sure. Only we'll get old Doc Erminius to hitch you *in* your plane. Get it? Wedding *over* the field. In the air. Microphones for everybody in the plane. Broadcast through a radio telephone hook-up via the field station right to the thousands on the field as the plane circles it. Do it right, and with that Jack-Blythe background it'll be the biggest stunt this or any other town ever saw!"

"My God," yelled Ty, rising, "if you think—"

"Go on, Sam, get out of here," said Bonnie hurriedly, pushing him. "It'll be all right. I promise. Go on now."

Vix grinned and said: "Sure. Got plenty to do. Be seein' you," and he dashed out.

"Ty Royle, you listen to me," said Bonnie fiercely. "I *hate* it. But we're caught, and we're going to do it. I don't want to hear another word out of you. It's settled, do you hear? Whatever they want!"

Ellery detached himself from the support of the doorway and said dryly: "Now that all the master-minds have had their say, may I have mine?"

Inspector Glücke came in with him. He said, frowning: "I don't know. I'm not sure I like it. What do you think, Queen?"

"I don't give a damn what anybody thinks," said Ty, going over to a liquor cabinet. "Will you guys please clear out and leave Bonnie and me alone?"

"I think," said Ellery grimly, "that I'll find myself a nice deep hole, crawl into it, and pull it after me. I don't want to be around when the explosion comes."

"Explosion? What are you talking about?" said Ty, tossing off a quick one. "You and your riddles!"

"Oh, this is a lovely one. Don't you realize yet what you've done?" cried Ellery. "Announcing your marriage was bad enough, but now this! Spare me these Hollywood heroes and heroines."

"But I don't understand," frowned Bonnie. "What have we done? We've only decided to get married. That's our right, and it's nobody's business, either!" Her lip trembled. "Oh, Ty," she wailed, "and it was going to be so beautiful, too."

"You'll find out very shortly whose business it is," snapped Ellery.

"What's this all about?" demanded Glücke.

"You're like the sorcerer's apprentice, you two, except that you're a pair. Sorcerer goes away and you start fiddling with things you don't understand—dangerous things. Result, grief. And plenty of it!"

"What grief?" growled Ty.

"You've done the worst thing you could have done. You've just agreed to do the one thing, in fact, that's absolutely fatal to both of you."

"Will you get to the point?"

"I'll get to the point. Oh, yes, I'll get to the point. Hasn't it occurred to either of you that you're designs in a pattern?"

"Pattern?" said Bonnie, bewildered.

"A pattern formed by you and Ty and your mother and Ty's father. Hang it all, it's so obvious it simply shrieks." Ellery raced up and down the room, muttering. Then he waved his arms. "I'm not going to launch into a long analysis now. I'm just going to open your eyes to a fundamental fact. What happened to Blythe and Jack when *they* married? What happened to them, eh? Only an hour *after* they married?"

Intelligence leaped into Inspector Glücke's eyes; and Ty and Bonnie gaped.

"Ah, you see it now. They were both murdered, that's what happened. Then what? Bonnie gets warnings, winding up with one which tells her in so many words to have nothing more to do with Ty. What does that mean? It means lay off—no touch—hands off. And what do you idiots do? You promptly decide to be married—in such loud tones that the whole world will know not only the fact but the manner, too, in a matter of hours!"

"You mean—" began Bonnie, licking her lips. She whirled on Ty and buried her face in his coat. "Oh, Ty."

"I mean," said Ellery tightly, "that the pattern is repeating itself. I mean that if you marry tomorrow the same thing will happen to you that happened to Jack and Blythe. I mean that you've just signed your death warrant—that's what I mean!"

PART FOUR

Chapter XIX

The Four of Hearts

Ty RECOVERED a little of his color, or perhaps it was the Scotch. At any rate, he said: "I don't believe it. You're trying to frighten us with a bogeyman."

"Doesn't want us to be *married?*" said Bonnie in a daze. "You mean mother . . . too? That that—"

"It's nonsense," scoffed Ty. "I'm through listening to you, anyway, Queen. All you've ever done to me is mix me up."

"You poor fool," said Ellery. "You don't know what I've done to you. You don't know what I've done *for* you. How can people be so blind?"

"That's me," said the Inspector. "Not just blind; stiff. Queen, talk some sense, will you? Give me facts, not a lot of curly little fancies."

"Facts, eh?" Ellery glowered. "Very well, I'll give you—"

The front doorbell rang. Bonnie called wearily: "Clotilde, see who it is." But Ellery and the Inspector jostled each other crowding through the doorway. They pushed the Frenchwoman out of their way. Ty and Bonnie stared after them as if the two men were insane.

Ellery jerked open the door. A stout lady, hatless but wearing a broadtail coat over a flowered house-dress, stood indignantly on the *Welcome* mat trying to shake off the grip of one of Glücke's detectives.

"You let go of me!" panted the lady. "Of all things! And all I wanted to do—"

"In or out?" asked the detective of his superior.

Glücke looked helplessly at Ellery, who said: "I daresay we may invite the lady in." He stared at the woman with unmoving eyes. "Yes, madam?"

"Of course," sniffed Madam, "if a person can't be *neighborly* . . ."

Bonnie asked from behind them: "What is it? Who is it?"

"Oh, Miss *Stuart,*" gushed the stout lady instantly, barging between Ellery and the Inspector and bobbing before Bonnie in a ponderous figure that was almost a curtsy. "You *do* look just the way you look in pictures. I've always remarked to my husband that you're one of the *loveliest—*"

"Yes, yes, thank you," said Bonnie hurriedly. "I'm a little busy just now—"

"What's on your mind, Madam?" demanded Inspector Glücke. For some reason of his own Ellery kept watching the stout lady's hands.

"Well, I *hope* you won't think I'm intruding, Miss Stuart, but the funniest thing just happened. I'm Mrs. Stroock—you know, the *big* yellow house around the corner? Well, a few minutes ago my doorbell rang and the second maid answered it after a delay and there was nobody there, but an envelope was lying on my mat outside the door, and it wasn't for me at all, but was addressed to *you*, Miss Stuart, and to Mr. Royle, and I thought to myself: 'Isn't that the queerest mistake?' Because after all your address is plain enough, and the names of our streets are so different—"

"Yes, yes, envelope," said Ellery impatiently, extending his hand. "May I have it, please?"

"I *beg* your pardon," said Mrs. Stroock with a glare. "This happens to be *Miss Stuart's* letter, not yours, *whoever* you are, and you aren't Mr. Royle, I know *that*. Anyway, Miss Stuart," she said, turning to Bonnie again, all smiles, "here it is, and I assure you I ran over here just as fast as I could, which isn't fast," she giggled, "because my doctor says I *am* running the least bit to flesh these days. How *do* you keep your figure? I've always said that you—"

"Thank you, Mrs. Stroock," said Bonnie. "May I?"

The stout lady regretfully took an envelope out of her coat pocket and permitted Bonnie to take it from her. "And may I congratulate you on your engagement to Mr. Royle? I just heard the announcement over the radio. I'm sure it's the nicest, sweetest thing for two young people—"

"Thank you," murmured Bonnie. She was staring with a sort of horror at the envelope.

"By the way," said Ellery, "did you or your maid see the person who rang your bell, Mrs. Stroock?"

"No, indeed. When Mercy went to the door there was nobody there."

"Hmm. Thank you again, Mrs. Stroock." Ellery shut the door politely in the stout lady's face. She sniffed again and marched down the steps, followed to the gate by the detective, who watched her until she turned the corner and then drifted away.

"Thank you," said Bonnie for the fourth time in a stricken voice to the closed door.

Ellery took the envelope from her fingers and, frowning, returned to the drawing-room. Inspector Glücke gently took Bonnie's arm.

Ty said: "What's the matter now?"

Ellery opened the too familiar envelope, addressed in pencilled block letters to "Miss Bonnie Stuart and Mr. Tyler Royle"—no stamp, no other writing except Bonnie's address—and out tumbled two playing-cards with the blue-backed design.

"The . . . four of hearts?" said Bonnie faintly.

Ty snatched both cards. "Four of hearts? And the ace of spades!" He went to Bonnie and pulled her close to him suddenly.

"I told you this morning, Glücke, we were dealing with a playful creature," remarked Ellery. He stared at the cards in Ty's fist. "Perhaps now you'll believe me."

"The ace of *spades*," said the Inspector, as if he could not credit the evidence of his own eyesight.

"What does it mean?" asked Bonnie piteously.

"It means," said Ellery, "that the interview you two gave the press today has already borne fruit. I suppose the extras have been on the streets for an hour, and you heard that awful woman mention the radio. Our friend Egbert was in such haste to get this message to you he refused to wait for the regular mails, which would have brought the cards Monday, or even a special delivery, which would have brought them some time tomorrow."

"But what's it *mean*?"

"As an intelligible message?" Ellery shrugged. "Together the cards say: 'Bonnie Stuart and Tyler Royle, break your engagement or prepare to die.'"

The Inspector made a sound deep in his throat and nervously looked about the room.

Bonnie was pale, too; paler than Ty. Her hand crept into his.

"Then it *is* true," she whispered. "There *is* a pattern. Ty, what are we going to do?"

"The reason," Mr. Queen remarked, "that Egbert delivered this message in such haste is that Monday—obviously—will be too late. Even tomorrow may be too late. I trust you get his implication?"

Ty sat down on the sofa, his shoulders sagging. He said wearily: "I get it, all right. It's true, and we're not to marry, and if we do it's curtains for us. So I guess we've got to satisfy everybody—Butch, the studio, Egbert L. Smith —and drop our marriage plans."

Bonnie moaned: "Oh, Ty. . . ."

"Why kid ourselves, honey?" Ty scowled. "If I was the only one concerned, I'd say the hell with Egbert. But I'm not; you're in it, too. I won't marry you and lay you wide open to an attack on your life."

"Oh, you *are* stupid!" cried Bonnie, stamping. "Don't you see that isn't so? *I* received threats even before we announced our plans. Those threats were mailed to *me*. The only time *you* were threatened was just now, *after* we'd announced our intention to be married!"

"Hurrah for the female intelligence," said Ellery. "I'm afraid Bonnie scores there, Ty. That's perfectly true. I refrained from mentioning it before, but I can't hold it back any longer. All my efforts to keep you two apart have been exerted in *your* behalf, Ty, not Bonnie's. It's your life that's involved in this association with Bonnie. Bonnie's life, with or without you, has been in danger from the day her mother died."

Ty looked confused. "And I socked you!"

"Marry Bonnie and you're on the spot. Don't marry Bonnie and you're not on the spot. But she is whether you marry her or not. It's a pretty thought."

"In again, out again." Ty grinned a twisted grin. "I've given up trying to make sense out of this thing. If what you say is true, we're going to be married. I'm not going to let her face this alone. Let that sneaking son try to kill me—let him try."

"No, Ty," said Bonnie miserably. "I can't have you doing that. I can't. Why should you endanger your life? I don't pretend to understand it, either, but how can I let you share a danger that's apparently directed at me alone?"

"You," said Ty, "are marrying me tomorrow, and no arguments."

"Oh, Ty," whispered Bonnie, creeping into his arms. "I'd hoped you'd say that. I *am* afraid."

Inspector Glücke was prowling about in a baffled sort of way. "If we only knew who it was," he muttered. "If we knew, we might be able to do something."

"Oh, but we do know," said Ellery. He looked up at their exclamations. "I forgot you didn't know. I do, of course, and I tell you we can do nothing—"

"'Of course,' he says!" shouted the Inspector. He pounced on Ellery and shook him. "Who is it?"

"Yes," said Ty in a funny voice. "Who is it, Queen?"

"Please, Glücke. Just knowing who it is doesn't solve this problem." He began to pace up and down, restlessly.

"Why not?"

"Because there's not an atom of evidence to bring into court. The case wouldn't get past a Grand Jury, if it ever got to a Grand Jury at all. It would be thrown out for lack of evidence, and you'd have missed your chance to pin the crimes on the one who committed them."

"But, good God, man," cried Ty, "we can't just sit around here waiting for the fellow to attack. We've got to do something to trim his claws!"

"Let me think," said Ellery irritably. "You're making too much noise, all of you."

He walked up and down, head bent. There was no sound at all except the sound of his march about the room.

"Look," interrupted the Inspector. "A cop has just as great a responsibility protecting life as investigating death. You say you know who's behind all this, Queen. All right. Let's go to this bird, tell him we know, warn him he'll be watched until the day he dies by a squad of detectives on twenty-four-hour duty. He'd be a bigger fool than any one could be if he didn't give up his plans then and there."

"I've thought of that, of course," said Ellery crossly. "But it has one nasty drawback. It means Egbert will never hang for the murder of Jack and Blythe; and if there's one little fellow I'd have no objection to seeing hanged, it's Egbert."

"If it means safety for Bonnie," said Ty, "let him go. Let him go! Glücke's right."

"Or why couldn't we," began Bonnie, and stopped. "*That's* it! Why couldn't Ty and I be married right this minute and then vanish? Go off somewhere without anybody's knowing where. *Anybody.* Then we'd be safe!"

"And go through the rest of a long life looking over your shoulder every time you heard a sound behind you?" asked Ellery. And then he stared at Bonnie. "Of course! That's it. Vanish! Exactly. Exactly. Force his hand. He'd have to . . ." His voice trailed off and he began to run about madly, like an ant, his lips moving silently.

"Have to what?" demanded the Inspector.

"Try to murder them, of course. . . . Yes, he would. Let's see now. If we pulled the stunt—"

"Try to *murder* us?" repeated Bonnie, blinking.

Ellery stopped racing. "Yes," he said briskly. "That's exactly what we'll do. We'll jockey this bird into the position of *trying* to murder you. If the compulsion is strong enough—and I think we can make it strong enough—he *must* try to murder you . . . Bonnie." Ellery's eyes were shining. "Would you be willing to run the risk of an open attack on your life if by running that risk we stood a good chance of catching your mother's murderer red-handed?"

"You mean," said Bonnie slowly, "that if it were successful I'd be free? Ty and I—we'd both be *free?*"

"Free as the air."

"Oh, yes. Oh, yes, I'll do anything for that!"

"Not so fast," said Ty. "What's the plan?"

"To go through with the announced marriage, to utilize it as a trap for the murderer."

"And use Bonnie as a guinea-pig? Nuts."

"But I tell you Bonnie's life is in danger in any event," said Ellery impatiently. "Even if she's surrounded by armed guards day and night, do you want her to spend the rest of her life waiting for the ax to fall? I assure you, Ty, it's either Egbert or Bonnie. Take my word for that. The creature's gone too far to stop now. *His plans make it mandatory for Bonnie to die.*"

"It's a hell of a decision to make," muttered Ty.

"Ty, will you listen to me? I tell you it's the safest course in the long run. Don't you see that by setting a trap we force his hand? We make him attempt Bonnie's life when *we* want him to, under conditions *we* have established—yes, lure him unsuspecting right into a spot where we know what he'll do and be prepared for him. By taking the bold step we reduce the danger to a minimum. Don't you see?"

"How do you know," said Glücke intently, "he'll attack?"

"He's got to. He can't wait too long; I'm positive of that, never mind how. If part of our plan is to announce that immediately after the wedding tomorrow Bonnie and Ty are taking off for an unknown destination, to be gone an indefinite length of time, he *must* attack; I know he must. He can't let Bonnie, living, vanish; he'll have to try to kill her tomorrow or give up his whole plan."

"Why shouldn't he give up his whole plan?"

"Because," said Ellery grimly, "he's already killed two people in pursuance of his objective. Because we'll give him another opportunity he can't pass up. Because he's desperate, and cold-blooded, and his motive—to him—is overwhelming."

"Motive? What motive? I thought he was crazy."

"Yes, what motive?" asked Bonnie tensely. "Nobody could possibly have a reason for killing me."

"Obviously some one has, as this last message indicates. Let's not go down byroads now. The big point is: Are you game to try?"

Bonnie laid her head on Ty's shoulder. Ty twisted his head to look down at her. She smiled back at him faintly.

"All right, Queen," said Ty. "Let's go."

"Good! Then we've got to understand this clearly, all four of us. You, too, Glücke. You'll have an important job.

"We'll let Sam Vix's plans for the wedding stand; in fact, we use them. As it's turned out, that studio mix-up just now was a break for us; it happened naturally, and that's what we need most—natural events arousing no possible suspicion on the part of . . . let's continue to call him Egbert.

"All right. We can depend on Sam to ring the welkin tonight; there will be plenty of ballyhoo between now and tomorrow afternoon. We make it clear that you two are to be married in the plane; we make it even clearer—this is vital—that you two are leaving for an unannounced destination, for an indefinite stay. That no one, not even the studio, will know where you're going or when you're coming back. That you're sick and tired of it all, and want to be alone, to chuck Hollywood and all its sorrows for a while. If possible you must tell that to the press . . . convincingly."

"The way I feel," grinned Ty, "don't worry about that."

"Now what does Egbert do? He's got to murder Bonnie—yes, and after the wedding you, too, Ty—before you slip out of his grasp. How is he going to do it? Not by poisoning food or drink, as in the case of Jack and Blythe; he'll realize that, with the manner of their deaths so fresh in your minds, you just won't touch untested gifts of food or drink. So he'll have to plan a more direct assault; that's inevitable. The most direct is a gun."

"But—" began the Inspector, frowning.

"Let me finish. To shoot and get away safely, he can't attack on the field; even if he succeeded in taking two accurate potshots from the crowd, he'd never live to leave the field. So," snapped Ellery, "he'll have only one course to follow. In order to make sure of a successful double murder and a successful getaway, *he'll have to get into that plane with you.*"

"Oh . . . I see," said Bonnie in a small voice. Then she set her smooth jaw.

"I get it, I get it," mumbled Glücke.

"Moreover, since we know he'll try to get into that plane, we also know how. He can get in, reasonably, only as *the pilot.*"

"The way he did it in the case of Jack and Blythe!" exclaimed the Inspector.

"Since we're reasonably certain he'll take the opportunity if he's given the opportunity, all we have to do is give it to him. So we engage a professional aviator. That's part of our announcement. We see to it that the pilot isn't openly under surveillance, we permit Egbert to decoy the pilot into a dark corner, to incapacitate him—I don't believe he'll be in serious danger, but we can take steps to keep it down to a minimum—and we permit Egbert to take the pilot's place in the plane."

"Why a pilot at all? I run my own ship. Won't that sound phony?" asked Ty.

"No, because you're taking a pilot in order to have him drop you off somewhere to make connections with a train or a boat—not even the pilot, we'll announce, will know where he's going until after the take-off. So of course you'll need a pilot, ostensibly, to bring the plane back after he dumps you. That's all right. At any rate, friend Egbert will hop into the plane and take off, secure in the feeling that he's left no trail and will be able to commit his crime in mid-air."

"Wait a minute," said Glücke. "I like your scheme, but it means putting these two youngsters in a plane with a dangerous criminal, alone except for some fool of a minister who'll probably only make things worse."

"This minister won't."

"Erminius is an old woman."

"But it won't be Erminius. It will be some one who just looks like Erminius," said Ellery calmly.

"Who?"

"Your obedient servant. Erminius has a beautiful set of black whiskers, which makes him a cinch to impersonate. Besides, Egbert won't be paying much attention to the preacher, I can promise you that. He'll be too intent on getting that plane off the ground unsuspected. Anyway, Ty and I will both be armed. At the first sign of trouble, we shoot."

"Shoot," repeated Bonnie, licking her lips and trying to look brave.

"We'll subdue him if we can, but we must give him the opportunity to show his hand. And *that* can be brought out in court."

"Hell," protested the Inspector, "you ought to know even catching the guy in an attempted homicide won't pin the murders of Jack and Blythe on him."

"I rather think it won't make any difference. I think that, once caught, our friend will collapse like a straw man and tell all. If the stunt works, sheer surprise at finding himself trapped at a moment when he thought his plans were about to be consummated will put him off guard. At any rate, it's our only chance to catch him at all."

There was a little uncomfortable interval, and then Glücke said: "It sounds screwy as the devil, but it might work, it might work. What do you say, you two?"

"I say yes," said Bonnie quickly, as if she were afraid that if she hesitated she might not say yes at all. "What do *you* say, darling?"

And Ty kissed her and said, "I love you, Pug Nose." Then he said to

Ellery in an altogether different tone of voice: "But if anything goes wrong, Queen, I swear I'll strangle you with my bare hands. If it's the last thing I do."

"It probably will be," muttered Ellery. "Because Egbert's plan will undoubtedly be to stage a second St. Valentine's Day massacre in that plane with his popgun and then bail out, leaving the plane to crash in the desert somewhere."

Chapter XX

Castle in the Air

TIME, WHICH HAD been floating by, suddenly took on weight and speed. Ellery kept looking at his wrist-watch in despair as he went into the details of his plan, instructing Ty and Bonnie over and over in their rôles.

"Remember, Ty, you'll have to handle all the arrangements; Glücke and I can't possibly appear in this. In fact, we'll stay as far away from you as we can until tomorrow. Have you a gun?"

"No."

"Glücke, give him yours." The Inspector handed his automatic over to Ty, who examined it expertly and dropped it into his jacket pocket. "Now what's your story to the press?"

"Bonnie has received a warning to break our engagement, but we both agree it's the work of some crank and intend to be married at once. I show the cards."

"Right. Not a word about our real plans to any one. In a half-hour call Erminius and engage him to perform the ceremony. Bonnie."

Bonnie peeped out from the cradle of Ty's arms.

"You're all right?"

"I'm feeling f-fine," said Bonnie.

"Good girl! Now do a little of that acting Butch pays you for. You're happy—just the proper combination of happiness and grief. You're marrying Ty because you love him, and you also know that Blythe and Jack must be happy somewhere knowing what you're about to do. The feud is over, never to be resurrected. You've got all that?"

"Yes," said Bonnie in a shaky little voice.

"By George, I feel like a director!" Ellery grinned with a confidence he did not feel and stuck his hand out to Ty. "Good luck. By this time tomorrow night the nightmare will be over."

"Don't worry about us, Queen," said Ty, shaking hands soberly. "We'll come through. Only—get into that plane!"

Glücke said abruptly: "Stay here. Send for your duds, Ty. Don't leave this house. It's surrounded right now, but I'll send two men in here to watch from a hiding-place—just in case. Don't do anything foolish, like those heroes you play in the movies. At the first suspicion of trouble, yell like the devil."

"I'll take care of that part of it," said Bonnie with a grimace; then she tried to smile, and they shook hands all around, and Ellery and the Inspector slipped out by the back way.

The next twelve hours were mad on the surface and madder underneath. The necessity for boring from within was a bother; Ellery was constantly answering telephone calls in his hotel apartment and giving cautious instructions. He could only pray that Ty and Bonnie were carrying off their end successfully.

The first assayable results came booming in via radio late that night. Towards the end of an expensive Saturday-night program a studio announcer interrupted with the detailed news of the projected wedding. Apparently Sam Vix had sailed into his assignment with his customary energy. Within two hours four of the largest radio stations on the Pacific Coast had broadcast the announcement of the Sunday airplane wedding of Tyler Royle and Bonnie Stuart. A famous female studio commentator climbed panting on the air to give the palpitating public the intimate details of the plan, as transmitted directly from the mouths of the lovers themselves. The interview, reported this lady, had been too, too sweet. Somebody, she said sternly, had had the bad taste to "warn" Bonnie against marriage. This was, it seemed, a frank and brutal case of lèse majesté. Those two, poor, sorrowing children! panted the lady. She hoped every friend Ty and Bonnie had within driving distance of Griffith Park airport would be on hand Sunday to show Ty and Bonnie what the world thought of their coming union.

The newspapers erupted with the news late Saturday night, chasing a scarehead concerning the Japanese war in China off the front page.

And so on, interminably, far into the night.

Ellery and the Inspector met secretly at Police Headquarters at two o'clock in the morning to discuss developments. So far, so good. Dr. Erminius had been duly, and unsuspectingly, engaged to perform the unique ceremony. Dr. Erminius was delighted, it appeared, at this heaven-sent opportunity to join two fresh young souls in holy wedlock with God's pure ether as a background, although he fervently prayed the Lord that there would be no repetition of the ghastly aftermath of the first Royle-Stuart wedding at which he had officiated.

The pilot had also been engaged; he had been selected without his knowledge more for his character than for his skill as an aviator. He was known to have a healthy respect for firearms.

In his office at Headquarters Glücke had several photographs of the eminent divine ready for Ellery, who came down with a make-up box stolen from one of the Magna dressing-rooms; and the two men spent several anxious hours making Ellery up and comparing him with Dr. Erminius's photographs. They agreed finally that a bundling, muffling overcoat with a beaver collar, such as Dr. Erminius affected in brisk weather, would help; and parted with plans to meet early in the morning.

Ellery returned to Hollywood, snatched three hours of uneasy sleep, and at eight Sunday morning met the Inspector and two detectives outside Dr. Erminius's expensive house in Inglewood. They went in; and when they came out they were minus the two detectives and richer by a fur-collared coat. The good man howled ungodly imprecations from within.

Several telephone calls, a final check-up. . . . Ellery crossed his fingers. "Nothing more for us to do," he sighed. "Well, so long, Glücke. See you in the Troc or in hell."

At noon Sunday the parking spaces about the Griffith Park airport were almost filled. At one o'clock there was a jam over which a hundred policemen sweated and cursed. At one-fifteen all cars were halted at the intersection of Los Feliz and Griffith Park Boulevards and detoured; and at one-thirty it seemed as if every automobile-owner in the State of California had come to see Ty and Bonnie married.

Ty's red-and-gold plane stood in a cleared area considerably larger than the area in which it had stood a week before. But the jam threatened to burst the ropes on the field, and the police heaved against them, shouting. When Dr. Erminius's royal-blue limousine rolled onto the field under motorcycle escort and the good dominie descended, complete with shiny black whiskers and beaver-collared coat, muffled to the ears—the doctor had a bad cold, it appeared—a cheer shook the heavens. And when Ty and Bonnie arrived, pale but smiling, the din frightened a flock of pigeons into swooping for cover.

Cameras were leveled, reporters yelled themselves hoarse, and Ty and Bonnie and Dr. Erminius were photographed from every conceivable angle and in every position commensurate with the moral tone of the family newspaper.

Meanwhile, the pilot who had been engaged, very natty in his flying suit, received a puzzling message and wandered off to the empty hangar in which only a week before Ty and Bonnie had been held up. He went into the hangar and looked about.

"Who wants me?" he called.

Echo answered; but answer also materialized, and the man's jaw dropped as a bulky, shapeless figure in flying togs, wearing a face-concealing pair of goggles and a helmet, stepped from behind a tarpaulined airplane and leveled a revolver at the pilot's chest.

"Huh?" gasped the pilot, elevating his arms.

The revolver waved an imperious order. The pilot stumbled forward, fascinated. The butt described a short, gentle arc and the pilot crumpled to the floor, no longer interested in the proceedings.

And from a rent in the tarpaulin, behind which he had been suffocating for two hours, Inspector Glücke, automatic in hand, watched the pilot fall, watched the bundled figure stoop over the man and drag him into a corner.

The Inspector did not so much as stir a finger; the tap had been gentle, and interference just then would have been disastrous to the plan.

Because of his position, Glücke could see only the inert body. He did see a pair of hands begin to undress the pilot, divesting him of his outer clothing; it struck Glücke suddenly that the two flying-suits were of different cut; of course, little Egbert would have to put on his victim's suit and helmet and goggles.

It was all over in two minutes. Glücke saw the flying-suit of the attacker flung down on the unconscious pilot, then the helmet, the goggles; and the quick disappearance of the pilot's rig.

Then the attacker appeared again, dressed as the pilot, goggled and un-recognizable; he appeared stooping over the motionless figure. He began to bind and gag the pilot. Still the Inspector did not move.

The attacker pushed his bound victim under the very tarpaulin behind which Glücke crouched, pocketed the revolver, and with a certain grim jaunti-ness strode out of the hangar.

Glücke moved then, quickly. He clambered out of the covered ship, made a low warning sound, and three plain-clothesmen stepped out of steel lockers. Leaving the unconscious man in their hands, he ducked out of the hangar by a rear door and strolled around the building to merge briefly with the crowd. Then he sauntered casually up to the group of shouting, gesticulating people around the red-and-gold plane.

The "pilot" was busily engaged in picking up the tumbled luggage and depositing it, piece by piece, in the plane. No one paid any attention to him. Finally he climbed into the plane and a moment later the propeller turned over and began to spin with a roar.

He looked out the window and waved his arm impatiently.

The Reverend Dr. Erminius looked startled. But he caught the eye of Inspector Glücke, who nodded, and heaved a relieved sigh.

"All set," he said in Ty's ear.

"What?" yelled Ty above the roar of the motor.

Dr. Erminius gave him a significant look. Bonnie caught it, too, and closed her eyes for a second; and then she smiled, and waved, and Ty, looking rather grim, picked her slender figure up in his arms and carried her into the plane to the howling approval of the mob. The Reverend Dr. Erminius followed more sedately. The pilot came out of his cubicle, shut the door securely, went back to his cubicle; the police and field attendants cleared the runway; and finally the signal came, and the red-and-gold plane began slowly to taxi down the field, picking up speed . . . its tail lifting, its wings gripping the air. And then it left the solid ground and soared into the blue, and they were alone with their destiny.

Afterwards, in recollection, it all seemed to have happened quickly. But at the time there was an interminable interval, during which the thousands on the field below grew smaller and smaller as the plane circled the field, and finally became only animated dots, and the hangars and administration buildings looked like toys, and the runway, the crowd released, suddenly took on the appearance of a gray patch overrun with bees.

Bonnie kept looking out the window as Ty adjusted the speaking tube to her head, and put one on himself, and gave one to Dr. Erminius. Bonnie was trying to look gay, waving idiotically at the mobs below, steadfastly keeping her eyes averted from the cubicle in which the pilot sat quietly at the controls.

Ty's arms were tightly about her, and his right hand gripped the automatic in his pocket. And his eyes never left the back of the pilot's helmeted head.

As for the Reverend Dr. Erminius, that worthy beamed on the earth and on the sky, and fumbled with the Word of God, obviously preparing to preside over the coming union of two young, untried souls.

And the plane began imperceptibly to nose towards the northeast, where the desert lay, leveling off at eight thousand feet and throbbing steadily.

"I believe," announced Dr. Erminius solemnly, and at his words the bees being left behind stopped swarming and froze to the ground as the amplifiers on the field caught his voice, "that the time has come to join you children in the ineffable bliss of matrimony."

"Yes, Doctor," said Bonnie in a low voice. "I'm ready." And she turned around, and gulped, and the gulp was audible as a hollow thunder below. She rose to stand at Ty's knee and clutch his shoulder. Ty rose quickly then, placing her behind him. His right hand was still in his pocket.

"Oh, pilot," called Dr. Erminius over the mutter of the motor.

The pilot turned his goggled head in inquiry.

"You have automatic controls there, have you not?"

Ty answered in a flat voice: "Yes, Doctor. This is my plane, you know. The Sperry automatic pilot."

"Ah. Then if you will come back here, pilot, after locking the controls you may act as the witness to this ceremony. It will be more comfortable than crowding about your cockpit, or whatever it is called."

The pilot nodded and they saw him adjust something on the complex control-board in front of him. He spent a full minute there, his back to them; and none of them spoke.

Then he got out of his seat, and turned, and stooped, and came into the body of the plane with a swift lurch of his bulky body, looking like a hunchback with the protuberance of the unopened parachute between his shoulder-blades. The Reverend Dr. Erminius had his Book open and ready, and he was beaming on Ty and Bonnie. Ty's hand was still in his pocket, Bonnie was by his side and yet somehow a little behind him, sheltered by his body and the body of the beaming preacher.

And the preacher said: "Let us begin. Bless my soul, we're leaving the field! Weren't we supposed—"

The pilot's hand darted into his pocket and emerged with a snub-nosed automatic, and he brought his hand up very swiftly, his finger tightening on the trigger as the muzzle came up to aim directly at Bonnie's heart.

At the same moment there was a flash of fire from Ty's right pocket, and a flash of fire as if miraculously from the pages of the Good Book in the no longer beaming dominie's hands; and the pilot coughed and lurched forward, dropping the snub-nosed automatic from a gloved hand which suddenly spouted blood.

Bonnie screamed, once, and fell back; and Ty and Dr. Erminius pounced on the swaying figure.

The pilot lashed out, catching Ty with his good fist on the jaw and sending him staggering back against Bonnie. Dr. Erminius snarled and fell on the cursing man. The two tumbled to the floor of the plane, pummeling each other.

Ty lunged forward again.

But somehow, by exactly what means they never knew, the pilot managed to shake them off. One moment they were all struggling on the floor and the next he was on his feet, goggles and helmet torn away from his flushed face, screaming: "You'll never hang *me!*"

And before either of the men on the floor could get to his feet, the pilot darted to the door, wrenched it open, and flung himself out into the sky.

He bounced once on the metal wing.

His body hurtled toward the distant wrinkled face of the earth.

They watched that plummet dive with the paralysis of horror.

The tumbling figure waved frantic arms, growing smaller and smaller.

But no parachute blossomed, and the body became a shrinking mote that suddenly stopped shrinking and spread infinitesimally on the earth.

Chapter XXI

Excursion into Time

THE FIELD WAS the surface of a bubbling pot when they landed. Police were using their night-sticks. Men with cameras and men with notebooks were fighting openly to break through the cordon.

Ellery, one whisker askew, cooing over Bonnie, saw Inspector Glücke in a small army of detectives gesticulating near the hangar; and he grinned with the satisfaction of sheer survival.

"It's all right, Bonnie," he said. "It's all over now. You've got nothing more to worry about. That's right. Cry it out. It's all right."

"Just wait," growled Ty. "Wait till I get this damned thing standing still."

"I'm waiting," sobbed Bonnie. "Oh, Ty, I'm waiting!" And she shuddered over the palpable sight of a small leggy figure tumbling end over end through empty air, like a dead bug.

The Inspector hurried them into the hangar, out of sight of the frenzied crowd. He was red-faced and voluble, and he grinned all over as he pumped Ty's hand, and Ellery's hand, and Bonnie's hand, and listened to details, and shouted instructions, and swore it had all come in like a movie. Outside a police plane managed to find a space clear enough for a take-off; it headed northeast on the funereal mission of locating and gathering the splattered remains of the one who had sought escape and found death.

Ty seized Bonnie and began shoving through the crowd of detectives to the hangar door.

"Here, where are you going?" demanded Ellery, grabbing his arm.

"Taking Bonnie home. Can't you see the poor kid's ready to collapse? Here, you men, get us off this field!"

"You wouldn't run out on me now, Bonnie?" smiled Ellery, chucking her chin. "Come on, square your shoulders and get set for another sky-ride."

"Another?" yelled Ty. "What now, for the love of Mike? Haven't you had enough sky-riding for one day?"

"No," said Ellery, "I have not." He began to rip off his false whiskers, glancing inquiringly at the Inspector; and the Inspector nodded with a certain grimness, and before Ty could open his mouth to protest he and Bonnie were hurried onto the field and through lanes of police into a large transport plane drawn up on the line with its motor spitting.

"Hey, for God's sake!" shouted a reporter. "Glücke! Give us a break. Glücke!"

"Ty!"

"Bonnie!"

But the Inspector shook his head, and followed Ty and Bonnie into the plane; and there, huddled in a pale-faced group, were several familiar faces.

They were looking at Ty and Bonnie, and Ty and Bonnie were looking at them; and Glücke hauled Ellery in and said something in a low voice to the pilot.

And then they all stared at the rushing, congested field as the plane took off and headed southeast.

And soon they were settling down on the little landing-field near Tolland Stuart's mountain mansion; and as they landed another plane, which had been following from Los Angeles, settled down after them.

Ellery, his face his own, jumped to the ground almost before the plane stopped. He waved to its oncoming pursuer, and ran over to the hangar before which the emaciated figure of Dr. Junius was waiting. The doctor's mouth was open and his eyes were glary with confusion.

Police poured out of the second plane and scattered quickly into the woods.

"What's this?" stammered Dr. Junius, staring at the numerous figures getting out of the first plane. "Mr. Royle? Miss Stuart? What's happened?"

"All in good time, Doctor," said Ellery brusquely, taking his arm. He shouted to the others: "Up to the house!" and began to march the physician along.

"But . . ."

"Now, now, a little patience."

And when they reached the house, Ellery said: "Where's the old fire-eater? We can't leave him out of this."

"Mr. Stuart? In his room, sulking with a cold. He thinks he's catching the grippe. Wait, I'll tell him—" Dr. Junius broke away and ran up the living-room steps. Ellery watched him go, smiling.

"Upstairs," he said cheerfully to the others. "The old gentleman's indisposed for a change."

When they got upstairs they found Dr. Junius soothing the old man, who sat propped up in bed against two enormous pillows, wrapped in an Indian blanket almost to the hairline, his two bright eyes glaring out at them.

"I thought I told you," he began to complain, and then he spied Bonnie. "Oh, so you've come back, hey?" he snarled.

"Yes, indeed," said Ellery, "and with a considerable escort, as you see. I trust, Mr. Stuart, you won't be as inhospitable this time as you were the last. You see, I've got a little tale to tell, and it did seem a pity to keep it from you."

"Tale?" said the old man sourly.

"The tale of an escapade just now in the California clouds. We've captured the murderer of John Royle and your daughter Blythe."

Dr. Junius said incredulously: "What?"

And the old man opened his toothless mouth, and closed it again, and then reopened it as he stared from Ellery to Inspector Glücke. His mouth remained open.

"Yes," said Ellery, nodding over a cigaret, "the worst is over, gentlemen. A very bad hombre's come to the end of the line. I shouldn't have said 'captured.' He's dead, unless he learned somewhere to survive an eight-thousand foot drop from a plane with a parachute that didn't open."

"Dead. Oh, I see; he's dead." Dr. Junius blinked. "Who was he? I can't imagine. . . ." His eyes, bulging out of their yellow-violet sockets, began timidly to reconnoitre the room.

"I think it would be wisest," said Ellery, blowing a cloud of smoke, "to clean this sad business up in an orderly manner.

"So I'll begin at the beginning. There were two elements in the double murder of John Royle and Blythe Stuart which pointed to our now departed friend as the only possible culprit: motive and opportunity.

"It was in a consideration of motive that this case has been most interesting. In one way, unique. Let's see what we had to work with.

"Neither Blythe nor Jack left an estate worth killing for, so murder for monetary gain was out. Since there were no romantic entanglements, such as jealous inamoratos of either victim—Blythe was stainless morally and all of Jack's lady-friends have been eliminated by Glücke because of alibis—then the only possible emotional motive would have had to arise out of the Royle-Stuart feud. But I have been able, as some of you know, to rule out the feud as the motive behind these crimes.

"If the feud is eliminated, then neither Jack Royle nor Ty Royle could have been criminally involved—the feud being their only possible motive.

"But if the feud is eliminated, we're faced with a puzzling situation. No one gained by the double murder, either materially or emotionally. In other words, a double murder was committed *apparently without motive.*

"Now this is palpably absurd. The only kind of crime which can even be conceived to lack motivation is the crime of impulse, the passion of a moment—and even this kind of crime, strictly speaking, has some deep-seated motive, even though the motive may manifest itself only in a sudden emotional eruption. But the murder of Jack and Blythe did not fall into even this classification. It was clearly a crime of great deliberation, of much planning in advance of the event—the warnings, the hamper, the frame-ups of Ty and Jack, the poison, and so on.

"Why, then, was Blythe Stuart, against whom the crime was originally and exclusively directed, marked for death? We agree there must have been a motive in so deeply premeditated a crime. But what?

"This raises," said Ellery slowly, "one of the most extraordinary questions in my experience. The question being: How is it possible for a murder-motive to exist and yet elude the most searching analysis? It's there; we know it's there; and yet we can't see it, we can't even glimpse its ghost; it lies in pure darkness, in the vacuum of the void.

"Well," said Ellery, "maybe we can't see the motive for the simplest reason imaginable. Maybe we can't see it because it doesn't exist . . . yet."

He paused, and Inspector Glücke said with an exasperation which flicked the hide from his words: "You just said there must be a motive, that Blythe Stuart was murdered because of that motive, that all we have to do is find that motive. And now you say we can't find the motive because it doesn't exist yet! But if it didn't exist when the murderer planned his crime, why the devil did he plan it? Do you know what you're talking about?"

"This fascinating discussion," drawled Ellery, "shows the limitations of language. Glücke, it's so simple it's absurd. It's merely a question of *time*—I used the word 'yet,' you'll recall."

"Time?" repeated Bonnie, bewildered.

"Time—you know, that invisible thing made visible by your wrist-watch. The background of *The Magic Mountain* and Albert Einstein's mathematical researches. Time—what time is it? have you the time? I'm having a great time."

He laughed. "Look. Whatever the great intellects may call time, mankind has divided it for practical purposes into three classifications: the past, the present, and the future. All living is motivated by one, two, or all of these classifications. The business man pays a sum of money to his bank because he took a loan *in the past*; certainly his current headaches are directly attributable to a past event. I am smoking this cigaret because I have the impulse to satisfy a craving for tobacco *in the present*. But isn't the future just as important in our lives? In many ways, more important? A man scrimps to provide against the rainy day—our way of nominating the future. A woman buys a steak at the butcher's in the morning because she knows her husband will be hungry in the evening. Magna plans a football picture in May because they know that in October people will be excited about football. Future, future, future; it dictates ninety percent of our actions."

He said sharply: "In the same way, it struck me that crime—murder—is dictated by time just as inexorably as any other human activity. A man might murder his wife because she was unfaithful to him yesterday. Or a man might murder his wife if he catches her in the act of being unfaithful to him—which means the present. But mightn't a man also murder his wife because he overhears her planning to be unfaithful to him tomorrow?"

And Ellery cried: "So, not having found a past event to account for Blythe Stuart's murder; not having found a present event, one contemporaneous with the crime, to account for it—it struck me with force that Blythe Stuart might have been murdered *because of an event which was destined to happen in the future!*"

Inspector Glücke said queerly: "You mean . . ." He did not finish. But after that he kept his gaze riveted on one person in the room with a vague curiosity that was half suspicion.

"But what event," Ellery went on swiftly, "was destined to happen in the future which could have provided a strong motive for the murder of Blythe Stuart? Of all the factors which made up Blythe Stuart—the woman, the actress, the member of a social unit we call 'family'—one factor stood out. Some day . . . in the future . . . some day Blythe Stuart's father would die. And when Blythe Stuart's father died *she would inherit a large fortune*. She was not yet an heiress, but *she was destined to be*."

The old man in the bed sank deeper into his swathings, fixing his eyes bitterly on Bonnie.

And Bonnie grew paler and said: "But that means . . . If mother died, *I* would inherit . . ."

"Queen, are you crazy?" cried Ty.

"Not at all; your hands are clean, Bonnie. For after your mother's death wasn't it apparent that you, too, were marked for death? Those threatening messages? The ace of spades?

"No," said Ellery, "you were the only one who would *directly* gain by your mother's death, from the standpoint of a future inheritance. But, equally as restrictive, there was only one person who would gain by the deaths of both your mother *and* you, the only one who stood in the direct line after you two women should have died.

"And that was how I knew that the sole living relation of Tolland Stuart, once you and your mother were dead, must be the driving force behind the entire plot. That was how I knew the murderer was Lew Bascom."

Chapter XXII

Beginning of the End

AND THERE WAS an interval in time in which the only sound was the asthmatic breathing of the old man in the bed.

And then he muttered: "Lew? My cousin Lew Bascom?"

And Dr. Junius kept blinking, saying nothing.

But Ellery said: "Yes, Mr. Stuart, your cousin Lew Bascom, who conceived and was well on his way to executing a brilliant reversal of the usual procedure in murder-to-gain-a-fortune. A strange creature, Lew. Always broke, too erratic to settle down and put his undeniable talents to a humdrum and sustained economic use, Lew planned murder as the easy way. Of course it was the hard way, but you could never have convinced a man like Lew of that.

"Lew was no sentimentalist, and naturally he was cracked. All deliberate killers are out of plumb somewhere. But the rift in his psychological make-up did not prevent him from seeing that a man stood a much better chance of getting away with murder *if he concealed the motive.* Usually, in murders for gain through inheritance, the rich man is killed first, to insure the passing of the estate. Then the heir or heirs are eliminated, the estate passing legally from one to the other until finally, with no one left but the last legal heir, it becomes his property. There are numerous cases on record of such crimes. But the trouble with them, as many murderers have discovered to their sorrow, is that the method leaves a plain motive trail.

"It was too plain for Lew. If your daughter Blythe were killed while her father Tolland Stuart remained alive, he saw that the real motive for her murder would be a hopeless enigma to the police. Originally, of course, he hoped the frame-up of Jack Royle would provide an instant motive to the police. But even when he had to kill Jack and destroy the force of his own frame-up, he still felt safe; Tolland Stuart was still alive. Then he planned to kill Bonnie, and again it would seem as if Bonnie's death had been a result of the Royle-Stuart feud; the whole childish business of the card-messages had only this purpose—to lay a trail which led back to the Royles. And all the while Tolland Stuart would live, not suspecting that it was *his* death, and not the deaths of his daughter and granddaughter, that was the ultimate goal of the murderer."

"Oh, grandfather!" said Bonnie, and she went to him and sat down on the bed. He sank back on the pillows, exhausted.

"He meant to kill me, then?" mumbled the old man.

"I think not, Mr. Stuart. I think—I know—he meant to let Nature take her course. You are an old man. . . . Well, we'll get to that in a moment.

"Now for element two—opportunity. How had Lew Bascom committed the murders at the airport? That took a bit of figuring."

"That's right, too," said Alan Clark suddenly, from his position between Sam Vix and silent, grim Jacques Butcher. "Lew was with you and me last Sunday, Ellery, when this fake pilot made off with the plane. So Lew couldn't possibly have been that pilot. I don't understand."

"True, Alan; he couldn't have been the kidnaper of the plane. I saw that, if I could clear the kidnaper of complicity in the murder, I could pin the actual poisoning by a stringent process of elimination on Lew.

"Well, who was the kidnaper? One thing I knew beyond question, as you've just pointed out: whoever the kidnaper was, he wasn't Lew."

"How did you know," asked Inspector Glücke, "that he mightn't have been Bascom's accomplice? That's the way I would figure it."

"No, he couldn't have been Lew's accomplice, either, Inspector. Paula Paris gave me the necessary information—the first of the two clues which I got through her."

"The Paris woman? You mean she's mixed up in this, too?"

"Lord, no! But Paula *was* tipped off to the kidnaping before it happened by some one who phoned her from the airport—she didn't tell you that, but she told it to me. Who could have known of the kidnaping and phoned Paula *before* it took place? Only the person who planned, or was involved in the plan, to do it. But this person, in tipping off Paula, *made no secret of his identity*—she admitted that to me, although she wouldn't for ethical reasons divulge the name."

"The interfering little snoop!" snarled Glücke. "I'll break her now. Suppressing evidence!"

"Oh, no, you won't," said Ellery. "Before we're finished you'll thank her, Glücke; if not for her this case would never have been solved.

"Now, if the kidnaper had been involved in the murders as Lew's accomplice, would he have revealed his identity to a newspaperwoman, especially before the crime occurred? Absurd. And if he had been the criminal himself —not Lew—would he have revealed himself to Paula, putting himself in her power? Utterly incredible. No, indeed; his telephone call to her, his willingness to let her know who he was, indicated that he had no idea murder was about to occur, eliminated him either as the poisoner or as the poisoner's accomplice; *or even, for that matter, as a kidnaper.*"

"This gets worse and worse," groaned Glücke. "Say that again?"

"I'll get around to it," grinned Ellery. "For the moment let me push along on the Lew tack. I was satisfied that the kidnaper wasn't involved in the murders in any way. That meant he didn't poison the thermos bottles.

"If the kidnaper didn't, who did? Well, who could have? The bottles were all right when the last round of cocktails was drunk before the plane—obvious from the fact that no one who drank, and many did, suffered any ill effects. Therefore the morphine-sodium allurate mixture must have been slipped into the bottles *after* the last round was poured.

"Exactly when? Well, it wasn't done in the plane, because we've eliminated Jack, Blythe, and the kidnaper as the possible murderers, and they were the only three who entered the plane between the last round of drinks and the take-off. Then the bottles were poisoned before the hamper was stowed away in the plane, but after the last round. But after the last round I myself sat on that hamper, and I got up only to hand it to the kidnaper when he was stowing the luggage away in the plane.

"So you see," murmured Ellery, "I arrived by sheer elimination to only one conceivable time and only one conceivable person. The bottles must have been poisoned *between the time the last round was poured and the time I sat down on the hamper.* Who suggested the last round? Lew Bascom. Who poured the last round? Lew Bascom. Who immediately after returned the bottles to the hamper? Lew Bascom. Therefore it must have been Lew Bascom who dropped the poison into the bottles, probably as he was screwing the caps back on after pouring the last round."

The Inspector grunted a little crossly.

"So both elements—motive and opportunity—pointed to Lew as the only possible criminal. But what proof did I have that would satisfy a court? Absolutely none. I had achieved the truth through a process of reasoning; there was no confirmatory evidence. Therefore Lew had to be caught red-handed, trapped into giving himself away. Which occurred today."

"But who the hell *was* the kidnaper?" asked Butch.

"I said, you'll recall, that he wasn't even that, really. Had the kidnaper seriously intended to spirit Jack and Blythe away by force, hold them for ransom, or whatever, would he have told a newspaperwoman first? Naturally not. So I saw that it wasn't intended to be a real kidnaping at all. The wraith we were chasing had staged a *fake* kidnaping!"

"Fake?" shouted Glücke. "The hell you say! After we've worn our eyes out looking for him?"

"Of course, Inspector. For who would stage a kidnaping and inform a famous newspaper columnist about it in advance? Only some one who was interested in a news story, publicity. And who could have been interested in a publicity splash centering about Jack Royle and Blythe Stuart?" Ellery grinned. "Come on, Sam; talk. You're caught with the goods."

Vix grew very pale. He gulped, his one eye rolling wildly, looking for an avenue of escape.

The Inspector gasped: "*You?* Why, you ornery, one-eyed baboon—"

"Peace," sighed Ellery. "Who can quell the instincts of the buzzard or the dyed-in-the-wool publicity man? It was the opportunity of a lifetime, wasn't it, Sam?"

"Yeah," said Vix with difficulty.

"The marriage of two world-famous figures, the gigantic splash of that airport send-off . . . why, if those two were thought to be kidnaped, the Magna picture Butch was going to make would get a million dollars' worth of publicity."

"A million dollars' worth of misery to me, as it turned out," groaned Vix. "It was to be a surprise; I didn't even tell Butch. I figured I'd let on to Jack and Blythe once we were safely away, and then we'd hide out somewhere for a few days. They wanted a little peace and quiet, anyway. . . . Oh, nuts. When I turned around and saw those two dead, my stomach turned over. I knew I was in the worst kind of jam. If I gave myself up and told the truth, nobody'd believe me, certainly not a one-cylinder flattie like Glücke. I could see myself tagged for a twin killing and going out by the aerial route, kicking. What could I do? I set the plane down on the first flat place I could find and took it on the lam."

"You," said Inspector Glücke venomously, "are going up on charges. I'll give you publicity!"

"Take it easy, Inspector," growled Jacques Butcher. "Why make the studio suffer? It was a dumb stunt, but Sam can't be considered in any way responsible for what happened; if there'd been no murder there wouldn't have been any harm done. He'll take his rap in the papers, anyway; and you've got your man."

"Not only have you got your man," said Ellery pleasantly, "but if you're a good doggie, Glücke, maybe I'll give you something else."

"Isn't this nightmare over yet?" Glücke threw up his hands.

"Well, what forced Lew to change his plans?" asked Ellery. "What forced him to kill not only Blythe, but Jack Royle? What happened between the inauguration of his playing-card threats against Blythe and the day of the murder?

"Only one important thing happened—Blythe buried the hatchet, gave up her long feud with Jack; in fact, announced her intention to marry him, and did so.

"But how could Blythe's marriage have forced Lew to kill not only Blythe but the man she married? Well, what was behind his whole scheme? To get for himself the entire Stuart estate. Who were his obstacles? Blythe and Bonnie. But when Blythe married Jack Royle, then Jack Royle became an obstacle, too! For by the terms of Tolland Stuart's will half the estate went to Blythe, if living, *or to Blythe's heirs if dead*; and her heirs in that case would be her daughter Bonnie and her husband Jack. Only if Jack Royle died, too, before the estate passed would Jack cease to be an heir; living, he would inherit, but if dead his own estate would collect nothing and Bonnie, Blythe's only heir, would consequently get everything.

"So Lew killed Jack, too. Now he must kill Bonnie. But what happened before he got the opportunity to kill Bonnie? History repeated itself: Bonnie announced her intention to marry Ty. Therefore Ty became an obstacle in the way of Lew, for if Bonnie married Ty and Lew killed only Bonnie, Ty would get the entire estate, since according to the will if Bonnie pre-deceased her grandfather her portion would go to *her* heirs . . . or Ty, her surviving husband.

"Therefore Lew tried to prevent the marriage, because if he could scare Bonnie into not marrying Ty he would have to kill only Bonnie; whereas if she did marry Ty he would have to kill both of them; and one murder was preferable to two for obvious reasons."

"That's all very well," muttered Glücke, "but what I can't understand is how Bascom expected to be able to control Mr. Stuart's will. How could he be sure Mr. Stuart, when he saw his daughter murdered, wouldn't write a new will which would make it impossible for Lew ever to collect a cent, murders or not?"

"Ah," said Ellery. "A good point, Glücke. In discussing that, and Mr. Bascom's good fortune, I'm forced to refer again to my invaluable friend, Paula Paris. A pearl, that woman! The very first time I met her she painted an interesting word-picture of Tolland Stuart. She told me of his hypochondria, of his pamphlets inveighing against the evils of stimulants, even unto coffee and tea; of his drinking cold water with a teaspoon, obviously because he was afraid of what cold water would do, drunk normally, to his stomach—chill it, I suppose; of his diatribes against white bread."

"But I don't see what that—"

"That's quite true," said Dr. Junius unexpectedly, clearing his throat. "But I, too, fail to see the relevance—"

"I imagine, Doctor," said Ellery, "that you're due for a nasty shock. Your faith in humanity is about to be destroyed. Can you imagine Tolland Stuart being inconsistent in a matter like that?"

Dr. Junius's face looked like a yellow paste. "Well, now, of course—"

"That disconcerts you, naturally. You're amazed to learn that Tolland Stuart *could* be inconsistent in his hypochondriasis?"

"No, really, it happens. I mean I don't know what you're referring to—"

"Well, Doctor," said Ellery in a hard voice, "let me enlighten you. Friday afternoon Miss Stuart and I, as you will recall, came up here to visit her grandfather. You were away—shopping, I believe? Too bad. Because when we came upon Mr. Tolland Stuart lying in this room—yes, in this very bed— what was he doing? The man who had a horror of white bread was eating a cold meat sandwich made of white bread. The man who sipped cold water from a teaspoon because he was afraid of chilling his stomach, the man who avoided stimulants as he would the plague, that man was *gulping* down quite callously large quantities of *iced tea!*"

The old man in the bed whimpered, and Dr. Junius shrank within himself like a withering weed. As for the others, they stared in perplexity from Ellery to the old man. Only Inspector Glücke looked aware; and he gave a signal to one of his men. The detective went to the bed and motioned Bonnie away. Ty jumped forward to grasp Bonnie's arm and draw her from the bed.

And the man in the bed dropped the Indian blanket with the swiftness of desperate purpose and reached for the shotgun which stood close to his hand. But Ellery was swifter.

"No," he said, handing the gun to the Inspector, "not yet, sir."

"But I don't understand," cried Bonnie, her glance wavering between the old man and Ellery. "It doesn't make sense. You talk as if . . . as if this man weren't my grandfather."

"He isn't," said Ellery. "I have every reason to believe that he's a man supposed to have committed suicide—an old and desperate and dying man known to the Hollywood colony of extras as Arthur William Park, the actor."

If Inspector Glücke had seen the revelation coming, at least he had not seen it in its entirety, for he gaped at the cowering old man in the bed, who covered his face with his wrinkled hands.

"Because of that sandwich and iced drink," continued Ellery, "I saw that it was possible Tolland Stuart was being impersonated. I began to put little bits together; bits that had puzzled me, or passed me by, but that coalesced into a significant whole once my suspicions were aroused.

"For one thing, an imposture was not difficult; in this case it was of the essence of simplicity. The improbability of most impostures lies in the fact that doubles are rare, and that even expert make-up will not stand the test of constant inspection by people who knew the one impersonated well.

"But—" and Ellery shrugged "—who knew Tolland Stuart well? Not even his daughter, who had visited him only two or three times in the last ten years. But granting that Blythe might have seen through an imposture, Blythe was dead. Bonnie? Hardly; she had not seen her grandfather since her pinafore days. Only Dr. Junius of the survivors. Dr. Junius saw Tolland Stuart every day and had seen him every day for ten years. . . . No, no, Doctor; I assure you that's futile. The house is surrounded, and there's a detective just outside the door."

Dr. Junius stopped in his slow sidle toward the door, and he wet his lips.

"Then there was the incident last Sunday, when we flew up here after the discovery of the bodies in Ty's plane on that plateau. I thought I heard the motors of a plane during the thunder-and-lightning storm. I went out and, while I couldn't see the plane, I did see this man, now in bed, crouching outside the house with a *flyer's helmet* on his head. At the time it merely puzzled me; but when I suspected an imposture, I saw that the explanation was simple: this man had just been landed on the Stuart estate by an airplane, whose motors I had heard. Undoubtedly piloted by Lew Bascom, who had departed from the plateau that Sunday before we did in an Army plane. Lew flew a plane, as I knew because he offered to pilot the wedding plane when the original Royle-Stuart wedding stunt was being discussed; moreover, he even offered the use of his own plane. So Lew must have returned to the airport with the Army pilot, picked up Park at his rooms, landed Park on this estate, and returned quietly to Los Angeles. You *are* Park, aren't you?"

The old man in the bed uncovered his face. Dr. Junius started to cry out, but closed his mouth without uttering the cry.

"You aren't Tolland Stuart."

The old man said nothing, did nothing. His face was altered; the sharp lines were even sharper than before, but no longer irascible, no longer lines of evil; he merely looked worn out, like an old stone, and weary to death.

"There's a way of proving it, you know," said Ellery with a sort of pity. "In the desk in the study downstairs there's Tolland Stuart's will, and that will is signed with Tolland Stuart's signature. Shall we ask you, Mr. Park, to write the name Tolland Stuart for comparison purposes?"

Dr. Junius said: "Don't!" in a despairing burst, but the old man shook his head. "It's no use, Junius. We're caught." He lay back on the pillows, closing his eyes.

"And there were other indications," said Ellery. "The way Dr. Junius acted last Sunday. He put up a colossal bluff. He knew there was no Tolland Stuart upstairs. He was expecting Park; our sudden appearance must have made him frantic. When we finally came up here and found Park, who must have blundered about after sneaking into a house he'd never been in before, found Stuart's room, and hastily got into Stuart's night-clothes, Junius was so surprised he fled. He hadn't heard those airplane engines. Oh, it was all cleverly done; Mr. Park is an excellent actor, and he was told everything he must know to play his part perfectly. After Sunday, of course, he was given further instruction."

"Then the doctor here was Bascom's confederate?" asked the Inspector, open-mouthed.

"Of course. As was Mr. Park, although he's the least culpable, I suspect, of the three.

"Now, convinced that Tolland Stuart was being impersonated, I could find only one plausible reason for it. Lew's plans depended on Stuart's remaining alive until after the murder of Blythe and Bonnie; if Tolland Stuart was being impersonated, then it could only mean that Tolland Stuart was dead. When had he died? Well, I knew Stuart had been alive four days before the murder of Jack—"

"How did you know that?"

"Because on that day, when Blythe and Jack visited here, she saw him, for one thing; she might have spotted an impersonation. But more important, he gave her a check for a hundred and ten thousand dollars, which she turned over to Jack. Would Stuart's bank have honored Stuart's signature if it had not been genuine? So I knew that four days before the murders Stuart had still been in the land of the living.

"Apparently, then, Stuart had died between that day and the following Sunday. Probably Saturday night, the night before the crime, because we know Lew got hold of Park Sunday, hurried him up here under the most difficult and dangerous conditions—something he would not have done Sunday had he been able to do it before Sunday. So I imagine Dr. Junius telephoned Lew Saturday night to say Tolland Stuart had suddenly died, and Lew thought of Park, and instructed the doctor to bury his benefactor in a very deep hole, and immediately got busy on the Park angle. Park left a suicide note to efface his trail and vanished—to turn up here the next day as Bonnie's grandfather."

"This is—extraordinary," said Jacques Butcher, staring from Junius to Park. "But why? What did Park and Junius hope to get out of it?"

"Park? I believe I can guess. Park, as I knew from Lew himself long ago, is dying of cancer. He's penniless, has a wife and crippled son back East dependent on him. He knew he couldn't last long, and for his family a man will do almost anything—a certain type of man—if there's enough money in it to insure his family's security.

"Dr. Junius? I have the advantage of you there; I've read Tolland Stuart's will. In it he engaged to pay the doctor a hundred thousand dollars if the doctor kept him alive until the age of seventy. From the wording of the will and its date—it was made out at the age of sixty and was dated nine and a half years ago—it was obvious that Stuart had died at the age of *sixty-nine and a half*. Dr. Junius had spent almost ten years of his life in a living hell to earn that hundred thousand. He wasn't going to let a mere matter of a couple of murders stand in the way of his getting it. Nevertheless, he wouldn't have risked his neck unless he felt reasonably certain Stuart wouldn't live to reach the age of seventy. Consequently, I was convinced that, far from being a healthy man, Stuart was really a very sick man; and that Junius was putting on an act when he claimed his patient was just a hypochondriac. I was convinced that Stuart, who I knew had died suddenly, had died probably of his illness—not accidentally or through violence, since violence was the last thing Lew wanted in the case of the old man."

"There's something," whispered Dr. Junius, "of the devil in you."

"I imagine the shoe fits you rather better," replied Ellery. "And, of course, it must have been you who supplied Lew Bascom with the morphine and the sodium allurate in the proper dose—no difficult feat for a physician."

"I went into it with Bascom," said Dr. Junius in the same whisper, "because I knew Stuart wouldn't survive. When he engaged me nine and a half years ago he had a badly ulcerated condition of the stomach. I treated him faithfully, but he developed a cancer, as so often occurs. I felt . . . cheated; I knew he probably wouldn't live to reach seventy. When Bascom approached me, I fell in with his scheme. Bascom knew, too, that the old man was dying. In a sense our—interests lay in the same direction: I wanted Stuart to live to seventy, and Bascom wanted him to live until after Blythe and Bonnie Stuart were . . ." He stopped and wet his lips. "Bascom had got the coöperation of Park, here, in advance, just in case the old man died prematurely, as he did. Park had plenty of time to study his physical rôle."

"You animal," said Bonnie.

Dr. Junius said nothing more; he turned his face to the wall. And the old man in the bed seemed asleep.

"And since Park had a cancer, too," said Ellery, "and couldn't live very long, it was just dandy all around, wasn't it? When he died, there'd be nobody to suspect he wasn't Stuart; and even an autopsy would merely have revealed that he died of cancer, which was perfectly all right. And by that time, too, he'd have grown real hair, instead of the false hair and spirit gum he's got on his face now. Oh, an ingenious plan." He paused, and then he said: "It makes me feel a little sick. Do you sleep well at night, Dr. Junius?"

And after a moment Glücke asked doggedly: "But Bascom didn't know exactly when Stuart would die. You still haven't answered the question of how he could control the old man before he died, how he could be sure the old man wouldn't make out a new will."

"That was simple. The old will, the present will, existed; all Lew had to do was see—probably through Junius—that the old man didn't get his hands on his own will. Then, even if he did make out a new will, they could always destroy it, leaving the old will in force.

"When Stuart died prematurely, it was even simpler. There would be no question of a new will at all. Park, playing Stuart's rôle, couldn't make out a new one, even if he wanted to. The old will would remain, as it has remained, the will in force.

"Incidentally, I was sure Lew would fall for our trap today. With Park dying of cancer, his survival for even a short time doubtful, Lew couldn't permit Bonnie and Ty to vanish for an indefinite period. If Park died while they were off on their honeymoon at an unknown place, Lew's whole scheme was nullified. His scheme was based on Bonnie's dying before her grandfather, to conceal the true motive. If he killed Bonnie—and Ty, as he would have to—after the death of Park-acting-as-Stuart, his motive would be clearly indicated. So I knew he would take any risk to kill Bonnie and Ty before they went away and while Park was still alive."

Ellery sighed and lit a fresh cigaret, and no one said anything until Inspector Glücke, with a sudden narrowing of his eyes, said: "Park. You there —Park!"

But the old man in the bed did not answer, or move, or give any sign that he had heard.

Ellery and Glücke sprang forward as one man. Then they straightened up without having touched him. For in his slack hand there lay a tiny vial, and he was dead.

And Dr. Junius turned from the wall and collapsed in a chair, whimpering like a child.

Chapter XXIII

End of the Beginning

WHEN ELLERY TURNED the key in his apartment door Sunday night, and let himself in, and shut the door, and flung aside his hat and coat, and sank into his deepest chair, it was with a spent feeling. His bones ached, and so did his head. It was a relief just to sit there in the quiet living-room thinking of nothing at all.

He always felt this way at the conclusion of a case—tired, sluggish, his vital energies sapped.

Inspector Glücke had been gruff with praises again; and there had been invitations, and thanks, and a warm kiss on the lips from Bonnie, and a silent handshake from Ty. But he had fled to be alone.

He closed his eyes.

To be alone?

That wasn't quite true. Damn, analyzing again! But this time his mind dwelt on a more pleasant subject than murder. Just what *was* his feeling for Paula Paris? Was he sorry for her because she was psychologically frustrated, because she shut herself up in those sequestered rooms of hers and denied the world the excitement of her company? Pity? No, not pity, really. To be truthful about it, he rather enjoyed the feeling when he went to see her that they were alone, that the world was shut out. Why was that?

He groaned, his head beginning to throb where it had only ached dully before. He was mooning like an adolescent boy. Tormenting himself this way! Why think? What was the good of thinking? The really happy people didn't have a thought in their heads. That's why they were happy.

He rose with a sigh and stripped off his jacket; and as he did so his wallet fell out. He stooped to pick it up and suddenly recalled what was in it. That envelope. Queer how he had forgotten it in the excitement of the last twenty-four hours!

He took the envelope out of the wallet, fingering its creamy vellum face with appreciation. Good quality. Quality, that was it. She represented a special, unique assortment of human values, the tender and shy and lovable ones, the ones that appealed mutely to the best in a man.

He smiled as he tore the envelope open. Had she really guessed who had murdered Jack Royle and Blythe Stuart?

In her free, clear script was written: "Dear Stupid: It's inconceivable to you that a mere woman could do by intuition what it's taken you Siegfriedian writhings of the intellect to achieve. Of course it's Lew Bascom. Paula."

Damn her clever eyes! he thought angrily. She needn't have been so brash about it. He seized the telephone.

"Paula! This is Ellery. I've just read your note—"

"Mr. Queen," murmured Paula. "Back from the wars. I suppose I should offer you the congratulations owing to the victor?"

"Oh, that. We were lucky it all went off so well. But Paula, about this note—"

"It's hardly necessary for me to open your envelope now."

"But I've opened yours, and I must say you made an excellent stab in the dark. But how—"

"You might also," said Paula's organ voice, "congratulate *me* for having made it."

"Well, of course. Congratulations. But that's not the point. Guessing! That's the point. Where does it get you? Nowhere."

"Aren't you being incoherent?" Paula laughed. "It gets you the answer. Nor is it entirely a matter of guesswork, O Omniscience. There was reason behind it."

"Reason? Oh, come now."

"It's true I didn't understand why Lew did it—his motives and things; the murder of Jack didn't fit in . . . you'll have to explain those things to me—"

"But you just said," growled Ellery, "you had a *reason*."

"A feminine sort of reason." Paula paused. "But do we have to discuss it over the phone?"

"Tell me!"

"Yes, sir. You see, I did know the kind of person Lew was, and it struck me that Lew's character exactly matched the character of the crime."

"What? What's that?"

"Well, Lew was an idea man, wasn't he? He conceived brilliantly, executed poorly—that was characteristic not only of him but of his work, too."

"What of it?"

"But the whole crime, if you stop to think of it, as I did, was exactly like that—brilliantly conceived and poorly executed!"

"You mean to say," spluttered Ellery, "that *that* sort of dishwater is what you call reasoning?"

"Oh, but it's so true. Have you stopped," said Paula sweetly, "to think it out? The playing-card scheme was very, very clever—a true Lew Bascom idea; but it was also fantastic and devious, and wasn't it carried out shoddily? Lew all over. Then the frame-up of Jack, followed by the frame-up of Ty . . . two frame-ups that didn't jibe at all. And that clumsy device of filing those typewriter keys! Poor execution."

"Lord," groaned Ellery.

"Oh, dozens of indications. That hamper with the bottles of cocktails. Suppose it hadn't been delivered? Suppose, if it were delivered in that crush, it weren't taken along? Or suppose Jack and Blythe were too wrapped up in each other, even if it were taken along, to bother about a drink? Or suppose only one of them drank? So awfully *chancy*, Ellery; so poorly thought out. Now Jacques Butcher, had he been the criminal, would *never*—"

"All right, all right," said Ellery. "I'm convinced—yes, I'm not. You saw a clever idea with fantastic overtones and poor craftsmanship, and because Lew was that way you said it was Lew. I'll have to recommend the method to Glücke; he'll be delighted. Now, Miss Paris, how about paying off that bet of ours?"

"The bet," said Paula damply.

"Yes, the bet! You said I'd never catch the criminal. Well, I have caught him, so I've won, and you've got to take me out tonight to the *Horseshoe Club*."

"Oh!" And Paula fell silent. He could sense her panic over the wires. "But . . . but that *wasn't* the bet," she said at last in a desperate voice.

"The bet was that you'd bring him to justice, into court. You didn't. He committed suicide, he tried to escape and his parachute didn't open—"

"Oh, no, you don't," said Ellery firmly. "You don't welch on me, Miss Paris. You lost that bet, and you're going to pay off."

"But, Ellery," she wailed, "I *can't*! I—I haven't set foot outside my house for years and years! You don't know how the very thought of it makes me shrivel up inside—"

"You're taking me to the *Club* tonight."

"I think . . . I'd faint, or something. I know it sounds silly to a normal person," she cried, "but why can't people understand? They'd understand if I had measles. It's something in me that's *sick*, only it doesn't happen to be organic. This fear of people—"

"Get dressed."

"But I've got nothing to wear," she said triumphantly. "I mean, no evening gowns. I've never had occasion to wear them. Or even—I've no wrap, no—no nothing."

"I'm dressing now. I'll be at your house at eight-thirty."

"Ellery, no!"

"Eight-thirty."

"Please! Oh, please, Ellery—"

"Eight-thirty," repeated Mr. Queen inflexibly, and he hung up.

At eight-thirty precisely Mr. Queen presented himself at the front door of the charming white house in the Hills, and a pretty young girl opened the door for him. Mr. Queen saw, with some trepidation, that the young lady was star-eyed and pink-cheeked with excitement. She was one of Paula's elfin secretaries, and she regarded his lean, tuxedo-clad figure with a keenness that made him think of a mother inspecting her daughter's first swain come a-calling.

It was absurd, too absurd, blustered Mr. Queen inwardly. Out of my way, wench.

But the wench said: "Oh, Mr. Queen," in an ecstatic whisper, "it's simply *wonderful*! Do you think she'll *do* it?"

"Why, of course she'll do it," pooh-poohed Mr. Queen. "All this blather about crowd phobia. Nonsense! Where is she?"

"She's been crying and laughing and—oh, she looks *beautiful*! Wait till you see her. It's the most marvelous thing that's ever happened to her. I do hope nothing . . ."

"Now, now," said Mr. Queen brusquely. "Less chatter, my dear. Let's have a look at this beauty."

Nevertheless, he approached Paula's door with a quaking heart. What was the matter with him? All this fuss and nervousness over a little thing like going to a night-club!

He knocked and the secretary, looking anxious, faded away; and Paula's voice came tremulously: "Come . . . come in."

Mr. Queen touched his black tie, coughed, and went in.

Paula was standing, tall and tense, against the closed glass doors of the farthest wall, staring at him. She was wearing elbow-length red evening gloves, and her braceleted hands were pressed to her heart. She was wearing . . . well, it shimmered and crinkled where the light struck it—cloth of gold? What the devil was it?—and a long white fur evening cape over her shoulders, caught at the neck with a magnificent marcasite brooch, and her hair done up in—well, it looked like the hair of one of those court pages of the time of Elizabeth; simply exquisite. Simply the last word. Simply—there was no last word.

"Holy smoke," breathed Mr. Queen.

She was white to the lips. "Do I—do I look all right?"

"You look," said Mr. Queen reverently, "like one of the Seraphim. You look," said Mr. Queen, "like the popular conception of Cleopatra, although Cleo had a hooked nose and probably a black skin, and *your* nose and skin . . . You look," said Mr. Queen, "you look like one of those godlike beings from Aldebaran, or some place, that H. G. Wells likes to describe. You look swell."

"Don't be funny," she said with a little angry glance. "I mean the clothes."

"The clothes? Oh, the clothes. Incidentally, I thought you said you didn't have any evening clothes. Liar!"

"I didn't, and don't; that's why I asked," she said helplessly. "I've had to borrow the cape from Bess, and the dress from Lilian, and the shoes from a neighbor down the street whose feet are as big as mine, and I feel like the original Communist. Oh, Ellery, are you *sure* I'll do?"

Ellery advanced across the room with determined strides. She shrank against the glass doors.

"Ellery. What are you . . ."

"May I present the loveliest lady I know," said Mr. Queen with fierce gallantry, "with these?" And he held out a little cellophane box, and in the box there lay an exquisite corsage of camellias.

Paula gasped: "Oh!" and then she said softly, "That was sweet," and suddenly she was no longer tense, but pliant, and a little abstracted, and she pinned the corsage to her bodice with swift, flashing, red-swathed fingers.

And Mr. Queen said, wetting his lips: "Paula."

"Yes?"

Mr. Queen said again: "Paula."

"Yes?" She looked up, frowning.

Mr. Queen said: "Paula, will you . . . May I . . . Oh, hell, there's only one way to do it, and that's to *do* it!"

And he seized her and pulled her as close to his stiff shirt as the shirt would permit and clumsily kissed her on the mouth.

She lay still in his arms, her eyes closed, breathing quickly. Then, without opening her eyes, she said: "Kiss me some more."

And after a while Mr. Queen said thickly: "I think— Let's not go out and say we did. Let's sort of—stay here."

"Yes," she whispered. "Oh, yes."

But there was iron in that man's soul, after all. He sternly put aside temptation. "No, we *are* going out. It's the very soul of the treatment."

"Oh, I can't. I mean . . . I don't think I can."

Mr. Queen took her by the arm and marched her straight across the room to the closed door.

"Open that door," he said.

"But I'm . . . now I'm all messed!"

"You're beautiful. Open that door."

"You mean . . . open it?"

"Open it. Yourself. With your own hands."

The twin imps of fear peeped out of her wide, grave eyes. She gulped like a little girl and her red-gloved right hand crept forward to touch the knob. She looked at Ellery in distress.

"Open it, darling," said Mr. Queen in a low voice.

Slowly her hand turned the knob until it would turn no more. Then, quickly, like little Lulu about to swallow her cod-liver oil, Paula closed her eyes and jerked the door open.

And, her eyes still closed, stumbled blindly across the threshold into the world.

THE ORIGIN OF EVIL

ELLERY WAS SPREAD over the ponyskin chair before the picture window, *huarachos* crossed on the typewriter table, a ten-inch frosted glass in his hand, and the corpse at his feet. He was studying the victim between sips and making not too much out of her. However, he was not concerned. It was early in the investigation, she was of unusual proportions, and the *ron* consoled.

. He took another sip.

It was a curious case. The victim still squirmed; from where he sat he could make out signs of life. Back in New York they had warned him that these were an illusion, reflexes following the death rattle. Why, you won't believe it, they had said, but corruption's set in already and anyone who can tell a stinkweed from a camellia will testify to it. Ellery had been skeptical. He had known deceased in her heyday—a tumid wench, every man's daydream, and the laughing target of curses and longing. It was hard to believe that such vitality could be exterminated.

On the scene of the crime—or rather above it, for the little house he had taken was high over the city, a bird's nest perched on the twig tip of an upper branch of the hills—Ellery still doubted. There she lay under a thin blanket of smog, stirring a little, and they said she was dead.

Fair Hollywood.

Murdered, ran the post-mortem, by Television.

He squinted down at the city, sipping his rum and enjoying his nakedness. It was a blue-white day. The hill ran green and flowered to the twinkled plain, simmering in the sun.

There had been no technical reason for choosing Hollywood as the setting for his new novel. Mystery stories operate under special laws of growth; their beginnings may lie in the look in a faceless woman's eye glimpsed in a crowd for exactly the duration of one heartbeat, or in the small type on page five of a life insurance policy; generally the writer has the atlas to pick from. Ellery had had only the gauziest idea of where he was going; at that stage of the game it could as well have been Joplin, Missouri, or the kitchens of the Kremlin. In fact, his plot was in such a cloudy state that when he heard about the murder of Hollywood he took it as a sign from the heavens and made immediate arrangements to be present at the autopsy. His trade being violent death, a city with a knife in its back seemed just the place to take his empty sample cases.

Well, there was life in the old girl yet. Of course, theaters with *MOVIES ARE BETTER THAN EVER* on their marquees had crossbars over their portals saying *CLOSED*; you could now get a table at the Brown Derby without waiting more than twenty minutes; that eminent haberdasher of the

Strip, Mickey Cohen, was out of business; movie stars were cutting their prices for radio; radio actors were auditioning tensely for television as they redesigned their belts or put their houses up for sale; shopkeepers were complaining that how could anybody find money for yard goods or nail files when the family budget was mortgaged to Hoppy labels, the new car, and the television set; teen-age gangs, solemnly christened "wolf packs" by the Los Angeles newspapers, cruised the streets beating up strangers, high school boys were regularly caught selling marijuana, and "Chicken!" was the favorite highway sport of the hot-rodders; and you could throttle a tourist on Hollywood Boulevard between Vine and La Brea any night after 10:30 and feel reasonably secure against interruption.

But out in the San Fernando Valley mobs of little cheap stuccos and redwood fronts were beginning to elbow the painted hills, paint-fresh signal lights at intersections were stopping cars which had previously known only the carefree California conscience, and a great concrete ditch labeled "Flood Control Project" was making its way across the sandy valley like an opening zipper.

On the ocean side of the Santa Monica Mountains, from Beverly Glen to Topanga Canyon, lordlier mansions were going up which called themselves "estates"—disdaining the outmoded "ranch" or "rancho," which more and more out-of-state ex-innocents were learning was a four-or-five-and-den on a 50×100 lot containing three callow apricot trees. Beverly Hills might be biting its perfect fingernails, but Glendale and Encino were booming, and Ellery could detect no moans from the direction of Brentwood, Flintridge, Sunland, or Eagle Rock. New schools were assembling; more oldsters were chugging in from Iowa and Michigan, flexing their arthritic fingers and practicing old age pension-check-taking; and to drive a car in downtown Los Angeles at noontime the four blocks from 3rd to 7th along Broadway, Spring, Hill, or Main now took thirty minutes instead of fifteen. Ellery heard tell of huge factories moving in; of thousands of migrants swarming into Southern California through Blythe and Indio on 60 and Needles and Barstow on 66 —latter-day pioneers to whom the movies still represented Life and Love and "television" remained a highfalutin word, like "antibiotic." The carhops were more beautiful and numerous than ever; more twenty-foot ice cream cones punctuated the skyline; Tchaikovsky under the stars continued to fill Hollywood Bowl with brave-bottomed music lovers; Grand Openings of hardware stores now used two giant searchlights instead of one; the Farmers' Market on Fairfax and 3rd chittered and heaved like an Egyptian bazaar in the tourist season; Madman Muntz had apparently taken permanent possession of the skies, his name in mile-high letters drifting expensively away daily; and the newspapers offered an even more tempting line of cheesecake than in the old days—Ellery actually saw one photograph of the routine well-stacked cutie in a Bikini bathing suit perched zippily on a long flower-decked box inscribed *Miss National Casket Week.* And in three days or so, according to the reports, the Imperial Potentate would lead a six-hour safari of thirteen thousand red-fezzed, capering, elderly Penrods, accompanied by fifty-one bands, assorted camels, clowns, and floats, along Figueroa Street to the Memorial Coliseum to convene the seventy-umpth Imperial Session of the Ancient Arabic Order of the Nobles of the Mystic Shrine—a civic event guaranteed to rouse even the dead.

It became plain in his first few days in Hollywood and environs that what the crapehangers back East were erroneously bewailing was not the death of the angelic city but its exuberant rebirth in another shape. The old order changeth. The new organism was exciting, but it was a little out of his line; and Ellery almost packed up and flew back East. But then he thought, It's all hassle and hurly-burly, everybody snarling or making hay; and there's still the twitching nucleus of the old Hollywood bunch—stick around, old boy, the atmosphere is murderous and it may well inspire a collector's item or two for the circulating library shelves.

Also, there had been the press and its agents. Ellery had thought to slip into town by dropping off at the Lockheed field in Burbank rather than the International Airport in Inglewood. But he touched Southern California soil to a bazooka fire of questions and lenses, and the next day his picture was on the front page of all the papers. They had even got his address in the hills straight, although his pal the real estate man later swore by the beard of Nature Boy that he'd had nothing to do with the leak. It had been that way for Ellery ever since the publicity explosion over the Cat case. The newspaper boys were convinced that, having saved Manhattan from a fate equivalent to death, Ellery was in Los Angeles on a mission at least equally large and torrid. When he plaintively explained that he had come to write a book they all laughed, and their printed explanations ascribed his visit to everything from a top-secret appointment by the Mayor as Special Investigator to Clean Up Greater L.A. to the turning of his peculiar talents upon the perennial problem of the Black Dahlia.

How could he run out?

At this point Ellery noticed that his glass was as empty as his typewriter.

He got up from the ponyskin chair and found himself face to face with a pretty girl.

As he jumped nudely for the bedroom doorway Ellery thought, The *huarachos* must look ridiculous. Then he thought, Why didn't I put on those ten pounds Barney prescribed? Then he got angry and poked his head around the door to whine, "I told Mrs. Williams I wasn't seeing anybody today, not even her. How did you get in?"

"Through the garden," said the girl. "Climbed up from the road below. I tried not to trample your marigolds. I hope you don't mind."

"I do mind. Go away."

"But I've got to see you."

"Everybody's got to see me. But I don't have to see everybody. Especially when I look like this."

"You are sort of pale, aren't you? And your ribs stick out, Ellery." She sounded like a debunked sister. Ellery suddenly remembered that in Hollywood dress is a matter of free enterprise. You could don a parka and drive a team of Siberian huskies from Schwab's Drugstore at the foot of Laurel Canyon to NBC at Sunset and Vine and never turn a head. Fur stoles over slacks are acceptable if not *de rigueur*, the exposed navel is considered conservative, and at least one man dressed in nothing but Waikiki trunks may be found poking sullenly among the avocados at any vegetable stand. "You ought to put on some weight, Ellery. And get out in the sun."

"Thank you," Ellery heard himself saying.

His Garden of Eden costume meant absolutely nothing to her. And she was even prettier than he had thought. Hollywood prettiness, he thought sulkily; they all look alike. Probably Miss Universe of Pasadena. She was dressed in zebra-striped culottes and bolero over a bra-like doodad of bright green suède. Green open-toed sandals on her tiny feet. A matching suède jockey cap on her cinnamon hair. Skin toast-colored where it was showing, and *no* ribs. A small and slender number, but three-dimensional where it counted. About nineteen years old. For no reason at all she reminded him of Meg in Thorne Smith's *The Night Life of the Gods*, and he pulled his head back and banged the door.

When he came out safe and suave in slacks, Shantung shirt, and burgundy corduroy jacket, she was curled up in his ponyskin chair smoking a cigaret.

"I've fixed your drink," she said.

"Kind of you. I suppose that means I must offer you one." No point in being too friendly.

"Thanks. I don't drink before five." She was thinking of something else.

Ellery leaned against the picture window and looked down at her with hostility. "It's not that I'm a prude, Miss—"

"Hill. Laurel Hill."

"—Miss Laurel Hill, but when I receive strange young things *au naturel* in Hollywood I like to be sure no confederate with a camera and an offer to do business is skulking behind my drapes. Why do you think you have to see me?"

"Because the police are dummies."

"Ah, the police. They won't listen to you?"

"They listen, all right. But then they laugh. I don't think there's anything funny in a dead dog, do you?"

"In a what?"

"A dead dog."

Ellery sighed, rolling the frosty glass along his brow. "Your pooch was poisoned, of course?"

"Guess again," said the set-faced intruder. "He wasn't my pooch, and I don't know what caused his death. What's more, dog-lover though I am, I don't care a curse. . . . They said it was somebody's idea of a rib, and I know they're talking through their big feet. I don't know what it meant, but it was no rib."

Ellery had set the glass down. She stared back. Finally he shook his head, smiling. "The tactics are primitive, Laurel. E for Effort. But no dice."

"No tactics," she said impatiently. "Let me tell you—"

"Who sent you to me?"

"Not a soul. You were all over the papers. It solved my problem."

"It doesn't solve mine, Laurel. My problem is to find the background of peaceful isolation which passeth the understanding of the mere, dear reader. I'm here to do a book, Laurel—a poor thing in a state of arrested development, but writing is a habit writers get into and my time has come. So, you see, I can't take any cases."

"You won't even listen." Her mouth was in trouble. She got up and started across the room. He watched the brown flesh below the bolero. Not his type, but nice.

"Dogs die all the time," Ellery said in a kindly voice.

"It wasn't the dog, I tell you. It was the way it happened." She did not turn at the front door.

"The way he died?" Sucker.

"The way we found him." The girl suddenly leaned against the door, sidewise to him, staring down at her cigaret. "He was on our doorstep. Did you ever have a cat who insisted on leaving tidily dead mice on your mat to go with your breakfast eggs? He was a . . . gift." She looked around for an ashtray, went over to the fireplace. "And it killed my father."

A dead dog killing anybody struck Ellery as worth a tentative glance. And there was something about the girl—a remote, hardened purpose—that interested him.

"Sit down again."

She betrayed herself by the quick way in which she came back to the ponyskin chair, by the way she folded her tense hands and waited.

"How exactly, Laurel, did a dead dog 'kill' your father?"

"It murdered him."

He didn't like the way she sat there. He said deliberately, "Don't build it up for me. This isn't a suspense program. A strange dead hound is left on your doorstep and your father dies. What's the connection?"

"It frightened him to death!"

"And what did the death certificate say?" He now understood the official hilarity.

"Coronary something. I don't care what it said. Getting the dog did it."

"Let's go back." Ellery offered her one of his cigarets, but she shook her head and took a pack of Dunhills from her green pouch bag. He held a match for her; the cigaret between her lips was shaking. "Your name is Laurel Hill. You had a father. Who was he? Where do you live? What did he do for a living? And so on." She looked surprised, as if it had not occurred to her that such trivia could be of any interest to him. "I'm not necessarily taking it, Laurel. But I promise not to laugh."

"Thank you . . . Leander Hill. Hill & Priam, Wholesale Jewelers."

"Yes." He had never heard of the firm. "Los Angeles?"

"The main office is here, though Dad and Roger have—I mean had . . ."

She laughed. "What tense *do* I use? . . . branch offices in New York, Amsterdam, South Africa."

"Who is Roger?"

"Roger Priam. Dad's partner. We live off Outpost, not far from here. Twelve acres of lopsided woods. Formal gardens, with mathematical eucalyptus and royal palms, and plenty of bougainvillea, bird-of-paradise, poinsettia—all the stuff that curls up and dies at a touch of frost, which we get regularly every winter and which everybody says can't possibly happen again, not in Southern California. But Dad liked it. Made him feel like a Caribbean pirate, he used to say. Three in help in the house, a gardener who comes in every day, and the Priams have the adjoining property." From the carefully scrubbed way in which she produced the name Priam it might have been Hatfield. "Daddy had a bad heart, and we should have lived on level ground. But he liked hills and wouldn't hear of moving."

"Mother alive?" He knew she was not. Laurel had the motherless look. The self-made female. A man's girl, and there were times when she would insist on being a man's man. Not Miss Universe of Pasadena or anywhere else, he thought. He began to like her. "She isn't?" he said, when Laurel was silent.

"I don't know." A sore spot. "If I ever knew my mother, I've forgotten."

"Foster mother, then?"

"He never married. I was brought up by a nurse, who died when I was fifteen—four years ago. I never liked her, and I think she got pneumonia just to make me feel guilty. I'm—I was his daughter by adoption." She looked around for an ashtray, and Ellery brought her one. She said steadily as she crushed the cigaret, "But really his daughter. None of that fake pal stuff, you understand, that covers contempt on one side and being unsure on the other. I loved and respected him, and—as he used to say—I was the only woman in his life. Dad was a little on the old-school side. Held my chair for me. That sort of thing. He was . . . solid." And now, Ellery thought, it's jelly and you're hanging on to the stuff with your hard little fingers. "It happened," Laurel Hill went on in the same toneless way, "two weeks ago. June third. We were just finishing breakfast. Simeon, our chauffeur, came in to tell Daddy he'd just brought the car around and there was something 'funny' at the front door. We all went out, and there it was—a dead dog lying on the doorstep with an ordinary shipping tag attached to its collar. Dad's name was printed on it in black crayon: *Leander Hill.*"

"Any address?"

"Just the name."

"Did the printing look familiar? Did you recognize it?"

"I didn't really look at it. I just saw one line of crayon marks as Dad bent over the dog. He said in a surprised way, 'Why, it's addressed to me.' Then he opened the little casket."

"Casket?"

"There was a tiny silver box—about the size of a pillbox—attached to the collar. Dad opened it and found a wad of thin paper inside, folded over enough times so it would fit into the box. He unfolded it and it was covered with writing or printing—it might have been typewriting; I couldn't really see because he half turned away as he read it.

"By the time he'd finished reading his face was the color of bread dough, and his lips looked bluish. I started to ask him who'd sent it to him and what was wrong, when he crushed the paper in a sort of spasm and gave a choked cry and fell. I'd seen it happen before. It was a heart attack."

She stared out the picture window at Hollywood.

"How about a drink, Laurel?"

"No. Thanks. Simeon and—"

"What kind of dog was it?"

"Some sort of hunting dog, I think."

"Was there a license tag on his collar?"

"I don't remember seeing any."

"An anti-rabies tag?"

"I saw no tag except the paper one with Dad's name on it."

"Anything special about the dog collar?"

"It couldn't have cost more than seventy-five cents."

"Just a collar." Ellery dragged over a chartreuse latticed blond chair and straddled it. "Go on, Laurel."

"Simeon and Ichiro, our houseman, carried him up to his bedroom while I ran for the brandy and Mrs. Monk, our housekeeper, phoned the doctor. He lives on Castilian Drive and he was over in a few minutes. Daddy didn't die—that time."

"Oh, I see," said Ellery. "And what did the paper in the silver box on the dead dog's collar say, Laurel?"

"That's what I don't know."

"Oh, come."

"When he fell unconscious the paper was still in his hand, crumpled into a ball. I was too busy to try to open his fist, and by the time Dr. Voluta came, I'd forgotten it. But I remembered it that night, and the first chance I got—the next morning—I asked Dad about it. The minute I mentioned it he got pale, mumbled, 'It was nothing, nothing,' and I changed the subject fast. But when Dr. Voluta dropped in, I took him aside and asked him if he'd seen the note. He said he had opened Daddy's hand and put the wad of paper on the night table beside the bed without reading it. I asked Simeon, Ichiro, and the housekeeper if they had taken the paper, but none of them had seen it. Daddy must have spotted it when he came to, and when he was alone he took it back."

"Have you looked for it since?"

"Yes, but I haven't found it. I assume he destroyed it."

Ellery did not comment on such assumptions. "Well, then, the dog, the collar, the little box. Have you done anything about them?"

"I was too excited over whether Daddy was going to live or die to think about the dog. I recall telling Itchie or Sim to get it out of the way. I only meant for them to get it off the doorstep, but the next day when I went looking for it, Mrs. Monk told me she had called the Pound Department or some place and it had been picked up and carted away."

"Up the flue," said Ellery, tapping his teeth with a fingernail. "Although the collar and box . . . You're sure your father didn't react to the mere sight of the dead dog? He wasn't afraid of dogs? Or," he added suddenly, "of dying?"

"He adored dogs. So much so that when Sarah, our Chesapeake bitch, died of old age last year he refused to get another dog. He said it was too hard losing them. As far as dying is concerned, I don't think the prospect of death as such bothered Daddy very much. Certainly not so much as the suffering. He hated the idea of a lingering illness with a lot of pain, and he always hoped that when his time came he'd pass away in his sleep. But that's all. Does that answer your question?"

"Yes," said Ellery, "and no. Was he superstitious?"

"Not especially. Why?"

"You said he was frightened to death. I'm groping."

Laurel was silent. Then she said, "But he was. I mean frightened to death. It wasn't the dog—at first." She gripped her ankles, staring ahead. "I got the feeling that the dog didn't mean anything till he read the note. Maybe it didn't mean anything to him even then. But whatever was in that note terrified him. It came as a tremendous shock to him. I'd never seen him look *afraid* before. I mean the real thing. And I could have sworn he died on the way down. He looked really dead lying there . . . That note did something devastating." She turned to Ellery. Her eyes were greenish, with brown flecks in them; they were a little bulgy. "Something he'd forgotten, maybe. Something so important it made Roger come out of his shell for the first time in fifteen years."

"What?" said Ellery. "What was that again?"

"I told you—Roger Priam, Dad's business partner. His oldest friend. Roger left his house."

"For the first time in fifteen years?" exclaimed Ellery.

"Fifteen years ago Roger became partly paralyzed. He's lived in a wheelchair ever since, and ever since he's refused to leave the Priam premises. All vanity; he was a large hunk of man in his day, I understand, proud of his build, his physical strength; he can't stand the thought of having people see him helpless, and it's turned him into something pretty unpleasant.

"Through it all Roger pretends he's as good as ever and he brags that running the biggest jewelry business on the West Coast from a wheelchair in the hills proves it. Of course, he doesn't do any such thing. Daddy ran it all, though to keep peace he played along with Roger and pretended with him—gave Roger special jobs to do that he could handle over the phone, never took an important step without consulting him, and so on. Why, some of the people at the office and showrooms downtown have been with the firm for years and have never even laid eyes on Roger. The employes hate him. They call him 'the invisible God,'" Laurel said with a smile. Ellery did not care for the smile. "Of course—being employes—they're scared to death of him."

"A fear which you don't share?"

"I can't stand him." It came out calmly enough, but when Ellery kept looking at her she glanced elsewhere.

"You're afraid of him, too."

"I just dislike him."

"Go on."

"I'd notified the Priams of Dad's heart attack the first chance I got, which was the evening of the day it happened. I spoke to Roger myself on the phone. He seemed very curious about the circumstances and kept insisting he had to talk to Daddy. I refused—Dr. Voluta had forbidden excitement of any kind. The next morning Roger phoned twice, and Dad seemed just as anxious to talk to *him*. In fact, he was getting so upset I let him phone. There's a private line between his bedroom and the Priam house. But after I got Roger on the phone Dad asked me to leave the room."

Laurel jumped up, but immediately she sat down again, fumbling for another Dunhill. Ellery let her strike her own match; she failed to notice.

She puffed rapidly. "Nobody knows what he said to Roger. Whatever it was, it took only a few minutes, and it brought Roger right over. He'd been lifted, wheelchair and all, into the back of the Priams' station wagon, and Delia—Roger's wife—drove him over herself." And Laurel's voice stabbed at the name of Mrs. Priam. So another Hatfield went with this McCoy. "When he was carried up to Dad's bedroom in his chair, Roger locked the door. They talked for three hours."

"Discussing the dead dog and the note?"

"There's no other possibility. It couldn't have been business—Roger had never felt the necessity of coming over before on business, and Daddy had had two previous heart attacks. It was about the dog and note, all right. And if I had any doubts, the look on Roger Priam's face when he wheeled himself out of the bedroom killed them. He was as frightened as Daddy had been the day before, and for the same reason.

"And that was something to see," said Laurel softly. "If you were to meet Roger Priam, you'd know what I mean. Frightened looks don't go with his face. If there's any fright around, he's usually dishing it out . . . He even talked to me, something he rarely bothers to do. 'You take good care of your father,' he said to me. I pleaded with him to tell me what was wrong, and he pretended not to have heard me. Simeon and Itchie lifted him into the station wagon, and Delia drove off with him.

"A week ago—during the night of June tenth—Daddy got his wish. He died in his sleep. Dr. Voluta says that last shock to his heart did it. He was cremated, and his ashes are in a bronze drawer fifteen feet from the floor at Forest Lawn. But that's what he wanted, and that's where he is. The sixty-four dollar question, Ellery, is: Who murdered him? And I want it answered."

Ellery rang for Mrs. Williams. When she did not appear, he excused himself and went downstairs to the miniature lower level to find a note from his housekeeper describing minutely her plan to shop at the supermarket on North Highland. A pot of fresh coffee on the range and a deep dish of whipped avocado and bacon bits surrounded by crackers told him that Mrs. Williams had overheard all, so he took them upstairs.

Laurel said, surprised, "How nice of you," as if niceness these days were a quality that called for surprise. She refused the crackers just as nicely, but then she changed her mind and ate ten of them without pausing, and she drank three cups of coffee. "I remembered I hadn't eaten anything today."

"That's what I thought."

She was frowning now, which he regarded as an improvement over the stone face she had been wearing. "I've tried to talk to Roger Priam half a dozen times since then, but he won't even admit he and Dad discussed anything unusual. I told him in words of one syllable where I thought his obligations lay—certainly his debt to their lifelong friendship and partner-ship—and I explained my belief that Daddy was murdered by somebody who knew how bad his heart was and deliberately shocked him into a heart attack. And I asked for the letter. He said innocently, 'What letter?' and I realized I'd never get a thing out of him. Roger's either over his scare or he's being his usual Napoleonic self. There's a big secret behind all this and he means to keep it."

"Do you think," asked Ellery, "that he's confided in Mrs. Priam?"

"Roger doesn't confide in anybody," replied Laurel grimly. "And if he did, the last person in the world he'd tell anything to would be Delia."

"Oh, the Priams don't get along?"

"I didn't say they don't get along."

"They do get along?"

"Let's change the subject, shall we?"

"Why, Laurel?"

"Because Roger's relationship with Delia has nothing to do with any of this." Laurel sounded earnest. But she was hiding something just the same. "I'm interested in only one thing—finding out who wrote that note to my father."

"Still," said Ellery, "what was your father's relationship with Delia Priam?"

"Oh!" Laurel laughed. "Of course you couldn't know. No, they weren't having an affair. Not possibly. Besides, I told you Daddy said I was the only woman in his life."

"Then they were hostile to each other?"

"Why do you keep on the subject of Delia?" she asked, a snap in her voice.

"Why do you keep off it?"

"Dad got along with Delia fine. He got along with everybody."

"Not everybody, Laurel," said Ellery.

She looked at him sharply.

"That is, if your theory that someone deliberately scared him to death is sound. You can't blame the police, Laurel, for being fright-shy. Fright is a dangerous weapon that doesn't show up under the microscope. It takes no fingerprints and it's the most unsatisfactory kind of legal evidence. Now the letter . . . if you had the letter, that would be different. But you don't have it."

"You're laughing at me." Laurel prepared to rise.

"Not at all. The smooth stories are usually as slick as their surface. I like a good rough story. You can scrape away at the uneven places, and the dust tells you things. Now I know there's something about Delia and Roger Priam. What is it?"

"Why must you know?"

"Because you're so reluctant to tell me."

"I'm not. I just don't want to waste any time, and to talk about Delia and Roger is wasting time. Their relationship has nothing to do with my father."

Their eyes locked.

Finally, with a smile, Ellery waved.

"No, I don't have the letter. And that's what the police said. Without the letter, or some evidence to go on, they can't come into it. I've asked Roger to tell them what he knows—knowing that what he knows *would* be enough for them to go on—and he laughed and recommended Arrowhead or Palm Springs as a cure for my 'pipe dream,' as he called it. The police point to the autopsy report and Dad's cardiac history and send me politely away. Are you going to do the same?"

Ellery turned to the window. To get into a live murder case was the last thing in the world he had bargained for. But the dead dog fascinated him. Why a dead dog as a messenger of bad news? It smacked of symbolism. And murderers with metaphoric minds he had never been able to resist. If, of course, there was a murder. Hollywood was a playful place. People produced practical jokes on the colossal scale. A dead dog was nothing compared with some of the elaborations of record. One he knew of personally involved a race horse in a bathroom, another the employment for two days of seventy-six extras. Some wit had sent a cardiac jeweler a recently deceased canine and a fake Mafia note, and before common sense could set in the victim of the dogplay had a heart attack. Learning the unexpected snapper of his joke, the joker would not unnaturally turn shy. The victim, ill and shaken, summoned his oldest friend and business partner to a conference. Perhaps the note threatened Sicilian tortures unless the crown jewels were deposited in the oily crypt of the pterodactyl pit in Hancock Park by midnight of the following day. For three hours the partners discussed the note, Hill nervously insisting it might be legitimate, Priam reasonably poohing and boshing the very notion. In the end Priam came away, and what Laurel Hill had taken to be fear was probably annoyance at Hill's womanish obduracy. Hill was immobilized by his partner's irritation, and before he could rouse himself his heart gave out altogether. End of mystery. Of course, there were a few dangling ends . . . But you could sympathize with the police.

It was a lot likelier than a wild detective-story theory dreamed up by deceased's daughter. They had undoubtedly dismissed her as either a neurotic girl tipped over by grief or a publicity hound with a yen for a starlet contract. She was determined enough to be either.

Ellery turned about. She was leaning forward, the forgotten cigaret sending up question marks.

"I suppose," said Ellery, "your father had a closetful of bony enemies?"

"Not to my knowledge."

This astonished him. To run true to form she should have come prepared with names, dates, and vital statistics.

"He was an easy, comfortable sort of man. He liked people, and people liked him. Dad's personality was one of the big assets of Hill & Priam. He'd have his moments like everybody else, but I never knew anyone who could stay mad at him. Not even Roger."

"Then you haven't the smoggiest notion who could be behind this . . . fright murder?"

"Now you *are* laughing." Laurel Hill got to her feet and dropped her cigaret definitely into the ashtray. "Sorry I've taken up so much of your time."

"You might try a reliable agency. I'll be glad to—"

"I've decided," she smiled at him, "to go into the racket personally. Thanks for the avocado—"

"Why, Laurel."

Laurel turned quickly.

A tall woman stood in the doorway.

"Hello, Delia," said Laurel.

Chapter II

NOTHING IN Laurel Hill's carefully edited remarks had prepared him for Delia Priam. Through his only available windows—the narrow eyes of Laurel's youth—he had seen Delia's husband as a pompous and tyrannical old cock, crippled but rampant, ruling his roost with a beak of iron; and from this it followed that the wife must be a gray-feathered hennypenny, preening herself emptily in corners, one of Bullock's elderly barnyard trade . . . a dumpy, nervous, insignificant old biddy.

But the woman in his doorway was no helpless fowl, to be plucked, swallowed, and forgotten. Delia Priam was of a far different species, higher in the ranks of the animal kingdom, and she would linger on the palate.

She was so much younger than his mental sketch of her that only much later was Ellery to recognize this as one of her routine illusions, among the easiest of the magic tricks she performed as professionally as she carried her breasts. At that time he was to discover that she was forty-four, but the knowledge remained as physically meaningless as—the figure leaped into his mind—learning the chronological age of Ayesha. The romantic nonsense of this metaphor was to persist. He would even be appalled to find that he was identifying himself in his fantasy with that hero of his adolescence, Allan Quatermain, who had been privileged to witness the immortal strip-tease of She-Who-Must-Be-Obeyed behind her curtain of living flame. It was the most naked juvenility, and Ellery was duly amused at himself. But there she was, a glowing end in herself; it took only imagination, a commodity with which he was plentifully provided, to supply the veils.

Delia Priam was big game; one glance told him that. His doorway framed the most superbly proportioned woman he had ever seen. She was dressed in a tawny peasant blouse of some sheer material and a California print skirt of bold colors. Her heavy black hair was massed to one side of her head, sleekly, in the Polynesian fashion; she wore plain broad hoops of gold in her ears. Head, shoulders, bust, hips—he could not decide which pleased him more. She stood there not so much in an attitude as in an atmosphere—an atmosphere of intense repose, watchful and disquieting.

By Hollywood standards she was not beautiful: her eyes were too deep and light-tinted, her eyebrows too lush; her mouth was too full, her coloring too high, her figure too heroic. But it was this very excessiveness that excited—a tropical quality, humid, brilliant, still, and overpowering. Seeing her for the first time was like stepping into a jungle. She seized and held the senses; everything was leashed, lovely, and dangerous. He found his ears trying to recapture her voice, the sleepy growl of something heard from a thicket.

Ellery's first sensible thought was, *Roger, old cock, you can have her.* His second was, *But how do you keep her?* He was on his third when he saw the chilly smile on Laurel Hill's lips.

Ellery pulled himself together. This was evidently an old story to Laurel.

"Then Laurel's . . . mentioned me." A dot-dot-dot talker. It had always annoyed him. But it prolonged the sound of that bitch-in-a-thicket voice.

"I answered Mr. Queen's questions," said Laurel in a warm, friendly voice. "Delia, you don't seem surprised to see me."

"I left my surprise outside with your car." Those lazy throat tones were warm and friendly, too. "I could say . . . the same to you, Laurel."

"Darling, you never surprise me."

They smiled at each other.

Laurel turned suddenly and reached for another cigaret.

"Don't bother, Ellery. Delia always makes a man forget there's another woman in the room"

"Now, Laurel." She was indulgent. Laurel slashed the match across the packet.

"Won't you come in and sit down, Mrs. Priam?"

"If I'd had any idea Laurel was coming here . . ."

Laurel said abruptly, "I came to see the man about the dog, Delia. *And* the note. Did you follow me?"

"What a ridiculous thing to say."

"Did you?"

"Certainly not, dear. I read about Mr. Queen in the papers and it coincided with something that's been bothering me."

"I'm sorry, Delia. I've been upset."

"I'll come back, Mr. Queen."

"Mrs. Priam, does it concern Miss Hill's father's death?"

"I don't know. It may."

"Then Miss Hill won't mind your sitting in. I repeat my invitation."

She had a trick of moving slowly, as if she were pushing against something. As he brought the chartreuse chair around he watched her obliquely. When she sat down she was close enough so that he could have touched her bare back with a very slight movement of his finger. He almost moved it.

She did not seem to have taken him in at all. And yet she had looked him over; up and down, as if he had been a gown in a dress shop. Perhaps he didn't interest her. As a gown, that is.

"Drink, Mrs. Priam?"

"Delia doesn't drink," said Laurel in the same warm, friendly voice. Two jets spurted from her nostrils.

"Thank you, darling. It goes to my head, Mr. Queen."

And you wouldn't let anything go to your head, wherefore it stands to reason, thought Ellery, that one way to get at you is to pour a few extra-dry Martinis down that red gullet . . . He was surprised at himself. A married woman, obviously a lady, and her husband was a cripple. But that wading walk was something to see.

"Laurel was about to leave. The facts interest me, but I'm in Hollywood to do a book . . ."

The shirring of her blouse rose and fell. He moved off to the picture window, making her turn her head.

"If, however, you have something to contribute, Mrs. Priam . . ."

He suspected there would be no book for some time.

Delia Priam's story penetrated imperfectly. Ellery found it hard to concentrate. He tended to lose himself in details. The curves of her blouse. The promise of her skirt, which molded her strongly below the waist. Her large, shapely hands rested precisely in the middle of her lap, like compass points. "*Mistresses with great smooth marbly limbs . . .*" Right out of Browning's Renaissance. She would have brought joy to the dying Bishop of Saint Praxed's.

"Mr. Queen?"

Ellery said guiltily, "You mean, Mrs. Priam, the same day Leander Hill received the dead dog?"

"The same morning. It was a sort of gift. I don't know what else you'd call it."

Laurel's cigaret hung in the air. "Delia, you didn't tell me Roger had got something, too!"

"He told me not to say anything, Laurel. But you've forced my hand, dear. Kicking up such a fuss about that poor dog. First the police, now Mr. Queen."

"Then you did follow me."

"I didn't have to." The woman smiled. "I saw you looking at Mr. Queen's photo in the paper."

"Delia, you're wonderful."

"Thank you, darling." She sat peaceful as a lady tiger, smiling over secrets . . . Here, Brother Q!

"Oh. Oh, yes, Mrs. Priam. Mr. Priam's been frightened—"

"Ever since the day he got the box. He won't admit it, but when a man keeps roaring that he won't be intimidated it's pretty clear that he is. He's broken things, too, some of his own things. That's not like Roger. Usually they're mine."

Delightful. What a pity.

"What was in the box, Mrs. Priam?"

"I haven't any idea."

"A dead dog," said Laurel. "Another dead dog!" Laurel looked something like a little dog herself, nose up, testing the air. It was remarkable how meaningless she was across from Delia Priam. As sexless as a child.

"It would have to have been an awfully small one, Laurel. The box wasn't more than a foot square, of cardboard."

"Unmarked?" asked Ellery.

"Yes. But there was a shipping tag attached to the string that was tied around the box. 'Roger Priam' was printed on it in crayon." The beautiful woman paused. "Mr. Queen, are you listening?"

"In crayon. Yes, certainly, Mrs. Priam. Color?" What the devil difference did the color make?

"Black, I think."

"No address?"

"No. Nothing but the name."

"And you don't know what was in it. No idea."

"No. But whatever it was, it hit Roger hard. One of the servants found the box at the front door and gave it to Alfred—"

"Alfred."

"Roger's . . . secretary."

"Wouldn't you call him more of a . . . companion, Delia?" asked Laurel, blowing a smoke ring.

"I suppose so, dear. Companion, nurse, handyman, secretary—what-have-you. My husband, you know, Mr. Queen, is an invalid."

"Laurel's told me. All things to one man, eh, Mrs. Priam? I mean Alfred. We now have the versatile Alfred with the mysterious box. He takes it to Mr. Priam's room. And then?" Why was Laurel laughing? Not outwardly. But she was. Delia Priam seemed not to notice.

"I happened to be in Roger's room when Alfred came in. We didn't know then about . . . Leander and *his* gift, of course. Alfred gave Roger the box, and Roger lifted a corner of the lid and looked inside. He looked angry, then puzzled. He slammed the lid down and told me to get out. Alfred went out with me, and I heard Roger lock his door. And that's the last . . . I've seen of the box or its contents. Roger won't tell me what was in it or what he's done with it. Won't talk about it at all."

"When did your husband begin to show fear, Mrs. Priam?"

"After he talked to Leander in the Hill house the next day. On the way back home he didn't say a word, just stared out the window of the station wagon. Shaking. He's been shaking . . . ever since. It was especially bad a week later when Leander died . . ."

Then what was in Roger Priam's box had little significance for him until he compared gifts with Leander Hill, perhaps until he read the note Hill had found in the collar of the dog. Unless there had been a note in Priam's box as well. But then . . .

Ellery fidgeted before the picture window, sending up a smoke screen. It was ridiculous, at his age . . . pretending to be interested in a case because a respectable married woman had the misfortune to evoke the jungle. Still, he thought, what a waste.

He became conscious of the two women's eyes and expelled a mouthful of smoke, trying to appear professional. "Leander Hill received a queer gift, and he died. Are you afraid, Mrs. Priam, that your husband's life is in danger, too?"

Now he was more than a piece of merchandise; he was a piece of merchandise that interested her. Her eyes were so empty of color that in the sunlight coming through the window she looked eyeless; it was like being looked over by a statue. He felt himself reddening and it seemed to him she was amused. He immediately bristled. She could take her precious husband and her fears elsewhere.

"Laurel darling," Delia Priam was saying with an apologetic glance, "would you mind terribly if I spoke to Mr. Queen . . . alone?"

Laurel got up. "I'll wait in the garden," she said, and she tossed her cigaret into the tray and walked out.

Roger Priam's wife waited until Laurel's slim figure appeared beyond the picture window, among the shaggy asters. Laurel's head was turned away. She was switching her thigh with her cap.

"Laurel's sweet," said Delia Priam. "But so young, don't you think? Right now she's on a crusade and she's feeling ever so knightly. She'll get over it. . . . Why, about your question, Mr. Queen. I'm going to be perfectly frank with you. I haven't the slightest interest in my husband. I'm not afraid that he may die. If anything, it's the other way around."

Ellery stared. For a moment her eyes slanted to the sun and they sparkled in a mineral way. But her features were without guile. The next instant she was eyeless again.

"You're honest, Mrs. Priam. Brutally so."

"I've had a rather broad education in brutality, Mr. Queen."

So there was that, too. Ellery sighed.

"I'll be even franker," she went on. "I don't know whether Laurel told you specifically . . . Did she say what kind of invalid my husband is?"

"She said he's partly paralyzed."

"She didn't say what part?"

"What part?" said Ellery.

"Then she didn't. Why, Mr. Queen, my husband is paralyzed," said Delia Priam with a smile, "from the waist down."

You had to admire the way she said that. The brave smile. The smile that said *Don't pity me.*

"I'm very sorry," he said.

"I've had fifteen years of it."

Ellery was silent. She rested her head against the back of the chair. Her eyes were almost closed and her throat was strong and defenseless.

"You're wondering why I told you that."

Ellery nodded.

"I told you because you can't understand why I've come to you unless you understand that first. Weren't you wondering?"

"All right. Why have you come to me?"

"For appearance's sake."

Ellery stared. "You ask me to investigate a possible threat against your husband's life, Mrs. Priam, for appearance's sake?"

"You don't believe me."

"I do believe you. Nobody would invent such a reason!" Seating himself beside her, he took one of her hands. It was cool and secretive, and it remained perfectly lax in his. "You haven't had much of a life."

"What do you mean?"

"You've never done any work with these hands."

"Is that bad?"

"It could be." Ellery put her hand back in her lap. "A woman like you has no right to remain tied to a man who's half-dead. If he were some saintly character, if there were love between you, I'd understand it. But I gather he's a brute and that you loathe him. Then why haven't you done something with your life? Why haven't you divorced him? Is there a religious reason?"

"There might have been when I was young. Now . . ." She shook her head. "Now it's the way it would look. You see, I'm stripping myself quite bare."

Ellery looked pained.

"You're very gallant to an old woman." She laughed. "No, I'm serious, Mr. Queen. I come from one of the old California families. Formal upbringing. Convent-trained. Duennas in the old fashion. A pride of caste and tradition. I could never take it as seriously as they did . . .

"My mother had married a heretic from New England. They ostracized her and it killed her when I was a little girl. I'd have got away from them completely, except that when my mother died they talked my father into giving me into their custody. I was brought up by an aunt who wore a mantilla. I married the first man who came along just to get away from them.

He wasn't their choice—he was an 'American,' like my father. I didn't love him, but he had money, we were very poor, and I wanted to escape. It cut me off from my family, my church, and my world. I have a ninety-year-old grandmother who lives only three miles from this spot. I haven't seen her for eighteen years. She considers me dead."

Her head rolled. "Harvey died when we'd been married three years, leaving me with a child. Then I met Roger Priam. I couldn't go back to my mother's family, my father was off on one of his jaunts, and Roger attracted me. I would have followed him to hell." She laughed again. "And that's exactly where he led me.

"When I found out what Roger really was, and then when he became crippled and I lost even that, there was nothing left. I've filled the vacuum by trying to go back where I came from.

"It hasn't been easy," murmured Delia Priam. "They don't forget such things, and they never forgive. But the younger generation is softer-bottomed and corrupted by modern ways. Their men, of course, have helped . . . Now it's the only thing I have to hang on to."

Her face showed a passion not to be shared or relished. Ellery was glad when the moment passed. "The life I lead in Roger Priam's house isn't even suspected by these people. If they knew the truth, I'd be dropped and there'd be no return. And if I left Roger, they'd say I deserted my husband. Upper caste women of the old California society don't do that sort of thing, Mr. Queen; it doesn't matter what the husband is. So . . . I don't do it.

"Now something is happening, I don't know what. If Laurel had kept her mouth shut, I wouldn't have lifted a finger. But by going about insisting that Leander Hill was murdered, Laurel's created an atmosphere of suspicion that threatens my position. Sooner or later the papers will get hold of it—it's a wonder they haven't already—and the fact that Roger is apparently in the same danger might come out. I can't sit by and wait for that. My people will expect me to be the loyal wife. So that's what I'm being. Mr. Queen, I ask you to proceed as if I'm terribly concerned about my husband's safety." Delia Priam shrugged. "Or is this all too involved for you?"

"It would seem to me far simpler," said Ellery, "to clear out and start over again somewhere else."

"This is where I was born." She looked out at Hollywood. Laurel had moved over to a corner of the garden. "I don't mean all that popcorn and false front down there. I mean the hills, the orchards, the old missions. But there's another reason, and it has nothing to do with me, or my people, or Southern California."

"What's that, Mrs. Priam?"

"Roger wouldn't let me go. He's a man of violence, Mr. Queen. You don't—you can't—know his furious possessiveness, his pride, his compulsion to dominate, his . . . depravity. Sometimes I think I'm married to a maniac."

She closed her eyes. The room was still. From below Ellery heard Mrs. Williams's Louisiana-bred tones complaining to the gold parakeet she kept in a cage above the kitchen sink about the scandalous price of coffee. An

invisible finger was writing in the sky above the Wilshire district: MUNTZ
TV. The empty typewriter nudged his elbow.

But there she sat, the jungle in batiste and colored cotton. His slick and
characterless Hollywood house would never be the same again. It was exciting
just to be able to look at her lying in the silly chair. It was dismaying to
imagine the chair empty.

"Mrs. Priam."

"Yes?"

"Why," asked Ellery, trying not to think of Roger Priam, "didn't you
want Laurel Hill to hear what you just told me?"

The woman opened her eyes. "I don't mind undressing before a man,"
she said, "but I do draw the line at a woman."

She said it lightly, but something ran up Ellery's spine.

He jumped to his feet. "Take me to your husband."

Chapter III

WHEN THEY CAME out of Ellery's house Laurel said pleasantly, "Has a contract been drawn up, Ellery? And if so, with which one of us? Or is the
question incompetent and none of my business?"

"No contract," said Ellery testily. "No contract, Laurel. I'm just going to
take a look around."

"Starting at the *Priam* house, of course."

"Yes."

"In that case, since we're all in this together—aren't we, Delia?—I suppose
there's no objection if I trail along?"

"Of course not, darling," said Delia. "But do try not to antagonize Roger.
He always takes it out on me afterwards."

"What do you think he's going to say when he finds out you've brought
a detective around?"

"Oh, dear," said Delia. Then she brightened. "Why, darling, *you're* bring-
ing Mr. Queen around, don't you see? Do you mind very much? I know
it's yellow, but I have to live with him. And you did get to Mr. Queen first."

"All right," said Laurel with a shrug. "We'll give you a head start, Delia.
You take Franklin and Outpost, and I'll go around the long way, over
Cahuenga and Mulholland. Where have you been, shopping?"

Delia Priam laughed. She got into her car, a new cream Cadillac convertible, and drove off down the hill.

"Hardly a substitute," said Laurel after a moment. Ellery started. Laurel
was holding open the door of her car, a tiny green Austin. "Either car *or*
driver. Can you see Delia in an Austin? Like the Queen of Sheba in a row-
boat. Get in."

"Unusual type," remarked Ellery absently, as the little car shot off.

"The adjective, yes. But as to the noun," said Laurel, "there is only one Delia Priam."

"She seems remarkably frank and honest."

"Does she?"

"I thought so. Don't you?"

"It doesn't matter what I think."

"By which you tell me what you think."

"No, you don't! But if you must know . . . You never get to the bottom of Delia. She doesn't lie, but she doesn't tell the truth, either—I mean the whole truth. She always keeps something in reserve that you dig out much, much later, if you're lucky to dig it out at all. Now I'm not going to say anything more about Delia, because whatever I say you'll hold, not against her, but against me. Delia bowls over big shots especially . . . I suppose it's no use asking you what she wanted to talk to you alone about?"

"Take—it—easy," said Ellery, holding his hat. "Another bounce like that and my knees will stab me to death."

"Nice try, Laurel," said Laurel; and she darted into the Freewaybound traffic on North Highland with a savage flip of her exhaust.

After a while Ellery remarked to Laurel's profile: "You said something about Roger Priam's 'never' leaving his wheelchair. You didn't mean that literally, by any chance?"

"Yes. Not ever. Didn't Delia tell you about the chair?"

"No."

"It's fabulous. After Roger became paralyzed he had an ordinary wheelchair for a time, which meant he had to be lifted into and out of it. Daddy told me about it. It seems Roger the Lion-Hearted couldn't take that. It made him too dependent on others. So he designed a special chair for himself."

"What does it do, boost him in and out of bed on mechanical arms?"

"It does away with a bed altogether."

Ellery stared.

"That's right. He sleeps in it, eats in it, does his work in it—everything. A combination office, study, living room, dining room, bedroom and bathroom on wheels. It's quite a production. From one of the arms of the chair hangs a small shelf which he can swing around to the front and raise; he eats on that, mixes drinks, and so on. Under the shelf are compartments for cutlery, napkins, cocktail things, and liquor. There's a similar shelf on the other arm of the chair which holds his typewriter, screwed on, of course, so it won't fall off when it's swung aside. And under that shelf are places for paper, carbon, pencils and Lord knows what else. The chair is equipped with two phones of the plug-in type—the regular line and a private wire to our house—and with an intercom system to Wallace's room."

"Who's Wallace?"

"Alfred Wallace, his secretary-companion. Then—let's see." Laurel frowned. "Oh, he's got compartments and cubbyholes all around the chair for just about everything imaginable—magazines, cigars, his reading glasses, his toothbrush; everything he could possibly need. The chair's built so that it can be lowered and the front raised, making a bed out of it for daytime napping or sleeping at night. Of course, he needs Alfred to help him sponge-bathe and dress and undress and so on, but he's made himself as self-suf-ficent as possible—hates help of any kind, even the most essential. When I was there yesterday his typewriter had just been sent into Hollywood to be repaired and he had to dictate business memoranda to Alfred instead of doing them himself, and he was in such a foul mood because of it that even Alfred got mad. Roger in a foul mood can be awfully foul . . . I'm sorry, I thought you wanted to know."

"What?"

"You're not listening."

"I am, though not with both ears." They were on Mulholland Drive now, and Ellery was clutching the side of the Austin to avoid being thrown clear as Laurel zoomed the little car around the hairpin curves. "Tell me, Laurel. Who inherits your father's estate? I mean besides yourself?"

"Nobody. There isn't anyone else."

"He didn't leave anything to Priam?"

"Why should he? Roger and Daddy were equal partners. There are some small cash bequests to people in the firm and to the household help. Every-thing else goes to me. So you see, Ellery," said Laurel, soaring over a rise, "I'm your big suspect."

"Yes," said Ellery, "and you're also Roger Priam's new partner. Or are you?"

"My status isn't clear. The lawyers are working on that now. Of course I don't know anything about the jewelry business and I'm not sure I want to. Roger can't chisel me out of anything, if that's what's in your mind. One of the biggest law firms in Los Angeles is protecting my interests. I must say Roger's been surprisingly decent about that end of it—for Roger, I mean. Maybe Daddy's death hit him harder than he expected—made him realize how important Dad was to the business and how unimportant *he* is. Actually, he hasn't much to worry about. Dad trained a very good man to run things, a Mr. Foss, in case anything happened to him . . . Anyway, there's one item on my agenda that takes priority over everything else. And if you won't clear it up for me, I'll do it myself."

"Because you loved Leander Hill very much?"

"Yes!"

"And because, of course," remarked Ellery, "you *are* the big suspect?"

Laurel's little hands tightened on the wheel. Then they relaxed. "That's the stuff, Ellery," she laughed. "Just keep firing away at the whites of our eyes. I love it.—There's the Priam place."

The Priam place stood on a private road, a house of dark round stones and blackish wood wedged into a fold of the hills and kept in forest gloom by a thick growth of overhanging sycamore, elm, and eucalyptus. Ellery's first thought was that the grounds were neglected, but then he saw evidences of both old and recent pruning on the sides away from the house and he realized that nature had been coaxed into the role she was playing. The hopeless matting of leaves and boughs was deliberate; the secretive gloom was wanted. Priam had dug into the hill and pulled the trees over him. Who was it who had defied the sun?

It was more like an isolated hunting lodge than a Hollywood house. Most of it was hidden from the view of passers-by on the main road, and by its character it transformed a suburban section of ordinary Southern California canyon into a wild Scottish glen. Laurel told Ellery that the Priam property extended up and along the hill for four or five acres and that it was all like the area about the house.

"Jungle," said Ellery as Laurel parked the car in the driveway. There was no sign of the cream Cadillac.

"Well, he's a wild animal. Like the deer you flush occasionally up behind the Bowl."

"He's paying for the privilege. His electric bills must be enormous."

"I'm sure they are. There isn't a sunny room in the house. When he wants—you can't say more *light*—when he wants less gloom, and air that isn't so stale, he wheels himself out on that terrace there." To one side of the house there was a large terrace, half of it screened and roofed, the other open not to the sky but a high arch of blue gum eucalyptus leaves and branches which the sun did not penetrate. "His den—den is the word—is directly off the terrace, past those French and screen doors. We'd better go in the front way; Roger doesn't like people barging in on his sacred preserves. In the Priam house you're announced."

"Doesn't Delia Priam have anything to say about the way her house is run?"

"Who said it's her house?" said Laurel.

A uniformed maid with a tic admitted them. "Oh, Miss Hill," she said nervously. "I don't think Mr. Priam . . . He's dictatin' to Mr. Wallace. I better not . . ."

"Is Mrs. Priam in, Muggs?"

"She just got in from shoppin', Miss Hill. She's upstairs in her room. Said she was tired and was not to be disturbed."

"Poor Delia," said Laurel calmly. "I know Mr. Queen is terribly disappointed. Tell Mr. Priam I want to see him."

"But, Miss Hill—"

A muffled roar of rage stopped her instantly. She glanced over her shoulder in a panic.

"It's all right, Muggsy. I'll take the rap. *Vamos*, Ellery."

"I wonder why she—" Ellery began in a mumble as Laurel led him up the hall.

"Yours not to, where Delia is concerned."

The house was even grimmer than he had expected. They passed shrouded

rooms with dark paneling, heavy and humorless drapes, massive uncomfort-
able-looking furniture. It was a house for secrets and for violence.

The roar was a bass snarl now. "I don't give a damn what Mr. *Hill* wanted
to do about the Newman-Arco account, Foss! Mr. *Hill's* locked in a drawer
in Forest Lawn and he ain't in any condition to give us the benefit of his
advice . . . No, I won't wait a minute, Foss! I'm running this — business,
and you'll either handle things my way or get the hell out!"

Laurel's lips thinned. She raised her fist and hammered on the door.

"Whoever that is, Alfred—! Foss, you still there?"

A man opened the heavy door and slipped into the hall, pulling the door
to and keeping his hand on the knob behind him.

"You picked a fine time, Laurel. He's on the phone to the office."

"So I hear," said Laurel. "Mr. Queen, Mr. Wallace. His other name ought
to be Job, but it's Alfred. The perfect man, I call him. Super-efficient. Discreet as all get-out. Never slips. One side, Alfred. I've got business with my
partner."

"Better let me set him up," said Wallace with a smile. As he slipped back
into the room, his eyes flicked over Ellery. Then the door was shut again,
and Ellery waved his right hand tenderly. It still tingled from Wallace's grip.

"Surprised?" murmured Laurel.

Ellery was. He had expected a Milquetoast character. Instead Alfred Wallace was a towering, powerfully assembled man with even, rather sharp, features, thick white hair, a tan, and an air of lean distinction. His voice was
strong and thoughtful, with the merest touch of . . . superiority? Whatever
it was, it was barely enough to impress, not quite enough to annoy. Wallace
might have stepped out of a set on the M-G-M lot labeled *High Society
Drawing Room*; and, in fact, "well-preserved actor" had been Ellery's impulsive characterization—Hollywood leading-men types with Athletic Club tans
were turning up these days in the most unexpected places, swallowing their
pride in order to be able to swallow at all. But a moment later Ellery was not
so sure. Wallace's shoulders did not look as if they came off with his coat.
His physique, even his elegance, seemed home-grown.

"I should think you'd be smitten, Laurel," said Ellery as they waited.
"That's a virile character. Perfectly disciplined, and dashing as the devil."

"A little too old," said Laurel. "For me, that is."

"He can't be much more than fifty-five. And he doesn't look forty-five,
white hair notwithstanding."

"Alfred would be too old for me if he were twenty.—Oh. Well? Do I
have to get Mr. Queen to brush you aside, Alfred, or is the Grand Vizier
going to play gracious this morning?"

Alfred Wallace smiled and let them pass.

The man who slammed the phone down and spun the steel chair about
as if it were a studio production of balsa wood was a creature of immensities.
He was all bulge, spread, and thickness. Bull eyes blazed above iron cheekbones; the nose was a massive snout; a tremendous black beard fell to his

chest. The hands which gripped the wheels of the chair were enormous; forearms and biceps strained his coat sleeves. And the whole powerful mechanism was in continuous movement, as if even that great frame was unable to contain his energy. Something by Wolf Larsen out of Captain Teach, on a restless quarter-deck. Besides that immense torso Alfred Wallace's strong figure looked frail. And Ellery felt like an underfed boy.

But below the waist Roger Priam was dead. His bulk sat on a withered base, an underpinning of skeletal flesh and atrophied muscle. He was trousered and shod—and Ellery tried not to imagine the labor that went into that operation twice daily—but his ankles were visible, two shriveled bones, and his knees were twisted projections, like girders struck by lightning. The whole shrunken substructure of his body hung useless.

It was all explicable, Ellery thought, on ordinary grounds: the torso overdeveloped by the extraordinary exertions required for the simplest movement; the beard grown to eliminate one of the irksome processes of his daily toilet; the savage manner an expression of his hatred of the fate that had played such a trick on him; and the restlessness a sign of the agony he endured to maintain a sitting position. Those were the reasons; still, they left something unexplained . . . Ferocity—fierce strength, fierce emotions, fierce reaction to pain and people—ferocity seemed his center. Take everything else away, and Ellery suspected it would still be there. He must have been fierce in his mother's womb, a wild beast by nature. What had happened to him merely brought it into play.

"What d'ye want, Laurel? Who's this?" His voice was a coarse, threatening bass, rumbling up from his chest like live lava. He was still furious from his telephone conversation with the hapless Foss; his eyes were filled with hate. "What are you looking at? Why don't you open your mouth?"

"This is Ellery Queen."

"Who?"

Laurel repeated it.

"Never heard of him. What's he want?" The feral glance turned on Ellery. "What d'ye want? Hey?"

"Mr. Priam," said the beautiful voice of Alfred Wallace from the doorway, "Ellery Queen is a famous writer."

"Writer?"

"And detective, Mr. Priam."

Priam's lips pushed out, dragging his beard forward. The great hands on the wheel became clamps.

"I told you I wasn't going to let go, Roger," said Laurel evenly. "My father was murdered. There must have been a reason. And whatever it was, you were mixed up in it as well as Daddy. I've asked Ellery Queen to investigate, and he wants to talk to you."

"He does, does he?" The rumble was distant; the fiery eyes gave out heat. "Go ahead, Mister. Talk away."

"In the first place, Mr. Priam," said Ellery, "I'd like to know—"

"The answer is no," said Roger Priam, his teeth showing through his beard. "What's in the second place?"

"Mr. Priam," Ellery began again, patiently.

"No good, Mister. I don't like your questions. Now you listen to me, Laurel." His right fist crashed on the arm of the chair. "You're a damn busybody. This ain't your business. It's mine. I'll tend to it. I'll do it my way, and I'll do it myself. Can you get that through your head?"

"You're afraid, Roger," said Laurel Hill.

Priam half-raised his bulk, his eyes boiling. The lava burst with a roar.

"Me afraid? Afraid of what? A *ghost*? What d'ye think I am, another Leander Hill? The snivelin' dirt! Shaking in his shoes—looking over his shoulder—creeping on his face! He was born a —— yellowbelly, and he died the same—"

Laurel hit him on the cheek with her fist. His left arm came up impatiently and brushed her aside. She staggered backward halfway across the room into Alfred Wallace's arms.

"Let go of me," she whispered. "Let go!"

"Laurel," said Ellery.

She stopped, breathing from her diaphragm. Wallace silently released her. Laurel walked out of the room.

"*Afraid!*" A spot swelled on Priam's cheekbone. "You think so?" he bellowed after her. "Well, a certain somebody's gonna find out that *my* pump don't go to pieces at the first blow! Afraid, am I? I'm ready for the goddam ——! Any hour of the day or night, understand? Any time he wants to show his scummy hand! He'll find out I got a pretty good pair myself!" And he opened and closed his murderous hands, and Ellery thought again of Wolf Larsen.

"Roger. What's the matter?"

And there she was in the doorway. She had changed to a hostess gown of golden silk which clung as if it loved her. It was slit to the knee. She was glancing coolly from her husband to Ellery.

Wallace's eyes were on her. They seemed amused.

"Who is this man?"

"Nobody. Nothing, Delia. It don't concern you." Priam glared at Ellery. "You. Get out!"

She had come downstairs just to establish the fact that she didn't know him. As a point in character, it should have interested him. Instead, it annoyed him. Why, he could not quite make out. What was he to Hecuba? Although she was making clear enough what Hecuba was to *him*. He felt chagrined and challenged, and at the same time he wondered if she affected other men the same way . . . Wallace was enjoying himself discreetly, like a playgoer who has caught a point which escaped the rest of the audience and is too polite to laugh aloud . . . Her attitude toward her husband was calm, without fear or any other visible emotion.

"What are you waiting for? You ain't wanted, Mister. Get out!"

"I've been trying to make up my mind, Mr. Priam," said Ellery, "whether you're a bag of wind or a damned fool."

Priam's bearded lips did a little dance. His rage, apparently always in shallow water, was surfacing again. Ellery braced himself for the splash. Priam *was* afraid. Wallace—silent, amused, attentive Wallace—Wallace saw it. And Delia Priam saw it; she was smiling.

"Alfred, if this fella shows up again, break his —— back!"

Ellery looked down at his arm. Wallace's hand was on it.

"I'm afraid, Mr. Queen," murmured Wallace, "that I'm man enough to do it, too."

The man's grip was paralyzing. Priam was grinning, a yellow hairy grin that jarred him. And the woman—that animate piece of jungle—watching. To his amazement, Ellery felt himself going blind-mad. When he came to, Alfred Wallace was sitting on the floor chafing his wrist and staring up at Ellery. He did not seem angry; just surprised.

"That's a good trick," Wallace said. "I'll remember it."

Ellery fumbled for a cigaret, decided against it. "I've made up my mind, Mr. Priam. You're a bag of wind and a damned fool."

The doorway was empty . . .

He was furious with himself. Never lose your temper. Rule One in the book; he had learned it on his father's lap. Just the same, she must have seen it. Wallace flying through the air. And the gape on Priam's ugly face. Probably set her up for the week . . .

He found himself searching for her out of the corners of his eyes as he strode down the hall. The place was overcrowded with shadows; she was certainly waiting in one of them. With the shades of her eyes pulled down but everything else showing.

The hall was empty, too . . .

Slit to the knee! That one was older than the pyramids. And how old was his stupidity? It probably went back to the primordial slime.

Then he remembered that Delia Priam was a lady and that he was behaving exactly like a frustrated college boy, and he slammed the front door.

Laurel was waiting for him in the Austin. She was still white; smoking with energy. Ellery jumped in beside her and growled, "Well, what are we waiting for?"

"He's cracking," said Laurel tensely. "He's going to pieces, Ellery. I've seen him yell and push his weight around before, but today was something special. I'm glad I brought you. What do you want to do now?"

"Go home. Or get me a cab."

She was bewildered. "Aren't you taking the case?"

"I can't waste my time on idiots."

"Meaning me?"

"Not meaning you."

"But we found out something," she said eagerly. "He admitted it. You heard him. A 'ghost,' he said. A 'certain somebody'—I heard that on my way out. I wasn't being delirious, Ellery. Roger thinks Daddy was deliberately shocked to death, too. And, what's more, he knows what the dog meant—"

"Not necessarily," grunted Ellery. "That's the trouble with you amateurs. Always jumping to conclusions. Anyway, it's too impossible. You can't get anywhere without Priam, and Priam isn't budging."

"It's Delia," said Laurel, "isn't it?"

"Delia? You mean Mrs. Priam? Rubbish."

"Don't tell me about Delia," said Laurel. "Or about men, either. She's catnip for anything in pants."

"Oh, I admit her charms," muttered Ellery. "But they're a bit obvious, don't you think?" He was trying not to look up at the second-story windows, where her bedroom undoubtedly was. "Laurel, we can't park here in the driveway like a couple of adenoidal tourists—" He had to see her again. Just to see her.

Laurel gave him an odd look and drove off. She turned left at the road, driving slowly.

Ellery sat embracing his knees. He had the emptiest feeling that he was losing something with each spin of the Austin's wheels. And there was Laurel, seeing the road ahead and something else, too. Sturdy little customer. And she must be feeling pretty much alone. Ellery suddenly felt himself weakening.

"What do you intend to do, Laurel?"

"Keep poking around."

"You're determined to go through with this?"

"Don't feel sorry for me. I'll make out."

"Laurel, I'll tell you what I'll do."

She looked at him.

"I'll go as far as that note with you—I mean, give you a head start, anyway. If, of course, it's possible."

"What are you talking about?" She stopped the car with a bump.

"The note your father found in that silver box on the dog's collar. You thought he must have destroyed it."

"I told you I looked for it and it wasn't there."

"Suppose I do the looking."

Laurel stared. Then she laughed and the Austin jumped.

The Hill house spread itself high on one of the canyon walls, cheerfully exposing its red tiles to the sun. It was a two-story Spanish house, beautifully bleached, with black wrought-iron tracery, arched and balconied and patioed and covered with pyracantha. It was set in two acres of flowers, flowering shrubs, and trees—palm and fruit and nut and bird-of-paradise. Around the lower perimeter ran the woods.

"Our property line runs down the hill," Laurel said as they got out of the car, "over towards the Priams'. A little over nine additional acres meeting the Priam woods. Through the woods it's no distance at all."

"It's a very great distance," mumbled Ellery. "About as far as from an eagle's nest to an undersea cave. True Spanish, I notice, like the missions, not the modern fakes so common out here. It must be a punishment to Delia Priam—born to this and condemned to *that*."

"Oh, she's told you about that," murmured Laurel; then she took him into her house.

It was cool with black Spanish tile underfoot and the touch of iron. There was a sunken living room forty feet long, a great fireplace set with Goya tiles, books and music and paintings and ceramics and huge jars of flowers everywhere. A tall Japanese in a white jacket came in smiling and took Ellery's hat.

"Ichiro Sotowa," said Laurel. "Itchie's been with us for ages. This is Mr. Queen, Itchie. He's interested in the way Daddy died, too."

The houseman's smile faded. "Bad—bad," he said, shaking his head. "Heart no good. You like a drink, sir?"

"Not just now, thanks," said Ellery. "Just how long did you work for Mr. Hill, Ichiro?"

"Sixteen year, sir."

"Oh, then you don't go back to the time of . . . What about that chauffeur—Simeon, was it?"

"Shimmie shopping with Mis' Monk."

"I meant how long Simeon's been employed here."

"About ten years," said Laurel. "Mrs. Monk came around the same time."

"That's that, then. All right, Laurel, let's begin."

"Where?"

"From the time your father had his last heart attack—the day the dog came—until his death, did he leave his bedroom?"

"No. Itchie and I took turns nursing him. Night and day the entire week."

"Bedroom indicated. Lead the way."

An hour and a half later, Ellery opened the door of Leander Hill's room. Laurel was curled up in a window niche on the landing, head resting against the wall.

"I suppose you think I'm an awful sissy," she said, without turning. "But all I can see when I'm in there is his marbly face and blue lips and the crooked way his mouth hung open . . . not my daddy at all. Nothing, I suppose."

"Come here, Laurel."

She jerked about. Then she jumped off the ledge and ran to him.

Ellery shut the bedroom door.

Laurel's eyes hunted wildly. But aside from the four-poster bed, which was disarranged, she could see nothing unusual. The spread, sheets, and quilt were peeled back, revealing the side walls of the box spring and mattress.

"What—?"

"The note you saw him remove from the dog's collar," Ellery said. "It was on thin paper, didn't you tell me?"

"Very. A sort of flimsy, or onionskin."

"White?"

"White."

Ellery nodded. He went over to the exposed mattress. "He was in this room for a week, Laurel, between his attack and death. During that week did he have many visitors?"

"The Priam household. Some people from the office. A few friends."

"Some time during that week," said Ellery, "your father decided that the note he had received was in danger of being stolen or destroyed. So he took out insurance." His finger traced on the side wall of the mattress one of the perpendicular blue lines of the ticking. "He had no tool but a dull penknife from the night table there. And I suppose he was in a hurry, afraid he might be caught at it. So the job had to be crude." Half his finger suddenly vanished. "He simply made a slit here, where the blue line meets the undyed ticking. And he slipped the paper into it, where I found it."

"The note," breathed Laurel. "You've found the note. Let me see!"

Ellery put his hand in his pocket. But just as he was about to withdraw it, he stopped. His eyes were on one of the windows.

Some ten yards away there was an old walnut tree.

"Yes?" Laurel was confused. "What's the matter?"

"Get off the bed, yawn, smile at me if you can, and then stroll over to the door. Go out on the landing. Leave the door open."

Her eyes widened.

She got off the bed, yawned, stretched, showed her teeth, and went to the door. Ellery moved a little as she moved, so that he remained between her and the window.

When she had disappeared, he casually followed. Smiling in profile at her, he shut the bedroom door.

And sprang for the staircase.

"Ellery—"

"Stay here!"

He scrambled down the black-tiled stairs, leaving Laurel with her lips parted.

A man had been roosting high in the walnut tree, peering in at them through Leander Hill's bedroom window from behind a screen of leaves. But the sun had been on the tree, and Ellery could have sworn the fellow was mother-naked.

Chapter IV

THE NAKED MAN was gone. Ellery thrashed about among the fruit and nut trees feeling like Robinson Crusoe. From the flagged piazza Ichiro gaped at him, and a chunky fellow with a florid face and a chauffeur's cap, carrying a carton of groceries, was gaping with him.

Ellery found a large footprint at the margin of the orchard, splayed and deeptoed, indicating running or jumping, and it pointed directly to the woods. He darted into the underbrush and in a moment he was nosing past trees and scrub on a twisting but clear trail. There were numerous specimens of the naked print on the trail, both coming and going.

"He's made a habit of this," Ellery mumbled. It was hot in the woods and he was soon drenched, uncomfortable, and out of temper.

The trail ended unceremoniously in the middle of a clearing. No other footprints anywhere. The trunk of the nearest tree, an ancient, oakish-looking monster, was yards away. There were no vines.

Ellery looked around, swabbing his neck. Then he looked up. The giant limbs of the tree covered the clearing with a thick fabric of small spiny leaves, but the lowest branch was thirty feet from the ground.

The creature must have flapped his arms and taken off.

Ellery sat down on a corrupting log and wiped his face, reflecting on this latest wonder. Not that anything in Southern California ever really surprised him. But this was a little out of even God's country's class. Flying nudes!

"Lost?"

Ellery leaped. A little old man in khaki shorts, woolen socks, and a T-shirt was smiling at him from a bush. He wore a paper topee on his head and he carried a butterfly net; a bright red case of some sort was slung over one skinny shoulder. His skin was a shriveled brown and his hands were like the bark of the big tree, but his eyes were a bright young blue and they seemed keen.

"I'm not lost," said Ellery irritably. "I'm looking for a man."

"I don't like the way you say that," said the old man, stepping into the clearing. "You're on the wrong track, young fellow. People mean trouble. Know anything about the Lepidoptera?"

"Not a thing. Have you seen—?"

"You catch 'em with this dingbat. I just bought the kit yesterday—passed a toy shop on Hollywood Boulevard and there it was, all new and shiny, in the window. I've caught four beauties so far." The butterfly hunter began to trot down the trail, waving his net menacingly.

"Wait! Have you seen anyone running through these woods?"

"Running? Well, now, depends."

"Depends? My dear sir, it doesn't depend on a thing! Either you saw somebody or you didn't."

"Not necessarily," replied the little man earnestly, trotting back. "It depends on whether it's going to get him—or you—in trouble. There's too much trouble in this world, young man. What's this runner look like?"

"I can't give you a description," snapped Ellery, "inasmuch as I didn't see enough of him to be able to. Or rather, I saw the wrong parts.—Hell. He's naked."

"Ah," said the hunter, making an unsuccessful pass at a large, paint-splashed butterfly. "Naked, hm?"

"And there was a lot of him."

"There was. You wouldn't start any trouble?"

"No, no, I won't hurt him. Just tell me which way he went."

"I'm not worried about your hurting him. He's much more likely to hurt you. Powerful build, that boy. Once knew a stoker built like him—could bend a coal shovel. That was in the old *Susie Belle*, beating up to Alaska—"

"You sound as if you know him."

"Know him? I darned well ought to. He's my grandson. There he is!" cried the hunter.

"Where?"

But it was only the fifth butterfly, and the little old man hopped between two bushes and was gone.

Ellery was morosely studying the last footprint in the trail when Laurel poked her head cautiously into the clearing.

"There you are," she said with relief. "You scared the buttermilk out of me. What happened?"

"Character spying on us from the walnut tree outside the bedroom window. I trailed him here—"

"What did he look like?" frowned Laurel.

"No clothes on."

"Why, the lying mugwump!" she said angrily. "He promised on his honor he wouldn't do that any more. It's got so I have to undress in the dark."

"So you know him, too," growled Ellery. "I thought California had a drive on these sex cases."

"Oh, he's no sex case. He just throws gravel at my window and tries to get me to talk drool to him. I can't waste my time on somebody who's preparing for Armageddon at the age of twenty-three. Ellery, let's see that note!"

"Whose grandson is he?"

"Grandson? Mr. Collier's."

"Mr. Collier wouldn't be a little skinny old gent with a face like a sun-dried fig?"

"That's right."

"And just who is Mr. Collier?"

"Delia Priam's father. He lives with the Priams."

"Her *father*." You couldn't keep her out of anything. "But if this Peeping Tom is Delia Priam's father's grandson, then he must be—"

"Didn't Delia tell you," asked Laurel with a *soupçon* of malice, "that she has a twenty-three year old son? His name is Crowe Macgowan. Delia's child by her first husband. Roger's stepson. But let's not waste any time on him—"

"How does he disappear into thin air? He pulled that miracle right here."

"Oh, that." Laurel looked straight up. So Ellery looked straight up, too. But all he could see was a leafy ceiling where the great oak branched ten yards over his head.

"Mac!" said Laurel sharply. "Show your face."

To Ellery's amazement, a large young male face appeared in the middle of the green mass thirty feet from the ground. On the face there was a formidable scowl.

"Laurel, who is this guy?"

"You come down here."

"Is he a reporter?"

"Heavens, no," said Laurel disgustedly. "He's Ellery Queen."

"Who?"

"Ellery Queen."

"You're kidding!"

"I wouldn't have time."

"Say. I'll be right down."

The face vanished. At once something materialized where it had been and hurtled to the ground, missing Ellery's nose by inches. It was a rope ladder. A massive male leg broke the green ceiling, then another, then a whole young man, and in a moment the tree man was standing on the ground on the exact spot where the trail of naked footprints ended.

"I'm certainly thrilled to meet you!"

Ellery's hand was seized and the bones broken before he could cry out. At least, they felt broken. It was a bad day for the Master's self-respect: he could not decide which had the most powerful hands, Roger Priam, Alfred Wallace, or the awesome brute trying to pulverize him. Delia's son towered six inches above him, a handsome giant with an impossible spread of shoulder, an unbelievable minimum of waist, the muscular development of Mr. America, the skin of a Hawaiian—all of which was on view except a negligible area covered by a brown loincloth—and a grin that made Ellery feel positively aged.

"I thought you were a newshound, Mr. Queen. Can't stand those guys—they've made my life miserable. But what are we standing here for? Come on up to the house."

"Some other time, Mac," said Laurel coldly, taking Ellery's arm.

"Oh, that murder foolitchness. Why don't you relax, Laur?"

"I don't think I'd be exactly welcome at your stepfather's, Mac," said Ellery.

"You've already had the pleasure? But I meant come up to *my* house."

"He really means 'up,' Ellery," sighed Laurel. "All right, let's get it over with. You wouldn't believe it secondhand."

"House? Up?" Feebly Ellery glanced aloft; and to his horror the young giant nodded and sprang up the rope ladder, beckoning them hospitably to follow.

It really was a house, high in the tree. A one-room house, to be sure, and not commodious, but it had four walls and a thatched roof, a sound floor, a beamed ceiling, two windows, and a platform from which the ladder dangled —this dangerous-looking perch young Macgowan referred to cheerfully as his "porch," and perfectly safe if you didn't fall off.

The tree, he explained, was *Quercus agrifolia,* with a bole circumference of eighteen feet, and "watch those leaves, Mr. Queen, they bite." Ellery, who was gingerly digging several of the spiny little devils out of his shirt, nodded sourly. But the structure was built on a foundation of foot-thick boughs and seemed solid enough underfoot.

He poked his head indoors at his host's invitation and gaped like a tourist. Every foot of wall- and floor-space was occupied by—it was the only phrase Ellery could muster—aids to tree-living.

"Sorry I can't entertain you inside," said the young man, "but three of us would bug it out a bit. We'd better sit on the porch. Anybody like a drink? Bourbon? Scotch?" Without waiting for a reply Macgowan bent double and slithered into his house. Various liquid sounds followed.

"Laurel, why don't they put the poor kid away?" whispered Ellery.

"You have to have grounds."

"What do you call this?" cried Ellery. "Sanity?"

"Don't blame you, Mr. Queen," said the big fellow amiably, appearing with two chilled glasses. "Appearances are against me. But that's because you people live in a world of fantasy." He thrust a long arm into the house and it came out with another glass.

"Fantasy. We." Ellery gulped a third of the contents of his glass. "You, of course, live in a world of reality?"

"Do we have to?" asked Laurel wearily. "If he gets started on this, Ellery, we'll be here till sundown. That note—"

"I'm the only realist I know," said the giant, lying down at the edge of his porch and kicking his powerful legs in space. "Because, look. What are you people doing? Living in the same old houses, reading the same old newspapers, going to the same old movies or looking at the same old television, walking on the same old sidewalks, riding in the same old new cars. That's a dream world, don't you realize it? What price business-as-usual? What price, well, sky-writing, Jacques Fath, Double-Crostics, murder? Do you get my point?"

"Can't say it's entirely clear, Mac," said Ellery, swallowing the second third. He realized for the first time that his glass contained bourbon, which he loathed. However.

"We are living," said young Mr. Macgowan, "in the crisis of the disease commonly called human history. You mess around with your piddling murders while mankind is being set up for the biggest homicide since the Flood. The atom bomb is already fuddy-duddy. Now it's hydrogen bombs, guaranteed to make the nuclear chain reaction—or whatever the hell it is—look like a Fourth of July firecracker. Stuff that can poison all the drinking water on a continent. Nerve gases that paralyze and kill. Germs there's no protection against. And only God knows what else. They won't use it? My friend, those words constitute the epitaph of Man. Somebody'll pull the cork in a place like Yugoslavia or Iran or Korea and, whoosh! that'll be that.

"It's all going to go," said Macgowan, waving his glass at the invisible world below. "Cities uninhabitable. Crop soil poisoned for a hundred years.

Domestic animals going wild. Insects multiplying. Balance of nature upset. Ruins and plagues and millions of square miles radioactive and maybe most of the earth's atmosphere. The roads crack, the lines sag, the machines rust, the libraries mildew, the buzzards fatten, and the forest primeval creeps over Hollywood and Vine, which maybe isn't such a bad idea. But there you'll have it. Thirty thousand years of primate development knocked over like a sleeping duck. Civilization atomized and annihilated. Yes, there'll be some survivors—I'm going to be one of them. But what are we going to have to do? Why, go back where we came from, brother—to the trees. That's logic, isn't it? So here I am. All ready for it."

"Now let's have the note," said Laurel.

"In a moment." Ellery polished off the last third, shuddering. "Very logical, Mac, except for one or two items."

"Such as?" said Crowe Macgowan courteously. "Here, let me give you a refill."

"No, thanks, not just now. Why, such as these." Ellery pointed to a network of cables winging from some hidden spot to the roof of Macgowan's tree house. "For a chap who's written off thirty thousand years of primate development you don't seem to mind tapping the main power line for such things as—" he craned, surveying the interior—"electric lights, a small electric range and refrigerator, and similar primitive devices; not to mention—" he indicated a maze of pipes—"running water, a compact little privy connected with—I assume—a septic tank buried somewhere below, and so on. These things—forgive me, Mac—blow bugs through your logic. The only essential differences between your house and your stepfather's are that yours is smaller and thirty feet in the air."

"Just being practical," shrugged the giant. "It's my opinion it'll happen any day now. But I can be wrong—it may not come till next year. I'm just taking advantage of the civilized comforts while they're still available. But you'll notice I have a .22 rifle hanging there, a couple of .45s, and when my ammunition runs out or I can't rustle any more there's a bow that'll bring down any deer that survives the party. I practice daily. And I'm getting pretty good running around these treetops—"

"Which reminds me," said Laurel. "Use your own trees after this, will you, Mac? I'm no prude, but a girl likes her privacy sometimes. Really, Ellery—"

"Macgowan," said Ellery, eying their host, "what's the pitch?"

"Pitch? I've just told you."

"I know what you've just told me, and it's already out the other ear. What character are you playing? And in what script by whom?" Ellery set the glass down and got to his feet. The effect he was trying to achieve was slightly spoiled, as he almost fell off the porch. He jumped to the side of the house, a little green. "I've been to Hollywood before."

"Go ahead and sneer," said the brown giant without rancor. "I promise to give you a decent burial if I can find the component parts."

Ellery eyed the wide back for a moment. It was perfectly calm. He shrugged. Every time he came to Hollywood something fantastic happened. This was the screwiest yet. He was well out of it.

But then he remembered that he was still in it.

He put his hand in his pocket.

"Laurel," he said meaningly, "shall we go?"

"If it's about that piece of paper I saw you find in Leander's mattress," said young Macgowan, "I wouldn't mind knowing myself what's in it."

"It's all right, Ellery," said Laurel with an exasperated laugh. "Crowe is a lot more interested in the petty affairs of us dreamers than he lets on. And in a perverted sort of way I trust him. May I *please* see that note?"

"It isn't the note you saw your father take from the collar of the dog," said Ellery, eying Macgowan disapprovingly as he took a sheet of paper from his pocket. "It's a copy. The original is gone." The sheet was folded over once. He unfolded it. It was a stiff vellum paper, tinted green-gray, with an embossed green monogram.

"Daddy's personal stationery."

"From his night table. Where I also found this bi-colored pencil." Ellery fished an automatic pencil from his pocket. "The blue lead is snapped. The note starts in blue and ends in red. Evidently the blue ran out halfway through his copying and he finished writing with the red. So the pencil places the copying in his bedroom, too." Ellery held out the sheet. "Is this your father's handwriting?"

"Yes."

"No doubt about it?"

"No."

In a rather peculiar voice, Ellery said, "All right, Laurel. Read it."

"But it's not signed." Laurel sounded as if she wanted to punch somebody.

"Read it."

Macgowan knelt behind her, nuzzling her shoulder with his big chin. Laurel paid no attention to him; she read the note with a set face.

You believed me dead. Killed, murdered. For over a score of years I have looked for you—for you and for him. And now I have found you. Can you guess my plan? You'll die. Quickly? No, very slowly. And so pay me back for my long years of searching and dreaming of revenge. Slow dying . . . unavoidable dying. For you and for him. Slow and sure—dying in mind and in body. And for each pace forward a warning . . . a warning of special meaning for you—and for him. Meanings for pondering and puzzling. Here is warning number one.

Laurel stared at the notepaper.

"That," said Crowe Macgowan, taking the sheet, "is the unfunniest gag of the century." He frowned over it.

"Not just that." Laurel shook her head. "Warning number one. Murder. Revenge. Special meanings . . . It—it has a long curly mustache on it. Next week *Uncle Tom's Cabin.*" She looked around with a laugh. "Even in Hollywood."

"Why'd the old scout take it seriously?" Crowe watched Laurel a little anxiously.

Ellery took the sheet from him and folded it carefully. "Melodrama is a matter of atmosphere and expression. Pick up any Los Angeles newspaper and you'll find three news stories running serially, any one of which would make this one look like a work by Einstein. But they're real because they're couched in everyday terms. What makes this note incredible is not the contents. It's the wording."

"The wording?"

"It's painful. Actually archaic in spots. As if it were composed by someone who wears a ruff, or a tricorn. Someone who speaks a different kind of English. Or writes it. It has a . . . bouquet, an archive smell. A something that would never have been put into it purely for deception, for instance . . . like the ransom note writers who deliberately misspell words and mix their tenses to give the impression of illiteracy. And yet—I don't know." Ellery slipped the note into his pocket. "It's the strangest mixture of genuineness and contrivance. I don't understand it."

"Maybe," suggested the young man, putting his arm carelessly around Laurel's shoulders, "maybe it's the work of some psycho foreigner. It reads like somebody translating from another language."

"Possible." Ellery sucked his lower lip. Then he shrugged. "Anyway, Laurel, there's something to go on. Are you sure you wouldn't rather discuss this—?"

"You mean because it involves Roger?" Laurel laughed again, removing Macgowan's paw. "Mac isn't one of Roger's more ardent admirers, Ellery. It's all right."

"What did he do now?" growled Roger Priam's stepson.

"He said he wasn't going to be scared by any 'ghost,' Mac. Or rather roared it. And here's a clue to someone from his past and, apparently, Leander Hill's. 'For you and for him . . .' Laurel, what do you know of your father's background?"

"Not much. He'd led an adventurous life, I think, but whenever I used to ask him questions about it—especially when I was little—he'd laugh, slap me on the bottom, and send me off to Mad'moiselle."

"What about his family?"

"Family?" said Laurel vaguely.

"Brothers, sisters, uncle, cousins—family. Where did he come from? Laurel, I'm fishing. We need some facts."

"I'm no help there. Daddy never talked about himself. I always felt I couldn't pry. I can't remember his ever having any contact with relatives. I don't even know if any exist."

"When did he and Priam go into business together?"

"It must have been around twenty, twenty-five years ago."

"Before Delia and he got married," said Crowe. "Delia—that's my mother, Mr. Queen."

"I know," said Ellery, a bit stiffly. "Had Priam and Hill known each other well before they started the jewelry business, Macgowan?"

"I don't know." The giant put his arm about Laurel's waist.

"I suppose they did. They must have," Laurel said in a helpless way, absently removing the arm. "I realize now how little I know about Dad's past."

"Or I about Roger's," said Crowe, marching two fingers up Laurel's back. She wriggled and said, "Oh, stop it, Mac." He got up. "Neither of them ever talked about it." He went over to the other end of the platform and stretched out again.

"Apparently with reason. Leander Hill and Roger Priam had a common enemy in the old days, someone they thought was dead. *He* says they tried to put him out of the way, and he's spent over twenty years tracking them down."

Ellery began to walk about, avoiding Crowe Macgowan's arms.

"Dad tried to murder somebody?" Laurel bit her thumb.

"When you yell bloody murder, Laurel," said Ellery, "you've got to be prepared for a certain echo of nastiness. This kind of murder," he said, lighting a cigaret and placing it between her lips, "is never nice. It's usually rooted in pretty mucky soil. Priam means nothing to you, and your father is dead. Do you still want to go through with this? *You're* my client, you know, not Mrs. Priam. At her own suggestion."

"Did Mother come to you?" exclaimed Macgowan.

"Yes, but we're keeping it confidential."

"I didn't know she cared," muttered the giant.

Ellery lit a cigaret for himself.

Laurel was wrinkling her nose and looking a little sick.

Ellery tossed the match overside. "Whoever composed that note is on a delayed murder spree. He wants revenge badly enough to have nursed it for over twenty years. A quick killing doesn't suit him at all. He wants the men who injured him to suffer, presumably, as he's suffered. To accomplish this he starts a private war of nerves. His strategy is all plotted. Working from the dark, he makes his first tactical move . . . the warning, the first of the 'special meanings' he promises. Number one is—of all things—a dead pooch, number two whatever was in the box to Roger Priam—I wonder what it was, by the way! You wouldn't know, Mac, would you?"

"I wouldn't know *anything* about my mother's husband," replied Macgowan.

"And he means to send other warnings with other 'gifts' which have special meanings. To Priam exclusively now—Hill foxed him by dying at once. He's a man with a fixed idea, Laurel, and an obsessive sense of injury. I really think you ought to keep out of his way. Let Priam defy him. It's his skin, and if he needs help he knows where he can apply for it."

Laurel threw herself back on the platform, blowing smoke to the appliquéd sky.

"Don't you feel you have to act like the heroine of a magazine serial?"

Laurel did not reply.

"Laurel, drop it. Now."

She rolled her head. "I don't care what Daddy did. People make mistakes, even commit crimes, who are decent and nice. Sometimes events force you, or other people. I knew him—as a human being—better than anyone in creation. If he and Roger Priam got into a mess, it was Roger who thought up the dirty work . . . The fact that he wasn't my real father makes it even more important. I owe him everything." She sat up suddenly. "I'm not going to stay out of this, Ellery. I can't."

"You'll find, Queen," scowled young Macgowan in the silence that followed, "that this is a very tough number."

"Tough she may be, my Tarzanian friend," grumbled Ellery, "but this sort of thing is a business, not an endurance contest. It takes know-how and connections and a technique. And experience. None of which Miss Strongheart has." He crushed his cigaret out on the platform vindictively. "Not to mention the personal danger . . . Well, I'll root around a little, Laurel. Do some checking back. It shouldn't be too much of a job to get a line on those two and find out what they were up to in the Twenties. And who got caught in the meat-grinder . . . You driving me back to the world of fantasy?"

Chapter V

THE NEXT MORNING Ellery called the Los Angeles Police Department and asked to speak to the officer in charge of the Public Relations Department.

"Sergeant Lordetti."

"Sergeant, this is Ellery Queen . . . Yes, how do you do. Sergeant, I'm in town to write a Hollywood novel—oh, you've seen that . . . no, I can't make the newspapers believe it and, frankly, I've given up trying. Sergeant Lordetti, I need some expert advice for background on my book. Is there anyone in, say, the Hollywood Division who could give me a couple hours of his time? Some trouble-shooter with lots of experience in murder investigation and enough drag in the Department so I could call on him from time to time? . . . Exposé? So you fell for that, too, haha! Me, the son of a cop? No, no, Sergeant, nothing like that, believe me . . . Who? . . . K-e-a-t-s. Thanks a lot . . . Not at all, Sergeant. If you can make a little item out of it, you're entirely welcome."

Ellery called the Hollywood Division on Wilcox below Sunset and asked to speak to Lieutenant Keats. Informed that Lieutenant Keats was on another phone, Ellery left his telephone number with the request that Lieutenant Keats call back as soon as he was free.

Twenty minutes later a car drew up to his house and a big lean man in a comfortable-looking business suit got out and rang the bell, glancing around at Ellery's pint-sized garden curiously. Hiding behind a drape, Ellery decided he was not a salesman, for he carried nothing and his interest had something amused in it. Possibly a reporter, although he seemed too carefully dressed for that. He might have been a sports announcer or a veteran airline pilot off duty.

"It's a policeman, Mr. Queen," reported Mrs. Williams nervously. "You done something?"

"I'll keep you out of it, Mrs. Williams. Lieutenant Keats? The service staggers me. I merely left a message for you to phone back."

"Sergeant Lordetti phoned and told me about it," said the Hollywood detective, filling the doorway. "Thought I'd take the shortcut. No, thanks, don't drink when I'm working."

"Working—? Oh, Mrs. Williams, close the door, will you? . . . Working, Lieutenant? But I explained to Lordetti—"

"He told me." Keats placed his hat neatly on the chartreuse chair. "You want expert advice for a mystery novel. Such as what, Mr. Queen? How a homicide is reported in Los Angeles? That was for the benefit of the *Mirror* and *News*. What's really on your mind?"

Ellery stared. Then they both grinned, shook hands, and sat down like old friends.

Keats was a sandy-haired man of thirty-eight or forty with clear, rather distant gray eyes below reddish brows. His hands were big and well-kept, with a reliable look to them; there was a gold band on the fourth finger of the left. His eyes were intelligent and his jaw had been developed by adversity. His manner was slightly standoffish. A smart cop, Ellery decided, and a rugged one.

"Let me light that for you, Lieutenant."

"The nail?" Keats laughed, taking a shredded cigaret from between his lips. It was unlit. "I'm a dry smoker, Mr. Queen. Given up smoking." He put the ruin on an ashtray and fingered a fresh cigaret, settling back. "Some case you're interested in? Something you don't want to get around?"

"It came my way yesterday morning. Do you know anything about the death of a wholesale jeweler named Leander Hill?"

"So she got to you." Keats lipped the unlit cigaret. "It passed through our Division. The girl made a pest of herself. Something about a dead dog and a note that scared her father to death. But no note. An awfully fancy yarn. More in your line than ours."

Ellery handed Keats the sheet of Leander Hill's stationery.

Keats read it slowly. Then he examined the notepaper, front and back.

"That's Hill's handwriting, by the way. Obviously a copy he made. I found it in a slit in his mattress."

"Where's the original of this, Mr. Queen?"

"Probably destroyed."

"Even if this were the McCoy." Keats put the sheet down. "There's nothing here that legally connects Hill's death with a murder plot. Of course, the revenge business . . ."

"I know, Lieutenant. It's the kind of case that gives you fellows a hard ache. Every indication of a psycho, and a possible victim who won't co-operate."

"Who's that?"

"The 'him' of the note." Ellery told Keats about Roger Priam's mysterious box, and of what Priam had let slip during Ellery's visit. "There's something more than a gangrenous imagination behind this, Lieutenant. Even though no one's going to get anywhere with Priam, still . . . it ought to be looked into, don't you agree?"

The detective pulled at his unlit cigaret.

"I'm not sure I want any part of it myself," Ellery said, glancing at his typewriter and thinking of Delia Priam. "I'd like a little more to go on before I commit myself. It seemed to me that if we could find something in Hill's past, and Priam's, that takes this note out of the ordinary crackpot class . . ."

"On the q.t.?"

"Yes. Could you swing it?"

For a moment Keats did not reply. He picked up the note and read it over again.

"I'd like to have this."

"Of course. But I want it back."

"I'll have it photostated. Tell you what I'll do, Mr. Queen." Lieutenant Keats rose. "I'll talk to the Chief and if he thinks it's worth my time, I'll see what I can dig up."

"Oh, Keats."

"Yes, sir?"

"While you're digging . . . Do a little spadework on a man who calls himself Alfred Wallace. Roger Priam's secretary-general."

Delia Priam phoned that afternoon. "I'm surprised you're in."

"Where did you think I'd be, Mrs. Priam?" The moment he heard her throaty purr his blood began stewing. Damn her, she was like the first cocktail after a hard day.

"Out detecting, or whatever it is detectives do."

"I haven't taken the case." He was careful to keep his voice good-humored. "I haven't made up my mind."

"You're angry with me about yesterday."

"Angry? Mrs. Priam!"

"Sorry. I thought you were." Oh, were you? "I'm afraid I'm allergic to messes. I usually take the line of least resistance."

"In everything?"

"Give me an example." Her laugh was soft.

He wanted to say, *I'd be glad to specify if you'd drop in on me, say, this afternoon.* Instead, he said innocuously, "Who's questioning whom?"

"You're such a careful man, Mr. Queen."

"Well, I haven't taken the case—yet, Mrs. Priam."

"Do you suppose I could help you make up your mind?"

There's the nibble. Reel 'er in . . .

"You know, Mrs. Priam, that might be a perilous offer . . . Mrs. Priam? . . . Hello!"

She said in a low voice, quickly, "I must stop," and the line went dead.

Ellery hung up perspiring. He was so annoyed with himself that he went upstairs and took a shower.

Laurel Hill dropped in on him twice in the next twenty-four hours. The first time she was "just passing by" and thought she would report that nothing was happening, nothing at all. Priam wouldn't see her and as far as she could tell he was being his old bullying, beastly self. Delia had tried to pump her about Ellery and what he was doing, and as a matter of fact she couldn't help wondering herself if . . .

Ellery's glance kept going to his typewriter and after a few moments Laurel left abruptly.

She was back the next morning, recklessly hostile.

"Are you taking this case, or aren't you?"

"I don't know, Laurel."

"I've talked to my lawyers. The estate isn't settled, but I can get the money together to give you a retainer of five thousand dollars."

"It isn't the money, Laurel."

"If you don't want to bother, say so and I'll get someone else."

"That's always the alternative, of course."

"But you're just sitting here!"

"I'm making a few preliminary inquiries," he said patiently.

"From this—this ivory tower?"

"Stucco. What I'll do, Laurel, depends entirely on what I find out."

"You've sold out to Delia, that's what you've done," Laurel cried. "She doesn't really want this investigated at all. She only followed me the other day to see what I was up to—the rest was malarkey! She *wants* Roger murdered! And that's all right with me, you understand—all I'm interested in is the case of Leander Hill. But if Delia's standing in the way—"

"You're being nineteen, Laurel." He tried not to let his anger show.

"I'll admit I can't offer you what *she* can—"

"Delia Priam hasn't offered me a thing, Laurel. We haven't even discussed my fee."

"And I *don't* mean money!" She was close to tears.

"Now you're hysterical." His voice came out sharp, not what he had intended at all. "Have a little patience, Laurel. Right now there's nothing to do but wait."

She strode out.

The next morning Ellery spread his newspaper behind a late breakfast tray to find Roger Priam, Leander Hill, and Crowe Macgowan glaring back at him. Mac was glaring from a tree.

$$$aire Denies Murder Threat;
Says Partner Not Slain

Denying that he has received a threat against his life, Roger Priam, wealthy wholesale gem merchant of L.A., barred himself behind the doors of his secluded home above Hollywood Bowl this morning when reporters investigated a tip that he is the intended victim of a murder plot which allegedly took the life of his business partner, Leander Hill, last week . . .

Mr. Priam, it appeared, after ousting reporters had issued a brief statement through his secretary, Alfred Wallace, repeating his denial and adding that the cause of Hill's death was "a matter of official record."

Detectives at the Hollywood Division of the L.A.P.D. admitted this morning that Hill's daughter, Laurel, had charged her father was "frightened to death," but said that they had found no evidence to support the charge, which they termed "fantastic."

Miss Hill, interviewed at her home adjoining the Priam property, said: "If Roger Priam wants to bury his head in the sand, it's his head." She intimated that she "had reason to believe" both her father and Priam were slated to be murdered "by some enemy out of their past."

The story concluded with the reminder that "Mr. Priam is the stepfather of twenty-three year old Crowe Macgowan, the Atomic Age Tree Boy, who broke into print in a big way recently by taking off his clothes and bedding down in a tree house on his stepfather's estate in preparation for the end of the world."

Observing to himself that Los Angeles journalism was continuing to maintain its usual standards, Ellery went to the phone and called the Hill home.

"Laurel? I didn't expect you'd be answering the phone in person this morning."

"I've got nothing to hide." Laurel laid the slightest stress on her pronoun. Also, she was cold, very cold.

"One question. Did you tip off the papers about Priam?"

"No."

"Cross your heart and—?"

"I said no!" There was a definite *snick!*

It was puzzling, and Ellery puzzled over it all through breakfast, which Mrs. Williams with obvious disapproval persisted in calling lunch. He was just putting down his second cup of coffee when Keats walked in with a paper in his pocket.

"I was hoping you'd drop around," said Ellery, as Mrs. Williams set another place. "Thanks, Mrs. W, I'll do the rest . . . Not knowing exactly what is leaking where, Keats, I decided not to risk a phone call. So far I've been kept out of it."

"Then you didn't feed the kitty?" asked Keats. "Thanks. No cream or sugar."

"Of course not. I was wondering if it was you."

"Not me. Must have been the Hill girl."

"Not she. I've asked her."

"Funny."

"Very. How was the tip tipped?"

"By phone call to the city room. Disguised voice, and they couldn't trace it."

"Male or female?"

"They said male, but they admitted it was pitched in a queer way and might have been female. With all the actors floating around this town you never know." Keats automatically struck a match, but then he shook his head and put it out. "You know, Mr. Queen," he said, scowling at his cigaret, "if there's anything to this thing, that tip might have come . . . I know it sounds screwy . . ."

"From the writer of the note? I've been dandling that notion myself, Lieutenant."

"Pressure, say."

"In the war on Priam's nerves."

"If he's got an iron nerve himself." Keats rose. "Well, this isn't getting us anywhere."

"Anything yet on Hill and Priam?"

"Not yet." Keats slowly crumpled his cigaret. "It might be a toughie, Mr. Queen. So far I haven't got to first base."

"What's holding you up?"

"I don't know yet. Give me another few days."

"What about Wallace?"

"I'll let you know."

Late that afternoon—it was the twenty-first, the day after the Shriners parade—Ellery looked around from his typewriter to see the creamy nose of Delia Priam's convertible in profile against his front window.

He deliberately forced himself to wait until Mrs. Williams answered the door.

As he ran his hand over his hair, Mrs. Williams said: "It's a naked man. You in?"

Macgowan was alone. He was in his Tree Boy costume—one loincloth, flame-colored this time. He shook Ellery's hand limply and accepted a Scotch on the Rocks, settling himself on the sofa with his bare heels on the sill of the picture window.

"I thought I recognized the car," said Ellery.

"It's my mother's. Mine was out of gas. Am I inconvenient?" The giant glanced at the typewriter. "How do you knock that stuff out? But I had to see you." He seemed uneasy.

"What about, Mac?"

"Well . . . I thought maybe the reason you hadn't made up your mind to take the case was that there wasn't enough money in it for you."

"Did you?"

"Look. Maybe I could put enough more in the pot to make it worth your while."

"You mean *you* want to hire me, too, Mac?"

"That's it." He seemed relieved that it was out. "I got to thinking . . . that note, and then whatever it was Roger got in that box the morning old man Hill got the dead dog . . . I mean, maybe there's something in it after all, Mr. Queen."

"Suppose there is." Ellery studied him with curiosity. "Why are you interested enough to want to put money into an investigation?"

"Roger's my mother's husband, isn't he?"

"Touching, Mac. When did you two fall in love?"

Young Macgowan's brown skin turned mahogany. "I mean . . . It's true Roger and I never got along. He's always tried to dominate me as well as everybody else. But he means well, and—"

"And that's why," smiled Ellery, "you call yourself Crowe Macgowan instead of Crowe Priam."

Crowe laughed. "Okay, I detest his lazy colon. We've always fought like a couple of wild dogs. When Delia married him he wouldn't adopt me legally; the idea was to keep me dependent on him. I was a kid, and it made me hate him. So I kept my father's name and I refused to take any money from Roger. I wasn't altogether a hero—I had a small income from a trust fund my father left for me. You can imagine how that set with Mr. Priam." He laughed again. But then he finished lamely, "The last few years I've grown up, I guess. I tolerate him for Mother's sake. That's it," he added, brightening, "Mother's sake. That's why I'd like to get to the bottom of this. You see, Mr. Queen?"

"Your mother loves Priam?"

"She's married to him, isn't she?"

"Come off it, Mac. I intimated to you myself the other day, in your tree, that your mother had already offered to engage my services. Not to mention Laurel. What's this all about?"

Macgowan got up angrily. "What difference does my reason make? It's an honest offer. All I want is this damned business cleaned up. Name your fee and get going on it!"

"As they say in the textbooks, Mac," said Ellery, "I'll leave you know. It's the best I can do."

"What are you waiting for?"

"Warning number two. If this business is on the level, Mac, there will be a warning number two, and I can't do a thing till it comes. With Priam being pigheaded, you and your mother can be most useful by simply keeping your eyes open. I'll decide then."

"What do we watch for," sneered the young man, "another mysterious box?"

"I've no idea. But whatever it turns out to be—and it may not be a thing, Mac, but an event—whatever happens out of the ordinary, no matter how silly or trivial it may seem to you—let me know about it right away. You," and Ellery added, as if in afterthought, "or your mother."

The phone was ringing. He opened his eyes, conscious that it had been ringing for some time.

He switched on the light, blinking at his wristwatch.

4:35. He hadn't got to bed until 1:30.

"Hello?" he mumbled.

"Mr. Queen—"

Delia Priam.

"Yes?" He had never felt so wakeful.

"My son Crowe said to call you if—" She sounded far away, a little frightened.

"Yes? Yes?"

"It's probably nothing at all. But you told Crowe—"

"Delia, what's happened?"

"Roger's sick, Ellery. Dr. Voluta is here. He says it's ptomaine poisoning. But—"

"I'll be right over!"

Dr. Voluta was a floppy man with jowls and a dirty eye, and it was a case of hate at first sight. The doctor was in a bright blue yachting jacket over a yellow silk undershirt and his greasy brown hair stuck up all over his head. He wore carpet slippers. Twice Ellery caught himself about to address him as Captain Bligh and it would not have surprised him if, in his own improvised costume of soiled white ducks and turtleneck sweater, he had inspired Priam's doctor to address him in turn as Mr. Christian.

"The trouble with you fellows," Dr. Voluta was saying as he scraped an evil mess from a rumpled bedsheet into a specimen vial, "is that you really enjoy murder. Otherwise you wouldn't see it in every bellyache."

"Quite a bellyache," said Ellery. "The stopper's right there over the sink, Doctor."

"Thank you. Priam is a damn pig. He eats too much for even a well man. His alimentary apparatus is a medical problem in itself. I've warned him for years to lay off bedtime snacks, especially spicy fish."

"I'm told he's fond of spicy fish."

"I'm fond of spicy blondes, Mr. Queen," snapped Dr. Voluta, "but I keep my appetite within bounds."

"I thought you said there's something wrong with the tuna."

"Certainly there's something wrong with it. I tasted it myself. But that's not the point. The point is that if he'd followed my orders he wouldn't have eaten any in the first place."

They were in the butler's pantry, and Dr. Voluta was looking irritably about for something to cover a plastic dish into which he had dumped the remains of the tuna.

"Then it's your opinion, Doctor—?"

"I've given you my opinion. The can of tuna was spoiled. Didn't you ever hear of spoiled canned goods, Mr. Queen?" He opened his medical bag, grabbed a surgical glove, and stretched it over the top of the dish.

"I've examined the empty tin, Dr. Voluta." Ellery had fished it out of the tin can container, thankful that in Los Angeles you had to keep cans separate from garbage. "I see no sign of a bulge, do you?"

"You're just assuming that's the tin it came from," the doctor said disagreeably. "How do you know?"

"The cook told me. It's the only tuna she opened today. She opened it just before she went to bed. And I found the tin at the top of the waste can."

Dr. Voluta threw up his hands. "Excuse me. I want to wash up."

Ellery followed him to the door of the downstairs lavatory. "Have to keep my eye on that vial and dish, Doctor," he said apologetically. "Since you won't turn them over to me."

"You don't mean a thing to me, Mr. Queen. I still think it's all a lot of nonsense. But if this stuff has to be analyzed, I'm turning it over to the police personally. Would you mind stepping back? I'd like to close this door."

"The vial," said Ellery.

"Oh, for God's sake." Dr. Voluta turned his back and opened the tap with a swoosh.

They were waiting for Lieutenant Keats. It was almost six o'clock and through the windows a pale farina-like world was taking shape. The house was cold. Priam was purged and asleep, his black beard jutting from the blankets on his reclining chair with a moribund majesty, so that all Ellery had been able to think of—before Alfred Wallace shut the door politely in his face—was Sennacherib the Assyrian in his tomb; and that was no help. Wallace had locked Priam's door from the inside. He was spending what was left of the night on the daybed in Priam's room reserved for his use during emergencies.

Crowe Macgowan had been snappish. "If I hadn't made that promise, Queen, I'd never have had Delia call you. All this stench about a little upchucking. Leave him to Voluta and go home." And he had gone back to his oak, yawning.

Old Mr. Collier, Delia Priam's father, had quietly made himself a cup of tea in the kitchen and trotted back upstairs with it, pausing only long enough to chuckle to Ellery: "A fool and his gluttony are soon parted."

Delia Priam . . . He hadn't seen her at all. Ellery had rather built himself up to their middle-of-the-night meeting, although he was prepared to be perfectly correct. Of course, she couldn't know that. By the time he arrived she had returned to her room upstairs. He was glad, in a way, that her sense of propriety was so delicately tuned to his state of mind. It was, in fact, astoundingly perceptive of her. At the same time, he felt a little empty.

Ellery stared gritty-eyed at Dr. Voluta's blue back. It was an immense back, with great fat wrinkles running across it.

He could, of course, get rid of the doctor and go upstairs and knock on her door. There was always a question or two to be asked in a case like this.

He wondered what she would do.

And how she looked at six in the morning.

He played with this thought for some time.

"Ordinarily," said the doctor, turning and reaching for a towel, "I'd have told you to go to hell. But a doctor with a respectable practice has to be cagey in this town, Mr. Queen, and Laurel started something when she began to talk about murder at Leander Hill's death. I know your type. Publicity-happy." He flung the towel at the bowl, picked up the vial and the plastic dish, holding them firmly. "You don't have to watch me, Mr. Queen. I'm not going to switch containers on you. Where the devil is that detective? I haven't had any sleep at all tonight."

"Did anyone ever tell you, Doctor," said Ellery through his teeth, "that you look like Charles Laughton in *The Beachcomber?*"

They glared at each other until a car drew up outside and Keats hurried in.

At four o'clock that afternoon Ellery pulled his rented Kaiser up before the Priam house to find Keats's car already there. The maid with the tic, which was in an active state, showed him into the living room. Keats was standing before the fieldstone fireplace, tapping his teeth with the edge of a sheet of paper. Laurel Hill, Crowe Macgowan, and Delia Priam were seated before him in a student attitude. Their heads swiveled as Ellery came in, and it seemed to him that Laurel was coldly expectant, young Macgowan uneasy, and Delia frightened.

"Sorry, Leiutenant. I had to stop for gas. Is that the lab report?"

Keats handed him the paper. Their eyes followed. When Ellery handed the paper back, their eyes went with it.

"Maybe you'd better line it up for these folks, Mr. Queen," said the detective. "I'll take it from there."

"When I got here about five this morning," nodded Ellery, "Dr. Voluta was sure it was food poisoning. The facts were these: Against Voluta's medical advice, Mr. Priam invariably has something to eat before going to sleep. This habit of his seems to be a matter of common knowledge. Since he doesn't sleep too well, he tends to go to bed at a late hour. The cook, Mrs. Guittierez, is on the other hand accustomed to retiring early. Consequently, Mr. Priam usually tells Mr. Wallace what he expects to feel like having around midnight, and Mr. Wallace usually transmits this information to the cook before she goes to bed. Mrs. Guittierez then prepares the snack as ordered, puts it into the refrigerator, and retires.

"Last night the order came through for tuna fish, to which Mr. Priam is partial. Mrs. Guittierez got a can of tuna from the pantry—one of the leading brands, by the way—opened it, prepared the contents as Mr. Priam likes it—with minced onion, sweet green pepper, celery, lots of mayonnaise, the juice of half a freshly squeezed lemon, freshly ground pepper and a little salt, a dash of Worcestershire sauce, a half-teaspoon of dried mustard, and a pinch of oregano and powdered thyme—and placed the bowl, covered, in the refrigerator. She then cleaned up and went to bed. Mrs. Guittierez left the kitchen at about twenty minutes of ten, leaving a night light burning.

"At about ten minutes after midnight," continued Ellery, speaking to the oil painting of the Spanish grandee above the fireplace so that he would not be disturbed by a certain pair of eyes, "Alfred Wallace was sent by Roger Priam for the snack. Wallace removed the bowl of tuna salad from the refrigerator, placed it on a tray with some caraway-seed rye bread, sweet butter, and a sealed bottle of milk, and carried the tray to Mr. Priam's study. Priam ate heartily, although he did not finish the contents of the tray. Wallace then prepared him for bed, turned out the lights, and took what remained on the tray back to the kitchen. He left the tray there as it was, and himself went upstairs to his room.

"At about three o'clock this morning Wallace was awakened by the buzzer of the intercom from Mr. Priam's room. It was Priam, in agony. Wallace ran downstairs and found him violently sick. Wallace immediately phoned Dr. Voluta, ran upstairs and awakened Mrs. Priam, and the two of them did what they could until Dr. Voluta's arrival, which was a very few minutes later."

Macgowan said irritably, "Damned if I can see why you tell us—"

Delia Priam put her hand on her son's arm and he stopped.

"Go on, Mr. Queen," she said in a low voice. When she talked, everything in a man tightened up. He wondered if she quite realized the quality and range of her power.

"On my arrival I found the tray in the kitchen, where Wallace said he had left it. When I had the facts I phoned Lieutenant Keats. While waiting for him I got together everything that had been used in the preparation of the midnight meal—the spices, the empty tuna tin, even the shell of the lemon, as well as the things on the tray. There was a quantity of the salad, some rye bread, some of the butter, some of the milk. Meanwhile Dr. Voluta preserved what he could of the regurgitated matter. When Lieutenant Keats arrived, we turned everything over to him."

Ellery stopped and lit a cigaret.

Keats said: "I took it all down to the Crime Laboratory and the report just came through." He glanced at the paper. "I won't bother you with the detailed report. Just give you the highlights.

"Chemical analysis of the regurgitated matter from Mr. Priam's stomach brought out the presence of arsenic.

"Everything is given a clean bill—spices, tuna tin, lemon, bread, butter, milk—everything, that is, but the tuna salad itself.

"Arsenic of the same type was found in the remains of the tuna salad.

"Dr. Voluta was wrong," said Keats. "This is not a case of ptomaine poisoning caused by spoiled fish. It's a case of arsenical poisoning caused by the introduction of arsenic into the salad. The cook put the salad in the refrigerator about 9:40 last night. Mr. Wallace came and took it to Mr. Priam around ten minutes after midnight. During that period the kitchen was empty, with only a dim light burning. During those two and a half hours someone sneaked into the kitchen and poisoned the salad."

"There can't have been any mistake," added Ellery. "There is a bowl of something for Mr. Priam in the refrigerator every night. It's a special bowl, used only for his snacks. It's even more easily identified than that—it has the name *Roger* in gilt lettering on it, a gift to Roger Priam from Alfred Wallace last Christmas."

"The question is," concluded Keats, "who tired to poison Mr. Priam."

He looked at the three in a friendly way.

Delia Priam, rising suddenly, murmured, "It's so incredible," and put a handkerchief to her nose.

Laurel smiled at the older woman's back. "That's the way it's seemed to me, darling," she said, "ever since Daddy's death."

"Oh, for Pete's sake, Laur," snapped Delia's son, "don't keep smiling like Lady Macbeth, or Cassandra, or whoever it was. The last thing in the world Mother and I want is a mess."

"Nobody's accusing you, Mac," said Laurel. "My only point is that now maybe you'll believe I wasn't talking through clouds of opium."

"All *right!*"

Delia turned to Keats. Ellery saw Keats look her over uncomfortably, but with that avidity for detail which cannot be disciplined in the case of certain women. She was superb today, all in white, with a large wooden crucifix on a silver chain girdling her waist. No slit in this skirt; long sleeves; and the dress came up high to the neck. But her back was bare to the waist. Some Hollywood designer's idea of personalized fashion; didn't she realize how shocking it was? But then women, even the most respectable, have the wickedest innocence in this sort of thing, mused Ellery; it really wasn't fair to a hard-working police officer who wore a gold band on the fourth finger of his left hand. "Lieutenant, do the police have to come into this?" she asked.

"Ordinarily, Mrs. Priam, I could answer a question like that right off the bat." Keats's eyes shifted; he put an unlit cigaret between his lips and rolled it nervously to the corner of his mouth. A note of stubbornness crept into his voice. "But this is something I've never run into before. Your husband refuses to co-operate. He won't even discuss it with me. All he said was that he won't be caught that way again, that he could take care of himself, and that I was to pick up my hat on the way out."

Delia went to a window. Studying her back, Ellery thought that she was relieved and pleased. Keats should have kept her on a hook; he'd have to have a little skull session with Keats on the best way to handle Mrs. Priam. But that back *was* disturbing.

"Tell me, Mrs. Priam, is he nuts?"

"Sometimes, Lieutenant," murmured Delia without turning, "I wonder."

"I'd like to add," said Keats abruptly, "that Joe Dokes and his Ethiopian brother could have dosed that tuna. The kitchen back door wasn't locked. There's gravel back there, and woods beyond. It would have been a cinch for anyone who'd cased the household and found out about the midnight snack routine. There seems to be a tie-up with somebody from Mr. Priam's and Mr. Hill's past—somebody who's had it in for both of them for a long time. I'm not overlooking that. But I'm not overlooking the possibility that that's a lot of soda pop, too. It could be a cover-up. In fact, I think it is. I don't go for this revenge-and-slow-death business. I just wanted everybody to know that. Okay, Mr. Queen, I'm through."

He kept looking at her back.

Brother, thought Ellery with compassion.

And he said, "You may be right, Keats, but I'd like to point out a curious fact that appears in this lab report. The quantity of arsenic apparently used, says the report, was 'not sufficient to cause death.'"

"A mistake," said the detective. "It happens all the time. Either they use way too much or way too little."

"Not all the time, Lieutenant. And from what's happened so far, I don't see this character—whoever he is—as the impulsive, emotional type of killer. If this is all tied up, it has a pretty careful and coldblooded brain behind it. The kind of criminal brain that doesn't make simple mistakes like underdosing. 'Not sufficient to cause death' . . . that was deliberate."

"But why?" howled young Macgowan.

" 'Slow dying,' Mac!" said Laurel triumphantly. "Remember?"

"Yes, it connects with the note to Hill," said Ellery in a glum tone. "Nonlethal dose. Enough to make Priam very sick, but not fatally. 'Slow and sure . . . For each pace forward a warning.' The poisoning attack is a warning to Roger Priam to follow up whatever was in the box he received the morning Hill got the dead dog. Priam's warning number one—unknown. Warning number two—poisoned tuna. Lovely problem."

"I don't admire your taste in problems," said Crowe Macgowan. "What's it mean? All this—this stuff?"

"It means, Mac, that I'm forced to accept your assignment," replied Ellery. "And yours, Laurel, and yours, Delia. I shouldn't take the time, but what else can I do?"

Delia Priam came to him and took his hands and looked into his eyes and said, with simplicity, "Thank you, Ellery. It's such a . . . relief knowing it's going to be handled . . . by you."

She squeezed, ever so little. It was all impersonally friendly on her part; he felt that. It had to be, with her own son present. But he wished he could control his sweat glands.

Keats lipped his unlit cigaret.

Macgowan looked down at them, interested.

Laurel said, "Then we're all nicely set," in a perfectly flat voice, and she walked out.

Chapter VI

THE NIGHT WAS chilly, and Laurel walked briskly along the path, the beam of her flashlight bobbing before her. Her legs were bare under the long suède coat and they felt goose-pimply.

When she came to the great oak she stabbed at the green ceiling with her light.

"Mac. You awake?"

Macgowan's big face appeared in her beam.

"Laurel?" he said incredulously.

"It's not Esther Williams."

"Are you crazy, walking alone in these woods at night?" The rope ladder hurtled to her feet. "What do you want to be, a sex murder in tomorrow's paper?"

"You'd be the natural suspect." Laurel began to climb, her light streaking about the clearing.

"Wait, will you! I'll put on the flood." Macgowan disappeared. A moment later the glade was bright as a studio set. "That's why I'm nervous," he grinned, reappearing. His long arm yanked her to the platform. "Boy, is this cosy. Come on in."

"Turn off the flood, Mac. I'd like some privacy."

"Sure!" He was back in a moment, lifting her off her feet. She let him carry her into his tree house and deposit her on the rollaway bed, which was made up for the night. "Wait till I turn the radio off." When he straightened up his head barely missed the ceiling. "And the light."

"Leave the light."

"Okay, okay. Aren't you cold, baby?"

"That's the only thing you haven't provided for, Mac. The California nights."

"Didn't you know I carry my own central heating? Shove over."

"Sit down, Mac."

"Huh?"

"On the floor. I want to talk to you."

"Didn't you ever hear of the language of the eyes and so forth?"

"Tonight it has to come out here." Laurel leaned back on her arms, smiling at him. He was beginning to glower. But then he folded up at her feet and put his head on her knees. Laurel moved him, drew her coat over her legs, and replaced his head.

"All right, then, let it out!"

"Mac," said Laurel, "why did *you* hire Ellery Queen?"

He sat still for a moment. Then he reached over to a shelf, got a cigaret, lit it, and leaned back.

"That's a hell of a question to ask a red-blooded man in a tree house at twelve o'clock at night."

"Just the same, answer it."

"What difference does it make? You hired him, Delia hired him, everybody was doing it, so I did it too. Let's talk about something else. If we've got to talk."

"Sorry. That's my subject for tonight."

He encircled his mammoth legs, scowling through the smoke at his bare feet. "Laurel, how long have we known each other?"

"Since we were kids." She was surprised.

"Grew up together, didn't we?"

"We certainly did."

"Have I ever done anything out of line?"

"No," Laurel laughed softly, "but it's not because you haven't tried."

"Why, you little squirt, I could break you in two and stuff both halves in my pants pocket. Don't you know I've been in love with you ever since I found out where babies come from?"

"Why, Mac," murmured Laurel. "You've never said that to me before. Used that word, I mean."

"Well, I've used it," he growled. "Now let me hear your side of it."

"Say it again, Mac?"

"Love! I love you!"

"In that tone of voice?"

She found herself off the bed and on the floor, in his arms. "Damn you," he whispered, "I love you."

She stared up at him. "Mac—"

"I love you . . ."

"Mac, let go of me!" She wriggled out of his arms and jumped to her feet. "I suppose," she cried, "that's the reason you hired him! Because you love me, or—or something like that. Mac, what's the *reason*? I've got to know!"

"Is that all you have to say to a guy who tells you he loves you?"

"The reason, Mac."

Young Macgowan rolled over on his back and belched smoke. Out of the reek his voice mumbled something ineffectual. Then it stopped. When the smoke cleared, he was lying there with his eyes shut.

"You won't tell me."

"Laur, I can't. It's got . . . nothing to do with anything. Just some cock-eyed thing of my own."

Laurel seated herself on the bed again. He was very long, and broad, and brown and muscular and healthy-looking. She took a Dunhill from her coat pocket and lit it with shaky fingers. But when she spoke, she sounded calm. "There are too many mysteries around here, Chesty. I know there's one about you, and where you're concerned . . ."

His eyes opened.

"No, Mac, stay there. I'm not entirely a fool. There's something behind this tree house and all this learned bratwurst about the end of civilization, and it's not the hydrogen bomb. Are you just lazy? Or is it a new thrill for some of your studio girls—the ones who want life with a little extra something they can't get in a motel?" He flushed, but his mouth continued sullen. "All right, we'll let that go. Now about this love business."

She put her hand in his curly hair, gripping. He looked up at her thoroughly startled. She leaned forward and kissed him on the lips.

"That's for thanks. You're such a beautiful man, Mac . . . you see, a girl has her secrets, too—No! Mac, no. If we ever get together, it's got to be in a clean house. On the ground. Anyway, I have no time for love now."

"No time!"

"Darling, something's happening, and it's ugly. There's never been any ugliness in my life before . . . that I can remember, that is. And he was so wonderful to me. The only way I can pay him back is by finding whoever murdered him and seeing him die. How stupid does that sound? And maybe I'm kind of bloodthirsty myself. But it's all in the world I'm interested in right now. If the law gets him, fine. But if . . ."

"For God's sake!" Crowe scrambled to his feet, his face bilious. A short-nosed little automatic had materialized in Laurel's hand and it was pointing absently at his navel.

"If they don't, I'll find him myself. And when I do, Mac, I'll shoot him as dead as that dog. If they send me to the gas chamber for it."

"Laurel, put that blamed thing back in your pocket!"

"No matter who it is." Her green, brown-flecked eyes were bright. The gun did not move. "Even if it turned out to be you, Mac. Even if we were married—had a baby. If I found out it was you, Mac, I'd kill you, too."

"And I thought Roger was tough." Macgowan stared at her. "Well, if you find out it was me, it'll serve me right. But until you do—"

Laurel cried out. The gun was in his hand. He turned it over curiously. "Nasty little beanshooter. Until you do, Red, don't let anybody take this away from you," and he dropped it politely into her pocket, picked her up, and sat down on the bed with her.

A little later Laurel was saying faintly, "Mac, I didn't come here for this."

"Surprise."

"Mac, what do you think of Ellery Queen?"

"I think he's got a case on Ma," said the giant. "Do we have to talk?"

"How acute of you. I think he has, too. But that's not what I meant. I meant professionally."

"Oh, he's a nice enough guy . . ."

"Mac!"

"Okay, okay." He got up sullenly, dumping her. "If he's half as good as his rep—"

"That's just it. Is he?"

"Is he what? What are we talking about?" He poured himself a drink.

"Is he even *half* as good?"

"How should I know? You want one?"

"No. I've dropped in on him twice and phoned him I don't know how many times in the past couple of days, and he's always there. Sitting in his crow's nest, smoking and scanning the horizon."

"Land ho. It's a way of life, Laurel." Macgowan tossed it off and made a face. "That's the way these big-shot dicks work sometimes. It's all up here."

"Well, I'd like to see a little activity on the other end." Laurel jumped up suddenly. "Mac, I can't stand this doing nothing. How about you and me taking a crack at it? On our own?"

"Taking a crack at what?"

"At what he ought to be doing."

"Detecting?" The big fellow was incredulous.

"I don't care what you call it. Hunting for facts, if that sounds less movie-ish. Anything that will get somewhere."

"Red Hill, Lady Dick, and Her Muscle Man," said young Macgowan, touching the ceiling with both hands. "You know? It appeals to me."

Laurel looked up at him coldly. "I'm not gagging, Mac."

"Who's gagging? Your brain, my sinews—"

"Never mind. Good night."

"Hey!" His big hand caught her in the doorway. "Don't be so half-cocky. I'm really going birdy up here, Laurel. It's tough squatting in this tree waiting for the big boom. How would you go about it?"

She looked at him for a long time. "Mac, don't try to pull anything cute on me."

"My gosh, what would I pull on *you!*"

"This isn't a game, like your apeman stunt. We're not going to have any code words in Turkish or wear disguises or meet in mysterious bistros. It's going to be a lot of footwork and maybe nothing but blisters to show for it. If you understand that and still want to come in, all right. Anything else, I go it solo."

"I hope you'll put a skirt on, or at least long pants," the giant said morosely. "Where do we start?"

"We should have started on that dead dog. Long ago. Where it came from, who owned it, how it died, and all that. But now that's as cold as I am . . . I'd say, Mac," said Laurel, leaning against the jamb with her hands in her pockets, "the arsenic. That's fresh, and it's something to go on. Somebody got into the kitchen over there and mixed arsenic in with Roger's tuna. Arsenic can't be too easy to get hold of. It must leave a trail of some sort."

"I never thought of that. How the dickens would you go about tracing it?"

"I've got some ideas. But there's one thing we ought to do before that. The tuna was poisoned in the house. So that's the place to start looking."

"Let's go." Macgowan reached for a dark blue sweater.

"*Now?*" Laurel sounded slightly dismayed.

"Know a better time?"

Mrs. Williams came in and stumbled over a chair. "Mr. Queen? You in here?"

"Present."

"Then why don't you put on a light?" She found the switch. Ellery was bunched in a corner of the sofa, feet on the picture window, looking at Hollywood. It looked like a fireworks display, popping lights in all colors. "Your dinner's cold."

"Leave it on the kitchen table, Mrs. Williams. You go on home."

She sniffed. "It's that Miss Hill and the naked man, only he's got clothes on this evening."

"Why didn't you say so!" Ellery sprang from the sofa. "Laurel, Mac! Come in."

They were smiling, but Ellery thought they both looked a little peaked. Crowe Macgowan was in a respectable suit; he even wore a tie.

"Well, well, still communing with mysterious thoughts, eh, Queen? We're not interrupting anything momentous?"

"As far as I can see," said Laurel, "he hasn't moved from one spot in sixty hours. Ellery," she said abruptly, "we have some news for you."

"News? For me?"

"We've found out something."

"I wondered why Mac was dressed," said Ellery. "Here, sit down and tell me all about it. You two been on the trail?"

"There's nothing to this detective racket," said the giant, stretching his legs. "You twerps have been getting away with mayhem. Tell him, Red."

"We decided to do a little detecting on our own—"

"That sounds to me," murmured Ellery, "like the remark of a dissatisfied client."

"That's what it is." Laurel strode around smoking a cigaret. "We'd better have an understanding, Ellery. I hired you to find a killer. I didn't expect you to produce him in twenty-four hours necessarily, but I did expect *something—some* sign of interest, maybe even a twitch or two of activity. But what have you done? You've sat here and smoked!"

"Not a bad system, Laurel," said Ellery, reaching for a pipe. "I've worked that way for years."

"Well, I don't care for it!"

"Am I fired?"

"I didn't say that—"

"I think all the lady wants to do," said young Macgowan, "is give you a jab, Queen. She doesn't think thinking is a substitute for footwork."

"Each has its place," Ellery said amiably—"sit down, Laurel, won't you? Each has its place, and thinking's place can be very important. I'm not altogether ignorant of what's been going on, seated though I've remained. Let's see if I can't—er—think this out for you . . ." He closed his eyes. "I would say," he said after a moment, "that you two have been tracking down the arsenic with which Priam's tuna was poisoned." He opened his eyes. "Is that right so far?"

"That's right," cried Macgowan.

Laurel glared. "How did you know?"

Ellery tapped his forehead. "Never sell cerebration short. Now! What exactly have you accomplished? I look into my mental ball and I see . . . you and Mac . . . discovering a . . . can of . . . a can of rat poison in the Priam cellar." They were open-mouthed. "Yes. Rat poison. And you found that this particlar rat poison contains arsenic . . . arsenic, the poison which was also found in Priam's salad. How'm I doin'?"

Laurel said feebly, "But I can't imagine how you . . ."

Ellery had gone to the blondewood desk near the window and pulled a drawer open. Now he took out a card and glanced over it. "Yes. You traced the purchase of that poison, which bears the brand name of D-e-t-h hyphen o-n hyphen R-a-t-z. You discovered that this revoltingly named substance was purchased on May the thirteenth of this year at . . . let me see . . . at Kepler's Pharmacy at 1723 North Highland."

Laurel looked at Macgowan. He was grinning. She glared at him and then back at Ellery.

"You questioned either Mr. Kepler himself," Ellery went on, "or his clerk, Mr. Candy—unfortunately my crystal ball went blank at this point. But one of them told you that the can of Deth-on-Ratz was bought by a tall, handsome man whom he identified—probably from a set of snapshots you had with you—as Alfred Wallace. Correct, Laurel?"

Laurel said tightly, "How did you find out?"

"Why, Red, I leave these matters to those who can attend to them far more quickly and efficiently than I—or you, Red. Or the Atomic Age Tree Boy over here. Lieutenant Keats had all that information within a few hours and he passed it along to me. Why should I sauté myself in the California sun when I can sit here in comfort and think?"

Laurel's lip wiggled and Ellery burst into laughter. He shook up her hair and tilted her chin. "Just the same, that was enterprising of you, Laurel. That was all right."

"Not so all right." Laurel sank into a chair, tragic. "I'm sorry, Ellery. You must think I'm an imbecile."

"Not a bit of it. It's just that you're impatient. This business is a matter of legs, brains, and bottoms, and you've got to learn to wait on the last-named with philosophy while the other two are pumping away. What else did you find out?"

"Nothing," said Laurel miserably.

"I thought it was quite a piece," said Crowe Macgowan. "Finding out that Alfred bought the poison that knocked Roger for a loop . . . that ought to mean something, Queen."

"If you jumped to that kind of conclusion," said Ellery dryly, "I'm afraid you're in for a bad time. Keats found out something else."

"What's that?"

"It was your mother, Mac, who thought she heard mice in the cellar. It was your mother who told Wallace to buy the rat poison."

The boy gaped, and Laurel looked down at her hands suddenly.

"Don't be upset, Mac. No action is going to be taken. Even though the mice seem to have been imaginary—we could find no turds or holes . . . The fact is, we have nothing positive. There's no direct evidence that the arsenic in Priam's tuna salad came from the can of rat poison in the cellar. There's no direct evidence that either your mother or Wallace did anything but try to get rid of mice who happen not to have been there."

"Well, of course not." Macgowan had recovered; he was even looking pugnacious. "Stupid idea to begin with. Just like this detective hunch of yours, Laurel. Everything's under control. Let's leave it that way."

"All right," said Laurel. She was still studying her hands.

But Ellery said, "No. I don't see it that way. It's not a bad notion at all for you two to root around. You're on the scene—"

"If you think I'm going to rat on my mother," began Crowe angrily.

"We seem to be in a rodent cycle," Ellery complained. "Are you worried that your mother may have tried to poison your stepfather, Mac?"

"No! I mean—you know what I mean! What kind of rat—skunk do you think I am?"

"I got you into this, Mac," Laurel said. "I'm sorry. You can back out."

"I'm *not* backing out! Seems to me you two are trying to twist every word I say!"

"Would you have any scruples," asked Ellery with a smile, "where Wallace is concerned?"

"Hell, no. Wallace doesn't mean anything to me. Delia does." Her son added, with a sulky shrewdness, "I thought she did to you, too."

"Well, she does." The truth was, Keats's information about Delia Priam and the rat poison had given him a bad time. "But let's stick to Wallace for the moment. Mac, what do you know about him?"

"Not a thing."

"How long has he been working for your stepfather?"

"About a year. They come and go. Roger's had a dozen stooges in the last fifteen years. Wallace is just the latest."

"Well, you keep your eye on him. And Laurel—"

"On Delia," said Macgowan sarcastically.

"Laurel on everything. Keep giving me reports. Anything out of the ordinary. This case may prove to be a series of excavations, with the truth at the bottom level. Dig in."

"I could go back to the beginning," mumbled Laurel, "and try to trace the dead dog . . ."

"Oh, you don't know about that, do you?" Ellery turned to the writing desk again.

"About the *dog?*"

He turned around with another card. "The dog belonged to somebody named Henderson who lives on Clybourn Avenue in the Toluca Lake district. He's a dwarf who gets occasional work in films. The dog's name was Frank. Frank disappeared on Decoration Day. Henderson reported his disappearance to the Pound Department, but his description was vague and unfortunately Frank had no license—Henderson, it seems, is against bureaucracy and regimentation. When the dog's body was picked up at your house,

Laurel, in view of its lack of identification it was disposed of in the usual way. It was only afterward that Henderson identified the collar, which was returned to him.

"Keats has seen the collar, although Henderson refuses to part with it for sentimental reasons. Keats doubts, though, that anything can be learned from it. There's no trace of the little silver box which was attached to the collar. The receipt Henderson signed at the Pound Department mentions it, but Henderson says he threw it away as not belonging to him.

"As for what the dog died of, an attendant at the Pound remembered the animal and he expressed the opinion that Frank had died of poisoning. Asked if it could have been arsenic poisoning, the man said, yes, it could have been arsenic poisoning. In the absence of an analysis of the remains, the opinion is worthless. All we can do is speculate that the dog was fed something with arsenic in it, which is interesting as speculation but meaningless as evidence. And that's the story of the dead dog, Laurel. You can forget it."

"I'll help wherever I can," said Laurel in a subdued voice. "And again, Ellery—I'm sorry."

"No need to be. My fault for not having kept you up to date." Ellery put his arm around her, and she smiled faintly. "Oh, Mac," he said. "There's something personal I want to say to Laurel. Would you mind giving me a couple of minutes with her alone?"

"Seems to me," grumbled the giant, rising, "as a bloodhound you've got a hell of a wolf strain in you, Queen." His jaw protruded. "Lay off my mother, hear me? Or I'll crack your clavicles for soup!"

"Oh, stop gibbering, Mac," said Laurel quickly.

"Laur, do you want to be alone with this character?"

"Wait for me in the car."

Mac almost tore the front door off its hinges.

"Mac is something like a great Dane himself," Laurel murmured, her back to the door. "Huge, honest, and a little dumb. What is it, Ellery?"

"Dumb about what, Laurel?" Ellery eyed her. "About me? That wasn't dumb. I admit I've found Delia Priam very attractive."

"I didn't mean dumb about you." Laurel shook her head. "Never mind, Ellery. What did you want?"

"Dumb about Delia? Laurel, you know something about Mac's mother—"

"If it's Delia you want to question me about, I—I can't answer. May I go now, please?"

"Right away." Ellery put his hand on the doorknob, looking down at her cinnamon hair. "You know, Laurel, Lieutenant Keats has done some work at your house, too."

Her eyes flew to his. "What do you mean?"

"Questioning your housekeeper, the chauffeur, the houseman."

"They didn't say anything about me!"

"You're dealing with a professional, Laurel, and a very good one. They didn't realize they were being pumped." His eyes were grave. "A few weeks ago you lost or mislaid a small silver box, Laurel. A sort of pillbox."

She had gone pale, but her voice was steady. "That's right."

"From the description Mrs. Monk, Simeon, and Ichiro gave—you'd asked them to look for it—the box must have been about the same size and shape as the one you told me contained the warning note to your father. Keats wanted to quiz you about it immediately, but I told him I'd handle it myself. Laurel, was it your silver box that was attached to the collar of Henderson's defunct dog?"

"I don't know."

"Why didn't you mention to me the fact that a box of the same description belonging to you had disappeared shortly before June second?"

"Because I was sure it couldn't have been the same one. The very idea was ridiculous. How could it have been my box? I got it at the May Company, and I think The Broadway and other department stores have been carrying it, too. It's advertised for carrying vitamin tablets and things like that. There must have been thousands of them sold all over Los Angeles. I really bought it to give to Daddy. He had to take certain pills and he could have carried this around in his watch pocket. But I mislaid it—"

"Could it have been your pillbox?"

"I suppose it could, but—"

"And you never found the one you lost?"

She looked at him, worried. "Do you suppose it was?"

"I'm not supposing much of anything yet, Laurel. Just trying to get things orderly. Or just trying to get things." Ellery opened the door and looked out cautiously. "Be sure to tell your muscular admirer that I'm returning you to him *virgo intacto*. I'm sort of sentimental about my clavicles." He smiled and squeezed her fingers.

He watched until they were out of sight around the lower curve of the hill, not smiling at all.

Ellery went down to his cold supper and chewed away. The cottage was cheerlessly silent. His jaws made sounds.

Then there was a different sound.

A tap on the kitchen door?

Ellery stared. "Come in?"

And there she was.

"Delia." He got out of his chair, still holding the knife and fork.

She was in a long loose coat of some dark blue material. It had a turned-up collar which framed her head. She stood with her back against the door, looking about the room.

"I've been waiting in the back garden in the dark. I saw Laurel's car. And after Laurel and . . . Crowe drove away I thought I'd better wait a little longer. I wasn't sure that your housekeeper was gone."

"She's gone."

"That's good." She laughed.

"Where is your car, Delia?"

"I left it in a side lane at the bottom of the hill. Walked up. Ellery, this is a darling kitchen—"

"Discreet," said Ellery. He had not stirred.

"Aren't you going to ask me in?"

He said slowly, "I don't think I'm going to."

Her smile withered. But then it burgeoned again. "Oh, don't sound so serious. I was passing by and I thought I'd drop in and see how you were getting on—"

"With the case."

"Of course." She had dimples. Funny, he had never noticed them before.

"This isn't a good idea, Delia."

"*What* isn't?"

"This is a small town, Delia, and it's all eyes and ears. It doesn't take much in Hollywood to destroy a woman's reputation."

"Oh, that." She was silent. Then she showed her teeth. "Of course, you're right. It was stupid of me. It's just that sometimes . . ." She stopped, and she shivered suddenly.

"Sometimes what, Delia?"

"Nothing. I'm going.—Is there anything new?"

"Just that business about the rat poison."

She shrugged. "I really thought there were mice."

"Of course."

"Good night, Ellery."

"Good night, Delia."

He did not offer to walk her down the hill and she did not seem to expect it.

He stared at the kitchen door for a long time.

Then he went upstairs and poured himself a stiff drink.

At three in the morning Ellery gave up trying to sleep and crawled out of bed. He turned on the lights in the living room, loaded and fired his brier, turned the lights out, and sat down to watch Hollywood glimmer scantily below. Light always disturbed him when he was groping in the dark.

And he was groping, and this was darkness.

Of course, it was a puzzling case. But puzzle was merely the absence of answer. Answer it, and the puzzle vanished. Nor was he bothered by the nimbus of fantasy which surrounded the case like a Los Angeles daybreak fog. All crimes were fantastic insofar as they expressed what most people merely dreamed about. The dream of the unknown enemy had been twenty years or more in the making . . .

He clucked to himself in the darkness. Back to the writer of the note.

The wonder was not that he made gifts of poisoned dogs and wrote odd notes relishing slow death and promising mysterious warnings with special meanings. The wonder was that he had been able to keep his hatred alive for almost a generation; and that was not fantasy, but sober pathology.

Fantasy was variance from normal experience, a matter of degree. Hollywood had always attracted its disproportionate quota of variants from the norm. In Vandalia, Illinois, Roger Priam would have been encysted in the community like a foreign substance, but in the Southern California canyons he was peculiarly soluble. There might be Delia Priams in Seattle, but in the houri paradise of Hollywood she belonged, the female archetype from whom all desire sprang. And Tree Boy, who in New York would have been dragged off to the observation ward of Bellevue Hospital, was here just another object of civic admiration, rating columns of good-natured newspaper space.

No, it wasn't the fantasy.

It was the hellish scarcity of facts.

Here was an enemy out of the past. What past? No data. The enemy was preparing a series of warnings. What were they? A dead dog had been the first. Then the unknown contents of a small cardboard box. Then a deliberately nonlethal dose of arsenic. The further warnings, the warnings that were promised, had not yet come forth. How many would there be? They were warnings of "special meaning." A series, then. A pattern. But what connection could exist between a dead dog and an arsenic-salted tunafish salad? It would help, help greatly, to know what had been in that box Roger Priam had received at the same moment that Leander Hill was stooping over the body of the dog and reading the thin, multi-creased note. Yes, greatly. But . . . no data. It was probable that, whatever it was, Priam had destroyed it. But Priam knew. How could the man be made to talk? He must be made to talk.

The darkness was darker than even that. Ellery mused, worrying his pipe. There was a pattern, all right, but how could he be sure it was the only pattern? Suppose the dead hound had been the first warning of special meaning in a proposed series to Hill, the other warnings of which were forever lost in the limbo of an unknown mind because of Hill's premature death? And suppose whatever was in Priam's box was the first warning of a *second* series, of which the second warning was the poisoning—a series having no significant relation to the one aborted by Hill's heart attack? It was possible. It was quite possible that there was no connection in *meaning* between Hill's and Priam's warnings.

The safest course for the time being was to ignore the dead dog received by Hill and to concentrate on the living Priam, proceeding on the assumption that the unknown contents of Priam's box and the poisoning of his salad constituted a separate series altogether. . . .

Ellery went back to bed. His last thought was that he must find out at any cost what had been in that box, and that he could only wait for the third warning to Priam.

But he dreamed of Delia Priam in a jungle thicket, showing her teeth.

Chapter VII

As ELLERY WAS able to put it together when he arrived at Delia Priam's summons that fabulous Sunday morning—from the stories of Delia, Alfred Wallace, and old Mr. Collier—Delia had risen early to go to church. Beyond remarking that her church attendance was "spotty," she was reticent about this; Ellery gathered that she could not go as regularly as she would like because of the peculiar conditions of her life, and that only occasionally was she able to slip away and into one of the old churches where, to "the blessed mutter of the mass," she returned to her childhood and her blood. This had been such a morning, five days after the poisoning attack on her husband, two after her strange visit to Ellery's cottage.

While Delia had been up and about at an early hour, Alfred Wallace had risen late. He was normally an early riser, because Priam was a demanding charge and Wallace had learned that if he was to enjoy the luxury of breakfast he must get it over with before Priam awakened. On Sundays, however, Priam preferred to lie in bed until mid-morning, undisturbed, and this permitted Wallace to sleep until nine o'clock.

Delia's father was invariably up with the birds. On this morning he had breakfasted with his daughter, and when she drove off to Los Angeles Mr. Collier went out for his early morning tramp through the woods. On his way back he had stopped before the big oak and tried to rouse his grandson, but as there was no answer from the tree house beyond Crowe's Brobdingnagian snores the old man had returned to the Priam house and gone into the library. The library was downstairs off the main hall, directly opposite the door to Roger Priam's quarters, with the staircase between. This was shortly after eight, Mr. Collier told Ellery; his son-in-law's door was shut and there was no light visible under the door; all seemed as it always was at that hour of a Sunday morning; and the old man had got his postage stamp albums out of a drawer of the library desk, his stamp hinges, his tongs, and his Scott's catalogue, and he had set to work mounting his latest mail purchases of stamps. "I've done a lot of knocking about the world," he told Ellery, "and it's corking fun to collect stamps from places I've actually been in. Want to see my collection?" Ellery had declined; he was rather busy at the time.

At a few minutes past nine Alfred Wallace came downstairs. He exchanged greetings with Delia's father—the library door stood open—and went in to his breakfast without approaching Priam's door.

Mrs. Guittierez served him, and Wallace read the Sunday papers, which were always delivered to the door, as he ate. It was the maid's and chauffeur's Sunday off and the house was unusually quiet. In the kitchen the cook was getting things ready for Roger Priam's breakfast.

Shortly before ten o'clock Alfred Wallace painstakingly restored the Sunday papers to their original state, pushed back his chair, and went out into the hall carrying the papers. Priam liked to have the newspapers within arm's reach when he awakened Sunday mornings, and he flew into a rage if they were crumpled or disarranged.

Seeing a line of light beneath Priam's door, Wallace quickened his step. He went in without knocking.

The first *he* knew anything out of the ordinary had occurred, said Mr. Collier, he heard Wallace's cry from Roger Priam's room: "Mr. Collier! Mr. Collier! Come here!" The old man jumped up from his stamp albums and ran across the hall. Wallace was rattling the telephone, trying to get the operator. Just as he was shouting to Collier, "See about Mr. Priam! See if he's all right!" the operator responded, and Wallace—who seemed in a panic—babbled something about the police and Lieutenant Keats. Collier picked his way across the room to his son-in-law's wheelchair, which was still made up as a bed. Priam, in his night clothes, was up on one elbow, glaring about with a sort of vitreous horror. His mouth was open and his beard was in motion, but no sound passed them. As far as the old man could see, there was nothing wrong with Priam but stupefying fright. Collier eased the paralyzed man backward until he was supine, trying to soothe him; but Priam lay rigid, as if in a coma, his eyes tightly shut to keep out what he had seen, and the old man could get no response from him.

At this moment, Delia Priam returned from church.

Wallace turned from the phone and Collier from Priam at a choked sound from the doorway. Delia was staring into the room with eyes sick with disbelief. She was paler than her husband and she seemed about to faint.

"All this . . . all these . . ."

She began to titter.

Wallace said roughly, "Get her out of here."

"He's dead. He's dead!"

Collier hurried to her. "No, no, daughter. Just scared. Now you go upstairs. We'll take care of Roger."

"He's not dead? Then why—? How do these—?"

"Delia." The old man stroked her hand.

"Don't touch anything. Anything!"

"No, no, daughter—"

"Nothing must be touched. It's got to be left exactly as you found it. *Exactly*." And Delia stumbled up the hall to the household telephone and called Ellery.

When Ellery pulled up before the Priam house a radio patrol car was already parked in the driveway. A young officer was in the car, making a report to headquarters by radio, his mouth going like a faucet. His mate was apparently in the house.

"Here, you." He jumped out of the car. "Where you going?" His face was red.

"I'm a friend of the family, Officer. Mrs. Priam just telephoned me." Ellery looked rather wild himself. Delia had been hysterical over the phone and the only word he had been able to make out, "fogs," had conveyed nothing reasonable. "What's happened?"

"I wouldn't repeat it," said the patrolman excitedly. "I wouldn't lower myself. They think I'm drunk. What do they think I am? Sunday morning! I've seen a lot of crosseyed things in this town, but—"

"Here, get hold of yourself, Officer. Has Lieutenant Keats been notified, do you know?"

"They caught him at home. He's on his way here now."

Ellery bounded up the steps. As he ran into the hall he saw Delia. She was dressed for town, in black and modest dress, hat, and gloves, and she was leaning against a wall bloodlessly. Alfred Wallace, disheveled and un-nerved, was holding one of her gloved hands in both of his, whispering to her. The tableau dissolved in an instant; Delia spied Ellery, said something quickly to Wallace, withdrawing her hand, and she ran forward. Wallace turned, rather startled. He followed her with a hasty shuffle, almost as if he were afraid of being left alone.

"Ellery."

"Is Mr. Priam all right?"

"He's had a bad shock."

"Can't say I blame him," Wallace mumbled. The handsome man passed a trembling handkerchief over his cheeks. "The doctor's on his way over. We can't seem to snap Mr. Priam out of it."

"What's this about 'fogs,' Delia?" Ellery hurried up the hall, Delia cling-ing to his arm. Wallace remained where he was, still wiping his face.

"Fogs? I didn't say fogs. I said—"

Ellery stopped in the doorway.

The other radio car patrolman was straddling a chair, cap pushed back on his head, looking about helplessly.

Roger Priam lay stiffly on his bed staring at the ceiling.

And all over Priam's body, on his blanket, on his sheet, in the shelves and compartments of his wheelchair, on his typewriter, strewn about the floor, the furniture, Wallace's emergency bed, the window sills, the cornices, the fireplace, the mantelpiece—everywhere—were frogs.

Frogs and toads.

Hundreds of frogs and toads.

Tiny tree toads.

Yellow-legged frogs.

Bullfrogs.

Each little head was twisted.

The room was littered with their corpses.

Ellery had to confess to himself that he was thrown. There was a nonsense quality to the frogs that crossed over the line of laughter into the darker regions of the mind. Beyond the black bull calf of the Nile with the figure of an eagle on his back and the beetle upon his tongue stood Apis, a god; beyond absurdity loomed fear. Fear was the timeless tyrant. At mid-twentieth century it took the shape of a gigantic mushroom. Why not frogs? With frogs the terrible Wrath of the Hebrews had plagued the Egyptian, with frogs and blood and wild beasts and darkness and the slaying of the first-born . . . He could hardly blame Roger Priam for lying frozen. Priam knew something of the way of gods; he was by way of being a minor one himself.

While Keats and the patrolmen tramped about the house, Ellery drifted around the Priam living room trying to get a bearing. The whole thing irritated and enchanted him. It made no sense. It related to nothing. There lay its power over the uninitiated; that was its appearance for the mob. But Priam was of the inner temple. He knew something the others did not. He knew the sense this nonsense made. He knew the nature of the mystery to which it related. He knew the nature of this primitive god and he grasped the meaning of the god's symbolism. Knowledge is not always power; certainty does not always bring peace. This knowledge was paralyzing and this certainty brought terror.

Keats found him nibbling his thumb under the Spanish grandee.

"Well, the doctor's gone and the frogs are all collected and maybe you and I had better have a conference about this."

"Sure."

"This is what you'd call Priam's third warning, isn't it?"

"Yes, Keats."

"Me," said the detective, seating himself heavily on a heavy chair, "I'd call it broccoli."

"Don't make that mistake."

Keats looked at him in a resentful way. "I don't go for this stuff, Mr. Queen. I don't believe it even when I see it. Why does he go to all this trouble?" His tone said he would have appreciated a nice, uncomplicated bullet.

"How is Priam?"

"He'll live. The problem was this doctor, Voluta. It seems we took him away from a party—a blonde party—at Malibu. He took the frogs as a personal insult. Treated Priam for shock, put him to sleep, and dove for his car."

"Have you talked to Priam?"

"I talked to Priam, yes. But he didn't talk to me."

"Nothing?"

"He just said he woke up, reached for that push-button-on-a-cord arrangement he's got for turning on the lights, saw the little beasties, and knew no more."

"No attempt at explanation?"

"You don't think he knows the answer to *this* one!"

"The strong man type represented by our friend Priam, Lieutenant," said Ellery, "doesn't pass out at the sight of a few hundred frogs, even when they're strewn all over his bed. His reaction was *too* violent. Of course he knows the answer. And it scares the wadding out of him."

Keats shook his head. "What do we do now?"

"What did you find out?"

"Not a thing."

"No sign of a point of entry?"

"No. But what sign would there be?. You come from the suspicious East, Mr. Queen. This is the great West, where men are men and nobody locks his door but Easterners." Keats rolled a tattered cigaret to the other side of his mouth. "Not even," he said bitterly, "taxpayers who are on somebody's knock-off list." He jumped up with a frustrated energy. "The trouble is, this Priam won't face the facts. Poison him, and he looks thoughtful. Toss a couple hundred dead frogs around his bedroom and he shakes his head doubtfully. You know what I think? I think everybody in this house, present company excepted, is squirrel food."

But Ellery was walking a tight circle, squinting toward some hidden horizon. "All right, he got in without any trouble—simply by walking in. Presumably in the middle of the night. Priam's door isn't locked at night so that Wallace or the others can get at him in an emergency, consequently he enters Priam's room with equal facility. So there he is, with a bag or a suitcase full of murdered frogs. Priam is asleep—not dead, mind you, just asleep. But he might just as well have been dead, because his visitor distributed two or three hundred frogs about the premises—in the dark, mind you—without disturbing Priam in the least. Any answers, Lieutenant?"

"Yes," said Keats wearily. "Priam polished off a bottle last night. He *was* dead—dead to the world."

Ellery shrugged and resumed his pacing. "Which takes us back to the frogs. A cardboard box containing . . . we don't know what; that's warning number one. Food poisoning . . . that's warning number two. Warning number three . . . a zoo colony of dead frogs. One, unknown; two, poisoned food; three, strangled frogs. It certainly would help to know number one."

"Suppose it was a fried coconut," suggested Keats. "Would it help?"

"There's a connection, Lieutenant. A pattern."

"I'm listening."

"You don't just pick frogs out of your hat. Frogs *mean* something."

"Yeah," said Keats, "warts." But his laugh was unconvincing. "Okay, so they mean something. So this *all* means something. I don't give a damn what it means. I said, what kind of maniac is this Priam? Does he *want* to shove off? Without putting up a battle?"

"He's putting up a battle, Lieutenant," frowned Ellery. "In his peculiar way, a brave one. To ask for help, even to accept help without asking for it would be defeat for Priam. Don't you understand that? He has to be top man. He has to control his own destiny. He *has* to, or his life has no meaning. Remember, Keats, he's a man who's living his life away in a chair. You say he's asleep now?"

"With Wallace guarding him. I offered a cop, and I nearly got beaned with the *Examiner*. It was all I could do to make Priam promise he'd keep his doors locked from now on. At that, he didn't promise."

"How about that background stuff? On the partners?"

The detective crushed the stained butt in his fist and flipped it in the fireplace. "It's like pulling teeth," he said slowly. "I don't get it. I put two more men on it yesterday." He snapped a fresh cigaret into his mouth. "The way I see it, Mr. Queen, we're doing this like a couple of country constables. We've got to go right to the horse's mouth. Priam's got to talk. He knows the whole story, every answer. Who his enemy is. Why the guy's nursed a grudge for so many years. Why the fancy stuff—"

"And what was in the box," murmured Ellery.

"Correct. I promised Dr. Voluta I'd lay off Priam today." Keats clapped his hat on his head. "But tomorrow I think I'm going to get tough."

When the detective had left, Ellery wandered out into the hall. The house was moody with silence. Crowe Macgowan had gone loping over to the Hill house to tell Laurel all about the amphibian invasion. The door to Priam's quarters was shut.

There was no sign or sound of Delia. She was going to her room to lock herself in, she had said, and lie down. She had seemed to have no further interest in her husband's condition. She had looked quite ill.

Ellery turned disconsolately to go, but then—or perhaps he was looking for an excuse to linger—he remembered the library, and he went back up the hall to the doorway opposite Priam's.

Delia's father sat at the library desk intently examining a postage stamp for its watermark.

"Oh, Mr. Collier."

The old man looked up. Immediately he rose, smiling. "Come in, come in, Mr. Queen. Everything all right now?"

"Well," said Ellery, "the frogs are no longer with us."

Collier shook his head. "Man's inhumanity to everything. You'd think we'd restrict our murderous impulses to our own kind. But no, somebody had to take his misery out on some harmless little specimens of *Hyla regilla*, not to mention—"

"Of what?" asked Ellery.

"*Hyla regilla*. Tree toads, Mr. Queen, or tree frogs. That's what most of those little fellows were." He brightened. "Well, let's not talk about that any more. Although why a grown man like Roger Priam should be afraid of them —with their necks wrung, too!—I simply don't understand."

"Mr. Collier," said Ellery quietly, "have you any idea what this is all about?"

"Oh, yes," said the old man. "I'll tell you what this is all about, Mr. Queen." He waved his stamp tongs earnestly. "It's about corruption and wickedness. It's about greed and selfishness and guilt and violence and hatred and lack of self-control. It's about black secrets and black hearts, cruelty, confusion, fear. It's about not making the best of things, not being satisfied with what you have, and always wanting what you haven't. It's about envy and suspicion and malice and lust and nosiness and drunkenness and unholy excitement and a thirst for hot running blood. It's about man, Mr. Queen."

"Thank you," said Ellery humbly, and he went home.

And the next morning Lieutenant Keats of the Hollywood Division put on his tough suit and went at Roger Priam as if the fate of the city of Los Angeles hung on Priam's answers. And nothing happened except that Keats lost his temper and used some expressions not recommended in the police manual and had to retreat under a counterattack of even harder words, not to mention objects, which flew at him and Ellery like mortar fire. Priam quite stripped his wheelchair of its accessories in his furious search for ammunition.

Overnight the bearded man had bounced back. Perhaps not all the way: his eyes looked shaft-sunken and he had a case of the trembles. But the old fires were in the depths and the shaking affected only his aim, not his strength—he made a bloodless shambles of his quarters.

Keats had tried everything in ascending order—reason, cajolery, jokes, appeals to personal pride and social responsibility, derision, sarcasm, threats, curses, and finally sheer volume of sound. Nothing moved Priam but the threats and curses, and then he responded in kind. Even the detective, who was left livid with fury, had to admit that he had been out-threatened, out-cursed, and out-shouted.

Through it all Alfred Wallace stood impeccably by his employer's wheelchair, a slight smile on his lips. Mr. Wallace, too, had ricocheted. It occurred to Ellery that in Wallace's make-up there was a great deal of old Collier's *Hyla regilla*—a chameleon quality, changing color to suit his immediate background. Yesterday Priam had been unnerved, Wallace had been unnerved. Today Priam was strong, Wallace was strong. It was a minor puzzle, but it annoyed him.

Then Ellery saw that he might be wrong and that the phenomenon might have a different explanation altogether. As he crossed the threshold to the echo of Priam's last blast, with Wallace already shutting the door, Ellery glimpsed for one second a grotesquely different Priam. No belligerent now. No man of wrath. His beard had fallen to his chest. He was holding on to the arms of his wheelchair as if for the reassurance of contact with reality. And his eyes were tightly closed. Ellery saw his lips moving; and if the thought had not been blasphemous, Ellery would have said Priam was praying. Then Wallace slammed the door.

"That was all right, Keats." Ellery was staring at the door. "That got somewhere."

"Where?" snarled the detective. "You heard him. He wouldn't say what was in the cardboard box, he wouldn't say who's after him, he wouldn't say why—he wouldn't say anything but that he'll handle this thing himself and let the blanking so-and-so come get him if he's man enough. So where did we get, Mr. Queen?"

"Closer to the crackup."

"What crackup?"

"Priam's. Keats, all that was the bellowing of a frightened steer in the dark. He's even more demoralized than I thought. He played a big scene just now for our benefit—a very good one, considering the turmoil he's in.

"Maybe one more, Keats," murmured Ellery. "One more."

Chapter VIII

LAUREL SAID THE frogs were very important. The enemy had slipped. So many hundreds of the warty beasts must have left a trail. All they had to do was pick it up.

"What trail? Pick it up where?" demanded Macgowan.

"Mac, where would you go if you wanted some frogs?"

"I wouldn't want some frogs."

"To a pet shop, of course!"

The giant looked genuinely admiring. "Why can't I think of things like that?" he complained. "To a pet shop let us go."

But as the day wore on young Macgowan lost his air of levity. He began to look stubborn. And when even Laurel was ready to give up, Macgowan jeered, "Chicken!" and drove on to the next shop on their list. As there are a great many pet emporia in Greater Los Angeles, and as Greater Los Angeles includes one hundred towns and thirty-six incorporated cities, from Burbank north to Long Beach south and Santa Monica west to Monrovia east, it became apparent by the end of an endless day that the detective team of Hill and Macgowan had assigned themselves an investigation worthy of their high purpose, if not their talents.

"At this rate we'll be at it till Christmas," said Laurel in despair as they munched De Luxe Steerburgers at a drive-in in Beverly Hills.

"You can give up," growled Crowe, reaching for his Double-Dip Giant Malted. "Me, I'm not letting a couple of hundred frogs throw me. I'll go it alone tomorrow."

"I'm not giving up," snapped Laurel. "I was only going to say that we've gone at this like the couple of amateurs we are. Let's divide the list and split up tomorrow. That way we'll cover twice the territory in the same time."

"Functional idea," grunted the giant. "Now how about getting something to eat? I know a good steak joint not far from here where the wine is on the house."

Early next morning they parceled the remaining territory and set out in separate cars, having arranged to meet at 6:30 in the parking lot next to Grauman's Chinese. At 6:30 they met and compared notes while Hollywood honked its homeward way in every direction.

Macgowan's notes were dismal. "Not a damn lead, and I've still got a list as long as your face. How about you?"

"One bite," said Laurel gloomily. "I played a hunch and went over to a place in Encino. They even carry zoo animals. A man in Tarzana had ordered frogs. I tore over there and it turned out to be some movie star who'd bought two dozen—he called them 'jug-o'-rums'—for his rock pool. All I got out of it was an autograph, which I didn't ask for, and a date, which I turned down."

"What's his name?" snarled Crowe.

"Oh, come off it and let's go over to Ellery's. As long as we're in the neighborhood."

"What for?"

"Maybe he'll have a suggestion."

"Let's see what the Master has to say, hey?" hissed her assistant. "Well, I won't wash his feet!"

He leaned on his horn all the way to the foot of the hill.

When Laurel got out of her Austin, Crowe was already bashing Ellery's door.

"Open up, Queen! What do you lock yourself in for?"

"Mac?" came Ellery's voice.

"And Laurel," sang out Laurel.

"Just a minute."

When he unlocked the front door Ellery looked rumpled and heavy-eyed. "Been taking a nap, and Mrs. Williams must have gone. Come in. You two look like the shank end of a hard day."

"Brother," scowled Macgowan. "Is there a tall, cool drink in this oasis?"

"May I use your bathroom, Ellery?" Laurel started for the bedroom door, which was closed.

"I'm afraid it's in something of a mess, Laurel. Use the downstairs lavatory . . . Right over there, Mac. Help yourself."

When Laurel came back upstairs her helper was showing Ellery their lists. "We can't seem to get anywhere," Crowe was grumbling. "Two days and nothing to show for them."

"You've certainly covered a lot of territory," applauded Ellery. "There are the fixings, Laurel—"

"Oh, yes."

"You'd think it would be easy," the giant went on, waving his glass. "How many people buy frogs? Practically nobody. Hardly one of the pet shops even handles 'em. Canaries, yes. Finches, definitely. Parakeets, by the carload. Parakeets, macaws, dogs, cats, tropical fish, monkeys, turkeys, turtles, even snakes. And I know now where you can buy an elephant, cheap. But no frogs to speak of. And toads—they just look at you as if you were balmy."

"Where did we go wrong?" asked Laurel, perching on the arm of Crowe's chair.

"In not analyzing the problem before you dashed off. You're not dealing with an idiot. Yes, you could get frogs through the ordinary channels, but they'd be special orders, and special orders leave a trail. Our friend is not leaving any trails for your convenience. Did either of you think to call the State Fish and Game Commission?"

They stared.

"If you had," said Ellery with a smile, "you'd have learned that most of the little fellows we found in Priam's room are a small tree frog or tree toad— *Hyla regilla* is the scientific name—commonly called spring peepers, which are found in great numbers in this part of the country in streams and trees, especially in the foothills. You can even find bullfrogs here, though they're not native to this part of the country—they've all been introduced from the East. So if you wanted a lot of frogs and toads, and you didn't want to leave a trail, you'd go out hunting for them."

"Two whole days," groaned Macgowan. He gulped what was left in his glass.

"It's my fault, Mac," said Laurel miserably. But then she perked up. "Well, it's all experience. Next time we'll know better."

"Next time he won't use frogs!"

"Mac." Ellery was tapping his teeth with the bit of his pipe. "I've been thinking about your grandfather."

"Is that good?" Mac immediately looked bellicose.

"Interesting man."

"You said it. And a swell egg. Keeps pretty much to himself, but that's because he doesn't want to get in anybody's way."

"How long has he been living with you people?"

"A few years. He knocked around all his life and when he got too old for it he came back to live with Delia. Why this interest in my grandfather?"

"Is he very much attached to your mother?"

"Well, I'll put it this way," said Crowe, squinting through his empty glass. "If Delia was God, Gramp would go to church. He's gone on her and she's the only reason he stays in Roger's vicinity. And I'm not gone on these questions," said Crowe, looking at Ellery, "so let's talk about somebody else, shall we?"

"Don't you like your grandfather, Mac?"

"I love him! Will you change the subject?"

"He collects stamps," Ellery went on reflectively. "And he's just taken to hunting and mounting butterflies. A man of Mr. Collier's age, who has no business or profession and takes up hobbies, Mac, usually doesn't stop at one or two. What other interests has he?"

Crowe set his glass down with a smack. "Damned if I'm going to say another word about him. Laurel, you coming?"

"Why the heat, Mac?" asked Ellery mildly.

"Why the questions about Gramp!"

"Because all I do is sit here and think, and my thoughts have been covering a lot of territory. Mac, I'm feeling around."

"Feel in some other direction!"

"No," said Ellery, "you feel in all directions. That's the first lesson you learn in this business. Your grandfather knew the scientific name of those spring peepers. It suggests that he may have gone into the subject. So I'd like to know: In those long tramps he takes in the foothill woods, has he been collecting tree frogs?"

Macgowan had gone rather pale and his handsome face looked pained and baffled. "I don't know."

"He has a rabbit hutch somewhere near the house, Mac," said Laurel in a low voice. "We could look."

"We could, but we're not going to! *I'm* not going to! What do you think I am?" His fists were whistling over their heads. "Anyway, suppose he did? It's a free country, and you said yourself there's lots of these peepers around!"

"True, true," Ellery soothed him. "Have another drink. I've fallen in love with the old gent myself. Oh, by the way, Laurel."

"Do I brace myself?" murmured Laurel.

"Well," grinned Ellery, "I'll admit my thoughts have sauntered in your direction too, Laurel. The first day you came to me you said you were Leander Hill's daughter by adoption."

"Yes."

"And you said something about not remembering your mother. Don't you know anything at all about your real parents, where you came from?"

"No."

"I'm sorry if this distresses you—"

"You know what you are?" yelled Macgowan from the sideboard. "You're equally divided between a bottom and a nose!"

"It doesn't distress me, Ellery," said Laurel with a rather unsuccessful smile. "I don't know a thing about where I came from. I was one of those storybook babies—really left on a doorstep. Of course, Daddy had no right to keep me—a bachelor and all. But he hired a reliable woman and kept me for about a year before he even reported me. Then he had a lot of trouble. They took me away from him and there was a long court squabble. But in the end they couldn't find out a thing about me, nobody claimed me, and he won out in court and was allowed to make it a legal adoption. I don't remember any of that, of course. He tried for years afterwards to trace my parents, because he was always afraid somebody would pop up and want me back and he wanted to settle the matter once and for all. But," Laurel made a face, "he never got anywhere and nobody ever did pop up."

Ellery nodded. "The reason I asked, Laurel, was that it occurred to me that this whole business . . . the circumstances surrounding your foster father's death, the threats to Roger Priam . . . may somehow tie in with your past."

Laurel stared.

"Now there," said Macgowan, "there is a triumph of the detectival science. How would that be, Chief? Elucidate."

"I toss it into the pot for what it's worth," shrugged Ellery, "admitting as I toss that it's probably worth little or nothing. But Laurel," he said, "whether that's a cockeyed theory or not, your past may enter this problem.

In another way. I've been a little bothered by *you* in this thing. Your drive to get to the bottom of this, your wanting revenge—"

"What's wrong with that?" Laurel sounded sharp.

"What's wrong with it is that it doesn't seem altogether normal. No, wait, Laurel. The drive is overintense, the wish for revenge almost neurotic. I don't get the feeling that it's like you—like the you I think you are."

"I never lost my father before."

"Of course, but—"

"You don't know me." Laurel laughed.

"No, I don't." Ellery tamped his pipe absently. "But one possible explanation is that the underlying motivation of your drive is not revenge on a murderer at all, but the desire to find yourself. It could be that you're nursing a subconscious hope that finding this killer will somehow clear up the mystery of your own background."

"I never thought of that." Laurel cupped her chin and was silent for some time. Then she shook her head. "No, I don't think so. I'd like to find out who I am, where I came from, what kind of people and all that, but it wouldn't mean very much to me. They'd be strangers and the background would be . . . not home. No, I loved him as if he were my father. He *was* my father. And I want to see the one who drove him into that fatal heart attack get paid back for it."

When they had gone, Ellery opened his bedroom door and said, "All right, Delia."

"I thought they'd never go."

"I'm afraid it was my fault. I kept them."

"You wanted to punish me for hiding."

"Maybe." He waited.

"I like it here," she said slowly, looking around at the pedestrian blond furniture.

She was seated on his bed, hands gripping the spread. She had not taken her hat off, or her gloves.

She must have sat that way all during the time they were in the other room, Ellery thought. Hanging in midair. Like her probable excuse for leaving the Priam house. A visit somewhere in town. Among the people who wore hats and gloves.

"Why do you feel you have to hide, Delia?"

"It's not so messy that way. No explanations to give. No lies to make up. No scenes. I hate scenes." She seemed much more interested in the house than in him. "A man who lives alone. I can hardly imagine it."

"Why did you come again?"

"I don't know. I just wanted to." She laughed. "You don't sound any more hospitable this time than you did the last. I'm not very quick, but I'm beginning to think you don't like me."

He said brutally, "When did you get the idea that I did?"

"Oh, the first couple of times we met."

"That was barnyard stuff, Delia. You make every man feel like a rooster."

"And what's your attitude now?" She laughed again. "That you don't feel like a rooster any more?"

"I'll be glad to answer that question, Delia, in the living room."

Her head came up sharply.

"You don't have to answer any questions," she said. She got up and strolled past him. "In your living room or anywhere else." As he shut the bedroom door and turned to her, she said, "You really don't like me?" almost wistfully.

"I like you very much, Delia. That's why you mustn't come here."

"But you just said in there—"

"That was in there."

She nodded, but not as if she really understood. She went to his desk, ignoring the mirror above it, and picked up one of his pipes. She stroked it with her forefinger. He concentrated on her hands, the skin glowing under the sheer nylon gloves.

He made an effort. "Delia—"

"Aren't you ever lonely?" she murmured. "I think I die a little every day, just from loneliness. Nobody who talks to you really *talks*. It's just words. People listening to themselves. Women hate me, and men . . . At least when they talk to me!" She wheeled, crying, "Am I that stupid? You won't talk to me, either! Am I?"

He had to make the effort over again. It was even harder this time. But he said through his teeth, "Delia, I want you to go home."

"Why?"

"Just because you're lonely, and have a husband who's half-dead—in the wrong half—and because I'm not a skunk, Delia, and you're not a tramp. Those are the reasons, Delia, and if you stay here much longer I'm afraid I'll forget all four of them."

She hit him with the heel of her hand. The top of his head flew off and he felt his shoulderblades smack against the wall.

Through a momentary mist he saw her in the doorway.

"I'm sorry," she said in an agonized way. "You're a fool, but I'm sorry. I mean about coming here. I won't do it again."

Ellery watched her go down the hill. There was fog, and she disappeared in it.

That night he finished most of a bottle of Scotch, sitting at the picture window in the dark and fingering his jaw. The fog had come higher and there was nothing to see but a chaos. Nothing made sense.

But he felt purged, and safe, and wryly noble.

Chapter IX

JUNE TWENTY-NINTH was a Los Angeles special. The weather man reported a reading of ninety-one and the newspapers bragged that the city was having its warmest June twenty-ninth in forty-three years.

But Ellery, trudging down Hollywood Boulevard in a wool jacket, was hardly aware of the roasting desert heat. He was a man in a dream these days, a dream entirely filled with the pieces of the Hill-Priam problem. So far it was a meaningless dream in which he mentally chased cubist things about a crazy landscape. In that dimension temperature did not exist except on the thermometer of frustration.

Keats had phoned to say that he was ready with the results of his investigation into the past of Hill and Priam. Well, it was about time.

Ellery turned south into Wilcox, passing the post office.

You could drift about in your head for just so long recognizing nothing. There came a point at which you had to find a compass and a legible map or go mad.

This ought to be it.

He found Keats tormenting a cigaret, the knot of his tie on his sternum and his sandy hair bristling.

"I thought you'd never get here."

"I walked down." Ellery took a chair, settling himself. "Well, let's have it."

"Where do you want it," asked the detective, "between the eyes?"

"What do you mean?" Ellery straightened.

"I mean," said Keats, plucking shreds of tobacco from his lips—"damn it, they pack cigarets looser all the time!—I mean we haven't got a crumb."

"A crumb of what?"

"Of information."

"You haven't found out *anything*?" Ellery was incredulous.

"Nothing before 1927, which is the year Hill and Priam went into business in Los Angeles. There's nothing that indicates they lived here before that year; in fact, there's reason to believe they didn't, that they came here that year from somewhere else. But from where? No data. We've tried everything from tax records to the Central Bureau fingerprint files. I'm pretty well convinced they had no criminal record, but that's only a guess. They certainly had no record in the State of California."

"They came here in '27," said Keats bitterly, "started a wholesale jewelry business as partners, and made a fortune before the crash of '29. They weren't committed to the market and they rode out the depression by smart manipulation and original merchandising methods. Today the firm of Hill & Priam is rated one of the big outfits in its line. They're said to own one of the largest stocks of precious stones in the United States. And that's a lot of help, isn't it?"

"But you don't come into the wholesale jewelry business from outer space," protested Ellery. "Isn't there a record somewhere of previous connections in the industry? At least of one of them?"

"The N.J.A. records don't show anything before 1927."

"Well, have you tried this? Certainly Hill, at least, had to go abroad once in a while in connection with the firm's foreign offices—Laurel told me they have branches in Amsterdam and South Africa. That means a passport, a birth certificate—"

"That was my ace in the hole." Keats snapped a fresh cigaret to his lips. "But it turns out that Hill & Priam don't own those branches, although they do own the one in New York. They're simply working arrangements with established firms abroad. They have large investments in those firms, but all their business dealings have been, and still are, negotiated by and through agents. There's no evidence that either Hill or Priam stepped off American soil in twenty-three years, or at least during the twenty-three years we have a record of them." He shrugged. "They opened the New York branch early in 1929, and for a few years Priam took care of it personally. But it was only to get it going and train a staff. He left it in charge of a man who's still running it there, and came back here. Then Priam met and married Delia Collier Macgowan, and the next thing that happened to him was the paralysis. Hill did the transcontinental hopping for the firm after that."

"Priam's never had occasion to produce a birth certificate?"

"No, and in his condition there's no likelihood he ever will. He's never voted, for instance, and while he might be challenged to prove his American citizenship—to force him to loosen up about his place of birth and so on—I'm afraid that would take a long, long time. Too long for this merry-go-round."

"The war—"

"Both Priam and Hill were over the military age limit when World War II conscription began. They never had to register. Search of the records on World War I failed to turn up their names."

"You're beginning to irritate me, Lieutenant. Didn't Leander Hill carry any insurance?"

"None that antedated 1927, and in the photostats connected with what insurance he did take out after that date his place of birth appears as Chicago. I've had the Illinois records checked, and there's none of a Leander Hill; it was a phony. Priam carries no insurance at all. The industrial insurance carried by the firm, of course, is no help.

"In other words, Mr. Queen," said Lieutenant Keats, "there's every indication that both men deliberately avoided leaving, or camouflaged, the trail to their lives preceding their appearance in L.A. It all adds up to one thing—"

"That there was no Leander Hill or Roger Priam in existence before 1927," muttered Ellery. "Hill and Priam weren't their real names."

"That's it."

Ellery got up and went to the window. Through the glass, darkly, he saw the old landscape again.

"Lieutenant." He turned suddenly. "Did you check Roger Priam's paralysis?"

Keats smiled. "Got quite a file on that if you want to read a lot of medical mumbo jumbo. The sources are some of the biggest specialists in the United States. But if you want it in plain American shorthand, his condition is on the level and it's hopeless. By the way, they were never able to get anything out of Priam about his previous medical history, if that's what you had in mind."

"You're disgustingly thorough, Keats. I wish I could find the heart to congratulate you. Now tell me you couldn't find anything on Alfred Wallace and I'll crown you."

Keats picked up an inkstand and offered it to Ellery. "Start crowning."

"Nothing on Wallace *either?*"

"That's right." Keats spat little dry sprigs of tobacco. "All I could dig up about Mr. Alfred W. dates from the day Priam hired him, just over a year ago."

"Why, that can't be!" exploded Ellery. "Not three in the same case."

"He's not an Angeleno, I'm pretty well convinced of that. But I can't tell you what he *is*. I'm still working on it."

"But . . . it's such a short time ago, Keats!"

"I know," said Keats, showing his teeth without dropping the cigaret, "you wish you were back in New York among the boys in the big league. Just the same, there's something screwy about Wallace, too. And I thought, Mr. Queen, having so little to cheer you up with today, I'd cut out the fancy stuff and try a smash through the center of the line. I haven't talked to Wallace. How about doing it now?"

"You've got him here?" exclaimed Ellery.

"Waiting in the next room. Just a polite invitation to come down to the station here and have a chat. He didn't seem to mind—said it was his day off anyway. I've got one of the boys keeping him from getting bored."

Ellery pulled a chair into a shadowed corner of the office and snapped, "Produce."

Alfred Wallace came in with a smile, the immaculate man unaffected by the Fahrenheit woes of lesser mortals. His white hair had a foaming wave to it; he carried a debonair slouch hat; there was a small purple aster in his lapel.

"Mr. Queen," said Wallace pleasantly. "So you're the reason Lieutenant Keats has kept me waiting over an hour."

"I'm afraid so." Ellery did not rise.

But Keats was polite. "Sorry about that, Mr. Wallace. Here, have this chair . . . But you can't always time yourself in a murder investigation."

"You mean what *may* be a murder investigation, Lieutenant," said Wallace, seating himself, crossing his legs, and setting his hat precisely on his knee. "Or has something new come up?"

"Something new could come up, Mr. Wallace, if you'll answer a few questions."

"Me?" Wallace raised his handsome brows. "Is that why you've placed this chair where the sun hits my face?" He seemed amused.

Keats silently pulled the cord of the Venetian blind.

"Thanks, Lieutenant. I'll be glad to answer any questions you ask. If, of course, I can."

"I don't think you'll have any trouble answering this one, Mr. Wallace: Where do you come from?"

"Ah." Wallace looked thoughtful. "Now that's just the kind of question, Lieutenant, I can't answer."

"You mean you won't answer."

"I mean I can't answer."

"You don't know where you come from, I suppose."

"Exactly."

"If that's going to be Mr. Wallace's attitude," said Ellery from his corner, "I think we can terminate the interview."

"You misunderstand me, Mr. Queen. I'm not being obstructive." Wallace sounded earnest. "I can't tell you gentlemen where I come from because I don't know myself. I'm one of those interesting cases you read about in the papers. An amnesia victim."

Keats glanced at Ellery. Then he rose. "Okay, Wallace. That's all."

"But that's not all, Lieutenant. This isn't something I can't prove. In fact, now that you've brought it up, I insist on proving it. You're making a recording of this, of course? I would like this to go into the record."

Keats waved his hand. His eyes were intent and a little admiring.

"One day about a year and a half ago—the exact date was January the sixteenth of last year—I found myself in Las Vegas, Nevada, on a street corner," said Alfred Wallace calmly. "I had no idea what my name was, where I came from, how I had got there. I was dressed in filthy clothing which didn't fit me and I was rather banged up. I looked through my pockets and found nothing—no wallet, no letters, no identification of any kind. There was no money, not even coins. I went up to a policeman and told him of the fix I was in, and he took me to a police station. They asked me questions and had a doctor in to examine me. The doctor's name was Dr. James V. Cutbill, and his address was 515 North Fifth Street, Las Vegas. Have you got that, Lieutenant?

"Dr. Cutbill said I was obviously a man of education and good background, about fifty years old or possibly older. He said it looked like amnesia to him. I was in perfect physical condition, and from my speech a North American. Unfortunately, Dr. Cutbill said, there were no identifying marks of any kind on my body and no operation scars, though he did say I'd had my tonsils and adenoids out probably as a child. This, of course, was no clue. There were some fillings in my teeth, of good quality, he thought, but I'd had no major dental work done. The police photographed me and sent my picture and a description to all Missing Persons Bureaus in the United States. There must be one on file in Los Angeles, Lieutenant Keats."

Keats grew fiery red. "I'll check that," he growled. "And lots more."

"I'm sure you will, Lieutenant," said Wallace with a smile. "The Las Vegas police fixed me up with some clean clothes and found me a job as a handyman in a motel, where I got my board and a place to sleep, and a few dollars a week. The name of the motel is the 711, on Route 91 just north of town. I worked there for about a month, saving my pay. The Las Vegas police told me no one of my description was listed as missing anywhere in the country. So I gave up the job and hitchhiked into California.

"In April of last year I found myself in Los Angeles. I stayed at the Y, the Downtown Branch on South Hope Street; I'm surprised you didn't run across my name on their register, Lieutenant, or haven't you tried to trace me? —and I got busy looking for employment. I'd found out I could operate a typewriter and knew shorthand, that I was good at figures—apparently I'd had business training of some sort as well as a rather extensive education— and when I saw an ad for a secretarial companion-nurse job to an incapaci- tated businessman, I answered it. I told Mr. Priam the whole story, just as I've told it to you. It seems he'd been having trouble keeping people in recent years and, after checking back on my story, he took me on for a month's trial. And here," said Wallace with the same smile, "here I am, still on the job."

"Priam took you on without references?" said Keats, doodling. "How des- perate was he?"

"As desperate as he could be, Lieutenant. And then Mr. Priam prides himself on being a judge of character. I was really glad of that, because to this day I'm not entirely sure what my character is."

Ellery lit a cigaret. Wallace watched the flame of the match critically. When Ellery blew the flame out, Wallace smiled again. But immediately Ellery said, "How did you come to take the name Alfred Wallace if you remembered nothing about your past? Or did you remember that?"

"No, it's just a name I plucked out of the ether, Mr. Queen. Alfred, Wallace—they're very ordinary names and more satisfying than John Doe. Lieutenant Keats, aren't you going to check my story?"

"It's going to be checked," Keats assured him. "And I'm sure we'll find it happened exactly as you've told it, Wallace—dates, names, and places. The only thing is, it's all a dodge. That's something I feel in my bones. As one old bone-feeler to another, Mr. Queen, how about it?"

"Did this doctor in Las Vegas put you under hypnosis?" Ellery asked the smiling man.

"Hypnosis? No, Mr. Queen. He was just a general practitioner."

"Have you seen any other doctor since? A psychiatrist, for example?"

"No, I haven't."

"Would you object to being examined by a psychiatrist of—let's say— Lieutenant Keats's choosing?"

"I'm afraid I would, Mr. Queen," murmured Wallace. "You see, I'm not sure I want to find out who I really am. I might discover, for example, that I'm an escaped thief, or that I have a bowlegged wife and five idiot children somewhere. I'm perfectly happy where I am. Of course, Roger Priam isn't the easiest employer in the world, but the job has its compensations. I'm living in royal quarters. The salary Priam pays me is very large—he's a generous employer, one of his few virtues. Old, fat Mrs. Guittierez is an excellent cook, and even though Muggs, the maid, is a straitlaced virgin with halitosis who's taken an unreasonable dislike to me, she does keep my room clean and polishes my shoes regularly. And the position even solves the problem of my sex life—oh, I shouldn't have mentioned that, should I?" Wallace looked distressed; he waved his muscular hand gently. "A slip of the tongue, gentlemen. I do hope you'll forget I said it."

Keats was on his feet. Ellery heard himself saying, "Wallace. Just what did you mean by that?"

"A gentleman, Mr. Queen, couldn't possibly have the bad taste to pursue such a question."

"A gentleman couldn't have made the statement in the first place. I ask you again, Wallace: How does your job with Priam take care of your sex life?"

Wallace looked pained. He glanced up at Keats. "Lieutenant, must I answer that question?"

Keats said slowly, "You don't have to answer anything. You brought this up, Wallace. Personally, I don't give a damn about your sex life unless it has something to do with this case. If it has, you'd better answer it."

"It hasn't, Lieutenant. How could it have?"

"I wouldn't know."

"Answer the question," said Ellery in a pleasant voice.

"Mr. Queen seems more interested than you, Lieutenant."

"Answer the question," said Ellery in a still pleasanter voice.

Wallace shrugged. "All right. But you'll bear witness, Lieutenant Keats, that I've tried my best to shield the lady in the case." He raised his eyes suddenly to Ellery and Ellery saw the smile in them, a wintry shimmer. "Mr. Queen, I have the great good luck to share my employer's wife's bed. As the spirit moves. And the flesh being weak, and Mrs. Priam being the most attractive piece I've yet seen in this glorious state, I must admit that the spirit moves several times a week and has been doing so for about a year. Does that answer your question?"

"Just a minute, Wallace," Ellery heard Keats say.

And Keats was standing before him, between him and Wallace. Keats was saying in a rapid whisper, "Queen, look, let me take it from here on in. Why don't you get out of here?"

"Why should I?" Ellery said clearly.

Keats did not move. But then he straightened up and stepped aside.

"You're lying, of course," Ellery said to Wallace. "You're counting on the fact that no decent man could ask a decent woman a question like that, and so your lie won't be exposed. I don't know what slimy purpose your lie serves, but I'm going to step on it right now. Keats, hand me that phone."

And all the time he was speaking Ellery knew it was true. He had known it was true the instant the words left Wallace's mouth. The story of the amnesia was true only so far as the superficial facts went; Wallace had prepared a blind alley for himself, using the Las Vegas police and a mediocre doctor to seal up the dead end. But this was all true. He knew it was all true and he could have throttled the man who sat halfway across the room smiling that iced smile.

"I don't see that that would accomplish anything," Keats was saying. "She'd only deny it. It wouldn't prove a thing."

"He's lying, Keats."

Wallace said with delicate mockery, "I'm happy to hear you take that attitude, Mr. Queen. Of course. I'm lying. May I go, Lieutenant?"

"No, Wallace." Keats stuck his jaw out. "I'm not letting it get this far without knowing the whole story. You say you've been cuckolding Priam for almost a year now. Is Delia Priam in love with you?"

"I don't think so," said Wallace. "I think it's the same thing with Delia that it is with me. A matter of convenience."

"But it stopped some time ago, didn't it?" Keats had a wink in his voice; man-to-man stuff. "It's not still going on."

"Certainly it's still going on. Why should it have stopped?"

Keats's shoulders bunched. "You must feel plenty proud of yourself, Wallace. Eating a man's food, guzzling his liquor, taking his dough, and sleeping with his wife while he's helpless in a wheelchair on the floor below. A cripple who couldn't give you what you rate even if he knew what was going on."

"Oh, didn't I make that clear, Lieutenant?" said Alfred Wallace, smiling. "Priam does know what's going on. In fact, looking back, I can see that he engineered the whole thing."

"What are you giving me!"

"You gentlemen apparently don't begin to understand the kind of man Priam is. And I think you ought to know the facts of life about Priam, since it's his life you're knocking yourselves out to save."

Wallace ran his thumb tenderly around the brim of his hat. "I don't deny that I didn't figure Priam right myself in the beginning, when Delia and I first got together. I sneaked it, naturally. But Delia laughed and told me not to be a fool, that Priam knew, that he wanted it that way. Although he'd never admit it or let on—to me, or to her.

"Well," said Wallace modestly. "Of course I thought she was kidding me. But then I began to notice things. Looks in his eye. The way he kept pushing us together. That sort of thing. So I did a little investigating on the quiet.

"I found out that in picking secretaries Priam had always hired particularly virile-looking men.

"And I remembered the questions he asked me when I applied for the job—how he kept looking me over, like a horse." Wallace took a cigar from his pocket and lit it. Puffing with enjoyment, he leaned back. "Frankly, I've been too embarrassed to put the question to Delia directly. But unless I'm mistaken, and I don't think I am, Priam's secretaries have always done double duty. Well, for the last ten years, anyway. It also explains the rapid turnover. Not every man is as virile as he looks," Wallace said with a laugh, "and then there are always some mushy-kneed lads who'd find a situation like that uncomfortable . . . But the fact remains. Priam's hired men to serve not only the master of the house, you might say, but the mistress too."

"Get him out of here," Ellery said to Keats. But to his surprise no words came out.

"Roger Priam," continued Alfred Wallace, waving his cigar, "is an exaggerated case of crudity, raw power, and frustration. The clue to his character—and, gentlemen, I've had ample opportunity to judge it—is his compulsive need to dominate everything and everyone around him. He tried to dominate old Leander Hill through the farce of pretending he, Roger Priam, was running a million-dollar business from a wheelchair at home. He tried to dominate Crowe Macgowan before Crowe got too big for him, according to Delia. And he's always dominated Delia, who doesn't care enough about anything to put up a scrap—dominated her physically until he became paralyzed, Delia's told me, with the most incredible vulgarities and brutalities.

"Now imagine," murmured Wallace, "what paralysis from the waist down did to Priam's need to dominate his woman. Physically he was no longer a man. And his wife was beautiful; to this day every male who meets her begins strutting like a bull. Priam knew, knowing Delia, that it was only a question of time before one of them made the grade. And then where would he be? He might not even know about it. It would be entirely out of his control. Unthinkable! So Priam worked out the solution in his warped way—to dominate Delia by proxy.

"By God, imagine that! He deliberately picks a virile man—the substitute for himself physically and psychologically—and flings them at each other's heads, letting nature take its course."

Wallace flicked an ash into the tray on Keats's desk. "I used to think he'd taken a leaf out of Faulkner's *Sanctuary*, or Krafft-Ebing, except that I've come to doubt if he's read a single book in forty-five years. No, Priam couldn't explain all this—to himself least of all. He's an ignorant man; he wouldn't even know the words. Like so many ignorant men, he's a man of pure action. He throws his wife and hand-picked secretary together, thus performing the function of a husband vicariously, and by pretending to be deaf to what goes on with domestic regularity over his head he retains his mastery of the situation. He's the god of the machine, gentlemen, and there is no other god but Roger Priam. That is, to Roger Priam." Wallace blew a fat ring of cigar smoke and rose. "And now, unless there's something else, Lieutenant, I'd like to salvage what's left of my day off."

Keats said in a loud voice, "Wallace, you're a fork-tongued female of a mucking liar. I don't believe one snicker of this dirty joke. And when I prove you're a liar, Wallace, I'm going to leave my badge home with my wife and kids, and I'm going to haul you into some dark alley, and I'm going to kick the — out of you."

Wallace's smile thinned. His face reassembled itself and looked suddenly old. He reached over Keats's desk and picked up the telephone.

"Here," he said, holding the phone out to the detective. "Or do you want me to get the number for you?"

"Scram."

"But you want proof. Delia will admit it if you ask her in the right way, Lieutenant. Delia's a very civilized woman."

"Get out."

Wallace laughed. He replaced the phone gently, adjusted his fashionable hat on his handsome head, and walked out humming.

Keats insisted on driving Ellery home. The detective drove slowly through the five o'clock traffic.

Neither man said anything.

He had seen them for that moment in the Priam hallway, the day he had come at her summons to investigate the plague of dead frogs. Wallace had been standing close to her, far closer than a man stands to a woman unless he knows he will not be repulsed. And she had not repulsed him. She had stood there accepting his pressure while Wallace squeezed her hand and whispered in her ear . . . He remembered one or two of Wallace's glances at her, the glances of a man with a secret knowledge, glances of amused power . . . "I always take the line of least resistance . . ." He remembered the night she had hidden herself in his bedroom at the sound of her son's and Laurel's arrival. She had come to him that night for the purpose to which her life in the Priam house had accustomed her. Probably she had a prurient curiosity about "celebrities" or she was tired of Wallace. (And this was Wallace's revenge?) He would have read the signs of the nymph easily enough if he had not mistaken her flabbiness for reserve—

"We're here, Mr. Queen," Keats was saying.

They were at the cottage.

"Oh. Thanks." Ellery got out automatically. "Good night."

Keats failed to drive away. Instead he said, "Isn't that your phone ringing?"

"Yes. Why doesn't Mrs. Williams answer it?" Ellery said with irritation. Then he laughed. "She isn't answering it because I gave her the afternoon off. I'd better go in."

"Wait." Keats turned his motor off and vaulted to the road. "Maybe it's my office. I told them I might be here."

Ellery unlocked the front door and went in. Keats straddled the threshold.
"Hello?"

Keats saw him stiffen.

"Yes, Delia."

Ellery listened in silence. Keats heard the vibration of the throaty tones, faint and warm and humid.

"Keats is with me now. Hide it till we get there, Delia. We'll be right over."

Ellery hung up.

"What does the lady want?" asked Keats.

"She says she's just found another cardboard box. It was in the Priam mailbox on the road, apparently left there a short time ago. Priam's name handprinted on it. She hasn't told Priam about it, asked what she ought to do. You heard what I told her."

"Another warning!"

Keats ran for his car.

Chapter X

KEATS STOPPED HIS car fifty feet from the Priam mailbox and they got out and walked slowly toward it, examining the road. There were tire marks in profusion, illegibly intermingled. Near the box they found several heelmarks of a woman's shoe, but that was all.

The door of the box hung open and the box was empty.

They walked up the driveway to the house. Keats neither rang nor knocked. The maid with the tic came hurring toward them as he closed the door.

"Mrs. Priam said to come upstairs," she whispered. "To her room." She glanced over her shoulder at the closed door of Roger Priam's den. "And not to make any noise, she said, because *he's* got ears like a dog."

"All right," said Keats.

Muggs fled on tiptoe. The two men stood there until she had disappeared beyond the swinging door at the rear of the hall. Then they went upstairs, hugging the balustrade.

As they reached the landing, a door opposite the head of the stairs swung in. Keats and Ellery went into the room.

Delia Priam shut the door swiftly and sank back against it.

She was in brief tight shorts and a strip of sun halter. Her thighs were long and heavy and swelled to her trunk; her breasts spilled over the halter. The glossy black hair lay carelessly piled; she was barefoot—her high-heeled shoes had been kicked off. The rattan blinds were down and in the gloom her pale eyes glowed sleepily.

Keats looked her over deliberately.

"Hello, Ellery." She sounded relieved.

"Hello, Delia." There was nothing in his voice, nothing at all.

"Don't you think you'd better put something on, Mrs. Priam?" said Keats. "Any other time this would be a privilege and a pleasure, but we're here on business." He grinned with his lips only. "I don't think I could think."

She glanced down at herself, startled. "I'm sorry, Lieutenant. I was up on the sun deck before I walked down to the road. I'm very sorry." She sounded angry and a little puzzled.

"No harm done, Delia," said Ellery. "This sort of thing is all in the eye of the beholder."

She glanced at him quickly. A frown appeared between her heavy brows. "Is something wrong, Ellery?"

He looked at her.

The color left her face. Her hands went to her naked shoulders and she hurried past them into a dressing room, slamming the door.

"Bitch," said Keats pleasantly. He took a cigaret out of his pocket and jammed it between his lips. The end tore and he spat it out, turning away.

Ellery looked around.

The room was overpowering, with dark Spanish furniture and wallpaper and drapes which flaunted masses of great tropical flowers. The rug was a sullen Polynesian red with a two-inch pile. There were cushions and hassocks of unusual shapes and colors. Huge majolicas stood about filled with lilies. On the wall hung heroic Gauguin reproductions and above the bed a large black iron crucifix that looked very old. Niches were crowded with ceramics, woodcarvings, metal sculptures of exotic subjects, chiefly modern in style and many of them male nudes. There was an odd bookshelf hanging by an iron chain, and Ellery strolled over to it, his legs brushing the bed. Thomas Aquinas, Kinsey, Bishop Berkeley, Pierre Loti, Havelock Ellis. *Lives of the Saints* and *Fanny Hill* in a Paris edition. The rest were mystery stories; there was one of his, his latest. The bed was a wide and herculean piece set low to the floor, covered with a cloth-of-gold spread appliquéd, in brilliant colors of metallic thread, with a vast tree of life. In the ceiling, directly above the bed and of identical dimensions, glittered a mirror framed in fluorescent tubing.

"For some reason," remarked Lieutenant Keats in the silence, "this reminds me of that movie actor, What's-His-Name, of the old silent days. In the wall next to his john he had a perforated roll of rabbit fur." The dressing room door opened and Keats said, "Now that's a relief, Mrs. Priam. Thanks a lot. Where's this box?"

She went to a trunk-sized teak chest covered with brasswork chased intricately in the East Indian manner, which stood at the foot of the bed, and she opened it. She had put on a severe brown linen dress and stockings as well as flat-heeled shoes; she had combed her hair back in a knot. She was pale and frigid, and she looked at neither man.

She took out of the chest a white cardboard box about five inches by nine and an inch deep, bound with ordinary white string, and handed it to Keats.

"Have you opened this, Mrs. Priam?"

"No."

"Then you don't know what's in it?"

"No."

"You found it exactly where and how, again?"

"In our mailbox near the road. I'd gone down to pick some flowers for the dinner table and I noticed it was open. I looked in and saw this. I took it upstairs, locked it in my chest, and phoned."

The box was of cheap quality. It bore no imprint. To the string was attached a plain Manila shipping tag. The name "Roger Priam" was lettered on the tag in black crayon, in carefully characterless capitals.

"Dime store stock," said Keats, tapping the box with a fingernail. He examined the tag. "And so is this."

"Delia." At the sound of his voice she turned, but when she saw his expression she looked away. "You saw the box your husband received the morning Hill got the dead dog. Was it like this? In quality, kind of string, tag?"

"Yes. The box was bigger, that's all." There was a torn edge to the furry voice.

"No dealer's imprint?"

"No."

"Does the lettering on this tag look anything like the lettering on the other tag?"

"It looks just like it." She put her hand on his arm suddenly, but she was looking at Keats. "Lieutenant, I'd like to speak to Mr. Queen privately for a minute."

"I don't have any secrets from Keats." Ellery was glancing down at his arm.

"Please?"

Keats walked over to one of the windows with the box. He lifted the blind, squinting along the slick surface of the box.

"Ellery, is it what happened the other night?" Her voice was at its throatiest, very low.

"Nothing happened the other night."

"Maybe that's the trouble." She laughed.

"But a great deal has happened since."

She stopped laughing. "What do you mean?"

He shrugged.

"Ellery. Who's been telling you lies about me?"

Ellery glanced again at her hand. "It's my experience, Delia, that to label something a lie before you've heard it expressed is to admit it's all too true."

He took her hand between his thumb and forefinger as if it were something sticky, and he dropped it.

Then he turned his back on her.

Keats had the box to his ear and he was shaking it with absorption. Something inside rustled slightly. He hefted the box.

"Nothing loose. Sounds like a solid object wrapped in tissue paper. And not much weight." He glanced at the woman. "I don't have any right to open this, Mrs. Priam. But there's nothing in the statutes to stop you . . . here and now."

"I wouldn't untie that string, Lieutenant Keats," said Delia Priam in a trembling voice, "for all the filth in your mind."

"What did I do?" Keats raised his reddish brows as he handed the box to Ellery. "That puts it up to you, Mr. Queen. What do you want to do?"

"You can both get out of my bedroom!"

Ellery said, "I'll open it, Keats, but not here. And not now. I think this ought to be opened before Roger Priam, with Mrs. Priam there, and Laurel Hill, too."

"You can get along without me," she whispered. "Get out."

"It's important for you to be there," Ellery said to her.

"You can't tell me what to do."

"In that case I'll have to ask the assistance of someone who can."

"No one can."

"Not Wallace?" smiled Ellery. "Or one of his numerous predecessors?"

Delia Priam sank to the chest, staring.

"Come on, Keats. We've wasted enough time in this stud pasture."

Laurel was over in ten minutes, looking intensely curious. Padding after her into the cavelike gloom of the house came the man of the future. Young Macgowan had returned to the Post-Atomic Age.

"What's the matter now?" he inquired plaintively.

No one replied.

By a sort of instinct, he put a long arm about his mother and kissed her. Delia smiled up at him anxiously, and when he straightened she kept her grasp on his big hand. Macgowan seemed puzzled by the atmosphere. He fixed on Keats as the cause, and he glared murderously from the detective to the unopened box.

"Loosen up, boy," said Keats. "Tree life is getting you. Okay, Mr. Queen?"

"Yes."

Young Macgowan didn't know. Laurel knew—Laurel had known for a long time—but Delia's son was wrapped in the lamb's wool of mother-adoration. I'd hate to be the first one, Ellery thought, to tell him.

As for Laurel, she had glanced once at Delia and once at Ellery, and she had become mousy.

Ellery waited on the threshold to the hall as Keats explained about the box.

"It's the same kind of tag, same kind of crayon lettering, as on the dead dog," Laurel said. She eyed the box grimly. "What's inside?"

"We're going to find that out right now." Ellery took the box from Keats and they all followed him up the hall to Priam's door.

"Furl your mains'l," said a voice. It was old Mr. Collier, in the doorway across the hall.

"Mr. Collier. Would you care to join us? There's something new."

"I'll sit up in the rigging," said Delia's father. "Hasn't there been enough trouble?"

"We're trying to prevent trouble," said Keats mildly.

"So you go looking for it. Doesn't make sense to me," said the old man, shaking his head. "Live and let live. Or die and let die. If it's right one way, it's right the other." He stepped back and shut the library door emphatically.

Ellery tried Priam's door. It was locked. He rapped loudly.

"Who is it?" The bull voice sounded slurry.

Ellery said, "Delia, you answer him."

She nodded mechanically. "Roger, open the door, won't you?" She sounded passive, almost bored.

"Delia? What d'ye want?" They heard the trundling of his chair and some glassy sounds. "Damn this rug! I've told Alfred a dozen times to tack it down—" The door opened and he stared up at them. The shelf before him supported a decanter of whisky, a siphon, and a half empty glass. His eyes were bloodshot. "What's this?" he snarled at Ellery. "I thought I told you two to clear out of my house and stay out." His fierce eyes lighted on the box in Ellery's hand. They contracted, and he looked up and around. His glance passed over his wife and stepson as if they had not been there. It remained on Laurel's face for a moment with a hatred so concentrated that Crowe Macgowan made an unconscious growling sound. Laurel's lips tightened.

He put out one of his furry paws. "Give me the box."

"No, Mr. Priam."

"That tag's got my name on it. Give it to me!"

"I'm sorry, Mr. Priam."

He raised the purplish ensign of his rage, his eyes flaming. "You can't keep another man's property!"

"I have no intention of keeping it, Mr. Priam. I merely want to see what's inside. Won't you please back into the room so that we can come in and do this like civilized people?"

Ellery kept looking at him impassively. Priam glared back, but his hands went to the wheels of his chair. Grudgingly, they pushed backwards.

Keats shut the door very neatly. Then he put his back against it. He remained there, watching Priam.

Ellery began to untie the box.

He seemed in no hurry.

Priam's hands were still at the sides of his chair. He was sitting forward, giving his whole attention to the untying process. His beard rose and fell with his chest. The purple flag had come down, leaving a sort of gray emptiness, like a foggy sky.

Laurel was intent.

Young Macgowan kept shifting from foot to naked foot, uneasily.

Delia Priam stood perfectly still.

"Lieutenant," said Ellery suddenly, as he worked over the last knot, "what do you suppose we'll find in here?"

Keats said, "After those dead frogs I wouldn't stick my chin out." He kept looking at Priam.

"Do you have to take out the knots?" cried Crowe. "Open it!"

"Would anyone care to guess?"

"*Please.*" Laurel, begging.

"Mr. Priam?"

Priam never stirred. Only his lips moved, and the beard around them. But nothing came out.

Ellery whipped the lid off.

Roger Priam threw himself back, almost upsetting the chair. Then, conscious of their shock, he fumbled for the glass of whisky. He tilted his head, drinking, not taking his glance from the box.

All that had been exposed was a layer of white tissue.

"From the way you jumped, Mr. Priam," said Ellery conversationally, "anyone would think you expected a hungry rattler to pop out at you, or something equally live and disagreeable. What is it you're afraid of?"

Priam set the glass down with a bang. His knuckles were livid. "I ain't afraid," he spluttered. "Of anything!" His chest spread. "Stop needling me, you ——! Or I swear—"

He brought his arm up blindly. It struck the decanter and the decanter toppled from the shelf, smashing on the floor.

Ellery was holding the object high, stripped of its tissue wrapping. He held it by its edges, between his palms.

His own eyes were amazed, and Keats's.

Because there was nothing in what he was displaying to make a man cringe.

It was simply a wallet, a man's wallet of breast pocket size made of alligator leather, beautifully grained and dyed forest green. There were no hideous stains on it; it had no history; it was plainly brand-new. And highpriced; it was edged in gold. Ellery flipped it open. Its pockets were empty. There had been no note or card in the box.

"Let me see that," said Keats.

Nothing to make a man cower, or a woman grow pale.

"No initials," said Keats. "Nothing but the maker's name." He scratched his cheek, glancing at Priam again.

"What is it, Lieutenant?" asked Laurel.

"What is what, Miss Hill?"

"The maker's name."

"Leatherland, Inc., Hollywood, California."

Priam's beard had sunk to his chest.

Paler than Priam. For Delia Priam's eyes had flashed to their widest at sight of the wallet, all the color running out of her face. Then the lids had come down as if to shut out a ghost.

Shock. But the shock of what? Fear? Yes, there was fear, but fear followed the shock; it did not precede.

Suddenly Ellery knew what it was.

Recognition.

He mulled over this, baffled. It was a new wallet. She couldn't possibly have seen it before. Unless . . . For that matter, neither could Priam. Did it mean the same thing to both of them? Vaguely, he doubted this. Their reactions had thrown off different qualities. Lightning had struck both of them, but it was as if Priam were a meteorologist who understood the nature of the disaster, his wife an ignorant bystander who knew only that she had been stunned. I'm reading too much into this, Ellery thought. You can't judge the truth of anything from a look . . . It's useless to attempt to talk to her now . . . In an indefinable way he was glad. It was remarkable how easily passion was killed by a dirty fact. He felt nothing when he looked at her now, not even revulsion. The sickness in the pit of his stomach was for himself and his gullibility.

"Delia, where you going?"

She was walking out.

"Mother."

So Crowe had seen it, too. He ran after her, caught her at the door.

"What's the matter?"

She made an effort. "It's all too silly, darling. It's getting to be too much for me. A wallet! And such a handsome one, too. Probably a gift from someone who thinks it's Roger's birthday. Let me go, Crowe. I've got to see Mrs. Guittierez about dinner."

"Oh. Sure." Mac was relieved.

And Laurel . . .

"The only thing that would throw me," Keats was drawling, "I mean if I was in Mr. Priam's shoes—"

Laurel had been merely puzzled by the wallet.

"—is what the devil I'd be expected to do with it. Like a battleship getting a lawnmower."

Laurel had been merely puzzled by the wallet, but when she had glimpsed Delia's face her own had reflected shock. The shock of recognition. Again. But this was not recognition of the object per se. This was recognition of Delia's recognition. A chain reaction.

"When you stop and think of it, everything we know about these presents so far shows one thing in common—"

"In common?" said Ellery. "What would that be, Keats?"

"Arsenic, dead frogs, a wallet for a man who never leaves his house. They've all been so damned useless."

Ellery laughed. "There's a theory, Mr. Priam, that's in your power to affirm or deny. Was your first gift useless, too? The one in the first cardboard box?"

Priam did not lift his head.

"Mr. Priam. What was in that box?"

Priam gave no sign that he heard.

"What do these things mean?"

Priam did not reply.

"May we have this wallet for examination?" asked Keats.

Priam simply sat there.

"Seems to me I caught the flicker of one eyelash, Mr. Queen." Keats wrapped the wallet carefully in the tissue paper and tucked it back in the box. "I'll drop you off at your place and then take this down to the Lab."

They left Roger Priam in the same attitude of frozen chaos.

Keats drove slowly, handling the wheel with his forearms and peering ahead as if answers lay there. He was chewing on a cigaret, like a goat.

"Now I'm wrong about Priam," laughed Ellery. "Perfect score."

Keats ignored the addendum. "Wrong about Priam how?"

"I predicted he'd blow his top and spill over at warning number four. Instead of which he's gone underground. Let's hope it's only a temporary recession."

"You're sure this thing is a warning."

Ellery nodded absently.

"Me, I'm not," Keats complained. "I can't seem to get the feel of this case. It's like trying to catch guppies with your bare hands. Now the arsenic, that I could hold on to, even though I couldn't go anywhere with it. But all the rest of it . . ."

"You can't deny the existence of all the rest of it, Keats. The dead dog was real enough. The first box Priam got was real, and whatever was in it. There was nothing vapory about those dead frogs and toads, either. Or about the contents of this box. Or, for that matter," Ellery shrugged, "about the thing that started all this, the note to Hill."

"Oh, yes," growled the detective.

"Oh yes what?"

"The note. What do we know about it? Not a thing. It's not a note, it's a copy of a note. Or is it even that? That might be only what it *seems*. Maybe the whole business was dreamed up by Hill."

"The arsenic, froglets, and wallet weren't dreamed up by Hill," said Ellery dryly, "not in the light of his current condition and location. No, Keats, you're falling for the temptation to be a reasonable man. You're not dealing with a reasonable thing. It's a fantasy, and it calls for faith." He stared ahead. "There's something that links these four 'warnings,' as the composer of the note calls them, links them in a series. They constitute a group."

"How?" Bits of tobacco flew. "Poisoned food, dead frogs, a seventy-five dollar wallet! And God knows what was in that first box to Priam—judging by what followed, it might have been a size three Hopalong Cassidy suit, or a bock beer calendar of the year 1897. Mr. Queen, you *can't* connect those things. They're not connectable." Keats waved his arms, and the car swerved. "The most I can see in this is that each one stands on its own feet. The arsenic? That means: Remember how you tried to poison *me?*—this is a little reminder. The frogs? That means . . . Well, you get the idea."

But Ellery shook his head. "If there's one thing in this case I'm sure of, it's that the warnings have related meanings. And the over-all meaning ties up with Priam's past and Hill's past and their enemy's past. What's more, Priam knows its significance, and it's killing him.

"What we've got to do, Lieutenant, is crack Priam, or the riddle, before it's too late."

"I'd like to crack Priam," remarked Keats. "On the nut."

They drove the rest of the way in silence.

Keats phoned just before midnight.

"I thought you'd like to know what the Lab found out from examination of the wallet and box."

"What?"

"Nothing. The only prints on the box were Mrs. Priam's. There were no prints on the wallet at all. Now I'm going home and see if I'm still married. How do you like California?"

Chapter XI

OUTSIDE HER GARAGE, Laurel looked around. Her look was furtive. He hadn't been in the walnut tree this morning, thank goodness, and there was no sign of him now. Laurel slipped into the garage, blinking as she came out of the sun, and ran to her Austin.

"Morning, Little Beaver."

"Mac! Damn you."

Crowe Macgowan came around the big Packard, grinning. "I had a hunch you had a little something under your armpit last night when you told me how late you were going to sleep this morning. Official business, hm?" He was dressed. Mac looked very well when he was dressed, almost as well as when he wasn't. He even wore a hat, a Swiss yodeler sort of thing with a little feather. "Shove over."

"I don't want you along today."

"Why not?"

"Mac, I just don't."

"You'll have to give me a better reason than that."

"You . . . don't take this seriously enough."

"I thought I was plenty serious on the frog safari."

"Well . . . Oh! all right. Get in."

Laurel drove the Austin down to Franklin and turned west, her chin northerly. Macgowan studied her profile in peace.

"La Brea to Third," he said, "and west on Third to Fairfax. Aye, aye, Skipper?"

"Mac! You've looked it up."

"There's only one Leatherland, Inc., of Hollywood, California, and it's in Farmers' Market."

"I wish you'd let me drop you!"

"Nothing doing. Suppose you found yourself in an opium den?"

"There are no opium dens around Fairfax and Third."

"Then maybe a gangster. All the gangsters are coming west, and you know how tourists flock to Farmers' Market."

Laurel said no more, but her heart felt soggy. Between her and the traffic hung a green alligator.

She parked in the area nearest Gilmore Stadium. Early as they were, the paved acres were jammed with cars.

"How are you going to work this?" asked Crowe, shortening his stride as she hurried along.

"There's nothing much to it. Their designs are exclusive, they make everything on the premises, and they have no other outlets. I'll simply ask to see some men's wallets, work my way around to alligator, then to green alligator—"

"And then what?" he asked dryly.

"Why . . . I'll find out who's bought one recently. They certainly can't sell many green alligator wallets with gold trimming. Mac, what's the idea? Let go!"

They were outside The Button Box. Leatherland, Inc., was nearby, a double-windowed shop with a ranchhouse and corral fence décor, bannered with multicolored hides and served by a bevy of well-developed cowgirls.

"And how are *you* going to get one of those babes to open up?" asked Crowe, keeping Laurel's arm twisted behind her back with his forefinger. "In the first place, they don't carry their customers' names around in their heads; they don't have that kind of head. In the second place, they're not going to go through their sales slips—for you, that is. In the third place, what's the matter with me?"

"I might have known."

"All I have to do is flash my genuine Red Ryder sheriff's badge, turn on the charm, and we're in. Laurel, I'm type-casting."

"Take off your clothes," said Laurel bitterly, "and you'll get more parts than you can handle."

"Watch me—fully dressed and lounging-like."

He went into the shop confidently.

Laurel pretended to be interested in a handtooled, silver-studded saddle in the window.

Although the shop was crowded, one of the cowgirls spotted Crowe immediately and cantered up to him. Everything bouncing, Laurel observed, hoping one of the falsies would slip down. But it was well-anchored, and she could see him admiring it. So could the cowgirl.

They engaged in a dimpled conversation for fully two minutes. Then they moved over to the rear of the shop. He pushed his hat back on his head the way they did in the movies and leaned one elbow on the showcase. The rodeo Venus began to show him wallets, bending and sunfishing like a bronc. This went on for some time, the sheriff's man leaning farther and farther over the case until he was practically breathing down her sternum. Suddenly he straightened, looked around, put his hand in his pocket, and withdrew it cupped about something. The range-type siren dilated her eyes . . .

When Crowe strolled out of the shop he passed Laurel with a wink.

She followed him, furious and relieved. The poor goop still didn't catch on, she thought. But then men never noticed anything but women; men like Mac, that is. She turned a corner and ran into his arms.

"Come to popsy," he grinned. "I've got all the dope."

"Are you sure that's all you've got?" Laurel coldly swept past him.

"And I thought you'd give me a gold star!"

"It's no make-up off my skin, but as your spiritual adviser—if you're lining up future mothers of the race for the radioactive new world, pick specimens who look as if they can climb a tree. You'd have to send that one up on a breeches buoy."

"What do you mean, is that all I've got? You saw me through the window. Could anything have been more antiseptic?"

"I saw you take down her phone number!"

"Shucks, gal. That was professional data. Here." He picked Laurel up, dropped her into the Austin, and got in beside her. "They made up a line of men's wallets in alligator leather last year, dyed three or four different colors. All the other colors sold but the green—they only unloaded three of those. Two of the three greens were bought before Christmas, almost seven months ago, as gifts. One by a Broadway actor to be sent to his agent back in New York, the other by a studio executive for some bigshot French producer—the shop mailed that one to Paris. The third and only other one they've sold is unaccounted for."

"It would be," said Laurel morosely, "seeing that that's the one we're interested in. How unaccounted for, Mac?"

"My cowgirl dug out the duplicate sales slip. It was a cash-and-carry and didn't have the purchaser's name on it."

"What was the date?"

"This year. But what month this year, or what day of what month this year, sales slip showeth not. The carbon slipped or something and the date was smudged."

"Well, didn't she remember what the purchaser looked like? That might tell us something."

"It wasn't my babe's customer, because the initials of the salesgirl on the slip were of someone else."

"Who? Didn't you find out?"

"Sure I found out."

"Then why didn't you speak to her? Or were you too wrapped up in Miss Falsies?"

"Miss who? Say, I thought those were too good to be true. I couldn't speak to the other gal. The other gal quit last week."

"Didn't you get her name and address?"

"I got her name, Lavis La Grange, but my babe says it wasn't Lavis's real name and she doesn't know what Lavis's real name is. Certainly not Lavis or La Grange. Her address is obsolete, because she decided she'd had enough of the glamorous Hollywood life and went back home. But when I asked my babe where Lavis's home is, she couldn't say. For all she knows it could be Labrador. And anyway, even if we could locate Lavis, my babe says she probably wouldn't remember. My babe says Lavis has the brain of a barley seed."

"So we can't even fix the buyer's sex," said Laurel bitterly. "Some man-hunters we are."

"What do we do now, report to the Master?"

"You report to the Master, Mac. What's there to report? He'll probably know all this before the day's out, anyway. I'm going home. You want me to drop you?"

"You've got more sex appeal. I'll stick with you."

Young Macgowan stuck with Laurel for the remainder of the day; technically, in fact, until the early hours of the next, for it was five minutes past two when she climbed down the rope ladder from the tree house to the floodlit clearing. He leaped after her and encircled her neck with his arm all the way to her front door.

"Sex fiends," he said cheerfully.

"You're doing all right," said Laurel, who felt black and blue; but then she put her mouth up to be kissed, and he kissed it, and that was a mistake because it took her another fifteen minutes to get rid of him.

Laurel waited behind the closed door ten minutes longer to be sure the coast was clear.

Then she slipped out of her house and down to the road.

She had her flashlight and the little automatic was in her coat pocket.

Just before she got to the Priam driveway she turned off into the woods. Here she stopped to put a handkerchief over the lens of her flash. Then, directing the feeble beam to the ground, she made her way toward the Priam house.

Laurel was not feeling adventurous. She was feeling sick. It was the sickness not of fear but of self-appraisal. How did the heroines of fiction do it? The answer was, she decided, that they were heroines of fiction. In real life when a girl had to let a man make love to her in order to steal a key from him she was nothing but a tramp. Less than a tramp, because a tramp got something out of her trampery—money, or an apartment, a few drinks, or even, although less likely, fun. It was a fairly forthright transaction. But she . . . she had had to pretend, all the while searching desperately for the key. The worst part of it was trying to dislike it. That damned Macgowan was so purely without guile and he made love so cheerfully—and he was such a darling—that the effort to hate him, it, and herself came off poorly. What a bitchy thing to do, Laurel moaned as her fingers tightened about the key in her pocket.

She stopped behind a French lilac bush. The house was dark. No light anywhere. She moved along the strip of lawn below the terrace.

Even then it wouldn't have been so nasty if it hadn't concerned his *mother*. How could Mac have lived with Delia all these years and remained blind to what she was? Why did Delia have to be *his* mother?

Laurel tried the front door carefully. It was locked, sure enough. She unlocked it with the key, silently thankful that the Priams kept no dogs. She closed the door just as carefully behind her. Wielding the handkerchief-covered flashlight for a moment, she oriented herself; then she snapped it off.

She crept upstairs close to the banisters.

On the landing she used the flash again. It was almost three o'clock. The four bedroom doors were closed. There was no sound either from this floor or the floor above, where the chauffeur slept. Mrs. Guittierez and Muggs occupied two servants' rooms off the kitchen downstairs.

Laurel tiptoed across the hall and put her ear against a door. Then, quickly and noiselessly, she opened the door and went into Delia Priam's bedroom. How co-operative of Delia to go up to Santa Barbara, where she was visiting "some old Montecito friends" for the weekend. The cloth-of-gold tree of life spread over the bed immaculately. In whose bed was she sleeping tonight?

Laurel hooked the flash to the belt of her coat and began to open dresser drawers. It was the weirdest thing, rummaging through Delia's things in the dead of night by the light of a sort of dark lantern. It didn't matter that you weren't there to take anything. What chiefly made a sneak thief was the technique. If Delia's father, or the unspeakable Alfred, were to surprise her now . . . Laurel held on to the thought of the leaden, blue-lipped face of Leander Hill.

It was not in the dresser. She went into Delia's clothes closet.

The scent Delia used was strong, and it mingled disagreeably with the chemical odor of mothproofing and the cedar lining of the walls. Delia's perfume had no name. It had been created exclusively for her by a British Colonial manufacturer, a business associate of Roger Priam's, after a two-week visit to the Priam house years before. Each Christmas thereafter Delia received a quart bottle of it from Bermuda. It was made from the essence of the passionflower. Laurel had once suggested sweetly to Delia that she name it *Prophetic*, but Delia had seemed not to think that very funny.

It was not in the closet. Laurel came out and shut the door, inhaling.

Had she been wrong after all? Maybe it was an illusion, built on the substructure of her loathing for Delia and that single, startling look on Delia's face as Ellery had held up the green wallet.

But suppose it wasn't an illusion. Then the fact that it wasn't where she would ordinarily have kept such a thing might be significant. Because Delia had hurried out of Roger's den immediately. She might have gone directly upstairs to her bedroom, taken it from among the others, and stowed it away where it was unlikely to be found. By Muggs, for instance.

Where might Delia have hidden it? All Laurel wanted was to see it, to verify its existence . . .

It was not in the brassbound teak chest at the foot of the bed. Laurel took everything out and then put everything back.

After conquering three temptations to give it up and go home and crawl into bed and pull the bedclothes of oblivion over her head, Laurel found it. It was in the clothes closet after all. But not, Laurel felt, in an honest place. It was wedged in the dolman sleeve of one of Delia's winter coats, a luxurious white duvetyn, which in turn was encased in a transparent plastic bag. Innocent and clever. Only a detective, Laurel thought, would have found it. Or another woman.

Laurel felt no triumph, just a shooting pain, like the entry of a hypodermic needle; and then a hardening of everything.

She had been right. She *had* seen Delia carrying one. Weeks before.

It was a woman's envelope bag of forest green alligator leather, with gold initials. The maker's name was Leatherland, Inc., of Hollywood, California.

A sort of Eve to the Adam of the wallet someone had sent to Roger Priam. A mate to the fourth warning.

"I suppose I should have told you yesterday," Laurel said to Ellery in the cottage on the hill, "that Mac and I were down to Farmers' Market on the trail of the green wallet. But we didn't find out anything, and anyway I knew you'd know about it."

"I've had a full report from Keats." Ellery looked at Laurel quizzically. "We had no trouble identifying Tree Boy from the salesgirl's description, and it stood to reason you'd put him up to it."

"Well, there's something else you don't know."

"The lifeblood of this business is information, Laurel. Is it very serious? You look depressed."

"Me?" Laurel laughed. "It's probably a result of confusion. I've found out something about somebody in this case that *could* mean . . ."

"Could mean what?" Ellery asked gravely, when she paused.

"That we've found the right one!" Laurel's eyes glittered. "But I can't quite put it into place. It seems to mean so much, only . . . Ellery, last night—really in the early hours of this morning—I did something dishonest and—and horrible. Since Roger was poisoned Alfred Wallace has been locking the doors at night. I stole a key from Mac and in the middle of the night I let myself in, sneaked upstairs—"

"And you went into Delia Priam's bedroom and searched it."

"How did you know!"

"Because I caught the look on your face day before yesterday when *you* saw the look on *Delia's* face. That man's alligator wallet meant something to her. She either recognized it or something about it reminded her directly of something like it. And her start of recognition produced some sort of recognition in you, too, Laurel. Delia left the room at once, and before we went away we made sure of where she'd gone. She'd gone right up to her bedroom.

"She left for Santa Barbara yesterday afternoon, and last night—while you were luring the key out of young Macgowan, probably—I pulled a second-story job and gave the bedroom a going-over. Keats, of course, couldn't risk it; the L.A. police have had to lean over backwards lately, and if Keats had been caught housebreaking there might have been a mess that would spoil everything. There wasn't enough, of course, to justify a warrant and an open search.

"I left Delia's alligator bag in the sleeve of the white coat, where I found it.

And where, I take it, you found it a few hours later. I hope you left everything exactly as it was."

"Yes," moaned Laurel. "But all that breast-beating for nothing."

Ellery lit a cigaret. "Now let me tell you something *you* don't know,
Laurel." His eyes, which had not laughed at all, became as smoky as his
cigaret. "That green alligator pocketbook of Delia's was a gift. She didn't
buy it herself. Luckily, the salesgirl who sold it remembered clearly what
the purchaser looked like, even though it was a cash sale. She gave an excellent and recognizable description, and when she was shown the correspond-
ing photograph she identified it as the man she had described. The purchase
was made in mid-April of this year, just before Delia's birthday, and the
purchaser was Alfred Wallace."

"Alfred—" Laurel was about to go on, but then her teeth closed on her
lower lip.

"It's all right, Laurel," said Ellery. "I know all about Delia and Alfred."

"I wasn't sure." Laurel was silent. Then she looked up. "What do you think
it means?"

"It could mean nothing at all," Ellery said slowly. "Coincidence, for example, although coincidence and I haven't been on speaking terms for years.
More likely whoever it is we're after may have noticed Delia's bag and,
consciously or unconsciously, it suggested to him the nature of the fourth
warning to Priam. Delia's suspicious actions can be plausibly explained, in
this interpretation, as the fear of an innocent person facing a disagreeable
involvement. Innocent people frequently act guiltier than guilty ones.

"It could mean that," said Ellery, "or . . ." He shrugged. "I'll have to
think about it."

Chapter XII

BUT ELLERY'S THOUGHTS were forced to take an unforeseen turn. In this he
was not unique. Suddenly something called the 38th Parallel, half a planet
away, had become the chief interest in the lives of a hundred and fifty million Americans.

Los Angeles particularly suffered a bad attack of the jitters.

A few days before, Koreans from the north had invaded South Korea with
Soviet tanks and great numbers of Soviet 7.63-millimeter submachine guns.
The explosive meaning of this act took some time to erupt the American
calm. But when United States occupation troops were rushed to South Korea
from Japan and were overwhelmed, and the newspapers began printing reports of American wounded murdered by the invaders, conviction burst. The
President made unpleasantly reminiscent announcements, reserves were being
called, the United Nations were in an uproar, beef and coffee prices soared,

THE ORIGIN OF EVIL

427

there were immediate rumors about sugar and soap scarcities, hoarding began, and everyone in Los Angeles was saying that World War III had commenced and that Los Angeles would be the first city on the North American continent to feel the incinerating breath of the atom bomb—and how do we know it won't be tonight? San Diego, San Francisco, and Seattle were not sleeping soundly, either, but that was no consolation to Los Angeles.

It was impossible to remain unaffected by the general nervousness. And, absurd as the thought was, there was always the possibility that it was only too well grounded.

The novel, which had been sputtering along, coughed and went into a nose dive. Ellery hounded the radio, trying to shut out the prophecies of doom which streaked up from his kitchen like flak in wailing Louisiana accents from eight to five daily. His thoughts kept coming back to Tree Boy. Crowe Macgowan no longer seemed funny.

He had not heard from Lieutenant Keats for days.

There was no word from the Priam establishment. He knew that Delia had returned from Montecito, but he had not seen or heard from her.

Laurel phoned once to seek, not give, information. She was worried about Macgowan.

"He just sits and broods, Ellery. You'd think with what's happening in Korea he'd be going around saying I told you so. Instead of which I can't get him to open his big mouth."

"The world of fantasy is catching up with Crowe, and it's probably a painful experience. There's nothing new at the Priams'?"

"It's quiet. Ellery, what do you suppose this lull means?"

"I don't know."

"I'm so confused these days!" Laurel's was something of a wail, too. "Sometimes I think what's going on in the world makes all this silly and unimportant. And I suppose in one way it is. But then I think, no, it's not silly and it is important. Aggressive war is murder, too, and you don't take that lying down. You have to fight it on every front, starting with the picayune personal ones. Or else you go down."

"Yes," said Ellery with a sigh, "that makes sense. I only wish this particular front weren't so . . . fluid, Laurel. You might say we've got a pretty good General Staff, and a bang-up army behind us, but our Intelligence is weak. We have no idea where and when the next attack is coming, in what form and strength—or the meaning of the enemy's strategy. All we can do is sit tight and keep on the alert."

Laurel said quickly, "Bless you," and she hung up quickly, too.

The enemy's next attack came during the night of July 6–7. It was, surprisingly, Crowe Macgowan who notified Ellery. His call came at a little after one in the morning, as Ellery was about to go to bed.

"Queen. Something screwy just happened. I thought you'd want to know." Macgowan sounded tired, not like himself at all.

"What, Mac?"

"The library's been broken into. One of the windows. Seems like a case of ordinary housebreaking, but I dunno."

"The *library*? Anything taken?"

"Not as far as I can see."

"Don't touch anything. I'll be over in ten minutes."

Ellery rang up Keats's home, got a sleepy "What, again?" from the detective, and ran.

He found young Macgowan waiting for him in the Priam driveway. There were lights on upstairs and down, but Roger Priam's French windows off the terrace were dark.

"Before you go in, maybe I'd better explain the setup . . ."

"Who's in there now?"

"Delia and Alfred."

"Go on. But make it snappy, Mac."

"Last couple of nights I've been sleeping in my old room here at the house—"

"What? No more tree?"

"You wanted it presto, didn't you?" growled the giant. "I hit the sack early tonight, but I couldn't seem to sleep. Long time later I heard sounds from downstairs. Seemed like the library; my room's right over it. I thought maybe it was Gramp and I felt a yen to talk to him. So I got up and went down the hall and at the top of the stairs I called, 'Gramp?' No answer, and it was quiet down there. Something made me go back up the hall and look in the old gent's room. He wasn't there; bed hadn't been slept in. So I went back to the head of the stairs and there was Wallace."

"Wallace?" repeated Ellery.

"In a robe. He said he'd heard a noise and was just going to go downstairs." Macgowan sounded odd; his eyes were hard in the moonlight. "But you know something, Queen? I got a queer feeling as I spotted Wallace at the head of those stairs. I couldn't make up my mind whether he was about to go down . . . or had just come up."

He stared at Ellery defiantly.

A car was tearing up the road.

Ellery said, "Life is full of these dangling participles, Mac. Did you find your grandfather?"

"No. Maybe I'd better take a look in the woods." Crowe sounded casual. "Gramp often takes a walk in the middle of the night. You know how it is when you're old."

"Yes." Ellery watched Delia's son stride off, pulling a flashlight from his pocket as he went.

Keats's car slammed to a stop a foot from Ellery's rear.

"Hi."

"What is it this time?" Keats had a leather jacket on over an undershirt, and he sounded sore.

Ellery told him, and they went in.

Delia Priam was going through the library desk, looking baffled. She was in a brown monkish negligee of some thick-napped material, girdled by a heavy brass chain. Her hair hung down her back and there were purplish shadows, almost welts, under her eyes. Alfred Wallace, in a Paisley dressing gown, was seated comfortably in a club chair, smoking a cigaret.

Delia turned, and Wallace rose, as the two men came into the library, but neither said anything.

Keats went directly to the only open window. He examined the sash about the catch without touching it.

"Jimmied. Have any of you touched this window?"

"I'm afraid," said Wallace, "we all did."

Keats mumbled something impolite and went out. A few moments later Ellery heard him outside, below the open window, and saw the beam of his flash.

Ellery looked around. It was the kind of library he liked; this was one room in which the prevailing Priam gloom was mellow. Leather shone, and the black oak paneling was a friendly background for the books. Books from floor to ceiling on all four walls, and a fieldstone fireplace with a used look. It was a spacious room, and the lamps were good.

"Nothing missing, Delia?"

She shook her head. "I can't understand it." She turned away, pulling her robe closer about her.

"Crowe and I probably scared him off." Alfred Wallace sat down again, exhaling smoke.

"Your father's stamp albums?" Ellery suggested to Delia's back. He had no idea why he thought of old Collier's treasures, except that they might be valuable.

"As far as I know, they haven't been touched."

Ellery wandered about the room.

"By the way, Crowe tells me Mr. Collier hasn't been to bed. Have you any idea where he is, Delia?"

"No." She wheeled on him, eyes flashing. "My father and I don't check up on each other. And I can't recall, Mr. Queen, that I ever gave you permission to call me by my first name. Suppose you stop it."

Ellery looked at her with a smile. After a moment she turned away again. Wallace continued to smoke.

Ellery resumed his ambling.

When Keats returned he said shortly, "There's nothing out there. Have you got anything?"

"I think so," said Ellery. He was squatting before the fireplace. "Look here." Delia Priam turned at that, and Wallace.

The fireplace grate held the remains of a wood fire. It had burned away to a fine ash. On the ashes lay a heat-crimped and badly charred object of no recognizable shape.

"Feel the ashes to the side, Keats."

"Stony cold."

"Now the ashes under that charred thing."

The detective snatched his hand away. "Still hot!"

Ellery said to Delia, "Was there a wood fire in this grate tonight . . . Mrs. Priam?"

"No. There was one in the morning, but it burned out by noon."

"This object was just burned here, Keats. On top of the cold ashes."

The lieutenant wrapped a handkerchief around his hand and cautiously removed the charred thing. He laid it on the hearth.

"What was it?"

"A book, Keats."

"Book?" Keats glanced around at the walls. "I wonder if—"

"Can't tell any more. Pages all burned away and what's left of the binding shows nothing."

"It must have been a special binding." Most of the volumes on the shelves were leatherbound. "Don't they stamp the titles into these fancy jobs?" Keats prodded the remains of the book, turning it over. "Ought to be some indication left."

"There would have been, except that whoever burned this indulged in a little vandalism before he set fire to it. Look at these slashes on the spine— and here. The book was mutilated with a sharp instrument before it was tossed into the grate."

Keats looked up at Delia and Wallace, who were stooping over them. "Any idea what this book was?"

"Damn you! Are you two here again?"

Roger Priam's wheelchair blocked the doorway. His hair and beard were threatening. His pajama coat gaped, exposing his simian chest; a button was missing, as if he had torn at himself in a temper. His chair was made up as a bed and the blankets trailed on the floor.

"Ain't nobody going to open his mouth? Man can't get any shut-eye in his own house! Alfred, where the hell have you been? Not in your room, because I couldn't get you on the intercom!" He did not glance at his wife.

"Something's happened down here, Mr. Priam," said Wallace soothingly.

"Happened! What now?"

Ellery and Keats were watching Priam closely. The library desk and a big chair stood between the wheelchair and the fireplace; Priam had not seen the burned book.

"Somebody broke into your library here tonight, Mr. Priam," rasped Keats, "and don't think I'm happy about it, because I'm as sick of you as you are of me. And if you're thinking of blasting me out again, forget it. Breaking and entering is against the law, and I'm the cop on the case. Now you're going to answer questions about this or, by God, I'll pull you in on a charge of obstructing a police investigation. Why was this book cut up and burned?"

Keats stalked across the room carrying the charred remains. He thrust the thing under Priam's nose.

"Book . . . burned?"

All his rage had fled, exposing the putty color beneath. Priam glared down at the twisted cinder in Keats's hand, pulling away a little.

"Do you recognize this?"

Priam's head shook.

"Can't you tell us what it is?"

"No." The word came out cracked. He seemed fascinated by the binding. Keats turned in disgust. "I guess he doesn't know at that. Well—"

"Just a moment, Lieutenant." Ellery was at the shelves, riffling through books. They were beautiful books, the products of private presses chiefly—handmade paper, lots of gold leaf, colored inks, elaborate endpaper designs, esoteric illustrations, specially designed type fonts; each was hand-bound and expensively hand-tooled. And the titles were impeccable, all the proper classics. The only thing was, after riffling through two dozen books, Ellery had still to find one in which the pages had been cut.

The books had never been read. It was likely, from their stiff pristine condition, that they had not been opened since leaving the hands of the bookbinder.

"How long have you had these books, Mr. Priam?"

"How long?" Priam licked his lips. "How long is it, Delia?"

"Since shortly after we were married."

"Library means books," Priam muttered, nodding. "Called in a fancy dealer and had him measure the running feet of shelf space and told him to go out and get enough books to fill the space. Highbrow stuff, I told him; only the best." He seemed to gain confidence through talking; a trace of arrogance livened his heavy voice. "When he lugged them around, I threw 'em back in his face. 'I said the best!' I told him. 'Take this junk back and have it bound up in the most expensive leather and stuff you can find. It's got to look the money or you don't get a plugged nickel.'"

Keats had dropped his impatience. He edged back.

"And a very good job he did, too," murmured Ellery. "I see they're in the original condition, Mr. Priam. Don't seem to have been opened, any of them."

"Opened! And crack those bindings? This collection is worth a fortune, Mister. I've had it appraised. Won't let *nobody* read 'em."

"But books are made to be read, Mr. Priam. Haven't you ever been curious about what's in these pages?"

"Ain't read a book since I played hooky from public school," retorted Priam. "Books are for women and longhairs. Newspapers, that's different. And picture magazines." His head jerked up with a belligerent reflex. "What are you getting at?"

"I'd like to spend about an hour here, Mr. Priam, looking over your collection. I give you my word, I'll handle your books with the greatest care. Would you have any objection to that?"

Cunning pinpointed Priam's eyes. "You're a book writer yourself, ain't you?"

"Yes."

"Ever write articles like in the Sunday magazine sections?"

"Occasionally."

"Maybe you got some idea about writing up an article on the Priam Book Collection. Hey?"

"You're a shrewd man, Mr. Priam," said Ellery with a smile.

"I don't mind," the bearded man said with geniality. There was color in his cheekbones again. "That bookdealer said no millionaire's library ought to be without its own special catalogue. 'It's too good a collection, Mr. Priam,' he says to me. 'There ought to be a record of it for the use of bib-bib-' "

"Bibliophiles?"

"That's it. Hell, it was little enough, and besides I figured it might come in handy for personal publicity in my jewelry business. So I told him to go ahead. You'll find a copy of the catalogue right there on that stand. Cost me a lot of money—specially designed, y' know, four-color job on special paper. And there's a lot of technical stuff in it, in the descriptions of the books. Words I can't even pronounce," Priam chuckled, "but, God Almighty, you don't have to be able to pronounce it if you can pay for it." He waved a hairy hand. "Don't mind at all, Mister—what was the name again?"

"Queen."

"You go right ahead, Queen."

"Very kind of you, Mr. Priam. By the way, have you added any books since your catalogue was made up?"

"Added any?" Priam stared. "I got all the good ones. What would I want with more? When d'ye want to do it?"

"No time like the present, I always say, Mr. Priam. The night is killed, anyway."

"Maybe tomorrow I'll change my mind, hey?" Priam showed his teeth again in what he meant to be a friendly grin. "That's all right, Queen. Shows you're no dope, even if you do write books. Go to it!" The grin faded as he turned his animal eyes on Wallace. "You push me back, Alfred. And better bunk downstairs for the rest of the night."

"Yes, Mr. Priam," said Alfred Wallace.

"Delia, what are you standing around for? Go back to bed."

"Yes, Roger."

The last they saw of Priam he was waving amiably as Wallace wheeled him across the hall. From his gesture it was apparent that he had talked himself out of his fears, if indeed he had not entirely forgotten their cause.

When the door across the hall had closed, Ellery said: "I hope you don't mind, Mrs. Priam. We've got to know which book this was."

"You think Roger's a fool, don't you?"

"Why don't you go to bed?"

"Don't ever make that mistake. Crowe!" Her voice softened. "Where've you been, darling? I was beginning to worry. Did you find your grandfather?"

Young Macgowan filled the doorway; he was grinning. "You'll never guess where." He yanked, and old Collier appeared. There was a smudge of chemical stain along his nose and he was smiling happily. "Down in the cellar."

"Cellar?"

"Gramp's fixed himself up a dark room, Mother. Gone into photography."

"I've been using your Contax all day, daughter. I hope you don't mind. I've got a great deal to learn," said Collier, shaking his head. "My pictures didn't come out very well. Hello there! Crowe tells me there's been more trouble."

"Have you been in the cellar all this time, Mr. Collier?" asked Lieutenant Keats.

"Since after supper."

"Didn't you hear anything? Somebody jimmied that window."

"That's what my grandson told me. No, I didn't hear anything, and if I had I'd probably have locked the cellar door and waited till it was all over! Daughter, you look all in. Don't let this get you down."

"I'll survive, Father."

"You come on up to bed. Good night, gentlemen." The old man went away.

"Crowe." Delia's face set. "Mr. Queen and Lieutenant Keats are going to be working in the library for a while. I think perhaps you'd better stay . . . too."

"Sure, sure," said Mac. He stooped and kissed her. She went out without a glance at either of the older men. Macgowan shut the door after her. "What's the matter?" he asked Ellery in a plaintive tone. "Don't you two get along any more? What's happened?"

"If you must keep an eye on us, Mac," snapped Ellery, "do it from that chair in the corner, where you'll be out of the way. Keats, let's get going."

The "Priam collection" was a bibliographic monstrosity, but Ellery was in a scientific, not an esthetic, mood and his methodology had nothing to do with art or even morals; he simply had the Hollywood detective read off the titles on Priam's shelves and he checked them against the gold-crusted catalogue.

It took them the better part of two hours, during which Crowe Macgowan fell asleep in the leather chair.

When at last Keats stopped, Ellery said: "Hold it," and he began to thumb back along the pages of the catalogue.

"Well?" said Keats.

"You failed to read just one title." Ellery set the catalogue down and picked up the charred corpse of the book. "This used to be an octavo volume bound in laminated oak, with handblocked silk endpapers, of *The Birds*, by Aristophanes."

"The what, by whom?"

"*The Birds*. A play by Aristophanes, the great satirical dramatist of the fifth century before Christ."

"I don't see the joke."

Ellery was silent.

"You mean to tell me," demanded the detective, "that the burning of this book by a playwright dead a couple of dozen centuries is another of these warnings?"

"It must be."

"How can it be?"

"Mutilated and burned, Keats. At least two of the four previous warnings also involved violence in some form: the food poisoning, the murder of the frogs . . ." Ellery sat up.

"What's the matter?"

"Frogs. Another play by Aristophanes has that exact title. *The Frogs.*" Keats looked pained.

"But that's almost certainly a coincidence. The other items wouldn't begin to fit . . . *The Birds.* An unknown what's-it, food poisoning, dead toads and frogs, an expensive wallet, and now a plushy edition of a Greek social satire first performed—unless I've forgotten my Classics II—in 414 B.C."

"And I'm out of cigarets," grunted Keats. Ellery tossed a pack over. "Thanks. You say there's a connection?"

" 'And for each pace forward a warning . . . a warning of special meaning for you—and for him,' " Ellery quoted. "That's what the note said. 'Meanings for pondering and puzzling.' "

"How right he was. I still say, Queen, if this stuff means anything at all, each one stands on its own tootsies."

" 'For each pace forward,' Keats. It's *going* somewhere. No, they're tied. The whole thing's a progression." Ellery shook his head. "I'm not even sure any more that Priam knows what they mean. This one tonight really balls things up. Priam is virtually an illiterate. How could he possibly know what's meant by the destruction of an old Greek play?"

"What's it about?"

"The play? Well . . . to the best of my recollection, two Athenians talk the Birds into building an aerial city, in order to separate the Gods from Man."

"That helps."

"What did Aristophanes call his city in the air? Cloud . . . Cloudland . . . Cloud-Cuckoo-Land."

"That's the first thing I've heard in this case that rings the bell." Keats got up in disgust and went to the window.

A long time passed. Keats stared out at the night, which was beginning to boil and show a froth. But the room was chilly, and he hunched his shoulders under the leather jacket. Young Macgowan snored innocently in the club chair. Ellery said nothing.

Ellery's silence lasted for so long that after a time Keats, whose brain was empty and wretched, became conscious of its duration. He turned around tiredly and there was a gaunt, unshaven, wild-eyed refugee from a saner world staring back at him with uninvited joy, grudgingly delirious, like a girl contemplating her first kiss.

"What in the hell," said the Hollywood detective in alarm, "is the matter with you?"

"Keats, they have something in common!"

"Sure. You've said that a dozen times."

"*Not one thing, but two.*"

Keats came over and took another of Ellery's cigarets. "What do you say we break this up? Go home, take a shower, and hit the hay." Then he said, "*What?*"

"Two things in common, Keats!" Ellery swallowed. His mouth was parched and there was a tuneful fatigue in his head, but he knew he had it, he had it at last

"You've *got* it?"

"I know what it means, Keats. I know."

"What? What?"

But Ellery was not listening. He fumbled for a cigaret without looking.

Keats struck a match for him and then, absently, held it to his own cigaret; he went to the window again, inhaling, filling his lungs. The froth on the night had bubbled down, leaving a starchy mass, glimmering like soggy rice. Keats suddenly became aware of what he was doing. He looked startled, then desperate, then defiant. He smoked hungrily, waiting.

"Keats."

Keats whirled. "Yes?"

Ellery was on his feet. "The man who owned the dog. What were his name and address again?"

"Who?" Keats blinked.

"The owner of the dead dog, the one you have reason to believe was poisoned before it was left on Hill's doorstep. What was the owner's name? I've forgotten it."

"Henderson. Clybourn Avenue, in Toluca Lake."

"I'll have to see him as soon as I can. You going home?"

"But why—"

"You go on and get a couple of hours' sleep. Are you going to be at the station later this morning?"

"Yeah. But what—?"

But Ellery was walking out of Roger Priam's library with stiff short steps, a man in a dream.

Keats stared after him.

When he heard Ellery's Kaiser drive away, he put Ellery's pack of cigarets in his pocket and picked up the remains of the burned book.

Crowe Macgowan awoke with a snort.

"You still here? Where's Queen?" Macgowan yawned. "Did you find out anything?"

Keats held his smoldering butt to a fresh cigaret, puffing recklessly. "I'll send you a telegram," he said bitterly, and he went away.

Sleep was impossible. He tossed for a while, not even hopefully.

At a little after six Ellery was downstairs in his kitchen, brewing coffee.

He drank three cups, staring into the mists over Hollywood. A dirty gray world with the sun struggling through. In a short time the mist would be gone and the sun would shine clear.

The thing was sharply brilliant. All he had to do was get rid of the mist.

What he would see in that white glare Ellery hardly dared anticipate. It was something monstrous, and in its monstrous way beautiful; that, he could make out dimly.

But first there was the problem of the mist.

He went back upstairs, shaved, took a shower, changed into fresh clothing, and then he left the cottage and got into his car.

Chapter XIII

IT WAS ALMOST eight o'clock when Ellery pulled up before a small stucco house tinted cobalt blue on Clybourn Avenue off Riverside Drive.

A handcolored wooden cutout resembling Dopey, the Walt Disney dwarf, was stuck into the lawn on a stake, and on it a flowery artist had lettered the name HENDERSON.

The uniformly closed Venetian blinds did not look promising.

As Ellery went up the walk a woman's voice said, "If you're lookin' for Henderson, he's not home."

A stout woman in an orange wrapper was leaning far over the railing of her red cement stoop next door, groping with ringed fingers for something hidden in a violet patch.

"Do you know where I can reach him?"

Something swooshed, and six sprinklers sent up watery bouquets over the woman's lawn. She straightened, red-faced and triumphant.

"You can't," she said, panting. "Henderson's a picture actor. He's being a pirate mascot on location around Catalina or somewhere. He expected a few weeks' work. You a press agent?"

"Heaven forbid," muttered Ellery. "Did you know Mr. Henderson's dog?"

"His dog? Sure I knew him. Frank, his name was. Always tearin' up my lawn and chasin' moths through my pansy beds—though don't go thinkin'," the fat woman added hastily, "that I had anything to do with poisonin' Frank, because I just can't abide people who do things like that to animals, even the destroyin' kind. Henderson was all broke up about it."

"What kind of dog was Frank?" Ellery asked.

"Kind?"

"Breed."

"Well . . . he wasn't very big. Nor so little, neither, when you stop to think of it—"

"You don't know his breed?"

"I think some kind of a hunting dog. Are you from the Humane Society or the Anti-Vivisection League? I'm against experimentin' with animals myself, like the *Examiner's* always sayin'. If the good Lord—"

"You can't tell me, Madam, what kind of hunting dog Frank was?"

"Well . . ."

"English setter? Irish? Gordon? Llewellyn? Chesapeake? Weimaraner?"

"I just guess," said the woman cheerfully, "I don't know."

"What color was he?"

"Well, now, sort of brown and white. No, black. Come to think of it, not really white, neither. More creamy, like."

"More creamy, like. Thank you," said Ellery. And he got into his car and moved fifty feet, just far enough to be out of his informant's range.

After thinking for a few minutes, he drove off again.

He cut through Pass and Olive, past the Warner Brothers studio, into Barham Boulevard to the Freeway. Emerging through the North Highland exit into Hollywood, he found a parking space on McCadden Place and hurried around the corner to the Plover Bookshop.

It was still closed.

He could not help feeling that this was inconsiderate of the Plover Bookshop. Wandering up Hollywood Boulevard disconsolately, he found himself opposite Coffee Dan's. This reminded him vaguely of his stomach, and he crossed over and went in for breakfast. Someone had left a newspaper on the counter and as he ate he read it conscientiously. When he paid his check, the cashier said, "What's the news from Korea this morning?" and he had to answer stupidly, "Just about the same," because he could not remember a word he had read.

Plover was open!

He ran in and seized the arm of a clerk. "Quick," he said fiercely. "A book on dogs."

"Book on dogs," said the clerk. "Any particular kind of book on dogs, Mr. Queen?"

"Hunting dogs! With illustrations! In color!"

Plover did not fail him. He emerged carrying a fat book and a charge slip for seven and a half dollars, plus tax.

He drove up into the hills rashly and caught Laurel Hill a moment after she stepped into her stall shower.

"Go away," Laurel said, her voice sounding muffled. "I'm naked."

"Turn that water off and come out here!"

"Why, Ellery."

"Oh . . . ! I'm not the least bit interested in your nakedness—"

"Thanks. Did you ever say that to Delia Priam?"

"Cover your precious hide with this! I'll be in the bedroom." Ellery tossed a bath towel over the shower door and hurried out. Laurel kept him waiting five minutes. When she came out of the bathroom she was swaddled in a red, white, and blue robe of terry cloth.

"I didn't know you cared. But next time would you mind at least knocking? Gads, look at my hair—"

"Yes, yes," said Ellery. "Now Laurel, I want you to project yourself back to the morning when you and your father stood outside your front door and looked at the body of the dead dog. Do you remember that morning?"

"I think so," said Laurel steadily.

"Can you see that dog right now?"

"Every hair of him."

"Hold on to him!" Ellery yanked her by the arm and she squealed, grabbing at the front of her robe. She found herself staring down at her bed. Upon it, open to an illustration in color of a springer spaniel, lay a large book. "Was he a dog like this?"

"N-no . . ."

"Go through the book page by page. When you come to Henderson's pooch, or a reasonable facsimile thereof, indicate same in an unmistakable manner."

Laurel looked at him suspiciously. It was too early in the morning for him to have killed a bottle, and he was shaved and pressed, so it wasn't the tag end of a large night. Unless . . .

"Ellery!" she screamed. "You've found out something!"

"Start looking," hissed Ellery viciously; at least it sounded vicious to his ears, but Laurel only looked overjoyed and began to turn pages like mad.

"Easy, easy," he cried. "You may skip it."

"I'll find your old hound." Pages flew like locust petals in a May wind. "Here he is—"

"Ah."

Ellery took the book.

The illustration showed a small, almost dumpy, dog with short legs, pendulous ears, and a wiry upcurving tail. The coat was smooth. Hindlegs and forequarters were an off-white, as was the muzzle; the little dog had a black saddle and black ears with secondary pigmentation of yellowish brown extending into his tail.

The caption under the illustration said: *Beagle*.

"Beagle." Ellery glared. "Beagle . . . Of course. Of *course*. No other possibility. None whatever. If I'd had the brain of a wood louse . . . Beagle, Laurel, beagle!" And he swept her off her feet and planted five kisses on top of her wet head. Then he tossed her on her unmade bed and before her horrified eyes went into a fast tap—an accomplishment which was one of his most sacred secrets, unknown even to his father. And Ellery chanted, "*Merci*, my pretty one, my she-detective. You have follow ze clue of ze ar-sen-ique, of ze little frog, of ze wallette, of ze everysing but ze sing you know all ze time—zat is to say, ze beagle. Oh, ze beagle!" And he changed to a soft-shoe.

"But what's the breed of dog got to do with anything, Ellery?" moaned Laurel. "The only connection I can see with the word 'beagle' is its slang meaning. Isn't a 'beagle' a detective?"

"Ironic, isn't it?" chortled Ellery; and he exited doing a Shuffle-Off-to-Buffalo, blowing farewell kisses and almost breaking the prominent nose of Mrs. Monk, Laurel's housekeeper, who had it pressed in absolute terror to the bedroom door.

Twenty minutes later Ellery was closeted with Lieutenant Keats at the Hollywood Division. Those who passed the closed door heard the murmur of the Queen voice, punctuated by a weird series of sounds bearing no resemblance to Keats's usual tones.

The conference lasted well over an hour.

When the door opened, a suffering man appeared. Keats looked as if he had just picked himself up from the floor after a kick in the groin. He kept shaking his head and muttering to himself. Ellery followed him briskly. They vanished in the office of Keats's chief.

An hour and a half later they emerged. Keats now looked convalescent, even robust.

"I still don't believe it," he said, "but what the hell, we're living in a funny world."

"How long do you think it will take, Keats?"

"Now that we know what to look for, not more than a few days. What are you going to do in the meantime?"

"Sleep and wait for the next one."

"By that time," grinned the detective, "maybe we'll have a pretty good line on this inmate."

They shook hands solemnly and parted, Ellery to go home to bed and Keats to set the machinery of the Los Angeles police department going on a twenty-four hour a day inquiry into a situation over twenty years old . . . this time with every prospect of success.

In three days not all the moldy threads were gathered in, but those they had been able to pick up by teletype and long distance phone tied snugly around what they already knew. Ellery and Keats were sitting about at the Hollywood Division trying to guess the lengths and textures of the missing ends when Keats's phone rang. He answered it to hear a tense voice.

"Lieutenant Keats, is Ellery Queen there?"

"It's Laurel Hill for you."

Ellery took the phone. "I've been neglecting you, Laurel. What's up?"

Laurel said with a rather hysterical giggle, "I've committed a crime."

"Serious?"

"What's the rap for lifting what doesn't belong to you?"

Ellery said sharply, "Something for Priam again?"

He heard a scuffle, then Crowe Macgowan's voice saying hastily, "Queen, she didn't swipe it. I did."

"He did not!" yelled Laurel. "I don't care, Mac! I'm sick and tired of hanging around not knowing—"

"*Is it for Roger Priam?*"

"It is," said Macgowan. "A pretty big package this time. It was left on top of the mailbox. Queen, I'm not giving Roger a hold over Laurel. I took it and that's that."

"Have you opened it, Mac?"

"No."

"Where are you?"

"Your house."

"Wait there and keep your hands off it." Ellery hung up. "Number six, Keats!"

They found Laurel and Macgowan in Ellery's living room, hovering hostilely over a package the size of a men's suit box, wrapped in strong Manila paper and bound with heavy string. The now-familiar shipping tag with Priam's name lettered on it in black crayon—the now-familiar lettering—was attached to the string. The package bore no stamps, or markings of any kind.

"Delivered in person again," said Keats. "Miss Hill, how did you come to get hold of this?"

"I've been watching for days. Nobody tells me anything, and I've got to do *something*. And, darn it, after hours and hours of hiding behind bushes I missed her after all."

"Her?" said Crowe Macgowan blankly.

"Well, her, or him, or whoever it is." Laurel turned old rose.

Crowe stared at her.

"Let's get technical," said Keats. "Go ahead and open it, Macgowan. Then we won't have to lie awake nights with a guilty conscience."

"Very humorous," mumbled Delia's son. He snapped the string and ripped off the wrapping in silence.

The box was without an imprint, white, and of poor quality. It bulged with its contents.

Mac removed the lid.

The box was crammed with printed documents in a great variety of sizes, shapes, and colored inks. Many were engraved on banknote paper.

"What the devil." Keats picked one out at random. "This is a stock certificate."

"So is this," said Ellery. "And this . . ." After a moment they stared at each other. "They all seem to be stock certificates."

"I don't get it." Keats worried his thumbnail. "This doesn't fit in with what you figured out, Queen. It couldn't."

Ellery frowned. "Laurel, Mac. Do these mean anything to you?"

Laurel shook her head, staring at a name on the certificate she had picked up. Now she put it down, slowly, and turned away.

"Why, this must represent a fortune," exclaimed Crowe. "Some warning!"

Ellery was looking at Laurel. "We'd better have a breakdown on the contents of this box, Keats, and then we can decide how to handle it.—Laurel, what's the matter?"

"Where you going?" demanded Macgowan.

Laurel turned at the door. "I'm sick of this. I'm sick of the whole thing, the waiting and looking and finding and doing absolutely nothing. If you and the lieutenant have anything, Ellery, what is it?"

"We're not through making a certain investigation, Laurel."

"Will you ever be?" She said it drearily. Then she went out, and a moment later they heard the Austin scramble away.

About seven o'clock that evening Ellery and Keats drove up to the Priam house in Keats's car, Ellery carrying the box of stock certificates. Crowe Macgowan was waiting for them at the front door.

"Where's Laurel, Mac? Didn't you get my phone message?" said Ellery.

"She's home." Crowe hesitated. "I don't know what's the matter with her. She's tossed off about eight Martinis and I couldn't do a thing with her. I've never seen Laurel act like that. She doesn't take a drink a week. I don't like it."

"Well, a girl's entitled to a bender once in a while," jeered Keats. "Your mother in?"

"Yes. I've told her. What did you find out?"

"Not much. The wrappings and box were a washout. Our friend likes gloves. Did you tell Priam?"

"I told him you two were coming over on something important. That's all."

Keats nodded, and they went to Roger Priam's quarters.

Priam was having his dinner. He was wielding a sharp blade and a fork on a thick rare steak. Alfred Wallace was broiling another on a portable barbecue. The steak was smothered with onions and mushrooms and barbecue sauce from several chafing dishes, and a bottle of red wine showed three-quarters empty on the tray. Priam ate in character: brutally, teeth tearing, powerful jaws crunching, eyes bulging with appetite, flecks of sauce on his agitated beard.

His wife, in a chair beside him, watched him silently, as one might watch a zoo animal at feeding time.

The entrance of the three men caught the meat-laden fork in midair. It hung there for a moment, then it completed its journey, but slowly, and Priam's jaws ground away mechanically. His eyes fixed and remained on the box in Ellery's hands.

"Sorry to interrupt your dinner, Mr. Priam," said Keats, "but we may as well have this one out now."

"The other steak, Alfred." Priam extended his plate. Wallace refilled it in silence. "What's this, now?"

"Warning number six, Mr. Priam," said Ellery.

Priam attacked his second steak.

"I see it's no use," he said in almost a friendly tone, "trying to get you two to keep your noses out of my business."

"I took it," said Crowe Macgowan abruptly. "It was left on the mailbox and I lifted it."

"Oh, you did." Priam inspected his stepson.

"I live here, too, you know. I'm getting pretty fed up with this and I want to see it cleaned out."

Priam hurled his plate at Crowe Macgowan's head. It hit the giant a glancing blow above the ear. He staggered, crashed back into the door. His face went yellow.

"*Crowe!*"

He brushed his mother aside. "Roger, if you ever do that again," he said in a low voice, "I'll kill you."

"Get out!" Priam's voice was a bellow.

"Not while Delia's here. If not for that I'd be in a uniform right now. God knows why she stays, but as long as she does, I do too. I don't owe you a thing, Roger. I pay my way in this dump. And I have a right to know what's going on . . . It's all right, Mother." Delia was dabbing at his bleeding ear with her handkerchief; her face was pinched and old-looking. "Just remember what I said, Roger. Don't do that again."

Wallace got down on his hands and knees and began to clean up the mess.

Priam's cheekbones were a violent purple. He had gathered himself in, bunched and knotted. His glare at young Macgowan was palpable.

"Mr. Priam," said Ellery pleasantly, "have you ever seen these stock certificates before?"

Ellery laid the box on the tray of the wheelchair. Priam looked at the mass of certificates for a long time without touching them—almost, Ellery would have said, without seeing them. But gradually awareness crept over his face and as it advanced it touched the purple like a chemical, leaving pallor behind.

Now he seized a stock certificate, another, another. His great hands began to scramble through the box, scattering its contents. Suddenly his hands fell and he looked at his wife.

"I remember these." And Priam added, with the most curious emphasis, "Don't you, Delia?"

The barb penetrated her armor. "I?"

"Look at 'em, Delia." His bass was vibrant with malice. "If you haven't seen them lately, here's your chance."

She approached his wheelchair reluctantly, aware of something unpleasant that was giving him a feeling of pleasure. If he felt fear at the nature of the sixth warning, he showed no further trace of it.

"Go ahead, Delia." He held out an engraved certificate. "It won't bite you."

"What are you up to now?" growled Crowe. He strode forward.

"You saw them earlier today, Macgowan," said Keats. Crowe stopped, uneasy. The detective was watching them all with a brightness of eye he had not displayed for some time . . . watching them all except Wallace, whom he seemed not to be noticing, and who was fussing with the barbecue as if he were alone in the room.

Delia Priam read stiffly, "Harvey Macgowan."

"Sure is," boomed her husband. "That's the name on the stock, Delia. Harvey Macgowan. Your old man, Crowe." He chuckled.

Macgowan looked foolish. "Mother, I didn't notice the name at all."

Delia Priam made an odd gesture. As if to silence him. "Are they all—?"

"Every one of them, Mrs. Priam," said Keats. "Do they mean anything to you?"

"They belonged to my first husband. I haven't seen these for . . . I don't know how many years."

"You inherited these stocks as part of Harvey Macgowan's estate?"

"Yes. If they're the same ones."

"They're the same ones, Mrs. Priam," Keats said dryly. "We've done a bit of checking with the old probate records. They were turned over to you at the settlement of your first husband's estate. Where have you kept them all these years?"

"They were in a box. Not this box . . . It's so long ago, I don't remember."

"But they were part of your effects? When you married Mr. Priam, you brought them along with you? Into this house?"

"I suppose so. I brought everything." She was having difficulty enunciating clearly. Roger Priam kept watching her lips, his own parted in a grin.

"Can't you remember exactly where you've kept these, Mrs. Priam? It's important."

"Probably in the storeroom in the attic. Or maybe among some trunks and boxes in the cellar."

"That's not very helpful."

"Stop badgering her, Keats," said young Macgowan. Because he was bewildered, his jaw stuck out. "Do you remember where you put your elementary school diploma?"

"Not quite the same thing," said the detective. "The face value of these stocks amounts to a little over a million dollars."

"That's nonsense," said Delia Priam with a flare of asperity. "These shares are worthless."

"Right, Mrs. Priam. I wasn't sure everybody knew. They're worth far less than the paper they're printed on. Every company that issued these shares is defunct."

"What's known on the stock market," said Roger Priam with every evidence of enjoyment, "as cats and dogs."

"My first husband sank almost everything he had in these pieces of paper," said Delia in a monotone. "He had a genius for investing in what he called 'good things' that always turned out the reverse. I didn't know about it until after Harvey died. I don't know why I've hung on to them."

"Why, to show 'em to your loving second husband, Delia," said Roger Priam, "right after we were married; remember? And remember I advised you to wallpaper little Crowe's little room with them as a reminder of his father? I gave them back to you and I haven't seen them again till just now."

"They've been somewhere in the house, I tell you! Where anyone could have found them!"

"And where someone did," said Ellery. "What do you make of it, Mr. Priam? It's another of these queer warnings you've been getting—in many ways the queerest. How do you explain it?"

"These cats and dogs?" Priam laughed. "I'll leave it to you, my friends, to figure it out."

There was contempt in his voice. He had either convinced himself that the whole fantastic series of events was meaningless, the work of a lunatic, or he had so mastered his fears of what he knew to be a reality that he was able to dissemble like a veteran actor. Priam had the actor's zest; and, shut up in a room for so many years, he may well have turned it into a stage, with himself the star performer.

"Okay," said Lieutenant Keats without rancor. "That seems to be that."

"Do you think so?"

The voice came from another part of the room.

Everyone turned.

Laurel Hill stood inside the screen door to Priam's terrace.

Her face was white, nostrils pinched. Her murky eyes were fixed on Delia Priam.

Laurel wore a suède jacket. Both hands were in the pockets.

"That's the end of that, is it?"

Laurel shoved away from the screen door. She teetered for an instant, regained her balance, then picked her way very carefully half the distance to Delia Priam, her hands still in her pockets.

"Laurel," began Crowe.

"Don't come near me, Mac. Delia, I have something to say to you."

"Yes?" said Delia Priam.

"When that green alligator wallet came, it reminded me of something. Something that belonged to you. I searched your bedroom while you were in Montecito and I found it. One of your bags—alligator, dyed green, and made by the same shop as the wallet. So I was sure you were behind all this, Delia."

"You'd better get her out of here," said Alfred Wallace suddenly. "She's tight."

"Shut up, Alfred." Roger Priam's voice was a soft rumble.

"Miss Hill," said Keats.

"No!" Laurel laughed, not taking her eyes from Delia. "I was sure you were behind it, Delia. But Ellery Queen didn't seem to think so. Of course, he's a great man, so I thought I must be wrong. But these stock certificates belong to you, Delia. You put them away. You knew where they were. You're the only one who could have sent them."

"Laurel," began Ellery, "that's not the least bit logical—"

"Don't come near me!" Her right hand came out of her pocket with an automatic.

Laurel pointed its snub nose at Delia Priam's heart.

Young Macgowan was gaping.

"But if you sent this 'warning'—whatever in your poisoned mind it's supposed to mean—you sent the others too, Delia. And they won't do anything about it. It's washed up, they say. Well, I've given them their chance, Delia. You'd have got away with it if only men were involved; your kind always does. But I'm not letting you get away with killing my father! You're going to pay for that right now, Delia!—right n . . ."

Ellery struck her arm as the gun went off and Keats caught it neatly as it flew through the air. Crowe made a choking sound, taking a step toward his mother. But Delia Priam had not moved. Roger Priam was looking down at his tray. The bullet had shattered the bottle of wine two inches from his hand.

"By God," snarled Priam, "she almost got me. Me!"

"That was a dumb-bunny stunt, Miss Hill," said Keats. "I'm going to have to take you in for attempted homicide."

Laurel was looking in a glazed way from the gun in the detective's hand to the immobile Delia. Ellery felt the girl shrinking in his grip, in spasms, as if she were trying to compress herself into the smallest possible space.

"I'm sorry, Mrs. Priam," Keats was saying. "I couldn't know she was carrying a gun. She never seemed the type. I'll have to ask you to come along and swear out a complaint."

"Don't be silly, Lieutenant."

"Huh?"

"I'm not making any charge against this girl."

"But Mrs. Priam, she shot to kill—"

"Me!" yelled Roger Priam.

"No, it's me she shot at." Delia Priam's voice was listless. "She's wrong, but I understand how you can bring yourself to do a thing like this when you've lost somebody you've loved. I wish I had Laurel's spunk. Crowe, stop looking like a dead carp. I hope you're not going to be stuffy about this and let Laurel down. It's probably taken her weeks to work herself up to this, and at that she had to get drunk to do it. She's a good girl, Crowe. She needs you. And I know you're in love with her."

Laurel's bones all seemed to melt at once. She sighed, and then she was silent.

"I think," murmured Ellery, "that the good girl has passed out."

Macgowan came to life. He snatched Laurel's limp figure from Ellery's arms, looked around wildly, and then ran with her. The door opened before him; Wallace stood there, smiling.

"She'll be all right." Delia Priam walked out of the room. "I'll take care of her."

They watched her go up the stairs behind her son, back straight, head high, hips swinging.

Chapter XIV

By THE NIGHT of July thirteenth all the reports were in.

"If I'm a detective," Keats said unhappily to Ellery, "then you've got second sight. I'm still not sure how you doped this without inside information."

Ellery laughed. "What time did you tell Priam and the others?"

"Eight o'clock."

"We've just got time for a congratulatory drink."

They were in Priam's house on the stroke of eight. Delia Priam was there, and her father, and Crowe Macgowan, and a silent and drained-looking Laurel. Roger Priam had evidently extended himself for the occasion; he had on a green velvet lounging jacket and a shirt with starched cuffs, and his beard and hair had been brushed. It was as if he suspected something out of the ordinary and was determined to meet it full-dress, in the baronial manner. Alfred Wallace hovered in the background, self-effacing and ineffaceable, with his constant mocking, slightly irritating smile.

"This is going to take a little time," said Lieutenant Keats, "but I don't think anybody's going to be bored . . . I'm just along for atmosphere. It's Queen's show."

He stepped back to the terraceward wall, in a position to watch their faces.

"Show? What kind of show?" There was fight in the Priam tones, his old hairtrigger belligerence.

"Showdown would be more like it, Mr. Priam," said Ellery.

Priam laughed. "When are you going to get it through your heads that you're wasting your time, not to mention mine? I didn't ask for your help, I don't want your help, I won't take your help—and I ain't giving any information."

"We're here, Mr. Priam, to give you information."

Priam stared. Of all of them, he was the only one who seemed under no strain except the strain of his own untempered arrogance. But there was curiosity in his small eyes.

"Is that so?"

"Mr. Priam, we know the whole story."

"What whole story?"

"We know your real name. We know Leander Hill's real name. We know where you and Hill came from before you went into business in Los Angeles in 1927, and what your activities were before you both settled in California. We know all that, Mr. Priam, and a great deal more. For instance, we know the name of the person whose life was mixed up with yours and Hill's before 1927—the one who's trying to kill you today."

The bearded man held on to the arms of his wheelchair. But he gave no other sign; his face was iron. Keats, watching from the sidelines, saw Delia Priam sit forward, as at an interesting play; saw the flicker of uneasiness in old Collier's eyes; the absorption of Macgowan; the unchanging smile on Wallace's lips. And he saw the color of life creep back in Laurel Hill's cheeks.

"I can even tell you," continued Ellery, "exactly what was in the box you received the morning Leander Hill got the gift of the dead dog."

Priam exclaimed, "That's bull! I burned that box and what was in it the same day I got it. Right in that fireplace there! Is the rest of your yarn going to be as big a bluff as this?"

"I'm not bluffing, Mr. Priam."

"You know what was in that box?"

"I know what was in that box."

"Out of the zillions of different things it could have been, you know the one thing it was, hey?" Priam grinned. "I like your nerve, Queen. You must be a good poker player. But that's a game I used to be pretty good at myself. So suppose I call you. What was it?"

He raised a glass of whisky to his mouth.

"Something that looked like a dead eel."

Had Ellery said, "Something that looked like a live unicorn," Priam could not have reacted more violently. He jerked against the tray and most of the whisky sprayed out on his beard. He spluttered, swiping at himself.

As far as Keats could see, the others were merely bewildered. Even Wallace dropped his smile, although he quickly picked it up and put it on again.

"I was convinced from practically the outset," Ellery went on, "that these 'warnings'—to use the language of the original note to Hill—were interconnected; separate but integral parts of an all-over pattern. And they are. The pattern is fantastic—for instance, even now I'm sure Lieutenant Keats still suspects what Hollywood calls a weenie. But fantastic or not, it exists; and the job I set myself was to figure out what it was. And now that I've figured it out, it doesn't seem fantastic at all. In fact, it's straightforward, even simple, and it certainly expresses a material enough meaning. The fantasy in this case, as in so many cases, lies in the mind that evolved the pattern, not in the pattern itself.

"As the warnings kept coming in, I kept trying to discover their common denominator, the cement that was holding them together. When you didn't know what to look for—unlike Mr. Priam, who did know what to look for—it was hard, because in some of them the binding agent was concealed.

"It struck me, after I'd gone over the warnings innumerable times," said Ellery, and he paused to light a cigaret, so that nothing in the room was audible but the scratch of the match and Roger Priam's heavy breathing, "it struck me finally that *every warning centrally involved an animal.*"

Laurel said, "What?"

"I'm not counting the dog used to bring the warning note to Hill. Since it conveyed a warning to Hill and not to you, Mr. Priam, we must consider the dead dog entirely apart from the warnings sent to you. Still, it's interesting to note in passing that Hill's series of warnings, which never got beyond the first, began with an animal, too.

"Omitting for the moment the contents of the first box you received, Mr. Priam," Ellery said, "let's see how the concept 'animal' derives from the warnings we had direct knowledge of. Your second warning was a poisoning attack, a non-fatal dose of arsenic. The animal? *Tuna fish,* the medium by which the poison was administered.

"The third warning? *Frogs and toads.*

"The fourth warning was one step removed from the concept—a wallet. But the wallet was leather, and the leather came from an *alligator.*

"There was no mistaking the animal in the fifth warning. The ancient Greek comedy by Aristophanes—*The Birds*.

"And the sixth warning, Mr. Priam—some worthless old stock certificates —would have given me a great deal of trouble if you hadn't suggested the connection yourself. There's a contemptuous phrase applied to such stocks by market traders, you said—'*cats and dogs*.' And you were quite right—that's what they're called.

"So . . . fish, frogs, alligator, birds, cats and dogs. The fish, frogs, and alligator suggested literally, the birds and the cats and dogs suggested by allusion. All animals. That was the astonishing fact. What did you say, Mr. Priam?"

But Priam had merely been bumbling in his beard.

"Now the fact that each of the five warnings I'd had personal contact with concealed, like a puzzle, a different animal—astonishing as it was—told me nothing," continued Ellery, throwing his cigaret into Priam's fireplace. "I realized after some skull work that the meaning must go far deeper. It had to be dug out.

"But digging out the deeper meaning was another story.

"You either see it or you don't. It's all there. There's nothing up its sleeve. The trick lies in the fact that, like all great mystifications, it wears the cloak of invisibility. I do not use the word 'great' loosely. It's just that—a great conception—and it wouldn't surprise me if it takes its place among the classic inventions of the criminal mind."

"For God's sake," burst out Crowe Macgowan, "talk something that makes sense!"

"Mac," said Ellery, "what are frogs and toads?"

"What are frogs and toads?"

"That's right. What kind of animals are they?"

Macgowan looked blank.

"Amphibians," said old Mr. Collier.

"Thank you, Mr. Collier. And what are alligators?"

"Alligators are reptiles."

"The wallet derived from a reptile. And to which family of animals do cats and dogs belong?"

"Mammals," said Delia's father.

"Now let's restate our data, still ignoring the first warning, of which none of us had firsthand knowledge but Mr. Priam. The second warning was *fish*. The third warning was *amphibians*. The fourth warning was *reptiles*. The fifth warning was *birds*. The sixth warning was *mammals*.

"Immediately we perceive a change in the appearance of the warnings. From being an apparently unrelated, rather silly conglomeration, they've taken on a related, scientific character.

"Is there a science in which fish, amphibians, reptiles, birds, and mammals are related—what's more, *in exactly that order*?

"In fact, is there a science in which fish are regarded as coming—as it were—second, amphibians third, reptiles fourth, birds fifth, and mammals last?—exactly as the warnings came?

"Any high school biology student could answer the question without straining himself.

"They are progressive stages in the evolution of man."

Roger Priam was blinking steadily, as if there were a growing, rather too bright light.

"So you see, Mr. Priam," said Ellery with a smile, "there was no bluff involved whatever. Since the second warning, fish, represents the second stage in the evolution of man, and the third warning, amphibians, represents the third stage in the evolution of man, and so on, then plainly the first warning could only have represented the first stage in the evolution of man. It's the lowest class of what zoologists call, I believe, craniate vertebrates—the lamprey, which resembles an eel but belongs to a different order. So I knew, Mr. Priam, that when you opened that first box you found in it something that looked like an eel. There was no other possibility."

"I thought it was a dead eel," said Priam rigidly.

"And did you know what the thing that looked like a dead eel meant, Mr. Priam?"

"No, I didn't."

"There was no note in that first box giving you the key to the warnings?"

"No . . ."

"He couldn't have expected you to catch his meaning from the nature of the individual warnings themselves," said Ellery with a frown. "To see through a thing like this calls for a certain minimum of education which —unfortunately, Mr. Priam—you don't have. And he knows you don't have it; he knows you, I think, very well."

"You mean he sent all these things," cried Laurel, "not caring whether they were understood or not?"

The question was in Lieutenant Keats's eyes, too.

"It begins to appear," said Ellery slowly, "as if he preferred that they *weren't* understood. It was terror he was after—terror for its own sake." He turned slightly away with a worried look.

"I never did know what they meant," muttered Roger Priam. "It was not knowing that made me . . ."

"Then it's high time you did, Mr. Priam." Ellery had shrugged his worry off. "The kind of mentality that would concoct such an unusual series of warnings was obviously not an ordinary one. Granted his motive—which was to inspire terror, to punish, to make his victim die mentally over and over— he must still have had a mind which was capable of thinking in these specialized terms and taking this specific direction. Why did he choose the stages of evolution as the basis of his warnings? How did his brain come to take that particular path? Our mental processes are directly influenced by our capacities, training, and experience. To have founded his terror campaign on the evolution theory, to have worked it out in such systematic detail, the enemy of Leander Hill and Roger Priam must have been a man of scientific training—biologist, zoologist, anthropologist . . . or a naturalist.

"When you think of the stages of evolution," continued Ellery, "you automatically think of Charles Darwin. Darwin was the father of the evolutionary theory. It was Darwin's researches over a hundred years ago, his lecture before the Linnaean Society in 1858 on 'The Theory of Evolution,' his publication the following year of the amplification of his 'Theory' which he called On the Origin of Species, that opened a new continent of scientific knowledge in man's exploration of his own development.

"So when I saw the outline of a naturalist and accordingly thought of Darwin, the greatest naturalist of all, it was a logical step to think back to Darwin's historic voyage—one of the world's great voyages on perhaps science's most famous ship—the voyage of naturalistic exploration on which Darwin formulated his theory of the origin of species and their perpetuation by natural selection. And thinking back to that produced a really wonderful result." Ellery gripped the back of a chair, leaning over it. "Because the ship on which Charles Darwin set sail from Plymouth, England, in 1831 on that epic voyage was named . . . H.M.S. Beagle."

"Beagle." Laurel goggled. "The dead dog!"

"There were a number of possibilities," Ellery nodded. "In sending Hill a beagle, the sender might have been providing the master key which was to unlock the door of the warnings to come—beagle, Darwin's ship, Darwin, evolution. But that seemed pretty remote. Neither Hill nor Priam was likely to know the name of the ship on which Darwin sailed more than a hundred years ago, if indeed they knew anything at all about the man who had sailed on it. Or the plotter might have been memorializing in a general way the whole basis of his plot. But this was even unlikelier. Our friend the scientifically minded enemy hasn't wasted his time with purposeless gestures.

"There were other possibilities along the same line, but the more I puzzled over the dead beagle the more convinced I became that it was meant to refer to something specific and significant in the background of Hill, Priam, and their enemy. What could the connection have been? What simple, direct tie-up could have existed among a naturalist and two non-scientific men, and the word or concept 'beagle,' and something that happened about twenty-five years ago?

"Immediately a connection suggested itself, a connection that covered the premises in the simplest, most direct way. Suppose twenty-five years or so ago a naturalist, together with Hill and Priam, planned a scientific expedition. Today they would probably use a plane; twenty-five years ago they would have gone by boat. And suppose the naturalist, conscious of his profession's debt to the great naturalist Darwin, in embarking on this expedition had the problem of naming, or the fancy to rename, the vessel on which he, Hill, and Priam were to be carried on their voyage of naturalistic exploration . . .

"I suggested to Lieutenant Keats," said Ellery, "that he try to trace a small ship, probably of the coastal type, which was either built, bought, or chartered for purposes of a scientific expedition—a ship named, or renamed, *Beagle* which set sail from probably an American port in 1925 or so.

"And Lieutenant Keats, with the co-operation of various police agencies of the coastal cities, succeeded in tracing such a vessel. Shall I go on, Mr. Priam?"

Ellery paused to light a fresh cigaret.

Again there was no sound but the hiss of the match and Priam's breathing.

"Let's take the conventional interpretation of Mr. Priam's silence, Lieutenant," said Ellery, blowing out the match, "and nail this thing down."

Keats pulled a slip of paper from his pocket and came forward.

"The name of the man we want," the detective began, "is Charles Lyell Adam. Charles Lyell Adam came from a very wealthy Vermont family. He was an only child and when his parents died he inherited all their money. But Adam wasn't interested in money. Or, as far as we know, in women, liquor, or good times. He was educated abroad, he never married, and he kept pretty much to himself.

"He was a gentleman, a scholar, and an amateur scientist. His field was naturalism. He devoted all his time to it. He was never attached to a museum, or a university, or any scientific organization that we've been able to dig up. His money made it possible for him to do as he liked, and what he liked to do most was tramp about the world studying the flora and fauna of out-of-the-way places.

"His exact age," continued Keats, after referring to his notes, "isn't known. The Town Hall where his birth was recorded went up in smoke around 1910, and there was no baptismal record—at least, we haven't located one. Attempts to fix his age by questioning old residents of the Vermont town where he was born have produced conflicting testimony—we couldn't find any kin. We weren't able to find anything on him in the draft records of the First World War—he can't be located either as a draftee or an enlisted man. Probably he got some sort of deferment, although we haven't been able to turn up anything on this, either. About all we can be sure of is that, in the year 1925, when Adam organized an expedition bound for the Guianas, he was anywhere from twenty-seven to thirty-nine years old.

"For this expedition," said Keats, "Adam had a special boat built, a fifty-footer equipped with an auxiliary engine and scientific apparatus of his own design. Exactly what he was after, or what he was trying to prove scientifically, no one seems to know. But in the summer of '25 Adam's boat, *Beagle*, cleared Boston Harbor and headed down the coast.

"It stopped over in Cuba for repairs. There was a long delay. When the repairs were finished, the *Beagle* got under way again. And that was the last anybody saw or heard of the *Beagle*, or Charles Lyell Adam, or his crew. The delay ran them into hurricane weather and, after a thorough search turned up no trace of the vessel, the *Beagle* was presumed to have gone down with all hands.

"The crew," said Lieutenant Keats, "consisted of two men, each about forty years old at the time, each a deepwater sailor of many years' experience, like Adam himself. We've got their names—their real names—but we may as well keep calling them by the names they took in 1927: Leander Hill and Roger Priam."

Keats shot the name at the bearded man in the wheelchair as if it were a tennis ball; and, like spectators at the match, they turned their heads in unison to Priam. And Priam clutched the arms of his chair, and he bit his lip until a bright drop appeared. This drop he licked; another appeared and it oozed into his beard. But he met their eyes defiantly.

"All right," he rumbled. "So now you know it. What about it?"

It was as if he were grounded on a reef and gamely mustering his forces of survival against the winds.

"The rest," said Ellery, squarely to Priam, "is up to you."

"You bet it's up to me!"

"I mean whether you tell us the truth or we try to figure it out, Mr. Priam."

"You're doing the figuring, Mister."

"You still won't talk?"

"You're doing the talking," said Priam.

"We don't have much to go on, as you know very well," said Ellery, nodding as if he had expected nothing else, "but perhaps what we have is enough. You're here, twenty-five years later; and up to recently Leander Hill was here, too. And according to the author of the note that was left in the beagle's collar, Charles Lyell Adam was left for dead twenty-five years ago, under circumstances which justified him—in his own judgment, at any rate—in using the word 'murder,' Mr. Priam . . . except that he didn't die and *he's* here.

"Did you and Hill scuttle the *Beagle*, Mr. Priam, when you were Adam's crew and the *Beagle* was somewhere in West Indian waters? Attack Adam, leave him for dead, scuttle the *Beagle*, and escape in a dinghy, Mr. Priam? The Haitians sail six hundred miles in cockleshells as a matter of course, and you and Hill were good enough seamen for Adam to have hired in the first place.

"But seamen don't attempt murder and scuttle good ships for no reason, Mr. Priam. What was the reason? If it had been a personal matter, or mutiny, or shipwreck as a result of incompetence or negligence, or any of the usual reasons, you and Hill could always have made your way back to the nearest port and reported what you pleased to explain the disappearance of Adam and his vessel. But you and Hill didn't do that, Mr. Priam. You and Hill chose to vanish along with Adam—to vanish in your sailor personalities, that is, leading the world to believe that Adam's crew had died with him. You went to a great deal of trouble to bury yourselves, Mr. Priam. You spent a couple of years doing it, preparing new names and personalities for your resurrection. Why? Because you had something to conceal—*something you couldn't have concealed had you come back as Adam's crew.*

"That's the most elementary logic, Mr. Priam. Now will you tell us what happened?"

Nothing in Priam stirred, not even the hairs of his beard.

"Then I'll have to tell you. In 1927, you and Hill appeared in Los Angeles and set up a wholesale jewelry business. What did you know about the jewelry business? We know all about you and Hill now, Mr. Priam, from the time you were born until you signed on the *Beagle* for its one and only voyage. You both went to sea as boys. There was nothing in either of your backgrounds that remotely touched jewels or jewelry. And, like most sailors, you were poor men. Still, two years later, here you both were, starting a fabulous business in precious stones. *Was that what you couldn't have concealed had you come back as Adam's crew?* Because the authorities would have said, *Where did these two poor seamen get all this money—or all these jewels?* And that's one question, Mr. Priam, you didn't want asked—either you or Hill.

"So it's reasonable to conjecture, Mr. Priam," said Ellery, smiling, "that the *Beagle* didn't go down in a hurricane after all. That the *Beagle* reached its destination, perhaps an uninhabited island, and that in exploring for the fauna and flora that interested him as a naturalist, Adam ran across something far afield from his legitimate interests. Like an old treasure chest, Mr. Priam, buried by one of the pirate swarms who used to infest those waters. You can find descendants of those pirates, Mr. Priam, living in the Bahamas today . . . An old treasure chest, Mr. Priam, filled with precious stones. And you and Hill, poor sailors, attacked Adam, took the *Beagle* into blue water, sank her, and got away in her dinghy.

"And there you were, with a pirate's fortune in jewels, and how were you to live to enjoy it? The whole thing was fantastic. It was fantastic to find it, it was fantastic to own it, and it was fantastic to think that you couldn't do anything with it. But one of you got a brilliant idea, and about that idea there was nothing fantastic at all. Bury all trace of your old selves, come back as entirely different men—*and go into the jewelry business.*

"And that's what you and Hill did, Mr. Priam. For two years you studied the jewelers' trade—exactly where, we haven't learned. When you felt you had enough knowledge and experience, you set up shop in Los Angeles . . . and your stock was the chest of precious stones Adam had found on his island, for undisputed possession of which you'd murdered him. And now you *could* dispose of them. Openly. Legitimately. And get rich on them."

Priam's beard was askew on his chest. His eyes were shut, as if he were asleep . . . or gathering his strength.

"But Adam didn't die," said Ellery gently. "You and Hill bungled. He survived. Only he knows how he nursed himself back to health, what he lived on, how he got back to civilization, and where, and where he's been since. But by his own testimony, in the note, he dedicated the rest of his life to tracking you and Hill down. For over twenty years he kept searching for the two sailors who had left him for dead—for his two murderers, Mr. Priam. Adam didn't want the fortune—he had his own fortune; and, anyway, he was never very interested in money. What he wanted, Mr. Priam, was revenge. As his note says.

"And then he found you."

And now Ellery's voice was no longer gentle.

"Hill was a disappointment to him. The shock of learning that Adam, against all reason, was alive—and all that that implied—was too much for Hill's heart. Hill was rather different from you, I think, Mr. Priam; whatever he'd been in the old days at sea, he had grown into the semblance of a solid citizen. And perhaps he'd never been really vicious. You were always the bully-boy of the team, weren't you? Maybe Hill didn't do anything but acquiesce in your crime, dazzled by the reward you dangled before his eyes. You needed him to get away; I think you needed his superior intelligence. In any event, after that one surrender to you and temptation, Hill built himself up into what a girl like Laurel could learn to love and respect . . . and for the sake of whose memory she was even willing to kill.

"Hill was a man of imagination, Mr. Priam, and I think what killed him at the very first blow was as much his dread of the effect on Laurel of the revelation of his old crime as the knowledge that Adam was alive and hot for revenge.

"But you're made of tougher material, Mr. Priam. You haven't disappointed Adam; on the contrary. It's really a pleasure for Adam to work on you. He's still the scientist—his method is as scientifically pitiless as the dissection of an old cadaver. And he's having himself a whale of a time, Mr. Priam, with you providing the sport. I don't think you understand with what wonderful humor Charles Lyell Adam is chasing you. Or do you?"

But when Priam spoke, he seemed not to have been listening. At least, he did not answer the question. He roused himself and he said, "Who is he? What's he calling himself now? Do you know that?"

"That's what you're interested in, is it?" Ellery smiled. "Why, no, Mr. Priam, we don't. All we know about him today is that he's somewhere between fifty-two and sixty-four years of age. I'm sure you wouldn't recognize him; either his appearance has been radically changed by time or he's had it changed for him by, say, plastic surgery. But even if Adam looked today exactly as he looked twenty-five years ago, it wouldn't do you—or us, Mr. Priam—any good. Because he doesn't have to be on the scene in person, you see. He could be working through someone else." Priam blinked and blinked. "You're not precisely a well-loved man, Mr. Priam, and there are people very close to you who might not be at all repelled by the idea of contributing to your unhappiness. So if you have any idea that as long as you protect yourself against a middle-aged male of certain proportions you're all right, you'd better get rid of it as quickly as possible. Adam's unofficial accomplice, working entirely for love of the job, you might say, could be of either sex, of any age . . . and right here, Mr. Priam, in your own household."

Priam sat still. Not wholly in fear—with a reserve of desperate caution, it seemed, even defiance, like a treed cat.

"What a stinking thing to say—!"

"Shut up, Mac." And this was Keats, in a low voice, but there was a note in it that made Delia's son bring his lips together and keep them that way.

"A moment ago," said Ellery, "I mentioned Adam's sense of humor. I wonder if you see the point, Mr. Priam. Where his joke is heading."

"What?" said Priam in a mumble.

"All his warnings to you have had not one, but two, things in common. Not only has each warning involved an animal—but each animal was dead."

Priam's head jerked.

"His first warning was a dead lamprey. His second warning was a dead fish. His third consisted of dead frogs and toads. The next a dead alligator. The next—The Birds—a little symbolism here, because he mutilated and destroyed the book . . . the only way in which you can physically 'kill' a book! Even his last warning—the 'cats and dogs'—connotes death; there's nothing quite so 'dead' as the stock of a company that has folded up. Really a humorist, this Adam.

"Right up the ladder of evolution—from the lowest order of vertebrates, the lamprey, to one of the highest, cats and dogs. And every one, in fact or by symbol, was delivered dead.

"But Mr. Priam, Adam isn't finished." Ellery leaned forward. "He hasn't climbed Darwin's ladder to stop at the next-to-the-last rung. The top rung of that ladder is still to be put in evidence. The highest creature in the class of Mammalia.

"So it's perfectly certain that there's an exhibit yet to come, the last exhibit, and by inference from the preceding ones, a dead exhibit. Charles Lyell Adam is going to produce a dead man, Mr. Priam, and there wouldn't be much point to his Darwinian joke if that dead man weren't Roger Priam."

Priam remained absolutely motionless.

"We've gone all over this," said Lieutenant Keats sharply, "and we agree there's only one thing to do. You're tagged for murder, Priam, and it's going to come soon—tomorrow, maybe tonight, maybe an hour from now. I've got to have you alive, Priam, and I want Adam alive, too, if possible, because the law likes us to bring 'em back that way. You're going to have to be guarded night and day, starting right now. A man in this room. One on the terrace there. A couple around the grounds—"

Roger Priam filled his chest.

A roar came out that set the crystals in the chandelier jangling.

"Criminal, am I? On what evidence?" He brandished a clublike forefinger at Lieutenant Keats. "I'm not admitting a thing, you can't prove a thing, and I ain't asking for your protection or taking it!—d'ye get me?"

"What are you afraid of?" jeered the detective. "That we will lay our hands on Adam?"

"I've always fought my own scraps and, by God, I'll fight this one!"

"From a wheelchair?"

"From a wheelchair! Now get out of my house, you ——, and stay out!"

Chapter XV

THEY STAYED OUT. Anyone from the outside would have said they were finished with Roger Priam and all his works. Daily Lieutenant Keats might have been seen going about his business; daily Ellery might have been seen staring at his—a blank sheet of paper in a still typewriter—or at night dining alone, with an ear cocked, or afterwards hovering above the telephone. He rarely left the cottage during the day; at night, never. His consumption of cigarets, pipe tobacco, coffee, and alcohol gave Mrs. Williams a second subject for her interminable monologues; she alternated between predictions of sudden death for the world and creeping ulcers for Ellery.

At one time or another Laurel, Crowe Macgowan, Alfred Wallace, Collier —even Delia Priam—phoned or called in person, either unsolicited or by invitation. But each hung up or went away as worried or perplexed or thoughtful as he had been; and if Ellery unburdened himself to any of them, or vice versa, nothing seemed to come of it.

And Ellery lit another cigaret, or tormented another pipe, or gulped more hot coffee, or punished another highball, and Mrs. Williams's wails kept assailing the kitchen ceiling.

Then, one humid night at the beginning of the fourth week in July, just after midnight, the call came for which Ellery was waiting.

He listened, he said a few words, he broke the connection, and he called the number of Keats's house.

Keats answered on the first ring.

"Queen?"

"Yes. As fast as you can."

Ellery immediately hung up and ran out to his car. He had parked the Kaiser at the front door every night for a week.

He left it on the road near the Priam mailbox. Keats's car was already there. Ellery made his way along the bordering grass to the side of the house. He used no flashlight. In the shadow of the terrace a hand touched his arm.

"Quick." Keats's whisper was an inch from his ear.

The house was dark, but a faint night light was burning in Roger Priam's room off the terrace. The French door was open, and the terrace was in darkness.

They got down on their knees, peered through the screening of the inner door.

Priam's wheelchair was in its bed position, made up for the night. He lay on his back, motionless, beard jutting obliquely to the ceiling.

Nothing happened for several minutes.

Then there was the slightest metallic sound.

The night light was in an electric outlet in the wainscoting near the door which led into the hall. They saw the doorknob clearly; it was in motion. When it stopped, the door began to open. It creaked. Came to rest.

Priam did not move.

The door opened swiftly.

But the night light was beyond the doorway and when the door swung back to the farther wall it cut off most of the slight glow. All they could make out from the terrace was a formless blackness deeper than the darkness at the rear of the room. This gap in the void moved steadily from the doorway to Roger Priam's chair-bed. A tentacular something projected before it. The projection swam into the outermost edge of the night light's orbit and they saw that it was a revolver.

Beside Priam's chair the moving blackness halted.

The revolver came up a little.

Keats stirred. It was more a tightening of his muscles than a true movement; still, Ellery's fingers clamped on the detective's arm.

Keats froze.

And then the whole room exploded, motion gone wild.

Priam's arm flashed upward and his great hand closed like the jaws of a reptile on the wrist of the hand that held the revolver. The crippled man heaved his bulk upright, bellowing. There was the blurriest of struggles; they looked like two squids locked in battle at the bottom of the sea.

Then there was a soggy report, a smart thud, and quiet.

When Ellery snapped the wall switch Keats was already on his knees by the figure on the floor. It lay in a curl, almost comfortably, one arm hidden and the other outstretched. At the end of the outstretched arm lay the revolver.

"Chest," Keats muttered.

Roger Priam was glaring at the two men.

"It's Adam," he said hoarsely. "Where did you two come from? He came to kill me. It's Adam. I told you I could handle him!" He laughed with his teeth, but at once he began to shake, and he squinted at the fallen figure and rubbed his eyes with a trembling hand. "Who is he? Let me see him!"

"It's Alfred."

"*Alfred?*" The beard drooped.

Keats rose to go around Priam's chair. He plucked one of Priam's telephones from its hook and dialed a number.

"*Alfred is Adam?*" Priam sounded dazed, stupid. He recoiled quickly, but it was only Ellery removing his top blanket.

Ellery dropped the blanket over the thing on the floor.

"He's . . . ?" Priam's tongue came out. "Is he dead?"

"Headquarters?" said Keats. "Keats, Hollywood Division, reporting a homicide. The Hill-Priam case. Roger Priam just shot Alfred Wallace, his secretary-nurse-what-have-you, shot him to death . . . That's right. Through the heart. I witnessed the shooting myself, from the terrace—"

"To death," said Priam. "To death. He's dead! . . . But it was self-defense. You witnessed it—if you witnessed it . . . He pussyfooted into my room here. I heard him come in. I made believe I was sleeping. Oh, I was ready for him!" His voice cracked. "Didn't you see him point the gun at me? I grabbed it, twisted his hand! It was self-defense—"

"We saw it all, Mr. Priam," said Ellery in a soothing voice.

"Good, you saw it. He's dead. Damn him, he's dead! Wallace . . . Try to kill me, would he? By God, it's over. It's over."

"Yes," Keats was saying into the phone. "When? Okay, no hurry." He hung up.

"You heard Mr. Queen," Priam babbled. "He saw it all, Lieutenant—"

"I know." Keats went over to the blanket and lifted one corner. Then he dropped the blanket and took out a cigaret and lit it. "We'll have to wait." He inhaled.

"Sure, yes, Lieutenant." Priam fumbled with something. The upper half of his bed rose, the lower sank, to form the chair. He groped. "A drink," he said. "You join me? Celebration." He guffawed. "Besides, I'm a little wobbly."

Ellery was wandering around, pulling at an ear, rubbing the back of his neck. There was a ridge between his eyes.

Keats kept smoking and watching him.

"I've got to hand it to him," Priam was saying, busy with a bottle and a glass. "Alfred Wallace . . . Must have had his nose fixed. I never recognized him. Smooth, smooth operator. Gets right on the inside. Laughing up his sleeve all the time! But who's laughing now? Here's to him." He raised the glass, grinning, but the wild animal was still in his eyes. He tossed the whisky off. When he set the glass down, his hand was no longer shaking. "But there he is, and here I am, and it's all over." His head came down, and he was silent.

"Mr. Priam," said Ellery.

Priam did not reply.

"Mr. Priam?"

"Hey?" Priam looked up.

"There's one point that still bothers me. Now that it's over, would you straighten me out on it?"

Priam looked at him. Then, deliberately, he reached for the bottle and refilled his glass.

"Why, Mr. Queen, it all depends," he said. "If you expect me to admit a lot of guff—with maybe a stenographer taking it all down from my terrace—you can save your wind. All right, this man was after me. No idea why, friends, except that he went crazy. On that voyage. Absolutely nuts.

"On the *Beagle* he went after me and my shipmate with a machete. We were off some dirty island and we jumped overboard, swam to the beach, and hid in the woods. Hurricane blew up that night and swept the *Beagle* out to sea. We never saw the ship or Adam again. Shipmate and me, we then found a treasure on that island and we finally got it off on a raft we made.

"Reason we laid low and changed our names to Hill and Priam was so Adam could never come back and claim one third of the treasure—he'd been exploring that island. And maybe he'd still try to kill us even if he didn't claim a third. That's my story, friends. Not a crime in a cargo load." He grinned and tossed off the second glassful. "And I'm sticking to it."

Keats was regarding him with admiration. "It's a lousy story, Priam, but if you stick to it we're stuck with it."

"Anything else, Mr. Queen . . ." Priam waved genially. "All you got to do is ask. What's the point that's been giving you such a bad time?"

"The letter Adam sent to Leander Hill," said Ellery.

"The letter—?" Priam stared. "Why in hell would you be worrying about *that?*"

Ellery took a folded sheet of paper from his breast pocket.

"This is a copy of the note Hill found in the silver box on the beagle's collar," he said. "It's been some time and perhaps I'd better refresh your memory by reading it aloud."

"Go ahead." Priam still stared.

"*You believed me dead,*" read Ellery. "*Killed, murdered. For over a score of years I have looked for you—for you and for him. And now I have found you. Can you guess my plan? You'll die. Quickly? No, very slowly. And so pay me back for my long years of searching and dreaming of revenge. Slow dying . . . unavoidable dying. For you and for him. Slow and sure—dying in mind and in body. And for each pace forward a warning . . . a warning of special meaning for you—and for him. Meanings for pondering and puzzling. Here is warning number one.*"

"See?" said Priam. "Crazy as a bug."

"*Killed, murdered,*" said Keats. "By a hurricane, Mr. Priam?" But he was smiling.

"That was his craziness, Lieutenant. I remember when he was steaming after us on deck, waving the machete around his head, how he kept yelling we were trying to murder him. All the time he was trying to murder us. Ask your brain doctors. They'll tell you." Priam swung about. "Is that what's been bothering you, Mr. Queen?"

"What? Oh! No, not that, Mr. Priam." Ellery scowled down at the paper. "It's the phrasing."

"The what?"

"The way the message is worded."

Priam was puzzled. "What's the matter with it?"

"A great deal is the matter with it, Mr. Priam. I'll go so far as to say that this is the most remarkable collection of words I've ever been privileged to read. How many words are there in this message, Mr. Priam?"

"How the devil should I know?"

"Ninety-nine, Mr. Priam."

Priam glanced at Keats. But Keats was merely smoking with the gusto of a man who has denied himself too long, and there was nothing on Ellery's face but concern. "So it's got ninety-nine words. I don't get it."

"Ninety-nine words, Mr. Priam, comprising three hundred and ninety-seven letters of the English alphabet."

"I still don't get it." A note of truculence crept into Priam's heavy voice. "What are you trying to prove, that you can count?"

"I'm trying to prove—and I can prove, Mr. Priam—that there's something wrong with this message."

"Wrong?" Priam's beard shot up. "What?"

"The tools of my business, Mr. Priam," said Ellery, "are words. I not only write words of my own, but I read extensively—and sometimes with envy— the words of others. So I consider myself qualified to make the following observation: This is the first time I've ever run across a piece of English prose, deathless or otherwise, made up of as many as ninety-nine words, con- sisting of almost four hundred individual characters, *in which the writer failed to use a single letter T.*"

"Single letter *T*," repeated Priam. His lips moved after he stopped speak- ing, so that for a moment it looked as if he were chewing something with a foreign and disagreeable taste.

"It took me a long time to spot that, Mr. Priam," continued Ellery, walk- ing around the body of Alfred Wallace. "It's the sort of thing you can't see because it's so obvious. When we read, most of us concentrate on the sense of what we're reading, not its physical structure. Who looks at a building and sees the individual bricks? Yet the secret of the building lies precisely there. There are twenty-six basic bricks in the English language, some of them more important than the rest. There's no guesswork about those bricks, Mr. Priam. Their nature, their usability, their interrelationships, the fre- quency of their occurrence have been determined as scientifically as the com- position of stucco.

"Let me tell you about the letter *T*, Mr. Priam," said Ellery.

"The letter *T* is the second most frequently used letter in the English language. Only *E* occurs more frequently. *T* is the number two brick of the twenty-six.

"*T*, Mr. Priam, is the most frequently used *initial* letter in the English language.

"English uses a great many combinations of two letters representing a single speech sound. These are known as digraphs. The letter *T*, Mr. Priam, is part of the most frequently used digraph—*TH*.

"*T* is also part of the most frequently used trigraph—three letters spelling a single speech sound—*THE*, as in the word *BATHE*.

"*TT*, Mr. Priam, gives ground only to *SS* and *EE* as the most frequently used *double* letter.

"The same letters, S and E, are the only letters which occur more frequently than T as the *last* letters of words.

"But that isn't all, Mr. Priam," said Ellery. "The letter T is part of the most frequently used three-letter word in the English language—the word *THE*.

"The letter T is part of the most frequently used four-letter word—*THAT* —and also of the second most frequently used four-letter word—*WITH*.

"And as if that weren't enough, Mr. Priam," said Ellery, "we find T in the second most frequently used two-letter word—*TO*—and in the fourth most frequently used two-letter word—*IT*. Do you wonder now, Mr. Priam," said Ellery, "why I called Charles Adam's note to your partner remarkable?

"It's so remarkable, Mr. Priam, that it's impossible. No conceivable chance or coincidence could produce a communication of almost a hundred English words that was completely lacking in T's. *The only way you can get a hundred-word message without a single T is by setting out to do so. You have to make a conscious effort to avoid using it.*

"Do you want confirmation, Mr. Priam?" asked Ellery, and now something new had come into his voice; it was no longer thoughtful or troubled. "The writer of this note didn't use a single *TO* or *IT* or *AT* or *THE* or *BUT* or *NOT* or *THAT* or *WITH* or *THIS*. You simply can't escape those words unless you're trying to.

"The note refers to you and Leander Hill; that is, to two people. He says: *I have looked for you and for him.* Why didn't he write: *I have looked for the two of you,* or *I have looked for both of you?*—either of which would have been a more natural expression than *for you and for him?* The fact that in the word *TWO* and in the word *BOTH* the letter T occurs can hardly escape us. He just happened to express it that way? Perhaps once; even possibly twice; but he wrote *for you and for him* three times in the same message!

"He writes: *Slow dying . . . unavoidable dying.* And again: *dying in mind and in body.* He's no novelist or poet looking for a different way of saying things. And this is a note, not an essay for publication. Why didn't he use the common phrases: *Slow death . . . inevitable death . . . death mentally and physically?* Even though the whole message concerns death, the word itself—in that form—does not occur even once. If he was deliberately avoiding the letter T, the question is answered.

"*You believed me dead . . .* Had he expressed this in a normal, natural way he would have written: *You thought I was dead.* But *thought* contains two T's. We find the word *pondering*, for *to think over*, for obviously the same reason.

"And surely *Here is warning number one* is a circumlocution to avoid writing the more natural *This is the first warning*.

"Am I quibbling? Can this still have been a coincidence, dictated by an eccentric style? The odds against this mount astronomically when you consider two other examples from the note.

"*And for each pace forward a warning*, he writes. He's not talking about physical progress, where a *pace* might have a specialized meaning in the context. There is no reason on earth why he shouldn't have written *And for each step forward*, except that *step* contains a *T*.

"My last example is equally significant. He writes: *For over a score of years*. Why use the fancy word *score*? Why didn't he write: *For over twenty years*, or whatever the actual number of years was? Because the word *twenty*, or any combination including the word *twenty*—from twenty-one through twenty-nine—gets him involved in *T*'s."

Roger Priam was baffled. He was trying to capture something, or recapture it. All his furrows were deeper with the effort, and his eyes rolled a little. But he said nothing.

And, in the background, Keats smoked; and, in the foreground, Alfred Wallace lay under the blanket.

"The question is, of course," said Ellery, "why the writer of the note avoided using the letter *T*.

"Let's see if we can't reconstruct something useful here.

"How was the original of Leander Hill's copy written? By hand, or by mechanical means? We have no direct evidence; the note has disappeared. Laurel caught a glimpse of the original when Hill took it from the little silver box, but Hill half-turned away as he read it and Laurel couldn't specify the character of the writing.

"But the simplest analysis shows the form in which it must have appeared. The letter could not have been handwritten. It is just as easy to write the letter *T* as any other letter of the alphabet. The writer, considering the theme of his message, could hardly have been playing word games; and no other test but ease or difficulty makes sense.

"If the note wasn't handwritten, then it was typewritten. You saw that note, Mr. Priam—Hill showed it to you the morning after his heart attack. Wasn't it typewritten?"

Priam looked up, frowning in a peculiar way. But he did not answer.

"It was typewritten," said Ellery. "But the moment you assume a typewritten note, the answer suggests itself. The writer was composing his message on a typewriter. He used no *T*'s. Why look for complicated reasons? If he used no *T*'s, it's simply because *T*'s were not available to him. He *couldn't* use *T*'s. The *T* key on the machine he was using wouldn't function. It was broken."

Surprisingly, Priam lifted his head and said, "You're guessing."

Ellery looked pained. "I'm not trying to prove how clever I am, Mr. Priam, but I must object to your verb. Guessing is as obnoxious to me as swearing is to a bishop. I submit that I worked this out; I've had little enough fun in this case! But let's assume it's a guess. It's a very sound guess, Mr. Priam, and it has the additional virtue of being susceptible to confirmation.

"I theorize a typewriter with a broken key. Do we know of a typewriter—in this case—which wasn't in perfect working order?

"*Strangely enough, Mr. Priam, we do.*

"On my way to your house for the first time, in Laurel Hill's car, I asked

Laurel some questions about you. She told me how self-sufficient you've made yourself, how as a reaction to your disability you dislike help of the most ordinary kind. As an example, Laurel said that when she was at your house 'the day before' you were in a foul mood over having to dictate business memoranda to Wallace instead of doing them yourself—*your typewriter had just been sent into Hollywood to be repaired."*

Priam twisted. Keats stood by his wheelchair, lifting the attached typewriter shelf.

Priam choked a splutter, glancing painfully down at the shelf as Keats swung it up and around.

Ellery and Keats bent over the machine, ignoring the man in the chair. They glanced at each other.

Keats tapped the *T* key with a fingernail. "Mr. Priam," he said, "there's only one key on this machine that's new. It's the *T*. The note to Hill was typed right here." He spread his fingers over the carriage of Priam's typewriter, almost with affection.

A sound, formless and a little beastly, came out of Priam's throat. Keats stood by him, very close.

"And who could have typed a note on your machine, Mr. Priam?" asked Ellery in the friendliest of voices. "There's no guesswork here. If I'd never seen this typewriter shelf I'd have known the machine is screwed on. It would have to be, to keep it from falling off when the shelf is swung aside and dropped. Besides, Laurel Hill told me so.

"So, except for those times when the typewriter needs a major repair, it's a permanent fixture of your wheelchair. Was the original of the note to Hill typed on your machine after it was removed for repair but before the broken *T* key was replaced? No, because the note was delivered to Hill two weeks *before* you sent the machine into Hollywood. Did someone type the note on your machine while you were out of your wheelchair? No, Mr. Priam, because you're never out of your chair; you haven't left it for fifteen years. Was the note typed on your machine while you were—say—asleep? Impossible; when the chair is a bed the shelf obviously can't come up.

"So I'm very much afraid, Mr. Priam, there's only one conclusion we can reach," said Ellery. "*You typed that warning note yourself.*

"It's you who threatened your partner with death.

"The only active enemy out of your past and Hill's, Mr. Priam, is Roger Priam."

"Don't misunderstand me," said Ellery. "Charles Adam is not imaginary. He was an actual person, as our investigation uncovered. Adam disappeared in West Indian waters 'over a score of years ago,' as you wrote in the note, and he hasn't been seen or heard of since. It was only the note that made us believe Adam was still alive. Knowing now that you wrote the note, we can only conclude that Adam didn't survive the *Beagle's* voyage twenty-five years ago after all, that you and Hill did succeed in killing him, and that his reappearance here in Southern California this summer was an illusion you deliberately engineered.

"Priam," said Ellery, "you knew what a shock it would be to your partner Hill to learn that Adam was apparently alive after so many years of thinking he was dead. Not only alive but explicitly out for revenge. You knew that Hill would be particularly susceptible to such news. He had built a new life for himself. He was bound up emotionally with Laurel, his adopted daughter, who worshiped the man he seemed to be.

"So Adam's 'reappearance' threatened not only Hill's life but, what was possibly even more important to him, the whole structure of Laurel's love for him. There was a good chance, you felt, that Hill's bad heart—he had had two attacks before—could not survive such a shock. And you were right —your note killed him.

"If Hill had any doubts about the authenticity of the note, you dispelled them the morning after the heart attack, when for the first time in fifteen years you took the trouble of having yourself carted over to Hill's house. The cause could only have been a telephone agreement with Hill to have a confidential, urgent talk about the note. You had, I imagine, another and equally pressing reason for that unprecedented visit: You wanted to be sure the note was destroyed so that it couldn't be traced back to your typewriter. Either Hill gave it to you and you destroyed it then or later, or he destroyed it before your eyes. What you didn't know, Priam, and what he didn't tell you, was that he had already made a copy of the note in his own handwriting and hidden it in his mattress. Why? Maybe after the first shock, when Hill thought it over, he hadn't been *quite* convinced. Maybe a sixth sense told him before you got to him that something was wrong. Whether you convinced him during that visit or not, the note was probably already copied and in his mattress, and a native caution—despite all your arguments—made him leave it there and say nothing about it. We can't know and won't ever know just what went on in Hill's mind.

"But the damage was done by the sheer impact of the shock, Priam. Murder by fright," said Ellery. "Far colder-blooded and more deliberate than killing by gun or knife, or even poison. A murder calling for great pains of premeditation. One wonders why. Not merely why you wanted to kill Hill, but why you splashed your crime so carefully with that elaborate camouflage of 'the enemy out of the past.'

"Your motive must have been compelling. It couldn't have been gain, because Hill's death brought you no material benefits; his share of the business went to Laurel. It couldn't have been to avoid exposure as the murderer of Adam twenty-five years ago, for Hill was neck-deep in that crime with you and had benefited from it equally—he was hardly in a position to hold it over you. In fact, he was in a poorer position than you were to hold it over *him*, because Hill had the additional reason to want to keep it from Laurel. Nor is it likely that you killed him to avoid exposure for any other crime of which he might have gained knowledge, such as—I take the obvious theory—embezzlement of the firm's funds. Because the truth is you have had very little to do with the running of Hill & Priam; it was Hill who ran it, while you merely put up a show of being an equal partner in work and responsibility. Never leaving your house, you could hardly have been so in control of daily events as to have been able to steal funds, or falsify accounts, or anything like that. Nor was it trouble over your wife. Hill's relationship with Mrs. Priam was friendly and correct; besides," said Ellery rather dryly, "he was getting past the age for that sort of thing.

"There's only one thing you accomplished, Priam, by killing Leander Hill. So, in the absence of a positive indication in any other direction, I'm forced to conclude that that's why you wanted Hill out of the way.

"And it's confirmed by your character, Priam, the whole drive of your personality.

"By killing Hill *you got rid of your business partner*. That is one of the facts that emerge from his death. Is it the key fact? I think it is.

"Priam, you have an obsessive need to dominate, to dominate your immediate background and everyone in it. The one thing above all others that you can't stand is dependence on others. With you the alternative is not so much independence of others as making others dependent on you. Because physically you're helpless, you want power. You must be master—even if, as in the case of your wife, you have to use another man to do it.

"You hated Hill because he, not you, was master of Hill & Priam. He ran it and he had run it for fifteen years with no more than token help from you. The firm's employes looked up to him and loathed you. He made policy, purchases, sales; to accounts, big and small, Leander Hill was Hill & Priam and Roger Priam was a forgotten and useless invalid stuck away in a house somewhere. The fact that to Hill you owe your material security and the sound condition of Hill & Priam has festered inside of you for fifteen years. Even while you enjoyed the fruits of Hill's efforts, they left a bitter taste in your mouth that eventually poisoned you.

"You planned his death.

"With Hill out of the way, you would be undisputed master of the business. That you might run it into the ground probably never occurred to you. But if it did, I'm sure the danger didn't even make you hesitate. The big thing was to make everyone involved in or with Hill & Priam come crawling to you. The big thing was to be boss."

Roger Priam said nothing. This time he did not even make the beastly sound. But his little eyes roved.

Keats moved even closer.

"Once you saw what you had to do," continued Ellery, "you realized that you were seriously handicapped. You couldn't come and go as you pleased; you had no mobility. An ordinary murder was out of the question. Of course, you could have disposed of Hill right in this room during a business conference by a shot. But Hill's death wasn't the primary objective. He had to die and leave you free to run the business.

"You had to be able to kill him in such a way that you wouldn't be even suspected.

"It occurred to you, as it's occurred to murderers before, that the most effective way of diverting suspicion from yourself was to create the illusion that you were equally in danger of losing your life, and from the same source. In other words, you had to create a fictitious outside threat directed not merely at Hill but at both of you.

"Your and Hill's connection with Charles Lyell Adam twenty-five years ago provided a suitable, if daring and dangerous, means for creating such an illusion. If Adam were 'alive,' he could have a believable motive to seek the death of both of you. Adam's background could be traced by the authorities; the dramatic voyage of the *Beagle* was traceable to the point of its disappearance with all hands; the facts of your and Hill's existence and present situation in life, plus the hints you could let drop in 'Adam's' note, would lead any competent investigator to the conclusion you wanted him to reach.

"You were very clever, Priam. You avoided the psychological error of making things too obvious. You deliberately told not quite enough in 'Adam's' note. You repeatedly refused on demand to give any information that would help the police or make the investigation easier, although an examination of your 'refusals' show that you actually helped us considerably. But on the surface you made us work for what we got.

"You made us work hard, because you laid a fantastic trail for us to follow.

"But if your theory-of-evolution pattern was on the fancy side, your logic was made curiously more convincing because of it. To nurse a desire for revenge for almost a generation a man has to be a little cracked. Such a mind might easily run to the involved and the fanciful. At the same time, 'Adam' would naturally tend to think in terms of his own background and experience. Adam having been a naturalist, you created a trail such as an eccentric naturalist might leave—a trail you were sure we would sooner or later recognize and follow to its conclusion, which was that Naturalist Charles Adam was 'the enemy out of the past.'

"Your camouflage was brilliantly conceived and stroked on, Priam. You laid it so thickly on this case that, if you had not foolishly used that broken-T typewriter, we should probably have been satisfied to pin the crime on a man who's really been dead for a quarter of a century."

Priam's big head wavered a little, almost a nod. But it might have been a momentary trembling of the muscles of his neck. Otherwise, he gave no sign that he was even listening.

"In an odd sort of way, Priam, you were unlucky. You didn't realize quite how bad Hill's heart was, or you miscalculated the impact of your paper bullet. Because Hill died as a result of your very first warning. You had sent yourself a warning on the same morning, intending to divide the other warnings between you and Hill, probably, alternating them. When Hill died so immediately, it was too late to pull yourself out. You were in the position of the general who has planned a complicated battle against the enemy, finds that his very first sortie has accomplished his entire objective, but is powerless to stop his orders and preparation for the succeeding attacks. Had you stopped after sending yourself only one warning the mere stoppage would have been suspect. The warnings to yourself had to continue in order that the illusion of Adam-frightening-Hill-to-death should be completely credible.

"You sent six warnings, including the masterly one of having your tuna salad poisoned so that you could eat some, fall sick, and so call attention to your 'fish' clue. After six warnings you undoubtedly felt you had thoroughly fooled us as to the real source of the crime. On the other hand, you recognized the danger of stopping even at six with yourself still alive. We might begin to wonder why—in your case—'Adam' had given up. Murderers have been caught on a great deal less.

"You saw that, for perfect safety, you had to give us a convincing end to the whole business.

"The ideal, of course, was for us to 'catch' 'Adam.'

"A lesser man, Priam, wouldn't have wasted ten seconds wrestling with the problem of producing a man dead twenty-five years and handing his living body over to the police. But you didn't abandon the problem merely because it seemed impossible to solve. There's a lot of Napoleon in you.

"And you solved it.

"Your solution was tied up with another unhappy necessity of the case. To carry out your elaborate plot against Hill and yourself, you needed help. You have the use of your brain unimpaired, and the use of your hands and eyes and ears in a limited area, but these weren't enough. Your plans demanded the use of legs, too, and yours are useless. You couldn't possibly, by yourself, procure a beagle, poison it, deliver it and the note to Hill's doorstep; get cardboard boxes and string from the dime store, a dead lamprey from God knows where, poison, frogs, and so on. It's true that the little silver box must have been left here, or dropped, by Laurel; that the arsenic undoubtedly came from the can of Deth-on-Ratz in your cellar; that the tree frogs were collected in these very foothills; that the green alligator wallet must have been suggested by your wife's possession of a handbag of the same material and from the same shop; that you found the worthless stock from Mrs. Priam's first husband's estate in some box or trunk stored in this house; that to leave the bird clue you chose a book from your own library. Whenever possible you procured what you needed from as close by as you could manage, probably because in this way you felt you could control them better. But even for the things in and from this house, you needed a substitute for your legs.

"Who found and used these things at your direction?

"Alfred Wallace could. Secretary, nurse, companion, orderly, handyman . . . with you all day, on call all night . . . you could hardly have used anyone else. If for no other reason than that Wallace couldn't possibly have been kept ignorant of what was going on. Using Wallace turned a liability into an asset.

"Whether Wallace was your accomplice willingly because you paid him well, or under duress because you had something on him," said Ellery, looking down at the mound under the blanket, "is a question only you can answer now, Priam. I suppose it doesn't really matter any more. However you managed it, you persuaded Alfred to serve as your legs and as extensions of your eyes and hands. You gave Alfred his orders and he carried them out.

"Now you no longer needed Alfred. And perhaps—as other murderers have found out—tools like Alfred have a way of turning two-edged. Wallace was the only one who knew you were the god of the machine, Priam. No matter what you had on him—if anything—Wallace alive was a continuous danger to your safety and peace of mind.

"The more you mulled, the more feasible Wallace's elimination became. His death would remove the only outside knowledge of your guilt; as your wife's lover he ought to die to satisfy your peculiar psychological ambivalence; and, dead, he became a perfect Charles Adam. Wallace was within Adam's age range had Adam lived; Wallace's background was unknown because of his amnesic history; even his personality fitted with what we might have expected Adam to be.

"If you could make us flush Alfred Wallace from the mystery as Charles Adam, you'd be killing three birds with one stone.

"And so you arranged for Wallace's death."

Roger Priam raised his head. Color had come back into his cheekbones, and his heavy voice was almost animated.

"I'll have to read some of your books," Priam said. "You sure make up a good story."

"As a reward for that compliment, Priam," said Ellery, smiling, "I'll tell you an even better one.

"A few months ago you ordered Alfred Wallace to go out and buy a gun. You gave Wallace the money for it, but you wanted the gun's ownership traceable to him.

"Tonight you buzzed Wallace on the intercom, directly to his bedroom, and you told Wallace you heard someone prowling around outside the house. You told him to take the gun, make sure it was loaded, and come down here to your room, quietly—"

"That's a lie," said Roger Priam.

"That's the truth," said Ellery.

Priam showed his teeth. "You're a bluffer after all. Even if it was true— which it ain't—how could you know it?"

"Because Wallace told me so."

The skin above Priam's beard changed color again.

"You see," said Ellery, "I took Wallace into my confidence when I saw the danger he was in. I told him just what to expect at your hands and I told him that if he wanted to save his skin he'd be wise to play ball with Lieutenant Keats and me.

"Wallace didn't need much convincing, Priam. I imagine you've found him the sort of fellow who can turn on a dime; or, to change the figure, the sort who always spots the butter side of the bread. He came over to me without a struggle. And he promised to keep me informed; and he promised, when the time came, to follow not your instructions, Priam, but mine.

"When you told him on the intercom tonight to sneak down here with the loaded revolver, Wallace immediately phoned me. I told him to hold up going downstairs for just long enough to allow the lieutenant and me to get here. It didn't take us long, Priam, did it? We'd been waiting nightly for Wallace's phone call for some time now.

"I'm pretty sure you expected someone to be outside on guard, Priam, although of course you didn't know it would be Keats and me in person on Wallace's notification. You've put up a good show about not wanting police guards, in line with your shrewd performance all along, but you've known from the start that we would probably disregard your wishes in a crisis, and that was just what you wanted us to do.

"When Alfred stole into this room armed with a gun, you knew whoever was on guard—you hoped actually watching from the terrace—would fall for the illusion that Wallace was trying to kill you. If no one was watching, but a guard on the grounds heard the shot, within seconds he'd be in the room, and he'd find Wallace dead—in *your* room, with you obviously awakened from sleep, and only your story to listen to. With the previous buildup of someone threatening your life, he'd have no reason to doubt your version of what happened. If there were no guards at all, you would phone for help immediately, and between your version of the events and the fact that the gun was bought by Wallace you had every reason to believe the matter would end there. It was a bold, even a Bonapartist plan, Priam, and it almost worked."

Priam stirred, and with the stir a fluidity came over him, passing like a ripple. Then he said in a perfectly controlled voice, "Whatever Wallace told you was a damn lie. I didn't tell him to buy a gun. I didn't call him down here tonight. And you can't prove I did. You yourself saw him sneak in here a while back with a loaded gun, you saw me fight for my life, you saw him lose, and now he's *dead*." The bearded man put the lightest stress on the last word, as if to underscore Wallace's uselessness as a witness.

"I'm afraid you didn't listen very closely to what I said, Priam," said Ellery. "I said it *almost* worked. You don't think I'd allow Alfred to risk death or serious injury, do you? What he brought downstairs with him tonight, on my instructions, was a gun loaded with blanks. We've put on a show for you, Priam." And Ellery said, "*Get up, Wallace.*"

Before Priam's bulging eyes the blanket on the floor rose like the magic carpet, and there, under it, stood Alfred Wallace, smiling.

Roger Priam screamed.

Chapter XVI

WHAT NO ONE foresaw—including Ellery—was how Roger Priam would react to his arrest, indictment, and trial. Yet from the moment he showed his hand it was impossible to conceive that he might have acted otherwise. Alfred Wallace was a probable sole exception, but Wallace was being understandably discreet.

Priam took the blame for everything. His contempt for Wallace's part in the proceedings touched magnificence. Wallace, Priam said, had been the merest tool, not understanding what he was being directed to do. One would have thought, to hear Priam, that Wallace was an idiot. And Wallace acted properly idiotic. No one was fooled, but the law operates under the rules of evidence, and since there were only two witnesses, the accused and his accomplice, each—for different motives—minimizing Wallace and maximizing Priam, Wallace went scot-free.

As Keats said, in a growl, "Priam's got to be boss, by God, even at his own murder trial."

It was reported that Priam's attorney, a prominent West Coast trial lawyer, went out on the night of the verdict and got himself thoroughly fried, missing the very best part of the show. Because that same night Roger Priam managed to kill himself by swallowing poison. The usual precautions against suicide had been taken, and those entrusted with the safety of the condemned man until his execution were chagrined and mystified. Roger Priam merely lay there with his bearded mouth open in a grin, looking as fiercely joyful as a pirate cut down on his own quarter-deck. No one could dictate to *him*, his grin seemed to say, not even the sovereign State of California. If he had to die, he was picking the method and the time.

He had to be dominant even over death.

To everyone's surprise, Alfred Wallace found a new employer immediately after the trial, an Eastern writer by the name of Queen. Wallace and his suitcase moved into the little cottage on the hill, and Mrs. Williams and her two uniforms moved out, the cause leading naturally to the effect.

Ellery could not say that it was a poor exchange, for Wallace turned out a far better cook than Mrs. Williams had ever been, an accomplishment in his new employe Ellery had not bargained for, since he had hired Wallace to be his secretary. The neglected novel was still the reason for his presence in Southern California, and now that the Hill-Priam case was closed Ellery returned to it in earnest.

Keats was flabbergasted. "Aren't you afraid he'll put arsenic in your soup?"

"Why should he?" Ellery asked reasonably. "I'm paying him to take dictation and type my manuscript. And talking about soup, Wallace makes a mean *sopa de almendras, à Mallorquiña.* From Valldemosa—perfectly delicious. How about sampling it tomorrow night?"

Keats said thanks a lot but he didn't go for that gourmet stuff himself, his speed was chicken noodle soup, besides his wife was having some friends in for television, and he hung up hastily.

To the press Mr. Queen was lofty. He had never been one to hound a man for past errors. Wallace needed a job, and he needed a secretary, and that was that.

Wallace merely smiled.

Delia Priam sold the hillside property and disappeared.

The usual guesses, substantiated by no more than "a friend of the family who asks that her name be withheld" or "Delia Priam is rumored," had her variously in Las Vegas at the dice tables with a notorious underworld character; in Taos, New Mexico, under an assumed name, where she was said to be writing her memoirs for newspaper and magazine syndication; flying to Rome heavily veiled; one report insisted on placing her on a remote shelf in India as the "guest" of some wild mountain rajah well-known for his peculiar tastes in Occidental women.

That none of these pleasantly exciting stories was true everyone took for granted, but authoritative information was lacking. Delia Priam's father was not available for comment; he had stuffed some things in a duffel bag and gone off to Canada to prospect, he said, for uranium ore. And her son simply refused to talk to reporters.

To Ellery, privately, Crowe Macgowan confided that his mother had entered a retreat near Santa Maria; he spoke as if he never expected to see her again.

Young Macgowan was cleaning up his affairs preparatory to enlisting in the Army. "I've got ten days left," he told Ellery, "and a thousand things to do, one of which is to get married. I said it was a hell of a preliminary to a trip to Korea, but Laurel's stuck her chin out, so what can I do?"

Laurel looked as if she were recuperating from a serious illness. She was pale and thin but at peace. She held on to Macgowan's massive arm with authority. "I won't lose you, Mac."

"What are you afraid of, the Korean women?" jeered Crowe. "I'm told their favorite perfume is garlic."

"I'm joining the WACs," said Laurel, "if they'll ship me overseas. I suppose it's not very patriotic to put a condition to it, but if my husband is in Asia I want to be in the same part of the world."

"You'll probably wind up in West Germany," growled the large young man. "Why don't you just stay home and write me long and loving letters?"

Laurel patted his arm.

"Why don't *you* just stay home," Ellery asked Crowe, "and stick to your tree?"

"Oh, that." Crowe reddened. "My tree is sold."

"Find another."

"Listen, Queen," snarled Delia's son, "you tend to your crocheting and I'll tend to mine. I'm no hero, but there's a war on—beg pardon, a United Nations police action. Besides, they'll get me anyway."

"I understand that," said Ellery with gravity, "but your attitude seems so different these days, Mac. What's happened to the Atomic Age Tree Boy? Have you decided, now that you've found a mate, that you're not worth preserving for the Post-Atomic Era? That's hardly complimentary to Laurel."

Mac mumbled, "You let me alone . . . Laurel, no!"

"Laurel yes," said Laurel. "After all, Mac, you owe it to Ellery. Ellery, about that Tree Boy foolishness . . ."

"Yes," said Ellery hopefully. "I've been rather looking forward to a solution of that mystery."

"I finally worried it out of him," said Laurel. "Mac, you're fidgeting. Mac was trying to break into the movies. He'd heard that a certain producer was planning a series of Jungle Man pictures to compete with the Tarzan series, and he got the brilliant idea of becoming a jungle man in real life, right here in Hollywood. The Atomic Age silliness was bait for the papers. It worked, too. He got so much publicity that the producer approached him, and he was actually negotiating a secret contract when Daddy Hill died and I began to yell murder. The murder talk, and the newspaper stories involving Mac's stepfather—which I suppose Roger planted himself, or had Alfred plant for him—scared the producer and he called off the negotiations. Crowe was awfully sore at me, weren't you, darling?"

"Not as sore as I am right now. For Pete's sake, Laur, do you have to expose my moral underwear to the whole world?"

"I'm only a very small part of it, Mac," grinned Ellery. "So that's why you tried to hire me to solve the case. You thought if I could clear it up pronto, you could still have the deal with the movie producer."

"I did, too," said young Macgowan forlornly. "He came back at me only last week, asking questions about my draft status. I offered him the services of my grandfather, who'd have loved to be a jungle man, but the ungrateful guy told me to go to hell. And here I am, en route. Confidentially, Queen, does Korea smell as bad as they say it does?"

Laurel and Crowe were married by a Superior Court judge in Santa Monica, with Ellery and Lieutenant Keats as witnesses, and the wedding supper was ingested and imbibed at a drive-in near Oxnard, the newlyweds thereafter scooting off in Laurel's Austin in the general direction of San Luis Obispo, Paso Robles, Santa Cruz, and San Francisco. Driving back south on the Coast Highway, Ellery and Keats speculated as to their destination.

"I'd say Monterey," said Keats emotionally. "That's where I spent my honeymoon."

"I'd say, knowing Mac," said Ellery, "San Juan Capistrano or La Jolla, seeing that they lie in the opposite direction."

They were both misty-eyed on the New York State champagne which Ellery had traitorously provided for the California nuptials, and they wound up on a deserted beach at Malibu with their arms around each other, harmonizing "Ten Little Fingers and Ten Little Toes" to the silver-teared Pacific.

After dinner one night in late September, just as Alfred Wallace was touching off the fire he had laid in the living room, Keats dropped in. He apologized for not having phoned before coming, saying that only five minutes before he had had no idea of visiting Ellery; he was passing by on his way home and he had stopped on impulse.

"For heaven's sake, don't apologize for an act of Christian mercy," exclaimed Ellery. "I haven't seen any face but Wallace's now for more than a week. The lieutenant takes water in his Scotch, Wallace."

"Go easy on it," Keats said to Wallace. "I mean the water. May I use your phone to call my wife?"

"Wonderful. You're going to stay." Ellery studied Keats. The detective looked harassed.

"Well, for a while." Keats went to the phone.

When he came back, a glass was waiting for him on the coffee table before the fire, and Ellery and Wallace were stretching their legs in two of the three armchairs around it. Keats dropped between them and took a long sip. Ellery offered him a cigaret and Wallace held a match to it, and for a few moments Keats frowned into the fire.

"Something wrong, Keats?" Ellery asked finally.

"I don't know." Keats picked up his glass. "I'm an old lady, I guess. I've wanted to chin with you for a long time now. I kept resisting the temptation, feeling stupid. Tonight . . ." He raised his glass and gulped.

"What's bothering you?"

"Well . . . the Priam case. Of course, it's all over—"

"What about the Priam case?"

Keats made a face. Then he set the glass down with a bang. "Queen, I've been over that spiel of yours—to me at the Hollywood Division, to Priam that night in his room—it must be a hundred times. I don't know, I can't explain it . . ."

"You mean my solution to the case?"

"It never seems to come out as pat when I go over it as it did when you . . ." Keats stopped and rather deliberately turned to look at Alfred Wallace. Wallace looked back politely.

"It's not necessary for Wallace to leave, Keats," said Ellery with a grin. "When I said that night at Priam's that I'd taken Wallace into my confidence, I meant just that. I took him into my confidence completely. He knows everything I know, including the answers to the questions that I take it have been giving you a bad time."

The detective shook his head and finished what was left in his glass. When Wallace rose to refill it, Keats said, "No more now," and Wallace sat down again.

"It's not the kind of thing I can put my mitt on," said the detective uncomfortably. "No *mistakes*. I mean mistakes that you can . . ." He drew on his cigaret for support, started over. "For instance, Queen, a lot of the hoopla you attributed to Priam just doesn't *fit.*"

"Doesn't fit what?" asked Ellery mildly.

"Doesn't fit Priam. I mean, what Priam was. Take that letter he typed on the broken machine and put in the collar of the dead beagle for delivery to Hill . . ."

"Something wrong with it?"

"Everything wrong with it! Priam was an uneducated man. If he ever used a fancy word, I wasn't around to hear it. His talk was crude. But when he wrote that letter . . . How could a man like Priam have made such a letter up? To avoid using the letter *T,* to invent roundabout ways of saying things —that takes . . . a *feel* for words, doesn't it? A certain amount of practice in—in composition? And punctuation—the note was dotted and dashed and commaed and everything perfectly."

"What's your conclusion?" asked Ellery.

Keats squirmed.

"Or haven't you arrived at one?"

"Well . . . I have."

"You don't believe Priam typed that note?"

"He typed it, all right. Nothing wrong with your reasoning on that . . . Look." Keats flipped his cigaret into the fire. "Call me a halfwit. But the more I think about it, the less I buy the payoff. Priam typed that letter, but somebody else *dictated* it. Word for word. Comma for comma." Keats jumped out of the chair as if he felt the need of being better prepared for the attack that was sure to come. But when Ellery said nothing, merely looked thoughtful and puffed on his pipe, Keats sat down again. "You're a kindhearted character. Now tell me what's wrong with *me.*"

"No, you keep going, Keats. Is there anything else that's bothering you?"

"Lots more. You talked about Priam's shrewd tactics, his cleverness; you compared him to Napoleon. Shrewd? Clever? A tactician? Priam was about as shrewd as a bull steer in heat and as clever as a punch in the nose. He couldn't have planned a menu. The only weapon Priam knew was a club.

"He figured out a series of related clues, you said, that added up—for our benefit—to a naturalist. Evolution. The steps in the ladder. Scientific stuff. How could a roughneck smallbrain like Priam have done that? A man who bragged he hadn't read a book since he was in knee pants! You'd have to have a certain amount of technical knowledge even to *think* of that evolutionary stuff as the basis of a red herring, let alone get all the stages correct and in the right order. Then picking a fancy-pants old Greek drama to tie in birds! No, sir, I don't purchase it. Not Priam.

"Oh, I don't question his guilt. He murdered his partner, all right. Hell, he confessed. But he wasn't the bird who figured out the method and thought up the details. That was the work of somebody with a lot better equipment than Roger Priam ever hoped to have."

"In other words, if I get your thought, Keats," murmured Ellery, "you believe Priam needed not only someone else's legs but someone else's gray matter, too."

"That's it," snapped the detective. "And I'll go whole hog. I say the same man who supplied the legs supplied the know-how!" He glared at Alfred Wallace, who was slumped in the chair, hands clasped loosely about the glass on his stomach, eyes gleaming Keats's way. "I mean you, Wallace! You got a lucky break, my friend, Priam sloughing you off as a moron who trotted around doing what you were told—"

"Lucky nothing," said Ellery. "That was in the cards, Keats. Priam *did* believe Wallace was a stupid tool and that the whole brilliant plot was the product of his own genius; being Priam, he couldn't believe anything else—as Wallace, who knew him intimately, accurately foresaw. Wallace made his suggestions so subtly, led Priam about by his large nose so tactfully, that Priam never once suspected that *he* was the tool, being used by a master craftsman."

Keats glanced again at Wallace. But the man lay there comfortably, even looking pleased.

Keats's head ached. "Then—you mean—"

Ellery nodded. "The real murderer in this case, Keats, was not Priam. It's Wallace. Always was."

Wallace extended a lazy arm and snagged one of Ellery's cigarets. Ellery tossed him a packet of matches, and the man nodded his thanks. He lit up, tossed the packet back, and resumed his hammocky position.

The detective was confused. He glanced at Ellery, at Wallace, at Ellery again. Ellery was puffing peacefully away at his pipe.

"You mean," said Keats in a high voice, "Hill wasn't murdered by Priam after all?"

"It's a matter of emphasis, Keats. Gangster A, a shot big enough to farm out his dirty work, employs Torpedo C to kill Gangster B. Torpedo C does so. Who's guilty of B's murder? A *and* C. The big shot and the little shot. Priam and Alfred were both guilty."

"Priam hired Wallace to do his killing for him," said Keats foolishly.

"No." Ellery picked up a pipe cleaner and inserted it in the stem of his pipe. "No, Keats, that would make Priam the big shot and Wallace the little. It was a whole lot subtler than that. Priam *thought* he was the big shot and that Wallace was a tool, but he was wrong; it was the other way around. Priam *thought* he was using Wallace to murder Hill, when all the time Wallace was using Priam to murder Hill. And when Priam planned the clean-up killing of Wallace—planned it on his own—Wallace turned Priam's plan right around against Priam and used it to make Priam kill himself."

"Take it easy, will you?" groaned Keats. "I've had a hard week. Let's go at this in words of one syllable, the only kind I can understand.

"According to you, this monkey sitting here, this man you call a murderer— who's taking your pay, drinking your liquor, and smoking your cigarets, all with your permission—this Wallace planned the murders first of Hill, then of Priam, using Priam without Priam's realizing that he was being used—in fact, in such a way that Priam thought *he* was the works. All my pea-brain wants to know is: *Why?* Why should *Wallace* want to kill Hill and Priam? What did *he* have against 'em?"

"You know the answer to that, Lieutenant."

"Me?"

"Who's wanted to murder Hill and Priam from the start?"

"Who?"

"Yes, who's had that double motive throughout the case?"

Keats sat up gripping the arms of his chair. He looked at Alfred Wallace in a sickly way. "You're kidding," he said feebly. "This whole thing is a rib."

"No rib, Keats," said Ellery. "The question answers itself. The only one who had motive to kill both Hill *and* Priam was Charles Adam. Ditto Wallace? Then why look for two? Things equal to the same thing are equal to each other. Wallace is Adam. Refill now?"

Keats swallowed.

Wallace got up and amiably did the honors, Keats watching as if he half-expected to catch the tall man slipping a white powder into the glass. He drank, and afterward gazed glumly into the brown liquid.

"I'm not being specially obtuse," Keats said finally. "I'm just trying to wriggle out of this logic of yours. Let's forget logic. You say that proves this smoothie is Charles Adam. How about coincidence? Of all the millions of nose-wipers who *could* have been Priam's man Friday, it turns out to be the one man in the universe who wanted to kill him. Too neat, Queen, not to say gaudy."

"Why do you call it coincidence? There was nothing coincidental about Charles Adam's becoming Priam's wet nurse. *Adam planned it that way.*

"For twenty-five years he looked for Priam and Hill. One day he found them. Result: He became Priam's secretary-nurse-companion . . . not as Adam, of course, but as a specially created character whom he christened Alfred Wallace. My guess is that Adam had more than a little to do with the sudden resignations of several of his predecessors in the job, but it remains a guess—Wallace, quite reasonably, is close-mouthed on the subject. My guess is also that he's been around Los Angeles far longer than the amnesic trail to Las Vegas indicated. Maybe it's been years—eh, Wallace?"

Wallace raised his brows quizzically.

"In any event, he managed finally to land the job and to fool Roger Priam absolutely. Priam went to his death completely unaware that Wallace was *actually* Adam rather than the spurious substitute for Adam Priam thought he was palming off on the authorities. Priam never doubted for a moment that Adam's bones were still lying in the coral sand of that deserted West Indian island."

Ellery stared reflectively at Wallace, who was sipping his Scotch like a gentleman in his club. "I wonder what you really look like, Adam. The newspaper photos we dug up weren't much use . . . Of course, twenty-five years have made a big difference. But you wouldn't have trusted to that. Plastic work, almost certainly, and of the highest order; there isn't a sign of it. Maybe a little something to your vocal cords. And lots of practice with such things as gait, tricks of speech, 'characteristic' gestures, and so on. It was probably all done years ago, so that you had plenty of time to obliterate all trace of— forgive me—of the old Adam. Priam never had a chance. Or Hill. And you had the virility Priam demanded in a secretary. You'd undoubtedly found out about that in your preliminary reconnaissance. A glimpse of Delia Priam, and you must have been absolutely delighted. Plum pudding to go with your roast beef."

Wallace smiled appreciatively.

"I don't know when—or how—Priam first let on that he wanted to be rid of Leander Hill. Maybe he never said so at all, in so many words. At least in the beginning. You were with him night and day, and you were studying him. You could hardly have remained blind to Priam's hatred. I think, Wallace," said Ellery, setting his feet on the coffee table, "yes, I think you got hold of Priam's proboscis very early with your magnetic grip, and steered it this way and that. It would be a technique that appealed to you, feeling your victim's desires and directing them, unsuspected, according to your own. Sensing that Priam wanted Hill dead, you led him around to becoming actively conscious of it. Then you let him chew on it. It took months, probably. But you had plenty of time, and you'd proved your patience.

"In the end, it became a passion with him.

"Of course, to do anything at all along that line he needed an accomplice. There couldn't be any question as to who the accomplice might be. It wouldn't surprise me if you dropped a few hints that you weren't altogether unfamiliar with violence . . . you had vague 'memories,' perhaps, that came and went conveniently through the curtain of your 'amnesia' . . . It was all very gradual, but one day you got there. It was out. And you were to do the 'legwork.' "

Wallace surveyed the flames dreamily. Keats, watching him, listening to Ellery, had the most childish sense that all this was happening elsewhere, to other people.

"Priam had plans of his own. They would be Priam-like plans, crude and explosive—a Molotov cocktail sort of thing. And you 'admired' them. But perhaps something a little less direct . . . ? In discussing the possibilities you may have suggested that there might be something in the common background of Priam and Hill that would give Priam—always Priam—a psychologically sound springboard for a really clever plan. Eventually you got the story of Adam—of yourself—out of him. Because, of course, that's what you were after all along.

"After that, it was ridiculously easy. All you had to do was put ideas into Priam's head, so that they could come out of his mouth and, in doing so, convince him that they were original with him. In time you had the whole thing explicit. There was the plot that would give Priam the indestructible garment of innocence, Priam was convinced it was all his idea . . . and all the time it was the very plot you'd planned to use yourself. That must have been a great day, Wallace."

Ellery turned to Keats.

"From that point it was a mere matter of operations. He'd mastered the technique of cuckolding Priam, psychologically as well as maritally; at every stage he made Priam think Priam was directing events and that he, Wallace, was carrying them out; but at every stage it was Priam who was ordering exactly what Wallace wanted him to order.

"It was Wallace who dictated the note to Hill, with Priam doing the typing —just as you figured out, Keats. Wallace didn't call it dictation—he undoubtedly called it, humbly, 'suggestions.' And Priam typed away on a machine on which the *T* key was broken. Accident? There are no accidents where Wallace-Adam is concerned. He'd managed, somehow, and without Priam's knowledge, to break that key; and he managed to persuade Priam that there was no danger in using the typewriter that way, since a vital part of the plan was to see to it that Hill destroyed the note after he read it. Of course, what Wallace wanted was a record of that note *for us,* and if Hill hadn't secretly made a copy of it, you may be sure Wallace would have seen to it that a transcription was found—by me or by you or by someone like Laurel who would take it to us at once. In the end, the clue of the missing *T* would trap Priam through the new *T* on Priam's machine . . . just as Wallace planned."

The man beyond Keats permitted himself a slight smile. He was looking down at his glass, modestly.

"And when he realized what was at the back of Priam's mind," continued Ellery, "the plan to kill *him* . . . Wallace made use of that, too. He took advantage of events so that the biter would be bitten. When I told Wallace what I 'knew,' it coincided perfectly with his final move. The only trouble was—eh, Adam?—I knew a little too much."

Wallace raised his glass. Almost it was a salute. But then he put it to his lips and it was hard to say if the gesture had meant anything at all.

Keats stirred, shifting in the comfortable chair as if it were uncomfortable. There was a wagon track between his eyes, leaving his forehead full of ruts.

"I'm not going good tonight, Queen," he mumbled. "So far this all sounds to me like just theory. You say this man is Charles Adam. You put a lot of arguments together and it sounds great. Okay, so he's Charles Adam. But how could you have been sure? It's *possible* that he wasn't Charles Adam. That he was John Jones, or Stanley Brown, or Cyril St. Clair, or Patrick Silverstein. I say it's *possible.* Show me that it isn't."

Ellery laughed. "You're not getting me involved in a defense of what's been, not always admiringly, called the 'Queen method.' Fortunately, Keats, I *can* show you that it's *not* possible for this man to be anyone else *but* Charles Adam. Where did he tell us he got the name Alfred Wallace?"

"He said he picked it out of thin air when he got an amnesia attack and couldn't remember who he was." Keats glowered. "All of which was horse-radish."

"All of which was horse-radish," nodded Ellery, "except the fact that, whatever his name was, it certainly *wasn't* Alfred Wallace. He did pick that when he wanted an assumed name."

"So what? There's nothing unusual about the name Alfred Wallace."

"Wrong, Keats. There's something not only unusual and remarkable about the name Alfred Wallace, but unique.

"Alfred Wallace—Alfred Russel Wallace—was a contemporary of Charles Darwin's. Alfred Wallace was the naturalist who arrived at a formulation of the evolution theory almost simultaneously with Darwin, although independently. In fact, their respective announcements were first given to the world in the form of a joint essay read before the Linnaean Society in 1858, and published in the Society's *Journal* the same year. Darwin had drafted the outline of his 'Theory' in manuscript in 1842. Wallace, ill with fever in South America, came to the same conclusions and sent his findings to Darwin, which is how they came to be published simultaneously."

Ellery tapped his pipe against an ashtray. "And here we have a man up to his ears in the Hill-Priam case who carries the admittedly assumed name of Alfred Wallace. A case in which a naturalist named Charles Adam used the theory of evolution—fathered by Darwin and the nineteenth century Alfred Wallace—as the basis of a series of clues. Coincidence that the secretary of one of Adam's victims should select as his alias one of the two names associated with evolution? Out of the billions of possible name combinations? Just as Charles Adam founded his entire murder plan on his scientific knowledge, so he drew an alias out of his science's past. He would hardly have stooped to calling himself Darwin; the obviousness of that would have offended him. But the name Alfred Wallace is almost unknown to the general public. Perhaps the whole process was unconscious; it would be a delightful irony if this man, who prides himself on being the god of events, should be mortally tripped by his own unconscious mind."

Keats got up so suddenly that even Wallace was startled.

But the detective was paying no attention to Wallace. In the firelight his fair skin was a pebbled red as he scowled down at Ellery, who was regarding him inquiringly.

"So when you hired him as your secretary, Queen, you knew you were hiring Adam—a successful killer?"

"That's right, Keats."

"Why?"

Ellery waved his dead pipe. "Isn't it evident?"

"Not a bit. Why didn't you tell all this to me a long time ago?"

"You haven't thought it out, Lieutenant." Ellery stared into the fire, tapping his lips with the stem. "Not a word of this could have been brought out at the trial. Not a word of it constitutes legal evidence. None of it is proof as proof is construed in a court of law. Even if the story could have been spread before the court, on the record, in the absence of legal proof of any of its component parts it would certainly have resulted in a dismissal of a charge against Wallace, and it might even have so garbled things as to get Priam off too, or sentenced to a punishment that didn't fit his crime.

"I didn't want to chance Priam's squeezing out by reason of sheer complication and confusion, Keats. I preferred to let him get what was coming to him and try to deal with the gentleman in this chair later. And here he's been for a couple of months, Keats, under my eye and thumb, and I still haven't found the answer. Maybe you have a suggestion?"

"He's a damn murderer," grated Keats. "Granted he got a dirty deal twenty-five years ago . . . when he took the law into his own hands he became as bad as they were. And if that sounds like a Sunday school sermon, let it!"

"No, no, it's very true," said Ellery sadly. "There's no doubt about that at all, Lieutenant. He's a bad one. You know it, I know it, and he knows it. But he isn't talking, and what can you and I prove?"

"A rubber hose—"

"I don't believe would do it," said Ellery. "No, Keats, Wallace-Adam is a pretty special problem. Can we prove that he broke the T key on Priam's typewriter? Can we prove that he suggested the plan behind Priam's murder of Hill? Can we prove that he worked out the series of death threats against Priam . . . threats Priam boasted in court he'd sent to himself? Can we prove *anything* we know this fellow did or said or suggested or planned? A single thing, Keats?"

Wallace looked up at Lieutenant Keats of the Hollywood Division with respectful interest.

Keats glared back at him for fully three minutes.

Then the Hollywood detective reached for his hat, jammed it down over his ears, and stamped out.

The front door made a loud, derisive noise.

And Keats's car roared down the hill as if the devil were after it.

Ellery sighed. He began to refill his pipe.

"Damn you, Adam. What am I going to do with you?"

The man reached for another of Ellery's cigarets.

Smiling his calm, secretive, slightly annoying smile, he said, "You can call me Alfred."